QPB

MAMMOTH

BOOK OF

EROTICA

QPB

MAMMOTH

BOOK OF

EROTICA

EDITED BY MAXIM JAKUBOWSKI

QUALITY PAPERBACK BOOK CLUB
NEW YORK

CONTENTS

◆

DESIRE BEGINS

Kathy Acker

I

I ABSOLUTELY LOVE TO fuck. These longings, unexplainable longings deep within me, drive me wild, and I have no way of relieving them. Living them. I'm 27 and I love to fuck. Sometimes with people I want to fuck; sometimes, and I can't tell when but I remember these times, with anybody who'll touch me. These, I call them nymphomaniac, times have nothing to do with (are not caused by) physical pleasure, for my cunt could be sore, I could be sick, and yet I'd feel the same way. I'll tease you till you don't know what you're doing, honey, and grab; and then I'll do anything for you.

I haven't always been this way. Once upon a time I was an intelligent sedate girl, who, like every intelligent sedate girl, hated her parents and didn't care about money. O in those days I didn't care about anything! I dated boys, stayed out till 5.00 in the morning then snuck home, read a lot of books. I cared more for the books than anyone else and would kiss my books good-night when I went to sleep. Would never go anywhere without a book. But my downfall came. My parents kicked me out of the house because I wasn't interested in marrying a rich man, I didn't care enough about money to become a scientist or a prostitute, I couldn't even figure out how to make any money.

I didn't. I became poor and had to find a way of justifying my lousy attitude about money. At first, like all poor people, I had delusions about being a great artist, but that quickly passed. I never did have any talent.

I want to fuck these two fantastic artists even though I'm not an artist: that's what this is about. This is the only way I can get them: (I only want them for a few hours. Days.) Jewels hang from the tips of silver branches. I also want money.

My name is Kathy Acker.

The story begins by me being totally bored.

Sunny California is totally boring; there are too many blond-assed surf jocks. I was lying on my bed, wondering if I should go down to the beach or sun myself on the patio until I passed out. I watched the curly silky brown hair below the damp palm of my hand rise and fall, I watched the rise, the mound twist in agony, laughed at myself. No way, I muttered, among these creeps no way. I need to love someone who can, by lightly, lightly stroking my flesh, tear open this reality, rip my flesh open until I bleed. Red jewels running down my legs and branches. I need someone who knows everything and who'll love me endlessly; then stop. My cats leaped up to me and rubbed their delicious bodies against my body. My cats didn't exist.

Suddenly heard a knocking at the door. No one ever knocks at the door, they just walk in. I wondered if it was FBI agents, or the telephone Mafia after Art Povera. I opened the door and saw Dan, I didn't know his name then, looking bewildered. Then, seeing me, looking scared. I realized I had forgotten to put clothes on. That's how southern California is: hot.

"Excuse me, I'm looking for 46 uh Belvedere."

"Oh you mean up the hill where David and Elly live; I'll show you. I have to get some clothes on."

He followed me into my small bedroom.

As I slowly bent over, reaching for my jeans, I noticed him watching me. He had brown hair, couldn't see his eyes because he squints so much but they look red, some acne, short with a body I like: heavy enough to run into and feel its weight on me; about 30 years old. I hesitantly took hold of my jeans. He started to talk again: he talks too much. I wanted him to rip off my skin, take me away to where I'd always be insane. He didn't want to fuck with me, much less do anything else. I slowly lifted my leg to put on my jeans, changed my mind. I turned around; suddenly we grabbed each other: I felt his body: his lips wet and large against my lips, his arms pressing my back and stomach into his thick endless stomach, his mouth over me, sucking me, exploring me I want this

"I want you you lousy motherfucker I want you to do everything to me I want you to tell me you want me I want you any way I can get you. Do you understand?" We run screaming out into the night, other people don't exist, feet touching the cold store, then the sand, then the black ocean water. I look up: black; toward the sand: black; I reach up for him and fall. The water passes over us. We stand up, spouting water; our mouths' wetness into each other's mouth cling together to stay erect. I rise up on my toes, the black waves rising, carefully, press my thighs into his so that his cock can touch my cunt. His right hand caresses his cock, touches its tip to my cunt lips, moves upward, into me I hold him tighter we fall

My hand touches my wet curling hairs then the thick lips of my cunt. Takes sand, rubs the sand into the outer lips of my cunt. Two areas of softness wetness touch me, move back so the cold air swirls at, touch me I feel warm liquid trickling between the swelling lips I feel them swelling a tongue a burning center touches me harder, inside the swollen lips: I lift my legs and imprison him. My nipples are hard as diamonds. The inner skin of my knees presses against his rough hairs: now I feel roughness: sandpaper rubbing the screaming skin above my clit. The joining of my inner lips almost more sensitive than my clit. Now I feel soft surface wetnesses, gently lap, now the burning center which becomes my burning center: rhythmically pressing until time becomes burning as I do. I'm totally relaxed. I'm a tongue which I can't control: which I beg to touch me each time it stops so I can open wider, rise rise toward the black, I open rising screaming I feel it: I feel waves of senses screaming I want more and more.

At the peak, as I think I'm beginning to descend, he throws himself on me and enters me making me come again again. All I feel is his cock in me moving circling circling every inch of my cunt walls moving back forth every inch, he stops, I can't, he starts slamming in to me not with his cock but the skin around his cock slamming into my clit I come I come he moves his cock into me slowly even more slowly, and then leaves.

For the new life, I have to change myself completely.

* * *

The next artist I meet in a bar in New York. I'm sick of artists.
The next man I meet is tall, dark, and handsome. I was wearing
a black silk sheath slashed in the back to the ruby which signals
the delicate opening of my buttocks: tiny black diamonds in my
ears and on the center of my fingernails. I had come to the bar to
drink: it was an old transvestite bar East Village New York no one
goes during the week, rows upon rows of white-covered tables low
hanging chandeliers containing almost no light: mirrors which are
walls reflect back, reflections upon reflections, tiny stars of light.
The only people in the bar are the two women who run the bar,
tiny grey-haired women who look like men: incredibly sexy. One
or two Spanish hustlers. I wanted to be alone.

I had no background. I'm not giving you details about myself
because these two occurrences are the first events of my life.
Otherwise I don't exist: I'm a mirror for beauty. The man
walked up to me and sat down. He bought two beers. I wasn't
noticing him.

"What do you really want to happen?" he asked me. I couldn't
answer him because I don't reveal the truth to people I know
slightly, only to strangers and to people I know well and want
to become. "I used to act as a stud," he was trying to put me at
my ease. "Housewives would pick me up in their cars, pay me to
satisfy them. I didn't mind because I hate housewives: that class.
Then I used to work this motel: I'd knock on a door to a room, a
man would start screaming "don't come in don't come in" scream
louder and louder; after a while he'd throw a pair of semened-up
underpants out the door. In the pants would be ten dollars."

I couldn't say anything to him because I was starting to respect
him.

"I only like people of the working class," he went on. Underneath
the table, he was slowly pouring wine on the black silk of my thigh.
I moved my legs slightly, open, so the cold liquid would hit the
insides of my thighs. Then close my thighs, rubbing them slowly
together. "You have a lot of trouble with men, don't you?"

"Don't you love me?" I cried in anguish. "Don't you care
anything about me?"

He gently took me in his arms kissed me. Lightly and gently.
He didn't press me to him or touch me passionately. "Quick," he
whispered. "Before they notice."

He threw me back on the velvet ledge we had been sitting on, pulled up my shift, and entered me. I wanted more. As I feel his cock rotate slowly around the skins of my cunt walls, touching each inch slowly too slowly, he began again to pour wine on my body: liquid cooling all of my skin except the inside burning skin of my cunt. Putting ice in my mouth on my eyes, around the thick heavy ridges of my breasts. Cock slowly easing out of me, I can't stand that, I can't stand that absence I start to scream I see my mound rise upward: the heavy brown hairs surrounded by white flesh, the white flesh against the black silk: I see his cock enter me, slide into me like it belongs in my slimy walls, I tighten my muscles I tighten them around the cock, jiggling, thrust upward, thousands of tiny fingers on the cock, fingers and burning tongues: this is public I have to move fast: explodes I explode and my mound rises upward, toward the red-black ceiling, I see my mound rise upward, toward the red-black ceiling I see us come fast.

He quickly got out of me, and arranged our clothes. No one in the bar had noticed. We kissed goodbye, perfunctorily, and he left.

Every night now I dream of my two lovers. I have no other life. This is the realm of complete freedom: I can put down anything. I see Dan: The inner skin of my knees presses against his rough hairs: now I feel roughness: sand-paper rubbing the screaming skin above my clit. The joining of my inner lips almost more sensitive than my clit. Now I feel soft surface wetnesses, gently lap, now the burning center which becomes my burning center: rhythmically pressing until time becomes burning as I do. I'm totally relaxed. I'm a tongue which I can't control: which I beg to touch me each time it stops so I can open wider, rise rise toward the black, I open rising screaming

I see my second artist love: I can't stand that absence I start to scream I see my mound rise upward: the heavy brown hairs surrounded by white flesh, the white flesh against the black silk: I see his cock enter me, slide into me like it belongs in my slimy walls, I tighten my muscles I tighten them around the cock, jiggling, thrust upward, thousands of tiny fingers on the cock, fingers and burning tongues: this is public I have to move fast: explodes I explode and my mound rises upward, toward the red-black ceiling, I see

I want a woman.

I'm sick of dreaming.

I decide to find these two artists no matter what no matter where. I'll be the most beautiful and intelligent woman in the world to them.

II

I want to make something beautiful: an old-fashioned wish. To do this I must first accomplish four tasks, for the last one I must die: Then I'll have something beautiful, and can fuck the men I want to fuck because they'll want to fuck me.

For the first task I have to learn to be as industrious as possible: I have to work as hard as possible to make up for my lack of beauty and charm. Not that I'm not extremely beautiful. I have to learn what is the best love-sex possible, and separate those people whom I can love from those people I can't love. I have until nightfall to do this.

Last night I dreamt I was standing on a low rise of grassy ground; Dan was standing next to me facing me. He put his arms around my neck kissed me, said "I love you." I said "I love you." Two years later I'm riding through a forest with my four younger sisters, green and wet, leaves in our eyes and skin; we push leaves out of the way the brown horse's neck lowered. My next-to-youngest sister tells me Dan asked her to marry him two months ago. I'm galloping wildly through the woods branches tear at my eyes flakes of my skin hanging. I try to go faster and faster. It's night. Three days later I appear, night, the livingroom of my parents' house: we're moving to Boston, a bayview overlooking a black sky, where I go to college. The skin of my face is torn; bruises over my naked arms; one of my eyes is bloodshot. My family's glad I haven't died. My father greets me, then my older sister who's tall, blonde, beautiful, intelligent. We love each other most. The room in which we're standing is large browns on browns; my parents are rich, not very rich, and liberals. A thin dark-haired man asks me if I want to go to a party. I want to: I rush upstairs to dress: my sister and the man, who's a close family friend, look happy because I'm not going to kill myself. I (outside the dream) look at myself (inside the dream): I'm tall and thin, short waving black hair: I'm not beautiful until you look at me for a long time. I'm very severe. When we walk into a large grey-white house, we realize the party's an artist party. The tall, dark, handsome artist walks over to me and asks me to dance. I wonder if he's asking me because he wants to marry a rich girl. He tells me he's a successful artist makes a lot of money. We dance, dance out to a dark balcony; he starts to take off my black dress as I lean over the portico. I've got two glasses of champagne: one in each hand. He says "I could strangle you like this" I get pissed and walk away. As I begin to walk away, I see Dan and some woman on the balcony: Dan walks over to the man I'm with. They greet each other: Dan admires the stranger's work. I nod hello to Dan. He announces he's getting married: introduces the woman with whom he's going to get married. I walk away to get more champagne. As I return to the balcony, a blonde woman walks up to the group the stranger says "I didn't know you wanted to come here." He introduces his wife to us. I'm going crazy but withstraining myself admirably. If I don't fuck someone soon know someone wants me. I'll have to ride my horse for three days again: do something wilder. I can't stop myself. I get another drink. Mel someone walks up to us says "I'm the only man here who isn't married or about to be married" meaning I might as well fuck him because I'm so desperate. I ask him to marry me since I have a lot of money: I'll support him. I tell him how much money I have. He says "Yes." I tell him to go shit on himself. I'm in a lousy mood. An old friend of mine comes up to me, who I haven't seen for a few months. I tell him I need someone's shoulder to cry on. His new lover comes up to him: he can't do anything. This dream's repulsively hetero. I get a bottle of champagne and drink it. I have to ride my horse through the dark forest, the winds swirling around. I rush out of the party. As I'm descending the wide wood steps, I turn around, see the tall dark artist. He asks if he can see me again. He's very severe. I say yes. I fall down the steps I'm so drunk. He asks me if I intend to drive myself home. I'm going to drive myself to the ocean so I can go swimming I'm rich do whatever I want he lifts me up puts me in my car drives me home I end up fucking him quickly then his wife comes I never see him again, I'm lying in my bed with my older sister who's very "I'll take care of you" severe type and whom I love. As we're fucking, her boyfriend enters the room and stops us because we're not supposed to act soooo

Last night I dreamt I was standing on a low rise of grassy ground; Dan was standing next to me facing me. He put his arms around my neck kissed me, said "I love you." I said "I love you." Two years later I'm riding through a forest with my four younger sisters, green and wet, leaves in our eyes and skin; we push leaves out of the way the brown horse's neck lowered. My next-to-youngest sister tells me Dan asked her to marry him two months ago. I'm galloping wildly through the woods branches tear at my eyes flakes of my skin hanging. I try to go faster and faster. It's night. Three days later I appear, night, the livingroom of my parents' house: we're moving to Boston, a bayview overlooking a black sky, where I go to college. The skin of my face is torn; bruises over my naked arms; one of my eyes is bloodshot. My family's glad I haven't died. My father greets me, then my older sister who's tall, blonde, beautiful, intelligent. We love each other most. The room in which we're standing is large browns on browns; my parents are rich, not very rich, and liberals. A thin dark-haired man asks me if I want to go to a party. I want to: I rush upstairs to dress: my sister and the man, who's a close family friend, look happy because I'm not going to kill myself. I (outside the dream) look at myself (inside the dream): I'm tall and thin, short waving black hair: I'm not beautiful until you look at me for a long time. I'm very severe. When we walk into a large grey-white house, we realize the party's an artist party. The tall, dark, handsome artist walks over to me and asks me to dance. I wonder if he's asking me because he wants to marry a rich girl. He tells me he's a successful artist makes a lot of money. We dance, dance out to a dark balcony; he starts to take off my black dress as I lean over the portico. I've got two glasses of champagne: one in each hand. He says "I could strangle you like this" I get pissed and walk away. As I begin to walk away, I see Dan and some woman on the balcony: Dan walks over to the man I'm with. They greet each other: Dan admires the stranger's work. I nod hello to Dan. He announces he's getting married: introduces the woman with whom he's going to get married. I walk away to get more champagne. As I return to the balcony, a blonde woman walks up to the group the stranger says "I didn't know you wanted to come here." He introduces his wife to us. I'm going crazy but withstraining myself admirably. If I don't fuck someone soon know someone wants me, I'll have to ride my horse for three days again: do something wilder. I can't stop myself. I get another drink. My sister who's also drunk asks me to dance, she's wearing a low grey gown; we dance in each other's arms giggling. I lie close in her arms: I lie backwards over her left arm. We're leaning against a grey wall under a picture: she kisses me, as she looks down on me I wonder if she now feel sexually toward me I'm excited, I ask her and she says she'd like to fuck me. I look up at her and kiss her: I want us to fuck in front of all these creepy people. Her thin dark-haired boyfriend comes over tells us we can't act too wildly: do what we want in our bedroom. Mel someone walks up to us says "I'm the only man here who isn't married or about to be married" meaning I might as well fuck him because I'm so desperate. I ask him to marry me since I have a lot of money: I'll support him. I tell him how much money I have. He says "Yes." I tell him to go shit on himself. I'm in a lousy mood. An old friend of mine comes up to me, who I haven't seen for a few months. I tell him I need someone's shoulder to cry on. His new lover comes up to him: he can't do anything. This dream's repulsively hetero. I get a bottle of champagne and drink it. I have to ride my horse through the dark forest, the winds swirling around. I rush out of the party. As I'm descending the wide wood steps, I turn around, see the tall dark artist. He asks if he can see me again. He's very severe. I say yes. I fall down the steps I'm so drunk. He asks me if I intend to drive myself home. I'm going to drive myself to the ocean so I can go swimming I'm rich and do whatever I want he lifts me up puts me in my car drives me home I end up fucking him quickly then his wife comes I never see him again, I'm lying in my bed with my older sister who's very "I'll take care of you" severe type and whom I love. As we're fucking, her boyfriend enters the room and stops us because we're not supposed to act soooo

Last night I dreamt I was standing on a low rise of grassy ground; Dan was standing next to me facing me. He put his arms around my neck kissed me, said "I love you." I said "I love you." Two years later I'm riding through a forest with my four younger sisters, green and wet, leaves in our eyes and skin; we push leaves out of the way the brown horse's neck lowered. My next-to-youngest sister tells me Dan asked her to marry him two months ago. I'm galloping wildly through the woods branches tear at my eyes flakes of my skin hanging. I try to go faster and faster. It's night. Three days later I appear, night, the livingroom of my parents' house: we're

moving to Boston, a bayview overlooking a black sky, where I go
to college. The skin of my face is torn; bruises over my naked
arms; one of my eyes is bloodshot. My family's glad I haven't
died. My father greets me, then my older sister who's tall, blonde,
beautiful, intelligent. We love each other most. The room in which
we're standing is large browns on browns; my parents are rich, not
very rich, and liberals. A thin dark-haired man asks me if I want
to go to a party. I want to: I rush upstairs to dress: my sister and
the man, who's a close family friend, look happy because I'm not
going to kill myself. I (outside the dream) look at myself (inside
the dream): I'm tall and thin, short waving black hair: I'm not
beautiful until you look at me for a long time. I'm very severe.
When we walk into a large grey-white house, we realize the party's
an artist party. The tall, dark, handsome artist walks over to me and
asks me to dance. I wonder if he's asking me because he wants to
marry a rich girl. He tells me he's a successful artist makes a lot of
money. We dance, dance out to a dark balcony; he starts to take
off my black dress as I lean over the portico. I've got two glasses
of champagne: one in each hand. He says "I could strangle you like
this" I get pissed and walk away. As I begin to walk away, I see
Dan and some woman on the balcony: Dan walks over to the man
I'm with. They greet each other: Dan admires the stranger's work.
I nod hello to Dan. He announces he's getting married: introduces
the woman with whom he's going to get married. I walk away to
get more champagne. As I return to the balcony, a blonde woman
walks up to the group the stranger says "I didn't know you wanted
to come here." He introduces his wife to us. I'm going crazy but
withstraining myself admirably. If I don't fuck someone soon know
someone wants me, I'll have to ride my horse for three days again:
do something wilder. I can't stop myself. I get another drink. My
sister who's also drunk asks me to dance, she's wearing a low grey
gown; we dance in each other's arms giggling. I lie close in her
arms: I lie backwards over her left arm. We're leaning against a
grey wall under a picture: she kisses me, as she looks down on me
I wonder if she now feels sexually toward me I'm excited, I ask
her and she says she'd like to fuck me. I look up at her and kiss
her: I want us to fuck in front of all these creepy people. Her thin
dark-haired boyfriend comes over tells us we can't act too wildly:
do what we want in our bedroom. Mel someone walks up to us says
"I'm the only man here who isn't married or about to be married"

meaning I might as well fuck him because I'm so desperate. I ask
him to marry me since I have a lot of money: I'll support him.
I tell him how much money I have. He says "Yes." I tell him to go
shit on himself. I'm in a lousy mood. An old friend of mine comes
up to me, who I haven't seen for a few months. I tell him I need
someone's shoulder to cry on. His new lover comes up to him: he
can't do anything. This dream's repulsively hetero. I get a bottle of
champagne and drink it. I have to ride my horse through the dark
forest, the winds swirling around. I rush out of the party. As I'm
descending the wide wood steps, I turn around, see the tall dark
artist. He asks if he can see me again. He's very severe. I say yes.
I fall down the steps I'm so drunk. He asks me if I intend to drive
myself home. I'm going to drive myself to the ocean so I can go
swimming I'm rich do whatever I want he lifts me up puts me in
my car drives me home I end up fucking him quickly then his wife
comes I never see him again, I'm lying in my bed with my older
sister who's very "I'll take care of you" severe type and whom I
love. As we're fucking, her boyfriend enters the room and stops
us because we're not supposed to act soooo

Last night I dreamt I was standing on a low rise of grassy ground;
Dan was standing next to me facing me. He put his arms around my
neck kissed me, said "I love you." I said "I love you." Two years
later I'm riding through a forest with my four youngest sisters,
green and wet, leaves in our eyes and skin; we push leaves out of
the way the brown horse's neck lowered. My next-to-youngest sister
tells me Dan asked her to marry him two months ago. I'm galloping
wildly through the woods branches tear at my eyes flakes of my skin
hanging. I try to go faster and faster. It's night. Three days later I
appear, night, the livingroom of my parents' house: we're moving
to Boston, a bayview overlooking a black sky, where I go to college.
The skin of my face is torn; bruises over my naked arms; one of my
eyes is bloodshot. My family's glad I haven't died. My father greets
me, then my older sister who's tall, blonde, beautiful, intelligent.
We love each other most. The room in which we're standing is large
browns on browns; my parents are rich, not very rich, and liberals.
A thin dark-haired man asks me if I want to go to a party. I want
to: I rush upstairs to dress: my sister and the man, who's a close
family friend, look happy because I'm not going to kill myself. I
(outside the dream) look at myself (inside the dream): I'm tall and
thin, short waving black hair: I'm not beautiful until you look at

me for a long time. I'm very severe. When we walk into a large
grey-white house, we realize the party's an artist party. The tall,
dark, handsome artist walks over to me and asks me to dance. I
wonder if he's asking me because he wants to marry a rich girl. He
tells me he's a successful artist makes a lot of money. We dance,
dance out to a dark balcony; he starts to take off my black dress as
I lean over the portico. I've got two glasses of champagne: one in
each hand. He says "I could strangle you like this" I get pissed and
walk away. As I begin to walk away, I see Dan and some woman on
the balcony: Dan walks over to the man I'm with. They greet each
other: Dan admires the stranger's work. I nod hello to Dan. He
announces he's getting married: introduces the woman with whom
he's going to get married. I walk away to get more champagne. As
I return to the balcony, a blonde woman walks up to the group
the stranger says "I didn't know you wanted to come here." He
introduces his wife to us. I'm going crazy but withstraining myself
admirably. If I don't fuck someone soon know someone wants me,
I'll have to ride my horse for three days again: do something wilder.
I can't stop myself. I get another drink. My sister who's also drunk
asks me to dance, she's wearing a low grey gown; we dance in each
other's arms giggling. I lie close in her arms: I lie backwards over
her left arm. We're leaning against a grey wall under a picture:
she kisses me, as she looks down on me I wonder if she now feel
sexually toward me I'm excited, I ask her and she says she'd like to
fuck me. I look up at her and kiss her: I want us to fuck in front of
all these creepy people. Her thin dark-haired boyfriend comes over
tells us we can't act too wildly: do what we want in our bedroom.
Mel someone walks up to us says "I'm the only man here who isn't
married or about to be married" meaning I might as well fuck him
because I'm so desperate. I ask him to marry me since I have a lot of
money: I'll support him. I tell him how much money I have. He says
"Yes." I tell him to go shit on himself. I'm in a lousy mood. An old
friend of mine comes up to me, who I haven't seen for a few months.
I tell him I need someone's shoulder to cry on. His new lover comes
up to him: he can't do anything. This dream's repulsively hetero.
I get a bottle of champagne and drink it. I have to ride my horse
through the dark forest, the winds swirling around. I rush out of
the party. As I'm descending the wide wood steps, I turn around,
see the tall dark artist. He asks if he can see me again. He's very
severe. I say yes. I fall down the steps I'm so drunk. He asks me

if I intend to drive myself home. I'm going to drive myself to the ocean so I can go swimming I'm rich do whatever I want he lifts me up puts me in my car drives me home I end up fucking him quickly then his wife comes I see him again, I'm lying in my bed with my older sister who's very "I'll take care of you" severe type and whom I love. As we're fucking, her boyfriend enters the room and stops us because we're not supposed to act soooo

FROM CRASH

J. G. Ballard

I

The harsh blue lights of police cars revolved within my mind during the next three weeks as I lay in an empty ward of the casualty hospital near London Airport. In this quiet terrain of used-car marts, water reservoirs and remand centres, surrounded by the motorway systems that served London Airport, I began my recovery from the accident. Two wards of twenty-four beds – the maximum number of survivors anticipated – were permanently reserved for the possible victims of an air-crash. One of these was temporarily occupied by car-crash injuries.

Not all the blood which covered me had belonged to the man I killed. The Asian doctors in the emergency theatre found that both my knee-caps had been fractured against the instrument panel. Long spurs of pain reached along the inner surface of my thighs into my groin, as if fine steel catheters were being drawn through the veins of my legs.

Three days after the first surgery on my knees I caught some minor hospital infection. I lay in the empty ward, taking up a bed that belonged by rights to an air-crash victim, and thinking in a disordered way about the wounds and pains he would feel. Around me, the empty beds contained a hundred histories of collision and bereavement, the translation of wounds through the violence of

aircraft and automobile crashes. Two nurses moved through the
ward, tidying the beds and radio headphones. These amiable young
women ministered within a cathedral of invisible wounds, their
burgeoning sexualities presiding over the most terrifying facial
and genital injuries.

As they adjusted the harness around my legs, I listened to
the aircraft rising from London Airport. The geometry of this
complex torture device seemed in some way related to the slopes
and contours of these young women's bodies. Who would be the
next tenant of this bed – some middle-aged bank cashier en route
to the Balearics, her head full of gin, pubis moistening towards
the bored widower seated beside her? After a runway accident
at London Airport her body would be marked for years by the
bruising of her abdomen against the seat belt stanchion. Each
time she slipped away to the lavatory of her provincial restaurant,
weakened bladder biting at a worn urethra, during each sex act with
her prostatic husband she would think of the few seconds before
her crash. Her injuries fixed for ever this imagined infidelity.

Did my wife, when she visited the ward each evening, ever
wonder what sexual errand had brought me to the Western Avenue
flyover? As she sat beside me, her shrewd eyes itemizing whatever
vital parts of her husband's anatomy were left to her, I was certain
that she read the answer to her unspoken questions in the scars
on my legs and chest.

The nurses hovered around me, carrying out their painful chores.
When they replaced the drainage tubes in my knees I tried not to
vomit back my sedative, strong enough to keep me quiet but not
to relieve the pain. Only their sharp tempers rallied me.

A young, blond-haired doctor with a callous face examined the
wounds on my chest. The skin was broken around the lower edge
of the sternum, where the horn boss had been driven upwards
by the collapsing engine compartment. A semi-circular bruise
marked my chest, a marbled rainbow running from one nipple
to the other. During the next week this rainbow moved through
a sequence of tone changes like the colour spectrum of automobile
varnishes. As I looked down at myself I realized that the precise
make and model-year of my car could have been reconstructed
by an automobile engineer from the pattern of my wounds. The
layout of the instrument panel, like the profile of the steering wheel
bruised into my chest, was inset on my knees and shin-bones. The

impact of the second collision between my body and the interior compartment of the car was defined in these wounds, like the contours of a woman's body remembered in the responding pressure of one's own skin for a few hours after a sexual act.

On the fourth day, for no evident reason, the anaesthetics were withdrawn. All morning I vomited into the enamel pail which a nurse held under my face. She stared at me with good-humoured but unmoved eyes. The cold rim of the kidney pail pressed against my cheek. Its porcelain surface was marked by a small thread of blood from some nameless previous user.

I leaned my forehead against the nurse's strong thigh as I vomited. Beside my bruised mouth her worn fingers contrasted strangely with her youthful skin. I found myself thinking of her natal cleft. When had she last washed this moist gulley? During my recovery, questions like this one obsessed me as I talked to the doctors and nurses. When had they last bathed their genitalia, did small grains of faecal matter still cling to their anuses as they prescribed some antibiotic for a streptococcal throat, did the odour of illicit sex acts infest their underwear as they drove home from the hospital, the traces of smegma and vaginal mucus on their hands marrying with the splashed engine coolant of unexpected car-crashes? I let a few threads of green bile leak into the pail, aware of the warm contours of the young woman's thighs. A seam of her gingham frock had been repaired with a few loops of black cotton. I stared at the loosening coils lying against the round surface of her left buttock. Their curvatures seemed as arbitrary and as meaningful as the wounds on my chest and legs.

This obsession with the sexual possibilities of everything around me had been jerked loose from my mind by the crash. I imagined the ward filled with convalescing air-disaster victims, each of their minds a brothel of images. The crash between our two cars was a model of some ultimate and yet undreamt sexual union. The injuries of still-to-be-admitted patients beckoned to me, an immense encyclopaedia of accessible dreams.

Catherine seemed well aware of these fantasies. During her first visits I had been in shock and she had made herself familiar with the layout and atmosphere of the hospital, exchanging good-humoured banter with the doctors. As a nurse carried away my vomit Catherine expertly pulled the metal table from the foot of the bed and unloaded on to it a clutch of magazines.

She sat down beside me, casting a brisk eye over my unshaven face and fretting hands.

I tried to smile at her. The stitches in the laceration across my scalp, a second hairline an inch to the left of the original, made it difficult for me to change my expression. In the shaving mirror the nurses held up to my face I resembled an alarmed contortionist, startled by his own deviant anatomy.

"I'm sorry." I took her hand. "I must look rather sunk in myself."

"You're fine," she said. "Absolutely. You're like someone's victim in Madame Tussaud's."

"Try to come tomorrow."

"I will." She touched my forehead, gingerly peering at the scalp wound. "I'll bring some make-up for you. I imagine the only cosmetic attention given to the patients here is at Ashford Mortuary."

I looked up at her more clearly. Her show of warmth and wifely concern pleasantly surprised me. The mental distance between my work at the television commercial studios in Shepperton and her own burgeoning career in the overseas tours section of Pan American had separated us more and more during the past years. Catherine was now taking flying lessons, and with one of her boyfriends had started a small air-tourist charter firm. All these activities she pursued with a single mind, deliberately marking out her independence and self-reliance as if staking her claim to a terrain that would later soar in value. I had reacted to all this like most husbands, quickly developing an extensive repertory of resigned attitudes. The small but determined drone of her light aircraft crossed the sky over our apartment house each weekend, a tocsin that sounded the note of our relationship.

The blond-haired doctor walked through the ward, nodding to Catherine. She turned away from me, her bare legs revealing her thighs as far as her plump pubis, shrewdly summing up the sexual potential of this young man. I noticed that she was dressed more for a smart lunch with an airline executive than to visit her husband in hospital. Later I learned that she had been badgered at the airport by police officers investigating the road-death. Clearly the accident and any possible manslaughter charges against me had made her something of a celebrity.

"This ward is reserved for air-crash victims," I told Catherine. "The beds are kept waiting."

"If I groundloop on Saturday you might wake up and find me next to you." Catherine peered at the deserted beds, presumably visualizing each imaginary injury. "You're getting out of bed tomorrow. They want you to walk." She looked down at me solicitously. "Poor man. Have you antagonized them in any way?"

I let this pass, but Catherine added, "The other man's wife is a doctor – Dr Helen Remington."

Crossing her legs, she began the business of lighting a cigarette, fumbling with an unfamiliar lighter. From which new lover had she borrowed this ugly machine, all too clearly a man's? Tooled from an aircraft cannon shell, it was more like a weapon. For years I had been able to spot Catherine's affairs within almost a few hours of her first sex act simply by glancing over any new physical or mental furniture – a sudden interest in some third-rate wine or film-maker, a different tack across the waters of aviation politics. Often I could guess the name of her latest lover long before she released it at the climax of our sexual acts. This teasing game she and I needed to play. As we lay together we would describe a complete amatory encounter, from the first chit-chat at an airline cocktail party to the sexual act itself. The climax of these games was the name of the illicit partner. Held back until the last moment, it would always produce the most exquisite orgasms for both of us. There were times when I felt that these affairs took place merely to provide the raw material for our sexual games.

Watching her cigarette smoke move away across the empty ward, I wondered with whom she spent the past few days. No doubt the thought that her husband had killed another man lent an unexpected dimension to their sex acts, presumably conducted on our bed in sight of the chromium telephone which had brought Catherine the first news of my accident. The elements of new technologies linked our affections.

Irritated by the aircraft noise, I sat up on one elbow. The bruises across my chest wall made it painful for me to breathe. Catherine peered down at me with a worried gaze, obviously concerned that I might die on the spot. She put the cigarette between my lips. I drew uncertainly on the geranium-flavoured smoke. The warm tip of the cigarette, stained with pink lipstick, carried with it the

unique taste of Catherine's body, a flavour I had forgotten in the
phenol-saturated odour of the hospital. Catherine reached for the
cigarette, but I held on to it like a child. The grease-smeared
tip reminded me of her nipples, liberally painted with lipstick,
which I would press against my face, arms and chest, secretly
imagining the imprints to be wounds. In a nightmare I had once
seen her giving birth to a devil's child, her swollen breasts spurting
liquid faeces.

A dark-haired student nurse came into the ward. Smiling at my
wife, she pulled back the bedclothes and dug the urine bottle from
between my legs. Inspecting its level, she flipped back the sheets.
Immediately my penis began to dribble; with an effort I controlled
the sphincter, numbed by the long succession of anaesthetics.
Lying there with a weak bladder, I wondered why, after this
tragic accident involving the death of an unknown young man –
his identity, despite the questions I asked Catherine, remained an
enigma to me, like an anonymous opponent killed in a pointless
duel – all these women around me seemed to attend only to my
most infantile zones. The nurses who emptied my urinal and
worked my bowels with their enema contraption, who steered
my penis through the vent of my pyjama shorts and adjusted
the drainage tubes in my knees, who cleansed the pus from the
dressings on my scalp and wiped my mouth with their hard hands
– these starched women in all their roles reminded me of those who
attended my childhood, commissionaires guarding my orifices.

A student nurse moved around my bed, sly thighs under her
gingham, eyes fixed on Catherine's glamorous figure. Was she
calculating how many lovers Catherine had taken since the
accident, excited by the strange posture of her husband in
his bed, or – more banal – the cost of her expensive suit and
jewellery? By contrast, Catherine gazed frankly at this young girl's
body. Her assessment of the contours of thigh and buttock, breast
and armpit, and their relationship with the chromium bars of my
leg harness, an abstract sculpture designed to show off her slim
figure, was open and interested. An interesting lesbian streak ran
through Catherine's mind. Often as we made love she asked me
to visualize her in intercourse with another woman – usually her
secretary Karen, an unsmiling girl with silver lipstick who spent
the entire office party before Christmas staring motionlessly at my
wife like a pointer in rut. Catherine often asked me how she could

allow herself to be seduced by Karen. She soon came up with the
suggestion that they visit a department store together, where she
would ask Karen's help in choosing various kinds of underwear.
I waited for them among the racks of nightdresses outside their
cubicle. Now and then I glanced through the curtains and
watched them together, their bodies and fingers involved in the
soft technology of Catherine's breasts and the brassières designed
to show them off to this or that advantage. Karen was touching
my wife with peculiar caresses, tapping her lightly with the tips
of her fingers, first upon the shoulders along the pink grooves
left by her underwear, then across her back, where the metal
clasps of her brassière had left a medallion of impressed skin,
and finally to the elastic-patterned grooves beneath Catherine's
breasts themselves. My wife stood through this in a trance-like
state, gabbling to herself in a low voice, as the tip of Karen's right
forefinger touched her nipple.

I thought of the bored glance which the assistant, a middle-aged
woman with the small face of a corrupt doll, had given me as the two
young women had left, flicking back the curtain as if some little sexual playlet had ended. In her expression was the clear assumption
that not only did I know what had been going on, and that these
booths were often used for these purposes, but that Catherine and
I would later exploit the experience for our own complex pleasures.
As I sat in the car beside my wife, my fingers moved across the
control panel, switching on the ignition, the direction indicator,
selecting the drive lever. I realized that I was almost exactly
modelling my responses to the car on the way in which Karen
had touched Catherine's body. Her sullen eroticism, the elegant
distance she placed between her fingertips and my wife's nipples,
were recapitulated in the distance between myself and the car.

Catherine's continuing erotic interest in her secretary seemed
an interest as much in the idea of making love to her as in the
physical pleasures of the sex act itself. Nonetheless, these pursuits
had begun to make all our relationships, both between ourselves
and with other people, more and more abstract. She soon became
unable to reach an orgasm without an elaborate fantasy of a lesbian
sex-act with Karen, of her clitoris being tongued, nipples erected,
anus caressed. These descriptions seemed to be a language in
search of objects, or even, perhaps, the beginnings of a new
sexuality divorced from any possible physical expression.

I assumed that she had at least once made love to Karen, but we had now reached the point where it no longer mattered, or had any reference to anything but a few square inches of vaginal mucosa, fingernails and bruised lips and nipples. Lying in my hospital ward, I watched Catherine summing up the student nurse's slim legs and strong buttocks, the deep-blue belt that outlined her waist and broad hips. I half expected Catherine to reach out and put her hand on this young woman's breast, or slip it under her short skirt, the edge of her palm sliding between the natal cleft into the sticky perineum. Far from giving a squeal of outrage, or even pleasure, the nurse would probably continue folding her hospital corner, unmoved by this sexual gesture, no more significant than the most commonplace spoken remark.

Catherine pulled a manila folder from her bag. I recognized the treatment of a television commercial I had prepared. For this high-budget film, a thirty-second commercial advertising Ford's entire new sports car range, we hoped to use one of a number of well-known actresses. On the afternoon of my accident I had attended a conference with Aida James, a freelance director we had brought in. By chance, one of the actresses, Elizabeth Taylor, was about to start work on a new feature film at Shepperton.

"Aida telephoned to say how sorry she was. Can you look at the treatment again? She's made a number of changes."

I waved the folder away, gazing at the reflection of myself in Catherine's hand-mirror. The severed nerve in my scalp had fractionally lowered my right eyebrow, a built-in eye-patch that seemed to conceal my new character from myself. This marked tilt was evident in everything around me. I stared at my pale, mannequin-like face, trying to read its lines. The smooth skin almost belonged to someone in a science-fiction film, stepping out of his capsule after an immense inward journey on to the overlit soil of an unfamiliar planet. At any moment the skies might slide . . .

On an impulse I asked, "Where's the car?"

"Outside – in the consultants' car-park."

"What?" I sat up on one elbow, trying to see through the window behind my bed. "*My* car, not yours." I had visualized it mounted as some kind of cautionary exhibit outside the operating theatres.

"It's a complete wreck. The police dragged it to the pound behind the station."

"Have you seen it?"

"The sergeant asked me to identify it. He didn't believe you'd got out alive." She crushed her cigarette. "I'm sorry for the other man – Dr Hamilton's husband."

I stared pointedly at the clock over the door, hoping that she would soon leave. This bogus commiseration over the dead man irritated me, merely an excuse for an exercise in moral gymnastics. The brusqueness of the young nurses was part of the same pantomime of regret. I had thought for hours about the dead man, visualizing the effects of his death on his wife and family. I had thought of his last moments alive, frantic milliseconds of pain and violence in which he had been catapulated from a pleasant domestic interlude into a concertina of metallized death. These feelings existed within my relationship with the dead man, within the reality of the wounds on my chest and legs, and within the unforgettable collisi‿n between my own body and the interior of my car. By comparison, Catherine's mock-grief was a mere stylization of a gesture – I waited for her to break into song, tap her forehead, touch every second temperature chart around the ward, switch on every fourth set of radio headphones.

At the same time, I knew that my feelings towards the dead man and his doctor wife were already overlaid by certain undefined hostilities, half-formed dreams of revenge.

Catherine watched me trying to catch my breath. I took her left hand and pressed it to my sternum. In her sophisticated eyes I was already becoming a kind of emotional cassette, taking my place with all those scenes of pain and violence that illuminated the margins of our lives – television newsreels of wars and student riots, natural disasters and police brutality which we vaguely watched on the colour TV set in our bedroom as we masturbated each other. This violence experienced at so many removes had become intimately associated with our sex acts. The beatings and burnings married in our minds with the delicious tremors of our erectile tissues, the spilt blood of students with the genital fluids that irrigated our fingers and mouths. Even my own pain as I lay in the hospital bed, while Catherine steered the glass urinal between my legs, painted fingernails pricking my penis, even the vagal flushes that seized at my chest seemed extensions of that real world of violence calmed and tamed within our television programmes and the pages of news magazines.

Catherine left me to rest, taking with her half the flowers she had brought. As the elder of the Asian doctors watched her from the doorway she hesitated at the foot of my bed, smiling at me with sudden warmth as if unsure whether she would ever see me again.

A nurse came into the ward with a bowl in one hand. She was a new recruit to the casualty section, a refined-looking woman in her late thirties. After a pleasant greeting, she drew back the bedclothes and began a careful examination of my dressings, her serious eyes following the bruised contours. I caught her attention once, but she stared back at me evenly, and went on with her work, steering her sponge around the central bandage that ran from the waistband between my legs. What was she thinking about – her husband's evening meal, her children's latest minor infection? Was she aware of the automobile components shadowed like contact prints in my skin and musculature? Perhaps she was wondering which model of the car I drove, guessing at the weight of the saloon, estimating the rake of the steering column.

"Which side do you want it?"

I looked down. She was holding my limp penis between thumb and forefinger, waiting for me to decide whether I wanted it to lie to right or left of the central bandage.

As I thought about this strange decision, the brief glimmer of my first erection since the accident stirred through the cavernosa of my penis, reflected in a slight release of tension in her neat fingers.

II

The traffic multiplied, concrete lanes moving laterally across the landscape. As Catherine and I drove from the coroner's inquest the flyovers overlaid one another like copulating giants, immense legs straddling each other's backs. A verdict of accidental death had been returned, without any show of interest or ceremony; no charges of manslaughter or negligent driving were brought against me by the police. After the inquest I let Catherine drive me to the airport. For half an hour I sat by the window in her office, looking down at the hundreds of cars in the parking lot. Their roofs formed a lake of metal. Catherine's secretary stood behind her shoulder, waiting for me to leave. As she handed Catherine's glasses to her I saw that she was wearing a white lipstick, presumably an ironic concession to this day of death.

Catherine walked me to the lobby. "James, you must go to the office – believe me, love, I'm trying to be helpful." She touched my right shoulder with a curious hand, as if searching for some new wound which had flowered there. During the inquest she had held my arm in a peculiar grip, frightened that I might be swept sideways out of the window.

Unwilling to haggle with the surly and baronial taxi-drivers only interested in taking London fares, I walked through the car-park opposite the air-freight building. Overhead, across the metallized air, a jet-liner screamed. When the aircraft had passed I raised my head and saw Dr Helen Remington moving among the cars a hundred yards to my right.

At the inquest I had been unable to take my eyes away from the scar on her face. I watched her walk calmly through the lines of cars towards the entrance of the immigration department. Her strong jaw was held at a jaunty angle, her face turned away from me as if she were ostentatiously blotting out all traces of my existence. At the same time I had the strong impression that she was completely lost.

A week after the inquest she was waiting at the taxi rank of the Oceanic Terminal as I drove away from Catherine's office. I called to her and stopped behind an airline bus, beckoning her into the passenger seat. Swinging her handbag from a strong wrist, she came across to my car, recognizing me with a grimace.

As we headed towards Western Avenue she surveyed the traffic with frank interest. She had brushed her hair back from her face, openly wearing the fading scar-line.

"Where can I take you?"

"Can we drive a little?" she asked. "There's all this traffic – I like to look at it."

Was she trying to taunt me? I guessed that in her matter-of-fact way she was already assessing the possibilities I had revealed to her. From the concrete aprons of the parking lots and the roofs of the multi-storey car-parks she was now inspecting with a clear and unsentimental eye the technology which had brought about the death of her husband.

She began to chatter with contrived animation. "Yesterday I hired a taxi-driver to drive me around for an hour. 'Anywhere,' I said. We sat in a massive traffic jam near the underpass. I don't think we moved more than fifty yards. He wasn't in the least put out."

We drove along Western Avenue, the service buildings and perimeter fence of the airport on our left. I kept the car in the slow lane as the high deck of the flyover receded in the rear-view mirror. Helen talked about the second life she was already planning for herself.

"The Road Research Laboratory need a medical officer – the salary is larger, something I've got to think about now. There's a certain moral virtue in being materialistic."

"The Road Research Laboratory . . ." I repeated. The news-reels of simulated car-crashes were often shown in television documentaries; these mutilated machines were haunted by a strange pathos. "Isn't that rather too close . . .?"

"That's the point. Besides, I know I can give something now that I wasn't remotely aware of before. It's not a matter of duty so much as of commitment."

Fifteen minutes later, as we moved back towards the flyover, she came and sat beside me, watching my hands on the controls as we once again entered the collision course.

The same calm but curious gaze, as if she were still undecided how to make use of me, was fixed on my face shortly afterwards as I stopped the car on a deserted service road among the reservoirs to the west of the airport. When I put my arm around her shoulders she smiled briefly to herself, a nervous rictus of the upper lip which exposed her gold-tipped right incisor. I touched her mouth with my own, denting the waxy carapace of pastel lipcoat, watching her hand reach out to the chromium pillar of the quarter window. I pressed my lips against the bared and unmarked dentine of her upper teeth, fascinated by the movement of her fingers across the smooth chrome of the window pillar. Its surface was marked along its forward edge by a smear of blue paint left by some disaffected production-line worker. The nail of her forefinger scratched at this fretline, which rose diagonally from the window-sill at the same angle as the concrete ledge of the irrigation ditch ten feet from the car. In my eyes this parallax fused with the image of an abandoned car lying in the rust-stained grass on the lower slopes of the reservoir embankment. The brief avalanche of dissolving talc that fell across her eyes as I moved my lips across their lids contained all the melancholy of this derelict vehicle, its leaking engine oil and radiator coolant.

Six hundred yards behind us the traffic waited on the raised deck of the motorway, the afternoon sunlight crossing the windows of the airline buses and cars. My hand moved around the outer curvature of Helen's thighs, feeling the open zip of her dress. As these razor-like links cut my knuckles I felt her teeth across my ear. The sharpness of these pains reminded me of the bite of the windshield glass during my crash. She opened her legs and I began to stroke the nylon mesh that covered her pubis, a glamorous veil for the loins of this serious-minded woman doctor. Looking into her face, with its urgent mouth gasping as if trying to devour itself, I moved her hand around her breasts. She was now talking to herself, rambling away like some demented accident casualty. She lifted her right breast from her brassière, pressing my fingers against the hot nipple. I kissed each breast in turn, running my teeth across the erect nipples.

Seizing me with her body in this arbour of glass, metal and vinyl, Helen moved her hand inside my shirt, feeling for my nipples. I took her fingers and placed them around my penis. Through the rear-view mirror I saw a water-board maintenance truck approaching. It moved past in a roar of dust and diesel exhaust that drummed against the doors of my car. This surge of excitement drew the first semen to my penis. Ten minutes later, when the truck returned, the vibrating windows brought on my orgasm. Helen knelt across me, elbows pressed into the seat on either side of my head. I lay back, feeling the hot, scented vinyl. My hands pushed her skirt around her waist so that I could see the curve of her hips. I moved her slowly against me, pressing the shaft of my penis against her clitoris. Elements of her body, her square kneecaps below my elbows, her right breast jacked out of its brassière cup, the small ulcer that marked the lower arc of her nipple, were framed within the cabin of the car. As I pressed the head of my penis against the neck of her uterus, in which I could feel a dead machine, her cap, I looked at the cabin around me. This small space was crowded with angular control surfaces and rounded sections of human bodies interacting in unfamiliar junctions, like the first act of homosexual intercourse inside an Apollo capsule. The volumes of Helen's thighs pressing against my hips, her left fist buried in my shoulder, her mouth grasping at my own, the shape and moisture of her anus as I stroked it with my ring finger, were each overlaid by the inventories of a benevolent technology – the moulded binnacle of the instrument dials, the jutting carapace of the steering column shroud, the extravagant pistol grip of the handbrake. I felt the warm vinyl of the seat beside me, and then stroked the damp aisle of Helen's perineum. Her hand pressed against my right testicle. The plastic laminates around me, the colour of washed anthracite, were the same tones as her pubic hairs parted at the vestibule of her vulva. The passenger compartment enclosed us like a machine generating from our sexual act an homunculus of blood, semen and engine coolant. My finger moved into Helen's rectum, feeling the shaft of my penis within her vagina. These slender membranes, like the mucous septum of her nose which I touched with my tongue, were reflected in the glass dials of the instrument panel, the unbroken curve of the windshield.

Her mouth bit my left shoulder, blood marking my shirt like the imprint of a mouth. Without thinking, I struck the side of her head with the palm of my hand.

"I'm sorry!" she gasped into my face. "Please, don't move!" She steered my penis back into her vagina. Holding her buttocks with both hands, I moved rapidly towards my orgasm. Above me, Helen Remington's serious faced gazed down at me as if she were resuscitating a patient. The sheen of moisture on the skin around her mouth was like the bloom on a morning windshield. She pumped her buttocks rapidly, forcing her pubic bone against mine, then leaned back against the dashboard as a Land-Rover thudded past along the track, sending a cloud of dust against the windows.

She lifted herself off my penis when it had gone, letting the semen fall on to my crotch. She sat herself behind the steering wheel, holding the wet glans in her hand. She looked around the compartment of the car, as if speculating on any other uses to which she could put our sexual act. Lit by the afternoon sun, the fading scar on her face marked off these concealed motives like the secret frontier of an annexed territory. Thinking that I might reassure her in some way, I took her left breast from the brassière and began to stroke it, I gazed at the jewelled grotto of the instrument panel, at the jutting shroud of the steering assembly and the chromium heads of the control switches.

A police car appeared on the service road behind us, its white hull rolling heavily through the dips and ruts. Helen sat up and put away her breast with a deft hand. She dressed quickly, and began to remake her face in the mirror of her compact. As abrubtly as we has begun, she was now distanced from her own eager sexuality.

However, Helen Remington clearly felt no concern herself at these out-of-character actions, these sexual acts in the cramped compartment of my motor-car parked in various deserted service roads, culs-de-sac and midnight parkways. When I collected her during the following weeks from the house she had rented in Northolt, or waited for her in the reception lounge outside the airport immigration offices, it seemed incredible to me that I had any kind of sexual involvement with this sensitive woman doctor in her white coat, listening indulgently to the self-defeating arguments of some tubercular Pakistani.

Strangely, our sexual acts took place only within my automobile. In the large bedroom of her rented house I was unable even to mount an erection, and Helen herself would become argumentative and remote, talking endlessly about the more boring aspects of her work. Once together in my car, with the crowded traffic lanes through which we had moved forming an unseen and unseeing audience, we were able to arouse each other. Each time she revealed a growing tenderness towards myself and my body, even trying to allay my concern for her. In each sexual act together we recapitulated her husband's death, re-seeding the image of his body in her vagina in terms of the hundred perspectives of our mouth and thighs, nipples and tongues within the metal and vinyl compartment of the car.

I waited for Catherine to discover my frequent meetings with this lonely woman doctor, but to my surprise she showed only a cursory interest in Helen Remington. Catherine had rededicated herself to her marriage. Before my accident our sexual relationship was almost totally abstracted, maintained by a series of imaginary games and perversities. When she stepped out of bed in the

mornings she seemed like some efficient mechanic servicing
herself: a perfunctory shower; the night's urine discharged into the
lavatory pan; her cap extracted, regreased and once again inserted
(how and where did she make love during her lunch-hour, and with
which of the pilots and airline executives?); the news programme
played while she percolated the coffee . . .

All this had now passed, replaced by a small but growing
repertory of tenderness and affections. As she lay beside me,
willingly late for her office, I could bring myself to orgasm
simply by thinking of the car in which Dr Helen Remington
and I performed our sexual acts.

III

Were there any limits to Vaughan's irony? When I returned from
the bar he was leaning against the window-sill of the Lincoln,
rolling the last of four cigarettes with the hash kit kept in a
tobacco bag in the dashboard locker. Two sharp-faced airport
whores, barely older than schoolchildren, were arguing with him
through the window.

"Where the hell do you think you were going?" Vaughan took
from me the two wine bottles I had bought. He rolled the cigarettes
on to the instrument binnacle, then resumed his discussion with
the young women. They were arguing in an abstract way about
time and price. Trying to ignore their voices, and the massed
traffic moving below the supermarket, I watched the aircraft
taking off from London Airport across the western perimeter
fence, constellations of green and red lights that seemed to be
shifting about large pieces of the sky.

The two women peered into the car, sizing me up in a
one-second glance. The taller of the two, whom Vaughan had
already assigned to me, was a passive blonde with unintelligent
eyes focused three inches above my head. She pointed to me with
her plastic handbag.

"Can he drive?"

"Of course – a few drinks always make a car go better."

Vaughan twirled the wine bottles like dumb-bells, herding the
women into the car. As the second girl, with short black hair and

a boy's narrow-hipped body, opened the passenger door, Vaughan handed a bottle to her. Lifting her chin, he put his fingers in her mouth. He plucked out the knot of gum and flicked it away into the darkness. "Let's get rid of that – I don't want you blowing it up my urethra."

Adjusting myself to the unfamiliar controls, I started the engine and crossed the forecourt to the slip road. Above us, along Western Avenue, the traffic stream edged its way towards London Airport. Vaughan opened a wine bottle and passed it to the blonde sitting beside me in the front seat. He lit the first of the four cigarettes he had rolled. Already one elbow was between the dark-haired girl's thighs, raising her skirt to reveal her black crotch. He drew the cork from the second bottle and pressed the wet end against her white teeth. In the rear-view mirror I could see her avoiding Vaughan's mouth. She inhaled the cigarette smoke, her hand resting on Vaughan's groin. Vaughan lay back, inspecting her small features with a detached gaze, looking her body up and down like an acrobat calculating the traverses and impacts of a gymnastic feat involving a large amount of complex equipment. With his right hand he opened the zip of his trousers, then arched his hips forward to free his penis. The girl held it in one hand, the other steadying the wine bottle as I let the car surge away from the traffic lights. Vaughan unbuttoned her shirt with his scarred fingers and brought out her small breast. Examining the breast, Vaughan gripped the nipple between thumb and forefinger, extruding it forward in a peculiar manual hold, as if fitting together a piece of unusual laboratory equipment.

Brake-lights flared twenty yards ahead of me. Horns sounded from the line of cars in the rear. As their headlamps pulsed I moved the shift lever into drive and pressed the accelerator, jerking the car forward. Vaughan and the girl rolled back against the rear seat. The cabin was lit only by the instrument dials, and by the headlamps and tail-lights in the crowded traffic lanes around us. Vaughan had freed both the girl's breasts, nursing them with his palm. His scarred lips sucked at the thick smoke from the crumbling butt of the cigarette. He took the wine bottle and raised it to her mouth. As she drank he lifted her legs so that her heels rested on the seat, and began to move his penis against the skin of her thighs, drawing it first across the black vinyl and then pressing the glans against her heel and ankle bone, as if testing the possible continuity of these two materials before taking part in a sexual act involving both the car and this young woman. He lay against the rear seat, left arm stretched above the girl's head, embracing this slab of over-sprung black vinyl. His hand was raised at right-angles to his forearm, measuring out the geometry of the chromium roof sill, while his right hand moved down the girl's thighs and cupped her buttocks. Squatting there with her heels under her buttocks, the girl opened her thighs to expose her small pubic triangle, the labia open and protruded. Through the smoke lifting from the ashtray Vaughan studied the girl's body in a good-humoured way.

Beside him, the girl's small, serious face was lit by the headlamps of the cars creeping forwards in the traffic files. The damp, inhaled smoke of burnt resin filled the interior of the car. My head seemed to float on these fumes. Somewhere ahead, beyond these immense lines of nearly stationary vehicles, was the illuminated plateau of the airport, but I felt barely able to do more than point the large car along the centre lane. The blonde woman in the front seat offered me a drink from the wine bottle. When I declined she leaned her head against my shoulder, giving a playful touch to the steering wheel. I put my arm around her shoulder, aware of her hand on my thigh.

I waited until we stopped again, and adjusted the driving mirror so that I could see into the rear seat. Vaughan had moved his thumb into the girl's vagina, forefinger into her rectum, as she sat back with her knees against her shoulders, drawing mechanically at the second of the cigarettes.

His left hand took the girl's breast, his ring- and fore-fingers propping up the nipple like a miniature crutch. Holding these elements of the girl's body in his formalized pose, he began to rock his hips back and forth, driving his penis into the girl's hand. When she tried to move his fingers from her vulva Vaughan knocked her hand away with his elbow, holding the fingers securely in her body. He straightened his legs, rotating himself around the passenger compartment so that his hips rested on the edge of the seat. Braced on his left elbow, he continued to work himself against the girl's hand, as if taking part in a dance of severely stylized postures that celebrated the design and electronics, speed and direction of an advanced kind of automobile.

This marriage of sex and technology reached its climax as the traffic divided at the airport overpass and we began to move forwards in the northbound lane. As the car travelled for the first time at twenty miles an hour Vaughan drew his fingers from the girl's vulva and anus, rotated his hips and inserted his penis in her vagina. Headlamps flared above us as the stream of cars moved up the slope of the overpass. In the rear-view mirror I could still see Vaughan and the girl, their bodies lit by the car behind, reflected in the black trunk of the Lincoln and a hundred points of the interior trim. In the chromium ashtray I saw the girl's left breast and erect nipple. In the vinyl window gutter I saw deformed sections of Vaughan's thighs and her abdomen forming a bizarre anatomical junction. Vaughan lifted the young woman astride him, his penis entering her vagina again. In a triptych of images reflected in the speedometer, the clock and revolution counter, the sexual act between Vaughan and this young woman took place in the hooded grottoes of these luminescent dials, moderated by the surging needle of the speedometer. The jutting carapace of the instrument panel and the stylized sculpture of the steering column shroud reflected a dozen images of her rising and falling buttocks. As I propelled the car at fifty miles an hour along the open deck of the overpass Vaughan arched his back and lifted the young woman into the full glare of the headlamps behind us. Her sharp breasts flashed within the chromium and glass cage of the speeding car. Vaughan's strong pelvic spasms coincided with the thudding passage of the lamp standards anchored in the overpass at hundred-yard intervals. As each one approached his hips kicked into the girl, driving his penis into her vagina, his hands splaying her buttocks to reveal her anus as the yellow light filled the car. We reached the end of the overpass. The red glow of brake-lights burned the night air, touching the images of Vaughan and the young woman with a roseate light.

Controlling the car, I drove down the ramp towards the traffic junction. Vaughan changed the tempo of his pelvic motion, drawing the young woman on top of himself and extending her legs along his own. They lay diagonally across the rear seat, Vaughan taking first her left nipple in his mouth, then the right, his finger in her anus, stroking her rectum to the rhythm of the passing cars, matching his own movements to the play of light sweeping transversely across the roof of the car. I pushed away the blonde girl lying against my shoulder. I realized that I could almost control the sexual act behind me by the way in which I drove the car.

Playfully, Vaughan responded to different types of street furniture
and roadside trim. As we left London Airport, heading inwards
towards the city on the fast access roads, his rhythm became faster,
his hands under the girl's buttocks forcing her up and down as
if some scanning device in his brain was increasingly agitated by
the high office blocks. At the end of the orgasm he was almost
standing behind me in the car, legs outstretched, head against
the rear seat, hands propping up his own buttocks as he carried
the girl on his hips.

Half an hour later I had turned back to the airport and stopped
the car in the shadows of the multi-storey car-park facing the
Oceanic Terminal. The girl at last managed to pull herself from
Vaughan, who lay exhausted against the rear seat. Clumsily, she
reassembled herself, remonstrating with Vaughan and the drowsy
blonde in the front seat. Vaughan's semen ran down her left thigh
on to the black vinyl of the seat. The ivory globes searched for the
steepest gradient to the central sulcus of the seat.

I stepped from the car and paid the two women. When they had
gone, carrying their hard loins back to the neonlit concourses, I
waited beside the car. Vaughan was staring at the terraced cliff
of the car-park, his eyes following the canted floors, as if trying
to recognize everything that had passed between himself and the
dark-haired girl.

Later, Vaughan explored the possibilities of the car-crash in
the same calm and affectionate way that he had explored the
limits of that young prostitute's body. Often I watched him
lingering over the photographs of crash fatalities, gazing at their
burnt faces with a terrifying concern, as he calculated the most
elegant parameters of their injuries, the junctions of their wounded
bodies with the fractured windshield and instrument assemblies.
He would mimic these injuries in his own driving postures, turning
the same dispassionate eyes on the young women he picked up
near the airport. Using their bodies, he recapitulated the deformed
anatomies of vehicle crash victims, gently bending the arms of these
girls against their shoulders, pressing their knees against his own
chest, always curious to see their reactions.

THE AGE OF DESIRE

Clive Barker

THE BURNING MAN propelled himself down the steps of the Hume Laboratories as the police car – summoned, he presumed, by the alarm either Welles or Dance had set off upstairs – appeared at the gate and swung up the driveway. As he ran from the door the car screeched up to the steps and discharged its human cargo. He waited in the shadows, too exhausted by terror to run any further, certain that they would see him. But they disappeared through the swing doors without so much as a glance towards his torment. Am I on fire at all? he wondered. Was this horrifying spectacle – his flesh baptized with a polished flame that seared but failed to consume – simply an hallucination, for his eyes and his eyes only? If so, perhaps all that he had suffered up in the laboratory had also been delirium. Perhaps he had not truly committed the crimes he had fled from, the heat in his flesh licking him into ecstasies.

He looked down his body. His exposed skin still crawled with livid dots of fire, but one by one they were being extinguished. He was going out, he realized, like a neglected bonfire. The sensations that had suffused him – so intense and so demanding that they had been as like pain as pleasure – were finally deserting his nerve-endings, leaving a numbness for which he was grateful. His body, now appearing from beneath the veil of fire, was in a sorry condition. His skin was a panic-map of scratches, his clothes torn to shreds, his hands sticky with coagulating blood;

blood, he knew, that was not his own. There was no avoiding the bitter truth. He *had* done all he had imagined doing. Even now the officers would be staring down at his atrocious handiwork.

He crept away from his niche beside the door and down the driveway, keeping a lookout for the return of the two policemen; neither reappeared. The street beyond the gate was deserted. He started to run. He had managed only a few paces when the alarm in the building behind him was abruptly cut off. For several seconds his ears rang in sympathy with the silenced bell. Then, eerily, he began to hear the sound of heat – the surreptitious murmuring of embers – distant enough that he didn't panic, yet close as his heartbeat.

He limped on, to put as much distance as he could between him and his felonies before they were discovered; but however fast he ran, the heat went with him, safe in some backwater of his gut, threatening with every desperate step he took to ignite him afresh.

It took Dooley several seconds to identify the cacophony he was hearing from the upper floor now that McBride had hushed the alarm bell. It was the high-pitched chattering of monkeys, and it came from one of the many rooms down the corridor to his right.

"Virgil," he called down the stairwell. "Get up here."

Not waiting for his partner to join him, Dooley headed off towards the source of the din. Half-way along the corridor the smell of static and new carpeting gave way to a more pungent combination: urine, disinfectant and rotting fruit. Dooley slowed his advance: he didn't like the smell, any more than he liked the hysteria in the babble of monkey-voices. But McBride was slow in answering his call, and after a short hesitation, Dooley's curiosity got the better of his disquiet. Hand on truncheon, he approached the open door and stepped in. His appearance sparked off another wave of frenzy from the animals, a dozen or so rhesus monkeys. They threw themselves around in their cages, somersaulting, screeching and berating the wiremesh. Their excitement was infectious. Dooley could feel the sweat begin to squeeze from his pores.

"Is there anybody here?" he called out.

The only reply came from the prisoners: more hysteria, more

cage-rattling. He stared across the room at them. They stared back, their teeth bared in fear or welcome; Dooley didn't know which, nor did he wish to test their intentions. He kept well clear of the bench on which the cages were lined up as he began a perfunctory search of the laboratory.

"I wondered what the hell the smell was," McBride said, appearing at the door.

"Just animals," Dooley replied.

"Don't they ever wash? Filthy buggers."

"Anything downstairs?"

"Nope," McBride said, crossing to the cages. The monkeys met his advance with more gymnastics. "Just the alarm."

"Nothing up here either," Dooley said. He was about to add, *"Don't do that,"* to prevent his partner putting his finger to the mesh, but before the words were out one of the animals seized the proffered digit and bit it. McBride wrested his finger free and threw a blow back against the mesh in retaliation. Squealing its anger, the occupant flung its scrawny body about in a lunatic fandango that threatened to pitch cage and monkey alike on to the floor.

"You'll need a tetanus shot for that," Dooley commented.

"Shit!" said McBride, "what's wrong with the little bastard anyhow?"

"Maybe they don't like strangers."

"They're out of their tiny minds." McBride sucked ruminatively on his finger, then spat. "I mean, look at them."

Dooley didn't answer.

"I said, *look* . . ." McBride repeated.

Very quietly, Dooley said: "Over here."

"What is it?"

"Just come over here."

McBride drew his gaze from the row of cages and across the cluttered work-surfaces to where Dooley was staring at the ground, the look on his face one of fascinated revulsion. McBride neglected his finger-sucking and threaded his way amongst the benches and stools to where his partner stood.

"Under there," Dooley murmured.

On the scuffed floor at Dooley's feet was a woman's beige shoe; beneath the bench was the shoe's owner. To judge by her cramped position she had either been secreted there by the miscreant or had dragged herself out of sight and died in hiding.

"Is she dead?" McBride asked.

"Look at her, for Christ's sake," Dooley replied, "she's been torn open."

"We've got to check for vital signs," McBride reminded him. Dooley made no move to comply, so McBride squatted down in front of the victim and checked for a pulse at her ravaged neck. There was none. Her skin was still warm beneath his fingers however. A gloss of saliva on her cheek had not yet dried.

Dooley, calling his report through, looked down at the deceased. The worst of her wounds, on the upper torso, were masked by McBride's crouching body. All he could see was a fall of auburn hair and her legs, one foot shoeless, protruding from her hiding place. They were beautiful legs, he thought; he might have whistled after such legs, once upon a time.

"She's a Doctor or a technician," McBride said, "she's wearing a lab coat." Or she had been. In fact the coat had been ripped open, as had the layers of clothing beneath, and then, as if to complete the exhibition, the skin and muscle beneath that. McBride peered into her chest; the sternum had been snapped and the heart teased from its seat, as if her killer had wanted to take it as a keepsake and been interrupted in the act. He perused her without squeamishness; he had always prided himself on his strong stomach.

"Are you satisfied she's dead?"

"Never saw deader."

"Carnegie's coming down," Dooley said, crossing to one of the sinks. Careless of fingerprints, he turned on the tap and splashed a handful of cold water on to his face. When he looked up from his ablutions McBride had left off his tête-à-tête with the corpse and was walking down the laboratory towards a bank of machinery.

"What do they do here, for Christ's sake?" he remarked. "Look at all this stuff."

"Some kind of research faculty," Dooley said.

"What do they research?"

"How the hell do I know?" Dooley snapped. The ceaseless chatterings of the monkeys and the proximity of the dead woman, made him want to desert the place. "Let's leave it be, huh?"

McBride ignored Dooley's request; equipment fascinated him. He stared entranced at the encephalograph and electrocardiograph;

at the print-out units still disgorging yards of blank paper on to the floor; at the video display monitors and the consoles. The scene brought the *Marie Celeste* to his mind. This deserted ship of science – still humming some tuneless song to itself as it sailed on, though there was neither Captain nor crew left behind to attend upon it.

Beyond the wall of equipment was a window, no more than a yard square. McBride had assumed it led on to the exterior of the building, but now that he looked more closely he realized it did not. A test-chamber lay beyond the banked units.

'Dooley . . .?" he said, glancing round. The man had gone, however, down to meet Carnegie presumably. Content to be left to his exploration, McBride returned his attention to the window. There was no light on inside. Curious, he walked around the back of the banked equipment, until he found the chamber door. It was ajar. Without hesitation, he stepped through.

Most of the light through the window was blocked by the instruments on the other side; the interior was dark. It took McBride's eyes a few seconds to get a true impression of the chaos the chamber contained: the overturned table; the chair of which somebody had made matchwood; the tangle of cables and demolished equipment – cameras, perhaps, to monitor proceedings in the chamber? – clusters of lights which had been similarly smashed. No professional vandal could have made a more thorough job of breaking up the chamber than had been made.

There was a smell in the air which McBride recognized but, irritatingly, couldn't place. He stood still, tantalized by the scent. The sound of sirens rose from down the corridor outside; Carnegie would be here in moments. Suddenly, the smell's association came to him. It was the same scent that twitched in his nostrils when, after making love to Jessica and – as was his ritual – washing himself, he returned from the bathroom to the bedroom. It was the smell of sex. He smiled.

His face was still registering pleasure when a heavy object sliced through the air and met his nose. He felt the cartilage give, and a rush of blood come. He took two or three giddy steps backwards, thereby avoiding the subsequent slice, but lost his footing in the disarray. He fell awkwardly in a litter of glass shards, and looked up to see his assailant, wielding a metal bar, moving towards him. The man's face resembled one of the monkeys: the same yellowed teeth, the same rabid eyes. "*No!*" the man shouted, as he brought

his makeshift club down on McBride, who managed to ward off
the blow with his arm, snatching at the weapon in so doing. The
attack had taken him unawares but now, with the pain in his
mashed nose to add fury to his response, he was more than
the equal of the aggressor. He plucked the club from the man,
sweets from a babe, and leapt, roaring, to his feet. Any precepts
he might once have been taught about arrest techniques had fled
from his mind. He lay a hail of blows on the man's head and
shoulders, forcing him backwards across the chamber. The man
cowered beneath the assault, and eventually slumped, whimpering,
against the wall. Only now, with his antagonist abused to the verge
of unconsciousness, did McBride's furore falter. He stood in the
middle of the chamber, gasping for breath, and watched the beaten
man slip down the wall. He had made a profound error. The
assailant, he now realized, was dressed in a white laboratory coat;
he was, as Dooley was irritatingly fond of saying, on the side of
the angels.

"Damn," said McBride, "shit, hell and damn."

The man's eyes flickered open, and he gazed up at McBride.
His grasp on consciousness was evidently tenuous, but a look
of recognition crossed his wide-browed, sombre face. Or rather,
recognition's absence.

"You're not him," he murmured.

"Who?" said McBride, realizing he might yet salvage his
reputation from this fiasco if he could squeeze a clue from the
witness. "Who did you think I was?"

The man opened his mouth, but no words emerged. Eager to
hear the testimony, McBride crouched beside him and said: "Who
did you think you were attacking?"

Again the mouth opened; again no audible words emerged.
McBride pressed his suit. "It's important," he said, "just tell me
who was here."

The man strove to voice his reply. McBride pressed his ear to
the trembling mouth.

"In a pig's eye," the man said, then passed out, leaving McBride
to curse his father, who'd bequeathed him a temper he was afraid
he would probably live to regret. But then, what was living for?

Inspector Carnegie was used to boredom. For every rare moment
of genuine discovery his professional life had furnished him with,

he had endured hour upon hour of waiting. For bodies to be photographed and examined, for lawyers to be bargained with and suspects intimidated. He had long ago given up attempting to fight this tide of *ennui* and, after his fashion, had learned the art of going with the flow. The processes of investigation could not be hurried; the wise man, he had come to appreciate, let the pathologists, the lawyers and all their tribes have their tardy way. All that mattered, in the fullness of time, was that the finger be pointed and that the guilty quake.

Now, with the clock on the laboratory wall reading twelve fifty-three a.m., and even the monkeys hushed in their cages, he sat at one of the benches and waited for Hendrix to finish his calculations. The surgeon consulted the thermometer, then stripped off his gloves like a second skin and threw them down on to the sheet on which the decreased lay. "It's always difficult," the Doctor said, "fixing time of death. She's lost less than three degrees. I'd say she's been dead under two hours."

"The officers arrived at a quarter to twelve," Carnegie said, "so she died maybe half an hour before that?"

"Something of that order."

"Was she put in there?" he asked, indicating the place beneath the bench.

"Oh certainly. There's no way she hid herself away. Not with those injuries. They're quite something, aren't they?"

Carnegie stared at Hendrix. The man had presumably seen hundreds of corpses, in every conceivable condition, but the enthusiasm in his pinched features was unqualified. Carnegie found that mystery more fascinating in its way than that of the dead woman and her slaughterer. How could anyone possibly enjoy taking the rectal temperature of a corpse? It confounded him. But the pleasure was there, gleaming in the man's eyes.

"Motive?" Carnegie asked.

"Pretty explicit, isn't it? Rape. There's been very thorough molestation; contusions around the vagina; copious semen deposits. Plenty to work with."

"And the wounds on her torso?"

"Ragged. Tears more than cuts."

"Weapon?"

"Don't know." Hendrix made an inverted U of his mouth. "I

---

mean, the flesh has been *mauled*. If it weren't for the rape evidence I'd be tempted to suggest an animal."

"Dog, you mean?"

"I was thinking more of a tiger," Hendrix said.

Carnegie frowned. "Tiger?"

"Joke," Hendrix replied, "I was making a joke, Carnegie. My Christ, do you have *any* sense of irony?"

"This isn't funny," Carnegie said.

"I'm not laughing," Hendrix replied, with a sour look.

"The man McBride found in the test-chamber?"

"What about him?"

"Suspect?"

"Not in a thousand years. We're looking for a *maniac*, Carnegie. Big; strong. Wild."

"And the wounding? Before or after?"

Hendrix scowled. "I don't know. Post-mortem will give us more. But for what it's worth, I think our man was in a frenzy. I'd say the wounding and the rape were probably simultaneous."

Carnegie's normally phlegmatic features registered something close to shock. "Simultaneous?"

Hendrix shrugged. "Lust's a funny thing," he said.

"Hilarious," came the appalled reply.

As was his wont, Carnegie had his driver deposit him half a mile from his doorstep to allow him a head-clearing walk before home, hot chocolate and slumber. The ritual was observed religiously, even when the Inspector was dog-tired. He used to stroll to wind down before stepping over the threshold; long experience had taught him that taking his professional concerns into the house assisted neither the investigation nor his domestic life. He had learned the lesson too late to keep his wife from leaving him and his children from estrangement, but he applied the principle still.

Tonight, he walked slowly, to allow the distressing scenes the evening had brought to recede somewhat. The route took him past a small cinema which, he had read in the local press, was soon to be demolished. He was not surprised. Though he was no cineaste the fare the flea-pit provided had degenerated in recent years. The week's offering was a case in point: a double-bill of horror movies. Lurid and derivative stuff to judge by the posters, with their crude graphics and their unashamed hyperbole. '*You May Never Sleep*

Again!' one of the hook-lines read; and beneath it a woman –
very much awake – cowered in the shadow of a two-headed man.
What trivial images the populists conjured to stir some fear in their
audiences. The walking dead; nature grown vast, and rampant in a
miniature world; blood-eaters, omens, fire-walkers, thunderstorms
and all the other foolishness the public cowered before. It was
all so laughably trite: amongst that catalogue of penny dreadfuls
there wasn't one that equalled the banality of human appetite,
which horror (or the consequences of same) he saw every week
of his working life. Thinking of it, his mind thumbed through a
dozen snapshots: the dead by torchlight, face down and thrashed
to oblivion; and the living too, meeting his mind's eye with hunger
in theirs: for sex, for narcotics, for others' pain. Why didn't they
put *that* on the posters?

As he reached his home a child squealed in the shadows beside
his garage; the cry stopped him in his tracks. It came again, and
this time he recognized it for what it was. No child at all, but a
cat, or cats, exchanging love-calls in the darkened passageway. He
went to the place to shoo them off. Their venereal secretions made
the passage stink. He didn't need to yell; his footfall was sufficient
to scare them away. They darted in all directions, not two, but half
a dozen of them: a veritable orgy had been underway apparently.
He had arrived on the spot too late however; the stench of their
seductions was overpowering.

Carnegie looked blankly at the elaborate set-up of monitors and
video-recorders that dominated his office.

"What in Christ's name is this about?" he wanted to know.

"The video tapes," said Boyle, his number two, "from the
laboratory. I think you ought to have a look at them. Sir."

Though they had worked in tandem for seven months, Boyle
was not one of Carnegie's favourite officers; you could practically
smell the ambition off his smooth hide. In someone half his age
again such greed would have been objectionable; in a man of thirty
it verged on the obscene. This present display – the mustering of
equipment ready to confront Carnegie when he walked in at eight
in the morning – was just Boyle's style: flashy and redundant.

"Why so many screens?" Carnegie asked acidly. "Do I get it in
stereo too?"

"They had three cameras running simultaneously, sir. Covering
the experiment from several angles."

"*What* experiment?"

Boyle gestured for his superior to sit down. Obsequious to a fault, aren't you, thought Carnegie; much good it'll do you.

"Right," Boyle instructed the technician at the recorders, "roll the tapes."

Carnegie sipped at the cup of hot chocolate he had brought in with him. The beverage was a weakness of his, verging on addiction. On the days when the machine supplying it broke down he was an unhappy man indeed. He looked at the three screens. Suddenly, a title.

"*Project Blind Boy*", the words read, "*Restricted*."

"*Blind Boy?*" said Carnegie. "What, or *who*, is that?"

"It's obviously a code word of some kind," Boyle said.

"*Blind Boy. Blind Boy.*" Carnegie repeated the phrase as if to beat it into submission, but before he could solve the problem the images on the three monitors diverged. They pictured the same subject – a bespectacled male in his late twenties sitting in a chair – but each showed the scene from a different angle. One took in the subject full length, and in profile; the second was a three-quarter medium shot, angled from above; the third a straight forward close up of the subject's head and shoulders, shot through the glass of the test-chamber, and from the front. The three images were in black and white, and none were completely centred or focused. Indeed, as the tapes began to run, somebody was still adjusting such technicalities. A backwash of informal chatter ran between the subject and the woman – recognizable even in brief glimpses as the deceased – who was applying electrodes to his forehead. Much of the talk between them was difficult to catch; the acoustics in the chamber frustrated microphone and listener alike.

"The woman's Doctor Dance," Boyle offered. "The victim."

"Yes," said Carnegie, watching the screens intently, "I recognize her. How long does this preparation go on for?"

"Quite a while. Most of it's unedifying."

"Well, get to the edifying stuff, then."

"Fast forward," Boyle said. The technician obliged, and the actors on the three screens became squeaking comedians. "Wait!" said Boyle. "Back up a short way." Again, the technician did as instructed. "There!" said Boyle. "Stop there. Now run on at normal speed." The action settled back to its natural pace. "This is where it really begins, sir."

Carnegie had come to the end of his hot chocolate; he put his finger into the soft sludge at the bottom of the cup, delivering the sickly-sweet dregs to his tongue. On the screens Doctor Dance had approached the subject with a syringe, was now swabbing the crook of his elbow, and injecting him. Not for the first time since his visit to the Hume Laboratories did Carnegie wonder precisely what they did at the establishment. Was this kind of procedure *de rigueur* in pharmaceutical research? The implicit secrecy of experiment – late at night in an otherwise deserted building – suggested not. And there was that imperative on the title-card – *"Restricted"*. What they were watching had clearly never been intended for public viewing.

"Are you comfortable?" a man, off camera, now enquired. The subject nodded. His glasses had been removed, and he looked slightly bemused without them. An unremarkable face, thought Carnegie; the subject – as yet unnamed – was neither Adonis nor Quasimodo. He was receding slightly, and his wispy, dirty blond hair touched his shoulders.

"I'm fine, Doctor Welles," he replied to the off-camera questioner.

"You don't feel hot at all? Sweaty?"

"Not really," the guinea-pig replied, slightly apologetically. "I feel ordinary."

That you are, Carnegie thought; then to Boyle: "Have you been through the tapes to the end?"

"No, sir," Boyle replied. "I thought you'd want to see them first. I only ran them as far as the injection."

"Any word from the hospital on Doctor Welles?"

"At the last call he was still comatose."

Carnegie grunted, and returned his attention to the screens. Following the burst of action with the injection, the tapes now settled into non-activity: the three cameras fixed on their short-sighted subject with beady stares, the torpor occasionally interrupted by an enquiry from Welles as to the subject's condition. It remained the same. After three or four minutes of this eventless study even his occasional blinks began to assume major dramatic significance.

"Don't think much of the plot," the technician commented. Carnegie laughed; Boyle looked discomforted. Two or three more minutes passed in a similar manner.

"This doesn't look too hopeful," Carnegie said. "Run through it at speed, will you?"

The technician was about to obey when Boyle said: "*What*."

Carnegie glanced across at the man, irritated by his intervention, and then back at the screens. Something *was* happening: a subtle transformation had overtaken the insipid features of the subject. He had begun to smile to himself, and was sinking down in his chair as if submerging his gangling body in a warm bath. His eyes, which had so far expressed little but affable indifference, now began to flicker closed, and then, once closed, opened again. When they did so there was a quality in them not previously visible: a hunger that seemed to reach out from the screen and into the calm of the Inspector's office.

Carnegie put down his chocolate cup and approached the screens. As he did so the subject also got up out of his chair and walked towards the glass of the chamber, leaving two of the cameras' ranges. The third still recorded him however, as he pressed his face against the window, and for a moment the two men faced each other through layers of glass and time, seemingly meeting each other's gaze.

The look on the man's face was critical now, the hunger was rapidly outgrowing sane control. Eyes burning, he laid his lips against the chamber window and kissed it, his tongue working against the glass.

"What in Christ's name is going on?" Carnegie said.

A prattle of voices had begun on the soundtrack; Doctor Welles was vainly asking the testee to articulate his feelings, whilde Dance called off figures from the various monitoring instruments. It was difficult to hear much clearly – the din was further supplemented by an eruption of chatter from the caged monkeys – but it was evident that the readings coming through from the man's body were escalating. His face was flushed; his skin gleamed with a sudden sweat. He resembled a martyr with the tinder at his feet freshly lit; wild with a fatal ecstasy. He stopped french-kissing the window, tearing off the electrodes at his temples and the sensors from his arms and chest. Dance, her voice now registering alarm, called out for him to stop. Then she moved across the camera's view and out again; crossing, Carnegie presumed, to the chamber door.

"Better not," he said, as if this drama were played out at his behest, and at a whim he could prevent the tragedy. But the woman took no notice. A moment later she appeared in long shot as she stepped into the chamber. The man moved to greet her, throwing over equipment as he did so. She called out to him – his name, perhaps. If so, it was inaudible over the monkeys' hullabaloo. "Shit," said Carnegie, as the testee's flailing arms caught first the profile camera, and then the three-quarter medium shot: two of the three monitors went dead. Only the head-on shot, the camera safe outside the chamber, still recorded events, but the tightness of the shot precluded more than an occasional glimpse of a moving body. Instead, the camera's sober eye gazed on, almost ironically, at the saliva smeared glass of the chamber window, blind to the atrocities being committed a few feet out of range.

"What in Christ's name did they give him?" Carnegie said, as, somewhere off-camera, the woman's screams rose over the screeching of the apes.

Jerome woke in the early afternoon, feeling hungry and sore. When he threw the sheet off his body he was appalled at his state: his torso was scored with scratches, and his groin region was re-draw. Wincing, he moved to the edge of the bed and sat there for a while, trying to piece the previous evening back together again. He remembered going to the Laboratories, but very little after that. He had been a paid guinea-pig for several months, giving of his blood, comfort and patience to supplement his meagre earnings as a translator. The arrangement had begun courtesy of a friend who did similar work, but whereas Figley had been part of the Laboratories' mainstream programme, Jerome had been approached, after one week at the place, by Doctors Welles and Dance, who had invited him – subject to a series of psychological tests – to work exclusively for them. It had been made clear from the outset that their project (he had never even been told its purpose) was of a secret nature, and that they would demand his total dedication and discretion. He had needed the funds, and the recompense they offered was marginally better than that paid by the Laboratories, so he had agreed, although the hours they had demanded of him were unsociable. For several weeks now he had been required to attend the Research facility late at night and often working into the small hours of the morning as he endured Welles' interminable questions about his private life, and Dance's glassy stare.

Thinking of her cold look, he felt a tremor in him. Was it because once he had fooled himself that she had looked upon him more fondly than a doctor need? Such self-deception, he chided himself, was pitiful. He was not the stuff of which women dreamt, and each day he walked the streets reinforced that conviction. He could not remember one occasion in his adult life when a woman had looked his way, and kept looking; a time when an appreciative glance of his had been returned. Why this should bother him now, he wasn't certain: his loveless condition, was, he knew, commonplace. And Nature had been kind; knowing, it seemed, that the gift of allurement had passed him by, it had seen fit to minimize his libido. Weeks passed without his conscious thoughts mourning his enforced chastity.

Once in a while, when he heard the pipes roar, he might wonder what Mrs Morrisey, his landlady, looked like in her bath: might imagine the firmness of her soapy breasts, or the dark divide of her rump as she stooped to put talcum powder between her toes. But such torments were, blissfully, infrequent. And when his cup brimmed he would pocket the money he had saved from his sessions at the Laboratories, and buy an hour's companionship from a woman called Angela (he'd never learned her second name) in Greek Street.

It would be several weeks before he did so again, he thought: whatever he had done last night, or, more correctly, had done to him, the bruises alone had nearly crippled him. The only plausible explanation – though he couldn't recall any details – was that he'd been beaten up on the way back from the Laboratories; either that, or he'd stepped into a bar and somebody had picked a fight with him. It had happened before, on occasion. He had one of those faces that awoke the bully in drunkards.

He stood up and hobbled to the small bathroom adjoining his room. His glasses were missing from their normal spot beside the shaving mirror, and his reflection was woefully blurred, but it was apparent that his face was as badly scratched as the rest of his anatomy. And more: a clump of hair had been pulled out from above his left ear; clotted blood ran down to his neck. Painfully, he bent to the task of cleaning his wounds, then bathing them in a stinging solution of antiseptic. That done, he returned into his bedsitting-room to seek out his spectacles. But search as he might, he could not locate them. Cursing his idiocy, he rooted amongst his belongings for his old pair, and found them. Their prescription was out of date – his eyes had worsened considerably since he'd worn them – but they at least brought his surroundings into a dreamy kind of focus.

An indisputable melancholy had crept up on him, compounded of his pain and those unwelcome thoughts of Mrs Morrisey. To keep its intimacy at bay he turned on the radio. A sleek voice emerged, purveying the usual palliatives. Jerome had always had contempt for popular music and its apologists, but now, as he mooched around the small room, unwilling to clothe himself with chafing weaves when his scratches still pained him, the songs began to stir something other than scorn in him. It was as though he was hearing the words and music for the first time: as though all his life he had been deaf to their sentiments. Enthralled, he forgot his pain, and listened. The songs told one seamless and obsessive story: of love lost and found, only to be lost again. The lyricists filled the airwaves with metaphor – much of it ludicrous, but no less potent for that. Of paradise, of hearts on fire; of birds, bells, journeys, sunsets; of passion as lunacy, as flight, as unimaginable treasure. The songs did not calm him with their fatuous sentiments; they flayed him, evoking, despite feeble rhyme and trite melody, a world bewitched by desire. He began to tremble. His eyes, strained (or so he reasoned) by the unfamiliar spectacles, began to delude him. It seemed as though he could see traces of light in his skin: sparks flying from the ends of his fingers.

He stared at his hands and arms; the illusion, far from retreating in the face of this scrutiny, increased. Beads of brightness, like the traces of fire in ash, began to climb through his veins, multiplying even as he watched. Curiously, he felt no distress. This burgeoning fire merely reflected the passion in the story the songs were telling him: love, they said, was in the air, round every corner, waiting to be found. He thought again of the widow Morrisey in the flat below him, going about her business, sighing, no doubt, as he had done; awaiting her hero. The more he thought of her the more inflamed he became. She would not reject him, of that the songs convinced him; or if she did he must press his case until (again, as the songs promised) she surrendered to him. Suddenly, at the thought of her surrender, the fire engulfed him. Laughing, he left the radio singing behind him, and made his way downstairs.

*   *   *

It had taken the best part of the morning to assemble a list
of testees employed at the Laboratories; Carnegie had sensed a
reluctance on the part of the establishment to open their files to
the investigation, despite the horror that had been committed on
its premises. Finally, just after noon, they had presented him with
a hastily assembled Who's Who of subjects, four and a half dozen
in *toto*, and their addresses. None, the offices claimed, matched the
description of Welles' testee. The Doctors, it was explained, had
been clearly using Laboratory facilities to work on private projects.
Though this was not encouraged, both had been senior researchers,
and allowed leeway on the matter. It was likely, therefore, that the
man Carnegie was seeking had never even been on the Laboratories'
payroll. Undaunted, Carnegie ordered a selection of photographs
taken off the video recording and had them distributed – with the
list of names and addresses – to his officers. From then on, it was
down to footwork and patience.

Leo Boyle ran his finger down the list of names he had been
given. "Another fourteen," he said. His driver grunted, and Boyle
glanced across at him. "You were McBride's partner, weren't you?"
he said.
"That's right," Dooley replied. "He's been suspended."
"Why?"
Dooley scowled. "Lacks finesse, does Virgil. Can't get the hang
of arrest technique."
Dooley drew the car to a halt.
"Is this it?" Boyle asked.
"You said number eighty. This is eighty. On the door. Eight.
Oh."
"I've got eyes."
Boyle got out of the car and made his way up the pathway. The
house was sizeable, and had been divided into flats: there were
several bells. He pressed for J. Tredgold – the name on his list
– and waited. Of the five houses they had so far visited, two had
been unoccupied and the residents of the other three had borne
no resemblance to the malefactor.
Boyle waited on the step a few seconds and then pressed the
bell again; a longer ring this time.
"Nobody in," Dooley said from the pavement.
"Looks like it." Even as he spoke Boyle caught sight of a figure

flitting across the hallway, its outline distorted by the cobblestone glass in the door. "Wait a minute," he said.

"What is it?"

"Somebody's in there and not answering." He pressed the first bell again, and then the others. Dooley approached up the pathway, flitting away an over-attentive wasp.

"You sure?" he said.

"I saw somebody in there."

"Press the other bells," Dooley suggested.

"I already did. There's somebody in there and they don't want to come to the door." He rapped on the glass. "Open up," he announced. "Police."

Clever, thought Dooley; why not a loud-hailer, so Heaven knows too? When the door, predictably, remained unanswered, Boyle turned to Dooley. "Is there a side gate?"

"Yes, sir."

"Then get round the back, pronto, before he's away."

"Shouldn't we call –?"

"Do it! I'll keep watch here. If you can get in the back come through and open the front door."

Dooley moved; leaving Boyle alone at the front door. He rang the series of bells again, and, cupping his hand to his brow, put his face to the glass. There was no sign of movement in the hallway; was it possible that the bird had already flown? He backed down the path and stared up at the windows; they stared back vacuously. Ample time had now passed for Dooley to get round the back of the house; but so far he had neither reappeared nor called. Stymied where he stood, and nervous that his tactics had lost them their quarry, Boyle decided to follow his nose around the back of the house.

The side gate had been left open by Dooley. Boyle advanced up the side passage, glancing through a window into an empty living-room before heading round the back door. It was open. Dooley, however, was not in sight. Boyle pocketed the photograph and the list, and stepped inside, loath to the call Dooley's name for fear it alert any felon to his presence, yet nervous of the silence. Cautious as a cat on broken glass he crept through the flat, but each room was deserted. At the flat door, which let on to the hallway in which he had first seen the figure, he paused. Where had Dooley gone? The man had apparently disappeared from sight.

Then, a groan from beyond the door.

"Dooley?" Boyle ventured. Another groan. He stepped into the hallway. Three more doors presented themselves, all were closed; other flats, presumably, or bedsitting rooms. On the coconut mat at the front door lay Dooley's truncheon, dropped there as if its owner had been in the process of making his escape. Boyle swallowed his fear and walked into the body of the hall. The complaint came again, close by. He looked round and up the stairs. There, on the half-landing, lay Dooley. He was barely conscious. A rough attempt had been made to rip his clothes; large portions of his flabby lower anatomy were exposed.

"What's going on, Dooley?" Boyle asked, moving to the bottom of the stairs. The officer heard his voice and rolled himself over. His bleary eyes, settling on Boyle, opened in terror.

"It's all right," Boyle reassured him. "It's only me."

Too late, Boyle registered that Dooley's gaze wasn't fixed on *him* at all, but on some sight over his shoulder. As he pivoted on his heel to snatch a glance at Dooley's bugaboo a charging figure slammed into him. Winded and cursing, Boyle was thrown off his feet. He scrabbled about on the floor for several seconds before his attacker seized hold of him by jacket and hair and hauled him to his feet. He recognized at once the wild face that was thrust into his – the receding hair-line, the weak mouth, the *hunger* – but there was much too he had not anticipated. For one, the man was naked as a babe, though scarcely so modestly endowed. For another, he was clearly aroused to fever-pitch. If the beady eye at his groin, shining up at Boyle, were not evidence enough, the hands now tearing at his clothes made the assailant's intention perfectly apparent.

"Dooley!" Boyle shrieked as he was thrown across the hallway. "In Christ's name! Dooley!"

His pleas were silenced as he hit the opposite wall. The wild man was at his back in half a heartbeat, smearing Boyle's face against the wallpaper: birds and flowers, intertwined, filled his eyes. In desperation, Boyle fought back, but the man's passion lent him ungovernable strength. With one insolent hand holding the policeman's head, he tore at Boyle's trousers and underwear, leaving his buttocks exposed.

"God . . ." Boyle begged into the pattern of the wallpaper. "Please God, somebody help me . . ."; but the prayers were no more fruitful than his struggles. He was pinned against the wall like a butterfly spread on cork, about to be pierced through. He closed his eyes, tears of frustration running down his cheeks. The assailant left off his hold on Boyle's head and pressed his violation home. Boyle refused to cry out. The pain he felt was not the equal of his shame. Better perhaps that Dooley remained comatose; that this humiliation be done and finished with unwitnessed.

"Stop," he murmured into the wall, not to his attacker but to his body, urging it not to find pleasure in this outrage. But his nerve-endings were treacherous; they caught fire from the assault. Beneath the stabbing agony some unforgivable part of him rose to the occasion.

On the stairs, Dooley hauled himself to his feet. His lumbar region, which had been weak since a car accident the previous Christmas, had given out almost as soon as the wild man had sprung him in the hall. Now, as he descended the stairs, the least motion caused excruciating agonies. Crippled with pain, he stumbled to the bottom of the stairs and looked, amazed, across the hallway. Could this be Boyle – he the supercilious, he the rising man, being pummelled like a street-boy in need of dope money? The sight transfixed Dooley for several seconds before he unhinged his eyes and swung them down to the truncheon on the mat. He moved cautiously, but the wild man was too occupied with the deflowering to notice him.

Jerome was listening to Boyle's heart. It was a loud, seductive beat, and with every thrust into the man it seemed to get louder. He wanted it: the heat of it, the life of it. His hand moved round to Boyle's chest, and dug at the flesh.

"Give me your heart," he said. It was like a line from one of the songs.

Boyle screamed into the wall as his attacker mauled his chest. He'd seen photographs of the woman at the Laboratories; the open wound of her torso was lightning-clear in his mind's eye. Now the maniac intended the same atrocity. *Give me your heart.* Panicked to the ledge of his sanity he found new stamina, and began to fight afresh, reaching round and clawing at the man's torso: nothing – not even the bloody loss of hair from his scalp – broke the rhythm of his thrusts, however. In extremis, Boyle attempted to insinuate one of his hands between his body and the wall and reach between his legs to unman the bastard. As he did so, Dooley attacked, delivering a hail of truncheon blows upon the man's head. The diversion gave Boyle precious leeway. He pressed hard against the wall; the man, his grip on Boyle's chest slicked with blood, lost his hold. Again, Boyle pushed. This time, he managed to shrug the man off entirely. The bodies disengaged; Boyle turned, bleeding but in no danger, and watched Dooley follow the man across the hallway, beating at his greasy blond head. He made little attempt to protect himself however: his burning eyes (Boyle had never understood the physical accuracy of that image until now) were still on the object of his affections.

"Kill him!" Boyle said quietly, as the man grinned – grinned! – through the blows. "Break every bone in his body!"

Even if Dooley, hobbled as he was, had been in any fit state to obey the imperative, he had no chance to do so. His berating was interrupted by a voice from down the hallway. A woman had emerged from the flat Boyle had come through. She too had been a victim of this marauder, to judge by her state; but Dooley's entry into the house had clearly distracted her molester before he could do serious damage.

"Arrest him!" she said, pointing at the leering man. "He tried to rape me!"

Dooley closed in to take possession of the prisoner, but Jerome had other intentions. He put his hand in Dooley's face and pushed him back against the front door. The coconut mat slid from under him: he all but fell. By the time he'd regained his balance Jerome was up and away. Boyle made a wretched attempt to stop him, but the tatters of his trousers were wrapped about his lower legs and Jerome, fleet-footed, was soon half-way up the stairs.

"Call for help," Boyle ordered Dooley. "And make it quick."

Dooley nodded, and opened the front door.

"Is there any way out from upstairs?" Boyle demanded of Mrs Morrisey. She shook her head. "Then we've got the bastard trapped haven't we?" he said. "Go on, Dooley!" Dooley hobbled away down the path. "And you," he said to the woman, "fetch something in the way of weaponry. Anything solid." The woman nodded and returned the way she'd come, leaving Boyle slumped beside the open door. A soft breeze cooled the sweat on his face. At the car outside Dooley was calling up reinforcements.

All too soon, Boyle thought, the cars would be here, and the man upstairs would be hauled away to give his testimony. There would be no opportunity for revenge once he was in custody; the law would take its placid course, and he, the victim, would be only a by-stander. If he was ever to salvage the ruins of his manhood, *now* was the time. If he didn't – if he languished here, his bowels on fire – he would never shrug off the horror he felt at his body's betrayal. He must act now – must beat the grin off his ravisher's face once and for all – or else live in self-disgust until memory failed him.

The choice was no choice at all. Without further debate, he got up from his squatting position, and began up the stairs. As he reached the half-landing he realized he hadn't brought a weapon with him, he knew, however, that if he descended again he'd lose all momentum. Prepared, in that moment, to die if necessary, he headed on up.

There was only one door open on the top landing; through it came the sound of a radio. Downstairs, in the safety of the hall, he heard Dooley come in to tell him that the call had been made, only to break off in mid-announcement. Ignoring the distraction, Boyle stepped into the flat.

There was nobody there. It took Boyle a few moments only to check the kitchen, the tiny bathroom, and the living room: all were deserted. He returned to the bathroom, the window of which was open, and put his head out. The drop to the grass of the garden below was quite manageable. There was an imprint in the ground of the man's body. He had leapt. And gone.

Boyle cursed his tardiness, and hung his head. A trickle of heat ran down the inside of his leg. In the next room, the love-songs played on.

For Jerome, there was no forgetfulness, not this time. The encounter with Mrs Morrisey, which had been interrupted by Dooley, and the episode with Boyle that had followed, had all merely served to fan the fire in him. Now, by the light of those flames, he saw clearly what crimes he had committed. He remembered with horrible clarity the laboratory, the injection, the monkeys, the blood. The acts he recalled, however (and there were many), woke no sense of sinfulness in him. All moral consequence, all shame or remorse, was burned out by the fire that was even now licking his flesh to new enthusiasms.

He took refuge in a quiet cul-de-sac to make himself presentable. The clothes he had managed to snatch before making his escape were motley, but would serve to keep him from attracting unwelcome attention. As he buttoned himself up – his body seeming to strain from its covering as if resentful of being concealed – he tried to control the holocaust that raged between his ears. But the flames wouldn't be dampened. His every fibre seemed alive to the flux and flow of the world around him. The marshalled trees along the road, the wall at his back, the very paving stones beneath his bare feet were catching a spark from him, and burning now with their own fire. He grinned to see the conflagration spread. The world, in its every eager particular, grinned back.

Aroused beyond control, he turned to the wall he had been leaning against. The sun had fallen full upon it, and it was warm: the bricks smelt ambrosial. He laid kisses on their gritty faces, his hands exploring every nook and cranny. Murmuring sweet nothings, he unzipped himself, found an accommodating niche, and filled it. His mind was running with liquid pictures: mingled anatomies, female and male in one undistinguishable congress. Above him, even the clouds had caught fire; enthralled by their burning heads he felt the moment rise in his gristle. Breath was short now. But the ecstasy? Surely that would go on forever.

Without warning a spasm of pain travelled down his spine from cortex to testicles, and back again, convulsing him. His hands lost grip of the brick and he finished his agonizing climax on the air as he fell across the pavement. For several seconds he lay where he had collapsed, while the echoes of the initial spasm bounced back and forth along his spine, diminishing with each return. He could taste blood at the back of his throat; he wasn't certain if he'd bitten his lip or tongue, but he thought not. Above his head the birds circled on, rising lazily on a spiral of warm air. He watched the fire in the clouds gutter out.

He got to his feet and looked down at the coinage of semen he'd spent on the pavement. For a fragile instant he caught again a whiff of the vision he'd just had; imagined a marriage of his seed with the paving stone. What sublime children the world might boast, he thought, if he could only mate with brick or tree; he would gladly suffer the agonies of conception, if such miracles were possible. But the paving stone was unmoved by his seed's entreaties; the vision, like the fire above him, cooled and hid its glories.

He put his bloodied member away, and leaned against the wall, turning the strange events of his recent life over and over.

Something fundamental was changing in him, of that he had no doubt; the rapture that had possessed him (and would, no doubt, possess him again) was like nothing he had hitherto experienced. And whatever they had injected into his system it showed no signs of being discharged naturally; far from it. He could feel the heat in him still, as he had leaving the Laboratories; but this time the roar of its presence was louder than ever.

It was a new kind of life he was living, and the thought, though frightening, exulted him. Not once did it occur to his spinning, eroticized brain that this new kind of life would, in time, demand a new kind of death.

Carnegie had been warned by his superiors that results were expected; he was now passing the verbal beating he'd received to those under him. It was a line of humiliation, in which the greater was encouraged to kick the lesser man, and that man, in turn, his lesser.

Carnegie had sometimes wondered what the man at the end of the line took his ire out on; his dog presumably.

"This miscreant is still loose, gentlemen, despite his photograph in many of this morning's newspapers, and an operating method which is, to say the least, insolent. We *will* catch him, of course, but let's get the bastard before we have another murder on our hands —"

The phone rang. Boyle's replacement, Migeon, picked it up, while Carnegie concluded his pep-talk to the assembled officers.

"I want him in the next twenty-four hours, gentlemen. That's the time-scale I've been given, and that's what we've got. Twenty-four hours."

Migeon interrupted. "Sir? It's Johannson. He says he's got something for you. It's urgent."

"Right." The Inspector claimed the receiver. "Carnegie."

The voice at the other end was soft to the point of inaudibility. "Carnegie," Johannson said, "we've been right through the laboratory; dug up every piece of information we could find on Dance and Welles' tests —"

"And?"

"We've also analyzed traces of the agent from the hypo they used on the suspect. I think we've found the *Boy*, Carnegie."

"What boy?" Carnegie wanted to know; he found Johannson's obfuscation irritating.

"The *Blind Boy*, Carnegie."

"And?"

For some inexplicable reason Carnegie was certain the man *smiled* down the phone before replying: "I think perhaps you'd better come down and see for yourself. Sometime around noon suit you?"

Johannson could have been one of history's greatest poisoners: he had all the requisite qualifications. A tidy mind (poisoners were, in Carnegie's experience, domestic paragons), a patient nature (poison could take time), and, most importantly, an encyclopaedic knowledge of toxicology. Watching him at work, which Carnegie had done on two previous cases, was to see a subtle man at his subtle craft, and the spectacle made Carnegie's blood run cold.

Johannson had installed himself in the laboratory on the top floor, where Doctor Dance had been murdered, rather than use police facilities for the investigation, because, as he explained to Carnegie, much of the equipment the Hume organization boasted was simply not available elsewhere. His dominion over the place, accompanied by his two assistants had, however, transformed the laboratory from the clutter left by the experimenters, to a dream of order. Only the monkeys remained a constant. Try as he might Johannson could not control their behaviour.

"We didn't have much difficulty finding the drug used on your man," Johannson said, "we simply cross-checked traces remaining in the hypodermic with materials found in the room. In fact, they seem to have been manufacturing this stuff, or variations on the theme, for some time. The people here claim they know nothing about it, of course. I'm inclined to believe them. What the good doctors were doing here was, I'm sure, in the nature of a personal experiment."

"What sort of experiment?"

Johannson took off his spectacles and set about cleaning them with the tongue of his red tie. "At first, we thought they were developing some kind of hallucogen," he said. "In some regards the agent used on your man resembles a narcotic. In fact – methods apart – I think they made some very exciting discoveries. Developments which take us into entirely new territory."

"It's not a drug then?"

"Oh, yes, of course it's a drug," Johannson said, replacing the spectacles, "but one created for a very specific purpose. See for yourself."

Johannson led the way across the laboratory to the row of monkeys' cages. Instead of being confined separately, the toxicologist had seen fit to open the interconnecting doors between one cage and the next, allowing the animals free access to gather in groups. The consequence was absolutely plain: the animals were engaged in an elaborate series of sexual acts. Why, Carnegie wondered, did monkeys perpetually perform obscenities? It was the same torrid display whenever he'd taken his offspring, as children, to Regent's Park Zoo; the Ape Enclosure elicited one embarrassing question upon another. He'd stopped taking the children after a while. He simply found it too mortifying.

"Haven't they got anything better to do?" he asked of Johannson, glancing away and then back at a ménage à trois that was so intimate the eye could not ascribe member to monkey.

"Believe me," Johannson smirked, "this is mild by comparison with much of the behaviour we've seen from them since we gave them a shot of the agent. From that point on they neglected all normal behaviour patterns; they bypassed the arousal signals, the courtship rituals. They no longer show any interest in food. They don't sleep. They have become sexual obsessives. All other stimuli are forgotten. Unless the agent is naturally discharged, I suspect they are going to screw themselves to death."

Carnegie looked along the rest of the cages: the same pornographic scenes were being played out in each one. Mass-rape, homosexual liaisons, fervent and ecstatic masturbation.

"It's no wonder the Doctors made a secret project of their discovery," Johannson went on, "they were on to something that could have made them a fortune. An aphrodisiac that actually works."

"An aphrodisiac?"

"Most are useless, of course. Rhinoceros horn, live eels in cream sauce: symbolic stuff. They're designed to arouse by association."

Carnegie remembered the hunger in Jerome's eyes. It was echoed here, in the monkeys'. Hunger, and the desperation that hunger brings.

"And the ointments too, all useless. *Cantharis vesticatora* –"

"What's that?"

"You know the stuff as Spanish Fly, perhaps? It's a paste made from a beetle. Again, useless. At best these things are inflammatants. But this . . ." He picked up a phial of colourless fluid. "*This* is damn near genius."

"They don't look too happy with it to me."

"Oh, it's still crude," Johannson said. "I think the researchers were greedy, and moved into tests on living subjects a good two or three years before it was wise to do so. The stuff is almost lethal as it stands, no doubt of that. But it *could* be made to work, given time. You see, they've sidestepped the mechanical problems: this stuff operates directly on the sexual imagination, on the libido. If you arouse the *mind*, the body follows. That's the trick of it."

A rattling of the wire-mesh close by drew Carnegie's attention from Johannson's pale features. One of the female monkeys, apparently not satisfied with the attentions of several males, was spreadeagled against her cage, her nimble fingers reaching for Carnegie; her spouses, not to be left loveless, had taken to sodomy. "*Blind Boy?*" said Carnegie. "Is that Jerome?"

"It's Cupid, isn't it?" Johannson said: "'*Love looks not with the eyes but with the mind, And therefore is winged Cupid painted blind.*' It's *Midsummer Night's Dream.*"

"The Bard was never my strongest suit," said Carnegie. He went back to staring at the female monkey. "And Jerome?" he said.

"He has the agent in his system. A sizeable dose."

"So he's like this lot!"

I would presume – his intellectual capacities being greater – that the agent may not be able to work in quite such an *unfettered* fashion. But, having said that, sex can make monkeys out of the best of us, can't it?" Johannson allowed himself a half-smile at the notion. "All our so-called higher concerns become secondary to the pursuit. For a short time sex makes us obsessive; we can perform, or at least *think* we can perform, what with hindsight may seem extraordinary feats."

"I don't think there's anything so extraordinary about rape," Carnegie commented, attempting to stem Johannson's rhapsody. But the other man would not be subdued.

"Sex without end, without compromise or apology," he said. "Imagine it. The dream of Casanova."

The world had seen so many Ages. The Age of Enlightenment; of Reformation; of Reason. Now, at last, the Age of Desire. And after this, an end to Ages; an end, perhaps, to everything. For the fires that were being stoked now were fiercer than the innocent world suspected. They were terrible fires, fires without end, which would illuminate the world in one last, fierce light.

So Welles thought, as he lay in his bed. He had been conscious for several hours, but had chosen not to signify such. Whenever a nurse came to his room he would clamp his eyes closed and slow the rhythm of his breath. He knew he could not keep the illusion up for long, but the hours gave him a while to think through his itinerary from here. His first move had to be back to the Laboratories; there were papers there he had to shred; tapes to wipe clean. From now on he was determined that every scrap of information about *Project Blind Boy* exist solely in his head. That way he would have complete control over his masterwork, and nobody could claim it from him.

He had never had much interest in making money from the discovery, although he was well aware of how lucrative a workable aphrodisiac would be; he had never given a fig for material wealth. His initial motivation for the development of the drug – which they had chanced upon quite by accident while testing an agent to aid schizophrenics – had been investigative. But his motives had matured, through their months of secret work. He had come to think of himself as the bringer of the millenium. He would not have anyone attempt to snatch that sacred role from him.

So he thought, lying in his bed, waiting for a moment to slip away.

As he walked the streets Jerome would have happily yea-said Welles' vision. Perhaps he, of all men, was most eager to welcome the Age of Desire. He saw its portents everywhere. On advertising hoardings and cinema bill-boards, in shop-windows, on television screens: everywhere, the body as merchandise. Where flesh was not being used to market artifacts of steel and stone, those artifacts were taking on its properties. Automobiles passed him by with every voluptuous attribute but breath: their sinuous body-work

gleamed, their interiors invited, plushly; the buildings beleaguered
him with sexual puns. Spires; passageways; shadowed plazas with
white-water fountains. Beneath the raptures of the shallow – the
thousand trivial distractions he encountered in street and square
– he sensed the ripe life of the body informing every particular.

The spectacle kept the fire in him well-stoked; it was all that
will power could do to keep him from pressing his attentions on
every creature that he met eyes with. A few seemed to sense
the heat in him, and gave him wide berth. Dogs sensed it too.
Several followed him, aroused by *his* arousal. Flies orbited his
head in squadrons. But his growing ease with his condition gave
him some rudimentary control over it. He knew that to make a
public display of his ardour would bring the law down upon him,
and that in turn would hinder his adventures. Soon enough, the
fire that he had begun would spread: *then* he would emerge from
hiding and bathe in it freely. Until then, discretion was best.

He had on occasion bought the company of a young woman in
Soho; he went to find her now. The afternoon was stiflingly hot,
but he felt no weariness. He had not eaten since the previous
evening, but he felt no hunger. Indeed, as he climbed the narrow
stairway up to the room on the first floor which Angela had once
occupied, he felt as primed as an athlete, glowing with health. The
immaculately dressed and wall-eyed pimp who usually occupied a
place at the top of the stairs was absent. Jerome simply went to the
girl's room and knocked. There was no reply. He rapped again,
more urgently. The noise brought an early middle-aged woman to
the door at the end of the landing.

"What do you want?"

"The woman," he replied simply.

"Angela's gone. And you'd better get out of here too, in that
state. This isn't a doss-house."

"When will she be back?" he asked, keeping as tight a leash as
he could on his appetite.

The woman, who was as tall as Jerome and half as heavy again
as his wasted frame, advanced towards him. "The girl won't *be*
back," she said, "so you get the hell out of here, before I call
Isaiah."

Jerome looked at the woman; she shared Angela's profession,
no doubt, if not her youth or prettiness. He smiled at her. "I can
hear your heart," he said.

"I told you –'

Before she could finish the words Jerome moved down the landing towards her. She wasn't intimidated by his approach, merely repulsed.

"If I call Isaiah, you'll be sorry," she informed him. The pace of her heartbeat had risen, he could hear it.

"I'm burning," he said.

She frowned; she was clearly losing this battle of wits. "Stay away from me," she told. "I'm warning you."

The heartbeat was getting more rapid still. The rhythm, buried in her substance, drew him on. From that source: all life, all heat.

"Give me your heart," he said.

"Isaiah!"

Nobody came running at her shout, however. Jerome gave her no opportunity to cry out a second time. He reached to embrace her, clamping a hand over her mouth. She let fly a volley of blows against him, but the pain only fanned the flames. He was brighter by the moment: his every orifice let on to the furnace in belly and loins and head. Her superior bulk was of no advantage against such fervour. He pushed her against the wall – the beat of her heart loud in his ears – and began to apply kisses to her neck, tearing her dress open to free her breasts.

"Don't shout," he said, trying to sound persuasive. "There's no harm meant."

She shook her head, and said, "I won't," against his palm. He took his hand from her mouth, she dragged in several desperate breaths. Where was Isaiah? she thought. Not far, surely. Fearing for her life if she tried to resist this interloper – how his eyes shone! – she gave up any pretence to resistance and let him have his way. Men's supply of passion, she knew of long experience, was easily depleted. Though they might threaten to move earth and heaven too, half an hour later their boasts would be damp sheets and resentment. If the worst came to the worst, she could tolerate his inane talk of burning; she'd heard far obscener bedroom chat. As to the prong he was even now attempting to press into her, it and its comical like held no surprises for her.

Jerome wanted to touch the heart in her; wanted to see it splash up into his face, to bathe in it. He put his hand to her breast, and felt the beat of her under his palm.

"You like that, do you?" she said as he pressed against her bosom. "You're not the first."

He clawed her skin.

"Gently, sweetheart," she chided him, looking over his shoulder to see if there was any sign of Isaiah. "Be gentle. This is the only body I've got."

He ignored her. His nails drew blood.

"Don't do that," she said.

"Wants to be out," he replied digging deeply, and it suddenly dawned on her that this was no love-game he was playing.

"*Stop it*," she said, as he began to tear at her. This time, she screamed.

Downstairs, and a short way along the street, Isaiah dropped the slice of *tarte française* he'd just bought and ran to the door. It wasn't the first time his sweet tooth had tempted him from his post, but – unless he was quick to undo the damage – it might very well be his last. There were terrible noises from the landing. He raced up the stairs. The scene that met his eyes was in every way worse than that his imagination had conjured. Simone was trapped against the wall beside her door, with a man battened upon her. Blood was coming from somewhere between them, he couldn't see where.

Isaiah yelled. Jerome, hands bloody, looked round from his labours as a giant in a Savile Row suit reached for him. It took Jerome vital seconds to uproot himself from the furrow, by which time the man was upon him. Isaiah took hold of him, and dragged him off the woman. She took shelter, sobbing, in her room.

"Sick bastard," Isaiah said, launching a fusillade of punches. Jerome reeled. But he was on fire, and unafraid. In a moment's respite he leapt at his man like an angered baboon. Isaiah, taken unawares, lost balance, and fell back against one of the doors, which opened inwards against his weight. He collapsed into a squalid lavatory, his head striking the lip of the toilet bowl as he went down. The impact disoriented him, and he lay on the stained linoleum groaning, legs akimbo. Jerome could hear his blood, eager in his veins; could smell sugar on his breath. It tempted him to stay. But his instinct for self-preservation counselled otherwise; Isaiah was already making an attempt to stand up again. Before he could get to his feet Jerome about turned, and made a getaway down the stairs.

The dog-day met him at the doorstep, and he smiled. The street wanted him more than the woman on the landing, and he was eager to oblige. He started out on to the pavement, his erection still pressing from his trousers. Behind him, he heard the giant pounding down the stairs. He took to his heels, laughing. The fire was still uncurbed in him, and it lent speed to his feet; he ran down the street not caring if Sugar Breath was following or not. Pedestrians, unwilling, in this dispassionate age, to register more than casual interest in the blood-spattered satyr, parted to let him pass. A few pointed, assuming him an actor perhaps. Most took no notice at all. He made his way through a maze of back streets, aware without needing to look that Isaiah was still on his heels.

Perhaps it was accident that brought him to the street market; perhaps, and more probably, it was that the swelter carried the mingled scent of meat and fruit to his nostrils, and he wanted to bathe in it. The narrow thoroughfare was thronged with purchasers, sightseers, and stalls heaped with merchandise. He dove into the crowd happily, brushing against buttock and thigh, meeting the plaguing gaze of fellow flesh on every side. Such a day! He and his prick could scarcely believe their luck.

Behind him, he heard Isaiah shout. He picked up his pace, heading for the most densely populated areas of the market, where he could lose himself in the hot press of people. Each contact was a painful ecstasy. Each climax – and they came one upon the other as he pressed through the crowd – was a dry spasm in his system. His back ached, his balls ached: but what his body now? Just a plinth for that singular monument, his prick. Head was *nothing*; mind was *nothing*. His arms were simply made to bring love close, his legs to carry the demanding rod any place where it might find satisfaction. He pictured himself as a walking erection, the world gaping on every side: flesh, brick, steel, he didn't care: he would ravish it all.

Suddenly, without his seeking it, the crowd parted, and he found himself off the main thoroughfare and in a narrow street. Sunlight poured between the buildings, its zeal magnified. He was about to turn back to join the crowd again when he caught a scent and sight that drew him on. A short way down the heat-drenched street three shirtless young men were standing amid piles of fruit crates, each containing dozens of punnets of strawberries. There had been a glut of the fruit that year, and in the relentless heat much of it had begun to soften and rot. The trio of workers was going through the punnets, sorting bad fruit from good, and throwing the spoiled strawberries into the gutter. The smell in the narrow space was overpowering: a sweetness of such strength it would have sickened any interloper other than Jerome, whose senses had lost all capacity for revulsion or rejection. The world was the world was the world; he would take it, as in marriage, for better or worse. He stood watching the spectacle entranced; the sweating fruit-sorters bright in the fall of sun, hands, arms and torsoes spattered with scarlet juice; the air mazed with every nectar-seeking insect; the discarded fruit heaped in the gutter in seeping mounds. Engaged in their sticky labours the sorters didn't even see him at first. Then one of the three looked up, and took in the extraordinary creature watching them. The grin on his face died as he met Jerome's eyes.

"What the hell?"

Now the other two looked up from their work.

"Sweet," said Jerome; he could hear their hearts tremble.

"Look at him," said the youngest of the three, pointing at Jerome's groin. "Fucking exposing himself."

They stood still in the sunlight, he and they, while the wasps whirled around the fruit, and, in the narrow slice of blue summer sky between the roofs, birds passed over. Jerome wanted the moment to go on forever: his too-naked head tasted Eden here.

And then, the dream broke. He felt a shadow on his back. One of the sorters dropped the punnet he was sorting through; the decayed fruit broke open on the gravel. Jerome frowned, and half-turned. Isaiah had found the street; his weapon was steel and shone. It crossed the space between he and Jerome in one short second. Jerome felt an ache in his side as the knife slid into him.

"*Christ*," the young man said, and began to run; his two brothers, unwilling to be witnesses at the scene of a wounding, hesitated only moments longer before following.

The pain made Jerome cry out, but nobody in the noisy market heard him. Isaiah withdrew the blade; heat came with it. He made to stab again, but Jerome was too fast for the spoiler; he moved out of range and staggered across the street. The would-be assassin, fearful that Jerome's cries would draw too much attention, moved quickly in pursuit to finish the job. But the tarmac was slick with rotted fruit, and his fine suede shoes had less grip than Jerome's bare feet. The gap between them widened by a pace.

"No you don't," Isaiah said, determined not to let his humiliator escape. He pushed over a tower of fruit crates – punnets toppled and strewed their contents across Jerome's path. Jerome hesitated, to take in the bouquet of bruised fruit. The indulgence almost killed him. Isaiah closed in, ready to take the man. Jerome, his system taxed to near eruption by the stimulus of pain, watched the blade come close to opening up his belly. His mind conjured the wound: the abdomen slit – the heat spilling out to join the blood of the strawberries in the gutter. The thought was so tempting. He almost wanted it.

Isaiah had killed before, twice. He knew the wordless vocabulary of the act, and he could see the invitation in his victim's eyes. Happy to oblige, he came to meet it, knife at the ready. At the last possible moment Jerome recanted, and instead of presenting himself for slitting, threw a blow at the giant. Isaiah ducked to avoid it and his feet slid in the mush. The knife fled from his hand and fell amongst the debris of punnets and fruit. Jerome turned away as the hunter – the advantage lost – stooped to locate the knife. But his prey was gone before his ham-fisted grip had found it: lost again in the crowd-filled streets. He had no opportunity to pocket the knife before the uniform stepped out of the crowd and joined him in the hot passageway.

"What's the story?" the policeman demanded, looking down at the knife. Isaiah followed his gaze. The bloodied blade was black with flies.

In his office Inspector Carnegie sipped at his hot chocolate, his third in the past hour, and watched the processes of dusk. He had always wanted to be a detective, right from his earliest rememberings; and, in those rememberings, this had always been a charged and magical hour. Night descending on the city; myriad evils putting on their glad rags and coming out to play. A time for vigilance, for a new moral stringency.

But as a child he had failed to imagine the fatigue that twilight invariably brought. He was tired to his bones, and if he snatched any sleep in the next few hours he knew it would be here, in his chair, with his feet up on the desk amid a clutter of plastic cups.

The phone rang. It was Johannson.

"Still at work?" he said, impressed by Johannson's dedication to the job. It was well after nine. Perhaps Johannson didn't have a home worth calling such to go back to either.

"I heard our man had a busy day," Johannson said.

"That's right. A prostitute in Soho; then got himself stabbed."

"He got through the cordon, I gather?"

"These things happen," Carnegie replied, too tired to be testy. "What can I do for you?"

"I just thought you'd want to know: the monkeys have started to die."

The words stirred Carnegie from his fatigue-stupor. "How many?" he asked.

"Three from fourteen so far. But the rest, will be dead by dawn, I'd guess."

"What's killing them? Exhaustion?" Carnegie recalled the desperate saturnalia he'd seen in the cages. What animal – human or otherwise – could keep up such revelry without cracking up?

"It's not physical," Johannson said. "Or at least not in the way you're implying. We'll have to wait for the dissection results before we get any detailed explanations –"

"Your best guess?"

"For what it's worth . . ." Johannson said, ". . . which is quite a lot: I think they're going *bang*."

"What?"

"Cerebral over-load of some kind. Their brains are simply giving out. The agent doesn't disperse you see; *it feeds on itself*. The more fevered they get, the more of the drug is produced; the more of the drug there is, the more fevered they get. It's a vicious circle. Hotter and hotter, wilder and wilder. Eventually the system can't take it, and suddenly I'm up to my armpits in dead monkeys." The smile came back into the voice again, cold and wry. "Not that the others let that spoil their fun. Necrophilia's quite the fashion down here."

Carnegie peered at his cooling hot chocolate; it had acquired a thin skin, which puckered as he touched the cup. "So it's just a matter of time?" he said.

"Before our man goes for bust? Yes, I'd think so."

"All right. Thank you for the up-date. Keep me posted."

"You want to come down here and view the remains?"

"Monkey corpses I can do without, thank you."

Johannson laughed. Carnegie put down the receiver. When he turned back to the window, night had well and fallen.

In the laboratory Johannson crossed to the light switch by the door; in the time he'd been calling Carnegie the last of the daylight had fled. He saw the blow that felled him coming a mere heartbeat before it landed; it caught him across the side of his neck. One of his vertebrae snapped, and his legs buckled. He collapsed without reaching the lightswitch. But by the time he hit the ground the distinction between day and night was academic.

Welles didn't bother to check whether his blow had been lethal or not; time was at a premium. He stepped over the body and headed across to the bench where Johannson had been working. There, lying in a circle of lamplight as if for the final act of a simian tragedy, lay a dead monkey. It had clearly perished in a frenzy; its face was knitted up: mouth wide and spittle-stained, eyes fixed in a final look of alarm. Its fur had been pulled out in tufts in the throes of its copulations; its body, wasted with exertion, was a mass of contusions. It took Welles half a minute of study to recognize the implications of the corpse, and of the other two he now saw lying on a nearby bench.

"Love kills," he murmured to himself philosophically, and began his systematic destruction of *Blind Boy*.

I'm dying, Jerome thought, I'm dying of *terminal joy*. The thought amused him. It was the only thought in his head which made much sense. Since his encounter with Isaiah, and the escape from the police that had followed, he could remember little with any coherence. The hours of hiding and nursing his wounds – of feeling the heat grow again, and of discharging it – had long since merged into one midsummer dream, from which, he knew with pleasurable certainty, only death would wake him. The blaze was devouring him utterly, from the entrails out. If he were to be eviscerated now, what would the witnesses find? Only embers and ashes.

Yet still his one-eyed friend demanded *more*; still, as he wove his way back to the Laboratories – where else for a made man to go when the stitches slipped, but back to the first heat? – still the grids gaped at him seductively, and every brick wall offered up a hundred gritty invitations.

The night was balmy: a night for love-songs and romance. In

the questionable privacy of a parking lot a few blocks from his destination he saw two people making sex in the back of a car, the doors open to accommodate limbs and draught. Jerome paused to watch the ritual, enthralled as ever by the tangle of bodies, and the sound – so loud it was like thunder – of twin hearts beating to one escalating rhythm. Watching, his rod grew eager.

The female saw him first, and alerted her partner to the wreck of a human being who was watching them with such childish delight. The male looked around from his gropings to stare. Do I burn, Jerome wondered? Does my hair flame? At the last, does the illusion gain substance? To judge by the look on their faces, the answer was surely no. They were not in awe of him, merely angered and revolted.

"I'm on fire," he told them.

The male got to his feet and spat at Jerome. He almost expected the spittle to turn to steam as it approached him but instead it landed on his face and upper chest as a cooling shower.

"Go to hell," the woman said. "Leave us alone."

Jerome shook his head. The male warned him that another step would oblige him to break Jerome's head. It disturbed our man not a jot; no words, no blows, could silence the imperative of the rod.

Their hearts, he realized, as he moved towards them, no longer beat in tandem.

Carnegie consulted the map, five years out of date now, on his office wall, to pinpoint the location of the attack that had just been reported. Neither of the victims had come to serious harm, apparently; the arrival of a car-load of revellers had dissuaded Jerome (it was unquestionably Jerome) from lingering. Now the area was being flooded with officers, half a dozen of them armed; in a matter of minutes every street in the vicinity of the attack would be cordoned off. Unlike Soho, which had been crowded, the area would furnish the fugitive with few hiding places.

Carnegie pin-pointed the location of the attack, and realized that it was within a few blocks of the Laboratories. No accident, surely. The man was heading back to the scene of his crime. Wounded, and undoubtedly on the verge of collapse – the lovers had described a man who looked more dead than alive – Jerome would probably be picked up before he reached home. But there was always the risk of his slipping through the net, and getting to the Laboratories. Johannson was working there, alone; the guard on the building was, in these straitened times, necessarily small.

Carnegie picked up the phone and dialled through to Johannson. The phone rang at the other end, but nobody picked it up. The man's gone home, Carnegie thought, happy to be relieved of his concern, it's ten-fifty at night and he's earned his rest. Just as he was about to put the receiver down, however, it was picked up at the other end.

"Johannson?"

Nobody replied.

"Johannson? This is Carnegie." And still, no reply. "Answer, damn it. Who is this?"

In the Laboratories the receiver was forsaken. It was not replaced on the cradle but left to lie on the bench. Down the buzzing line, Carnegie could clearly hear the monkeys, their voices shrill.

"Johannson?" Carnegie demanded. "Are you there? Johannson?"

But the apes screamed on.

Welles had built two bonfires of the *Blind Boy* material in the sinks, and then set them alight. They flared up enthusiastically. Smoke, heat and smuts filled the large room, thickening the air. When the fires were fairly raging he threw all the tapes he could lay hands upon into the conflagration, and added all of Johannson's notes for good measure. Several of the tapes had already gone from the files, he noted. But all they could show any thief was some teasing scenes of transformation: the heart of the secret remained his. With the procedures and formulae now destroyed, it only remained to wash the small amounts of remaining agent down the drain, and kill and incinerate the animals.

He prepared a series of lethal hypodermics, going about the business with uncharacteristic orderliness. This systematic destruction gratified him. He felt no regret at the way things had turned out. From that first moment of panic, when he'd helplessly watched the *Blind Boy* serum work its awesome effects upon Jerome – to this final elimination of all that had gone before – had been, he now saw, one steady process of wiping clean. With these fires he brought an end to the pretence of scientific enquiry; after this he was indisputably the Apostle of Desire, its John in the wilderness. The thought blinded him to any other. Careless of the monkeys' scratchings he hauled them one by one, from their cages to deliver the killing dose. He had dispatched three, and was opening the cage of the fourth, when a figure appeared in the doorway of the laboratory. Through the smoky air it was impossible to see who. The surviving monkeys seemed to recognize him, however: they left off their couplings and set up a din of welcome.

Welles stood still, and waited for the newcomer to make his move.

"I'm dying," said Jerome.

Welles had not expected this. Of all the people he had anticipated here, Jerome was the last.

"Did you hear me?" the man wanted to know.

Welles nodded. "We're *all* dying, Jerome. Life is a slow disease, no more nor less. But such a *light*, eh? in the going."

"You *knew* this would happen," Jerome said. "You knew the fire would eat me away."

"No," came the sober reply. "No, I didn't. Really."

Jerome walked out of the door frame and into the murky light. He was a wasted shambles: a patchwork man, blood on his body, fire in his eyes. But Welles knew better than to trust the apparent vulnerability of this scarecrow. The agent in his system had made him capable of superhuman acts: he had seen Dance torn open with a few nonchalant strokes. Tact was required. Though clearly close to death, Jerome was still formidable.

"I didn't intend this, Jerome," Welles said, attempting to tame the tremor in his voice. "I wish, in a way, I could claim that I had. But I wasn't that farsighted. It's taken me time and pain to see the future plainly."

The burning man watched him, gaze intent.

"Such fires, Jerome, waiting to be lit."

"I know . . ." Jerome replied. "Believe me . . . I know."

"You and I; we are the end of the world."

The wretched monster pondered this for a while, and then nodded slowly. Welles softly exhaled a sigh of relief; the death-bed diplomacy was working. But he had little time to waste with talk. If Jerome was here, could the authorities be far behind?

"I have urgent work to do, my friend," he said calmly. "Would you think me uncivil if I continued with it?"

Without waiting for a reply he unlatched another cage and hauled the condemned monkey out, expertly turning its body round to facilitate the injection. The animal convulsed in his arms for a few moments, then died. Welles disengaged its wizened fingers from his shirt, and tossed the corpse and the discharged hypodermic on to the bench, turning with an executioner's economy to claim his next victim.

"Why?" Jerome asked, staring at the animal's open eyes.

"Act of mercy," Welles replied, picking up another primed hypodermic. "You can see how they're suffering." He reached to unlatch the next cage.

"Don't," Jerome said.

"No time for sentiment," Welles replied. "I beg you: an end to that."

Sentiment, Jerome thought, muddily remembering the songs on the radio that had first rewoken the fire in him. Didn't Welles understand that the processes of heart and head and groin were indivisible? That sentiment, however trite, might lead to undiscovered regions? He wanted to tell the Doctor that, to explain all that he had seen and all that he had loved in these desperate hours. But somewhere between mind and tongue the explanations absconded. All he could say, to state the empathy he felt for all the suffering world, was:

"*Don't*," as Welles unlocked the next cage. The Doctor ignored him, and reached into the wire-mesh cell. It contained three animals. He took hold of the nearest and drew it, protesting, from its companions' embraces. Without doubt it knew what fate awaited it; a flurry of screeches signalled its terror.

Jerome couldn't stomach this casual disposal. He moved, the wound in his side a torment, to prevent the killing. Welles, distracted by Jerome's advance, lost hold of his wriggling charge: the monkey scampered away across the bench-tops. As he went to re-capture it the prisoners in the cage behind him took their chance, and slipped out.

"Damn you," Welles yelled at Jerome, "don't you see we've no *time*? Don't you understand?"

Jerome understood everything, and yet nothing. The fever he and the animals shared, he understood; its purpose, to transform the world, he understood too. But why it should end like this – that joy, that vision – why it should all come down to a sordid room filled with smoke and pain, to frailty, to despair – *that* he did not comprehend. Nor, he now realized, did Welles, who had been the architect of these contradictions.

As the Doctor made a snatch for one of the escaping monkeys, Jerome crossed swiftly to the remaining cages and unlatched them all: the animals leapt to their freedom. Welles had succeeded with his recapture however, and had the protesting monkeys in his grip, about to deliver the panacea. Jerome made towards him.

"Let it be," he yelled.

Welles pressed the hypodermic into the monkey's body, but before he could depress the plunger Jerome had pulled at his wrist. The hypodermic spat its poison into the air, and then fell to the ground: the monkey, wresting itself free, followed.

Jerome pulled Welles close. "I told you to *let it be,*' he said.

Welles' response was to drive his fist into Jerome's wounded flank. Tears of pain spurted from his eyes, but he didn't release the Doctor. The stimulus, unpleasant as it was, could not dissuade him from holding that beating heart close. He wished, embracing Welles like a prodigal, that he could ignite himself: that the dream of burning flesh he had endured would now become a reality, consuming maker and made in one cleansing flame. But his flesh was only flesh; his bone, bone. What miracles he had seen had been a private revelation, and now there was no time to communicate their glories or their horrors. What he had seen would die with him, to be rediscovered (perhaps) by some future self, only to be forgotten and discovered again. Like the story of love the radio had told; the same joy lost and found, found and lost. He stared at Welles with new comprehension dawning, hearing still the terrified beat of the man's heart. The Doctor was *wrong.* If he left the man to live, he would come to know his error. They were not presagers of the millenium. They had both been dreaming.

"Don't kill me," Welles pleaded. "I don't want to die."

More fool you, Jerome thought, and let the man go.

Welles' bafflement was plain: he couldn't believe that his appeal for life had been answered. Anticipating a blow with every step he took, he backed away from Jerome, who simply turned his back on the Doctor and walked away.

From downstairs there came a shout, and then many shouts. Police, Welles guessed. They had presumably found the body of the officer who'd been on guard at the door. In moments only they would be coming up the stairs. There was no time now for finishing the tasks he'd come here to perform. He had to be away before they arrived.

On the floor below, Carnegie watched the armed officers disappear up the stairs. There was a faint smell of burning in the air; he feared the worst.

I am the man who comes after the act, he thought to himself; I am perpetually upon the scene when the best of the action is over. Used as he was to waiting, patient as a loyal dog, this time he could not hold his anxieties in check while the others went ahead. Disregarding the voices advising him to wait, he began up the stairs.

The laboratory on the top floor was empty, but for the monkeys and Johannson's corpse. The toxicologist lay on his face where he had fallen, neck broken. The emergency exit, which let on to the fire-escape, was open; smoky air was being sucked out through it. As Carnegie stepped away from Johannson's body officers were already on the fire-escape, calling to their colleagues below to seek out the fugitive.

"Sir?"

Carnegie looked across at the moustachioed individual who had approached him.

"What is it?"

The officer pointed to the other end of the laboratory: to the test-chamber. There was somebody at the window. Carnegie recognized the features, even though they were much changed. It was Jerome. At first he thought the man was watching him, but a short perusal scotched that idea. Jerome was staring, tears on his face, at his own reflection in the smeared glass. Even as Carnegie watched, the face retreated with the gloom of the chamber.

Other officers had noticed the man too. They were moving down the length of the laboratory, taking up positions behind the benches where they had a good line on the door, weapons at the ready. Carnegie had been present in such situations before; they had their own, terrible momentum. Unless he intervened, there would be blood.

"No," he said, "hold your fire."

He pressed the protesting officer aside and began to walk down the laboratory, making no attempt to conceal his advance. He walked past sinks in which the remains of *Blind Boy* guttered, past the bench under which, a short age ago, they'd found the dead Dance. A monkey, its head bowed, dragged itself across his path, apparently deaf to his proximity. He let it find a hole to die in, then moved on to the chamber door. It was ajar. He reached for the handle. Behind him the laboratory had fallen completely silent; all eyes were on him. He pulled the door open. Fingers tightened on triggers. There was no attack however. Carnegie stepped inside.

Jerome was standing against the opposite wall. If he saw Carnegie enter, or heard him, he made no sign of it. A dead monkey lay at his feet, one hand still grasping the hem of his trousers. Another whimpered in the corner, holding its head in its hands.

"Jerome?"

Was it Carnegie's imagination, or could he smell strawberries? Jerome blinked.

"You're under arrest," Carnegie said. Hendrix would appreciate the irony of that, he thought. The man moved his bloody hand from the stabwound in his side to the front of his trousers, and began to stroke himself.

"Too late," Jerome said. He could feel the last fire rising in him. Even if this intruder chose to cross the chamber and arrest him now, the intervening seconds would deny him his capture. *Death was here.* And what was it, now he saw it clearly? Just another seduction, another sweet darkness to be filled up, and pleasured and made fertile.

A spasm began in his perineum, and lightning travelled in two directions from the spot, up his rod and up his spine. A laugh began in his throat.

In the corner of the chamber the monkey, hearing Jerome's humour, began to whimper again. The sound momentarily claimed Carnegie's attention, and when his gaze flitted back to Jerome the short-sighted eyes had closed, the hand had dropped, and he was dead, standing against the wall. For a short time the body defied gravity. Then, gracefully the legs buckled and Jerome fell forward. He was, Carnegie saw, a sack of bones, no more. It was a wonder the man had lived so long.

Cautiously, he crossed to the body and put his finger to the man's neck. There was no pulse. The remnants of Jerome's last laugh remained on his face, however, refusing to decay.

"Tell me . . ." Carnegie whispered to the man, sensing that

despite his pre-emption he had missed the moment; that once again he was, and perhaps would always be, merely a witness of consequences. "Tell me. *What was the joke?*"

But the blind boy, as is the wont of his clan, wasn't telling.

A LONG LETTER FROM F.

Leonard Cohen

MY DEAR FRIEND,

Five years with the length of five years. I do not know exactly where this letter finds you. I suppose you have thought often of me. You were always my favorite male orphan. Oh, much more than that, much more, but I do not choose, for this last *written* communication, to expend myself in easy affection.

If my lawyers have performed according to my instructions, you are now in possession of my worldly estate, my soap collection, my factory, my Masonic aprons, my treehouse. I imagine you have already appropriated my style. I wonder where my style has led you. As I stand on this last springy diving board I wonder where my style has led me.

I am writing this last letter in the Occupational Therapy Room. I have let women lead me anywhere, and I am not sorry. Convents, kitchens, perfumed telephone booths, poetry courses – I followed women anywhere. I followed women into Parliament because I know how they love power. I followed women into the beds of men so that I could learn what they found there. The air is streaked with the smoke of their perfume. The world is clawed with their amorous laughter. I followed women into the world, because I loved the world. Breasts, buttocks, everywhere I followed the soft balloons. When women hissed at me from brothel windows, when they softly hissed at me over the shoulders of their dancing husbands,

I followed them and I sank down with them, and sometimes when I listened to their hissing I knew it was nothing but the sound of the withering and collapse of their soft balloons.

This is the sound, this hissing, which hovers over every woman. There is one exception. I knew one woman who surrounded herself with a very different noise, maybe it was music, maybe it was silence. I am speaking, of course, about our Edith. It is five years now that I have been buried. Surely you know by now that Edith could not belong to you alone.

I followed the young nurses to Occupational Therapy. They have covered the soft balloons with starched linen, a pleasant tantalizing cover which my old lust breaks as easily as an eggshell. I have followed their dusty white legs.

Men also give off a sound. Do you know what our sound is, dear frayed friend? It is the sound you hear in male sea shells. Guess what it is. I will give you three guesses. You must fill in the lines. The nurses like to see me use my ruler.

1.—
2.—
3.—

The nurses like to lean over my shoulder and watch me use my red plastic ruler. They hiss through my hair and their hisses have the aroma of alcohol and sandalwood, and their starched clothes crackle like the white tissue paper and artificial straw which creamy chocolate Easter eggs come in.

Oh, I am happy today. I know that these pages will be filled with happiness. Surely you did not think that I would leave you with a melancholy gift.

Well, what are your answers? Isn't it remarkable that I have extended your training over this wide gulf?

It is the very opposite of a hiss, the sound men make. It is Shhh, the sound made around the index finger raised to the lips. Shhh, and the roofs are raised against the storm. Shhh, the forests are cleared so the wind will not rattle the trees. Shhh, the hydrogen rockets go off to silence, dissent and variety. It is not an unpleasant noise. It is indeed a perky tune, like the bubbles above a clam. Shhh, will everybody listen, please. Will the animals stop howling, please. Will the belly stop rumbling, please. Will Time call off its ultrasonic dogs, please.

It is the sound my ball pen makes on the hospital paper as I run it down the edge of the red ruler. Shhh, it says to the billion unlines of whiteness. Shhh, it whispers to the white chaos, lie down in dormitory rows. Shhh, it implores the dancing molecules, I love dances but I do not love foreign dances, I love dances that have rules, my rules.

Did you fill in the lines, old friend? Are you sitting in a restaurant or a monastery as I lie underground? Did you fill in the lines? You didn't have to, you know. Did I trick you again?

Now what about this silence we are so desperate to clear in the wilderness? Have we labored, plowed, muzzled, fenced so that we might hear a Voice? Fat chance. The Voice comes out of the whirlwind, and long ago we hushed the whirlwind. I wish that you would remember that the Voice comes out of the whirlwind. Some men, some of the time, have remembered. Was I one?

I will tell you why we nailed up the cork. I am a born teacher and it is not my nature to keep things to myself. Surely five years have tortured and tickled you into that understanding. I always intended to tell you everything, the complete gift. How is your constipation, darling?

I imagine they are about twenty-four years old, these soft balloons that are floating beside me this very second, these Easter candies swaddled in official laundry. Twenty-four years of journey, almost a quarter of a century, but still youth for breasts. They have come a long way to graze shyly at my shoulder as I gaily wield my ruler to serve someone's definition of sanity. They are still young, they are barely young, but they hiss fiercely, and they dispense a heady perfume of alcohol and sandalwood. Her face gives nothing away, it is a scrubbed nurse's face, family lines mercifully washed away, a face prepared to be a screen for our blue home movies as we sink in disease. A compassionate sphinx's face to drip our riddles on, and, like paws buried in the sand, her round breasts claw and scratch against the uniform. Familiar? Yes, it is a face such as Edith often wore, our perfect nurse.

–Those are very nice lines you've drawn.

–I'm quite fond of them.

Hiss, hiss, run for your lives, the bombs are dying.

–Would you like some colored pencils?

–As long as they don't marry our erasers.

Wit, invention, shhh, shhh, now do you see why we've sound-proofed the forest, carved benches round the wild arena? To hear

the hissing, to hear wrinkles squeezing out the bounce, to attend
the death of our worlds. Memorize this and forget it. It deserves
a circuit, but a very tiny circuit, in the brain. I might as well tell
you that I exempt myself, as of now, from all these categories.

Play with me, old friend.

Take my spirit hand. You have been dipped in the air of our
planet, you have been baptized with fire, shit, history, love, and
loss. Memorize this. It explains the Golden Rule.

See me at this moment of my curious little history, nurse leaning
over my work, my prick rotten and black, you saw my worldly prick
decayed, but now see my visionary prick, cover your head and see
my visionary prick which I do not own and never owned, which
owned me, which was me, which bore me as a broom bears a witch,
bore me from world to world, from sky to sky. Forget this.

Like many teachers, a lot of the stuff I gave away was simply
a burden I couldn't carry any longer. I feel my store of garbage
giving out. Soon I'll have nothing left to leave around but stories.
Maybe I'll attain the plane of spreading gossip, and thus finish my
prayers to the world.

Edith was a promoter of sex orgies and a purveyor of narcotics.
Once she had lice. Twice she had crabs. I've written crabs very
small because there is a time and a place for everything, and a young
nurse is standing close behind me wondering whether she is being
drawn by my power or her charity. I appear to be engrossed in my
therapeutic exercises, she in the duties of supervision, but shhh,
hiss, the noise of steam spreads through O.T., it mixes with the
sunlight, it bestows a rainbow halo on each bowed head of sufferer,
doctor, nurse, volunteer. You ought to look up this nurse sometime.
She will be twenty-nine when my lawyers locate you and complete
my material bequest.

Down some green corridor, in a large closet among pails,
squeegees, antiseptic mops, Mary Voolnd from Nova Scotia will
peel down her dusty white stockings and present an old man with
the freedom of her knees, and we will leave nothing behind us but
our false ears with which to pick up the steps of the approaching
orderly.

Steam coming off the planet, clouds of fleecy steam as boy and
girl populations clash in religious riots, hot and whistling like a
graveyard sodomist our little planet embraces its fragile yo-yo
destiny, tuned in the secular mind like a dying engine. But

some do not hear it this way, some flying successful moon-shot eyes do not see it this way. They do not hear the individual noises shhh, hiss, they hear the sound of the sounds together, they behold the interstices flashing up and down the cone of the flowering whirlwind.

Do I listen to the Rolling Stones? Ceaselessly.

Am I hurt enough?

The old hat evades me. I don't know if I can wait. The river that I'll walk beside – I seem to miss it by a coin toss every year. Did I have to buy that factory? Was I obliged to run for Parliament? Was Edith such a good lay? My café table, my small room, my drugged true friends from whom I don't expect too much – I seem to abandon them almost by mistake, for promises, phone calls casually made. The old hat, the rosy ugly old face that won't waste time in mirrors, the uncombed face that will laugh amazed at the manifold traffic. Where is my old hat? I tell myself I can wait. I argue that my path was correct. Is it only the argument that is incorrect? Is it Pride that tempts me with intimations of a new style? Is it Cowardice that keeps me from an old ordeal? I tell myself: wait. I listen to the rain, to the scientific noises of the hospital. I get happy because of many small things. I go to sleep with the earplug of the transistor stuck in. Even my Parliamentary disgrace begins to evade me. My name appears more and more frequently among the nationalist heroes. Even my hospitalization has been described as an English trick to muzzle me. I fear I will lead a government yet, rotten prick and all. I lead men too easily: my fatal facility.

My dear friend, go beyond my style.

Something in your eyes, old lover, described me as the man I wanted to be. Only you and Edith extended that generosity to me, perhaps only you. Your baffled cries as I tormented you, you were the good animal I wanted to be, or failing that, the good animal I wanted to exist. It was I who feared the rational mind, therefore I tried to make you a little mad. I was desperate to learn from your bewilderment. You were the wall which I, batlike, bounced my screams off of, so I might have direction in this long nocturnal flight.

I cannot stop teaching. Have I taught you anything?

I must smell better with this confession, because Mary Voolnd has just awarded me a distinct signal of cooperation.

–Would you like to touch my cunt with one of your old hands?

–Which hand are you thinking of?

–Would you like to depress a nipple with a forefinger and make it disappear?

–And make it reappear too?

–If it reappears I will hate you forever. I will inscribe you in the Book of Fumblers.

—

–That's better.

—

–I'm dripping.

Do you see how I cannot stop teaching? All my arabesques are for publication. Can you imagine how I envied you, whose suffering was so traditional?

From time to time, I will confess, I hated you. The teacher of composition is not always gratified to listen to the Valedictorian Address delivered in his own style, especially if he has never been Valedictorian himself. Times I felt depleted: you with all that torment, me with nothing but a System.

When I worked among the Jews (you own the factory), regularly I saw a curious expression of pain cross the boss's Levantine face. This I observed as he ushered out a filthy coreligionist, bearded, shifty, and smelling of low Romanian cuisine, who visited the factory every second month begging on behalf of an obscure Yiddish physical-therapy university. Our boss always gave the creature a few groschen and hurried him through the shipping exit with awkward haste, as if his presence there might start something far worse than a strike. I was always kinder to the boss on those days, for he was strangely vulnerable and comfortless. We walked slowly between the great rolls of cashmere and Harris tweed and I let him have his way with me. (He, for one, did not resent my new muscles, achieved through Dynamic Tension. Why did you drive me away?)

–What is my factory today? A pile of rags and labels, a distraction, an insult to my spirit.

–A tomb of your ambition, sir?

–That's right, boy.

–Dust in the mouth, cinders in the eye, sir?

–I don't want that bum in here again, do you hear me? One of these days they're going to walk out of here with him. And I'll be at the head of the line. That poor wretch is happier than the whole caboodle.

But, of course, he never turned the loathsome beggar away, and suffered for it, regular as menstruation pain, which is how the female regrets life beyond the pale of lunar jurisdiction.

You plagued me like the moon. I knew you were bound by old laws of suffering and obscurity. I am fearful of the cripple's wisdom. A pair of crutches, a grotesque limp can ruin a stroll which I begin in a new suit, clean-shaven, whistling. I envied you the certainty that you would amount to nothing. I coveted the magic of torn clothes. I was jealous of the terrors I constructed for you but could not tremble before myself. I was never drunk enough, never poor enough, never rich enough. All this hurts, perhaps it hurts enough. It makes me want to cry out for comfort. It makes me stretch my hands out horizontally. Yes, I long to be President of the new Republic. I love to hear the armed teen-agers chant my name outside the hospital gates. Long live the Revolution! Let me be President for my last thirty days.

Where are you walking tonight, dear friend? Did you give up meat? Are you disarmed and empty, an instrument of Grace? Can you stop talking? Has loneliness led you into ecstasy?

There was a deep charity in your suck. I hated it, I abused it. But I dare to hope that you embody the best of my longings. I dare to hope that you will produce the pearl and justify these poor secreted irritations.

This letter is written in the old language, and it has caused me no little discomfort to recall the obsolete usages. I've had to stretch my mind back into areas bordered with barbed wire, from which I spent a life-time removing myself. However, I do not regret the effort.

Our love will never die, that I can promise you, I, who launch this letter like a kite among the winds of your desire. We were born together, and in our kisses we confessed our longing to be born again. We lay in each other's arms, each of us the other's teacher. We sought the peculiar tone of each peculiar night. We tried to clear away the static, suffering under the hint that the static was part of the tone. I was your adventure and you were my adventure. I was your journey and you were my journey, and Edith was our holy star. This letter rises out of our love like the sparks between dueling swords, like the shower of needles from flapping cymbals, like the bright seeds of sweat sliding through the center of our tight embrace, like the white feathers hung in the air by razored bushido cocks, like the shriek between two approaching puddles of mercury,

like the atmosphere of secrets which twin children exude. I was your
mystery and you were my mystery, and we rejoiced to learn that
mystery was our home. Our love cannot die. Out of history I come
to tell you this. Like two mammoths, tusk-locked in earnest sport
at the edge of the advancing age of ice, we preserve each other. Our
queer love keeps the lines of our manhood hard and clean, so that
we bring nobody but our own self to our separate marriage beds,
and our women finally know us.

Mary Voolnd has finally admitted my left hand into the creases
of her uniform. She watched me compose the above paragraph, so
I let it run on rather extravagantly. Women love excess in a man
because it separates him from his fellows and makes him lonely.
All that women know of the male world has been revealed to them
by lonely, excessive refugees from it. Raging fairies they cannot
resist because of their highly specialized intelligence.

–Keep writing, she hisses.

Mary has turned her back to me. The balloons are shrieking like
whistles signaling the end of every labor. Mary pretends to inspect
a large rug some patient wove, thus shielding our precious play.
Slow as a snail I push my hand, palm down, up the tight rough
stocking on the back of her thigh. The linen of her skirt is crisp and
cool against my knuckles and nails, the stockinged thigh is warm,
curved, a little damp like a loaf of fresh white bread.

–Higher, she hisses.

I am in no hurry. Old friend, I am in no hurry. I feel I shall be
doing this throughout eternity. Her buttocks contract impatiently,
like two boxing gloves touching before the match. My hand pauses
to ride the quiver on the thigh.

–Hurry, she hisses.

Yes, I can tell by the tension in the stocking that I am approaching
the peninsula which is hitched to the garter device. I will travel the
whole peninsula, hot skin on either side, then I will leap off the
nipple-shaped garter device. The threads of the stocking tighten.
I bunch my fingers together so as not to make premature contact.
Mary is jiggling, endangering the journey. My forefinger scouts
out the garter device. It is warm. The little metal loop, the rubber
button – warm right through.

–Please, please, she hisses.

Like angels on the head of a pin, my fingers dance on the
rubber button. Which way shall I leap? Toward the outside

thigh, hard, warm as the shell of a beached tropical turtle? Or toward the swampy mess in the middle? Or fasten like a bat on the huge soft over-hanging boulder of her right buttock? It is very humid up her white starched skirt. It is like one of those airplane hangars wherein clouds form and it actually rains indoors. Mary is bouncing her bum like a piggy bank which is withholding a gold coin. The inundations are about to begin. I choose the middle.

–Yesssss.

Delicious soup stews my hand. Viscous geysers shower my wrist. Magnetic rain tests my Bulova. She jiggles for position, then drops over my fist like a gorilla net. I had been snaking through her wet hair, compressing it between my fingers like cotton candy. Now I am surrounded by artesian exuberance, nipply frills, numberless bulby brains, pumping constellations of mucous hearts. Moist Morse messages move up my arm, master my intellectual head, more, more, message dormant portions of dark brain, elect happy new kings for the exhausted pretenders of the mind. I am a seal inventing undulations in a vast electric aquacade, I am wires of tungsten burning in the seas of bulb, I am creature of Mary cave, I am froth of Mary wave, bums of nurse Mary applaud greedily as she maneuvers to plow her asshole on the edge of my arm bone, rose of rectum sliding up and down like the dream of banister fiend.

–Slish slosh slish slosh.

Are we not happy? Loud as we are, no one hears us, but this is a tiny miracle in the midst of all this bounty, so are the rainbow crowns hovering over every skull but tiny miracles. Mary looks at me over her shoulder, greeting me with rolled-up eyes white as eggshells, and an open goldfish mouth amazed smile. In the gold sunshine of OT everyone believes he is a stinking genius, offering baskets, ceramic ashtrays, thong-sewn wallets on the radiant altars of their perfect health.

Old friend, you may kneel as you read this, for now I come to the sweet burden of my argument. I did not know what I had to tell you, but now I know. I did not know what I wanted to proclaim, but now I am sure. All my speeches were preface to this, all my exercises but a clearing of my throat. I confess I tortured you but only to draw your attention to this. I confess I betrayed you but only to tap your shoulder. In our kisses and sucks, this, ancient darling, I meant to whisper.

God is alive. Magic is afoot. God is alive. Magic is afoot. God is afoot. Magic is alive. Alive is afoot. Magic never died. God never sickened. Many poor men lied. Many sick men lied. Magic never weakened. Magic never hid. Magic always ruled. God is afoot. God never died. God was ruler though his funeral lengthened. Though his mourners thickened Magic never fled. Though his shrouds were hoisted the naked God did live. Though his words were twisted the naked Magic thrived. Though his death was published round and round the world the heart did not believe. Many hurt men wondered. Many struck men bled. Magic never faltered. Magic always led. Many stones were rolled but God would not lie down. Many wild men lied. Many fat men listened. Though they offered stones Magic still was fed. Though they locked their coffers God was always served. Magic is afoot. God rules. Alive is afoot. Alive is in command. Many weak men hungered. Many strong men thrived. Though they boasted solitude God was at their side. Nor the dreamer in his cell, nor the captain on the hill. Magic is alive. Though his death was pardoned round and round the world the heart would not believe. Though laws were carved in marble they could not shelter men. Though altars built in parliaments they could not order men. Police arrested Magic and Magic went with them for Magic loves the hungry. But Magic would not tarry. It moves from arm to arm. It would not stay with them. Magic is afoot. It cannot come to harm. It rests in an empty palm. It spawns in an empty mind. But Magic is no instrument. Magic is the end. Many men drove Magic but Magic stayed behind. Many strong men lied. They only passed through Magic and out the other side. Many weak men lied. They came to God in secret and though they left him nourished they would not tell who healed. Though mountains danced before them they said that God was dead. Though his shrouds were hoisted the naked God did live. This I mean to whisper to my mind. This I mean to laugh with in my mind. This I mean my mind to serve till service is but Magic moving through the world, and mind itself is Magic coursing through the flesh, and flesh itself is Magic dancing on a clock, and time itself the Magic Length of God.

Old friend, aren't you happy? You and Edith alone know how long I've waited for this instruction.

—Damn you, Mary Voolnd spits at me.

–What?

–Your hand's gone limp. Grab!

How many times must I be slain, old friend? I do not understand the mystery, after all. I am an old man with one hand on a letter and one hand up a juicy cunt, and I understand nothing. If my instruction were gospel, would it wither up my hand? Certainly not. It doesn't figure. I'm picking lies out of the air. They're aiming lies at me. The truth should make me strong. I pray you, dear friend, interpret me, go beyond me. I know now that I am a hopeless case. Go forth, teach the world what I meant to be.

–Grab.

Mary wiggles and the hand comes to life, like those ancestral sea ferns which turned animal. Now the soft elbows of her cunt are nudging me somewhere. Now her asshole is rubbing the ridge of my arm, not like rosy banister reverie as before, but like an eraser removing dream evidence, and now, alas, the secular message appears.

–Grab, please, please. They'll start to notice at any second.

That is true. The air in O.T. is restless, no longer golden sunshine, merely sunny and warm. Yes, I've let the magic die. The doctors remember that they are at work and refuse to yawn. A fat little lady issues a duchess command, poor thing. A teen-ager weeps because he has wet himself again. A former school principal farts hysterically, threatening us all with no gym. Lord of Life, is my pain sufficient?

–Hurry.

Mary bears down. My fingers brush something. It is not part of Mary. It is foreign matter.

–Grab it. Pull it out. It's from our friends.

–Soon.

Dear Friend,

It comes back to me.

I sent you the wrong box of fireworks. I did not include the Pimple Cure in my famous soap and cosmetic collection. I cured Edith's acne with it, you know. But of course you do not know, because you have no reason to believe that Edith's complexion was ever anything but lovable to kiss and touch. When I found her her complexion was not lovable to kiss and touch, nor even

to look at. She was in an ugly mess. In another part of this long
letter I will tell you how we, Edith and I, constructed the lovely
wife whom you discovered performing extraordinary manicures
in the barber shop of the Mount Royal Hotel. Begin to prepare
yourself.

The soap collection, though it includes transparent bars, ghosts
of pine, lemon and sandalwood, Willy jelly, is useless without the
Pimple Cure. All you will achieve is scrubbed, fragrant pimples.
Perhaps that is enough for you – a demoralizing speculation.

You always resisted me. I had a body waiting for you, but
you turned it down. I had a vision of you with 19-inch arms,
but you walked away. I saw you with massive lower pecs and
horseshoe triceps, with bulk and definition simultaneously. In
certain intimate embraces I saw exactly how low your buttocks
should descend. In no case, when you were squatting in front
of me, should your buttocks have been lowered so far down that
they sat on your heels, for once this occurs the thigh muscles are
no longer engaged *but the buttocks muscles are*, ergo your rocky
cheeks, a very selfish development that gave me no happiness and
is a factor in your bowel predicament. I saw you oiled and shining, a
classic midsection of washboard abdominals fluted with razor-edged
obliques and serratus. I had a way to cut up the serratus. I had
access to a Professional Greek Chair. I had the straps and stirrups
to blitz your knob into a veritable sledgehammer, mouthful for a
pelican. I had a Sphincter Kit that worked off the tap like washing
machines and bosom aggrandizers. Had you a notion of my Yoga?
Call it ruin, or call it creation, have you a notion of my work on
Edith? Are you aware of the Ganges you insulted with a million
mean portages?

Perhaps it is my own fault. I withheld certain vital items, an
apparatus here, a fact there – but only because (yes, this is closer
to truth) I dreamed you would be greater than me. I saw a king
without dominion. I saw a gun bleeding. I saw the prince of Paradise
Forgotten. I saw a pimpled movie star. I saw a racing hearse. I saw
the New Jew. I saw popular lame storm troopers. I wanted you
to bring pain to heaven. I saw fire curing headaches. I saw the
triumph of election over discipline. I wanted your confusion to
be a butterfly net for magic. I saw ecstasy without fun and vice
versa. I saw all things change their nature by mere intensification
of their properties. I wanted to discredit training for the sake of

purer prayer. I held things back from you because I wished you greater than my Systems conceived. I saw wounds pulling oars without becoming muscles.

Who is the New Jew?

The New Jew loses his mind gracefully. He applies finance to abstraction resulting in successful messianic politics, colorful showers of meteorites and other symbolic weather. He has induced amnesia by a repetitious study of history, his very forgetfulness caressed by facts which he accepts with visible enthusiasm. He changes for a thousand years the value of stigma, causing men of all nations to pursue it as superior sexual talisman. The New Jew is the founder of Magic Canada, Magic French Québec, and Magic America. He demonstrates that yearning brings surprises. He uses regret as a bulwark of originality. He confuses nostalgic theories of Negro supremacy which were tending to the monolithic. He confirms tradition through amnesia, tempting the whole world with rebirth. He dissolves history and ritual by accepting unconditionally the complete heritage. He travels without passport because powers consider him harmless. His penetration into jails enforces his supranationality, and flatters his legalistic disposition. Sometimes he is Jewish but always he is American, and now and then, Québecois.

These were my dreams for you and me, vieux copain – New Jews, the two of us, queer, militant, invisible, part of a possible new tribe bound by gossip and rumors of divine evidence.

I sent you the wrong box of fireworks, and this was not entirely by mistake. You got the Rich Brothers' All-American Assortment, which claims to be the largest selection offered at the price, over 550 pieces. Let us be charitable and say that I didn't know exactly how long the ordeal should last. I could have sent you the Famous Banner Fireworks Display, same price as the other, with over a *thousand* pieces of noise and beauty. I denied you the rocking Electric Cannon Salutes, the good old-fashioned Cherry Bombs, the Silver Rain Torch, the 16-report Battle in Clouds, the suicidal Jap Pop-Bottle Night Rockets. Let charity record that I did this out of charity. The explosions might have drawn malicious attention. But how can I justify withholding the Big Colorful Family Lawn Display, a special package made up for those tuned to a minimum of noise? Musical Vesuvius Flitter Fountains I hid from you, Comet Star Shells, Flower Pots with

Handles, Large Floral Shells, Triangle Spinning Wheels, Patriotic
Colored Fire Flag. Stretch your heart, darling. Let charity argue
that I spared you a domestic extravagance.

I am going to set you straight on everything: Edith, me, you,
Tekakwitha, the A——s, the firecrackers.

I didn't want you to burn yourself to suicide. On the other hand,
I didn't want the exodus to be too easy. This last from professional
teacher's pride, and also a subtle envy which I have previously
exposed.

What is more sinister is the possibility that I may have contrived
to immunize you against the ravages of ecstasy by regular inocu-
lations of homeopathic doses of it. A diet of paradox fattens the
ironist not the psalmist.

Perhaps I should have gone all the way and sent you the
sub-machine guns which the firecrackers concealed in my brilliant
smuggling operation. I suffer from the Virgo disease: nothing I
did was pure enough. I was never sure whether I wanted disciples
or partisans. I was never sure whether I wanted Parliament or a
hermitage.

I will confess that I never saw the Québec Revolution clearly,
even at the time of my parliamentary disgrace. I simply refused to
support the War, not because I was French, or a pacifist (which
of course I'm not), but because I was tired. I knew what they
were doing to the Gypsies, I had a whiff of Zyklon B, but I was
very, very tired. Do you remember the world at that time? A huge
jukebox played a sleepy tune. The tune was a couple of thousand
years old and we danced to it with our eyes closed. The tune was
called History and we loved it, Nazis, Jews, everybody. We loved
it because we made it up, because, like Thucydides, we knew that
whatever happened to us was the most important thing that ever
happened in the world. History made us feel good so we played
it over and over, deep into the night. We smiled as our uncles
went to bed, and we were glad to get rid of them, because they
didn't know how to do the H. in spite of all their boasts and old
newspaper clippings. Good night, old frauds. Someone worked the
rheostat and we squeezed the body in our arms, we inhaled the
perfumed hair, we bumped into each other's genitals. History was
our song, History chose us to make History. We gave ourselves to
it, caressed by events.

In perfect drowsy battalions we moved through the moonlight.

Its will be done. In perfect sleep we took the soap and waited for the showers.

Never mind, never mind. I've gone too deep into the old language. It may trap me there.

I was tired. I was sick of the inevitable. I tried to slip out of History. Never mind, never mind. Just say I was tired. I said no.

–Leave Parliament this instant!

–Frogs!

–They can't be trusted!

–Vote him dead!

I ran off with heavy heart. I loved the red chairs of Parliament. I cherished the fucks under the monument. I had cream in National Library. Too impure for empty future, I wept old jackpots.

Now my fat confession. I loved the magic of guns. I sneaked them in under the skin of firecrackers. My old monkey made me do it. I planted guns in Québec for I was hung between free and coward. Guns suck magic. I buried guns for future History. If History rule let me be Mr. History. The guns are green. The flowers poke. I let History back because I was lonely. Do not follow. Go beyond my style. I am nothing but a rotten hero.

Among the bars in my soap collection. Never mind.

Later.

Among the bars in my soap collection. I paid big cash for it. Argentine vacation hotel week-end shack-up with Edith. Never mind that. I paid equivalent U.S. $635. Waiter giving me the eye for days. He not cute little recent immigrant. Former Lord of few miserable European acres. Transaction beside swimming pool. I wanted it. I wanted it. My lust for secular gray magic. Human soap. A full bar, minus the wear of one bath in which I plunged myself, for better or for worse.

Mary, Mary, where are you, my little Abishag?

My dear friend, take my spirit hand.

I am going to show you everything *happening*. That is as far as I can take you. I cannot bring you into the middle of action. My hope is that I have prepared *you* for this pilgrimage. I didn't suspect the pettiness of my dream. I believed that I had conceived the vastest dream of my generation: I wanted to be a magician. That was my idea of glory. Here is a plea based on my whole experience: do not be a magician, be magic.

That weekend when I arranged for you to work in the Archives, Edith and I flew down to Argentine for a little sun and experiments. Edith was having trouble with her body: it kept changing sizes, she even feared that it might be dying.

We took a large air-conditioned room overlooking the sea, double-locking the door as soon as the porter had left with his hand full of tip.

Edith spread a large rubber sheet over the double bed, carefully moving from corner to corner to smooth it out. I loved to watch her bend over. Her buttocks were my masterpiece. Call her nipples an eccentric extravagance, but the bum was perfect. It's true that from year to year it required electronic massage and applications of hormone mold, but the conception was perfect.

Edith took off her clothes and lay down on the rubber sheet. I stood over her. Her eyes blazed.

−I hate you, F. I hate you for what you've done to me and my husband. I was a fool to get mixed up with you. I wish he'd known me before you.

−Hush, Edith. We don't want to go over all that again. You wanted to be beautiful.

−I can't remember anything now. I'm all confused. Perhaps I was beautiful before.

−Perhaps, I echoed in a voice as sad as hers.

Edith shifted her brown hips to make herself comfortable, and a shaft of sunlight infiltrated her pubic hair, giving it a rust-coloured tint. Yes, that was beauty beyond my craft.

> Sun on Her Cunt
> Wispy Rusty Hair
> Her Tunnels Sunk in Animal
> Her Kneecaps Round and Bare

I knelt beside the bed and lay one of my thin ears on the little sunlit orchard, listening to the tiny swamp machinery.

−You've meddled, F. You've gone against God.

−Hush, my little chicken. There is some cruelty even I cannot bear.

−You should have left me like you found me. I'm no good to anyone now.

−I could suck you forever, Edith.

She made the shaved hairs on the back of my neck tingle with the grazing of her lovely brown fingers.

–Sometimes I feel sorry for you, F. You might have been a great man.

–Stop talking, I bubbled.

–Stand up, F. Get your mouth off me. I'm pretending that you are someone else.

–Who?

–The waiter.

–Which one? I demanded.

–With the mustache and the raincoat.

–I thought so, I thought so.

–You noticed him, too, didn't you, F.?

–Yes.

I stood up too suddenly. Dizziness twirled my brain like a dial and formerly happy chewed food in my stomach turned into vomit. I hated my life, I hated my meddling, I hated my ambition. For a second I wanted to be an ordinary bloke cloistered in a tropical hotel room with an Indian orphan.

> Take from me my Camera
> Take from me my Glass
> The Sun the Wet Forever
> Let the Doctors Pass

–Don't cry, F. You knew it had to happen. You wanted me to go all the way. Now I'm no good to anyone and I'll try anything.

I stumbled to the window but it was hermetically sealed. The ocean was deep green. The beach was polka-dotted with beach umbrellas. How I longed for my old teacher, Charles Axis. I strained my eyes for an immaculate white bathing suit, unshadowed by topography of genitalia.

–Oh, come here, F. I can't stand watching a man vomit and cry.

She cradled my head between her bare breasts, stuffing a nipple into each ear.

–There now.

–Thankyou, thankyou, thankyou, thankyou.

–Listen, F. Listen the way you wanted us all to listen.

—I'm listening, Edith.

> Let me let me follow
> Down the Sticky Caves
> Where embryonic Cities
> Form Scum upon the Waves

—You're not listening, F.

—I'm trying.

—I feel sorry for you, F.

—Help me, Edith.

—Then get back to work. That's the only thing that can help you. Try to finish the work you began on all of us.

She was right. I was the Moses of our little exodus. I would never cross. My mountain might be very high but it rises from the desert. Let it suffice me.

I recovered my professional attitude. Her lower perfume was still in my nostrils but that was my business. I surveyed the nude girl from my Pisgah. Her soft lips smiled.

—That's better, F. Your tongue was nice but you do better as a doctor.

—All right, Edith. What seems to be the trouble now?

—I can't make myself come any more.

—Of course you can't. If we're going to perfect the pan-orgasmic body, extend the erogenous zone over the whole fleshy envelope, popularize the Telephone Dance, then we've got to begin by diminishing the tyranny of the nipples, lips, clitoris, and asshole.

—You're going against God, F. You say dirty words.

—I'll take my chances.

—I feel so lost since I can't make myself come any more. I'm not ready for the other stuff yet. It makes me too lonely. I feel blurred. Sometimes I forget where my cunt is.

—You make me weary, Edith. To think I've pinned all my hopes on you and your wretched husband.

—Give it back to me, F.

—All right, Edith. It's a very simple matter. We do it with books. I thought this might happen, so I brought the appropriate ones along. I also have in this trunk a number of artificial phalli (used by women), Vaginal Vibrators, the Rin-No-Tam and Godemiche or Dildo.

—Now you're talking.

—Just lie back and listen. Sink into the rubber sheet. Spread your legs and let the air-conditioning do its filthy work.

—O.K., shoot.

I cleared my famous throat. I chose a swollen book, frankly written, which describes various Auto-Erotic practices as indulged in by humans and animals, flowers, children and adults, and women of all ages and cultures. The areas covered included: Why Wives Masturbate, What We Can Learn From the Anteater, Unsatisfied Women, Abnormalities and Eroticism, Techniques of Masturbation, Latitude of Females, Genital Shaving, Clitoral Discovery, Club Masturbation, Female Metal, Nine Rubber, Frame Caress, Urethral Masturbation, Individual Experiments, Masturbation in and of Children, Thigh-Friction Technique, Mammary Stimulation, Auto-Eroticism in Windows.

—Don't stop, F. I feel it coming back.

Her lovely brown fingers inched down her silky rounded belly. I continued reading in my slow, tantalizing, weather-reporting tones. I read to my deep-breathing protégée of the unusual sex practices, when Sex Becomes "Different". An "Unusual" sex practice is one where there is some greater pleasure than orgasm through intercourse. Most of these bizarre practices involve a measure of mutilation, shock, voyeurism, pain, or torture. The sex habits of the average person are relatively free of such sadistic or masochistic traits. NEVERTHELESS, the reader will be shocked to see how abnormal are the tastes of the so-called normal person. CASE HISTORIES and intensive field work. Filled with chapters detailing ALL ASPECTS of the sex act. SAMPLE HEADINGS: Rubbing, Seeing, Silk Rings, Satyriasis, Bestiality in Others. The average reader will be surprised to learn how "Unusual" practices are passed along by seemingly innocent, normal sex partners.

—It's so good, F. It's been so long.

Now it was late afternoon. The sky had darkened somewhat. Edith was touching herself everywhere, smelling herself shamelessly. I could hardly keep still myself. The texts had got to me. Goose pimples rose on her young form. I stared dumbly at Original drawings: male and female organs, both external and internal, drawings indicating correct and incorrect methods of penetration. Wives will benefit from seeing how the penis is received.

–Please, F. Don't leave me like this.

My throat was burning with the hunger of it. Love fondled. Edith writhed under her squeezes. She flipped over on her stomach, wielding her small beautiful fists in anal stimulation. I threw myself into a Handbook of Semi-Impotence. There were important pieces woven into the theme: how to enlarge the erect penis, penis darkness, use of lubricants, satisfaction during menstruation, abusing the menopause, a wife's manual assistance in overcoming semi-impotence.

–Don't touch me, F. I'll die.

I blurted out a piece on Fellatio and Cunnilingus Between Brother and Sister, and others. My hands were almost out of control. I stumbled through a new concept for an exciting sex life. I didn't miss the section on longevity. Thrilling culminations possible for all. Lesbians by the hundreds interviewed and bluntly questioned. Some tortured for coy answers. Speak up, you cheap dyke. An outstanding work showing the sex offender at work. Chemicals to get hair off palms. Not models! Actual Photos of Male and Female Sex Organs and Excrement. Explored Kissing. The pages flew. Edith mumbling bad words through froth. Her fingers were bright and glistening, her tongue bruised from the taste of her waters. I spoke the books in everyday terms, the most sensitivity, cause of erection, Husband-Above 1–17, Wife-Above 18–29, Seated 30–34, On-The-Side 35–38, Standing & Kneeling Positions 39–53, Miscellaneous Squats 54–109, Coital Movement In All Directions, both for Husband and Wife.

– Edith! I cried. Let me have Foreplay.

– Never.

I sped through a glossary of Sexual Terms. In 1852, Richard Burton (d. aet. 69) submitted calmly to circumcision at the age of 31. "Milkers." Detailed Library of Consummated Incest. Ten Steps on Miscegenation. Techniques of Notorious Photographers. The Evidence of Extreme Acts. Sadism, Mutilation, Cannibalism, Cannibalism of Oralists, How To Match Disproportionate Organs. See the vivid birth of the new American woman. I shouted the recorded facts. She will not be denied the pleasures of sex. CASE HISTORIES show the changing trends. Filled with accounts of college girls eager to be propositioned. Women no longer inhibited by oral intimacy. Men masturbated to death. Cannibalism during Foreplay. Skull Coition. Secrets of "Timing" the Climax. Foreskin,

Pro, Con, and Indifferent. The Intimate Kiss. What are the benefits of sexual experimentation? Own and other's sexual make-up.
Sin has to be taught. Kissing Negroes on their Mouths. Thigh
Documents. Styles of Manual Pressure in Voluntary Indulgence.
Death Rides a Camel. I gave her everything. My voice cried
the Latex. I hid no laces, nor a pair of exciting open-front
pants, nor soft elasticized bra instead of sagging, heavy wide
bust, therefore youthful separation. O'er Edith's separate nipples
I blabbed the full record, Santa Pants, Fire Alarm Snow, Glamor
Tip, plain wrapper Thick Bust Jelly, washable leather Kinsey Doll,
Smegma Discipline, the LITTLE SQUIRT ash-tray, "SEND ME
ANOTHER Rupture-Easer so I will have one to change off with.
It is enabling me to work top speed at my press machine 8 hrs a
day," this I threw in for sadness, for melancholy soft flat groin
pad which might lurk in Edith's memory swamp as soiled lever,
as stretched switch to bumpy apotheosis wet rocket come out of
the fine print slum where the only trumpet solo is grandfather's
stringy cough and underwear money problems.

Edith was wiggling her saliva-covered kneecaps, bouncing on the
rivulets of lubrication. Her thighs were aglow with froth, and her
pale anus was excavated by cruel false fingernails. She screamed
for deliverance, the flight her imagination commanded denied by
a half-enlightened cunt.

    – Do something, F. I beg you. But don't touch me.
    – Edith, darling! What have I done to you?
    – Stand back, F!
    – What can I do?
    – Try.
    – Torture story?
    – Anything, F. Hurry.
    – The Jews?
    – No. Too foreign.
    – 1649? Brébeuf and Lalemant?
    – Anything.

So I began to recite my schoolboy lesson of how the Iroquois
killed the Jesuits Brébeuf and Lalemant, whose scorched and
mangled relics were discovered the morning of the twentieth by
a member of the Society and seven armed Frenchmen. "Ils y
trouuerent vn spectacle d'horreur. . . ."

On the afternoon of the sixteenth the Iroquois had bound

Brébeuf to a stake. They commenced to scorch him from head to foot.

– Everlasting flames for those who persecute the worshipers of God, Brébeuf threatened them in the tone of a master.

As the priest spoke the Indians cut away his lower lip and forced a red-hot iron down his throat. He made no sign or sound of discomfort.

Then they led out Lalemant. Around his naked body they had fastened strips of bark, smeared with pitch. When Lalemant saw his Superior, the bleeding unnatural aperture exposing his teeth, the handle of the heated implement still protruding from the seared and ruined mouth, he cried out in the words of St. Paul:

– We are made a spectacle to the world, to angels, and to men.

Lalemant flung himself at Brébeuf's feet. The Iroquois took him, bound him to a stake, and ignited the vegetation in which he was trussed. He screamed for heaven's help, but he was not to die so quickly.

They brought a collar made of hatchets heated redhot and conferred it on Brébeuf. He did not flinch.

An ex-convert, who had backslid, now shouldered forward and demanded that hot water be poured on their heads, since the missionaries had poured so much cold water on them. A kettle was slung, water boiled, and then poured slowly on the heads of the captive priests.

– We baptize you, they laughed, that you may be happy in heaven. You told us that the more one suffers on earth, the happier he is in heaven.

Brébeuf stood like a rock. After a number of revolting tortures they scalped him. He was still alive when they laid open his breast. A crowd came forward to drink the blood of so courageous an enemy and to devour his heart. His death astonished his murderers. His ordeal lasted four hours.

Lalemant, physically weak from childhood, was taken back to the house. There he was tortured all night, until, sometime after dawn, one Indian wearied of the extended entertainment and administered a fatal blow with his hatchet. There was no part of his body which was not burned, "even to his eyes, in the sockets of which these wretches had placed live coals." His ordeal lasted seventeen hours.

– How do you feel, Edith?

There was no need for me to ask. My recitals had served only to bring her closer to a summit she could not achieve. She moaned in terrible hunger, her gooseflesh shining in supplication that she might be freed from the unbearable coils of secular pleasure, and soar into that blind realm, so like sleep, so like death, that journey of pleasure beyond pleasure, where each man travels as an orphan toward an atomic ancestry, more anonymous, more nourishing than the arms of blood or foster family.

I knew she would never make it.

– F., get me out of this, she moaned pitifully.

I plugged in the Danish Vibrator. A degrading spectacle followed. As soon as those delicious electric oscillations occupied my hand like an army of trained seaweed, weaving, swathing, caressing – I was reluctant to surrender the instrument to Edith. Somehow, in the midst of her juicy ordeal, she noticed me trying to slip the Perfected Suction Bracers down into the shadows of my underwear.

She lifted herself out of her pools and lunged at me.

– Give me that. You rat!

Bearlike (some ancestral memory?) she swung at me. I had not had the opportunity to fasten the Improved Wonder Straps, and the Vibrator flew out of my embrace. Thus the bear, with a swipe of his clawed paw, scoops the fish from the bosom of the stream. Crablike, the D.V. scuttled across the polished floor, humming like an overturned locomotive.

–You're selfish, F., Edith snarled.

–That's the observation of a liar and an ingrate, I said as gently as possible.

–Get out of my way.

–I love you, I said as I inched my way toward the D.V. I love you, Edith. My methods may have been wrong, but I never stopped loving you. Was it selfish of me to try to end your pain, yours and his (you, dear old comrade)? I saw pain everywhere. I could not bear to look into your eyes, so maggoty were they with pain and desire. I could not bear to kiss either of you, for each of your embraces disclosed a hopeless, mordant plea. In your laughter, though it were for money or for sunsets, I heard your throats ripped with greed. In the midst of the high jump, I saw the body wither. Between the spurts of come, you launched your tidings of regret. Thousands built, thousands lay squashed beneath tubes of highway. You were not happy to brush your teeth. I gave you breasts with nipples: could you nourish anyone? I gave you prick with separate memory: could you train a race? I took you to a complete movie of the Second World War: did you feel any lighter when we walked out? No, you threw yourselves upon the thorns of research. I sucked you, and you howled to dispense me something more than poison. With every handshake you wept for a lost garden. You found a cutting edge for every object. I couldn't stand the racket of your pain. You were smeared with blood and tortured scabs. You needed bandages – there was no time to boil the germs out of them – I grabbed what was at hand. Caution was a luxury. There was no time for me to examine my motives. Self-purification would have been an alibi. Beholding such a spectacle of misery, I was free to try anything. I can't answer for my own erection.

I have no explanation for my own vile ambitions. Confronted with your pus, I could not stop to examine my direction, whether or not I was aimed at a star. As I limped down the street every window broadcast a command: Change! Purify! Experiment! Cauterize! Reverse! Burn! Preserve! Teach! Believe me, Edith, I had to act, and act fast. That was my nature. Call me Dr Frankenstein with a deadline. I seemed to wake up in the middle of a car accident, limbs strewn everywhere, detached voices screaming for comfort, severed fingers pointing homeward, all the debris withering like sliced cheese out of Cellophane – and all I had in the wrecked world was a needle and thread, so I got down on my knees, I pulled pieces out of the mess and I started to stitch them together. I had an idea of what a man should look like, but it kept changing. I couldn't devote a lifetime to discovering the ideal physique. All I heard was pain, all I saw was mutilation. My needle going so madly, sometimes I found I'd run the thread right through my own flesh and I was joined to one of my own grotesque creations – I'd rip us apart – and then I heard my own voice howling with the others, and I knew that I was also truly part of the disaster. But I also realized that I was not the only one on my knees sewing frantically. There were others like me, making the same monstrous mistakes, driven by the same impure urgency, stitching themselves into the ruined heap, painfully extracting themselves –

–F., you're weeping.

–Forgive me.

–Stop blubbering. See, you've lost your hard-on.

–It's all breaking down now. My discipline is collapsing. Have you any idea how much discipline I had to use in training the two of you?

We both leaped for the Vibrator at the same instant. Her fluids made her slippery. For a second in our struggle I wished we were making love, for all her nozzles were stiff and fragrant. I grabbed her around the waist, before I knew it her bum popped out of my bear hug like a wet watermelon seed, her thighs went by like a missed train, and there I was with empty lubricated arms, nose squashed against the expensive mahogany floor.

Old friend, are you still with me? Do not despair. I promised you that this would end in ecstasy. Yes, your wife was naked during this story. Somewhere in the dark room, draped over the back of a chair like a huge exhausted butterfly, her Gal panties, stiffened by the slightest masonry of sweat, dreamed of ragged fingernails, and I dreamed with them – large, fluttering, descending dreams crisscrossed with vertical scratches. For me it was the end of Action. I would keep on trying, but I knew I had failed the both of you, and that both of you had failed me. I had one trick left, but it was a dangerous one, and I'd never used it. Events, as I will show, would force me into it, and it would end with Edith's suicide, my hospitalization, your cruel ordeal in the treehouse. How many times did I warn you that you would be whipped by loneliness?

So I lay there in Argentine. The Danish Vibrator hummed like a whittler as it rose and fell over Edith's young contours. It was cold and black in the room. Occasionally one of her glistening kneecaps would catch a glint of moonlight as she jerked her box up and down in desperate supplication. She had stopped moaning; I assumed she had approached the area of intense breathless silence which the orgasm loves to flood with ventriloquist gasps and cosmic puppet plots.

–Thank God, she whispered at last.

–I'm glad you could come, Edith. I'm very happy for you.

–Thank God it's off me. I had to blow it. It made me do oral intimacy.

–Wha –?

Before I could question her further it was upon my buttocks,

its idiot hum revved up to a psychotic whine. The detachable
crotch piece inserted itself between my hairy thighs, ingeniously
providing soft support for my frightened testicles. I had heard
of these things happening before, and I knew it would leave me
bitter and full of self-loathing. Like a cyanide egg dropped into
the gas chamber the D.V. released a glob of Formula Cream at
the top of the muscular cleavage I had labored so hard to define.
As my body heat melted it to the trickle which would grease its
shameful entry, several comfortable Latex cups assumed exciting
holds here and there. The elastic Developer seemed to have a life
of its own, and the Fortune Straps spread everything apart, and I
felt the air-conditioning coolly evaporating sweat and cream *from
tiny surfaces I hardly knew existed*. I was ready to lie there for ten
days. I was not even surprised. I knew it would be insatiable but
I was ready to submit. I heard Edith faintly calling to me just as
the Foam Pad rose the full length. After that I heard nothing.
It was like a thousand Sex Philosophers working over me with
perfect cooperation. I may have screamed at the first thrust of the
White Club, but the Formula Cream kept coming, and I think a
cup was converted to handle excreta. It hummed in my ears like
alabaster lips.

I don't know how long it swarmed among my private pieces.

Edith made it to a light switch. She couldn't bear to look at
me.

–Are you happy, F.?

I did not answer.

–Should I do something, F.?

Perhaps the D.V. answered with a sated whir. It pulled in the
American Laces fast as an Italian eater, the suck went out of the
cups, my scrotum dropped unceremoniously, and the machine
slipped off my quivering body meat. I think I was happy. . . .

–Should I pull out the plug, F.?

–Do what you want, Edith. I'm washed up.

Edith yanked at the electric cord. The D.V. shuddered, fell
silent, and stopped. Edith sighed with relief, but too soon. The
D.V. began to produce a shattering sonic whistle.

–Does it have batteries?

–No, Edith. It doesn't have batteries.

She covered her breasts with crossed arms.

–You mean –?

—Yes. It's learned to feed itself.

Edith backed into a corner as the Danish Vibrator advanced toward her. She stooped queerly, as if she were trying to hide her cunt behind her thighs. I could not stir from the puddle of jelly in which I had been buggered by countless improvements. It made its way across the hotel room in a leisurely fashion, straps and cups flowing behind it, like a Hawaiian skirt made of grass and brassières.

It had learned to feed itself.

(O Father, Nameless and Free of Description, lead me from the Desert of the Possible. Too long I have dealt with Events. Too long I labored to become an Angel. I chased Miracles with a bag of Power to salt their wild Tails. I tried to dominate Insanity so I could steal its Information. I tried to program the Computers with Insanity. I tried to create Grace to prove that Grace existed. Do not punish Charles Axis. We could not see the Evidence so we stretched our Memories. Dear Father, accept this confession: we did not train ourselves to Receive because we believed there wasn't Anything to Receive and we could not endure with this Belief.)

—Help, help me, F.

But I was fastened to the floor with a tingling nail, the head of which was my anus.

It took its time getting to her. Edith, meanwhile, her back squeezed into the right angle, had sunk to a defenseless sitting position, her lovely legs spread apart. Numbed by horror and the prospect of disgusting thrills, she was ready to submit. I have stared at many orifices, but never have I seen one wear such an expression. The soft hairs were thrown back from the dripping lips like a Louis Quatorze sunburst. The layers of lip spread and gathered like someone playing with a lens opening. The Danish Vibrator mounted her slowly, and soon the child (Edith was twenty) was doing things with her mouth and fingers that no one, believe me, old friend, no one has ever done to you. Perhaps this was what you wanted from her. But you did not know how to encourage her, and this was not your fault. No one could. That is why I tried to lead the fuck away from mutual dialing.

The whole assault lasted maybe twenty-five minutes. Before the tenth minute passed she was begging the thing to perform in her armpits, specifying which nipple was hungriest, twisting her torso to offer it hidden pink terrain – until the Danish Vibrator began to command. Then Edith, quite happily, became nothing but a buffet of juice, flesh, excrement, muscle to serve its appetite.

Of course, the implications of her pleasure are enormous.

The Danish Vibrator slipped off her face, uncovering a bruised soft smile.

–Stay, she whispered.

It climbed onto the window sill, purring deeply, revved up to a sharp moan, and launched itself through the glass, which broke and fell over its exit like a fancy stage curtain.

–Make it stay.

–It's gone.

We dragged our strange bodies to the window. The perfumed sticky tropical night wafted into the room as we leaned out to watch the Danish Vibrator move down the marble stories of the hotel. When it reached the ground it crossed the parking lot and soon achieved the beach.

–Oh, God, F., it was beautiful. Feel this.

–I know, Edith. Feel this.

A curious drama began to unfold beneath us on the deserted moonlit sand. As the D.V. made slowly toward the waves breaking in dark flowers on the bright shore, a figure emerged from a grove of ghostly palms. It was a man wearing an immaculate white bathing suit. I do not know whether he was running to intercept the Danish Vibrator with the intention of violently disabling it, or merely wished to observe at closer range its curiously graceful progress toward the Atlantic.

How soft the night seemed, like the last verse of a lullaby. With one hand on his hip and the other scratching his head, the tiny figure beneath us watched, as did we, the descent of the apparatus into the huge rolling sea, which closed over its luminous cups like the end of a civilization.

–Will it come back, F.? To us?

–It doesn't matter. It's in the world.

We stood close to each other in the window, two figures on a rung of a high marble ladder built into the vast cloudless night, leaning on nothing.

A small breeze detached a wisp of her hair and I felt its tiny fall across my cheek.

–I love you, Edith.

–I love you, F.

–And I love your husband.

–So do I.

–Nothing is as I planned it, but now I know what will happen.

–So do I, F.

–Oh, Edith, something is beginning in my heart, a whisper of rare love, but I will never be able to fulfil it. It is my prayer that your husband will.

–He will, F.

–But he will do it alone. He can only do it alone.

–I know, she said. We must not be with him.

A great sadness overtook us as we looked out over the miles of sea, an egoless sadness that we did not own or claim. Here and there the restless water kept an image of the shattered moon. We said good-by to you, old lover. We did not know when or how the parting would be completed, but it began that moment.

There was a professional knock on the blond door.

–It must be him, I said.

–Should we put our clothes on?

–Why bother.

We did not even have to open the door. The waiter had a passkey. He was wearing the old raincoat and mustache, but underneath he was perfectly nude. We turned toward him.

–Do you like Argentine? I asked for the sake of civil conversation.

–I miss the newsreels, he said.

–And the parades? I offered.

–And the parades. But I can get everything else here. Ah!

He noticed our reddened organs and began to fondle them with great interest.

–Wonderful! Wonderful! I see you have been well prepared.

What followed was old hat. I have no intention of adding to any pain which might be remaindered to you, by a minute description of the excesses we performed with him. Lest you should worry for us, let me say that we had, indeed, been well prepared, and we hardly cared to resist his sordid exciting commands, even when he made us kiss the whip.

–I have a treat for you, he said at last.

—He has a treat for us, Edith.

—Shoot, she replied wearily.

From the pocket of his overcoat he withdrew a bar of soap.

—Three in a tub, he said merrily in his heavy accent.

So we splashed around with him. He lathered us from head to
foot, proclaiming all the while the special qualities of the soap,
which, as you must now understand, was derived from melted
human flesh.

That bar is now in your hands. We were baptized by it, your
wife and I. I wonder what you will do with it.

You see, I have shown you *how it happens*, from style to style,
from kiss to kiss.

There is more, there is the history of Catherine Tekakwitha —
you shall have all of it.

Wearily we dried each other with the opulent towels of the
hotel. The waiter was very careful with our parts.

—I had millions of these at my disposal, he said without a trace
of nostalgia.

He slipped into his raincoat and spent some time before the
full-length mirror playing with his mustache and slanting his hair
across his forehead in just the way he liked.

—And don't forget to inform the *Police Gazette*. We'll bargain
over the soap later.

—Wait!

As he opened the door to go, Edith threw her arms about his
neck, pulled him to the dry bed, and cradled his famous head
against her breasts.

—What did you do that for? I demanded of her after the waiter
had made his stiff exit, and nothing remained of him but the
vague stink of his sulphurous flatulence.

—For a second I thought he was an A —.

—Oh, Edith!

I sank to my knees before your wife and I laid my mouth on
her toes. The room was a mess, the floor spotted with pools of
fluid and suds, but she rose from it all like a lovely statue with
epaulets and nipple tips of moonlight.

—Oh, Edith! It doesn't matter what I've done to you, the tits, the
cunt, the hydraulic buttock failures, all my Pygmalion tampering,
it means nothing, I know now. Acne and all, you were out of my
reach, you were beyond my gadgetry. Who are you?

– Ισις ἐγῶ εἰμί πάντα γεγονός καί ὄν καί ἐσόμενον καί τό ἐμόν πέπλον οὐδείς τῶν θνητῶν ἀπεκαλυψεν!

–You're not joking? Then I'm only fit to suck your toes.
–Wiggle.

LEONE or
the buffet of the Gare de Lyon

Régine Deforges

Translated by Maxim Jakubowski

IT ALL BEGAN in the Train Bleu, the restaurant of the Gare de Lyon.

The Christmas holidays had just begun. The railway station was surrounded by busy crowds, rushing, laden with cases, bags and skis. Leone, having delivered her mother and children, was settling up with the grumpy cab driver moaning about the traffic jams he'd just driven through.

"And they still complain about the price of petrol, even at ten francs per litre, shouldn't be allowed to drive damn cars . . . Christ, retirement won't ever come too early."

Leone gave him a good tip, to calm him down and watched a faint smile transform his weary face.

"That's very kind of you, madam. Have a nice journey."

Her mother had managed to find a porter, the two kids were waiting quietly, pacified by the promise of dinner in the restaurant before they boarded the sleeping car. Their behaviour was particularly impressive seeing they were so excited by the coming disruption to their everyday life.

They followed the porter to the lift that went up to the restaurant. Passing under the great clock, her son remembered an episode from Tardi's *ADELE BLANSEC* that had greatly impressed him. The children were agog at the baroque decor of the place. The abundance of gold, the walls and ceilings so full of colourful paintings, the warm nudes, the heavy silver trolleys laden with roasts, and in particular those bearing an impressive stack of patisseries which made their mouths water.

The maitre d' found them a comfortable corner and brought the menus. Sophie, full of the assurance of her lone five years, declared peremptorily that she would not have soup but snails.

"That's very heavy for an evening meal," the grandmother said.

"It doesn't matter, mother," Leone said. "It's the holidays."

A grateful Sophie winked at her mum. Jacques, older, chose sausage and andouillette "with really a lot of chips" he added. Leone and her mother, less ambitiously, selected a consommé and grilled meat with a decent Bordeaux wine.

Once they had ordered, and the wine was promptly delivered to the table as requested, Leone chose to relax and lit up a cigarette while slowly sipping a glass of wine.

Two young men, in their early thirties, looking merry, both rather handsome and weighed down by luggage, came to sit across from them, picked up their menu and ordered. Then, like Leone, they each lit up a cigarette and looked around them. They noticed her simultaneously and smiled pleasingly, impressed by the spectacle of the unknown woman. Leone demurely smiled back. She knew she was pretty, draped in the soft, black wool outfit that showed off her pale complexion and her ash blonde hair. She looked away but still felt the men's gaze on her. Her son also noticed their interest and, with a distinct sense of ownership, remarked:

"Why are those two guys looking at you like that?"

"It's because they think mummy is very pretty," said Sophie, cuddling up to her mother, to demonstrate that Leone was hers and hers alone. Which provoked Jacques to stand up and come over to kiss his mother. She held them both tight against her, laughing, pleased with the proximity of their warm young bodies.

"Those are indeed very lucky kids," one of the men whispered rather loudly.

It was trite, but the sound of his voice was pleasing to Leone.

The waiters brought the dishes. Jacques sat down again and laid siege to his sausage with gluttony, while Sophie struggled with the snail tongs. For a few moments, they ate in silence.

From time to time, Leone would look up and across to the nearby table. On each occasion, she would catch the eyes of one or the other of the friends. Soon, she felt herself become increasingly uneasy. "What a pity I'm not alone . . . they're both rather handsome. I'd find it difficult to choose between them . . . but, why choose? . . . Oh, what a fool I am, anyway, they'll soon be leaving . . . I'd like to leave, too . . . How it would be nice to be alone in Paris for a few days . . . Strange how these men attract me . . . It's reciprocal, they both like me too . . . what should I do? . . . I'd like to see them again . . . know where they live . . . I just can't speak to them, not in front of mother and the children . . . Oh, how life can be awkward!"

She pulled out a cigarette from the pack. A flame was struck. One of the men was offering it to her. She lit up her cigarette and thanked him with a nod.

The plates were cleared away and the meat was brought on. Increasingly disturbed, she was rather tersely answering the children's questions. Sophie pulled her by the sleeve.

"You're not even listening to me. What are you thinking of?"

Leone kissed the child.

"I was thinking how bored I will be without you around."

She tried to feign interest in her own mother's discourse: she was worried how her daughter would spend the holidays. Heard Jacques asking whether he would be having the same instructor as the previous year, and if he could still go to the movies in the afternoon.

Once again, her eyes met the gaze of the two men. This time, she didn't break the contact. She could read their desire, it was the same as hers, brutal and transparent. She felt her face go all red and looked away. There was something obsessive about their presence, her heartbeat quickened, her hands were becoming clammy, the bottom half of her body turning to lead. Shards of lucidity kept on telling her she was mad, ill, a sexual pervert. She took another cigarette and broke three matches in a row in a futile attempt to light it. The man who had offered her the flame earlier stood up, his light shivering slightly as he approached it. Leone took hold of the young man's hand to bring it to the level of her cigarette.

This brief contact caused her turmoil. The lighter's flame went out under her breath.

"I'm sorry," she said, looking up.

Her emotion reached its pinnacle as she witnessed the pale and stirring face of the man. He switched the lighter back on. Leone breathed the smoke in deeply with great relief.

"Thank you."

He returned to his seat, said a few words to his friend who was smiling back at him. The arrival of the dessert trolley was a welcome diversion. The children wanted a taste of each single one: the chocolate mousse, the rum baba, the egg cream, the raspberry pie, the blackcurrant sorbet, the chocolate cake, the iced meringues, the tarte tatin, their eyes were all over the place. The two men chose their desserts under the admiring gaze of the kids. Leone took only a coffee, which provoked some witty remarks among the men about how women knew to protect their waistline. Even though it was all rather banal, Leone laughed along with them, pleased by this fortuitous contact which would very soon come to an end on the station platform.

The time was nearing, Leone requested the bill and a porter. They offered to carry her luggage, but gave up smiling when they saw how many she had.

"Where are you going?" one of them asked.

"Morzine," Sophie said.

"What a coincidence, so are we," they said together in such harmony that all three burst out laughing.

Her mother watched Leone with disapproval while the children looked jealous. They reached their sleeping car. The ticket controller opened the door connecting the children and the grandmother's cabin. They moved and jumped between the compartments with noisy glee. Leone walked out into the corridor, and noticed the two men coming towards her from the other end of the car. The same emotion that had overcome her in the restaurant returned, only more violent now. She had to admit to herself that she wanted both of them together, that their joint desire was inflaming hers. "I'm a complete freak," she thought. A good thing matters would go no further: them to Morzine or wherever, she in Paris. Sadness suddenly swirled over her at the thought of being alone in Paris, in the grey, cold and muddy December Paris, while others left for the snow and holidays, maybe even some sun.

"We were looking for you . . . You will come and have a glass of champagne with us?"

"No, thank you. It's not possible, the train is about to leave."

"But until Morzine we have all the time in the world."

"I'm not taking the train, I'm only seeing the children off."

"Oh, no . . ."

The harmony of how they expressed their disappointment and the sad look on their faces touched Leone so much she couldn't stop herself from chuckling gently.

"Don't pull such faces, you both look as if you've just lost your best friend."

"Yeah, I suppose it's a bit like that," whispered the darker-haired one.

"Come with us," said the other. "It's stupid to stay in Paris at Christmas."

"Yes, yes, why don't you come along?"

"But I can't, my job . . ."

"You can phone in tomorrow and say you're sick."

All the while, Sophie had been quietly listening to the conversation and watching her mother and the two young men in turn. She took her mother by the hand.

"They're right, it would be nice if you came along with us."

"You know it's not possible, my darling. Go and see your grandmother."

"Come, we'd so much like to know you better. Even if you can't stay for the whole holiday, come for two or three days."

"No, I tell you, it's not possible. Anyway, I'd have nothing to wear. I can't go to the mountains and the snow dressed like this."

She pointed at herself, showing them how her black shoes couldn't adequately replace decent après-ski and her thin grey stockings substitute for warm leggings; and her delicate kid gloves, they would fall apart in the snow.

"It doesn't matter, everything you need we can buy there."

She did not answer. All three of them kept on watching each other, twisted up in their desire to huddle together, to caress one another, to love. Leone felt a pang of anger: "They're right, what's so important in Paris? I was only staying behind because I didn't feel like going with mother and the children . . . But . . . Can one go like this, with people you don't even know? . . . The only thing I know of them, is that they want to screw me . . . It's getting on my nerves, after all . . . and then, what would mother think, if I stayed here, like that . . . she's not stupid . . . and the children? . . . oh, to hell with the kids . . . if I did go? . . . It's not possible, I haven't got my toothbrush . . . or any make-up . . . I'd be such a sorry sight tomorrow morning . . . but they are so handsome . . . why not give in to their lust . . . and mine . . . so?"

"Madam, time to get off, the train is about to depart."

The ticket controller stole her away from her thoughts. She waved farewell to the two men and walked into the compartment to kiss her mother and the children. Like on the occasion of every departure, Sophie cried, her tears soon dried by Leone's kisses. Jacques wanted to open the window onto the platform; his mother convinced him not to, because of the cold. She kissed her mob one last time and got off the train. The controller closed the door behind her.

Like most people, she hated farewells on station platforms, it made her cry. Without even waiting for the train's departure, the final kisses blown from her lips, she began moving towards the exit. She passed the wagon where the two men were standing on the running board.

"Come, you can go back tomorrow if you want."

She stopped, her whole body braced towards them, torn between the desire to jump aboard and conventional morality.

"I'd really like to, but . . ."

The train gave a jump and slowly set itself in motion. She moved as if to climb on. She mechanically walked alongside, like someone trying to postpone the moment of separation from a loved one embarking on a long journey.

"Come . . ."

She felt herself lifted up, torn off the ground by two strong sets of hands and found herself in the now accelerating train, between the two men now looking at her with both satisfaction and worry.

"But it's a kidnapping . . . you're mad!"

But the sound of her voice, her bright, cheerful eyes, her moist, half-open mouth, contradicted her words.

If looks could eat, they were already devouring each other, truly amazed by the formidable aura of desire now surrounding them.

The spell wasn't broken by the appearance of the ticket controller who did not appear surprised to have an extra passenger. There was a spare seat. Leone wanted to pay for her fare, they would not allow her. They ordered another bottle of champagne.

"To celebrate our journey."

They introduced themselves: Gérard, Dominique. She only remembered their first names.

"I'm Leone."

"Let us drink to Leone's health."

They raised their three glasses. The champagne was luke-warm, but it wasn't important; it was only a symbol of their understanding.

Leaning on their elbows in front of the corridor window, they silently watched the procession outside of dark buildings, broken here and there by some light from a window, as they travelled through the sad Paris suburbs. Gérard put his arm around Leone's waist, while Dominique took hold of her shoulder. Without shame or false modesty, Leone gave in to the reassuring sense of well-being running through her as well as the heat of the two men. They stayed that way for some tim... , savouring the certainty of pleasures to come. Soon, the lights outside were few and far between and there was only the black hole of the countryside.

They moved into one of the compartments and helped Leone take her coat off. She remained standing, arms on her side, confident, calm. Only her breath quickened. Dominique pulled her towards him, gently kissing her face, her neck. She felt her body harden against his, thrust her lips forward and this first kiss was so voluptuous she almost fainted out of joy. Gérard turned her round and also kissed her with voracious brutality. She moaned. While Gérard prolonged his kiss, she felt Dominique pulling the zip of her dress. Without interrupting their kiss, he helped the young woman's arms out of the garment and let it fall softly to the ground. She stepped out of it and now only wore a short grey silk slip, lined with ochre lace. The hands of the two men moved across the smooth surface of the slip. They rubbed each other against her and she felt their hard cocks against her stomach and buttocks. She moved slightly, to feel them better. She thought they were getting even harder. Gérard abandoned her mouth and, sitting on the bunk, pulled down the shoulder straps of Leone's slip and brassiere. Her breasts burst out, heavy and voluptuous. Gérard buried his face in them, his mouth squashed against her musky mounds. He took a step back to admire them better. The train's movements echoed through them, bringing the breasts alive, their raised nipples begging for kisses and bites.

"How beautiful you are!"

She pulled Gérard's head against her chest. He greedily nibbled one tip. Leone let out a small cry.

"Oh, I'm sorry. Did I hurt you?"

"No, no, go on."

Gérard resumed his caress while Leone abandoned herself, a glutton for more.

Dominique was watching the spectacle of Gérard's mouth moving from one breast to another while his hands roamed freely over her splendid chest. He slipped off the already crumpled slip and the already wet knickers. He brought them up to his nose. Leone was naked between the two still-clothed men, she now only wore her suspender belt, her stockings and her shoes. Dominique could no longer hold back. He pulled his penis out and, arching Leone back towards him, holding her by the hips, drove into her. She struggled a bit, but the young man strengthened his hold on her and thrust himself in even deeper. His sex must be quite large, for she had never felt herself as mightily invaded as this. He moved slowly inside her, whispering:

"I love you, you are so good."

Gérard's mouth and hands kept on bruising her breasts, Dominique's cock surged on ever harder, a deep, savage lust rose inside Leone who came with a scream as Dominique spurted inside her. He briefly stayed within her, holding her up, kissing and pecking her back. Gérard pulled her away from his friend's body and laid her down on the cot. He hurriedly tore off all his clothes, scattering them around the compartment and threw himself into Leone. He took her without consideration. She barely had enough time to register the surprise of her intense arousal before they climaxed together, in total silence.

Leone felt as if time was standing still. Her body, blissful, floated. The swinging movements of the train completed the illusion.

"I'm thirsty," she whispered.

Dominique poured her some of the tepid champagne, she swallowed it in one gulp. He ran a wet towel over her body, which she was grateful for, and assisted her in rolling down her stockings and suspender belt. He then undressed.

Gérard grumbled. He was beginning to doze, and looking at him, Leone and Dominique began laughing.

"Here, some champagne will do you good."

He took the bottle from Dominique's hands and drank straight from it. The foam slipped out of his mouth, down his neck and lost itself in the hairs on his chest. He burped and apologized, lit a cigarette that he handed over to Leone and offered Dominique another. They were sitting on the cot, their legs hanging over the edge, curled up together, smoking in silence.

It was Dominique who interrupted their daydreaming, sliding down to the floor between Leone's legs. His warm and skilful tongue soon awakened her senses again. She moaned as she held the young man's head against her stomach. With her free hand, she searched for Gérard's penis; aroused by his fingers, it rose. Kneeling on the bunk, he brought his cock to the level of Leone's mouth; she lapped at it gently like a cat drinking milk. Dominique helped her slide down on the cot, and pulling her up, lowered her down on his member. Gérard, disappointed, stroked himself gently. They all three climaxed together.

Leone fell asleep in the middle of a sentence. But her sleep didn't last long. She was woken by a cock moving inside her. Later, one of the young men sodomized her. She barely had time to register the pain before she came again, at excruciating length.

Early in the morning, when the ticket controller knocked at the door to announce their arrival in Morzine station, she thought she wouldn't even be able to stand up again, her whole body ached so much. Aching, but satisfied. She shrieked in horror when she saw herself in the mirror. The circles around her eyes spread all the way down to her cheeks, her lips were swollen from too many kisses and bites, her tangled hair gave her the look of a wild, wanton woman.

"I can't go out like this. It looks as if I've . . ."

"Yes, you did," the men answered, laughing.

She shrugged and tried to make herself presentable. Her night companions weren't much of an improvement on her. Once she had dressed, they pulled her towards them.

"You don't regret it? You know, it's the first time we've made love to the same woman, together."

"For me too, it was the first time," she said, still a bit red-faced.

Dominique cupped her chin.

"You musn't be ashamed. We fell for you at first sight and you for us and it was wonderful."

She gave them each a big fat kiss on the cheeks, like you give to good friends, or children.

"Yes, it was wonderful."

"So, are you staying on?" asked Gérard.

"No, it's not possible. I'll hire a cab to Geneva and will then catch the first plane back to Paris."

They insisted but understood that she had made her mind up. "Keep an eye on my mother and my children disembarking, I don't want them to see me like this."

Gérard was the look-out while Dominique and Leone stayed back, huddled together, holding each other's hand. Leone knew she could grow attached to this tender, handsome, blue-eyed boy who made love so well. But her own life was already so full, there was no place left for further adventures. She regretted it.

Gérard returned, he'd found a cab and seen the family leave in another.

"Are you sure you don't want us to come with you to Geneva?"

"No, thanks, I don't enjoy farewells."

She got into the taxi, turned back to wave at them. Dominique was running behind the car. She guessed what he was asking: "Your name, your address." She looked away, smiled and settled down in the comfort of the seat. It was warm in the car, the snow-covered landscape was pretty in the morning light, the driver ignored her and remained silent. Images from the previous night floated back to the surface of her memory, raising exquisite feelings of pleasure. It felt like the dawn of time: before the creation of sin. She slept all the way to Geneva, a smile of ecstasy on her lips.

EQUINOX

Samuel R. Delany

THE COLOR OF bell metal:

Longer than a big man's foot; thick as a small girl's wrist. Veins made low relief like vines beneath the wrinkled hood. His fingers climbed the shaft, dropped to hair tight as wire, moved under the canvas flaps to gouge the sac, black as an over-ripe avocado: spilled his palm (it is a big hand); climbed the shaft again.

There is little light.

What's here bars the shutters in gold. Water lisps and whispers outside. The cabin sways, rises. There is a wind out to sea, that means. That means here at port it is clear evening.

The dog on the floor claws the planks.

The captain's toes spread the footboard. His chin went back and his belly made black ridges. The long head rolled on the pillow, brass ring at his ear a-flash.

The hood slipped from the punctured helmet.

The knuckles, like knots in weathered cable, flexed on him. The rhythm started with the boat's sway. Increase: his hand and the boat syncopate. The doubled pace pulled his buttocks from the blanket. The rim of his fist beat the tenderer rim (one color with his palm). His breath got loud. It halted, and halted, and halted.

Stop action film: a white orchid from bud to bloom.

Breath regular.

Mucus drips his knuckles. Still stiff, the shaft glistens. Pearls on black wire.

"Kirsten?"

He swung his feet over the edge, his shoulders hunched (dull as cannon shot); his dirty shirt was sleeveless. Buttons: copper.

"Kirsten!"

His voice: maroons, purples, a nap between velvet and suede.

"Come down here!"

When the door cracked, he laughed.

Her hair was yellow, paler than the light. Her smock, torn at her neck, hung between her breasts. One dull aureole rose on the blue horizon. Her face moved with its laughter before she saw, "Captain, you . . .?" saw, and smothered it, to have it break again. Blue eyes widened in the half dark. "What do you want?"

She stepped on to the rug. A copper anklet sloped beneath the knob of her ankle, crossed low on her calloused heel. (Uneven hem brushes smudged knees.) A print sash bound her belly.

"Where is your brother?"

"In the wheelhouse, asleep."

"Where were you?"

"On deck. I was sitting in the sun."

"With the men on the docks all coming by to stare? How many with their hands in their pockets?"

"Oh . . .!"

"None of them with what I got." He leaned back. His fingers tracked his stomach. "Come here. Tell me what's for supper."

"Your thoughts have gone as high as your gut, now?"

"How do you and the boy get chores done if you sleep and sun all the time?"

"But what is there to do in port?" She stepped across the rug, laughing.

He grabbed her wrist. She stumbled and he caught: "How many times!"

She pushed his chest. Her wrist turned under slippery fingers.

"Five times? Six? I'll say seven –"

"But see, you've already –"

"Once already. Six more now." He kneaded her inner thigh.

"*Captain* . . .!" She tried to pull away.

His hand went beneath the hem.

She shrieked and bit the sound off. What spilled after was a giggle.

"How many years have I had you two, now?" His forearm shifted like bunched blacksnakes. She tried to push his hand from under her skirt. Stopped trying.

She opened her lips and caressed his arm.

"How many years? Seven. Now, once for each year you've worked on my boat." He looked down at himself.

She touched where he looked: she took it, slipping the loose skin from the head. When she fingered beneath the twice full bag, he arched his back.

"Pig. Sit on it. Little white pig . . ." Three calloused fingers were knuckle deep in her. She bent; her hair swept his face. He caught it in his yellow teeth, twisted his head. Kirsten grabbed at her hair, and made an ugly sound. His teeth opened on laughter; it and her hair spilled black lips mottled with cerise.

Barking.

Claws at wood.

Black paws and long muzzle lapped the bunk. The captain kicked the dog with his bare foot (the big chain around his ankle jangles). "Down, Niger! Down, you stupid dog!"

Down; then back, nuzzling between them: dog's tongue. One color: Kirsten's nipple, the dog's tongue, the captain's palm. Niger lapped her crotch for salt.

"Down, Niger!"

The dog barked.

Then the captain looked up: frowned.

One shutter had swung open. A woman's face pressed the glass (dock-side of the boat), tongue caught at the corner of her mouth. Her fingers tipped the sill. Sunlight behind her exploded in loose hair, dimmed her features. Niger barked at her once more.

Her eyes shifted; she saw the captain. Her mouth opened, her palm slapped the pane, a sail of sunlight slapped the far wall: the window cleared and burned.

Niger wheeled the room, leapt on the door. It banged the hatchway wall. Claws clicked at the ladder. The door swung slowly back.

The captain: frowning. But Kirsten's hair, brushing his neck, fell from his face like lame, swept back from hers: she had not seen.

One knee was beside his left hip, one beside his right. She swayed, pulling at her brush; dug in the lips. His head lodged. Her hair rasped the plum glans. He gasped and grabbed her head.

Her lips struck his. His mashed open and swallowed hers. His tongue troweled her teeth; her teeth opened. He licked the roof of her mouth. He pressed her neck, her shoulders. Her breasts, bared now, bulged between the black bars his fingers made.

Gold brush lowered to iron wool.

Their mouths were windy with one another's breath. He thrust, and caught her lips in his teeth. She fell, clutching him. Tried to push away. He took her buttocks, his thumb tobogganing her, moist. He opened the wrinkled bud. She tried to block his tongue with her tongue. She failed.

He rolled with her. His knuckles scraped the wall. When she was beneath him, he braced his feet on the footboard and twisted on her. His belly slapped her. She tried to hold him in with her legs, but he pulled up, to fall, and: her fingers arched his neck, mashed his rough hair, arched. He rocked faster than the boat around them.

In stop action: an ice shard melts in a copper cup.

He lay on her. Her hair was wet to brass blades on her neck. He touched them with his tongue. Then he pushed himself up.

She gargled and reached for him. He glistened above her. (She sees him glance at the porthole, does not understand why.)

Her fingers palped the gold and coral wound.

"Two!" he panted. "Turn over."

Her eyes were closed, her legs apart. She moved her head on the crushed blanket, hands on her stomach.

"Turn *over!*"

He grabbed her leg and pulled. She felt lazy, she felt hysterical. Opened her eyes as he yanked her ankle again. (Why was he staring at the porthole? The light, like blood, varnished his big lips, his flat nose, flamed on his sloping brow till rough, rough hair soaked it up.) "Owww . . .!"

Her knee struck the floor. She stretched her arms over the blanket, and rocked her face on the damp, hot wool. The smell of him: she moved her lips there, her tongue. The taste of him.

The captain breathed hard. He raised his hand, high, drew back lips and shoulder and hip.

Crack!

Her buttocks shook. Redness bloomed and faded. She gasped, then bit her tongue. His hand swung back the other way. She gasped again.

He pulled apart her cheeks, puckered his lips, and pushed out his saliva. It trailed in the discolored cleft. When the foamy tear reached the sphincter, he leaned on her. The hood peeled. Entrance, and her shoulders came up. The heat of her surprised him. He caught a breath: then let it chuckle from him as he eased. Kirsten clutched the end of the mattress. He grasped her wrists, fell. She screamed, and her back, wiggling, slid under his chest. He hissed, "Swing it." He whispered: "That's right, girl." He hissed again, "Dance on that black stick, little monkey!"

Soft things slipped and broke. Something with points crumbled as he tunneled and plunged. Her buttocks mashed and spread under the blades of his pelvis. He bit her shoulder, kneaded the skin in his big teeth till it bruised burgundy.

He let go of her arm, felt under her belly. He thumbed the dry hairs; thumbed the wet. Four bunched fingers, in and in further. He spread them in her slop.

She made sounds in her chest.

He felt his swollen passage beyond her, wet and tender. His thumb, again, slipped under the thickening tab folded in the roof.

Her sounds were between simper and growl. Her smock was a wet roll at her back's small. She heaved at him. When he withdrew, she butted up to impale. His down stroke pushed her to the bed. And again. And.

In marble: white rock crumbles from the freshet.

In the shadow his back shone. Heavy, twinned breath. Sweat ran Kirsten's side, curved at her breast bulging out.

". . . three," while cooler air came between her back and his belly when he pulled –

"No! Don't take it . . ."

He stood, panting. His shirt lay on the floor. His belt dangled at each hip. The canvas pants creased down over his buttocks. "Once more . . ."

"You're not tired yet?" She let herself slip to her knees beside the bed. The triangle of sheet by the bunched blanket was wet. He let his knees bend, touched her back. As his hand walked on her shoulder she dropped her head back. He scratched her neck, ran his forefinger in the damp troughs of her ear. He cradled her head when she rolled it over his palm. (It is a big hand.) Her hair fell in ingots on his forearm. His fingers deviled them to cloudy snarls.

Through the closed shutter bars of light reddened the bedding. The captain reached to close the other. It swung to, the catch failed, and it swung out again. He made a fist in her hair.

"You want more?"

". . . no," all breathy.

"You want it!"

"But Gunner has tired me out, all this morning –" her smile a grimace as he tugged. She let her face fall against his thigh.

"Kiss it. That little dirty-face has made you hot for more. Yes? You don't, and I'll beat you and that little brother of yours. Kiss it all over, with your tongue."

She swiveled her cheek on his hip. "But it's all . . ." She slid her hand into the sweaty fold between leg and sack. ". . . all soft."

"You make it hard." He pushed her into it.

"And dirty!" She tried to pull away.

"It's your dirt."

She made muffled contest, but he pressed her face in. When he took his hand away, she didn't pull back. Her tongue went warm in the crevice. He grinned, and fingered her hair back. She took the limp length in her hands, opened her mouth, and tongued him to the hilt hair.

"Underneath. Go down underneath. Get it all in, girl. Before it gets too big." He moved his legs.

"There's a lot of junk in the pockets. Tongue . . . hungry. Yeah! Be sweet to it. That's where I like to see you. Be hungry. Be hungry and eat me. Hey, don't back away! Take it, deep." He brushed her distended cheek with bunched knuckles. "It's going, yeah, down. All the way. Get ready. Yeah," and, "Yeah . . ." and, "Oh, yeah!" He held her hair. Hardness and then soft ridges over his thrust. He swiveled to mash his hair on her mouth, till he felt her gag constrict him. He let her retreat to breathe, then filled her throat again. "Yeah . . .

"Go underneath again." He took his shining stock in his left fist; his right pushed her down; pushed half of the sack in her mouth with his thumb.

"Tongue it. That's good –"

He tapped her. "Watch your teeth! No nutcrackers. A little tickle." His left fist swung the long arc, fell at her face. "Now the other one . . . fine!"

He breathed like a dog. She held his hips and rocked her face between his legs.

"In your mouth, girl. Or let me leak it on your face . . ."

She swallowed him, and felt the under tube swell down her tongue, retreat, swell again. In a geyser of black mud, a sudden eruption of white froth (Eruption . . .)

and he pushed: thrust, and gout, thrust, thrust, gout.

He held his breath, and let her fall against the bed's edge. The black, bright length wrinkled, sagged. Her lips glistened. Her eyes were closed.

He sat on the bed and began to take loud breaths. She moved between his legs to lay her head on his groin. He moved one finger over her forehead, wiping wet brass from beaded alabaster. She put her palm on it, pressed it on her cheek.

"Why are you so tired," he asked, "after so little?"

She opened her eyes. "Gunner worried at me all morning, I say. Please, Captain. Let me go up and rest for a while. I'll come back, maybe after only an hour or so."

"And leave me to make love to my fists? First the left, after that the right. What then? I can't lap myself like Niger."

"You've had me every way! What else do you –"

He squeezed her breast; Kirsten closed her eyes. "Oh, yes, I know the things you think of." She looked up again. "Let me go upstairs. I'll send Gunner down."

He frowned.

"Finish with him. I'm too tired."

"He tired you out for me?" The captain tongued his lower lip. "Wake him up."

"I will. Right now." She stood.

She tried not to let him see her smile as she bent to pull her bunched shift down her hips. She shrugged into the sleeve, tried to cover her breast.

The captain fingered himself.

The torn cloth would not cover her any more.

Suddenly Kirsten got a strange expression. She reached quickly, took his face in her hands and thrust her tongue way in his mouth. He licked it. But when he reached beneath her hem she pulled away.

"I'll send Gunner!"

She turned and ran through the lines of sun.

In the minute alone he thinks about the currents that have brought them here. He thinks about light, and suddenly he remembers the woman at the pane. He turns to look.

"Captain?"

Knuckling his eyes, sleepy Gunner came in. His hair, pale as his sister's, pawed his neck, rioted at his forehead.

"Come here."

The boy walked over the rug, paused. The captain patted the blanket, so the boy sat. He took the back of Gunner's neck between thumb and forefinger. Shook him.

Gunner grinned: there were twin acne spots left of his mouth. He touched the captain. "What am I gonna do with this elephant?"

The captain moved his palm on the boy's bony back. "You've done half of it already." And shook again. "Hey, little mule. Kirsten says you tried to climb her back and break into her with your Johnny stick.

Gunner looked at his lap. The captain slipped two fingers into the buttonless fly. Gunner looked up. "I did not!" But grinned.

"What did you do?"

"I nosed her to see if I could smell anything you'd left there." He touched the captain's knee. Small hand: it has callouses from boat work, the nails quick bitten. His grin fell open into a smile. "Got my face wet. And she wouldn't let go my head."

"Did she kiss you back between your legs?"

"She wanted to. But I hid him in my hands." Gunner pulled apart his fly. Johnny jumped. Little brass wires snarled through the captain's fingers. Gunner frowned. "It's not half as long as yours."

Maroon and purple: suede and velvet.

"You're not half as old as I am. He's big enough for you, boy. You still need both hands to hide him when he's hard. Hey, take care of me. A couple or three times."

Gunner picked the captain's up.

The captain pushed his fingers under Gunner's rope belt. Most loops were broken. The waist pulled down on the boys buttocks. The captain lay his finger in the hot slip.

"You want my mouth?" Gunner dug the black fruit up. "That's why you wake me up?"

"So."

"Suppose I'm not thirsty."

"You?"

Gunner bent. The head rose and blunted on his mouth. Black hand grapples gold hair, pulls the boy up, gasping. "That's not where I want it –"

"Captain . . .?"

The black hand, kneading Gunner's buttocks, worked to the boy's belly. White and black fingers worked on the knot. As it came loose, he pushed the boy's head forward. He swung his leg back and kicked. The boy fell on the small rug. Knot undone, his trousers slipped to his knees.

The captain stood. He worked his thumb into the sweaty crevice siding his groin; swung like a crane. He stepped from the eight his pants made at his ankles.

Brass ring in his left ear (leather banding his right wrist), the heavy black chain on his left ankle. (That's all.) He stood above the boy.

Gunner stared.

The captain put his foot between the boy's legs. The groin was hot on the knuckles of his toes. Toes rose to prod the crack. He got down on his knees.

Gunner licked his fingers and wiped between his legs. "Lemme stick it up before –"

The captain knocked Gunner's hand away. "It's slick enough." He pushed, swiveled forward inches more, pushed straight again.

Gunner stopped breathing.

The captain put his arms around Gunner's chest. Once the boy barked in pain. The captain slid his hand between their bellies. "You're stiff as a ten penny. It doesn't hurt that much." His hips hunched.

Gunner caught his breath again.

But no sound. Backed and squirmed on it.

The captain's breath roared around his head like a rasp in a clay pipe: Gunner puppy-pants.

Unable to the double weight, their arms bent. The captain pulled him onto the floor. On his side, first; then, with Gunner, breath nearly out of him, the captain flexed.

He lay on his side, thrust in Gunner's gut, while the boy, on his back, to the hips' rocking, pulled at himself. Gunner's head pressed back on the captain's chest. His feet bunched the rug between the black knees. Raised himself. Lowered himself.

Gas growled out around him. Something small gave before the plunging, became hot paste. The captain stirred in the tight tunnel. He had a mouth full of Gunner's hair; he held the boy with one hand. Two fingers from the other in Gunner's mouth, a tongue grazing their salt and horn.

In a salt cave the thrower flames.

The captain panted. "Five . . . for me, now."

Gunner's fist still swung at his groin.

The captain closed the boy's fist in his to stop it. "Hold off unless you want to go again."

Gunner, still now, asked, "You messed in Kirsten all day. You still want to squeeze more out of these?" Sitting on the captain's hips, he reached between both their legs and picked up the big sack.

The captain laughed. He pushed Gunner's cheeks. "Get up. Go on."

Making a face, the boy eased forward. Soft, it slapped the captain's thigh. Gunner turned and scratched himself. "How many more you got?"

The captain folded his arms behind his head. "Another couple." He stretched. "Work me over."

The boy blinked.

The captain raised his head. "Lick my foot. Come on, get that look off. I want to see you lick my foot. Last week I saw you lick at Niger behind the locker. You can with a dog, you can with my foot. Go on."

Gunner held the calloused rim, laid his cheek on it. The captain felt the lips tickle the instep. Tongue fell from the boy's mouth; moved on the rough ball, found the trough before the toes; bladed between the big toe and the next, moved over the thick nail. Gunner took three toes in his mouth. The captain wriggled them, laughed. "Niger left his pile on the foredeck. I stepped in it before I came down here – don't pull back. Clean it. Look at you. Look what that does to you. Look good for me, boy." His knee bent, and the boy's lips whispered on his ankle, wrapped the chain, stuck tongue in the links. Gunner's fingers spread on his belly, moved jerkily to his tight yellow hair. The head, grey as a pale grape, pushed from its ivory cap.

"Work, boy!" The captain pulled his foot back, kicked Gunner's face. He laughed.

Gunner's knees struck the rug. He opened his mouth on the dark thigh. The captain caught the boy's hair, yanked him down.

Claws on the passage steps –

–Niger sprang through the door, hind legs, pawed the captain's knee.

"Black devil! Down!" Niger backed up, then dropped his black muzzle beside Gunner's blond head in the dark fork. The captain's lips parted. His back rose from the rug. On shoulders and heels he pushed into Gunner's face. The boy put one arm around the dog's neck. He looked up, once, mouth, cheek and chin wet.

The captain rocked back and grabbed the hollow of his knees. Gunner's face pushed; stroke, probe. Niger's tongue rolled the captain's sack over to hang on his belly.

The captain bellowed, swung his legs down. His heels hit the floor. Niger and Gunner scampered.

On his feet the captain lurched to the bunk, turned, and sat. His knees were wide. Saliva made his thighs dark mirrors. He gripped the shining tower to beat. Up to the paler ring. "Six coming . . ." the captain panted. "First one here gets it."

Niger and Gunner raced the floor. Niger leapt on the captain's right knee, dug his snout beneath the loose bag. Gunner humped the left harder than the dog, fell to it.

The captain beat the boy's lips a half dozen strokes. Gunner held the edge of the bed and learned back. He tongued under the foreflesh. It rammed over his tongue, bruised palates, hard and soft, prodded in the softer throat. "Take it. Eat that charred meat all up, you white . . . Yeah . . ." He pressed the boy's head down, and down, ground upon the face while Niger nipped and nuzzled. "Here it . . . here . . ." he grunted at the ceiling. Heat swelled the shaft, stretched the boy's mouth.

The black crater, quiet the hour, erupts. Oceans boil. The captain sagged forward over Gunner's back. "Six . . ."

Gunner twisted under the captain's belly. "Get off my head."

"Six, you little white squirrel!"

Niger had pulled away, was lying on the rug. He worried something between his paws.

The captain sat up. Gunner hung over his knees. His face was wet. "What about seven?" Gunner asked.

"Give it a rest."

Gunner picked up the limp. "It's tired, now, you think?"

The captain roughed the boy's hair. "You'd lap after it whatever." He frowned at the dog. "What's Niger got?"

Gunner looked over his shoulder. "Something he must have picked up when he went out."

"Go get it."

Gunner went to the dog. He pulled and played it away. The jaws gave up; Niger started to lick at Gunner. "He's getting me all hard again." He pushed Niger's head down. "It's a wallet." He took it to the captain and sat down on the bed. While the captain paged through the leather folder, Gunner tugged up his pants and tried to get the rope back through the functioning loops. Once he leaned over the captain's arm. "Pictures?"

The captain was looking at the portal.

"Hey?" Gunner said. "What about seven?"

The captain pushed the boy's hand from his thigh. Gunner put his hand between his own legs. He leaned against the captain's arm.

There was a color polaroid of a woman one side of the wallet, one of a man on the other. Her hair was loose in a wind that had caused her the slightest squint. His was white, or very pale. The faces suggested age, or experience. But they were handsome, and strong. Perhaps it was the contrast to the pale hair – perhaps shadow and position – but the man's eyes looked black.

Gunner pushed his nose under the dark arm and nuzzled the hair. The captain stood. "I'm going on deck." He reached for his pants. "Come on, Niger." He shrugged into his shirt. He kicked at the dog, and his chain rang. Niger barked, then followed the captain to the door.

He stopped once, frowned at the portal; then he saw Gunner. "On deck when you're done."

Gunner sat on the bed, cross-legged. He ran his hand over the damp sheet. Let himself fall, to lay his cheek, roll his face and take the salty folds in his teeth. Elbow shaking, one hand worked in arcs. The other kneaded his belly. His lips kissed unvoiced exhortations. Closed lids and the loose hair shook with his fist.

The cabin door closed.

PURE PORN

Dion Farquhar

... [the uncanny as it is depicted in literature] is a much more fertile province than the uncanny in real life, for it contains the whole of the latter and something more besides, something that cannot be found in real life.

–Freud

ON THE EL from the airport, they sat next to each other in a molded plastic seat designed to boundary two strangers via a slightly raised bump that travelled down the middle. Which they could feel as they sat very close to each other, bodies pressed left to right, leaning slightly against each other's side. He reached up and across her chest, grazing the front of her leather jacket with a prickly wool sleeve to grasp the raw silk scarf that lay around her neck. He slowly pulled on it until her face was very close to his, never breaking the gaze. She inadvertently fanned her fingers out to touch the side of his body as he pulled her toward him, feeling his chest through layers of wool and cotton as they sat on the rattling train, thighs warm and pressed against each other. They could only get together every other week, living as they did in different cities during the school term. But they were relatively mobile and able to arrange four- and five-day weekends.

They walked together, hip to hip, through the courtyard right

up to the stairway of his building, where they separated to walk up
the two squeaky flights to his apartment. She watched him walk
ahead of her. In the apartment, she dropped her brown suede
backpack into a Breuer chair by the door. They watched each
other unzip and take off their jackets, flinging them onto the
backs of chairs. Holding the gaze. Unwavering control. Unsure
about what they were doing. In part. Playing with tropes. Mutual
recognition. He lifted her bag from the floor to place it on a chair,
saying, "You travel light. It's good." Then he walked away into
the kitchen to pour them each an ice-cold seltzer. Coming back
with two glasses, he handed one to her and then raised his glass in
a gesture of acknowledgement. Which she responded to by leaning
toward him, kissing his neck with a sweep of tongue and lips cooled
by the liquid.

He walked slowly toward her. His hand reached over to her
shoulder, gently pulling her body into contact with his. Her arms
met his, embracing him back, pulling him toward her, feeling him
along the length of their bodies. Noting her soft breasts against his
hard chest, pubic bone to hardening cock, the firmness of their
touching thighs. They began to kiss, slowly and gently at first.
With a sweep of his tongue, he took her entire mouth in his,
then resting his tongue at the entrance of her open mouth, poised,
moving it only when he felt her tongue envelop his. Then, opening
his mouth to contain hers, he sucked her in and released her, over
and over, resting his lips against hers, for a moment resisting her
tongue meeting his, then pushing against her with closed lips, now
seeking out and trying to suck her tongue into his mouth.

They loved to kiss, she thought, running her tongue along his
cheek all the way down to his chin. She licked the tiny ridge under
his lower lip, feeling the pull of the rough texture of his nascent
beard offer resistance. If she stayed more than a moment kissing
or licking a cheek, or lip, or eyelid, he couldn't bear it. His tongue
would then seek out her mouth, moving over her lips from side to
side, savoring their moist pliancy. Their tongues darted around
each other, slowing down and speeding up, drawing back, then
hurrying on for more. He would moan and move to nibble her ear,
to take the bird from her earlobe with his lips. In the same way he
would kiss and lick her belly down to the top of her underpants,
sometimes grasping the elastic band in his mouth and pulling them
off with his mouth.

Their bodies pressed into one another, seeking out the radiant center of their genitals. They move against each other. She cannot stop herself from moaning slightly. Suddenly he grasped her, hands squeezing her shoulders, and pushed her away. "Not so fast," he says, reaching for her scarf. Which he placed over her eyes, winding it around her head and tying a knot with an emphatic tug "Now, you will feel it more," he said, sucking and biting her lips before opening his mouth to kiss her deep and long and hard.

Then he stopped. Grasping her hand firmly by the wrist, he pulled her to walk with him, and led her around the apartment until she could feel her legs touch the side of the bed. He pushed her slightly so that she sat down, one hand caressing a breast with increasing firmness as he leaned into her until they were lying along side of, then under, and on top of each other for long intervals. Until one of them would indicate a desire to vary position. Slipping his hand underneath her blouse, he brushed her erect nipple with the side of his hand, running his fingers around the aureole. Then he pulled her shirt over her head, and nuzzled his head between her breasts, pillowing into her with a sweep of his head, then rising to take as much of a breast into his mouth as he could. He nibbled and sucked her breasts until she moaned, feeling some direct connection to her clitoris that pulsed in rhythm to the firm pressure of his tongue.

When he stopped, she would seek his mouth strongly, falling into him and opening herself to his eager lips. Their bodies pressed up hard against each other, moving their hips in sync with each other. She sighed to feel his hard cock through their clothes, delighted but almost alarmed by its hardness, her wetness, the power of their desire for each other. "Enough of this," she said suddenly, pulling the scarf-blindfold off her head and holding it as she looked at him, reaching over to stroke the outline of his erect cock through his jeans.

"Now, I will tie you up," she said to his moan, pushing against her hand. "Stand up," she said, grasping his belt and pulling him toward her. "Take your clothes off," she said, rubbing him through the thick jeans material. As he pulled off a cotton sweater and unbuttoned a flannel shirt, she unbuckled his belt and unzipped his fly. Then his hand met hers, cupping it and pressing it against him through his clothes for a moment before finally shedding his jeans. She sat down on the bed, savoring the sight of his body, naked now except for his shorts. She looked at his erection, tight up against the white cotton material, seeing a few drops of preejaculate, a circle of wet against the shorts. Lifting them over his cock in order to pull them off, she smiled, noticing a drop quivering on its glistening tip. Following her gaze, he smiled and said, "I'm very wet." Touching him lightly and smiling broadly, she said, "So I see." He moved closer to her, bringing his head close to hers. "Kiss me," he said, before wrapping her mouth in his.

Tying two long silk scarves together, she wrapped one scarf around his right wrist, running it like a chain under the mattress until it met his other wrist from the opposite side. Next, she attended to his legs, knotting old silk ties together to secure his feet. She made one loop gently but firmly around an ankle, proceeding under the mattress to the other. This way each wrist and ankle were held as widely spread as seemed comfortable. She looked at his legs spread far apart but held tightly in position, centering his outstretched body on his pelvis. She had tied him spreadeagle to the bed. She wanted to see him struggle, beg her to release him, entreat her to fuck him, to never let him loose.

He had watched her as she tied him up, a slight sweat bathing his forehead. "Kiss me," he said, "please." She watched him thrust his pelvis up as much as the bonds limiting his motion allowed, craning his neck up towards her. Coming over to the bed, she lay down next to him and began to kiss him, caressing his cock with her hand, as she rubbed herself against his leg, feeling her slippery wetness as she slid her hardening clitoris back and forth against the bone of his knee, noting that he moved slightly to meet her motion. "You're very hard," he said, with a deep sigh, head thrown back, as she moved to kiss him deeply in reply.

"What would you like to do?" she paused to ask, raising an eyebrow as she looked at him. She inclined her body towards his from her position stretched out next to him, resting her head on her hand, supported by an elbow. She had one leg slung over the "X" his body made on the middle of the double bed. Her knee slowly rubbed his penis lightly back and forth. With her free hand, she grazed his chest, stroking and pinching a nipple until it grew hard, bending over him to tongue it and suck it until he groaned. "So, are you going to tell me what you want to do?" she asked, moving her knee away from his hard penis and resting it on a thigh. "Well . . ." he said, casting a glance over his immobilized torso, the erection quivering slightly, delight and embarrassment mixing in his look.

She began to kiss him again, taking his lower lip between hers and sucking hard on it, then running her tongue over it from side to side, moving to his upper lip until his tongue came to meet hers. She opened her mouth to take him inside her, gulping him down with tiny sucking motions, their tongues finding each other and twisting around and around until one of them would alter the motion.

She moved over to lie on top of him, holding herself up with her arms so that their bodies were touching only at the groin. He thrust his hips up, pushing his cock hard up against her belly, and she leaned into him, savoring his hardness. "Fuck me," he said, "please. I can't stand it any more." "We'll see what you can stand," she said, moving herself over him so that his penis slid effortlessly against her totally slippery wet vulva, rippling against her hard clit with each stroke. "Oh. Fuck me," he moaned, straining to push his cock against her as far as his bonds would allow. "Take me inside you," he said, looking hard at her. "Stop torturing me."

"Not so fast," she said, as she rolled off of him and lay next to him. She reached for the seltzer bottle on the night table and filled her glass again, greedily sipping it because she was parched. "Do you want some," she offered. He nodded, so she refilled a glass and held it to his lips until he had drunk his fill. Then she slowly began to kiss his face, making her way down from his lips to his ears, then biting and sucking his neck until she rested at a nipple. "Oh, I love it when you do that," he said of her hardening a nipple with her tongue. She loved the absurdity of mouths on breasts.

Moving herself slowly over him, she changed directions on the bed to suck his toes, tickle and rub his feet, making her way to the center of his body, to nibble the inside of his thighs, alternately licking, sucking, kissing, and biting him there with her mouth while her hand kneaded and softly caressed his other thigh and leg.

Taking his balls into her mouth made her dizzy with his smell, anchored by their rougher texture. He moaned continuously now, moving his hips and straining against the scarves that spread him open, setting a rhythm to her sucking and biting, which had not yet reached his penis. "Oh, God. Suck me. I can't stand it. Not another minute." She nipped at the many tiny folds of skin around its base, then licked him from base to tip, first hard, then softly, alternating the top and then the underside of her tongue, back and forth. He lifted his pelvis to meet her mouth, emitting cries and tossing his head from side to side. His body shuddered in waves of desire.

She ran her tongue around and around the top of his penis, taking his head between her lips and making shallow thrusting motions with her mouth and tongue. With one hand, she grasped his penis, encircling it and taking special care to press hard against the ridged area just below its lip that connected the sides. She sucked him, especially forcefully down the backside of its shaft, which he had told her was particularly sensitive. With each thrust she would rest her half-closed mouth firmly around the lip of its head and pressing her lips against him for intervals that she varied, until his groans urged her on. "Oh, more. More, more," he said. Then she swept her tongue around the head of his penis, sucking him deeply into her mouth and moving her tongue over its length, while her hand ringed him at the same time, attentive to his most sensitive spot.

Sliding her hands under his ass on one of his lifting motions, she grasped his cheeks, rubbing and working them along with the motion of her mouth on his cock. "Put your fingers inside me," he moaned, "fuck me." In answer, she moved her fingers back and forth along the crack of his ass until she felt the tiny wrinkled opening, warm and moist, throb against her gently circling finger. Pausing to lubricate her fingers thoroughly with the bottle of almond massage oil they kept on the night table, her hand followed the line from the base of his balls right up to the crack of his ass.

He opened to meet her like a flower, and she eased her middle finger into him, hearing him cry out in pleasure, feeling his sphincter tighten around her finger, release, then tighten again. She worked it to his rhythms, never going further until invited, but stopping only when her finger could easily enter him no further. She moved her finger inside him, slowly back and forth, pressing up against the front of his rectum, allowing his thrusting to work her hand, setting the pace. "Now try two fingers," he said in between gasps. All the while her mouth and other hand never left his cock, moving over him, in rhythm to her fingers fucking him easily as he pressed his ass against her fingers with each inward motion, allowing her more deeply inside him.

They fucked each other like this for a long delicious while. She had no idea. Her awareness contracted almost completely to the sensate liquid cosmos of her mouth and fingers and the sounds of their pleasure. Her world the feel and heat of him between her lips, reaching deep into her throat, the rhythm of his cock back and forth at the same time her fingers slid deeply in and out of his ass, feeling his thrusts meet her fingers. Then, his cock reached all the way down into the curve of her throat at the same time his ass took her fingers all the way in. His body pushed against her hard, stilling into a strong thrusted orgasm that she felt go on for what seemed to be minutes. Her mouth registered the spurts of semen, warm and briny like seawater, flowing into her mouth in several short spasms at the same time she felt his anus contract in little pulses of ringing afterpleasure. After a moment, she swallowed the ejaculate, and slowly leaned over him to kiss him. "Taste," she said.

"Oh, God. Oh, God," he spat out, rolling his head from side to side, still breathing in gasps, "it's too much." "Untie me, so I can torture you." She kissed him on the lips. "Twist my arm," she said, fiddling with the silk knots around his wrist.

They took a break to pee, wash a little, and refill seltzers. "We forgot to smoke," he said, returning to the bedroom with a joint and an ashtray. "And here's an extra bathrobe in case you get chilled," he said, draping a terry robe over her shoulders, and pausing to kiss her neck. "It's a smooth strong green," he said, sitting down next to her and lighting the joint, taking a long, slow puff. He held it out to her. "Hmm," she said, reaching for the joint, "smells great." "What shall we do now?" he said, looking playfully at her. "That depends on what you want to know," she said, as she coughed, laughing and exhaling a mouthful of smoke. Leaning back into a cluster of pillows, she passed the joint back to him. "I can't smoke too much. I want to do some work later," she said. "Good, I have tons to do myself. You can have the computer if you want. I have stuff to read." "Great. And let's get some takeout, then we'll work." "Thai, all right?" "Fine." He put the joint out, moved the ashtray, and began to kiss her until they were rolling around again on the bed. It was so easy when they weren't cripples or psychos, she thought, her arms around him, tongues intertwined, completely happy being with him.

Never predictable, he chose to replicate for her the spreadeagle position from which he had recently been released. "It had a lot going for it," he thought, as he looked at her body extended in a classic "X". He loved the way she looked tied up – helpless and

completely open to him, her hipbones prominent and breasts flatter
and rounder because of her raised and out-stretched arms, her pubic
hair wet with surplus secretions. Maybe they liked the trust and the
hypothetical risk. Though they had each never felt safer.

After he had tied her up in the same spreadeagle position, he
sat up next to her, leaning down to kiss her, tonguing her deeply.
Pulling away slightly, he bent over her and kissed her belly,
continuing down to her pubic triangle. Moving his hand over
her body to cup her vulva, he rocked her with his hand. "Let's
see how turned on you are," he said, feeling her wetness even on
the longer pubic hair that he grasped and pulled at, twirling a small
clump around his fingers, absorbing its wetness.

Then he skilfully parted her inner lips with two fingers, sliding
his middle finger far inside her, feeling her wetness and the
ever-changing texture of her vagina. "Oh," he said, "very nice,"
working a second finger into her and moving in and out with harder
and faster thrusts until she moaned and strained against the scarves,
meeting his hand. Suddenly, he took his fingers out of her and
began to work the area just a tiny bit above her clitoris with gentle
firm rhythmic caresses that made her scream in pleasure. Moving
down to cover its length and circle the small knob of hard flesh,
he moved his middle finger higher up to grasp its hood. Then he
opened her inner lips with a separating sweep of his second and
fourth fingers, holding them apart as he slid his middle finger firmly
over her clit, a gesture he knew she loved because she would always
moan more. He worked his middle finger rhythmically back and
forth over her clit, rubbing it ever so slightly harder in time to her
increasing pelvic movement against his hand. With his other hand,
he thrust two, then three, fingers all the way up inside her, faster
and faster until her body tensed into immobility, lifting her into a
high-pitched moan of an orgasm that rippled through her, rising
and falling for a long time.

He immediately arranged himself on top of her in order to
enter her while her orgasm went on in wave after wave, which
his fucking now skimmed and rode, taking his cues from her
thrusting. After slowing to meet her subsiding motion, instead
of stopping altogether, he slowly began to increase the rhythm
knowing that she could often be brought back into another pitch of
pleasure following immediately upon a first. She opened further to
this quick thrust fucking, raising her hips to meet his cock, burning

with such exquisite feeling she felt almost faint. "Oh, God. Oh, God," she moaned, "it's so good."

He leaned over her, kissing and biting her breasts, sucking hard on one and then another as he thrust high into her, or licking her neck as he withdrew to the entrance of her vagina, then plunging all the way into her until she screamed with pleasure, rocking with him, tightening her vaginal muscles to grip him when he was deepest inside her, making him gasp, squeeze his eyes shut, and whisper, "Oh, God. It's so good."

He stopped for a moment to bend over and untie her legs so she would move more. They both reached for pillows to slide under her hips, and she lifted her legs high, wrapping them tightly around his neck, and guiding him back into her. Each thrust pleasured her differently. After a while, she lost the ability to know which one of them initiated a stroke or set of strokes. She couldn't feel their borders. Who was who. What was what. Sometimes it felt as if they moved in and out of each other fast, fast, fast, with strokes that were close together. Other times their fucking was long and slow, it reaching so deeply into her that she would cry out. Sometimes there was anger in the force of their fucking, and they fucked as much from need as from desire, hate as much as love. She never knew in advance of their bodies joining who or what would move the other or how. Loving invention.

They fucked for a long time until he pulled out of her in order to move to her mouth. "I love being inside all of you," he said as he straddled her, bringing his cock very near her mouth. Opening to him with a sucking kiss, she could taste the mixture of their secretions, licking and moving her mouth over him, taking him all the way into her, then pulling back on him. Just as she was falling into a smooth rhythm of taking him in and wrapping her mouth around him as he rocked back on each thrust, he pulled out of her mouth, saying, "It's getting very sensitive."

He began to kiss her mouth, running his hands over her entire body, pausing to slide his fingers over her vulva, again seeking her inner labia and finally, as she moaned more and more, her clitoris. He opened her slowly, separating the inner lips carefully with his fingers, and pulling the hood firmly back until her clit lay completely exposed to his tongue. He knelt over her, his erect cock resting against her belly, and began to lick her there with wide gulps, wrapping his mouth around her. Her entire body shuddered with pleasure. Then he held her lips apart with the fingers of one hand as he slowly worked the tip of his tongue back and forth over the length of her clit, returning to the spot just above its most sensitive area for a more intense tonguing.

With each motion, she moved to meet his tongue and lips, breathing herself into his mouth, and pushing her pelvis against him when she wanted him to suck her harder and stronger, and moving ever so slightly up or down in the bed to guide his tongue. His other hand reached into her, thrusting hard and slipping partly out of her, then thrusting into her again with gathering force while his tongue worked her clit steadily. He sensed her lifting herself up to him and pressed his tongue harder onto her, moving back and forth faster until her moaning looped itself into an orgasmic cry that seemed to go on for minutes. Her arms strained hard against the scarves that held her taut, his tongue blanketing her vulva hard and safe, and his fingers pressing up hard against her as far into her as he could go, evoking strong sensation inside her as well.

Again, he entered her, though this time their pleasure was even more strong, pushing himself all the way into her, thrusting up, over and over, coming partly out only to come hard back into her, sighing and moaning more with each motion. She could feel his sweat mix with hers as he nuzzled his face against her neck. They smelled of sex. Yum. When he finally came, crying out, she felt, not orgasm, but a series of tiny but pleasurable ripples in her vagina reverberating from the cessation of motion, that she could intensify by contracting her muscles against his ejaculating penis.

Their weekend continued much in the same vein, their being talking sex, *pace* Foucault.

THREE TIMES A WOMAN

Grushenka

THE REASON GRUSHENKA did not want to be coupled for her lifetime with the captain of the police was, no doubt, inspired by her physical aversion against him. He was round and fat, his arms, backside, legs; everything about him was stupidly rounded and unpleasantly self-satisfied. He was not a good lover and when, once or twice a week, he put his short and stubby shaft into her sheath and gave himself a good rubbing in her, without considering her desires, he felt well pleased with himself. He snored in bed, he did not believe in keeping himself clean, and he spit in the room as one might have done in a pig-stye. He exercised his duties brutally, and his means to justice was the whip. Even his jokes were vile, so why stay with him?

In order to break away, Grushenka needed money and she had none. The captain, however, had plenty. In the evening his pockets were always bulging with gold and silver; yet he left in the morning without a cent. The bribes he received were enormous. But what did he do with this money? Grushenka found out quickly enough. He had a big iron cash-box, standing on the floor, about three feet high and five long. There was no lock on this box but it would not open for Grushenka. She watched him and saw him move a little handle on the back of it. The next morning she lifted the lid and was amazed. The box was filled almost to the top with thousands of coins; gold, silver and copper. He had thrown them in carelessly, as they came his way.

Grushenka did some thinking. She then proceeded to rifle his pile of wealth systematically. Every day, while he was away, she helped herself to a few hundred rubles in gold. Of these she changed one or two pieces into silver and coppers and threw them back into the box so as not to leave any holes. The rest she kept. Soon she had accumulated many thousand rubles, without the pile of coins having become smaller. She transferred her treasure one fine day to a banker – it was enough for a good start.

All that was now left was to get away from the man. This she accomplished through weeks of careful manipulation. First she became apparently moody and sickly and wailed about her failing health. Then she refused to have him when she felt that way. Of course he would not stand for that, but mounted her against her protests. While he worked away on her, she would start a conversation with him, annoying him all the time by talk. She would ask him to come quickly or, out of a blue sky – when he was ready to come – would ask him what he wanted for dinner the next day.

Of course he in turn did not treat her too kindly. Often he would give her a sound slap, providing her with a good excuse for sulking. Once or twice he turned her over and spanked her bare behind with his hands. She stood it because she knew he would soon want her to leave him. He began to fuck his prisoners again, as he had been in the habit of doing when he had no whore who enticed him. She would hear, of course, that he was untrue to her, and would make scenes about it.

Simultaneously she spoke with him about the disorderly houses in Moscow, how excellent that business was, and how little the bribes were that he collected from them. Soon she approached him directly as to whether it would not be a good idea for him to run a whore-house himself, give it his whole protection, close all the other ones and – put her in charge of it. He would not listen to it, because he was not interested in money after all. But when she painted, in the brightest colors, how he would be master of it, how she would always provide him with very young girls who would put on great parties for him, he succumbed to her wiles and told her to go ahead and do what she liked. But she was to understand that he had no money whatsoever and that she would have to put the house on its feet by herself. She almost loved him for that and got busy at once.

Grushenka acquired a house in the best neighborhood, where without the captain's protection, nobody would have dared to open an establishment of this kind. The house, surrounded by a small garden in the front and by a large one in the back, consisted of three floors. The upper floors contained about a dozen rooms each, while the ground floor had a magnificent dining room and four or five very spacious drawing rooms, all leading to a big front hall. Grushenka modelled the whole mansion after the layout of the best whore-house in Rome, which she had visited quite often to get her pussy kissed.

She resolved that it would be best for to employ only serf girls who could train for her purposes without having to consider their wishes. She prepared all this without the captain's knowledge. And she had to make more loots on his cash-box, because she furnished her establishment with the best. There were a colorful carriage and four horses, a few stable men, an old housekeeper, and six sturdy peasant maids, lovely furniture, and of course, a well-selected choice of four-poster beds with canopies and silk sheets. All this assembled, she left the captain, settled down in the big house and began leisurely to buy her girls.

We see her now, going in her own carriage, to all parts of Moscow, looking over features and shapes the way Katerina had done about ten years before, in order to buy her for Nelidowa. But she had it easier than Katerina because she did not have to look for any special type of girl; she needed girls of all types and shapes to satisfy the taste of her prospective customers. The hunger in the poor sections of Moscow was responsible for her best finds. Not only foster-parents but also parents, would flock to her with their daughters. The girls, on their part, were delighted to enter the services of so fine and elegant a lady, where they would be safe from starvation.

Grushenka would send word through her housekeeper to one of the poorer streets that she was willing to buy a few young girls, between fifteen and twenty years of age, for her private service. She would be told where, for example, in the backroom of a certain inn, she could look over the merchandise. When her elegant carriage rolled into the street, there would be great excitement, the mothers flocking around her, kissing the hem of her garments and imploring her to take their daughters. After the near-riot of her arrival was over, Grushenka would be led into a large room, filled with twenty to thirty girls, all in rags, dirty and smelly. The chatter and shouting of the parents, anxious to sell, would make it impossible for her to select at ease. The first few times she was so helpless against all this, that she left without making an attempt to look the girls over. Throwing alms on the ground for which the mob scrambled gave her the opportunity to leave quickly. But then she found a better way; she removed all the parents from the room, resolutely locked the door from the inside, and went about her task in a business-like way.

The girls had to throw off their rags. Those she disliked she sent from the room, keeping the three or four who seemed likely. She submitted these to the most rigorous examination. Long hair, beautiful features, perfect teeth, well-formed bust, and small juicy cunts were not the only requirements. She wanted girls who showed vitality and resistance. She took them over her lap, she had them open up, she played with the tickler and watched the reaction. She pinched them with sharp nails on the inside of the thighs, and when they showed any softness she gave them a couple of coins and sent them away. For those she selected, she made a hard bargain, clothed them in garments she had brought for that purpose, and took them right away with her.

After a meal and bath in her mansion, she administered the first whipping herself. She took this very seriously. It was a further try-out as to whether the girl was to make good. She did not take them down to the black-chamber, which she had found in the house when she had bought it from an aristocrat. Nor did she tie them. She put them on the elegant bed which would be theirs for the love-business later on, and under the threat of sending them back, made them expose those parts of their bodies she wanted to hurt with the whip.

All of the girls had been beaten before, but they had mostly received rough blows and kicks and few of them had been submitted to a skillful whipping by the leather whip. After laying stinging blows on their buttocks and between their thighs, she would make them get up, stand erect, and order them to hold their breasts from underneath ready to receive punishment. Those who complied were not touched at all, but those who were not ready to follow this order, would feel the whip again and again on their backs, until complete submission was affected. Grushenka had lost her softness: she had forgotten the fear and terror of her own youth. And this made her a success.

When she had collected in this way about fifteen girls, she began careful instructions on how to keep the body clean, the nails in perfect shape, how to smile and walk, how to eat and to talk. She succeeded quickly, especially because she had the most magnificent clothes made for her charges, and fine clothes inspire every woman to refined behavior. Satisfied with this she also gave them special and delicate instructions in how to handle and satisfy the men, instructions which, if repeated here, would make a whole chapter by itself. She spoke to attentive but bewildered girls. They heard the words but did not get the meaning in full, for it turned out that one-third of her fifteen girls were still virgins. If they had been fucked previously at all, they had just lain still when the rough men of their sections were working in their pussies. They did not understand yet how there can be a great difference between an expert courtesan and a peasant girl who just holds her legs open. They should know better soon.

When Grushenka felt she was ready, she held the great and bois- terous opening of her establishment. According to the custom of her time, she had an invitation printed which was quite a document, prettily lithographed and adorned with vignettes displaying love scenes. Here you could read that the famous Madame Grushenka Pawlowksa, just returned from an extensive tour over Europe in search of new and never-dreamed-of sex excitements, was inviting the Honorable Dukes, Counts and Barons for the great opening of her establishment. Here the customer, from the moment that he passed the threshold, would be drowned in an ocean of pleasure, etc . . . followed by the most startling announcement, namely, that for the opening gala banquet, no charge would be made! On this night, every one of the famous beauties would satisfy every whim free of charge, and a free lottery would be played, the prizes being five virgins to be raped by the winners!

Here – according to the style of the time – a special specification was also made, that the winners could deflower their prizes either in private chambers or "in state". It must be known that most marriages of that time started with deflowering "in state", which means that the bridegroom put his prick into the little pussy in the presence of all the near relatives, often all the wedding guests, in order to give a proof by witness that the marriage had been consummated. This habit flourished in the families of reigning houses of Russia right through the better part of the nineteenth century.

The opening party turned out to be a riotous bacchanal. It lasted not only one day and one night, but more than three days and nights, until it was finally disbanded by the discreet and quiet interference of the police. Grushenka received the guests in a gorgeous gown, very audacious, as was becoming for this occasion. From the waist down she wore a purple brocade skirt with a long train which encircled her in gracious swirls wherever she went. From the waist up she had on only a thin silver veil, which left her magnificent breasts and full rounded back bare to the view of the admiring men. She wore a large white wig with many curls which, because she had no diamonds at that time, was adorned with dark red roses. Her girls wore smart evening gowns which just left the nipples free and which were close-fitting in the waist but wide around the hips and behind. They had no under-garments on whatsoever and while the men were eating, Grushenka introduced them on a platform, one after the other, lifting their gowns up in front and in the back, displaying and covering up their undercarriages from every angle.

Grushenka had counted on about seventy visitors. Over two hundred came. Two oxen had been slaughtered and had been roasted in the garden over an open fire, but she soon had to send out for more food. The battalion of bottles of wine and vodka drunk during those days will never be known. A small army of hired lackeys were busy opening bottles and piling empty ones in the corners.

The first feature after the dinner was the lottery for the virgins. After long, and more rowdy than witty speeches, the men decided between themselves that anyone who would not "fuck in state" should be excluded from participation. The men were all from the aristocratic class, mostly landowners or their offspring, officers of regiments, government officials, and so on. But they were drunk and found that this was one occasion to break down barriers.

They cleared a space in the middle of the great dining hall and herded the five young girls into the middle, where they stood sheepishly. Numbers were hung around their necks, and every man received a numbered card, the winners being those who held numbers corresponding with those of the girls. The girls were now told to slip out of their dresses, while the winners proudly stood next to them. The rest of the crowd lay, sat or stood all around the room in a circle. Some had climbed to the window sills to see better. The girls were frightened and began to cry. The crowd answered with cheers and boos.

Grushenka stepped into the circle and got her wards close together. She spoke to them with quiet determination, but threatening them if they did not cheerfully obey. They slipped out of their gowns and lay meekly down on the carpet, closed their eyes and kept a hand on their pussies. But their ravishers found themselves also in a predicament. Two, it is true, had nice hard shafts when they opened their trousers. The other three could not so quickly find the trick of how to raise an erection in this noisy crowd. They discarded their coats and opened their trousers and lay on top of their girls all right, but good intentions don't mean a job accomplished.

Mme Grushenka stepped into the breach. She devoted her services at first to those two who had their guns ready to fire. Soon enough a piercing cry came from one of the girls and the struggling of her bottom announced that Mme Grushenka had, with her apt fingers, put the prick of her first customer into a love-nest. The second outcry came soon afterwards. With the third one – the shaft belonged to a young lieutenant of the cavalry – she had more difficulty. While her left hand tickled his cleft, her right hand masturbated his balls and sword so cleverly that she soon inserted it into the sheath.

Number four proved a futile attempt. The gentleman in question was more than anxious, his prick full but flappy. As soon as Grushenka touched him he gushed into the air and over the hairy Venus Hill of the little bitch underneath. When he got up, crimson in face and ashamed of his misfortune, the watching crowd did not at first understand what had happened. When they finally did, all bedlam broke loose. Of course, a substitute was quickly found and the maidenhead of numbers four and five were duly pierced.

For a moment the half-clothed men lay heavily breathing on top of the nude white forms of the girls whom they covered. The heavy air in the room was filled with rankness. Each fellow, after the climax got up and proudly exhibited his throbbing prick covered with blood. Grushenka had a devilish time getting the freshly deflowered girls safely out of the room. She had to fight through the crowd of men who clutched and pawed the scared girls on whose thighs were smeared the blood of their rape. Grushenka turned them all over to the old housekeeper who administered to them in a room on the third floor.

When Grushenka came back, she got into another melee with the excited men. They wanted to auction off the other girls also. A suggestion came from some corner demanding another maidenhead, namely that of the backhole. Grushenka did not want to hear anything about that and tried to joke them out of it. They started to manhandle her and as she was about to leave the room, tore the thin veil, even her wide skirt, from her, so that she was left only in her lace pants. They crowded in on her, half good-heartedly and joking, half threatening. She became frightened and promised everything.

She reached her ten remaining girls who were waiting in a room upstairs to hear what was demanded of them. She made a resolution to bundle them all in a carriage and to hustle them out of the house, leaving the drunken men to get sober and to disperse. But on second thought she remembered how dependent she was on the success of this event. Her very last money had gone, even the house having been mortgaged to provide the food and the wine. Furthermore, it might be good to let the girls get some rough treatment from the start. They would not be the worse thereafter. She had them take their gowns off before she marched them into the room where the men waited impatiently. She did not care that her wig was crooked on her head and that she had only her trousers left to cover her body. She was now all energy, resolved to play the game, and to do it in great style.

The men behaved well when she brought the girls in nude. They had put ten chairs in a circle in the middle of the room and had arranged for a complete lottery which took some time to carry out. Meanwhile they stared at the ten naked beauties in their midst. Many randy comments and jests flew through the air. The girls in turn, stimulated by Madame and not knowing what was in store for them, answered the men with no less cheery remarks. They threw them kisses, touching their lips, and then their breasts, or cunts in salutation to the fellows who they said, they would like to win and get poked by.

The winners decided on, Grushenka picked out for every group two helpers who should stand by and give assistance. The girls were told to kneel down on the chairs and to hold their asses in the air ready for aggression. They did so laughingly and opened up their knees for of course they thought they were going to be poked in the pussy. It was a wise move of Madame's that she had selected those helpers. They now stood alongside each couple, held the girls' heads down, played with their nipples and made excursions towards their ticklers. It was lucky because every one of these simple girls, as soon as she felt that the prick tried to force her backdoor, howled and began fighting. They jumped from the chairs, rolled over the carpet, kicked with their legs, and were utterly inclined to put up a good fight.

And how the watched crowd enjoyed it! Bets were made on who would be the first man to succeed, and who would be the last girl to be ass-fucked. None of the men had ever seen such a spectacle and the party became a huge success. The gladiators took their pricks in their hands and rubbed them quite openly. Self-restraint or shame was by now entirely lost. Grushenka herself, standing in the middle of the circle, was caught by the atmosphere and if the men had demanded that the girls should first be whipped, she would have agreed to it gladly – for her own pleasure as well as that of her guests.

The girls were overpowered in different positions: some lying on the floor on their belly, others with their heads between the legs of a helper bending over them, one in such a way that the man sat on a chair while the two helpers put the girl on his lap, holding her in the air by her knees so that she could not stave off the attack.

Only one girl was still fighting on the floor; a small young girl, very blonde, her long hair loosened and dishevelled over her bust and shoulders. Grushenka stepped in and settled that matter herself. She waved away the man whom the girl had each time skilfully shaken off at the moment when he thought he was about to succeed.

Grushenka made the girl get up and took hold of her by the hair between her legs and by one breast. Hypnotizing her by putting the whole weight of her personality into a few commanding words, she subdued the girl completely. She made her kneel on the chair and bend very low. Then she opened up the cleft and cleverly fingered the tight ass-hole for a few moments. She now invited the winning man to come and take what was his. The girl did not stir and did not dare to make an outcry when she felt her back-entrance filled with a big love-instrument. She was, incidentally, the only girl who got fucked kneeling on a chair in the way the men had intended it for all of them. But nonetheless, every one of them lost the innocence of their back-parts.

When this spectacle was over, Grushenka ordered every girl to go to her room and to wait for visitors. She invited the men, after the girls had left, to go into the rooms and to have a good time with the girls. She computed that every girl would have to take care of about ten men, which they could do very well.

The men did not ask for a second invitation, and went not alone but in groups, friends and strangers together, just as it happened. For the next few hours some fellows were sitting in every girl's room. While one man lay on top of a beauty who wiggled her bottom strenuously in order to get through as quickly as possible, others were waiting their turn.

If the men had gone home afterwards, as Grushenka had planned, everything would have been fine. But after shooting their sperm, they returned downstairs and lay and sat around, drinking. Songs filled the air, jokes were told, glasses were emptied, food was devoured. Some slumbered for a while only to wake up ready to begin again. After they had beguiled themselves enough downstairs, they would house again watching the fucking and mixing in it themselves.

Many scenes of lust and depravity took place in the girls' chambers. One group of fellows, for example, remembering the deflowered virgins, broke into their rooms and let them have some ass-fucking, in spite of their tears and protests.

Grushenka was everywhere and anywhere, first animated and cheery, then weary and tired. She slumbered in an easy chair, took a drink or two again, comforted her girls, or got drunken men out of the way. Finally she sent a lackey to her captain, who tactfully succeeded in getting the drunken guests out. The mansion was in a state of disorder and dirt. The tired-out whores and their mistress slumbered in a deathlike sleep for forty-eight hours.

But the excitement, costs, and lasciviousness of the strenuous task had not been for nothing. Madame Grushenka Pawlowksa had put her establishment on the map, and she handled it afterwards in a spirit very much to the advantage of her purse. She became rich and famous. In fact, so much so that after her death and after her famous salon had long been closed, anyone in Moscow could point out her house, just as in Paris is still pointed out the famous establishment of Madame Gourdan, who one hundred and fifty years ago was known all over Europe as the best Madame in the word, under the pet name, "the little Countess".

How Madame Grushenka ended up her own love life is not known. It might be that she found her satisfaction through the aid of the friendly tongues of her girls; maybe she married a solid young man to whom she clung quietly without the public's knowledge. The last time that we hear of her is in the official document of the police, of which we told in the preface to this story where she is described as "a distinguished lady in her prime, well formed and refined, with bold blue eyes and a full, smiling mouth, which is able to talk adroitly to the point". May this description of her have been fitting to her until her end.

MARRIED LOVE

David Guy

I MET HER AT the airport while we were waiting for a flight home at the end of the school year. I had noticed her around campus. She always wore a sweatshirt and jeans, and looked – with her short compact body, her curly black hair cut short – a little like a boy. She also carried herself like a boy, shoulders hunched and hands stuffed into her pockets, a funny little swagger to her walk. She had a beautiful olive tint to her skin, a hopeful expression in her wide brown eyes. In a crowd she would always be gazing around, as if hopeful of finding a friend, but if somebody met her gaze she always looked down. She was gazing around that day at the airport, but was wearing – somewhat to my surprise – a bright red jumper. She looked like a different person. We got to talking, and arranged to sit together on the plane.

She told me she had just broken up with a guy, a graduate student in her field – studio art – who had been a mentor for her but had treated her badly. He'd had several other girlfriends while he saw her and was very condescending and controlling. He'd fool around with her when *he* felt like it but would never actually screw her because she was a virgin and he was afraid she'd get hopelessly attached to him. (There was an old sexual myth to that effect.) Finally she had given up. Her ambition now was to learn about sex and become a great lover, go back and give him a taste of what might have been, then dump on the stupid bastard. She seemed genuinely unhappy about what had happened – I realized now that she had looked crestfallen around campus in recent weeks – but she had such a whimsical way of talking about it that you had to laugh. I told her I would be writing stories that summer, working in a factory to make some money. She said she was going off to California to live with some friends and find a summer job.

It occurred to me to wonder if I might be able to help her in her ambition.

In August, before school started, she called and told me her father had given her a car over the summer, asked if I wanted a ride down with her. I said I did, and asked her out to dinner. That was the night of the kisses on Mellon Square, spray from the fountains blowing over us in a gusting wind.

Back at her house, we built a fire against the early autumn chill, then sat and watched it, her head on my shoulder. Her hair, after a while, smelled like smoke. Her face got all ruddy and hot. She smiled and closed her eyes as I covered it with kisses.

My dorm room was a tiny single, virtually filled by a bed, a desk, and a dresser. Sara and I had to sneak in, since women weren't allowed in men's dorms, but my room was on the first floor, next to the entrance. At night, with all the lights off, we could open the curtains and illumine the room by the lights on the quad. Nobody could see in. We would latch the door and ignore what went on around us. We didn't even answer a knock.

My only real sexual experience at that point had been with that blowsy, boozy woman poet, who had taken me back to her motel room after her reading. Her body was saggy, her kisses wet and tonguey, tasting of scotch and tobacco. She had been very funny, made me suck her tits for what seemed like an endless time, gave me explicit and detailed instructions in oral sex, but we'd had only the most perfunctory of couplings. She must have sensed it was my first time but was nice enough not to say anything. She praised my performance and my body, told me I was a beautiful boy. "You know, lovey," she said. "I really do like tongues better than cocks. And girls better than boys. But it's so hard to pick up a girl at a place like this. They're all so uptight. They don't know what you mean."

She's telling me.

My night with the poet had done nothing to prepare me for the experience of Sara's body.

For a long time Sara would get naked only down to the tights she wore under her jumpers. She liked what we were doing but didn't want to hurry the process. After seeing her only in a sweatshirt and jeans, or in one of the shapeless jumpers she wore on our dates, I couldn't believe what a beautiful body she had, with that olive tone to her skin, the smooth shapely muscles in her shoulders and arms, her flat taut belly, small breasts that were nevertheless beautifully shaped, with lovely brown nipples. She looked like a ballerina in her tights. We would hug and kiss for hours, bare skin to bare skin. I would kiss her breasts, but gently, because her nipples were extremely tender.

It was all right for me to get as naked as I wanted. She loved bare flesh, and had a particular thing for my penis, an organ with which she hadn't had much experience but that she liked for its novelty. She must have thought for a while that they were perpetually erect, because in those days my cock stayed that way – a huge red throbbing erection – by the hour. She was skittish about being asked to do anything in particular with a penis. She wanted to do what *she* liked. One night, when we were locked in an embrace, I started to move rhythmically against her tights. I couldn't help myself. "Is this all right?" I said, and she said it was, though I don't think she knew what I meant. In a few minutes I had the kind of copious gushing orgasm that you have when you're twenty. I got up and fumbled around for a towel.

"I'm sorry I got your tights wet," I said.

No I wasn't.

"It's all right," she said. While I wiped her off she looked at me and smiled. "It got small."

"Yes." Not for long.

"It's cute."

Not the word I would have chosen myself, but I'd take it.

"You know," she said, "I didn't really get all this before. How it was done, exactly. But now I do."

"It's kind of a mess," I said.

"It is. But I like it."

In time the tights came off. Her ass was as smooth and shapely and firm as her breasts. The hair between her legs was a brilliant black, shiny and abundant. I taught her to touch me with her hand, so it was my belly, not hers, that got splattered with semen. (Mine was used to it.) We waited to do more until she felt perfectly ready, and until it was a good time of the month. I couldn't believe, when the night finally came, the incredible intensity of entering her. I came in about five strokes, one of the most satisfying orgasms I'd ever had. She could feel it happen, she said, in my back. Where her hands rested on my back.

"It's so powerful," she said.

"Is it?"

"It's amazing. I've never felt anything like it." She was wearing a huge smile. "So manly." I lay on my back, and she traced her fingertips across my chest. "I loved it," she said. "It didn't hurt or anything." She laid her head on my chest. "I can't believe we finally did it."

I had not had much experience with sex, but I'd read up on the subject avidly and with great interest. Probably no one my age in the world had a greater theoretical knowledge of sex than I, though, as any student of biology knows, theory and practice can be far apart. I knew about the magic little button of flesh on a woman ("The good feeling spot," as a little girl of my acquaintance once described it), and I would gently touch that place with a finger during foreplay, to make Sara wet. One evening when I was touching her, before we made love, she said, "That really feels good tonight. It *really* feels good. I want you to do it for a long time."

Up until then, when we had made love, I would sometimes feel a little flutter in her, or a brief contraction, and say, "Is that an orgasm?" She'd say, "I don't know. I guess so." I knew that this phenomenon existed. I had read about it in any number of places (though some of the older books claimed that, while a man had a spine-snapping orgasm during intercourse, a woman just got a "warm glow" out of the experience).

On this particular evening, while I was touching Sara in a relaxed and desultory way, I could tell that something more was happening than had ever happened before. She was going to a deeper place. Her eyes were closed, and she seemed to be less present with me, more inside herself. She seemed, in fact, to be utterly oblivious of me, making quiet little moans and groans. Her cunt was flooded with moisture. It was all over my hand. Her body seemed to grow tense, like a spring that is being wound tighter and tighter. It felt as if she would snap. Suddenly she went into convulsions. Her hips bucked off the bed; her body jerked all over the place; every muscle she had seemed to be expanding and contracting at once. She had shouted when it started, now made a muffled shrieking sound. I got scared and took my hand away, but she shouted, "Don't stop!" The convulsions went on – though eventually growing milder – for twenty or thirty seconds. Finally they ended. Sara's face was drained, and she was breathless. She looked at me with startled eyes.

"I don't think those other things *were* orgasms," I said.

"No."

"Because I think that was one."

"Yes."

It sure as hell wasn't a warm glow.

A man's orgasm to that was like a pop gun to a cannon. And she had told me mine was powerful.

"What a neat thing," she said.

Sara never did come to like the big wet raunchy kisses that I liked. Her ideal kiss was a gentle one, just the tips of our tongues touching. Her nipples were extremely tender, so it was only with great care that you could suck them. You couldn't do it with passion. She didn't like me to go down on her; she thought that was dirty, and didn't like the sloppy wet feeling of a tongue down there. She didn't like that smell on my face and mouth. She also didn't like to blow me. She said my cock tasted like pee, and that the size of it gagged her. She wouldn't think of letting me come in her mouth, but there was no chance of that anyway, since she would only suck me for a few seconds. She also said, repeatedly – in the kind of whimsical way that was meant to convey an important truth – that if I ever touched her asshole she would leave me.

We would often, in those days, have elaborate and lengthy dates on the weekends. We would go out for dinner and have an enormous meal, half a young spring chicken, fried, with french fries and biscuits. Cheesecake and coffee for dessert. We'd take in a nine o'clock movie. Then we'd go to my room and make love three or four times, with long conversations in between, and still get to her dorm for the two o'clock curfew. It was nothing for us to do all that. We often did it on Friday and Saturday nights. Six or seven acts of intercourse per weekend.

By Monday we were ready to dash off to the dorm for a quick one.

Back home we lived forty-five minutes apart, and it was much harder to find privacy. I would visit her house in the country, but in the daytime her mother was around, in the evening both her parents. We were always incredibly hot for each other, would get behind a door and kiss like a couple of maniacs, feel each other up. Once we went for an afternoon drive and stopped by a grassy meadow, perhaps a hundred yards long. It was an out-of-the-way spot, largely surrounded by trees, but the place we walked to was clearly visible from the road. Nevertheless, we took off our pants and did it, humping away fiercely, with only our pants as a blanket against the wet ground. Another time we lay down in the grass behind the garage at her house. The spot we picked wasn't visible from the house, but if Sara's mother had come out to get in her car she would have caught us in the act. She would have been about ten feet away. The long grass tickled our legs. The dog ran around us and yipped. Afterward we pulled on our pants and lay on our backs for a while, staring up at the sky.

We had gotten together as friends – barely acquaintances, actually – who wanted to fuck. Sara wanted to lose her virginity and become a virtuoso lover, and I was more than happy to fuck my brains out. But in the midst of all that fucking, something else happened. We spent all that time in bed, in intimate connection. We were also inseparable out of bed, eating our meals and studying together. We became vital parts of each other's lives. Best friends. You wouldn't have said we fell in love, but we came to love each other, and when it was time to step out and face the world, we wanted to do that together. We hardly had to talk about it. We just knew. I wasn't the love of Sara's life, and she probably wasn't mine – that wasn't a concept I'd given much thought to, since I'd never expected to be loved anyway – but in the world we saw around us, what we had was good. We didn't want to lose it.

Married life was hard. Neither of us had any money from our families at that point, and I don't think we would have used it if we had. We wanted to make it on our own. We lived in a tiny boxlike four-room house, with a cat. Sara worked in a restaurant, I at various places – a library, a bookstore, a bar – where I could keep odd hours and have my mornings for writing. Often at night we would hardly have seen each other by the time we got into bed. We were wrung out and exhausted, too tired to make love, too tense to go to sleep, so we got into the habit – a funny little habit, when you think of it – of just touching each other with our hands. It seemed an activity of about the right intensity for the shape we were in. I had gradually learned from Sara, and no longer touched that one little spot, with my finger, but slowly rubbed the whole area with three or four fingers, moving in a little circle. Sara had gotten as expert at handling a cock as a thirteen-year-old boy. She could stroke it smoothly, intensify what she was doing as she felt the pressure start to build, put pressure on the glans and release it just as I was about to explode. We did it almost every night, right after we went to bed, often without saying a word. It was a nice thing to do for each other, a friendly gesture, like a back rub. It was fun to lie on each other's shoulder and feel the excitement start to build, hear the happy little gasp as it was released.

When I think of the early hard exhausted years of my marriage, I think of that one thing, lying in bed and making each other come so we could go to sleep.

When you are young you have so much energy, your dreams are so fresh and strong that they can take a terrific battering. They cannot take an endless battering. The realities of life wear you down over time. Time itself wears you down. I had written dozens of stories that had been rejected everywhere; I had written for that little newspaper that had a narrow prestige and almost no money; I had poured my heart into three hundred pages of a novel that wound up going nowhere. As I gradually, over the course of two or three months, saw that project dissolve in my hands, I found myself standing at the edge of an abyss. I looked into my future and saw an endless blackness. I felt tiny in the face of it. I felt it would swallow me up.

If you stare long enough into that abyss, you undergo a change. It isn't that you see something emerge. It is that you accept the emptiness. You realize that the emptiness is what *is*. It isn't supposed to be some other way. You really are tiny in the face of it. You are minuscule. But it doesn't swallow you up. You remain what you are. A minuscule being in the face of an endless blackness.

The trick is not to go out of your mind before you have that realization.

I grew a knot in my chest, just beneath my breastbone. It felt as if someone had reached into my chest and gripped the muscles there, not terribly hard, but persistently. Sometimes, in moments of stress, it tightened into a burning. Sometimes it diminished until I could barely feel it, just one finger, or two, pressing beneath my breastbone. But it never ended.

Who is this guy who has a hold of me? I thought. What does he want?

I saw several doctors, who had various names for what I had, various remedies. They filled me with medicines and put me on diets. One went so far as to take an X-ray, which involved elaborate machinery and hours of time. I lay strapped to a motorized table that moved around, tilted me at all kinds of bizarre angles, while doctors in another room looked at my insides on a screen. They sat forward in their seats and stared, looking for what was wrong. They saw nothing.

I was suffering from rage at the world. It doesn't show up in an X-ray. I'd had a dream of the way my life was supposed to be, and the world had betrayed me. It had broken my heart. What I needed was to roar and breathe fire, shout out my rage, beat the living piss out of the world. I could have used a shovel or something. It wouldn't have done the world much harm, and it would have done me a great deal of good. But I didn't know that then. I didn't know I was full of rage. I thought I just had a stomachache. I thought I had no right to be angry (anger doesn't ask about its rights), that I was just another lousy writer with delusions of grandeur. In order to quiet my rage, which was boiling beneath the surface like a volcano, I had to hold it in. I had to cut it off precisely at the spot where it would emerge, at the top of my stomach, beneath the breastbone.

I was the person doing the gripping. I was gripping myself.

Why didn't I let go?

The knot in my chest sometimes kept me from sleeping. It woke me up early (which left me tired and increased my stress and tightened the knot). One morning, as I lay beside Sara with all the ease and flexibility of a concrete slab, she opened her eyes and was immediately awake. I had been awake for hours. She had just had an incredibly sexy dream, which she proceeded to tell me in

glowing detail while she threw off her nightgown and turned my
way. We often made love in the morning. It was in many ways our
favorite time. Sara felt so good in my arms, and the morning felt
so good – a spring breeze drifting in the window – and I wanted
so much *to* feel good, that I pretended I did. I pretended I was
there in my body, which I wasn't (I had retreated up into my head,
away from the pain). As I rolled over on Sara, I pretended that
my three-quarters erect penis, which looked roughly like a real
erection, actually had some feeling in it, which it didn't. I wouldn't
have wanted to disappoint her, after all. I wouldn't have wanted to
let her down sexually. I wouldn't have wanted her to know how
much pain I was in. That might have scared her. (I tried to spare
my wife from the pain I was going through. I felt I should be able
to take it by myself. I thereby cut her off from the deepest part of
my life.) So when I slipped inside her and felt myself immediately
start to come, when I felt myself coming and getting smaller at the
same time, I thought, *What is this*? I came not with that enormous
surge that roars through your body, like a wave crashing against
the shore, but with a tiny little ripple, way off in some distant part
of my body (did a pin drop?). As I hovered above Sara, I felt myself
flush, sweat popping out all over my body. I wanted to hide my
head. I wanted to crawl into a hole somewhere. I felt shame.

"What's wrong?" Sara said, an air of concern in her eyes.

She meant, What's wrong with you? With your spirit? What's
this sudden flush, sweat popping out on your body?

I thought she meant, What the hell happened to your cock?

I collapsed beside her. "I don't know."

This phenomenon is what the world calls premature ejaculation.
It is about two steps up from the basement floor. The basement
floor is impotence.

I thought: I can't write, I can't eat what I want, I can't sleep.
Now I can't even fuck.

A man in this situation thinks, What happened to my penis? The
answer is: Nothing. Your penis is the center of your body, and your
body has a wisdom that your brain doesn't. It knows things that
your brain hasn't noticed. ("He thinks with his dick" should not
be an insult, if a man is whole.) My rage was coming between
me and my cock, and I kept trying to go around it, function as
if the rage didn't exist. My cock was saying, You can't do that
anymore. I won't let you do it. I don't need the whole person with

me to function, but I sure as hell need more than this. I can't do
anything when you're huddled off in your head, hiding from your
pain and your rage.

Accept your rage, my body was saying. Acknowledge it. Let
yourself feel it. But I was afraid to do that. It felt like pain, for
one thing. Nobody wants to feel pain. I was also afraid of what
it might lead me to. I was afraid of what I might do. I was afraid
that if I started to roar I would never stop.

A man whose penis isn't working, who is cut off from his sexuality,
will do anything to get that feeling back. He will go through any
contortion. His penis is *him*, as he knows at some deep level. If
he doesn't have that, what does he have? A man also, at difficult
moments in his life, has a way of getting things confused that don't
essentially have anything to do with each other. If he can't succeed
in *this* (his career), if all his hopes and dreams have been shattered,
he will by God succeed in *that* (the sexual realm – he will become
one of the great fuckers of women on earth). He takes energy from
the one and uses it for the other. It is also the case that, if he is
feeling rage in his body but doesn't want to admit its true source
– doesn't want to admit (it's so humiliating!) that the world has
shattered his hopes – he may direct that rage toward other people.
Writers who have succeeded, for example. Those crummy bastards
who have kept him from getting what he wants. Or people who are
close to him. Easily accessible objects of anger. His wife.

"I want to eat you," he said.

In anger, in fatigue – for the thousandth time – she closed her
eyes. "No."

"Why can't we at least try it?"

"Because I don't like it. I've told you a million times I don't
like it."

"I'm not everybody else."

"I wish you *were* everybody else."

How had he wound up with the one person in the world who
wouldn't do this thing he liked so much?

"When you want to do this," she said, "you're not really here
with me. You're off in your head with one of your dream women.
If you were really here with me, if you really wanted to be with
me, you'd want to do what I want."

"I want you to be my dream woman for a while. That would be so wonderful to me. I'd love you forever if you'd do that."

"I'd like you to love me for what I am."

"Couldn't you do this for me? Out of love?"

"That wouldn't be love. That would be make-believe. I'd be a whore."

"What's wrong with a little make-believe?"

"I want you to be *here*. With *me*. I never feel you here with me. If you could do that, if you could be more with me, it might be more like you want."

Bullshit. It would never be like what he wanted.

"Besides," she said. "If it weren't this it would be something else. I'd do this and you'd go to the next thing. You'd find another thing I don't want to do. And you'd harp on that. You'd keep going until you found something. You want to have something to be angry about."

He honestly believed he would be happy if he got that one thing. Or maybe two things, on the outside. He couldn't understand why she wouldn't at least try. Was he never going to have anything in this world that he wanted?

A woman feels love and wants to have sex. A man has sex and comes to feel love. In the normal course of things, this delicate distinction gets blurred over. It all just kind of happens together, love and sex. But if a man and woman grow too far apart, the distinction looms larger. There is no way to get them back together. It is what you call a Mexican stand-off. Nobody moves.

You can't suck her tits you can't eat her pussy you can't so much as brush by her asshole she won't suck your cock. What else is there? What's left?

Those long nights in the dorm room, the curtains open, moonlight streaming in on the rumpled bed, the endless conversations, quiet laughter, all that happy fucking. What happened?

When you are fucking a woman who no longer loves you, who doesn't want to fuck you, who doesn't want to be there beneath you, you can feel it. You can feel the boundaries on her body. Touch the wrong place and she goes dead. You can feel the body's profound uneasiness beneath you. It squirms. It sweats. It would

like to throw you off. It would like to throw you through the roof.
You are using this body. You can feel that you are using it. You
are not fucking a person. You are fucking a hole in the middle of
a body. You work hard above it – sweating, groaning – trying to
finish so you can get off and leave it alone. You have gotten the
message. Finally you gasp at your climax, and you hear the body
beneath you heave a large sigh. It is not a sigh of pleasure. It is a
sigh of relief. It says, Thank God *that's* over. I don't have to do
that anymore.

Such an act does not bring you closer to someone. It drives you
further away. Until finally, one day, she is gone altogether.

When my marriage had ended, when Sara had been gone for about
three months, I met my therapist late one afternoon when everyone
else had left the building. I'd been seeing him at that point for
almost a year. He closed the doors; I loosened my clothes; he
handed me a foam-rubber encounter bat. For the next forty
minutes, while he urged me on, I beat the living piss out of his
office. I roared. I screamed. I stomped the floor. I shouted out all
my irrational hatred and bitterness. I shouted at him. I shouted at
the world. I tore into it. When I finally finished, my voice was gone,
and every muscle in my body was exhausted – I could hardly stand
– but I also felt, for the first time in years, utterly relaxed. I felt
whole and together. My body was mine, in a way that it hadn't
been for as long as I could remember. And my cock felt heavy.
Hanging there like a slab of meat. There was much more to do.
There were many more feelings to explore, over a long period of
grief. But they all started in that blind wordless rage.

LUST

Elfriede Jelinek

Translated by Michael Hulse

IN ALL SERIOUSNESS I call upon you: air and lust for one and all!

The woman will be with you in a moment, can you hold? First she has to collect herself: for a kiss it'd be best to be collected, all five senses, collect the set. The student is well developed, a perfect picture of a man, no need for touching up, so she lets him touch her up. He places his arm between her thighs. With his eye on the way ahead and the main chance, he rummages under her clothes, which consist chiefly of a plain dressing-gown, which won't be in the way for long. Many have to take terrible buses and regret it terribly when they remain on the wrong genitals for too long. The owner, or rather the passenger of his three-in-one wishes, grows too used to us and won't let us out of his ground-level hospitable apartment. Let me explain that three-in-one: woman is a trinity of pleasures, to be grabbed up top, down below, or in the middle! Till at length they can move on to various amiable kinds of sport, possessing each other without understanding. Bawling and bawling. The woman is eager for the driver to drive her around a little, step on it.

It can't simply be because the toilet's in the corridor that we feel

impelled to go out at night and, in front of the door, look slyly
around to see if anyone's watching as we stand there with our
hands on our sex, as if we might be due to lose it before we can
place it in its hand-painted chipboard box.

Of the many kinds of accommodation he might choose, the young
man opts for this one alone. But the closet won't keep still, no,
it's even hurrying off ahead in the dark and the cold! This Gerti
beats him to the enclosure. Many a one has talked of kissing here.
Spread their torchlight wide. And cast great shadows on the walls,
so that for one other person they will be greater than just anyone,
just anyone on a ski lift. As if sheer carnal desire could make them
greater, bigger! As if they could draw themselves up so erect that
they'd slam the ball straight in the basket! Players can be mighty
fine specimens, tall and erect, and there they stand before their
partners, fully equipped, with all the necessary tackle. So many
requirements, all of them pressing, pressed into the service of
hygiene and filth alike, simply to possess each other. As the
phrase inaptly goes. This dusty junk shop's where we end up.
Two household objects. Of simple geometrical design. Wanting
to fit together and be good as new again! Now! Suddenly there's
a woman in combinations in the corridor, a jug of water in her
hand; has she been casting spells, calling forth a storm, or is she
only going to make some tea? In no time at all a woman can make
a home of the plainest, barest, most spartan of places. That is to
say, even the plainest of women can make a man feel at home by
baring all, in no time he places his spar. This young man who has
entered her life might be the great intellectual? Now everything
will be different from how it was planned. We'll make a new plan
on the spot. Our heads will swell good and proper. Oh, your boy
plays the violin as well? But not at this very moment, surely, since
no one's punching his start button.

Come on, she yells to Michael. As if she were demanding money
of a shopkeeper who hates us customers. And yet he can't get by
without us. He has to tempt us into his store or go penniless.
Now the woman wants a pleasure that lasts at last. First of all,
one! two! (you can do it too, sitting in your car, your speed as
limited as your mental horizons) we lunge at each other's mouths,
then we plunge into all the other orifices; in thy orifices may I be

remembered. And all of a sudden our partner means everything to us. Presently, in a minute or two, Michael will penetrate Gerti, whom he hardly knows and has barely taken a look at. Just as a sleeping car attendant always knocks first with a hard object. He lifts the woman's dressing-gown over her head and with his mouth, in an excitement of his own creation, prompts her who was without form and void to make a frightful commotion in the queue. The queue at the cash desk where we're all waiting, money clenched and balled behind our flies. We are our own worst enemies in matters of taste. People all like different things, isn't that so? But what if we want to be liked? What will we do, in our infinite indolence: call upon sex to do the work for us?

Michael yanks the woman's legs about him like the legs of high-tension masts. In his exploratory zeal he gives intermittent attention to her undouched cleft, a gnarled version of what every other woman has on her person in a discreet shade of lavender or lilac. He pulls back and takes a good look at the place where he is repeatedly disappearing, only to reappear, a huge great thing, fun for one and all. A funster, this fellow. But flawed. Sport being one of his flaws, and hardly the least. The woman is calling him. What's got into him? Why hasn't it got into her? Since Gerti didn't have an opportunity to wash, her hole looks murky, as if it were plastic-coated. Who can resist jamming a finger in (you can use peas, lentils, safety pins or marbles if you like), try it and see what an enthusiastic response you'll get from your lesser half. Woman's unyielding sex looks as if it were unplanned. And what is it used for? So that Man can tussle with Nature, and the children and grandchildren have somewhere to come trailing their clouds of glory from. Michael scrutinizes Gerti's complicated architecture and yells like a stuck pig. As if he were dissecting a corpse, he seizes her hairy cunt, stinking of secret dissatisfaction and dissatisfied secretions, and buries his face in it. You tell a horse's age by the teeth. This woman isn't so young any more either, but nonetheless this wrathful bird of prey is flapping at her door.

Michael laughs: he's terrific. Will we ever learn from these transactions? Will the one ever be able to cross the gap to the other, to talk and be understood and understand? Women's genitals, so outrageously located in a hillside, tend to be quite

distinct, claims the expert. Just as no two people are entirely
alike. They can wear quite different headgear, for instance. And
the ladies are particularly prone to difference. No two of them are
entirely alike. Not that a lover cares, when they lie prone: what he
sees is what he's used to seeing on other women. In the mirror he
sees himself reflected, his own deity. In the waters' depths. Fishing,
plenty of fish in the sea, just hang out your dripping rod and wait
for a catch, another woman to toss off your godhead in and then
toss back. Ah, the privy parts and privy arts of mankind! All that's
required of womankind is that she reck his rod (not wreck his rod),
rock his godhead, toss his rocks off.

Let observation with extended view survey mankind . . . and
what you'll see is the gaping gawp of somebody's integrated,
semi-conducted craving for ecstasy. Go ahead. Try for something
of real value! Feeling, perhaps, that guide who takes the tour party
into terrain he's unfamiliar with, burgeoning through your skull?
We don't have to watch him grow. We can choose another pupil
to waken and give us pleasure. Yet the ingredients are stirred as
we are. Our dough rises, puffed up with the sheer force of air, the
atomic cloud mushrooming over the mountaintop. A door slams
shut. And we're on our own again. Gerti's jolly husband, who is
forever dangling his hose with a nonchalant air, as if his waters
sprang from some precious source, isn't here right now to reach
out his hand to his wife or torment his offspring on the rack of
music. The woman laughs out loud at the thought. The young man
is ramming his piston forcefully home, every stroke an attempt to
get a little locomotion going, stoke her engine, can't you hear that
whistle blow? He is taking a lively interest at present. Well aware
of the changes even the least likely of women can undergo at the
hands of a red-hot fresh and scented wad of male sex. Sex is the
downtown of our lives, shopping precinct and leisure centre and
red light district all in one, but it isn't where we live. We prefer a
little elbow room, a bigger living room, with appliances we can turn
on and off. Within her, this woman has already done an about-turn
and is heading straight back for her own familiar allotment where
she can pick the fruits of sensuality from her private plot herself and
do the job with her own hands. Even alcohol becomes volatile at a
certain point. But still, almost blubbing with joy at the changes he
has wished upon himself, the young man is rummaging about the

cosy taxi. He even looks under the seat. He opens Gerti, and then snaps her shut again. Nothing there!

Of course we can don hygienic caps if we like, to avoid the risk of disease. Otherwise, we have everything we need. And though the lordsandmasters cock their legs and slash their waters into their women, they can't remain but must hurry on, restless, to the next tree, where they waggle their genital worms till someone takes an interest. Pain flashes like lightning into women, but it does no permanent damage, no need to cry over charred furniture or molten appliances. And out it dribbles once again. Your partner will be willing to forego anything but your feelings. After all, she likes to cook up feelings too. Poor people's food. I'd even say she's specialized in economy cooking, she's out to have men's hearts in a preserve jar at last. The poor prefer to turn away without being shoo'd about by tour guides. Their pricks even lay them down to rest before they do. And the source from which their waters spring is the heart. They leave the sheet unstained, and off we go.

At any rate, there are glasses that contain nothing of any greater sense than the wine. The Direktor likes looking into the glass: when it's raised to his lips he can see the bottom, and similarly he wants to drain his own immense tank, right into Gerti. The moment he sees her he exposes himself. His rain comes pouring from the cloudburst before she has a chance to run for shelter. His member is big and heavy and would fill the pan if you added his eggs. In the old days he used to invite many a woman to breakfast, they gobbled him up, slipped down a treat, but now he no longer calls in the hungry folk to eat at his table. Deformed by the opulence of leisure, humanity reclines in its deckchairs, resting its sex, or else strolls the gravel paths, sex in its pockets, hands in its pockets. Work restores humankind and all its attributes to the savage animal condition that was its original intended state. Thanks to one of Nature's whims, men's members are usually too small by the time they've got the knack of handling them. And there they go, leafing through the catalogues of exotic women, high-performance models that are more economical to run and need less fuel. The dipsticks plunge their dipsticks in the sump they know best, which happens to be their wives. Whom they wouldn't trust as far as they could throw them. So they stay home to keep a

watch on them. Then their gaze pans across to the factory in the mist. Though, if they applied themselves a little more patiently, they could take a holiday as far afield as the Adriatic. Where they could dip their sticks in other waters. Their gangling danglers, carefully packed in their elasticated bathing trunks. Their wives wear sawn-off swimsuits. Their breasts are close friends, but they also like making new acquaintances, how do you do, a firm grip, perhaps too firm, uncouthly dragging them from the recliners where they were lounging, lazy and tender, tearing them out, crumpling them in careless fingers and tossing them into the nearest wastepaper basket.

There are signposts along the roads, pointing the way to the towns. Only this woman has to go messing about where children are trying to get their first bearings in life. Calm down and carry on! Hereabouts it is distinctly frosty and foresty. There's a smell of hay. Of straw. Strewn for us, for the animal within. The dog in the manger. How often we've taken the mangy creature walkies! How many before us – who would gladly have buried their wives if they could harvest a goodly crop of women from the place – have splashed and sprayed here! Like winning a motor race! Or like giving it all away: someone, for instance, has thrown a condom away before turning homeward once again. Most men have no idea what you can perform on that keyboard, the clitoris. But they've all read the magazines that prove there's more to women than anyone ever imagined. A millimetre or so more, to be exact.

The student crushes the woman to him. The hissing that escapes from his pent valve can be stopped by the merest touch, he can do it himself. He doesn't want to squirt off yet, nor does he want the wait to have been in vain. As she reclines there in his upholstered crate, he clumsily paws and pinches the most unseemly parts of the woman's anatomy, so that she has to spread her legs further apart. He rummages in her slumbering sex, squeezes it into a pout and smacks it abruptly apart again. Oughtn't he to excuse himself, given that he's treating her worse than the furniture? He slaps her derrière and heaves her onto her back once more. He'll sleep well tonight, that's for sure, like anyone who's done an honest day's work and then taken his innocent rest and recreation.

*   *   *

His hands clawed tight in her hair, the student quickly fucks the woman shitless, it messes the car seats but what the fuck. As he services her, he does not look out at the world, where only the beautiful come in for care and maintenance, a major service every few thousand miles. He looks at her, trying to read something in that face which has been rendered indecipherable by her husband. Men are capable of detaching themselves from the world for as long as they want. Only to take a tighter grip on their own tour group afterwards. They have the option. Everyone who has any idea about men knows who we mean: that male world, a couple of thousand people involved in sport, politics, the economy, the arts. Where the rest come a cropper. And who will love them all, that crop of puffed-up flatulent bigmouths? What does the student see, beyond his own body's unctions and functions? The woman's mouth, a source from which streams well up, and the floor, from where her image laughs at him. They don't bother with any rubber protection. The man half turns away in order to watch his rigid member entering and exiting. The woman's socket gapes wide. The piggy bank squeaks, it's designed for paying in, only to pay everything promptly out again. Both transactions are of equal importance in this business, but you try telling that to any modern businessman, he'll raise his eyebrows in alarm, he'll raise the alarm, he'll lift his kids up so high so that they don't step in their inferiors' anger.

Gradually the spasms the man has set going in the woman calm and subside. She's had hers and perhaps she'll even get a second helping. Quiet! Now only the senses are doing the talking. But we don't understand what they're saying, because under the seat they've changed into something incomprehensible.

The student spills his packetful into the animals' cratch, fills his packet into the animal's snatch. Now it is deepest night. Clad in deepest black. Elsewhere, people are turning over, thinking of other more finely built specimens they've seen in magazines before they dock their bodies alongside for love. When Michael unbuckled his skis, he didn't pause to consider that sport, that eternal constant of our world, which hath its dwelling place in the TV set, doesn't simply stop when you've shot down your slope. The whole of life is sport. Sports dress enlivens our existence. All our relatives under the age of eighty wear tracksuits and T-shirts. Tomorrow's eggs are on sale today so you can count your chickens before they're hatched. There are others who are better-looking or cleverer than we are, for it is written. But what will become of those of whom no mention at all is made? And their inactive unattractive penises: where shall they channel their little rivers? Where is the bed for them to flow and lay their heads to rest? On this earth they are forever worrying about their wretched little organs, but where oh where shall they spray the antifreeze to afford protection in the winter to come, so their engines don't refuse to start? Will they negotiate union, or negotiate with a union? What ridges and ranges of perfumed flesh strew the path of dalliance, all the way till the stock feel the knife on the throat and the family feel the ramrod and lash? For those who are attractive, and who generally tend to be the most active too, are not mere décor in our lives. They want to plug their members into other people's sockets, and will do. Always bear in mind that, in their attempt to get what they want, people will hide away far inside each other, inseparable. So the atom doesn't split them.

Even before the minute hand of happiness can stroke the two of them, Michael has emitted a fluid, and that's it. But, in the woman, nuclear energy is powering her higher. These are the headwaters of which she has secretly dreamt for decades. Ah, the faithful old work-horse, pulling the man's body at the woman's whiplash behest! These forces are felt in even the tiniest remotest ramifications of the female. They spread like wildfire. The woman hugs the man tight as if he had become a part of her. She cries out. Presently, her head turned by what she feels, she'll be going on her way, dripping the seeds of discord in the petty principality of her household, and wherever the seed touches the earth mandrakes and other creatures will shoot up and grow, for her sake. This woman belongs to love. Now, for sure, she has to make certain she revisits this wonderful leisure centre. Again and again. Because this young man has hauled out his tool (now next to useless) and waved it about, see you again, Gerti suddenly sees his face with the pimple at the top right in a totally new and meaningful light. It is a face she'll have to see again, of course. Her future will depend on this go-getter's talent for gun-running, the secret arms trade hidden in his trousers. From now on, his one and only joy shall be to dwell inside Gerti. But here come the windy gusts. The breezy gusto. Bang on time. For holidays over the hills and far away are ruffling and dishevelling and tousling the desire of girls and women, so that they want a good hard regular brushing. In town, where you can go dancing in the cafés, the women on holiday congregate in deadened leaden droves. Ready to fall when night falls. Michael, who is interested in shooting off the lead in his pencil, will have to invest in rubber. And make his choice of the women dressed in their *après ski* best. All of them are natural beauties with natural tastes in natural sex, naturally, that's what he likes best. Make-up painted over pimples would blow him clean away.

Long before opening time, poor Gerti is sure to be at the telephone tomorrow, pestering it. This Michael, if the signals he's sending us and has himself received from various magazines can be relied on, is a blond creature off the cinema screen. Looking as if he'd been out in the sun for some time, with gel in his hair. Prompting us to finger our own sex, he's giving us the finger, he won't give us the finger for real. He is and always will be far away from us. Remote even when he's close. He enjoys nightlife. Keeping the night alive, lively. Not a man who cares for restraint. It's not easy to account for lightning, either: but in middle age we women are herded together in an enclosure of weekend assignations, and the bolt will strike one of us, that's for sure, before we have to leave.

Mind how you go. You may have something about your person that men like that would find a use for!

The animals are falling asleep, and desire has drawn Gerti out of herself, has struck a spark from her little pocket lighter, but where's this draught come from that's made the flame burn higher? From this heart-shaped peep-hole? From some other loving heart? In winter they go skiing, in summer they are the children of light, playing tennis or swimming or finding other reasons to undress, other smouldering fires to stamp out. When once a woman's senses are bespoke you can be sure she'll make other slips of the tongue. This woman hates her sex. Which once she was the finest flower of.

The simpler folk hidden away behind their front gardens will soon be silent. But the woman is crying out loud for her idol Michael, long promised her in photographs that look like him. He's just been for a fast drive in the Alps, now she roars and turns the vehicle of her body in every direction. It's a steep downhill stretch. But even as she lies there whining and pining the clever housewife is planning the next rendezvous with her hero, who will provide shade on hot days and warm her on cold. When will they be able to meet without the lugubrious shadow of Gerti's husband falling across them? You know how it is with the ladies: the immortal image of their pleasures means more to them than the mortal original, which sooner or later they will have to expose to life. To competition. When, fevering, chained to their bodies, they show up at a café in a new dress, to be seen in public with somebody new. They want to look at the picture of their loved one, that wonderful vision, in the peace and quiet of the marital bedroom, snuggled up side by side with the one who sometimes idly juggles his balls and pokes his poker in. Every one of these images is better accommodated in memory than life itself. On our own, we pick the memories from between our toes: how good it was to have properly unlocked oneself for once! Gerti can even bake herself anew and serve up her fresh rolls to the Man in the breadroom. And the children sing the praises of their Baker.

All of us earn the utmost we can carry.

The meadows are frozen entirely over. The senseless are beginning to think of going to bed, to lose themselves altogether. Gerti clings to Michael; let her climb every mountain, she still won't find another like him. In the school of life, this young man has often been a beacon of light to his fellows, who are already taking their bearings from his appearance and his nose, which can always sniff out the genuine article from among the column inches of untruth. Most of the houses hereabouts hang aslant the slope, the sheds and byres clinging on to the walls with the last of their strength. They have heard of love, true. But they never got round to the purchasing of property that goes with it. So now they're ashamed to be seen by their own TV screen. Where someone is just losing the memory game, the memory he wanted to leave with the viewers, the bill-and-cooers at home in their love-seats, hot-seats, forget-me-not-seats. Still, they have the power to preserve the image in their memories or reject it. Love it or shove it. Over the cliff. I can't figure it out: is this the trigger on the eye's rifle, this eyeful, is this the outrigger on the ship of courting senses, this sensitive courtship? Or am I completely wrong?

Michael and Gerti can't get enough of touching. Necking. Checking to see if they're still there. Clawing and pawing each other's genitalia, done up in festive regalia as if for a première. Gerti speaks of her feelings and how far she'd like to follow them. Michael gapes as he realizes what he's landed. Time to get out the rod and go fishing again. He hauls the woman round by the hair till she's flapping above him like a great bird. The woman, awoken from the sedation of sex, is about to use her gob for uninhibited talking, but while it's open Michael can think of better things to do with it and shoves his corncob in, amazing. The woman's dragged by the hair against Michael's firm belly, then skewered face-first on Michael's shish-kebab. This continues for a while. Scarcely conceivable, that thousands of other insensate beings are wallowing in their misery at this very moment, forced by a terrible God to be parted from their loved ones all week long, in his illuminated factory. I hope your fate can be loosened a notch or two, so you can fit more in!

These two want to wonder and wander and squander each other, they have plenty of themselves in store and all the latest catalogues of erotica at home. Just think of those who don't need the expensive extras, who hold each other dear without the sundries! Their special offers are themselves. They flood their banks and dykes, they won't be dammed or damned, they go with the flow of experience, the tide takes them where it will. Suddenly Gerti has an irresistible urge to piss, which she does, first hesitantly, then full force. The vapour fills the confined space. She wraps the dressing-gown about her thighs and it gets wet. Michael playfully cups his hands and catches some of the audible jet, laughing he washes his face and body, then thumps Gerti onto her back and chews at her dripping labia, sucking and wringing out the rags. Then he drags Gerti into her own puddle and splashes her in it. She rolls her eyes upward but there's no lightbulb up there, just the darkness inside her grinning skull. This is a feast. We're on our own, talking to our sex: our dearest of guests, though one who is forever wanting the choicest titbits. The dressing-gown, which the woman has pulled back on again, is torn off her once more, and she beds down deep in the hay. On the floorboards there's a wet patch. As if some superior being no one saw coming had made it. The only light is moonlight. Illuminating the present. Expecting a present in return.

The pallid bags of her breasts sag on her rigcage. Only one man and one child have ever made use of them. The Man back home ever bakes his impetuous daily bread anew. If your breasts hang right down on the table at dinner you can get an operation. They were made for the child and for the Man and for the child in the Man. Their owner is still writhing in her excreted fluid. Her bones and hinges are rattling with cold. Michael, racing down the slope, chomps at her privates and clutches and tugs at her dugs. Any moment now his God-given sap will rise in his stem, his cup will overflow. Hurry up, stuff that prick in its designated slot, no loitering. You can hear her shrieks, you can see the whites of her eyes, what are you waiting for?

The young man is suddenly alarmed at the totality with which he can spend himself without being spent. Again and again he reappears from within the woman, only to bury his little bird in the box again. He's now licked Gerti from top to toe. His tongue's still tart with the taste of her piss. Next her face. The woman snaps at him and bites. It hurts, but it's a language animals understand. He grabs her head, still by the hair, pulls it up off the floor and slams it back where he first found it. Gerti splays her mouth wide open and Michael's penis gives it a thorough go. Her eyes are shut. He jabs his knees in, forcing the woman to spread her thighs again. The novelty of this has worn off, unfortunately, since he did it the same way last time. So there you are, all skin and flick, and your desire is always the same old film! An endless chain of repetitions, less appealing every time because the electronic media and melodies have accustomed us to having something new home-delivered every day. Michael spreads Gerti wide as if he wanted to nail her to a cross and were not presently going to hang her in the wardrobe with the other clothes he rarely wears, which is what he'd actually intended. He stares at her cleft. This is familiar territory now. When she looks away, because she cannot bear his scrutiny and the groping, pinching hands that examine her, he hits her. He wants to see and do everything. He has a right to. There are details you can't see, and, in the event of there being a next time, a flashlight would come in handy. Before going in out of the night to the bodywork repairs shop. This woman had best learn to take the lordandmaster's examination of her sex. And not hang her feelings on his peg. For thereby hangs a tale.

Hay cascades over her, warming her slightly. The master is finished. The woman's wound is throbbing and swollen. Retracting his instrument abruptly, Michael signals that he wants to retire to the tidy quarters of his own body. Already he has become a platform for this woman, from which she will speak on the subject of her longing and his long thing. Thus, without so much as being photographed in underwear and framed, one can become the centre-piece of a well-appointed room. This young man created the white and awe-inspiring mountains of flesh before him. Like the evening sun, he has touched that face with red. He has taken a lease on the woman, and as far as she's concerned he can now grope under her dress whenever he likes.

Gerti covers Michael with soft and downy kisses. Soon she will return to her house and her lord and master, who has qualities of his own. For we always wish to return to the place of our old wounds and tear open the gift wrapping in which we have disguised the old as the new, to conceal it. And our declining star teaches us nothing at all.

WATCHING

J. P. Kansas

I   Brian

I'D ALWAYS WONDERED if my wife ever masturbated when she was alone. Since Lois worked at home, she had plenty of opportunity, but we had never discussed it.

I was almost certain she knew that I did. I subscribed to the most respectable of the so-called men's magazines. My collection of erotic videotapes, begun during my bachelor days, now residing on the top shelf in the den, was an open secret. And she sometimes made half-joking allusions to the practice of masturbation, when she wasn't in the mood for sex and declined my advances.

She played with herself sometimes when we made love, and I found that extremely exciting, but that was different, because I was there, because she knew that I was watching, because I was inside her as she did it.

But did she do it when she was alone? I had no idea.

That day at lunch I started to feel like I was coming down with something. Although by the time I got back from lunch, I felt all right again, I decided to go home early. It was a Friday in July and things were slow. I put a few things in my brief case and told my secretary that I was taking some work home.

Thinking it would be fun to surprise her, I unlocked the door and came into the apartment as quietly as I could. We're lucky enough to have one of those apartments that go on forever in a pre-War building facing Prospect Park. The room she uses as her office is separated from the rest of the apartment, in what was once the maid's quarters. When I went down the hall to her room, I found that she wasn't there. She hadn't mentioned that she was going out when I'd spoken to her just before lunch. Puzzled, I returned to the entrance foyer and saw that her keys were sitting on the side table, so I knew that she was home.

I realized that I was hearing the television, so I began to walk toward the den. I had only taken a step or two when I noticed that the voices seemed familiar. I stopped walking as I tried to place them. It took me a moment to recognize it as the soundtrack of one of the adult videotapes in my collection, and when I did I felt a sudden lurch in my stomach, of embarrassment and surprise and fear and anger and confusion and excitement – most of all excitement. I was very, very aroused.

The fact is, I was consumed with the desire to see what she was doing – to watch her watching that video without her knowing that I was watching her.

My heart pounding, I held my breath and looked down the hallway. From where I was standing, it appeared that the door to the den was open. The way the furniture in the room was arranged, if she was on the couch facing the television, I would be able to see her without her seeing me.

Ashamed of myself, but knowing I intended to ignore that feeling, I slipped out of my shoes and walked down the hall in my socks as quietly as I could.

I stopped just at the door to the den, as soon as I could see in. She was, as I had supposed, sitting on the couch with her back to me. I could see most of her body, but only the back and one side of her head. She would not be able to see me, even in her peripheral vision. She was wearing a loose skirt and a sleeveless blouse that buttoned up the front.

As I had thought, she was watching a videotape from my collection. The cardboard box I kept them in was on the floor next to the television. The cover of the one she was watching lay on the top of the box. She had selected one that had three or four relatively short episodes, unconnected by narrative or plot, all of one man and two women – as it happened, my favorite situation to watch. I looked at the screen, the performers were still dressed.

I wasn't sure, but I thought that it was the first episode on the tape. They – and apparently she – had just begun.

I realized that I was holding my breath, and let it out as silently as I could. I gripped the doorframe with my left hand.

Lois was watching without moving. Her left hand held the remote control for the video player. Her right hand lay on the couch beside her.

On the television, the man and the two women – one blonde, one redhead – were standing in a bedroom, embracing and kissing. The redhead, in front of the man, had unbuttoned his shirt. The blonde, standing behind him, helped him take it off, as he helped the redhead off with her blouse, her large breasts tumbling out as she unfastened her brassiere. She rubbed her breasts against his muscular chest while, behind him, the blonde took off her blouse and pressed her breasts – much smaller than the redhead's but still very beautiful – against his back.

I ached with arousal and I longed to touch myself, but I did nothing. Lois still sat unmoving, apparently unaffected by what she was seeing.

The man was stepping out of his shoes as the redhead knelt in front of him. She unfastened his belt and loosened his pants. I thought I heard Lois sigh as the man's penis was briefly visible, just before it largely disappeared again into the redhead's mouth. Considering how long it was, it was amazing that she could accommodate it as well as she could. Behind the man, the blonde went onto her knees and licked the man's buttocks. There was a close-up of the woman's tongue running up and down the cleavage.

I heard a sigh that did not come from the television, and now, finally, I saw movement on the couch. Lois had brought her right hand under her skirt between her legs. Her left hand abandoned the remote control and was cupping her right breast through her blouse. Inside my underwear, my penis was agonizingly erect. I could not remember ever being so aroused. Still, I did not touch myself.

On the video, the man had reluctantly pulled the redhead to her feet, and was now himself kneeling in front of her. He and the blonde removed her skirt, under which she was wearing stockings and a garterbelt but no panties. Her pubic hair was trimmed into a neat line, only about an inch wide. The man and the blonde both licked her at the same time, their tongues meeting between the redhead's labia, which she held open with both hands.

Lois shifted position on the couch and stood up. She unfastened her skirt and let it drop onto the rug in front of the couch. She sat down again and put her fingers into her panties. The sight of my wife playing with herself as she watched the same erotic video I had so often enjoyed was unbearably exciting. The skin of my face felt hot and taut.

On the screen, the blonde had taken off her skirt, and now all three performers were completely naked. They climbed onto the bed and arranged themselves into one of the many familiar configurations of such a grouping: the man was on his back; facing toward his head, the blonde straddled his mouth, and the redhead crouched between his legs with his penis in her mouth.

Ordinarily, the activity on screen would have held all my interest, but now I was even more fascinated by what my wife was doing than by the activities on the video. Lois was unbuttoning her blouse. Although I'd seen her breasts countless times, I now waited with almost maniacal anticipation. With one hand, she unfastened the front clasp of her brassiere and pushed the cups aside. I sighed silently to see her milky breasts, the nipples puffy and dark. She pinched them, one at a time, and made them hard. I exhaled silently and squeezed the doorframe harder.

On the video the trio had rearranged themselves. Now the blonde had turned around and straddled the man in the opposite direction. Curled over him, she joined the redhead in licking and mouthing his penis.

Lifting her hips, Lois used both hands to slip her panties off. I caught a brief glimpse of her beautiful bottom before she sat down again. Now I could see her finger move up and down along one side of her clitoris, as she sometimes did while I was inside her.

I was paralyzed with arousal and indecision. I wanted to continue watching, and I was ashamed of my voyeurism. I wanted to reach for myself, timing my orgasm to coincide with hers, and I wanted to end the agony of desire and make love with her. And what would happen if she noticed my presence? Would she be angry? Embarrassed? Ashamed? Excited? Amused? What would happen, especially, if I announced my presence by reaching orgasm, as might happen now at any moment?

Of course, I could try to steal away as quietly as I had come, and then return to the apartment at my normal time. I glanced down at the crotch of my pants, comically distorted by my erection, and decided that that was not a sensible idea. I could, perhaps, retreat to another part of the apartment, wait until I heard her turn off the television and put everything away, and then pretend to arrive home.

I was kidding myself: I wasn't going anywhere. As to what would happen when she realized I'd been watching her, I'd take my chances.

Between her legs, her fingers were moving faster. She lifted her feet to the edge of the couch and let her knees fall apart. It looked like she had inserted her fingers into her vagina and was using her thumb on her clitoris. I had never seen her do anything like that, and my groin tightened, my testicles feeling charged and ready to burst.

On the screen, the performers had changed positions again. Now, the two women were side by side on the bed, both on their knees and shoulders. Awkwardly, they kissed and caressed each other as the man, behind them, moved back and forth, stroking his long penis a few times in the one before quickly moving to the other. The soundtrack was filled with women's sighs.

Lois was sighing along with them. I ducked back into the hallway as she changed position again, and then cautiously peeked in to see that she was now standing on her knees on the couch, her left hand reaching between her legs from behind, her right from in front, both moving frenziedly.

I could no longer resist, and almost without thought I took a step forward into the room. At that moment, the sighs and the groans from the television reached their peak. There was a close-up of the man withdrawing his penis and ejaculating, moving his penis back and forth so that his semen would fall on both women's buttocks. The two women, each with one hand in the other's labia, reached or pretended to reach their climaxes, too.

As I walked toward her, Lois' hands stopped for a moment, and then moved even more quickly, and her entire body shuddered powerfully. Her orgasm was a beautiful sight, familiar yet suddenly completely new, and more arousing than ever.

Suddenly I was coming, too, and I was sorry I wasn't inside her. I reached her just as the last spasm coursed through me. I took her in my arms as I felt the thick wetness spreading against my groin. I kissed her deeply, running my hands over her wonderful naked body.

If she was surprised or embarrassed, she didn't indicate it. Still kissing her, I struggled out of my pants. We lay down on the couch without speaking and I entered her, still hard, more aroused than ever, my fluids mixing with her fluids. We let the videotape continue to play, now on the next episode, as we made love.

II Lois

For all the usual reasons that seem to come up after five years of marriage, Brian and I hadn't had sex in a few days, and after he'd left for work, I went back to bed and quickly made myself come. It left me feeling unsatisfied, and I was thinking about Brian all morning.

Brian called me just before lunch, as he usually did, and we had a brief, routine conversation. I wanted to ask him if he still loved me, but I didn't. Did he know that I made myself come when I was home alone? Did he wonder? Would it make him upset to know that I did, or would it excite him? I wished we could talk about things like that.

I called him in the early afternoon, telling myself I wanted his opinion about some work that I was doing, but really just because I wanted to hear his voice again. I was surprised when his secretary told me that he'd just left for home. He hadn't said anything about leaving early when I'd spoken to him in the morning. I asked his secretary if he was feeling sick, and she told me he'd seemed fine. I wondered if he was having an affair.

I doubted it, but the idea had made me angry and afraid and excited at the same time. I'd really done no work at all in the hour since I'd hung up the phone. I wanted to make myself come again. I thought about Brian discovering me in the middle of making myself come, and the thought only made me hotter.

If he'd really left from home when he'd told his secretary he was leaving, he'd be home at any minute. If not – if not, it didn't matter.

I wandered through our ridiculously large apartment, on my way back to our bedroom.

Of course, I knew Brian jerked off regularly. Ninety per cent of men admit it, another nine per cent lie about it, and there's something wrong with the other one per cent. Brian was a reluctant member of the ninety per cent. Whenever I teased him about it, he seemed embarrassed. Sometimes when I walked in on him in the bathroom without knocking, I found him suddenly careful to keep the towel around his waist, which he normally never was. He subscribed to a high-class girlie magazine, although he claimed to be interested in the articles. But he had never gotten rid of the collection of porno videos he'd accumulated before I met him, and from time to time I'd notice that the carton he kept them in had changed position on the shelf in the closet in the den. Sometimes I'd wake up in the middle of the night to find his side of the bed empty and the sound of the television coming from the den. I might have assumed that he was just watching late-night TV or a real movie, but you don't watch a real movie going back and forth between fast forward and normal speed.

I had reached the doorway to the den. I suddenly realized that I wanted to let him find me watching one of his porno tapes – that is, if he was really coming home. If he was off having an affair, then the hell with him. I'd just watch without him.

As I went to the closet, I felt frightened and excited. It reminded me of once when I was a child and I entered a toystore to shoplift a doll my mother wouldn't get for me. I'd been too afraid to do it, and I rushed out to the street sure that everyone in the store knew what I'd been planning to do.

Now I had the courage to carry my plans through, at least as far as taking the cardboard carton down from the shelf and opening it up. There seemed to be a lot more tapes than when I'd first seen it, two years before we got married. Was I misremembering? I picked up the one on top and looked for the copyright notice. The tape was from the previous year: he'd gotten it recently. *So he's still buying these things*, I thought, unsure what to feel. At least, I supposed, it was better than him having an affair. As if, I contradicted myself, he couldn't do both.

I looked at the pictures on the box. There were two pictures each of four different threesomes, each consisting of a man and two women. Almost every man's favorite fantasy, for reasons I've never really understood, and apparently Brian was no exception.

The setting was the same in each of the pictures: a bedroom. The decor was modern American motel.

The men all looked more or less alike: in their late twenties or early thirties; reasonably slim and fit; not particularly handsome; and endowed with a large cock. I wondered why the men in porno videos always had enormous cocks. I'd thought men were always worried about the size of their cocks. Wouldn't the sight of such large ones make them worry more? I realized that the men watching were supposed to identify with the performers in the videos, rather than compare themselves with them, but it seemed unlikely. Whenever I saw a beautiful woman in a movie, it sure didn't make *me* feel more beautiful. How, I wondered, did Brian feel about seeing such large cocks? And how would he feel if he saw me making myself come as I watched these men with cocks so much larger than his own?

The women were a lot more varied: the first threesome included a redhead with enormous breasts and a blonde with breasts I considered normal – no larger than my own; the second threesome, two brunettes, one large-breasted, one small-breasted; the third, two blondes, one large-breasted, one with average breasts, both without hair on their pussies; and the fourth, a blonde and a brunette, both large-breasted.

The pictures showed the threesomes having sex, and they were completely explicit. I had never found pictures like that exciting. I'd rather look at a photograph of a beautifully prepared meal than a close-up of someone's open mouth while they're chewing. Like most women, I suppose, I don't usually find pictures of cocks and pussies very exciting. But the thought that Brian watched these things made the pictures enticing.

Still feeling somewhat like the child who'd resolved to shoplift a doll, I turned on the TV and the VCR and put the cassette in the machine. Taking the VCR remote control with me, I sat down on the couch and started the tape rolling.

After I fast-forwarded through the credits, the first episode began. It starred the threesome featuring the redhead and the blonde.

As the sequence began, the three of them were still dressed, and I used the remote control to pause the tape. I felt a little ridiculous. Why did I want to make myself come watching Brian's porno video? What if he *did* walk in on me while I was doing it?

I sat and wondered whether I really wanted to go through with this, or whether I should just put everything away and wait to see if Brian was coming home or not.

I stared at the threesome on the screen, caught in the middle of an uncomfortable-looking embrace, and could not decide what to do.

Just then, I heard a faint sound from the front of the apartment. It was Brian unlocking the door. I sighed in relief, realizing that my fears of his having an affair had been ridiculous.

He closed the door. It seemed he was being unusually quiet, as if he was trying to surprise me. I smiled to myself. One way or another, *he* was the one who was going to be surprised.

The situation I'd put myself in was even more ridiculous. I had no time to put everything away. I listened to Brian's footsteps grow softer as he seemed to walk down the hall to my office, and then grow louder again as, I guessed, he returned to the front hall. Not finding me in my office, he'd explore the rest of the apartment. Without question, he'd find me within a few seconds.

I looked at the screen again. The performers were still frozen, and so was I.

But I'd be damned if I'd be caught in the middle of putting the tapes away – it would look like I'd just *finished* watching, rather than just *begun*, and if I was to be found guilty of the crime, so to speak – and what else would he possibly think? – I might as well enjoy the fruit of it.

So I pressed the play button. The performers continued their insipid conversation. It seemed that they were improvising the dialogue. They were terrible actors, but I wasn't paying too much attention to them because I was trying to figure out what Brian was doing.

His footsteps grew a little louder. He seemed to have reached the main hallway, which leads toward the bedroom and the room we use as our den. His footsteps stopped, and then, after a moment, resumed, but much more quietly. *He had taken off his shoes! He really was trying to sneak up on me!*

I felt indignant, although this situation was what had made me so hot to imagine. I still didn't know what to do. I had the dangerous sense that I was no longer in control. I was watching myself as if watching someone else, and I had no idea what I would do next.

The tape played on. The three performers had, mercifully, stopped talking, and bad music was playing as they kissed and fondled each other with all their clothes still on.

Keeping as still as I could, I listened to Brian sneak up the hall in his stockinged feet. It made me furious, and it made me hot.

I could no longer hear any movement from the hall. In the television screen, I could see a small reflection of part of the doorway. I could only see a little of one leg. I couldn't see his face, but I knew that he was watching me. He wasn't trying to subtly let me know he was there, and he wasn't boldly walking into the room, either. He wanted to watch me. He wanted to watch me watch his porno tape. He wanted to see what would happen. He wanted to watch me make myself come.

In an instant, the entire scene unfolded in my mind. I saw myself already naked on the couch, using both hands on my pussy, watching the porno, as Brian stood in the doorway, his pants at his knees, his fist around his hard cock. Imagining all that, I think I was unable to suppress a sigh.

If that's what he wants, I thought, *that's what he'll get*. But I was still frozen, unable to move.

I had always thought of making myself come as something very private and special, my little secret. When, at the age of thirteen, playing in the bathtub with one of the shower sprayers on the end of a flexible hose, I had first discovered how to do it, I had actually thought I had invented it, and that I was the only one in the entire world who did it. When I learned that it was completely normal, at first I just didn't believe it, and then I was disappointed. I still liked to pretend I was a young teenager discovering how to do it for the first time. I liked to tease myself, as if I didn't know exactly how to make myself come.

Sometimes when I needed the extra stimulation, I'd touch myself a little while Brian and I were having sex, but I didn't like to do that – I was afraid he'd feel that he wasn't adequate to satisfy me. And somehow that didn't count – it didn't have anything to do with the private act I kept for myself.

Now I wanted to show that act to him, but hot as I was, I was still doing nothing. Why couldn't I take even the first step? What was I afraid of?

The performers in the video were making a lot more progress than I was. I had never seen anything like what was happening on the screen. Both women were naked to the waist. The redhead, her large breasts waving to and fro, knelt in front of the man and took his cock out of his pants. It looked even larger on the television than in the pictures on the box. Incredibly, the redhead put most of it in her mouth. Even more incredibly, rather than gagging and choking, she seemed to be enjoying it.

The blonde was kneeling behind the man and kissing and licking his butt. In case anyone might have missed the point, the camera cut to a close shot of the woman's tongue moving up and down between his cheeks.

Where do they come up with these ideas? I asked myself. In seven years with Brian, I had never thought of doing something like that – and I had never gotten the idea that he was hoping I would. But maybe he was. Maybe he was secretly longing for me to stick my tongue up his butt. I thought I should be outraged at the very idea, but I wasn't. In fact, I couldn't believe how hot I was.

Almost without being aware of it, I reached under my skirt. My panties, soaking wet, had ridden up into my pussy, and they were tickling me. *I just need,* I told myself, *to adjust them.*

But as soon as my hand was at my pussy, I realized I was fooling myself. *I'm really going to go through with this,* I admitted to myself with a sigh. In fact, I was afraid it would all be over too quickly: I was already ready to come. Through my panties, my pussy felt hot and soft and full, like your eyes just before you start to cry. My breasts ached, and with my other hand I began to touch them.

I was so hot that I didn't know what I wanted. I wanted to close my eyes and I wanted to keep watching the porno tape. I wanted to make myself come as fast as I could, and I wanted to make it last forever. I wanted Brian to come into the room and make love to me, and I wanted him to stand there and watch me as I drove him completely crazy.

Was Brian as hot as I was? How could he just stand there? I wanted to turn and look at him, but I just kept staring at the television, where the man and the blonde were both kneeling in front of the redhead and licking her pussy.

Was Brian looking at the television, or looking at me? The thought that he might be watching the tape instead of me got me angry again. *I'll give him something to watch!* I thought.

Careful not to look in Brian's direction, I stood up and unfastened my skirt. It dropped to the floor, and I sat down again. Imagining Brian's face as he watched me, I slipped my fingers under the elastic of my panties and onto my pussy. It was all I could do not to come.

In the porno tape, the threesome were busy arranging and rearranging themselves, like skaters going through their required figures. I couldn't believe all the positions they found. I couldn't believe that people actually allowed themselves to be filmed doing what they were doing. The screen was filled with mouths and hands and breasts and pussies and cocks and butts.

I couldn't believe how hot it was making me. I got out of my top and opened my bra. It felt good finally to have my hands on my bare breasts. *Watch this*! I thought, and pinched the nipples, rolling them between my thumb and let my forefinger, as I'd just seen the redhead do on the tape. Each time I did it, a jolt of electricity ran down my body into my pussy.

Suddenly I didn't care that much about what Brian was seeing or feeling or doing. I just knew that I had to come. I stood up and took off my panties. My juices were all over my pussy lips. I couldn't believe how wet I was. I sat down again and rubbed myself in just the right place.

Usually, I didn't put my fingers inside myself. But on the screen, the two women were up on their knees, kissing each other and playing with each other. Behind them, the man was taking turns, going back and forth between them. There were close-ups of his big cock going from one pussy to the other. It made me feel empty inside, and I brought my feet up and let my legs fall apart and stuck two fingers inside and put my thumb on my clit.

It felt great, and I was almost there, but I wanted to feel it from behind, like the women. I got up onto my knees and reached behind myself and used both hands at once.

On the tape, everybody was coming. The man pulled out of the redhead and his cock began to spurt. He used his hand to make his come land all over the women's butts. The women were groaning and shaking and heaving.

Just at that moment, I heard a footstep, and suddenly I was filled with embarrassment, as if it was my mother who'd caught me, rather than my husband. Ridiculously, my hands stopped moving, as if I could deny what I was doing.

But it was too late. I was already starting to come. If I didn't keep stroking myself right then, it would be a fizzle instead of an explosion, but I would still come. After all that, I had to save it. I moved both hands as quickly as I could. I came so hard I think I passed out for a moment. The next thing I knew, Brian had his arms around me, kissing me, running his hands over me. I couldn't remember the last time he'd been so passionate. He lay me down on the couch, and he got out of his clothes like a magician. I glanced down at his cock and saw the semen smeared all over its head: he'd come in his pants, just from watching me. The thought made me hot all over again. And he was already hard again, or he'd never gotten soft. Either way, he entered me easily. He felt huge, as big as the man in the video. We didn't even bother to turn off the porno tape.

WE LIKE TO WATCH

Donald Katz

THE FIRST TIME I watched him watch her, I knew the voyeur was madly in love with the beautiful young woman he called 101. For three years he watched and filmed her through the window of her apartment as she dressed, undressed, talked on the phone, entertained guests, cooked meals, and, sometimes, as she masturbated gloriously. Unlike most of the many "stars" or prime "targets" featured in his several hundred hours of high-resolution videotape culled from thousands of hours of secret viewing – a massive body of weirdly erotic footage the voyeur refers to collectively as *The Neighbors* – he never once saw 101 making love. And perhaps because of this, he watched her night after night.

"Look at the way she turns," the voyeur whispered the first time he showed me a clip of 101. I saw his light-brown eyes widen at the sight of her slowly spreading lotion over her dancer's hips and small breasts. "Look at the elegance of her mannerisms. You see, I *know* this woman. Look at the way she moves, the way she unfolds her hands. . . . Look. Look at that ass!"

The woman in 101 never closed her window shades or drew the curtains, but then few of the voyeur's several hundred neighbors in his highly magnified line of sight could possibly have imagined that a man so professional in the ways of light and optical devices would have turned watching them into a high-tech obsession, into an enclosed way of life he has over the years adorned with a discrete vocabulary, with the best of cinematic technique, with the gloss of social science, and with the noblest associations of fine art.

"You don't ever see art like this," he whispered as 101 bent forward to massage a slightly arched instep, a strange horizontal light burnishing the form with a surreal nimbus, like something come to life from Degas. "When I look at this . . . it's so beautiful."

I turned away from the screen and walked over to the window near his powerful binoculars and cameras to stare out at the great vertical sprawl of apartment buildings rising to a glass, brick, and concrete horizon. The voyeur joined me and pointed out 101's window, a tiny aperture more than a third of a mile away.

"How far can you . . . how far does the technology reach?" I inquired.

"Well," he said, his face coiling around a huge grin. "Now and again I've gotten off at around ten blocks."

I first heard about the voyeur – the viewer, as he occasionally refers to himself – through the Hollywood grapevine tethering members of the elite fraternity of directors, producers, actors, and technicians who make movies. I heard that these reality-based, stay-at-home times had produced a gifted student of cutting-edge film technique who had turned his considerable talents and a variety of very fast lenses and high-light grab cameras to the creation of films that observers claimed included the most torrid and provocative images they'd ever seen. One producer told me that a clip the voyeur titled "Masturbate 3" was "like a religious experience. One of the best things I've seen." Mention of the voyeur's name in film circles often evoked the query "Have you seen the tapes?" or "Do you know him well enough to get me in to see the tapes?"

It was said that the voyeur only checked into certain hotel rooms in cities all over the world because of the views. He was apparently quite intellectually serious about his habit and given to technical talk of "pre-event behaviors" that most often lead to his neighbors – "the nabes" – performing intimate acts (the amount of wine with a dinner, a certain level of subdued light, the choice of makeup or perfume before an encounter).

For decades the male portion of several American generations had concentrated its fantasies of erotic experience on thousands of

images of "the girl next door," unselfconsciously naked and ready
to go, and now, it seemed – according to numerous sophisticated
specialists in the art and science of capturing images – one voyeur
had managed to repackage those fantasies as something real.

I had to meet the guy – which is what others tended to say
when they wanted to see the tapes.

I approached the voyeur through friends, and he told me that
he believed himself to live on the cutting edge of "one of the most
scintillating and important things happening in the culture". He
said he believed everyone had watched at one time or another.

"I'm just the best," he said.

Eventually, he invited me to watch him watch.

"Watching it live is the best," he said the night we met. "I usually
only get the recorders going if sex looks inevitable. And even
when I'm recording, I want to see it. I want it live. Right now.
Immediate."

He stood at the huge window at one end of his thin and darkened
apartment. He wore jeans and a T-shirt over a lean and athletic
frame. Strapped to his forehead was one of those rock-climber's
lamps that allowed him to see dials and gauges in the dark. He
methodically checked in with his subjects from behind a graphite
tripod holding a pair of $3,000 Siworski 30x75 binoculars replete
with external sighting scope and cross hairs as a Mahler symphony
played on the stereo.

On one of several video monitors, a voluptuous woman performed slow and what seemed to be thoughtful fellatio on a young
man, who lay on his back touching and stroking her hair with
a real appreciation that was somehow more palpable, despite the
grainy black-and-white character of the footage, than any full-color
depiction of sex I'd ever seen. After a while, the woman stopped
and gracefully swung a long leg over the top of her partner. Then
she bowed her head very slowly for a kiss.

It didn't look like pornography. It looked like two people
making love.

"Got these Siworskis after the Gulf war," the voyeur said,
still scanning the intricate matrix of high-potential windows he'd
memorized for signs of live action. "Saw a sailor looking through
a pair on CNN and had to have 'em."

On another tripod beside him, a very fast Canon 300-millimeter

F2.8 Fluoride lens fitted with a 2x tele-extender dwarfed a tiny Sony CCD video camera with a remote-control attachment protruding from the back. "I can't imagine anyone in this having a better system," the viewer said. "But I do think about dumping another thirty or forty thousand into the kit and upgrading to a smart system capable of going remote from anywhere. I'd love to add one of those Chilean Starlight scopes for light intensification, and sometimes I fantasize about a Questar MLF12 lens – the one with four handles because two people have to lift it."

Cables ran back from the window systems to a long table full of recorders, switching devices, and monitors – one of them still depicting the graceful woman with long hair making love. One box had a four-position toggle switch with labels that read UHF, RF, VHS, VCR, though in fact the switches were the right-left and up-down controls for the remote-control device on the Sony camera. The switches were camouflaged to "deter visitors' questions."

There was even a small monitor connected to a window camera in his kitchen, because missing "the event" during a food run can darken a serious voyeur's days and nights for a week.

"One night I came in and 101's sister, who was about eighteen, was lying asleep and naked on a bed. She was on her stomach, and she had one of the most beautiful asses I've ever seen. I mean, unimaginably beautiful, with hair down to her waist. And I didn't know what happened! Did she masturbate? What? What had gone on? I went nuts. One of the most beautiful creatures I've ever seen in my life, and I didn't know what happened!"

On another table the cardboard sleeves of carefully catalogued cassettes were piled high: "The Neighbors #9" and "The Neighbors #38" were typical of the large-type titles, below which descended a long list of short subject descriptions, each noting the spot on the grid of windows or one of the many names and nicknames the voyeur had bestowed upon his stars: "Dyke undressed," "Yuppie 3," "Clarisa with no top," "Homosexual 4," "Gretchen dressing."

Gretchen is a real name. One day the voyeur saw his subject on the street, just as a friend called to her from afar. Coming upon targets face-to-face unnerves the viewer, and though he tends to speak quickly and with an acute articulation usually adorned with clinical exactitude ("Target quality comes down to this," he explained from the far end of the apartment: "gender, age, and physical condition"), the rare chance meetings have rendered him speechless. "I saw 101 in a coffee shop, and I was so . . . well, fucked up. But I made myself approach her. I said, 'Excuse me, are you a dancer?' But I couldn't get another sentence out. I swooned. I had this gigantic history with her, a relationship with her. I'd lusted for her, but she didn't even know.

"But you see, that's what's so interesting – so ironic, I suppose. You are having this experience by yourself, and yet not by yourself. You are totally involved in the life of a stranger."

The voyeur strolled back past a lightweight racing bike set high on a stand, past various duffels full of lenses and tapes carefully wrapped in plastic bags, and past a coffee table bearing scrapbooks full of photos of the viewer posing with innumerable famous movie stars – only a few of whom *know*.

He looked down at the monitor connected to the window camera, and then at the one playing the tape. The lovely woman had commenced an atavistic rocking motion, a hugely undular and balletic arching and thrusting that began near her neck and rolled slowly and powerfully to her legs. Her breasts rose high into a beautiful light that revealed the muscles of her back flexing in waves. Then she would fall to the man's chest below her and begin to move again.

"Beautiful, huh?" said the voyeur. "So hot. And the thing is, you can feel it. You've been there, so you know what every move feels like. You can smell it. But capturing these images is only one thing. The hottest part is the anticipation, to see this thing beginning to evolve. It's visual foreplay. It's – oh, wait. Look!" he said, pointing at the screen, where the target had revved everything up into double time.

"Women see a scene like this, and they say, 'She's pretending.' But men . . . well, let's just say this is a male-dominated field.

"So interesting," he continued as the lovemaking on the screen suddenly got closer and larger. "Good, switch to 4x," he said. Then his voice rose over the sound of the symphony on the stereo. "Here is a small piece of the great puzzle. Here is the art of the frame. Look at the patina of electronic graininess. You'll never see lighting like this in a film. Look at the shades of gray. It's all about sex, but it has its own brilliant form. Oh, the beauty and the horror."

Now the man also began to rise from the bed. Soon both figures framed by the distant window began to rise and fall together in a shuddering crescendo. "There it is!" crowed the voyeur. "Death! The divine death!"

People have threatened their marriages by doing this," he said later. "A writer I know had this lady he watched through the living-room window. One night when his wife was in the hospital and his mother-in-law was asleep in the living room, he had to crawl on his belly across the room because he had to get to that window. . . . In truth, this is insanity. Not serial-killer insanity, but an obsessively hot insanity."

The viewer takes no issue with psychological analyses that characterize his avocational calling as deviant. "In fact, the term – *voyeur* – has been watered down by popular usage. It originally referred to an excessive and exaggerated interest in sexual objects or activities. And that's what this is. But it's more than the sex per se; it's also about the beauty of the obsession. It is a quest, an odyssey, though one with a downside – living in total darkness, for instance, and gearing your entire schedule around potential events."

"The first time is like the first time you took acid or had sex," he explained over dinner one night. "For me it happened in college, in the 1970s. One night I looked out a window and across the way there was a guy standing naked in a room. A light bulb went off. *If this was an attractive woman*, I thought, *I would be in the* Twilight Zone.

"Now I'm thirty-nine, and I happen to have the perfect lifestyle for what I do. I've never been married. I've never been close. I've never really wanted to get married, because my life is fun. I don't even have a girlfriend. I'm extremely free of the baggage other people accumulate in their lives.

"Two nights ago I slept with a woman. I *got involved*," he said with derisive irony, "and while it was nice, it didn't have . . . that hunger. Only waiting and frustration can give you that. Only then do you feel the glory, that stress that makes you feel so alive, that intensity of the search for the real thing! My whole life seems to be a struggle to live in the moment, to search out and finally discover the real thing."

*   *   *

Fucking gold mine, but you can't get at it!" The viewer trucked up Broadway from West Sixty-second Street, a small camera in his right hand. "These are the kind of apartment buildings that house young and attractive subjects, but there are no vantage points." He stopped and pointed up. "This kind of building construction indicates dining rooms on the corner and only one access window to the bedroom. And the angle between that hotel and the apartment building is just too steep."

Then he was off again, bounding between parked cars during a visit to Manhattan. He stopped often to stare up at hundreds of windows of opportunity, scouting out potential hotel perches for the next time he was in town. He circles hotels before checking in – always gazing skyward – and he even suggests carrying a compass so that you can figure out where you are as you ask to change rooms over and over again, until you face the right way. "Hotels are a wonderful challenge. Give yourself twenty minutes to figure out who lives in three hundred different apartments."

He went up to the lobbies of apartment buildings to ascertain the relative income requirements of rent or mortgages – and to look for bicycles and baby strollers. He tends to correlate income and lifestyle accoutrements to find likely habitats of the most attractive, sexually active, and least blind- and window-conscious population. In less populated areas the voyeur suggests checking for station wagons and looking at the accumulation of rust on a swing set to find youthful and sexually active subjects, though he adds that suburban and rural at-the-window viewing is the most dangerous voyeurism of all.

"But these are tactical considerations that pale before the real science of voyeurism," he said, snapping photos of single vistas loaded with several tall apartment buildings. "The science comes in reconstructing people's lives from brief moments of time, from little slivers of life narrowed by curtains and air-conditioners. And the beauty emanates from figuring out what real people do. The trick is to know where people are in the apartment, even when you can't see them – to figure out what's going on from artifacts. I love looking at the artifacts of people's lives. I love the perfection of somebody doing his taxes in one window, and then panning down to two people fucking their brains out in the window below. I will endlessly watch someone watching TV. I've seen people each night in precisely the same position, legs crossed and hands positioned in a certain place. Night after night.

"The thing is, people don't know what real people do. We are encircled by lies. Television lies. Advertising lies. Movies lie. We need to know what real people do to see that we're okay, to feel like real human beings. How do other people do it? Do they touch and fondle? The other night I watched a lady give a hand job, and she was just brilliant, the first violinist in the symphony. Creative beyond words.

"I once watched a guy screwing a transvestite, and as soon as they were done they both got up and got dressed. I've seen this often with homosexuals. No caressing; you come in and you go out. Heterosexuals actually make love for a longer period of time than you might think. I've learned so much about women by watching them – I never had a sister."

"Can you see love?" I asked him. We were standing at the corner of Fifty-eighth Street and Third Avenue, and the question seemed to knock some of the rigidity from his usual straight-backed bearing and to side-track his rapid-fire talk.

"Yes, you can," he said. "I've watched dozens of relationships deteriorate, and I've watched people who are truly in love. The sight of it makes me want to be as eloquent as the character who speaks at the end of *Blade Runner*, the one who says, 'I've seen ships afire off the sea of Orion, and all of this is like tears in the rain.'

"Seeing love makes you more hungry for real experience than sex could ever make you. You can have sex at any moment, but you may never have love."

By now he had stopped walking and looking up. "If it came down to watching my neighbors and being in love with somebody," he said, "I'd never look out the window again."

Another evening and the viewer was rolling bits and pieces of tape like a museum curator working at disc-jockey pace. The attendant intellectual theme for the evening was art. Another lovely woman lolled on a bed on the screen, her sweater pulled up above her breasts. Only the top of her torso was visible as her head rocked back and forth on a pillow. Eventually a young man moved very slowly into the frame, kissing his way up her belly to her breasts.

"Like a moving painting," the voyeur said. "A beautiful whiteout is coming, a visually exquisite moment. Who would ever compose a photograph like this? This is a special combination of realism and art. A form that nobody created."

Then he played the famous "Masturbate 3," the take I'd heard about from film-industry friends. A young girl comes into a well-lit room and practically leaps backward onto a bed, her legs, with pants still around the ankles, thrust high into the air. She immediately begins a two-handed self-administration that involves one hand sneaking up creatively from behind.

"It's capturing it," the voyeur said in a respectful whisper. "It's not having something you can jerk off to. It's just having it."

Now 101 was back on the screen – tape #20 – her glorious lower body highlighted by stretch pants, the image entirely reminiscent of Ann-Margret in the unforgettable dance sequence of *Bye Bye Birdie*. But 101 wore no top, just as tens of thousands of American boys and men had wished to be so of the young Ann-Margret.

"You should understand that I don't show these films as if they were trophies. I show them only to people who are truly interested. I'm respectful about this. Some voyeurs seek a macho visual-rape thing. I will go to any extreme to make sure the targets don't see me, because it's absolutely immoral to make their lives worse. While someone with the right heat-sensing or infrared outfit could spot me in a second, I know what's out there. I know they aren't watching me, because I'm watching them.

"One time I did pass an actress I watched on the street, and I smiled, but I must have also stared, because she looked back in a way that made me know that she knew. I must have telegraphed something – that I knew her. A face can be a repository of excitement. It was just too close for comfort.

"But if people understood how I feel about my voyeurism, they wouldn't be horrified or vengeful or fearful or insulted or degraded because I watched them. They are my babies. I am part of their lives.

"One or two of my girlfriends might have thought me a little strange over the years," he added. "But if they accepted me, they accepted someone who has a unique lifestyle, who is very independent, very self-absorbed, and in love with his own brain."

Heading back to his apartment one late-summer evening, the viewer stopped to joke with children hanging out in front of his building. He picked up ongoing strings of happy conversation with several couples strolling down the street, and various people from the neighborhood called to him from the other side of his street and waved.

"There are certainly conundrums in this," he said, taking his long strides into the building. "Violence, for instance. I haven't seen real violence, and I'm glad. The only violence for me has happened to my wienie. But what if I saw something and had to act? A friend who watched a lady across the alley – an ultrafox – saw a guy outside her window on the fire escape one night. He called the police, and she never had her blinds open again.

"And what if you meet and want to become involved with someone you've watched. How do you break it to her? I wouldn't be able to live with her and have a family without telling her. It's a deal-breaker.

"But then one of the luxuries of being a voyeur is that you don't have to deal with the baggage of a relationship. All of my life, I would hunger for someone sexually, but in the end I wouldn't be interested in the person's soul. I wouldn't be interested in the person intellectually, culturally, spiritually, or even as a human being."

"But what if you spent all of the time you apportion to watching out there?" I ventured, pointing out the window as he checked the grid for signs of action with the Siworskis. "Wouldn't you increase the chances of discovering romance in a real relationship?"

"I don't have the patience to get past it all," he said, somewhat more slowly than he usually replied. "I don't have time to convey that I'm okay, that I won't beat people up, or that I'm cool. Life's too short to sit in a bar, trying to hustle a lady into bed. And where are the relationships that make you feel that this is honest, where are there no lies? Well, I have the answer. There are no lies in those windows. The two people I see out there might be lying to each other, but they sure as hell aren't lying to me. They can't lie. They don't know I'm there."

Then he rolled another tape. But by now my fascination with the tapes had waned before an abiding fascination with the man who'd made them, this silent wooer, apparently so ecstatically unrequited – a man to whom relationships with people and sex and most of the rest of human experience appeared so completely scripted and disingenuously preordained that only the observed lives of others seemed real. I wondered constantly about this gifted man, who for some twenty years had watched glorious sex and love and loss and loneliness in the curtainless village of his imagination, all of it magnified seventy times with an expensive lens.

Another selection from *The Neighbors* began in low light, an image of a woman in bed at dusk, the covers drawn close to her chin. She wore glasses, so it was only at the point the voyeur spoke that I realized it was 101.

"Oh, no," he said softly, moving to the control panel of the digital video machine. "I don't really want to watch this."

"Please wait," I implored.

He slumped into a chair and observed his neighbor begin to cry. She began to weep so that her whole body throbbed in syncopation with her despair. She stopped every so often, blinking away at her thoughts, but then she would be overtaken again, her pretty face collapsing with pain and her arms limp at her sides, seemingly too weakened by grief even to wipe away her tears.

And the silence made it even more difficult to bear.

"It's so fucking sad!" the voyeur said, drawing in a quick breath. "This is one of the only times I felt embarrassed. There are moments when people should not be watched. Sex is not one of them. Sadness . . . sadness is.

"She cried all the time for a while," he continued, his athletic and energetic bearing suddenly lax, as if deflated. "Then I came back from a location one day, and I saw that the pictures were down from the wall. There were boxes all over the floor. And then she was gone. For three years I'd watched her, and . . . it felt like such a failure when she left."

Suddenly the voyeur looked to be entirely in the moment, just as he'd always desired. Without technical references and bawdy throwaway lines, the pain became entirely real. "That's what can be hard about this," he said. "I fell in love with her, I know I could have made her happy."

A LETTER

Jana Krejcarová

Translated by A. G. Brain

DARLING, DARLING, DARLING – that is to say – in a word – well you
know what I mean,

as far as I recall, I borrowed the typewriter to bash out a material
base for the children, for us, for everyone, in fact, and here I
sit writing a love letter – there's something wrong somewhere –
alternatively, everything is one hundred percent all right, except
that would mean things were in a bloody mess in another sense,
so it makes no odds either way.

But I can still feel your kiss on my lips – I could hardly put it
in a more banal way, but that's the way it is and I'm old enough
now to indulge in banalities. Old enough and in love enough –
I am, in addition to all the things we talked about and that are
related to us, in love – as I am discovering at my old age, rather
to my amazement and amusement. But since the world is totally
and absolutely beyond belief I take it for granted. Do likewise. If
I were the sort who went in for dramatisation I would become a
fatalist, convinced that fate had a hand in this relationship, but
I'm not a fatalist so I just tell myself that God is mighty and may
his will be done – particularly when it corresponds so perfectly to
my own predilections.

An outsider might say that if the two of us had not met we might have been spared a great deal, but I would not wish to be spared a single one of our joint cock-ups, nor would I wish to be spared the bad – or seemingly bad – things, which is probably why I wasn't, thank God.

You tell me I don't like your sentimentality – you're wrong there, my darling, truly very wrong. I like it very much and need it; it's just that it took me many years to learn to trust it. These days I want it not because sentimentality particularly appeals to me, but because it comes from you. It is quite simply part of you, part of us.

I never was one to act very sensibly, maybe quite simply because I totally lack common sense, or alternatively because I have an almost physical aversion to sensible behaviour. If ever I did things of which I was ashamed, then they were always things I did in an effort to be sensible. Save me from the plague, typhus and common sense. Common sense – that's anti-alcohol posters and State control, condoms and TV sets, and sterile poetry in a good cause. May God protect me from common sense. By maintaining my vitality I can put up with more than anyone else, but common sense would finish me off in a week, and it would be the most miserable death imaginable. Common sense destroys anything of meaning within me, common sense saps my vigour, erotic and intellectual alike. So you can believe me that when I say that common sense has no bearing at all on my theory that if the two of us eventually decide to remain together it will only be as a result of free and unhampered reflection. But precisely because I have not a trace of that abstruseness held in such high regard and esteem in this irrational world (and incidentally it is striking how much this irrational world relies on its own common sense), I am incapable of limiting myself, not that I have any desire to, anyway. Limitations are not part of my world. The moment I feel your kiss, I want another and I think there is nothing wrong with that.

I have been happy with you many times throughout this period – but the feeling keeps on getting stronger all the time. It's not normal, but it does. I don't think I have ever been as happy as I was today, walking through Letná Park, out shopping, at the post-office, on the telephone, knowing that you were waiting for me, then after leaving Holešovice, when I thought I would never tear myself away from you and I knew you couldn't tear yourself away from me, in the pub where we went ostensibly to get a beer and a lemonade, in the tram, at the moment when you waved me goodbye. Perhaps I'm crazy and perhaps I'm the insufferably "sentimental" one now, but I can't help it. The whole time I've been crazily, rashly, calmly, wonderfully happy. And I am now, even though you're not here and if you were here I would get on with writing my novel and you would sit opposite me, or by my side, or anywhere and do what you liked and it would be fine, really fine, and it would be a real home, a home as I imagine it, the sort of home I want and need. But even though it isn't and you're horribly elsewhere, I am still happy. It's just that there was no way I could come home and get on with something, just like that, so I started to write this letter which has no rhyme or reason and is not intended to say anything or solve anything. But that's something I don't think I need to explain. I'm sure you'll understand and you won't mind. I expect we'll often find ourselves in situations where we'll have to solve something and there's nothing wrong with that – it's something that can't be avoided even under socialism. But I expect we'll also frequently find ourselves in situations in which we can do things for their own sake, for the joy of it, out of a sense of happiness or whatever, like the way I'm writing this letter.

You don't know how proud I am (it was something I was always prone to be, as you probably know), but you don't know how proud I am that I have you, that you love me (at least, I think you do), that I love you, that you are the way you are and that you are who you are. I mean that very seriously, Zbyněk, more seriously than you will ever imagine, maybe. To tell you I respect you would be the truth, admittedly, but it would not be the whole truth, just a small part of it. It is something else besides, it is being sure of your unique individuality that makes me proud. I do not admire your intellect, I take it for granted, and there's nothing wrong with that. But what excites me – physically almost – is that fantastic amalgam of intellect and a 100 percent insanely logical irrationality, a sort of philosophical poetry or poetic philosophy, that we talked about a bit today, but which extends far beyond anything we dealt with in that conversation. You see it's not two things alongside each other – poetry and philosophy – but a third thing created by their fusion, something whose value I shouldn't think we are able to anticipate yet. Your fear of being a charlatan couldn't be more misplaced, although it is quite understandable.

It has its roots in the prejudice that philosophy is the arid product of erudition, and that poetry is "persevering toil on the Nation's ancestral plot". Neither the one nor the other is true: erudite philosophy is all right for academe and the sterile brains of people who try to use it to defend their own futility, and toilsome poetry is laboured nonsense for school anthologies, laboured nonsense for the titillation of industrial schoolmistresses who don't have a particularly pleasant life otherwise.

I can appreciate that it is not easy to rid yourself of such prejudices, but even so I would like to tell you that you must get rid of them, otherwise they will become an iron ball shackling you to the galleys of servility. You see they give rise to dependence on things which neither philosophy nor poetry can have anything to do with. The point is it's only a short step from those prejudices to the idea that philosophy should serve someone and poetry should gratify them, to the horrifying situation in which those two things lose their intrinsic meaning and thousands of extrinsic meanings start being attributed to them, and they start to be soiled by the sort of servility I have been talking about, a servility that is the plague of the present century and possibly of many earlier ones too. They start to be soiled so badly that they end up losing any meaning at all. Damn it, why do the majority of people involved in poetry production run away with the idea that this poetry has to be for someone's benefit, why do they get themselves into the absurd situation that they end up writing for people they couldn't give a damn about, people for whom they wouldn't even buy a shot of rum with the fee they get, and yet these are the very people they want to gratify at all costs with their creations? In such a situation, not only is the work distorted but so are the readers whose eagerness to gratify themselves with it is worthy of greater things. The reason is that they have had it drummed into them that this poetry, created by someone whose company they would not tolerate for more than half an hour, will bring them undreamt-of emotions and the infused and distilled happiness of a cultural experience.

It's even worse in the case of philosophy. If poetry is turned into a skivvy, then philosophy becomes a proletarized debutante turned house cleaner, a job she is incapable of doing but it helps improve her class profile.

On the one hand, such philosophy is actually required to be arid and indigestible, so that no decent person can consume it without embarrassment and the only person who is turned on by it is the kind of university professor for whom it is proof that the money spent on his education was not spent in vain. It is particularly suitable for lads from poorer homes who have worked their way up and is redolent of the pathetic ambitions of poor little mums who keep their gifted sons at college by laundering soldiers' underpants. On the other hand, it is required to defend and bear the entire burden of human imbecility; entire State establishments are built upon it; it is used as a brush for cleaning the latrines; it is made to justify the jailing of Ministers of State and the latest butter price increases: to justify these things to people who are neither willing nor able to understand a single one of its postulates. They are not able to because they lack the education. It's a vicious circle that engenders still greater horrors, such as the self-assured sense of supremacy and power felt by those who wrongly suppose they have understood something of it. All those Mr Average Creeps who happen by chance not to be wages clerks and whose only reason for not counting out wages for the greater prosperity and happiness of the State is that they have a speck of grey matter, albeit only just enough to stuff their enormous heads full of information which is partly superfluous and partly of no use to the heads in question. All those cretins have the deep-seated conviction that they ought to be running the world and if they were it would instantly be "the end of the rainbow". Just hand each of them a few kilos of philosophical literature and you'll see what they'll do with the world.

Fortunately, however, God truly is mighty and philosophy is the child of a very bad home. Mind you, quite a bit of damage has already been wreaked though.

However, in reality every philosophical postulate is meaningful in its own terms and every poetical definition is a thing of value on its own account and does not need assigning any further purpose. And this is precisely the point I wanted to make: that you are no charlatan. The real charlatans are the universities that turn out people with degrees in philosophy, licensed to engage in philosophical thinking – what a terrifying and inhuman nonsense: examining someone's knowledge of x number of textbooks as qualification for a degree in philosophy. What sort of lunacy is this for holyjesuschristsake?! It takes one's breath away and makes one double up in hysterical spasms of laughter, despair, dismay and cold fear! If that is philosophy, then I'm an exemplary housewife. It is something to steer strictly clear of; one cannot accept a single truth discovered by such people because it is discovered in a context in which it is not a truth even if it is, if you see what I mean.

In one of your letters you wrote that you had done your philosophical work in pubs or adjacent to my cunt, and in despairing, cynical or unprincipled frames of mind, but never in libraries. That's not entirely true, but it is to a considerable extent, i.e. it is entirely true apart from the fact that you occasionally visited the library during the period. Thanks to that, even as it stands – and as such it has served other than purely philosophical ends – it is something one can use as a starting point, something one can build on. I do not believe and I shouldn't think I'll ever be convinced that it is possible to get to the bottom of anything in philosophy by dryasdust scholasticism, by antiseptic instruction. For God's sake, what can be more stimulating than philosophy? So how can anyone do anything in it if they eliminate the orgiastic thrill of it all, tell me that? To my mind it is like screwing with the help of 100 percent disinfected and harmless pills – except that philosophy isn't harmless and can't be pursued that way. You must get rid of the inferiority complex you have about your philosophy, your feeling that it is not arid enough to adorn an academic library; that is its merit not a defect, and above all it is the greatest hope it has. For heaven's sake don't allow that hope to be drowned in beads of erudite sweat! You have God-given gifts that few possess. Wherever do you find the gall to regard them as a source of your complexes, or the impudence to want to discard them just because some idiots who lack these gifts have what they dare to call an opinion about this matter, and one that actually differs from you – not from your opinion, but from you, do you understand? The fact that you have so far felt the need to create your philosophy in pubs has proved itself. Why then this desperate need for laboriousness and erudition? If one day it becomes a truly spontaneous need, then there's no reason why not, of course: one of the gifts that you not only have but have bought and paid for at a great price is precisely this ability to combine need and purpose. What I mean is that you have mostly felt the need to do things that have some purpose, even when at a given moment it is a purpose you are unaware of, or one that emerges only later, and sometimes a good deal later. Learn to rely on that gift and thank the Good

Lord for it wherever you go. Don't return it to him covered in vomit from your spasms of laboriousness, that's not what he gave it to you for. He just might hear you and take it back. I'd be careful if I were you. It doesn't pay to take those sorts of chances with gifts, my love. Forgive me, I don't intend to be vulgar or rude, but you understand me, don't you, you understand why I'm writing this and what matters to me.

Learn to trust the Good Lord a bit. He already knows what he's up to. And trust yourself a bit too. Insufficient self-confidence and underestimation of one's own resources is one of the deadly sins, you know, truly and literally deadly sins that kill you. More so, perhaps, than over-confidence. The thing is you have to be aware of your resources if you are ever to use them, if you are to manage to do with them what you were given them for. You will have a hard time, one day, explaining that you allowed yourself to be blinded by something so dubious as an inferiority complex. Modesty in this respect is not a virtue, you know. Modesty in this respect is at best stupidity and I mean at best. You are gifted with the most amazing imagination – something whose place can't be taken by reading, whether good or bad (I read somewhere a charming little sentence to the effect that imagination is something that some people just can't imagine) and it's your imagination that gives you your immense advantage, an imagination that is the seedbed of your poetry and your philosophy, as well as of something which I do not yet have a name for, something that arises from a homogeneous fusion of the two. The worst thing you could do would be to bridle your imagination with precepts from philosophical vocabularies, to lock it up securely in a spare room so it won't disturb the work you're doing in the room next door. If there is a real and genuine hope of your publishing a mature work (and there is), then you yourself will have to be fully part of it, warts and all, i.e. your socks, your aversion to libraries, your beard, your beer-drinking, your imagination, your intellect, your prick, the lot. Nothing turns me on like my hopes for a work that will be created in immediate dependence on all those things, a work that will leave nothing out, a work that will be uncensored, raw, crude and monstrous – but absolute. A work that won't be harmless, one that will make people vomit and shit after they've consumed it, that will seize people with feelings of happiness and horror alike, a work that will know no limits and will not let limitations be placed

on it at any time or in any way. And if there is one thing I
am convinced of it is that you will publish this work in all its
sweetness and orgiastic convulsiveness. But that is precisely why
I don't want you to delay its fruition because of prejudices that
belong to another world, a different world from ours. And that's
why I'm writing all this, and if there is any way I can help this
embryo to be born, any way of using some of my own warmth
somewhere to help it mature (and I want to very much) then it
is precisely by roaring out loud every time a shadow or blemish
appears on its absoluteness. I have the detachment to do it. None
of the fixes you get into, none of your misdemeanours or crazy
behaviour, none of the crimes you might commit are blemishes.
But pettiness is a definite blemish. And inferiority complexes and
lack of confidence are pettiness, we both know that. Don't get me
wrong, love, it's all part and parcel of the same thing: my love for
you and my desire to sleep with you, my interest in your work.
It's hard to tell what turns me on most, your body that I know
so well, or our different discussions. I really can't tell for sure. I
am capable of lying in bed talking to you about philosophy and
by the same token, we can be sitting at a table talking philosophy
and my cunt will be standing at attention. It's hardly possible to
divorce the two and abstract one thing from another, is it? I want to
spend hours yacking away with you so that I can sleep with you and
I want to screw away the hours with you until it's time to talk again,
I have to know, you see, that the hours spent sleeping with
you and talking to you are bound up with your work. There'd be
no sense in it if it weren't so closely, intimately and tightly bound
up together the way I conceive it. Maybe one day we'll actually
end up being totally together in every possible sense and it will
transcend happiness. But I shall flee from it the moment it loses
this single, real, authentic purpose, I shall flee from it and marry a
commercial engineer with a two-door saloon, because then there
won't be any difference.

And I have to know everything about you, you must remember
that, my love, everything, but everything. I don't have to know
what you have been doing or that you've not been home for a
week. I don't have to know why you came home late for dinner,
and so drunk they had to carry you. They're not the things I have
to know. But I have to know what you acquired or lost as a result. I
have to know the essential things. I'm no Hussite and don't believe

in my own truthfulness or yours i.e. the sort of truthfulness usually found among couples: "You told me you'd be back at two and you didn't come in till eight – a week later. Now just you tell me the name of the whore who lured you away from the hearth!" and he tells her it was no whore but the Comrade Director who had a nameday celebration "and you must see, darling, that I could hardly refuse!", which she does until the moment someone tells her the whore is a bandy-legged blonde, at which point there is a tearful scene of the "how could you!" variety followed by reconciliation in bed, the outcome of which is a further increase in the size of the family and another whore, a brunette this time. Believe me that's something I need like a pain in the head.

But I always need to know that you share the essential things with me as far as they possibly can be shared and maybe a bit further. Not because I want it or even because you yourself have this need, but because you feel it is useful in some way, because you are aware that a close contact of this kind is part of you and hence of your work as well, and that it is creative. I have to know it so that I have the courage to live with you at all, so that I am conscious of having the right, don't you see?

I really love you very much – the word love here is a trifle absurd because it is something else as well. I relate to you with everything I have and that is something more than loving – but that is precisely why I am completely free in this relationship and have the power to cancel it – not the relationship but its manifestation – the moment it looks like descending to the banal level of marital atrocities committed against body and soul. And that is precisely why I am equipped with an intuition for what is good and what is bad.

You see I want you to trust me absolutely. I don't mean mindless connubial trust, that's not what we're about and there are moments when I actually laugh about it and say that's something we should be afraid of – i.e. that against all probability we shall wake up one day and discover to our amusement that we are totally and utterly faithful to each other quite simply because everything else will have lost its attraction and paled into insignificance alongside the possibility of having each other. But that's not the point.

I want you to have the assurance that I belong to you completely, i.e. that I won't do anything or think of anything that was not connected with you in some way and that would threaten you. What I would like – for the first time ever in my life – is that you should feel safe with me. As safe as I am with you – safer, in fact, in the sense that it would not just be an impersonal security related to goodness knows what – my intellect or my life-style, say. No, I'd like it to be a security related to you alone, that exists for you alone, the security of inviolable trust and sacred intimacy. As I said, I want it for the first time in my life, I never wanted it for anyone else before, and during all those years I was unable to want it for you. Apart from the material questions that we've talked about already, I regard this former inability of mine to have been one of the causes of our problems. I've been thinking about it a lot just recently and I don't think I'm mistaken. There is an art to loving and I had to learn it the hard way. Whether successfully or not, I don't know, but one thing I do know is that I have learned during this period to my cost what it really is to love someone, and that you're the only person with whom I could have a relationship worthy of that profaned and banal – albeit plain and precise – description. I wanted to tell you something about it today, but somehow I couldn't get the words out. I'm not afraid of banality nor am I terrified of long words, so long as they are appropriate, but my feelings were too intense during our meeting for me to talk much.

It has just struck me that this is all rather unintelligible but maybe you'll understand. It could perhaps be that only during our last encounters did the final vestiges of "Stromky" fall away, which is why the place scarcely got mentioned today. I doubt you're even aware how it was always around somewhere, how it twisted my words and deformed my actions, even though things had long changed from the way they were that time in forty-nine. I expect I had rid myself of it long before, but it still remained in my relationship with you (is this making any sense?) in my lack of humility towards that relationship. I hate the word "humility" but it fits here. Even though I knew how much I was bound up with you, I always left the back door open, and just lately I have not only shut that door, I have actually bricked it up. You have no idea how relieved I was when I realized it – you see I wasn't aware of it while it was still around – I realized it between our last two meetings, which is why I felt so incredibly happy with you, not at your side but with you, something I was never really able to be before because of all that, you see.

And that is also one reason for the lack of stress, why I'm

not rushing anywhere and when I say I love you today there is no impatience in the words, nor are they filled with fear and apprehension. They are not even feverish when I seriously consider the possibility of our being together. And even though they turn me on intensely, they are free of such provisos as "we love each other and for that reason we don't have to live together yet", or the panic-filled "we love each other and so we have to be together." It could be that we're moving towards something I never even dreamt of: a relationship in which nothing is demanded. Maybe we are moving towards something I didn't dare believe in – a situation where two are more than one if they become one. Maybe this possibility is concealed beneath the dead weight of moralities and legalized screwing stipulated by religions of all times and races, maybe we have been given the opportunity and we are expected to take it. It's hard to say when and also how, but maybe it is what you were talking about and what I was unable to grasp, hampered as I was by old errors and sins – and that's one thing the Catholics are right about, that sins cloud the mind.

You're not cross, my love, are you, at my writing so much and going into all these details and particulars, are you, my darling? You're not even a little annoyed, are you? I hope and believe that it is right to say these things even though you'd understand anyway without my saying them. After all, speech is a means of communication and that was why it was invented. And things like these need to be said quickly so as to get them out of the way and not waste time over them. We really do have better things to worry about.

I feel really good. I have no inkling how things will turn out nor the faintest idea how long it will be before this all finally bears fruit and we are able to achieve what we have been preparing during all these years of wondrous coexistence. I don't even have a clue what other obstacles might stand in the way nor what other difficulties we will have to overcome, but I feel good and am certain that everything is exactly the way it should be and nothing untoward will occur. By now there's no way I can lose you nor you me. We're out of reach of the surrounding reality and the people who wield it. Now we've come this far we can be sure of each other. How it will come about is not our concern. It doesn't worry me and I think I can afford to be carefree without fear.

At last I've got the word – sorry for jumping from one thing

to another – it's guilelessness. For the first time in my life I am
guilelessly in love. I'm guilelessly in love with you, my love, and
I'd like to crow over the realization, out loud, at the top of my
voice, except it's half past midnight and I have neighbours who
would be far from compassionate, not being guilelessly in love
and not being in love with you. (Their misfortune is no fault of
mine, but it would not be kind on them for me to rub it in.)

It's not to say that so far I have been sitting here guilefully
hatching plots against you. Not in the least, I should think that's
obvious. But never before have I had the courage to remain
vulnerable and defenceless against you, never before have I had
the courage to lose that last trace of my own sovereignty, to lose
myself in order to gain you. It seemed to me too high a price, too
much of a risk. The fact it has vanished is not due to a trust that was
formerly absent and I've only just acquired. I trust – and distrust –
you precisely as much as I ever did. What I've lost is my fear for
myself, for my self. How should I explain it so you understand
– I am not in any sense invulnerable, on the contrary, I'm more
vulnerable than I ever was. Nor am I a clinical masochist who
would enjoy any pain you might inflict on me in this situation.
Far from it, I would find it very difficult to bear. Nor is it that I
exclude this possibility – even though I don't envisage it, it is one of
the possibilities I have to bear in mind. I expect it's like this: should
anything painful or vexatious occur, I'm capable of accepting it like
anything else connected with our relationship, as another part of it,
which I do not have to avoid even if it's unwelcome. I don't need
to be precautious, not because I'm particularly strong, but because
my relationship with you is now too complete for anything to be
left out as if it were a gristly stew – I'll have this bit and spit that
one out. It is too complete not to accept anything it brings.

Listen, what kind of lunacy is it that you're not here? What sort
of nonsense that I'm unable to be kissing you, that I can't be lying
down at your side, that I can't be caressing you, arousing you and
being aroused by you, that I cannot be bringing you to orgasm
with my mouth and feeling you in my womb and then laughing
with you about your whiskers smelling so strong that the tram
conductor will get an erection when he comes to clip your ticket,
that I can't be placing my whole body at your mercy, from my tits
and cunt to my arse till you've screwed yourself silly and deftly
using my tongue within your arse to make you shoot, your face

twisted in a spasm. Why can't I have the feeling of you inside me almost motionless in the burning tenderness of love that is almost sentimental, why can't I be squeezing your prick between my tits and proudly wiping off the sticky sperm on them afterwards? Why for cryingoutloud don't I have your tongue in my cunt, now that I so desperately want it there, why aren't I feeling the ticklish pain of you chewing my feet, why can't I be thrusting out my arse at you for you to fuck it, bite it, slap it and cover in sperm, why can't I be lying alongside you afterwards and talking to you about anything from philosophy to the immortality of the cock-chafer with the effortless intimacy of belonging side by side, while playing with your prick from time to time just incidentally from sheer excess of high spirits? Why can't I be lying on you with joyful and almost unsexual tenderness and talking to you as we make love about what we had for supper or what the weather was like? Why can't I be laying you down on your belly and fucking your arse with my hands, my tits, my tongue, slabbering it with my cunt that's already wet from the very thought of it, pinching it gently and then slapping it until it blushes like an immature girl when some perverted old fucker suddenly exposes his prick to her in the park? Why can't I be playing with your arsehole, tenderly licking its wrinkles, poking my finger into it, shoving the nipples of both tits inside, and rubbing myself against both your cheeks so slowly that you get a prickstand and your balls swell up? Why can't I then be stretching you out on your back and nibbling your nipples, running my tongue round your navel, and taking your balls in my mouth one at a time until you groan and fart from the thrill? Why can't I now, right now, be taking your prick and thrusting it into my armpit, caressing it with my hair, tugging back its skin with the gap between my feet, rousing it with my teeth and then letting it droop again, sticking it into my arse, pulling it out and sticking it in my cunt, and then licking my own juice from it? Why can't I be sucking you off and carrying the spunk in my mouth to yours, so you swallow it and choke on its pungency that I can always taste in my mouth for a long time afterwards so that whatever I scoff afterwards tastes like the product of your prick, and when I eat bread and butter it tastes just like making love? Why can't I be laying you down on your back and shoving my tits in your gob for you to suck with a babylike expression, eyes closed and blissfully smacking your lips. Why can't I be kneeling on you next with my cunt engorged from arousal and let you lick it and knead it with your fingers until my whole body stiffens in a spasm and when all my muscles relax I piss in your mouth? Why can't I be tickling the soles of your feet with my tits and between your toes just now and then, sort of by the way, but persistently, until you lose your temper and stuff your prick in my gob, balls and all? Why can't I be putting my feet up on your shoulders to let you look in my hole and observe my cunt with impersonal impudence, tug its lips and its fur while your face is so close to me that I can feel your breath and I leak even without the touch of your tongue? Why can't I be giving you a lovebite on your arsehole, and continuing till you're writhing on the bed and biting the coverlet, until your cock stands and then subsides again without shooting, until you push me away with your hands and tug me by the hair, then I stick my tongue deep into your arse until I taste your shit and you pull your arse away for fear you'll shit yourself. Why, in fury at that fear, can't I be sticking my finger in your arse and bringing you to orgasm there so that every one of your holes releases its contents? Why aren't you here to lay me on my belly and use your fingernails to scratch Easter-egg decorations on my arse until it dribbles tiny drops of blood? And the droplets turn into little scabs that I feel on my backside for many days afterwards? Why aren't you here to give me a lovebite in the hollow of my collar-bone, so that while you're at it my cunt becomes engorged until it's as hard as stale bread and rustles when you suck it?

Why aren't you here to lie at my side afterwards and caress me and say "Hey, d'you know girl . . " with the expression you have sometimes when you say it, that expression and tone whose entire meaning I understand. Why aren't you here to stroke my hair and tickle me behind the ears a bit jokily, assuring me that if that Klíma-ologist lived in Prague instead of Brno you'd straight run off to her because this is all rather a bit much for you, and fuck it, things must be a bit calmer with a Klíma-ologist? That would make me blush with pride deep down in my soul, and I would almost wish just the littlest bit that you would actually try it and see what good that "calmer" relationship would do you. And I would chuckle to myself at the thought of you rushing back here and pulling out that prick fresh from the Klíma-ologist and you would fume over the fact that your "calmer" relationship was good for nothing but to send you straight back here to me.

Why can't I be fucking with you using all the dirtiest and obscurest words we know, the ones that are a real gobful, and then letting myself be taken modestly and almost bashfully, so that we suddenly burst out laughing and our bottoms and bellies collide in uncontrollable mirth? Why aren't we lying side by side licking each other, while concentrating not only on our own orgasm but the other's as well, not knowing which arouses us the more? Why can't I be hearing your "hold on" when I have your prick in my gob, why can't I be making fun of this parsimonious saving of sperm and orgasms, and as soon as you shoot it out prove to you that saving is more than pointless? Why can't I be licking you when you're tired and almost impotent, licking your prick and arousing you for a whole hour during a seemingly endless and torturous blow job that ends in a spasm that is more painful than orgasmic, an hour during which your senses will be provoked to nervousness and from time to time you will see everything so clearly as if someone else were lying on the bed and from time to time you will succumb slightly to the thrill of my efforts and wince a bit, partly from arousal and partly from an effort to arouse yourself by trying to demonstrate your arousal. And why can't I be waking up afterwards and sliding onto you while I'm still half asleep and bleary-eyed and fucking you under me using your morning erection that is only partly due to sexual arousal, fucking you while you lie half-asleep and a bit surprised, holding on to my tits with both hands? Why can't I be watching you get out of bed in the morning, and letting you get out thinking I have gone back to sleep, observing you naked in the act of scratching your arse as you calmly get ready to dress, letting you put on a few bits and bobs such as your underpants and socks, before jumping on to you, ripping them off you, and screwing you on the floor so vigorously that you don't feel like getting dressed any more, then lying on the floor caressing and arousing my tits and my cunt on my own, masturbating in front of you until you come all over my thighs or my backside. And then when you're turned on and horny, pretending I don't feel like fucking any more, just jiggling your prick and poking your balls, then licking you a bit, nonchalantly watching your prick rise up, leaving you awhile to try every means possible from attempts at arousal to almost whimpering supplications, while I maintain the same expression, tugging at your whiskers and your prick and blowing on your balls as tantalizingly as I know how, until at last

you are so pissed off that you slap my arse and shove your prick
in anywhere it will go, my gob, between my tits, my arsehole, my
cunt, before finally spraying me with your spunk from head to
foot and I have no other option but to rush off and have a bath,
standing under the shower and scrubbing myself, scalp and all
until you follow me into the bathroom and lick my cunt until you
shoot over me once more?

Why aren't we making a decent, full-scale breakfast afterwards,
the two of us naked, me waving my tits above the frying eggs,
while we discuss what to add to it to make it more interesting,
and then eating it, sprawled out comfortably side by side, relishing
our excellent cooking, and then wiping out the pan with bread, one
either side, and then lying down together once more, so replete we
can hardly breathe, holding hands and talking, and then making
love again, this time in such an absolutely normal fashion it is
almost unlike us, me underneath with my legs raised and you
above me in regular rhythm of the angel position that allows
us to kiss at the same time and our only perversion is touching
tongue-tips, lovemaking that is long-lasting but not tiring and
which allows the maximum contact, lovemaking whose rhythm
is broken from time to time for rest so as to delay the climax for
a moment – but it isn't a question of parsimony and it happens by
tacit mutual agreement, lovemaking during which we are so long
in contact that we end up being joined together and the space
between us is not even wide enough to admit a caressing hand,
lovemaking that only involves the smallest of spasms – just prior
to the final climax.

And why aren't we lying side by side afterwards with our eyes
fixed on the ceiling, with our minds on almost nothing, or on
matters that are totally unrelated to us here, not because we
don't want to think about ourselves, but because a half-dreaming
languor confuses us and negates the censorship of our wakeful
state. Why aren't we lying here like that, that's something I'd
really like to know, and if someone can explain it to me they'll
be rendering me an enormous service, because at this moment I
can find no explanation, because I'm damp and worked up and
I want you, now, straight away, immediately and most likely I'm
not particularly receptive to any explanation. Every time I move
my cunt can be smelled within a mile radius of here and I'm
supposed to listen to some explanation!! I could frig myself, but

I don't want to masturbate, I want you, I want your fingers not my
own, I want your tongue and your prick, my fingers won't help me
very much that way. I'd turn myself on for nothing, and it would
make things even worse, and they're unbearable as they are.

Tomorrow morning it'll all make sense to me again, don't worry.
But I'll still regret tonight, that's something I won't be able to
get over. I've never learnt to accept arousal as something to be
overcome by abstinence and to be exorcized like some demon,
and arousal such as I feel tonight just cries out to be satisfied
and not for some ascetic abstinence. I was not endowed with this
capacity for horniness – such that every inch of my skin yearns
uncontrollably for you – just in order to drive it out with a cold
shower and restraint – if you don't mind. And if they are the devil's
snares then they are pretty good snares and I'm beginning to find
that old devil rather appealing.

Only the devil has nothing to do with it, nor has perversity,
though one must admit it might seem so to an outside observer,
but they would be wrong. The fact is there's nothing at all wrong
with it and it is quite natural, the only unnatural thing is that
you're not here and it's not all happening to its full extent, as per
description, if not more so. That is seriously quite unnatural and
I can't stand unnatural things. Unnaturalness of that kind never
did me any good, and I am afraid it doesn't agree with you either.
And why ever should it? All it can do is addle your brain, the way
it'll shortly addle mine, and I'm curious to know the effect on me
that will have. And on you too. Well at least such unnatural things
don't strike one so much in the morning, so I have a faint hope
that when I get up early tomorrow and wash my old cunt in blue
whitener and rinse it well, I might actually be able to go out and
safely show myself in public, which is something I could hardly
do at the moment, though it would be quite funny to watch the
swelling crotches and those blonde hair-dos offendedly standing
on end. It would be worth doing in its way, nobody could touch
me for it, unless omnipotence is suddenly against the law, and if
it is, it has not come to my notice. It's just that I'd rather not
have to explain to a platoon of rutting recruits herded into the
mother of cities to view the graves of the Bohemian kings that my
omnipotence has nothing to do with them even though they have
the stink of it beneath their noses in the tram. I don't like being
rude about the very thing that people value most and I would not

find it easy to make rude comments about a set of swelling pricks
to an entire platoon, because I was taught to behave tactfully in
company, which was a mistake. But there would be nothing for it,
as the only prick I don't feel like being rude about and rejecting
is yours, but you've taken it off with you to Podolí. You've taken
the whole damned lot, leaving me here like an illustration out of
"Valérie" – "She felt abandoned" is precisely what I could write
beneath my cunt. And if things continue this way I will write
it beneath your prick too – that's if I feel like writing anything
beneath him when I see him again.

It's two in the afternoon. I did go to bed last night after all. During
the morning I virtuously borrowed a paint roller and walked back
with it across the bridge we crossed together yesterday. It was
bizarre and nostalgic and magic and silly and banal and splendid,
and I've just read what I wrote yesterday. I was expecting it to be
too silly to post it to you or get it to you some other way, but I
discovered that were I to write it again I would have to write it
exactly the same way, word for word, so it's clear and it's all right,
i.e. it's not all right in the least and the situation is desolate. It is
simply the way it should be.

It's an ordinary day again and I've a load of work on my plate
(work, that was always my weakness, God knows how Marx could
have regarded work as something constructive, maybe it was partly
because of his wife's factory, otherwise there's no explaining it)
so I shall assume the role of responsible artistic professional (I'll
demonstrate it for you one day, it's a hoot) and complete the novel
I'm writing. I hope I manage not to write anything that will offend
the moral censor, though in my present state that's something I
cannot altogether guarantee.

Apart from that I intend to paint the walls of my flat with some
dismal roller – incidentally it's amazing the sort of weird activities
people can get up to – while standing on a step-ladder and looking
so constructive that you'd be instantly rendered impotent to see me.
You'd be rendered impotent and start reciting out loud: "Should I
get married?" – because you'd have no other option.

If it were not my intention to make a living from writing, I'd
probably start to write those memoirs, but I'm afraid they could
fall into the wrong hands, and someone might get the idea I am not
the right sort of person to be purveying culture in a socialist society,
on the grounds that I might cause the premature completion of

the cultural revolution. But it would definitely stimulate me like
nothing else would and anyway I believe our lives are a specimen
of a perfect work of art and as such should be preserved for future
generations at least in the form of a juicy description. Apart from
that, I realized today yet again that even though they seemingly
differ in many aspects, they are in reality identical, i.e. each of
them is only half of the other and only together do they make
sense, in a way that I should think is unique at this time and in
this country. There was a time when our uniqueness filled me
with inordinate pride and there was a time also when I had an
almost mortal complex about it. These days I take it for granted
and merely acknowledge it, but I wouldn't swap it for anything
in the world.

And I also realized the enormous amount of vitality we both
have, and I'm not thinking at this moment of the fact we did
not pack it in during those most difficult days, what I mean is
that we not only got over them but we actually managed to put
them to good use, that we were actually capable of enjoying them
and extracting what was important from them. That's what I call
real vitality. When people survive their sojourn in this world even
in the circumstances in which we did, it is only the instinct of
self-preservation – an instinct, mind you, that can be really mighty
and powerful sometimes. But when you don't turn into a living
corpse as a result of all that, it is something to thank the Good
Lord for, with sincere and humble gratitude – life per se is no gift,
life per se is total hell – but this is more than a gift, this has to be
something for which I have only one word – grace.

And if there is anything that fills me with optimism and
genuine hope – not hope of something but hope per se, hope
in its profoundest sense, the kind one needs for salvation, the
kind that every human being must have because only in its name
can one be saved, then it is the certainty of grace, the empirically
acquired certainty not that grace is given to us, but that it exists at
all. Certainty of its existence in this cosmos, on this earth, for these
bizarre beings, endowed with all divine attributes and endowed
also with the inability to use them, for these beings who resemble
God and were created in his image, in order to disgrace and glorify
him, although none of them, none of us, no human being, is ever
being capable of imagining in the slightest the one with whom we
are alike as two peas. And that's the point of that hope I'm talking

about, i.e. it is the means whereby our fantastic blindness becomes something other than an undeserved and unjust punishment for the fact of existence. It becomes a sweet and delightful umbilical cord binding us to him and along which we can climb to him. Man does not have to have faith and he cannot be virtuous – where would he have come by it. Don't tell me God is a virtuous being, he's everything possible but not virtuous, perfection can't be virtuous, for heaven's sake! People require neither faith nor virtue for their salvation. I firmly believe that one day we shall be amazed to discover just how many were damned for their virtuous deeds. But there must be hope, real hope bereft of any kind of greed, hope that will not protect them from despair, that will not protect them from the monstrous loss of all human values, hope that will not protect them from anything, not even damnation, but through which they will one day ascend, descend or whatever, hope that will be weighed and not found wanting, because its weight is greater than we in our blindness can even imagine, I should think.

Not everyone is fortunate enough to receive it with such assurance as we have. That's why I talk about grace. Truly not everyone is this fortunate.

The next time you ask me to write you five or six lines I'll break your jaw without any sexual emotion, my darling. I hope that is clear to you after this letter. Or I really will send you six lines and love to see your face when you get them; it's a good idea sometimes to give people exactly what they ask for.

It's three o'clock again, of course. Last night I finished at four, I'm being a bit rash with time. But I don't regard this letter as a waste of time. In fact I consider it the best use I can make of time at this given moment. Besides, it will give you something to read. A pity I won't be there at that moment, it would increase the enjoyment for the two of us. Sometimes I would watch your face, and sometimes I'd steal a glance at your penis, in the firm belief that your reading of this paper will be visibly reflected in both places.

And we'll have to go off walking somewhere one of these days. The weather is getting fine and I love our walks more than almost anything else. We'll go and wander somewhere on the outskirts of town, reviving old atmospheres and creating new ones, the way we always used to on our walks. We'll take a break now and then and visit one of those dicey-looking suburban pubs. And the two of us,

you with your beer and me with a bottle of sacchariny lemonade –
which I find disgusting but it is an integral part of those walks –
will dawdle along dusty fieldpaths and return blissfully weary and
happy and I'll write in my diary the date of our next meeting, so
I can spend the next fortnight looking forward to it and reassure
myself that I will survive those fourteen days without prejudice to
my mental and physical health, so I can discover to my amazement
a fortnight later that I really have stood the test.

And we'll make plans for the future, not the customary way but
the way we do it: naively specific, but maybe at last with an eye
to their fulfilment – albeit in the very long term.

I called Oldřich this morning. He's still in the hospital so I have
no news to cheer you up. I don't even know how long he'll be there
because it was well past mid-day when I called and I didn't speak
to the editorial office but to the porter. I'll probably call the office
again on Monday and find out what hospital he's in, and if he's in
not too bad a state I'll try to do it the way we discussed yesterday,
even before he leaves hospital. It also depends, of course, how long
he'll remain there, if it'll only be a matter of days. But if he's going
to be there for several weeks then it would be a good idea to try to
do something regardless.

I'm going in to the publishers on Monday morning – around ten
– and as soon as I'm done there I'll go and take a look at that place
in Malá Strana to see what we can count on. I'm convinced that a
room would not only be good for the two of us, but chiefly and
above all it would be good for your mental state, which is such at
the present time that your need for it really is beyond doubt.

I'm quite curious to know the outcome of my meeting at the
publishers, even though it looks fairly clear and I'll be quite glad
to go there. There really is a good atmosphere there and the kind
of people I work well with – at that level, at least. That does make
things a bit easier for me. The fact is if I was obliged to work with
a complex-ridden band of young commies it would probably end
in a mammoth scandal which neither they nor I would survive.

So all the best then. It's only twelve days this time, so it'll be
two days easier. You'll have time for a bit of reading and I even
nurture the hope that you'll feel the urge to drop me a line, so
that will make things a bit easier and maybe everything will work
out all right. For fuck's sake, we've known each other for thirteen
years and here we are carrying on like the lovers in the Chartreuse

de Parme. I admit it's a gas, but that's the way it is and I'm afraid
that when the two of us will be a pair of old fogies we'll carry on
even worse than now; we'd be well qualified by then. I shall tear my
grey hair the day I don't see you and you'll tug at your snow-white
beard in nervous agitation if I have to go off somewhere in the
afternoon. Don't you think I'm exaggerating, you'll see. Really
fantastic prospects for the two of us as diligent, decently cynical
ageing intellectuals. We'll talk about nuclear wars and fall about
laughing as we recall what a gas it was when Národní Avenue was
awash with guts, and if we have to be apart for a couple of hours
the tears will gush from our blind old eyes.

Now go and have that beneficial wank, if you haven't had one
already, partly so you'll be fit to be seen in public at all and partly
so you don't have to take a taxi to Holešovice clutching your prick
in your fist, and if the fancy takes you, drop me a line during the
next twelve days – five or six lines, in fact, my darling . . .

– I have read over again what I wrote and it gave me a fright, but
I don't intend to add any further explanation except maybe to say
that as it stands – and lies – it contains everything, of course, i.e.
even the tenderest and most banal love-making, even the tenderest
holding of hands, caressing of hair, and all the other things that I
suppose usually go on when people are in love. Remember that and
bear it in mind, so that you don't get the idea from my letter that
it expresses a need to fulfil some largely neuro-pathologico-sexual
emotions or other – even though there is that, of course, but in
a curiously non-pathological fashion – from being in love, more
likely. But I expect you'll understand all that without the need for
comment and if you don't then it was a fucking waste of time and
comments would be pointless and I'll have to explain it to you in
a practical fashion, my darling.

Surely it's about time we were together. Surely your miserable
existence by the marital hearth has no other purpose but to titillate
your sense of your own responsibility – were it not for my father, I
expect I'd be a lot more progressive too. So I leave it up to you,
but don't drag it out too long. Admittedly we are vigorous enough
still, thanks to our philosophical thinking, and we have plenty of
time and lots of security because we love each other so much and
there's no need to rush into anything, but we are people, for fuck's
sake, not "only" people as they say, but on the contrary, people

with all the trimmings, including something as enormous as a love like ours, so perhaps we ought to take a bit more care of it and not take risks with it as if it were the worthless and meaningless state of being in love suffered by those who are "only" people.

Bye
Honza

ROSES

Evelyn Lau

THE PSYCHIATRIST CAME into my life one month after my eighteenth birthday. He came into my life wearing a silk tie, his dark eyes half-obscured by lines and wrinkles. He brought with him a pronounced upper-class accent, a futile sense of humor, books to educate me. *Lolita. The Story of O.* His lips were thin, but when I took them between my own they plumped out and filled my mouth with sweet foreign tastes.

He worshipped me at first because he could not touch me. And then he worshipped me because he could only touch me if he paid to do so. I understood that without the autumn leaves, the browns of the hundreds and the fiery scarlets of the fifties, the marble pedestal beneath me would begin to erode.

The first two weeks were tender. He said he adored my childlike body, my unpainted face, my long straight hair. He promised to take care of me, love me unconditionally. He would be my father, friend, lover – and if one was ever absent, the other two were large enough on their own to fill up the space that was left behind.

He brought into my doorway the slippery clean smell of rain, and he possessed the necessary implements – samples of pills tiny as seeds, a gold shovel. My body yielded to the scrapings of his hands.

He gave me drugs because, he said, he loved me. He brought the tablets from his office, rattling in plastic bottles stuffed to the

brim with cotton. I placed them under my tongue and sucked
up their saccharine sweetness, learning that only the strong ones
tasted like candy, the rest were chalky or bitter. He loved me
beyond morality.

The plants that he brought each time he came to visit – baby's
breath, dieffenbachia, jade – began to die as soon as they crossed
the threshold of my home. After twenty-four hours the leaves would
crinkle into tight dark snarls stooping towards the soil. They could
not be pried open, though I watered his plants, exposed them to
sunlight, trimmed them. It was as if by contact with him or with
my environment, they had been poisoned. Watching them die, I
was reminded of how he told me that when he first came to Canada
he worked for two years in one of our worst mental institutions.
I walked by the building once at night, creeping as far as I dared
up the grassy slopes and between the evergreens. It was a sturdy
beige structure, it didn't look so bad from the outside. In my
mind, though, I saw it as something else. In my mind it was a
series of black-and-white film stills; a face staring out from behind
a barred window. The face belonged to a woman with tangled hair,
wearing a nightgown. I covered my ears from her screams. When he
told me about this place I imagined him in the film, the woman
clawing at him where the corridors were gray, and there was the
clanking sound of tin and metal. I used to lie awake as a child on
the nights my father visited my bed and imagine scenes in which
he was terrorized, in pain, made helpless. This was the same. I
could smell the bloodstains the janitors had not yet scrubbed from
the floors. I could smell the human discharges and see the hands
that groped at him as he walked past each cell, each room. The
hands flapped disembodied in the air, white and supplicating and
at the same time evil.

He told me that when he was married to his first wife, she had
gone shopping one day and he had had to take their baby with him
on his hospital rounds, "I didn't know where to put him when I
arrived," he said. "So I put him in the wastepaper basket." When
he returned the child had upended the basket and crawled out,
crying, glaring at his father. "I had no other choice," he said, and
he reached into his trenchcoat and gave me a bottle of pills. "I
love you," he said, "that's why I'm doing this."

I believed that only someone with a limitless love would put
his baby in a trash can, its face squinched and its mouth pursing

open in a squawk of dismay. Only someone like that could leave it swaddled in crumpled scraps of paper so he could go and take care of his patients. I could not imagine the breadth of the love that lay behind his eyes, those eyes that became as clear as glass at the moment of orgasm.

He bought a mask yesterday from a Japanese import store. It had tangled human hair that he washed with an anti-dandruff shampoo, carefully brushing it afterwards so the strands would not snap off. It had no pupils; the corneas were circles of bone. He took it home with him and stared at it for half an hour during a thunderstorm, paralysed with fear. It stared back at him. It was supposed to scare off his rage, he said.

After two weeks his tenderness went the way of his plants – crisp, shriveled, closed. He stopped touching me in bed but grew as gluttonous as dry soil. I started to keep my eyes open when we kissed and to squeeze them shut all the other times, the many times he pulled my hand or my head down between his legs.

He continued to bring me magazines and books, but they were eclipsed by the part of him he expected me to touch. Some days, I found I could not. I thought it was enough that I listened to his stories. I fantasized about being his psychoanalyst and not letting him see my face, having that kind of control over him. I would lay him down on my couch and shine light into his eyes while I remained in shadow where he could not touch me.

His latest gift, a snake plant, looks like a cluster of green knives or spears. The soil is so parched that I keep watering it, but the water runs smartly through the pot without, it seems, having left anything of itself behind. The water runs all over the table and into my hands.

Tonight I did not think I could touch him. I asked him to hit me instead, thinking his slim white body would recoil from the thought. Instead he rubbed himself against my thigh, excited. I told him pain did not arouse me, but it was too late. I pulled the blankets around my naked body and tried to close up inside the way a flower wraps itself in the safety of its petals when night falls.

At first he stretched me across his knees and began to spank me. I wiggled obediently and raised my bottom high into the air, the way my father used to like to see me do. Then he moved up to rain blows upon my back. One of them was so painful that I saw colors even with my eyes open; it showered through my body like fireworks. It was like watching a sunset and feeling a pain in your chest at its wrenching beauty, the kind of pain that makes you gasp.

How loud the slaps grew in the small space of my apartment – like the sound of thunder. I wondered if my face looked, in that moment, like his Japanese mask.

The pain cleansed my mind until it breathed like the streets of a city after a good and bright rain. It washed away the dirt inside me. I could see the gutters open up to swallow the candy wrappers, newspaper pages, cigarette butts borne along on its massive tide. I saw as I had not seen before every bump and indentation on the wall beside my bed.

And then he wanted more and I fought him, dimly surprised that he wasn't stronger. I saw as though through the eye of a camera this tangle of white thighs and arms and the crook of a shoulder, the slope of a back. I scraped his skin with my fingernails. I felt no conscious fear because I was the girl behind the camera, zooming in for a close-up, a tight shot, an interesting angle. Limbs like marble on the tousled bed. His face contorted with strain. He was breathing heavily, but I, I was not breathing at all. I knew that if I touched his hair my hand would come away wet, not with the pleasant sweat of sexual exertion, but with something different. Something that would smell like a hospital, a hospital with disinfectant to mask the smells underneath.

And when he pushed my face against his thigh, it was oddly comforting, though it was the same thigh that belonged to the body that was reaching out to hit me. I breathed in the soft, soapy smell of his skin as his hand stung my back – the same hand that comforted crying patients, that wrote notes on their therapeutic progress, that had shaken with shyness when it first touched me. The sound of the slaps was amplified in the candlelit room. Nothing had ever sounded so loud, so singular in its purpose. I had never felt so far away from myself, not even with his pills.

I am far away and his thigh is sandy as a beach against my cheek. The sounds melt like gold, like slow Sunday afternoons. I think of cats and the baby grand piano in the foyer of my father's house. I think of the rain that gushes down the drainpipes outside my father's bathroom late at night when things begin to happen. I think of the queerly elegant black notes on sheets of piano music. The light is flooding generously through the windows and I am a little girl with a pink ribbon in my hair and a ruffled dress.

I seat myself on the piano bench and begin to play, my fingertips softening to the long ivory, the shorter ebony keys. I look down at my feet and see them bound in pink ballerina slippers, pressing intermittently on the pedals. Always Daddy's girl, I perform according to his instruction.

When it was over he stroked the fear that bathed my hands in cold sweat. He said that when we fought my face had filled with hatred and a dead coldness. He said that he had cured himself of his obsession with me during the beating, he had stripped me of my mystery. Slapped me human. He said my fear had turned him on. He was thirsty for the sweat that dampened my palms and willing to do anything to elicit more of that moisture so he could lick it and quench his tongue's thirst.

I understood that when I did not bleed at the first blow, his love turned into hatred. I saw that if I was indeed precious and fragile I would have broken, I would have burst open like a thin shell and discharged the rich sweet stain of roses.

Before he left he pressed his lips to mine. His eyes were open when he said that if I told anyone, he would have no other choice but to kill me.

Now that he is gone, I look between my breasts and see another flower growing: a rash of raspberry dots, like seeds. I wonder if this is how fear discharges itself when we leave our bodies in moments of pain.

The psychiatrist, when he first came, promised me a rose garden and in the mirror tomorrow morning I will see the results for the first time on my own body. I will tend his bouquets before he comes again, his eyes misty with fear and lust. Then I will listen to the liquid notes that are pleasing in the sunlit foyer and smile because somewhere, off in the distance, my father is clapping.

ORACLE OF THE THOUSAND HANDS

Barry Malzberg

D'ARCY'S GENITALIA: They were of unusual size; even in a state of purest flaccidity they measured several centimeters in the usual three directions. Under engorgement, the subject himself as well as several partners measured them as well over a foot in length. It is further attested that the unusual "slickness" and "warmth" of the organ made penetration unusually easy, even with "slightly built" companions.

D'ARCY'S SEXUAL PREDILECTIONS: They were, as we all know, completely heterosexual; any rumors to the contrary have been created by jealous and envious homosexuals whom D'Arcy again and again spurned to seek female companionship. He preferred normal intercourse in the seventh and eighth positions of Lilly, with certain pre-coital variations mostly involved with the buttocks and thighs of partners. Breast (buccal) tendencies were negligible, D'Arcy having been known to state often that he felt himself too well-endowed for "that preliminary nonsense."

D'ARCY'S SEXUAL PERFORMANCE: It was, as all sources have testified, facile and almost incredibly accomplished, leading partners again and again to the "sublime" peak and letting them down always at their own pace and without embarrassment. Ejaculation was plentiful, fluid was copious, sufficient to "open-up" partners so inclined. Pre- and post-coital maneuvers were swift, gracious and wholly respectful of companion and circumstances. It can be said, then, that the subject's sexual performance was excellent.

D'ARCY'S SOCIAL IMPORTANCE AS SEEN IN HISTORI-CAL PERSPECTIVE: It cannot be minimized. Dealing with the "quintessence of heterosexuality" (his phrase) raised to the "nth degree of pleasure" (words of Mademoiselle M, a lady of his acquaintance), it came along just at the right time to reverse the slow trend of the Age toward narcissism, masturbation and latent homosexuality. D'Arcy's contribution, infusing as it did, all of his sexual "mainstream" with "new blood," was nothing less than the reversal of history, the setting aright of the microcosm he knew.

WHY THIS STUDY IS WRITTEN: I must admit that there are some questions about that to be squarely faced.

This study will deal with the "lover" D'Arcy from the inception of that self-imposed role in December of 196— to its tragic – and unpremeditated conclusion – in October of 196—. It will in no fashion attempt definitive biography nor does it presume to be more than a documentary of the public years of D'Arcy's existence. The early years, the growing years, the dwindling years, even the brief but poignant dying day . . . little of this will be touched upon within the confines of these pages. The historian must delimit to better define the quintessence of his insight. So few of our contemporary "biographers" admit this simple fact. As we diffuse, so must we move ever further from that basic kernel of insight which may, for all we know, be the metaphor for the folly of life itself. Aha!

So delimited, this work will address itself to such primary questions as these: did the subject feel love? Did D'Arcy, in the last smoke and plumes of love's consummation, know emotional release beyond his gigantic physical bursts? Was he ever, during the public years, frustrated in his pursuit of sexual conjoinment? What did some of his partners think of him? What conclusions can be drawn? Exactly what was the breadth and length of a typical D'Arcy orgasm?

We will answer those questions all in due time. On hand we have documents and testimonies of many of the subject's partners, none of them ever before revealed, confidentially given to the one who transcribes this memoir. In tandem they will piece together, we promise, into a shattering picture of our protagonist, revealing wonders and implications hitherto never before revealed.

THE QUESTION OF QUALIFICATION: It is always asked of the historian: who are you? What, is your particular credential? Why do you presume to give the sense of this material to a gullible and easily misled audience? This is a painful century; the question of credibility perhaps in nexus.

Let me state modestly, therefore, that I knew D'Arcy well; far better than any other during the public years and during many of those years I stood by his side. Friend, confidant, partner, assistant, I lived in the closest conjoinment with the subject. The public prints do not indicate this, of course.

The reason for that is that I always demanded anonymity. "Not for me notoriety or exploitation, D'Arcy," I said to my friend once while we were drinking wine together during one of his periods of "convalescence." "I would be less a friend and more an agent of the opposition were I to attempt to benefit in any way from the fortunate fact of our interrelationship. I prize your friendship above all others, I will not have myself known. But, in my quiet way, I will stand by you always."

And my dear, dear friend said to me, sipping his wine slowly, stirring the sediment with his finger in the characteristic gesture, "Truly, you are a friend. But I cannot ask this of you. If there is profit to be made from our friendship without discredit or interference to me, then take it, I say. Give an interview. Let your face be known. Tell them what I say about women, when I am in a kindly mood, of course. Advise them of my culinary idiosyncrasies. This will keep my name as always before them and you will derive a small income from your ramblings. I give you permission to do all of this as long as you understand from whom the permission comes and from what high motives; that is all I ask." And lifted his glass in the sun so that the purple glittered as stone, mixing toward the purest refraction of his driven, absent face.

And once again I said, raising my own glass, my blunt features dwindling to infinitesimal condition as the sun darted behind a cloud, "Never, my friend; this will never be. As long as I have health and strength to continue on our mutual travels I will never lend you the betrayal of publicity."

Even so, it is with a heavy heart that I begin this journal. Well-qualified as I am, there are certainly others who would be equally so: having never, for instance, truly "known" the hot embrace of D'Arcy in bed nor felt the pressure of his massive, earnest thighs against mine, I am obviously less qualified than many to talk of some of the more explicit aspects of D'Arcy's performance. But who else – I say again, who else? – could possibly take up the wearisome pen, shuffle the papers and commence?

Most of those juxtaposed to D'Arcy in the way I mention can neither read nor write, some cannot spell, the majority cannot perform the simplest mathematical examples. Too, a large percentage of these people are missing, which is to say that they are beyond the efforts of local authorities and institutions to find them.

It is peculiar but it is so: a high percentage of D'Arcy's companions are so far on the margin of our society as to be beyond its devices. *Nothing*, an acquaintance of mine once said, *nothing is as unlocatable as a common tart; even in the bedroom it is often impossible to find one*. D'Arcy's career, then, like a rocket in full, booming flight, discharged a trail of gas and combustible matter which negated it origins to the exact degree that the major ascent opened up new territory. I have often found that this is a general rule; being, of course, a strong adherent of the great man theory of history.

Only I, then, an Ishmael of the post-coital ecstasy, remain to tell the tale. My whereabouts fixed firmly by due process of law and institutionalization, my literacy shaped by 18 years of tutors smuggled from the public schools, my credentials beyond dispute, my humility attested to by my years of close friendship with the subject. I would not think that a further apologia is necessary. Awash, then, in the sea of possibilities, tossed by the whale of retrospection. I cling to the flotsam and jetsam of total recall, trying to spare immersion to the thousands who wait cheerlessly on the sands.

Of course, I remain attuned to the possibility that I may be prohibited from the removal of these notes from my present confines. There is a rich precedent for this: so many of my companions and enemies within these gates are similarly "writers"; were all the tracts, correspondence, romanticized history and pseudo-legal writs composed daily in this place to be put in one stack, it would probably reach to half the height of the senior attendant who demands that all our written material be placed in his hands for censorship and approval. Since this senior attendant, a bulky man with large ears, can neither read nor write, it is suspected by many of my companions here that their writings are being instantly tossed to perdition, most likely after "taps," when scufflings and rustlings and billowings in the hall might suggest the lively flush of toilets sending handwriting on its way. Nevertheless, I discount the possibility. The press visits me now and then and also some acquaintances; surely I could place my jottings in their hands were I to feel an imminence of capture. The important thing, as has been truly said, is to do one's work; a good conscience is its own best reward.

THE CIRCUMSTANCES UNDER WHICH THE STUDY IS BEING WRITTEN: Art and craft, being inextricably linked to environment, it would be fair, perhaps, to describe what it's like here. It is not the most felicitous of ambiances.

For one thing it is wretchedly cold in these rooms and for another, it is almost unspeakably foul much of the time. My collaborants in this large institution are, to an incalculable extent, unbearably dull – their efforts at the written word to the contrary – and entrapped by their small, circular obsessions. They are incapable, in short, of the mildest form of self-amusement, let alone the divertissement of one as complex and sophisticated as I. (It might be said, then, that I have taken to these notes out of boredom but this is not half the fact of the case; the act of writing can be as offensive as that of self-abuse and far less interesting.) The two young men, for instance, who share these rooms with me, seem to have reached an accord of many years' standing – they preceded me here by a long time – not to address one another unless under the governor of extrinsic need, and then in some kind of bizarre code which appears to be the least inventive amalgamation of French, English and the arcane mumblings of the retarded. I find this a great burden upon an active sensibility, but I am completely unable to alter this.

Not that I have not tried. There was a time when I hammered upon the dense barrier of their sullen alliance repeatedly: did it with small jokes, quips, reminiscences and even – for their sake – the admission that I was a companion of D'Arcy's throughout his notable career. I had thought that this final revelation would, when all else had failed, break us through to a small network of feeling or (at least) remonstrance but, shockingly, neither of them had ever *heard* of D'Arcy, much less possessing the slightest knowledge of his travels. It was when they made offensive comments to me about this acquaintanceship and my dear friend himself that I gave up on further attempts to establish a normal relationship in these rooms.

I exemplify: the other evening I was on the way to the "dayroom" here, prepared for yet another desultory game of chess with the bearded fossil who sits silently in front of the board all day, so immobile that it is necessary for his partners to contribute both sets of moves and announce imminent captures, when the elder of my roommates, a fierce man with wild eyes and blond hair so sheer that it might have blazed, said to the other, *Monsieur ici est entrappe.*

Non, non, chattered the other who was under the best of circumstances, rather elfin, *il est disappointe.*

Entrappe and disappointe together. Un jolie homme despite tout, however, est that non vraiment?

"Listen," I said, "there's no need to discuss a man to his face, it isn't polite and it shows a lack of intelligence in the bargain. I'll be wandering down the hall just a bit and you can say all you choose but for the moment call it off, yes?"

Est uproarious, said the first, taking a comb from somewhere around the perimeter of his waist and running it through his hair, squeezing the dandruff pods as they sifted downward. This never failed to excite the elf who stood, then, to the limit of his short frame and, running his own hands through a rather ferocious beard, gestured at me.

Felon, he said.

At that moment, my aged, bottled temper, stirred to the sediment, burbled forth. "Look, gentlemen," I said, "I do not need such talk from you. The same institutions which committed me here have placed you as well and for a much longer period, I might observe. I tell you frankly that unless this behavior stops, I will be compelled to seek new quarters and whoever succeeds me will be far less tolerant of your display of manners. Does that seem clear?"

They laughed at that.

"Now look," I said, "if I must start at the beginning, I will. I am a close friend, perhaps the closest, of the late, honored Justin D'Arcy and in that regard – "

I could not finish. I heard, interchangeably from them, an explosion of guttural monosyllables which sounded vaguely like curses. *Ha, ha!*, they added, *ha, ha!*

"Ha yourself," I said then, and for the first time told them my secret. I had to, to quiet them.

They stopped laughing. The elf seized an ashtray instead and made with it a complex, obscene gesture involving three parts of his anatomy. The gyrations were quite intricate. Then he ceased and both stared, apparently assessing my countermove.

"Makes no difference," I said, grandly, and with enormous dignity folding me like a shroud – that dignity I can conjure up under almost any circumstances – I quit the room and their presence.

THE PHILOSOPHICAL AND PSYCHOLOGICAL BIAS OF THE STUDY: There is no point in concealing this final notation: this study will be, inevitably, composed of a set of digressions from D'Arcy and deal on the personal level. My condition, of course, is so inseparable from his that our circumstances – until his unfortunate disappearance, that is to say – conjoined completely; our obsessions were so linked that it would be presumptuous to even assume that I could part from him. No, I am no cool, detached biographer although, to be sure, I am a faintly bewhiskered one. But D'Arcy's *ficelle*; I see that now, despite my own considerable, prolonged and irreversible detumescence.

But by all means, let me proceed, wander into the sunset of recollection, the old, hollow features tilted wistfully to the horizon, the faithful old frame complying, possibly for the last time, to the Master's demands.

May I leap ahead rapidly in time, modestly discarding the expository necessities, leaving the bridge-work to the biographer who, if possessed of intelligence as you are not, would be able to work out the transitions with a minimum of wordage and a maximum of insight; the transitions being the most painful because least necessary part of all biography. I am poised over the girl in the heat and cove of my room under the doom of a November rainfall – the girl is somewhat older than I am and tragically overdeveloped, her large breasts, fascinating in armor, in a kind of flat, aimless repose with clothing removed, stretched out aimless to her sides and under her arms, the nipples almost invisible under the distension, to say nothing of my clasping mouth. She is muttering faintly, probably about the weather, while with a kind of desperation I try to find her opening, at the same time making polite comments about the disorder of the room, my embarrassment of her seeing it in such shambles, until finally with a moist clamor I feel myself sliding into her, sliding into her, and her arms go reluctantly around me, severing the connection of mouth and breast – which had never been that interesting anyway; I had been doing it only out of a sense of propriety – and with a series of horselike bucking movements not to say whinnies, she begins to carry me, carry me over the sliding eaves of her need.

I feel myself growing inside her and at the same time moving away; all this time birdsongs moving within my head, proud eaglets struggling to churn away from the surfaces of the sea, and the rain comes down unevenly, unevenly, so that I feel myself surrounded by a kind of disorder on all levels as I lie submissive at last in her embrace, feeling the slow steaming and then, as one particularly violent heave of her round body sets my magazines on the shelf above my bed to a kind of scuttling underneath their rubber band, I feel myself turned to them, turned to that attunement, and in a kind of explosion of feeling, all legs, all memory, I am devoured into her and expire slowly, reaching at this time for her breasts to support and inspect them. The feeling at the moment of orgasm has been that of girl-as-giant-fist clasped around my genitalia but underneath that has been something else; a profound undercurrent of woe, perhaps, an unscholarly feeling of mystery destroying the personality. When I came from without her limbs again with that peculiar slurping which seems, I have since discovered, to be the comma of intercourse, I lay atop her having no idea of what to say until finally she dislodged me and sat up, her breasts assuming their normal (or abnormal) proportions again, falling hugely to the area of her navel where she inspected the nipples carefully, apparently for lustre or change of color.

"You really bite, don't you?" she says – all postcoital conversations have now, for me, assumed the aspect of the present tense; this is one subgenre which, because of its hideous sameness, is always of the moment. "You could have hurt them if they weren't so tough."

"Well, it was nice of you to come to the room," I say, because there is nothing else at the moment I can think of and at that moment, the magazines which have been precarious enough, shift on their perch and topple, in a slow, drooling wobble, one by one to the bed, between us. I shrug and reach toward them, hopeful that it will be seen as a kind of joke.

"Are these those girl magazines?" she says, chewing on a fingernail and reaching the free hand out to caress them. "Oh yes, they are. That's what I thought they were. You see them all over. You keep them too?"

"Just for the articles."

"Oh, a lot of the boys use them to jerk off. You'd be surprised how many use them that way. The shy ones, mostly. Do you ever use the magazines to jerk off in?"

"Not really," I say, assembling them hurriedly and trying to get them back on the shelf without exposing my genitalia which have hardened in idiot need to the coincidence. "I don't think of them that way."

"Oh that's perfectly all right. There's nothing shameful about it. A lot of the fellows who can't seem to get laid use them all the time. Can you imagine anyone not getting laid around this place?" She ventures a tentative laugh which becomes, eventually, a giggle. "It's possible, of course. You're not very good, you know. You need a lot of practice."

"It's not my fault. You rushed."

"Who rushed who?" she says, inspecting the other breast carefully, putting a finger in the nipple as if to test it for responsiveness. "You asked me to come to your room and have a talk and the next minute I have my clothes off. All of my clothes off. Not that I mind, of course. What else is there to do when it rains?"

"Well," I say, still in that slow stun which seems to be the inevitable consequence of the aftersex and feeling now too that familiar combination of dread and eagerness which means that the real implications of an event may lie entirely before me, "I guess you'd better get back upstairs."

"What? They never check after seven o'clock anyway. I might as well stay here all night."

"But in the morning – "

"Who's going to look? It's a progressive place. You've got to work with it; why fight things?"

I take her clothes from under the bed where I have casually tossed them with a social director's ease; where, poised like an arrow, I had hidden her garments in the same gracious gesture with which I had bent my mouth to her breasts. "I want you to go, though. I want to be alone now."

"Oh well," she says, "that's different. If you want to be alone, I can't stop you. Just don't ask me back again."

"Why not?" I say, finding my own clothing in the form of the shapeless bathrobe in which I had greeted her and belting it snugly. "It isn't anything personal."

"You could have some conversation too. It isn't all sex."

"What isn't?"

Somehow, I get through the moments between her nakedness and her entrapment, somehow I guide her without lapse of courtesy to the door, smooth over things, justify the equity of our act, our relations, the role they occupy in some larger scheme. Somehow, I enable her to pass through the door without disgrace, looking at her large rump dwindle in the hall, her step, a series of diminutions. I stand like a bird between heaven and hell; then opt for the latter with a bound, turning the key in my privates like a deep wound, moving out to cover all the inner and outer spaces. I seize the magazines and spreading the largest and most culpable all over the bed, I expose my organ from the (conveniently falling askew) bathrobe and holding it with both hands in a frenzy of disgrace I pull and pull until the last grey waters of consciousness have passed from inside to the outside of me and then I fall into a collapsing sleep, unstifled by groans, the magazines acting as a pillow for the precious rectal cheeks.

The name of this girl has been Carole and Carole is only one of the ten or so girls at this very progressive institution with whom I have coupled; there were Vivian and Portia and a girl named Helen with sloping, almost concave buttocks, and Marcia and Grace and Carole herself who dwelt in a double room above me and had found me interesting. The true tenor and possibilities of this new residence had been unknown to me for the first several days; when they became appallingly clear in the context of the mixed-sexes dormitory and the caliber of most of the personnel, it was still several weeks before I could act upon it. For me generation had always been an unequivocal, inward act rather than the frantic outpouring which seemed to be the *raison d'être* (can you spell that you idiot?) of this place, and when it did finally become clear that there was but one justification, one underlay, it took my atrophied skills a little longer to adjust. But now I was locked into the scheme of things: by day abysmal "classes" instructed by confused personnel, who seemed to be transfixed by latent possibilities which they could barely apprehend and of which they could never partake, functioned as a suitable bridge to the afternoons and evenings, and the evenings were full, rich, rooted in that casuality which is the token aim of the most progressive of all education. While Carole had been correct in saying that a surprising number of my colleagues were probably masturbators, it was wrong to attribute this to sheer lack; one of the prime benefits of this institution as it contributed to my self-knowledge was to give me the apprehension that there were many like me: those who preferred rather than submitted to the sacred self-abuse as the rounding-out of the full man. No one of us could have felt simple lack there; the male-female ratio had been contrived by a demon in the administration office to function at a constant one to one and as an occasional girl would leave the school in a fit of depression, insanity or pregnancy; as an occasional male would find this astonishing gratification of all forbidden fantasies too much for his cautious consciousness to assemble; a member of the same sex would be brought in, almost instantly, as replacement. It appeared that the waiting list for this institution was incredibly long; it numbered in the hundreds or, perhaps, the thousands, there would have been no way of explaining how she had maneuvered me in on something less than two months' notice had I not found out that one of the executive personnel had the same middle and last names as those of the social director, which cleared up part of the mystery. The girls were viable, cooperative, almost instantly gratifying, so much so that it was hard to believe that they, like me, were paying students; it was as if they had assumed a kind of staff function. I found out a great deal about the intricacies of female flesh during that splendid period; all the time holding my rod firmly in the final embrace behind locked doors to bring to my researches the final order of insight which could only be achieved by reinforcement-through-masturbation. Now I can construct for you a series of vignettes, picturizations, actually, which taken in toto can approximate a picturization of that period although, alas, it would be little more than a metaphor; insufficient data always leading to this conclusion. The name of this school was Rock Point and like the other resort it sat somewhere in desiccated heartland, and the two peaks which gave it its sole appeal held it clumsily, as two uneven palms might grasp a cup, as two frantic, grasping hands might catch a breast and squeeze its length away. Rock Point was privately supported by what was known mysteriously in the

catalogue as "friends of the institution," which endowment, added
to the handsome sums paid for tuition and other benefits, enabled
the school to have purchased the small cemetery lying directly on its
westward flank. It had commissioned this cemetery as a "historical
site," so much of what occurred seems to have taken place within
its confines.

I am holding the girl named Vivian close, close in the small shelter I have made of chest and huddled thighs and she is burrowing
beneath me eagerly, seeking my privates, her free hand caressing
me aimlessly in the area of the nape of the neck. We are clutched
to the right of a small gravestone, the northern drizzle coming down
slantwise and I feel the guilt once again surging within me that I had
not taken her to my room, and insisted that we get a "breath of out
doors" despite all signals to the contrary and had subjected her to
what can only be a complex humiliation, her body dampened by
the unrelieving blanket of rain which I can feel chill on my exposed,
upturned buttocks. But she does not seem to mind for all of that;
she is embarked on a complex, careless journey of her own, her
hands gripping and squeezing with amazed and growing discovery;
her mouth also enlarged and slippery under mine as her tongue
whickers inside. *Wet, wet,* she is murmuring, her upturned body
careless in the slick moisture and I am reaching as best as I can,
squeezing as best I can, while trying to make that difficult contact.
She is open before me, a furnace stoked by its own heat, unneeding
of operation and for an instant, trying to make the contact, I can
feel the foolishness; the sheer pointlessness of it all as I try to
burrow inside her; the position always striking me, somehow,
as irrelevant and pointless, the supple ease and graciousness of
the masturbatory turn having conditioned me. Her mouth presses
against mine, unyielding rubber and I reach forward with my loins
to find her slender frame: as I do so we slide, gracelessly into the
very stones of the grave site so that the crown of her head touches
and obscures some chiseled letters. "Oh, oh," she mutters, "never
anything like this before," and I feel her rising to greet me, her
slight, superfluous breasts trembling and puckering with the cold
impact of the stone and still fighting, still pillowing within her,
I reach a damp palm up to grasp the gravestone for support and
feel the hollows of the letters pressed against my hand; apparently
it is the word BELOVED although I cannot be sure. "Inside,
inside, you ass," she is muttering to me – all of them curse at

the moment of gathering, I have learned this; their revulsion at the act being so deep that even the Magazines themselves could hardly explain it, make it comprehensible – and as best as I can I point myself within her, reaching the other hand also for the gravestone because without that clinging support surely I will fall from my kneecaps and strike myself a blow in a more vulnerable spot from the stone. So as I move over her I am not touching her but the polished slickness of an epitaph, eyeing her nipples with rolling eyes, the eyes distended and flattened against the palm of my skull by the enormous effort I am making; the seriousness of the commitment. I feel absent flashes of fire, a rumbling below and my glazed eyes, fastened upon the stone, close; now I see the images of The Magazine itself and the images are less what is upon the page, the familiar dismemberment and narrowed focus upon breast, thigh, buttock, but rather upon the pages themselves, their uneven glossiness, the slickness of their feel: the Words written under the pictures that are themselves part of the picture and as her nipples rise up toward me in a trembling of gratitude I bend slightly, my eyelids still fluttering and put the last inches into her; feeling then the steaming and rising, the entrapment itself and my palms graze against the stone, entrap the stone, feeling the stone itself and yet at that moment it is probably not the stone but the very pages of the Magazine that I am feeling and so I come that way in a small spot of gloom, a cove of misery too deep to be reached let alone filtered by the bucking motions of thighs, the sound of cries in the air around me, the rain sifting down. "Come on," she says, grabbing me when I have worked out the last agonized spurts, "come on now and *come* you bastard," and this works me through the storms and stones of another orgasm, my palms falling from the slippery surface of the epitaph and I crumble in her quite helpless, quite drained while in an orgy of pragmatism she draws me over her body to cover her completely while one semi-detached hand, possessed of its own cleverness, begins to search for her pants.

I am in the cemetery again on a late-winter evening but far from the gravesites this time with a huge-breasted, tiny-buttocked girl named Jane who says that she has always wanted to do it open in the cool air, tickled by trees. The tree we have found is a wispy remnant of some crazed itinerant's mission, its leaves rustling dimly around us and somewhere in its very center protected against all elements, we huddle, the two of us quite naked this time while the huge, glowing surfaces of her breast flop a merry drum against my chest, my lips having found fuller purchase on her forehead where, discovering a full head of skin, they suck and suck away. She is not cursing to me but singing this time; singing one of the popular tunes of the era in a voice which both missounds and subsumes its banality; the song is all about love and Jove, heart and start and her voice, an unpleasant contralto, lifts to the uneven pounding of my thighs. I have caught her hole the first time out for once; the practice of fucking outweighing its disadvantage in some cases, the tiny hole possessing rewards which the more easily found (because instantaneously adjustable) closed fist could never provide and as best as I can, I am fucking away my private fuck on her, listening at the same time to the toneless melody which, absurdly, shifts now and then to a whistle, searching for her breasts with thumb and closed forefinger, and what she is singing blends, finally, into the better part which is what she is not seeing and so I come that way, poised bird against her huntressy determination, flicking seeds from my bill into her pouch and she clasps me in an orgy of gratitude as my magazine-inspired sperm greets her ripening and eager Egg. "Oh boy," she says, "oh boy, oh boy, oh boy, you're all heart; that's what you are; a jove of love." My throat, crackling with retrospection's saliva, would tell her something, but I am obviously speechless.

Surrounded by darkness above and below, I am suspended on my bed, hands and knees to full flight, moving eagerly in the ascension and reversal of love, locked into a cell of sensation so private and interesting that I could as well be alone but underneath me is the girl named Margaret, her body spread like drifting water, porous on the surfaces of the bed and she is accommodating me; accommodating me as best she can in her slippery hole, her hands working idly on my chest. Margaret is one of the "less advantaged" members of the student body; she supplements her scholarship and meager allowance by doing "housekeeping" tasks in the dormitory, and it is in such circumstances that I have come to greet her, her mop, broom and housedress to the side of the bed, her industry forgotten as we move in another, intricate kind of cleaning-gesture. I have then, it seems, done it to the housekeeper here, as well as everybody else, but the housekeeper is 17 years old and is mumbling to me in a credulous voice: *this is terrific, this is really terrific; I didn't know you guys had beds like this; you couldn't imagine what we girls have to sleep in; I could lie like this forever.* And so she could, but I am pursuing her with unprecedented industry, unprecedented business, her breasts so superfluous in the welter of sensation I have aroused through our joining that I am barely conscious of their presence or appearance. *This is really the lap of luxury* she advised me as her thighs thrust in conformation.

Above me, the cheerful, rattling *thump! bump!* of my magazines in their locked pouch indicates perilous movement on the shelf, the possibility of collision, disaster, falling action at any time and the knowledge that these magazines could truly fall, right into the cup of my exposed buttocks, bringing a kind of triumphant finale to my researches, fills me with ever-quickening excitement; I can imagine how they would feel clouting me slowly like a large covey of emergent insects and the explanations I would have to give – *oh the explanations!* – all of this sending me even further and deeper into necessity's groin and her arms gather listlessly to drag me in. *I have to finish off the other rooms soon,* she reminds me behind her closed eyes, *otherwise I'll lose my stipend,* and I moan to her in a burst of cooperation and feel myself open and open above her, a reciprocal opening below; breezes seem to drift over my buttocks and I get it inside her to its fullest length, feeling her fingers scrapple on my shoulders and the tube of her gathers around me all ferocity, all obligement and I finish then to a feeling of slow scattering, thousands of sheets of paper drifting down around me; fall upon her in the rigidity of the corpse itself imagining how it would be indeed if all of this texture and stock, photography and art would come down over the hushed and tenanted spaces of my distantly bartered grave.

I am at a "drive-in" movie with tiny-buttocked Jane again; this time she wants to do it in a new and novel way during which she can examine celebrities and because of her help and attention I am in poor position to protest. There is no way in which I can tell her that the trunk of the rented car which we have jointly taken (but which I must pay for and which Jane must drive) is jammed, almost to the top, with magazines; a hasty room inspection during the morning had determined that these would have to be out of my premises before was conducted what was called there the "mid-semester audit." This procedure, nominally to determine whether or not students were living up to the health habits and

ways of the institution was actually, I long suspected, in search
of prophylactics or the remains of aborted fetuses but I judged it
unwise – oh, the cunning now that I had at last learned what they
really meant! – to have my magazines for discovery; masturbation
was the one excess which the school, even in its convocations,
would never imply. (*We must learn to love one another*, had been the
suggestion of the Headmaster during the mid-Christmas assembly,
even if some touching is required in the process; he had said nothing of
Loving Oneself.) So the magazines, carried from class to class in a
large imitation leather briefcase with a self-locking clasp, had been
unobtrusively tossed in the rented trunk during the conclusion of
the rental process; now as I jounced and bounced my lonely way
above Jane's watchful breasts I hoped that somewhere in the rear
there was no suggestion of reciprocal, less joyous, bouncing of the
hidden and more important load. Before my stunned eyes had
drifted the slight convexity of the screen, huge images locked with
one another in two or three colors, suspended above us, and in
the soundlessness acting out scenes far more intricate and beautiful
than we could ever conceive, but now I had turned down upon
her again, making rough work of the entrance because it would be
quickest and the quicker fruition would lead to quicker retrieval
of the magazines, but she wanted it slow, begged to me in her
small popular-singer's voice to extend it as far as possible, all the
time her eyes rolled to the screen where she absorbed the images
in a kind of placidity and contentment which I could only dimly
apprehend. Her mouth, working on some gum, chewed evenly,
her eyes calm and bright surveyed me with an owner's pride as I
jabbed and jabbed at her slender receiving reed and then, hastening
over her, my eyelids clamped and fluttering against her breasts, I
must have had an accident; I must have jabbed something with
an elbow because the speakers suddenly flicked on, both of them
and the voices began to boom and shatter in the car, words of love
and rage tumbling over one another in unbearable volume and I
reached out my hand, trembling, to smash or reduce the sound
but found it stayed by two tentative fingers she had raised to stay
it. "No," she murmured, "leave it on; it's nice," and I fought with
the cripple's weakness to free myself of that clasp and shatter the
sound, but, confident of what her thighs had done to take my
strength, she merely held the pressure and said again, "It's so
nice this way; what do you want to spoil all the fun for; it's just

like they're right in the car or we're up on the screen, isn't that more exciting?"

And confined now by a small and terrible rage, a rage which exerted a pressure which screamed only for Justice – whatever that must be – I found the resolve she wanted, which was only the resolve for perishment, for completion, for a connection so rapid as to lead to an immediate withdrawal, which would be the end of shame, but with her clever, fluttering box she held me off for a long long time and so I was forced to listen to strings and horns, shrieks and giggles, sobs and *scenis obligatoria* while my reluctant weapon ground out its few spurts of enthusiasm and I came mumbling against her, as contrite, humbled and profoundly embarrassed as any character in the *commedia* she was witnessing. Throughout she took me with a massive and almost sympathetic air of contrition, her thighs grinding against my organ, her hole exerting the last inch of pressure against myself and at the apocalyptic moment, as through memory I raged and bucked thinking of those lovelies in the trunk, her thumb rose to her mouth and she sucked it earnestly, her eyes averted as I spent into her. Finally free, I was able to turn down the sound, still clamped within her and as I did so she sighed and looked at me as if for the first time, her fingers winding, winding below to complete the circle of causation.

"It's really a good movie," she said, "you know that? There's so much sense to it, just good common sense. What did you do down there? Did you finish? I wasn't sure."

"You weren't sure?"

"Well, I wasn't really concentrating on the movie and like that. I mean, I hope you had a good time, I didn't want to stop you or anything like that. It's just that I'm not really in the mood."

"I guess I finished," I said. "Do you want me to go outside and pick up anything? You want something to eat?"

"Well, that wouldn't be a bad idea, I guess. I'd want some hamburgers and drinks and so on. Maybe some candy. You sure you won't get lost outside and not be able to come back? I'd hate to have to return this car alone; I'd owe the whole thing."

"I think I can make it."

"Make sure you remember what row we're in and what number car. That's the best way of doing it."

Still within her, I tried to withdraw. "Okay," I said, "but I have to get my pants on." For a fine, slender moment of panic I thought that some of the horrid blue-covered texts in my parents' dresser which I had once read had intimated the truth after all; that I was in the grip of *glans penis captivus*. The harder I tugged, the more snugly the conjoinment seemed to fit. Finally, I lost my balance and tumbled on top of her, her little jaws still earnestly compressing and contracting the gum. "What's wrong?"

"I can't get out."

"What do you mean, you can't get out?"

"I mean, it seems stuck in there." I guided her unwilling hand down, let her fondle the dilemma. "You see what I mean?"

"Oh," she said, "that's just the thighs. Nothing to worry about at all; I'll just move my legs a little." I felt her grunt underneath me, her body heave. "Of course it's difficult to move because you're on top of me."

"Well, I can't get off you, can I?"

"I know that. Gee, this is really kind of embarrassing." Her fingers pinched, brought a glimmer of pain. "Try it now."

I tried, seemed to be on the verge of a small but boisterous withdrawal, but felt the pressure even harder, somewhere near the tip. "No, that won't do it."

"Jesus, I'm getting all out of position. I can hardly see the screen. We'll miss the whole movie and all."

"I've still got to get out of there."

"Couldn't you just kind of lie around and nap for a little while, until the picture's over? Then we can both work. It isn't anything to worry about; this has happened to me before. I have a very small, nervous thing."

"But I thought you wanted me to go out for some food."

"Well, yeah. Yeah, that's right too. Okay, now. You know, once a boy got caught inside for an hour. Boy was he mad! He didn't know what to say; we just had to wait until he got small enough to get out. That wasn't you, was it, who got stuck?"

"No, this is the first time it's happened."

"Oh. I guess I was thinking of someone else. All right try it now."

"I can't. I can't move."

She giggled. "This could be very embarrassing. I told you, you'll cool off and get out if you'll only relax. Why don't you put my breasts in your mouth and just relax on them? Boys seem to like that."

"I want to get out," I said and at that moment, the Singing Strings, all 106 of them, apparently in some unprecedented cinematic transition, broke out into an unmuted throb, a series of pulses so sharp as to break the tenor equipment of the speaker and fill the car with rattlings of sound.

"My God," Jane said, "someone's trying to come and see us. We better really get out of here. Can you drive?"

"It's just the speaker. Now let me do this." I felt myself overcome by rage, but as profound as that was, the pain was still there at the rock-center of the scene, flooding into my organ, making it even more turgid, things more rigid. I managed to get both hands in position, squashing what little there was of her breasts with my upper arms and seized what I could find of my organ, pulling and pulling desperately. She gave a high wheeze, somewhere between a shriek and a sigh and began to settle under me like a blanket.

"God that's lovely," she said, "I don't know what you're doing there but it's just lovely. More, more."

"I'm trying to get out."

"With the fingers, squeeze around that way. Oh, God, that's really terrific now. I can see the movie and everything. The speaker is broken. The movie is good. You've got to squeeze more. Oh, I'm coming, I'm coming. That's it. That's it. I'm coming."

And come she did in a series of thick waves and flashes of thumping which somehow disgorged my prick at her moment of climax and left it, sopping wetly, on the shiny cushions of the rental car. The speaker clattered in the blackness and, rubbing my fingers in her hole, I obliged her to an orgasm. She felt back, her eyes gripped by the screen.

"That was good," she said. "That was really terrific."

Speechless, I used a shirttail to clean off the residue of my orgasm, managed to adjust my garments without undue rolling, poked an elbow against the window painfully and subsided in the seat, watching several ballerinas on the screen attempt to persuade a choreographer that they were usable. I was quite incapable of thought.

"Well?" she said when the ballerinas had made their case and, embracing one another, had vanished in favor of an operatic singer who appeared to be having romantic difficulties with the choreographer. "What about it?"

"What about what?"

"Aren't you going to go out and get us something to eat? You said you would, you know. I'm hungry. I fixed you and all, the least you can do is bring some food back."

I managed to get the door open and inspecting her for a considerable time – she had heaved herself to a sitting position and was working halfheartedly on her brassiere while searching the dashboard for a fresh piece of gum – I got out into the dirt of the enclosure itself, standing uneasily on the ragged ground, trying to find my balance. Now, in the speakerless silence the screen had assumed a kind of beauty, its figures in being devoid of noise seemed to lack context as well. Moving in a sea as mysterious and as possessed of its fulfilment as I had moved in my sea sleeps many years ago. I stumbled away from it, my back to the screen, my eyes to the moon, feeling a special tendril of fiery knowledge cross between my smuggled goods in the trunk and my exhausted loins as I trudged to the food counter.

And, too, I am with Marcia the redundant in a classroom this time in the pitch of a winter evening, the two of us huddled over the desk, quite naked, her eyes roaming the ceiling while I inspect her nipples with microscopic urgency and work on the alternating surfaces of her stomach and thighs with a woe compounded out of lust and fright. We have no business doing it in this building, but she has assured me that faculty and staff themselves are aware of the student need to disseminate knowledge in its oldest form in the very seat of learning and that to copulate in the classrooms is, in the last analysis, only to join in the hidden and therefore more necessary, purposes of the institution itself. I am sliding, sliding, all lost in the glistening wetness, my tool a tangle, my eyes bulging and behind them I am playing the pictures and images while I work at her with a fool's persistence.

"Higher, higher," she mutters and for a moment I think she means a greater thrust and I attempt to spread her deeper and deeper yet upon the desk but her frantic, tickling fingers below tell me that there is something else she has in mind and I find withdrawal forced, a sudden retraction, a sudden drawing. Pouring sweat and mingled juices, my prick looks for a better home and she guides me with her hands to the cleft between her breasts, centering me with an indulgent palm while with the other she tugs at a breast and then, the first hand freed, takes the other in her hand and forms for me a tight channel, a wedge almost, through which I guide the small, desperate prow of my ship.

And it is as close, then, as close as I can ever come, before or since, to the sensation of the magazines, for here it is all before me, her breasts, held in that full, cupped aspect, almost dislodged from her body, her face a disordered irrelevancy behind the spread of her hair, and I feel myself reaching, reaching, grown to enormous size and power within her and she reaches forward grateful lips to touch me with teeth-and-tongue, adding a slow insistence to my rhythm. I can see vaguely below her cupped and held breasts the shuddering of her thighs and trembling of that nervous skin caught between them but it means nothing to me; I am surrounded by breasts and breasts, nestled in them, lost in them and as she increases the tension on them to make a cylinder I feel myself lengthen toward a final extension and come easily, gratefully, missing her withdrawn face, my hands reaching to touch the side of her breasts with appreciation while she mutters encouragement to me and I leak out the last drops.

After a long time I fall away from her, my buttocks brushing chalk, sliding to a stop on the wood and she looks up at me easily, her eyes glistening with an emotion come close to tenderness. "Oh, wasn't that wonderful?" she says. "When my breasts are held that way, they look just like all the breasts in those magazines, don't they? Don't they?" I tell her this is so and bury my apologetic prick in her bush, waiting for the lights to come on, waiting for the assailant to come.

Somewhere in the middle of that year – I am not sure when and it hardly matters – I received a letter from Marie-Jean, the only piece of extra-familial correspondence which came into my mailbox that year:

". . . I obtained your address from my father who with no difficulty attained it from your mother. I guess you suppose you're lucky to be up there, ha, ha, but I wanted to write you this letter to tell you that although you are gone you are not forgotten, at least not by me although you would like to think so. For what you did to me I can never forgive you even though you can forgive yourself so easily for a thousand things; I want you to know that Marie-Jean thinks of you all

the time and that Marie-Jean will never relax for a moment
until she has paid you back in kind for what you did to her.
What form that payment will take and when it will happen
is none of your business; it could happen at any minute or
not for the next 100 years but it will happen and it will serve
you right. Not only did you dishonor and shame me, you
dishonored and shamed my father by having your mother
take up his time only because then you could be safe in
taking me into the cornfields. My father is a fine man, an
innocent man, a widower who means everything to me but is
not a man who knows people of your type and your mother's
and thus could not deal with you or protect himself but I can
protect him double and I will. No matter what happens to
us there will be a time of getting even. I do not want you
to answer this letter as if you do I will find it necessary for
me to tear it up . . ."

And yet another fulfilment: straight as an arrow, proud as a
blade, I am hunched on the main quadrangle of the "campus"
itself, giving it in this noon of the night to the proudest, most
preposterous of all the bitches I have met this year; a girl named
Elena with breasts which thrust up as squarely as they thrust out,
breasts whose resilience increases out of clothes, thighs whose slight
flabbiness only made more needful and urgent those muscular
exercises which comprised her special contribution to the craft of
copulation, her feet pointed at the moon at the same angle that my
buttocks were and there was, around us, no intimation of substance
or of presence, only the two of us in the spring night, the campus
hushed around us, all groans and quivers in the cathedral or the
cemetery. It was Elena's special innovation to do it in the center
of this quadrangle itself at safe hours; expressing, as she said, her
feelings for the environment in the best way possible and she was
extremely difficult, not out of prudence, but by virtue of sheer
weight of numbers; there was always a waiting list of 30 or more
for Elena's embrace and there was no way to hasten one's progress
on that list because she was strictly fair about the process; so fair that
some escorts, having painfully waited out their ascension, wanted to
do it a second time but on another night and Elena felt that not to
give an option would be to render herself a bit of a slut. So it was a
question of patience, patience, but in the last analysis she was worth

it; the most "special" of all the special people who inhabited the campus, she conceded darkly that she had been there for five years and had worked with difficulty to her position of queen ex-officio; a position whose only benefit was that she was able, in essence, to talk for the student body at the occasional faculty confrontations which were part of the progressive spirit. I had waited and waited, working out my time with the Janes and the Viviennes, waited for so long that it seemed to me that Elena was a hoax and the waiting list was a ploy, but one night she called me in my room to say that she was finally able to take me up on dinner the following evening and now at last I had her; I had the queen on her campus itself, and it was almost worth it because she not only did not block out my fantasies or twist her body unconsciously against them as some of the others had but rather, with a tenderness and understanding I had thought impossible in women, had seemingly understood almost from the start what I wanted and had allowed me to stretch out not on top but alongside her, a fist held in readiness, while she dwarfed my organ in her bulky pouch and produced her breasts, one by one, for me to nibble. I was as loose, swinging and free at ease as if I had been doing it into a magazine; her body, a long, coiled tube, seemed ready to spring to my convenience at any moment. So we sighed and mumbled the night away, our limbs tumbled like glass on the shores of that campus, her breasts bulging hugely and contentedly against all my surfaces and until the sun came we lay there, every confrontation a joy, every joy a refreshment and then, as the sun began to moan darkly in the distance she came upon the oldest, coldest and boldest variation of them all; what she did was to take her breasts in either hand and pointing them toward me, she –

BETWEEN SIGNS

Cris Mazza

Living legends of the Enchanted Southwest
Watch Authentic Indians.
Handmade crafts, Leather,
Pan for Gold with Real Prospectors

He'll drive with one hand. With the other, unbuttons her shirt. Then when trucks pass, close, going the opposite direction, he'll drive with no hands for a moment, waving to the truckers with his left hand, his right hand never leaving her breasts. She'll arch her back, smile, eyes closed. The wind of the passing trucks will explode against the car like split-second thunder-storms.

Swim
Ski
Relax
Play
In Lostlake City

DO NOT PARK
IN DESIGNATED
PARKING AREAS

Someday she'll return, using this same road, and it will be late spring, and the migrating desert showers will wash the windshield of collected bugs and dust over and over, and the smell of wet pavement will lift her drooping eyelids, and she'll not stop until she's knocking on his door and it's opening and he's standing there. She'll feel the explosion of his body or the explosion of the door slamming.

**15 Restaurants
11 Motels
Next 2 exits**

RATTLESNAKE-SKIN BOOTS
TURQUOISE BELT BUCKLES
BEADED MOCCASINS, SNO CONES

They took nothing. Credit cards bought gas and food, plastic combs, miniature toothbrushes, motel rooms, tourist T-shirts, foaming shaving cream and disposable razors. She watched him shaving as she lay in the bathtub. Then he shaved her. Rinsing her with the showerhead, soaping her over and over again. Shoved a blob of jelly, from a plastic single-serving container taken from the diner, far inside her, went to retrieve it with his tongue, drop by drop, taste by taste, but there was always more where that came from.

See Mystic Magic Of The Southwest . . . THE THING?

While she takes a turn driving, he'll lay his head in her lap and watch her play with herself. The sound is sticky and sweet like a child sucking candy. The sun will appear and disappear. A band of light across her bare knees. She'll hold his hand and his fingers will join hers moving in and out. The seat wet between her thighs. A cattle crossing will bounce his head in her lap and her legs will tighten around their joined hands. Air coming in the vents is humid, thick with the warm smell of manure, straw, the heat of bodies on the endless flat pasture under the sun. He'll roll to his back to let her wet fingers embrace his erection.

VISIT RUBY FALLS

Make a Bee-Line to **ROCK CITY**

Don't Miss CATFISH WILLIE'S RIVERBOAT
Restaurant, Lounge, Casino
Fresh Catfish & Hushpuppies
Beulah, Tennessee

Rip Van Winkle Motel just 35 miles

He has no sunglasses. His eyes are slits. Bright white sky and blinking lines on the road. Touches blistered chapped lips with his tongue. Digs into his pocket, sitting on one hip and easing up on the gas. Crackle of paper among the loose change. He unwraps the butter scotch and slips it into his mouth, rolls it with his tongue, coats his mouth with the syrup. When he passes a mailbox on the side of the road, he looks far up the dirt driveway beside it, but can't see where it leads. At the next mailbox, five miles later, he stops for a second. The name on the box says Granger, but, again, the driveway is too long to see what it leads to.

Triple-Dip ice cream cones
Camping, ice, propane
Truckers Welcome

SLIPPERY WHEN WET   **FALLING ROCK**

They weren't allowed to rent a shower together, so they paid for two but when no one was looking she slipped into his. Someone far away was singing. They stood for a while, back to back, turned and simultaneously leaned against the opposite walls of the shower stall, then slid down and sat facing each other, legs crossing. She told him he looked like he was crying, the water running down his face, but his tears would probably taste soapy. She said once she'd put dish detergent into a doll that was supposed to wet and cry. From then on it had peed foam and bawled suds. He reached out and put a hand on each of her breasts, holding her nipples between two fingers. A door slammed in the stall beside theirs. Water started and a man grunted. He rose to his knees, pulled on her arms so she slid the rest of the way to the floor of the shower, the drain under her back. He eased over her, his mouth moving from breast to breast. Then he lathered her all over, slowly, using almost the whole bar of soap, her ears and neck, toes, ankles, knees, lingering between her legs where the hair was growing back and sometimes itched so badly while they drove that she had to put her hand in her pants and scratch. She was slick to hold. He didn't rinse her before pushing his cock in. The sting of the soap made them open their eyes wide and dig their fingernails into each other's skin. Staring at each other but not smiling.

Taste Cactus Jack's Homestyle Cookin

Relax in Nature's Spa
CHICKEN HOLLER HOT SPRINGS
Sandwiches, Live Bait

ROAD CLOSED IN FLOOD SEASON

Finally she stops and buys half a cantaloupe at a roadside fruit stand. After eating as much as she can with a plastic spoon, she presses her face down into the rind and scrapes the remaining flesh with her teeth. The juice is cool on her cheek and chin. Part of a tattered map, blown by the wind, is propped against the base of a telephone pole. He had laughed at her for getting cantaloupe Marguaritas, but then he'd sipped some of hers, ordered one for himself, said it tasted like her. She breaks the rind in half and slips one piece into her pants, between her legs. The crescent shape fits her perfectly.

MARVEL AT MYTHICAL RELICS
INDIAN JEWELRY
VELVET PAINTINGS

TEXMEX CHICKEN-FRIED STEAK
TACOS, BURRITOS
FREE 72 OZ STEAK IF YOU CAN EAT IT ALL!

When the dirt road gets so bumpy he has to keep both hands on the wheel, she'll take over using the vibrator on herself. He'll watch her, and watch the road. The road always disappears around a bend or beyond a small rise. The car bounces over ruts and rocks. She

won't even have to move the vibrator, just hold it inside. She'll say
he chose a good road, and her laugh will turn into a long moan,
her head thrown over the back of the seat. One of her feet pressed
against his leg. Her toes will clutch his pants.

View of Seven States from Rock City

Poison Spring Battleground
next exit, south 12 miles

PIKE COUNTY DIAMOND FIELD
All The Diamonds You Find Are Yours!

For three days he's had a postcard to send home, but can't find the
words to explain. It's a picture of the four corners, where Colorado,
New Mexico, Arizona and Utah meet. He hadn't gotten down on
hands and knees to be in all four states simultaneously. But he had
walked around them, one step in each state, making a circle, three
times. When he arrives at Chief Yellowhorse's Trading Post and
Rock Museum, he buys another postcard, a roadrunner following
the dotted line on highway 160. This one's for *her*, wherever she
is, if she even left a forwarding address. The rock museum costs a
dollar. A square room, glass cases around the edges, dusty brown
pebbles with handwritten nametags. Some of the rocks are sawed
in half to show blue rings inside. A bin of rose quartz pieces for a
nickel each. Black onyx for a dime. Shark's teeth are a quarter.

HOGEYE, pop. 2011
Hogeye Devildogs Football
class D state champs 1971

**Behold! Prehistoric Miracles!
Indian Pottery, Sand Paintings
Cochina Dolls, Potted Cactus**

Found Alive!
THE THING?

They'll toss their clothes into the back seat. Their skin slippery with sweat. She'll dribble diluted soda over and between his bare legs. Tint of warm root beer smell lingering in the car. She'll hold an ice cube in her lips and touch his shoulder with it. Runs it down his arm. It'll melt in his elbow. She'll fish another ice out of her drink, move it slowly down his chest. When she gets to his stomach, the ice will be gone, her tongue on his skin. She'll keep his hard-on cool by pausing occasionally to slip her last piece of ice into her mouth, then sucking him while he slides a finger in and out of her. The last time she puts the ice into her mouth, his hand will be there to take it from her lips. He'll push the ice into her, roll it around inside with a finger until it's gone. The road lies on the rippling desert like a ribbon. Leaving the peak of each of the road's humps, the car will be airborne for a second.

Cowboy Steaks, Mesquite Broiled

Black Hills Gold, Arrowheads,
Petrified Wood, Chicken Nuggets,
Soda, Thick Milkshakes, Museum
WAGON MOUND TRAVELERS REST

He had to slow down, find a turnout, pull her from the car and half carry her to the shade of a locked utility shack. She dropped to her knees, then stretched out full length on her stomach. He sat beside her, stroking her back. Her body shuddered several more times, then calmed. When she rolled over, the hair on her temples was wet and matted with tears, her eyes thick, murky, glistening, open, looking at him. She smiled.

INDIAN BURIAL MOUNDS NEXT EXIT
GAS, FOOD, LODGING

Rattlesnake Roundup
Payne County Fairgrounds
2nd weekend in July

DUST STORMS NEXT 18 MILES

The waterpark is 48 miles off the main interstate. He's the only car going in this direction and passes no others coming the opposite way. The park was described in a tourbook but wasn't marked on the map. Bumper boats, olympic pool, 3 different corkscrew waterslides, high dive. The only other car in the lot has 2 flat tires. Small boats with cartoon character names painted on the sides are upside down beside an empty concrete pond, a layer of mud and leaves at the bottom. Another layer of dirt at the bottom of the swimming pool is enough to have sprouted grass which is now dry and brown, gone to seed. The scaffold for the waterslides is still standing, but the slides have been dismantled. The pieces are a big aqua-blue pile of fiberglass.

Ancient Desert Mystery...THE THING? 151 miles

Land of Enchantment
New Mexico T-Shirts

BULL HORNS
HANDWOVEN BLANKETS
CACTUS CANDY
NATURAL WONDERS

She'll look out the back windshield. The earth is a faint, rolling line against a blue-black sky. His hair tickling her cheek. She'll be on his lap, straddling him, her chin hooked over his shoulder, his cock has been inside her for miles and miles. Sometimes she'll rock slowly from side to side. Sometimes he'll push up from underneath. Sometimes they'll sit and feel the pulse of the engine, the powerful vibration. The air coming through the vent, splashing against her back before it spreads through the car, is almost slightly damp. Smells of rain on pavement, clean and dusty. Out the front windshield, both sky and land stay so dark, there's no line where they meet. No lights and no stars.

If we go west fast enough, will it stay predawn forever?

We can try.

Did you ever pester your parents, When'll we get there, daddy? And I'd've thought it was torture if he said *never*.

GOSPEL HARMONY HOUSE CHRISTIAN DINNER THEATRE

MERGING TRAFFIC   DEER XING   SHARPCURVES
                                         NEXT 10 MILES

They started walking toward the entrance of the WalMart store, but she turned off abruptly, crossed a road and climbed a small hill where someone had set up three crosses in the grass. They were plant stakes lashed together. Kite string was tangled on a tumbleweed. When she got back to the parking lot, five or six big cockleburs were clinging to each of her socks. She sat on the hood of the car picking them off. When he came from the store with two blankets, toilet paper, aspirin and glass cleaner, she said, There weren't any graves up there after all. He put the bag in the back seat, turned and smiled. Kiss me, she said.

Meteor Crater and gift shop, 3 miles ➡

WARNING:
THIS ROAD CROSSES A US
AIR FORCE BOMBING RANGE
FOR THE NEXT 12 MILES DANGEROUS
OBJECTS MAY DROP FROM AIRCRAFT

BIMBO'S FIREWORKS
Open all year

He spreads a map over his steering wheel. This road came forty-five miles off the interstate. He pays and follows the roped-off trail, stands looking at the cliff dwellings as the guide explains which was the steam room, which compartment stored food, which housed secret rituals, where the women were allowed to go and where they weren't, why they died off before white settlers ever arrived, and the impossibly straight narrow paths which connected them directly to other cliff dwelling cities and even now were still visible from the sky, spokes on a wheel converging on their religious center.

Bucksnort Trout Pond
Catch a Rainbow!

Krosseyed Kricket Kampground

Two Guns United Methodist Church
Sunday Worship 10 a.m.
Visitors Welcome

She doesn't even know how long she's been sitting by the side of the road. The car shakes when the semis go past. Sometimes she can see a face turned toward her for a split second. The last time she went behind a rock to pee, she found three big black feathers with white tips. Now she's holding one, brushing it lightly over her face. Her eyes are closed. Somehow the scent of the feather is faintly wild. When she returns – in a year, two years, five years – in heavy sleep long past midnight but long before dawn, he'll never know any time passed at all. Like so many nights before she left, her footsteps will pad down the sidewalk. The nurse who shares his life will long since have put on her white legs and horned hat and gone to the hospital. Using the key he made for her, which she still carries on her chain, she'll let herself in. Move past the odor of hairspray in the bathroom. Drop her clothes in a heap in the doorway – simple clothes she'll easily be able to pull on in the moments before she leaves him. Then she'll stand there, listen to his body resting. Watch the dim form of him under the sheet become clearer. She'll crawl to the bedside, lean her elbows and chin on the mattress, his hand lying open near her face. She'll touch his palm with the wild feather, watch the fingers contract and relax. Until his hand reaches for her, pulls her into the bed and remembers her. She opens her eyes and squints although dusk has deadened the glare on the road. Slips the feather behind one ear. She doesn't remember which direction she'd been going before she stopped here to rest.

Bridge Freezes in Cold Weather

The Unknown is Waiting For You!
See The Thing? just 36 more miles

STATE PRISON
Do Not Stop For Hitchhikers

Yield

The music channel hadn't had any music for a while. She sat up, stared at the screen, counted the number of times either the interviewer or musician said *man*, lost track quickly, changed to the weather station, turned the sound down. She massaged his shoulders and back, each vertebra, his butt, his legs, the soles of his feet, each toe. He said, I'm yours forever. Said it into the pillow. Anything you want, he said. She lay her cheek against his back and watched a monsoon, palm trees bending to touch the tops of cottages, beach furniture thrown through windows. He had rolled over and was looking at her. His eyes looked almost swollen shut. Anything, he said. She looked back at the screen, yachts tossed like toys, roofs blown off, an entire pier folded sideways along the beach. She said, I've never been in something like that.

He pinned her wrists in just one of his hands, hurled her face-down. She was open and ready as though panting heavy fogged air from her cunt, and he slammed himself in there, withdrew completely and slammed in again and again. With each thrust she said, Oh! And he answered when he came, a long, guttural cry, releasing her wrists to hold onto her hips and pump her body on his cock.

They lay separate for a while. Now, she said, hold me . . . with both hands. Hold me like something you'd never want to break. Tomorrow I'll drop you off at the nearest airport.

SPECIAL PERMIT REQUIRED FOR:
Pedestrians
Bicycles
Motor Scooters
Farm Implements
Animals on Foot

Home of Johnny Johnson
Little All-American 1981

Ice Cream, Divinity, Gas, Picnic Supplies
Real Indians Performing Ancient Rites

He'll set the car on cruise control and they'll each climb out a window, pull themselves to the roof of the car, to the luggage rack. Their hair and clothes lash and snap in the rushing wind. Dawn has been coming on for hours. The sun may never appear. The sky behind them pink-gold on the horizon, bleeding to greenish, but like wet blue ink straight above them. She'll unbutton her shirt and hold her arms straight up, lets the wind undress her. They'll take turns loosening their clothes and feeling thin, cool rushing air whip the material away. Bursting through low pockets of fog, they come out wet and sparkling, tingling, goosebumped. They'll slide their bodies together, without hurry and without holding back, no rush to get anywhere, saving nothing for later, passing the same rocks, bushes and fenceposts over and over. As the car leaves the road, leaping and bounding with naive zest, they'll pull each other closer and hold on, seeing the lovely sky in each other's eyes, tasting the sage and salty sand on each other's skin, hearing the surge of velocity in the other's shouted or breathless laughter, feeling the tug of joy in their guts, in their vigorous appetites. The sky still deep violet-black, the dawn still waiting, the car still soaring from butte to pinnacle to always higher peaks.

HER FIRST BRA

(excerpt from *A Body Chemical*)

Chris Mazza

1981

There was one more card from Millard in November, a Thanksgiving card that said *hope to see you again . . . someday . . . somewhere*. Dale picked it up from the floor under the kitchen card table and said, "Who's this from, your mother?"

"Yuckity yuk." Leala was slicing hotdogs to go into canned beans. Dale ate lunch at about 10 a.m. when he got home from delivering tortillas to restaurants.

"Well, who is it?"

"It's a photographer I did a session for. I guess he liked me. Whose mother should we visit for Thanksgiving?"

"A *session*? What's that mean? You're working as a model? Since when?"

"About six months."

"Why didn't you tell me?"

"I thought I did." She put a plate of tepid franks-n-beans in front of him then started sorting through the mail, putting the utility and credit card bills in one pile for Dale to pay from his checking account, the rent and food came from hers. She had a session that afternoon. The guy on the phone yesterday asked how old she was and she'd answered *I'm very bold, why'd you ask?*

then the guy digressed to something else, the color of her hair and eyes, how tall she was, her measurements. She'd changed her ad again. It said, *young, versatile female model for private photo sessions with imaginative photographers, you won't believe what your camera can do.*

"How much have you made?" Dale asked.

"Not much. The rent went up, remember?"

"Well let's make out a budget or something, maybe we don't have to sell anything to buy grass. Or Christmas presents for that matter."

"Sessions aren't predictable, Dale. We can't *budget* for them. I thought you were *off* grass, anyway."

"Well they use it for cancer patients, don't they? Maybe it'll help."

"Help *what*? God, what a hypochondriac, it really gets old."

"I'm getting this shortness of breath all the fucking time, dammit, I'm hot then cold, then I start sweating my fucking ass off. What would *you* call it?"

"Maybe it's menopause."

"Har-de-fucking-har." He put three huge spoonfuls into his mouth in rapid succession before chewing and swallowing. "So you wanna go away for Christmas vacation this year?"

"No, not now."

"Then when?"

She picked up his empty plate and put it with the dirty pan beside the sink. "Dale, I tried to tell you once what'll probably happen, what I'm saving for, but you wouldn't believe me. That's fine, you can pretend. Sure, everything's *normal*, right?" She boosted herself to the counter and swung her feet into the sink to shave her legs. "Luckily I don't even think you'll miss me."

The photographer handed her two fifties before she came through the door. The session was at his house – he had his living room furniture pushed to one side and a corner converted into a set resembling a dressing room in a fancy department store. A three-sided mirror and stool, clothes with tags draped over accordion partitions, big umbrella lamps preventing anything from showing a shadow anywhere.

"Okay, listen to this," the guy said. He had long hair parted in the middle, the kind that either looks dirty or if it's clean, is so fine it's like baby hair that was never cut. He also had one of those halfway mustaches that usually only sixteen-year-old boys can grow, more baby hair. "Okay, listen," he repeated, "it's like, you're shopping, it's a big day because . . . you've come to the store without your mother –"

"My *mother*?"

"Yeah, listen, you've come shopping, you took a bus or rode your bike, but you came to this upscale store where you get one of those personal shoppers. You see, you're here to get your first . . . training bra." Suddenly he ducked his head and looked through a camera on a tripod. She wasn't even on the set yet.

"Does anyone even *use* training bras anymore?"

"Sure they do, and listen, you're all excited, this is a big day for you, milestone, know what I mean? Today you become a woman . . . and all that." He stood up but continued to look at the set, not at Leala.

"And I suppose my dressing room has a hidden camera or two-way mirror. And then what, my personal shopper is a man?"

"Maybe," he said slowly. "We'll see. The important thing is, this is such a big day for a girl. It makes her feel like anything can happen. Um, hang your old clothes on the hook there, like you would in a dressing room. And here you go, try these on." He pulled a plastic Sears shopping bag from behind one of the partitions.

"I doubt Sears has personal shoppers," she said, looking inside. There were three or four practically cupless bras and matching underwear, one set white with purple flowers, one baby blue, one with pink polkadots, and one set basic white with lace. The bras were just stretchy material with elastic straps and hook in back.

"You can have them when we're finished," he said. "Do you have any that nice?"

"No I can't say that I have any like these. In fact, I don't have a bra."

"You don't?" His face and sad brown eyes and repulsive mustache seemed to leap at her, but he hadn't moved closer, just was looking at her. "Oh, good, that's great. Perfect. Like . . . this's *real*, isn't it? Your first bra."

"Yeah, whatever. Where should I change?"

"Well . . . the dressing room, of course."

She looked back at him for a moment while he touched his limp hair then touched his mustache then put three fingers over his lips and dropped his eyes.

"Of course, silly me."

He dragged another stool over so he was sitting behind the camera. After her jeans and t-shirt were hung on the hook and her socks stuffed into her shoes (he said leave them under the stool, and let one sock come trailing out of the shoe a little), she glanced at the camera while putting on the flowered bra and underwear with her back to him, but of course she showed in the mirror, tits and trimmed bush. "Your first bra," he murmured, the camera clicking, zipping to the next frame and clicking again. "How does it feel?"

She turned to hide a laugh as a small burp. The bra actually fit her but the underwear was not bikini style. She could see in the mirror that the high-waisted underwear made her tits look even smaller, the bra like an elastic headband put around her chest.

"Oh god," he moaned, "god-in-heaven." The camera clicking and clicking. Her adrenal gland released, the chemical shot through, leaving behind a vibrating hot jello-y place in her middle. She turned slowly back and forth in front of the mirror, stretching to check her ass over each shoulder which also stretched the bra.

"*Oops!*" One tit popped out when the bra rode up. "Where's my personal shopper, I need to know if this one fits."

The guy was huddled on his stool, his face almost to his lap, no longer clicking, sort of whimpering.

"Come on, please, mister? It's my big day, help me pick one that fits."

He slid off the stool onto his knees and shuffled towards her. His head came up to her stomach. His eyes were murky and glistening, sweat on his upper lip had dampened the disgusting little mustache. He held her around her waist with one hand, pulling the flowered underwear tight against his chest, bending her knees slightly and throwing her off balance so she had to hold onto his shoulders and lean backwards slightly. With two fingers he eased the bra back over her exposed tit.

"There, it fits like that," he breathed.

"Are you sure?"

He moved his hands slowly up her body until he was holding her around the ribcage, a thumb on each nipple. He moved the thumbs back and forth, hardening the nipples under the stretchy purple-flowered material. His face tilted up. His two watery eyes right behind each thumb. "Yes, this is how it goes. Like this. Like this."

"I know sixteen is a little too late for my first bra, but my mother said I wasn't old enough," she said, making her voice airy and higher. The flowered underwear were wet between her legs. She tried to grind her twat against his chest a little but the zingers of adrenalin were zapping her almost continuously and she was in danger of falling over backwards.

"No," he whispered, "sixteen isn't too old. Not too old at all. You had to be ready. You knew when you were ready."

"I'm ready."

"Today you were ready. Today was the day. Oh, but if only your little titties wouldn't grow any more," he sobbed, "so impatient for this day, but now they'll be ruined." He slid his hands to her back and pulled her stomach against his face, blubbering against her skin below the bra.

"Hey, mister," she breathed softly. "Today's not over yet." She touched a bald spot on his crown with a single finger. "Remember, today's my big day. And there's still a half hour of it left."

He lurched to his feet with her in his arms. "Like a baby," he smiled through his tears down into her face. He bent and kissed her gently, touching her lips with the awful mustache, while carrying her out of the set and down a hall. The room they went into was dim, but after placing her on the bed, he turned on the night stand lamp and she could see the white lace canopy, the matching white lace lampshade and bedspread and curtains, antique-looking dolls in white or peach or baby-blue satin dresses lined up on a shelf, plus little troll dolls and glass princesses, horses and china puppies, a brush and comb set on the dresser, a life-sized white teddy bear sitting in a corner.

"This isn't *your* room is it?" Leala asked, propping herself up on her elbows. He was kneeling again, beside the bed.

"No . . . it's yours."

"Huh? *Oh* . . ..," she lay back slowly. "It's the room my mother doesn't know I left to go buy my first bra, right?"

"That's right." He took off his shirt. He was as skinny as Dale but not a single hair on him, except his armpits. "Just touch them against mine while they're still little, while it's still the big day." He got on top of her, still wearing baggy green army-surplus pants.

She couldn't feel any hard-on, but his hips were far below hers, on the mattress between her knees, so she wouldn't've anyway. He pressed his gaunt chest against hers, his head down against her neck, then without raising his body eased the bra up so her bare breasts were against his chest. He rocked slightly so their nipples brushed back and forth. And he started to tremble. She could feel his heart like a fist on a windowpane, banging to get out. His swaying continued for five or ten minutes.

Leala's adrenalin buzz was long gone. She checked her watch by raising one arm in the air behind his shoulders.

Then he was easing the bra back over her, with his chest still pressed to hers. "Okay," he whispered in her ear. "I didn't hurt you." He backed up off her and stood beside the bed. "I'll leave you in your pretty room, with your bears and dolls." He clicked off the light and retreated toward the door.

"Hey!" Leala sat up. "I *would* like a doll like one of them. Where could I get one?"

"A doll shop." He was a shadowy form by the door, putting his shirt on.

"How much would it cost for me to get one?"

"Some of them are as much as $200."

"I could just get a $50 one, though, couldn't I?"

He didn't answer, buttoning his shirt, then he looked up, but she couldn't really see his eyes. It was too dark.

"A girl should have a doll like that before she gets too old . . . don't you think?"

He slowly reached for the door knob. "Too old?"

"Yeah, like . . . before she's . . . say, *eighteen* . . . don't you think?"

He opened the door and a crack of light lay on the floor between him and the bed. "I . . . guess so." Then he went out and closed the door.

She lay back on the bed with a suddenly thudding pulse, but not the same thing as the earlier neon lightning bolt of adrenalin. The wave of almost nauseous weakness passed, and she thought about the symptoms Dale described, then she got off the bed. Her clothes were folded on the sofa in the living room with exactly $100 in cash placed on top, a fifty, two twenties, a five and five ones. Maybe he'd forgotten about the two fifties he'd already given her at the start of the session.

*   *   *

December was a slow time for both student photographers and sickos. Leala got her hair cut into a pixie style and used some of her savings for white jeans, a white jean jacket, and several new tank tops. She had her ears pierced and wore just the two pearl studs which came with the piercing. She let Dale pay for the piercing and call it her Christmas present, but he also bought her a corduroy skirt and jacket set that was one size too big, so she exchanged it for a denim mini and peasant-style top with sequins, both from the girls department. Dale said she looked like a baby pop star in *Teen Beat* magazine.

"That'll work," she answered. "Maybe I'll get some cheap jewelry from a teeny-bopper accessory store."

"Whadda you mean?"

"Oh . . . I don't know . . . If I want to start a real modeling career, I hafta have an angle, you know? My own shtick."

"You can't start a real modeling career just because you get a few new clothes and *say* you want to be a model."

"You don't know anything about it, Dale. I've had some gigs. How many gigs have *you* had lately?"

Dale stared fixedly at the TV screen. It wasn't even on. He still had hair down to his collar, except where he didn't have hair at all, and it looked wet even when it wasn't. The flattened cushions in the chair that had come with the furnished apartment had stains now where his head rested. Sometimes he still tapped a drumstick on the coffee table while he sat there. It seemed the drumstick appeared and disappeared by magic, but she'd found it once, by accident, stashed under the seat cushion.

Leala loaded some celery sticks with peanut butter, wrapped them in a paper towel and placed them on Dale's lap on her way to the sofa. "Listen, Dale, this is really important."

"What, that I'm a failure?"

"No, but *we* are. You know? It's only been, what, three and a half years. We could just call it one of those things. We're both young, we could . . . you know, still be like our ages."

"Instead of old married farts?"

"Speak for yourself, but I guess that's the general idea."

The drumstick appeared, but he didn't start tapping. He held it up and placed the tip against his lips like a long finger saying *Shhhh*. "No."

"No? That's it, just *no*?"

He took a bite of celery then replaced the tip of the drumstick against his mouth while he chewed. It sounded like a horse chewing corn. It sounded kind of nice.

"Dale, it wouldn't be like we hate each other's guts and go to court to fight over the car and stereo. And it doesn't have to be *now*, we could do it when we're both ready, when we can both afford it, you know?"

"We can barely afford this shit *together*."

"I know, but I'm working on a plan."

"You mean becoming a famous cover girl by next week?"

"There's lots of types of modelling, Dale, and I may've found my niche, and I can even capitalize on it, expand the potential."

"Now you sound like a yuppie businessman." He swallowed what looked like a hard lump.

"I'm just saying I've discovered a way to make what I do more lucrative, and when I make enough of a stash, how about I share it with you and we, you know, go our separate ways?"

"What if I want to stay with you?"

He was just sitting there looking down into his lap like an imbecile who watches himself pee, holding a celery stick with globs of peanut butter in one hand and the drumstick in the other.

Leala stayed on the sofa for only a few seconds longer, then went into the bathroom, shook her short hair and watched it all fall into place. For the first time in her life she was glad for the strip of freckles across her nose. She wondered how much colored contact lenses would cost, because some pure green eyes would really complete the package.

Three more jobs popped up right away in January. The first just wanted her feet – feet walking, feet splashing puddles, feet showing over the side of a pick-up truck, feet on gas pedals, feet kicking a ball, feet in high heels. He said he'd done sessions with guys and older people and little kids, and some animals. When he took her out for lunch after the session, she touched his leg with her bare toes under the table, but nothing happened, so the *Feet!* exhibit he said he was working on must've been real. The second wanted her to hang laundry on a line – just white sheets and towels – on a very windy day, wearing a light cotton dress and bare feet, but the photographer was a woman and, as a matter of fact, almost didn't want Leala at all when she saw her short hair. The third worked out a little better because he said from the start he wanted a nude, but he also made her sign a form promising she was over eighteen. Still, he liked her newly shaved pussy and fucked her afterwards, but only gave her $20 for cab fare when she asked, although she was parked around the corner from his house.

BOFF

David Meltzer

THE EBB OF end, his old tool vined with pumping veins, lets it
all go into her muscle milking clutching friction. She's elsewhere;
but so's he. Who knows? Lost in orgasm braille. Hot gripping
glistening pink passageway, tropic seashell sworl of fantasy. Maybe
it's raining. TV's hissing snow. Drawn paper windowshade, light
seeps through its gold. Her breathing flutters; sour wine smell;
saliva cellophane sparkles at the corners of her mouth. Big Ben
alarmclock clacks steady on the bedtable next to a thick glass
amber ashtray. Four o'clock in the afternoon. My back hurts
from our championship bout. Small clotted snores rattle out of
her slightly open mouth. Luke's tripod still at the foot of the bed
and the minicam bent down looking at the dust on the motel-room
floor. He's gone; took the tape to our processor who'll punch out a
bunch of them for our next ad in *Swing Shift*. We got a good thing
going with our amateur videos and next week Luke's bringing the
Duke of Prong, a black bi-she-he freelancer on the circuit, for our
first interracial gang bang and triple penetration shoot. ("Hi, I'm
Penny and this is Danny, my husband, who likes to watch and is
letting me fulfill my fantasy . . . etc.")
   She turns, one leg outstretched, pushes me further off the bed.
Dismissed; I've done what I could. Her less than firm boobs flop
like sacks on either side of her chest as the sheet slides down.
Her red-brown hysterectomy scar tips into view. I guess I'm okay

wanting to go into fucking in a dream-like state. We've been videoing our sex for so long that part of me is a camera. Fucking her or watching her go down on me, I pretend a crane-shot like a fly on the ceiling, zoom into key spots: close-up of her face filled with my meat or slow pan into her spread legs with my dong pushing into her. Am always thinking of production values, want the light even, not that jailbreak bright spotlight with everything else is shadows.

I mean, goddamnit, I'm a fucking connoisseur. Don't you get sick of those amateur tapes where all you see is some anonymous cock gobbled by some chick, pumping it with her hands, groaning in mock echo of pro triple-X soundtracks. What those soundtracks have done to amateur flick fucking is nobody's business. You hear these babes moaning, groaning, slurping their chops and in between mouthfuls of disinterested anonymous prick, "Uhhmm . . . oh yes . . . I want to suck you off and drink your cum and gobble it all down . . . uhm uhm . . . yum . . . mmmm . . ." I'm a fuckin' *auteur* for chrissake. It's not just to see hunks of meat flanks pounding up and down; it's not just blazing light in face of squinting clit-licking guy, mouth open and drawbridge tongue planking twitchily into her button. I'm interested in production values and we got an editing machine so I can get some kind of sense of rhythm, build up to those climaxes. I want my amateur videos to be the real thing not that fake bullshit of pumped-up demigod hunks and stiff silicone jugged bimbos. Bimbos from limbo, hunks from hell. No, I got a vision; I want the amateurs to be realer than real yet shot with the eye of an artiste. Let's face it, that's what I really am.

Everytime she sits down on the toilet to pee she farts a ripply toot. I'm weird about sounds. Maybe I got overactive hearing but I don't miss a thing. Sometime sound keeps me up at night. Every little creak and tick and thump and squeak. I can hear through rooms into rooms. Like fucking Superman I got x-ray ears. Walls, floorboards, ceiling, I can zoom into any sound, isolate it, live in it, get hung up about where a sound's coming from and scout it down. If I want to spook myself I can zero-in to my blood moving through my veins, heart pumping and recirculating it through the entire unit. I'll listen to my bones starting from the tip of my big toe and work up through the skeleton to discs and chunks holding my head up, eyes shut, listening to my body.

Don't you get tired of either dumb fixed camera-on-tripod shoots? Or the third-wheel with video-cam getting disco fever and moving all over the place as a couple hump and pork away? The fixated camera stays stuck in real-time work of mama bear giving papa bear big gut head. All you see is her face and hands and boobs working him over; he stands still, never moves and only talks off-camera when cum's coming down the hot chute for the money shot. She's sucking, licking, jerking it, twisting it, lapping the shaft up and down like a popsicle, chewing on the inanimate burning tip, for what seems an eternity, trying all she knows to get him to give up the gob of jism and either spray her face with it in some kind of fucking blessing or shoot it into her mouth, her lips, and her tongue keeps darting out to get a splat of it but always seems to miss. It's supposed to be a fucking pleasure not a goddamned job. Toil, labor, fuck no!

"Maybe you should recharge the battery; the red light's getting dim," she says, long upgush of plumbing sounds behind her as the toilet spirals its bounty down three stories of tired pipes in a tired old hotel. Fucking tired ass afternoon or morning or dawn, who the fuck knows anymore? It's the weekend hotel shoot. We both got day jobs; she's still checking and bagging for Safeway and me, the genius, works the food booth (popcorn, candybars, soft drinks) at the local Pussycat Theater. I mean I've been working my way down in this job for maybe fifteen years or more and she's been at her job maybe ten years or more. She looks cute in her uniform but she's getting on and getting thick around the middle like me and her tits are sagging but still real, a full handful but, fuck it, everybody's getting older. Time marches on. Marches all over us. And we got a good thing going with our tape business. Make a small profit and cut costs by Xeroxing flyers on the machine at work and I got a deal with a pro who duplicates our tapes at cut-rate for free copies and an occasional starring role. It's underground, under the table, you know what I mean, no year-end tax ream.

"You wanna do something else?" she asks, beginning to straighten out her side of the bed, smooth the wrinkles out of the sheet, fluff the pillow. "I might not be able to give you head. Got a cold-sore inside my lower slip." She pulls down her lower lip to show me.

"Shit, I can't see anything without my glasses. I believe you. How about some rear action. Got the K-Y?"

"Oh, honey, you know it's not a good idea. My hemorrhoids have been acting up. It's the weather."

"Yeah, but some customers get turned on by them."

"Not me and it hurts, for chrissake."

"Jiggle the frigging handle, the toilet's out a whack."

She goes back into the bathroom.

"Y'know, some guys get turned on by flappy pussy lips too. It's a weird fucking world out there. And then it isn't. Y'know what I mean?"

She doesn't understand my concept, my vision; sometimes I don't either, it's something I see in my weird mind's eye, a fuck flick like no other that gets inside, outside, around, and down with the action, that *is* the action, that's like fucking poetry in motion, that zooms, backs away, pans, cranes, cuts fast, plays with sounds, flicks of the unglam proles like me and the old lady, not those sleek tweaking semi-pros chewing horse cock boyfriend with expensive haircut and mustache looking dopely down at the bimbo. Not two dorks poling disinterested fucking gumchewing implanted bunny reject. Not murky bad lit static camera out of focus face fuck.

"Why don't we get dressed and go home? We've done okay this weekend," she says, getting her clothes out of the mothball closet with its three demented dented hangers. "Remember tomorrow I got to work Nelda's shift, her kid's birthday, so we gotta get up around seven. Are you listening?"

"Yeah, I hear you but you know I'm thinking, planning new movies."

"You should've been a goddamned artist, the way you see things. Next weekend, more chances."

"Yeah, next weekend. Maybe I'll borrow Chuck's minicam so we can have two of 'em set up at different angles. Shit, I wish I could lay hands on a tape editing machine. You know, that's the way to go, to get things rhythmic."

Pushing her boobs into my favorite black bra, she looks funny, something passes, I can see it in her eyes.

"What what?"

"Oh I don't know. The same. You know."

"Ah we'll live forever or at least to be real old fuckers."

"I just don't want to go before you."

"Nah, we'll go together at the same time like in a bucking movie."

"Oh you," she says, swiping at me with a black nylon stocking, "you and your movies."

ORF

David Meltzer

I

SET OUT TO FISH, to catch her from a stream and have her sing to me. And I'd return her to the water when her song was done. Pulled my red cart to the lake and unraveled my line, let it go into the water until it was gone. Sat down with the dragonflies and watched the sky move around me.

II

Ah shit. (He lights another cigarette. It's a habit. Lights a cigarette when working, puts it in the ashtray and starts battling with the words, then reaches for the cigarette and its paper is greasy from glass and tars and he lights another one.) Fuck. (The smoke tastes of metal and burnt peyotal twigs.) It has to happen, the words gotta be right. (Magical act of faith. It'll all work out. It has to. The golem had a magic talisman in his forehead. Talisman, memento of faith. No time to run out on faith. It'll come. The words will come right. They have to.) Piss. Fucking speed crashing in my head opening all the doors, the faces pop out, ghosts. – Wanna talk, tell me something, what's

happening? – the movies of each word on each screen for each
eye – fly eyes; a million eyes seeing a million movies – at once!
Fuck. Fucking Ortega sisters. Tough spick chicks. Shave their
legs every night. Sure, it's cool, take the bills, fifty bucks in
my pants pocket, shit, to get rid of them. How many times can
I get head from two chicks. Switch hitters. Wow, what a stench
of junkie perfume to hide the embalming fluid in their hearts.
The kind of spick chicks who carry knives in their beehives.
Zipguns in their cunts. Rita licks my balls and Norma runs her
tongue along my cock's seam and my cock's been hard since I
smelled their perfume and the speed freezes it hard and they're
working on me and me, I'm stretched out on the extra-large
Hollywood bed, arms behind my head, my head sinking into a
dozen foamrubber pillows. – Sing us a song, says Rita. – Haha,
I answer in my sensual revel. Norma's busy gobbling up my
cock. I look down at her and she looks up at me, still sucking
the swollen stem, and I start chortling lasciviously, nothing is
more, can be more, absurd than sex, the way we feel, the way
we look. – Say something, Norma, I say. – Hey, sing me a song.
And she gags on my meat in laughter. Rita tires of lapping my
balls, her tongue tasting every hairy swell of them, and moves
down to lick the space behind them, to work down further with
that rattling spick tongue of hers, yeh. Work out, baby. Muff,
muff, muff. (Dark girls. Trips the speed mind into a logical slide-
show, all logic a sliding thing. When I was a fucked-up grub of
a punk kid crawling to and fro, on no fucking merry way, just
a gray, tongue-tied, gloombag, I was walking home from high
school torture rites, and walked thru the so-called scummy section,
near the railroad tracks, all the buildings shacks, old tin rusty
signs like NEHI, LUCKY STRIKE, MISSION ORANGE, BLATZ, &tc.
&tc., and paper signs torn and like geology glued upon time after
time of more paper signs like FIGHTS, RONALD COLMAN EATS
CLOUDS, &tc., &tc. – I was walking the wrong way, the wrong way
home, and the train goes by, the pig train, the slop train, all dirty
gray, rusty brown, black, freight cars with strange stencils cut and
sprayed on their hides, and chalk doodles – try to decipher the bum
code which I read about once in some asshole simple magazine like
TRUE or REAL or MAN &tc., &tc. – the goddamned powerful
steel bulk of the engine and cars attached to it made the sidewalk I
was walking on tremble beneath my feet – like an earthquake; – so

I'm walking home from school in this forbidden set, like opening
the door to the bedroom when the oldfolks are finding a few tired
laughs fucking each other as quickly as possible, dreaming, I'm
sure, of moviestars and burlesque tit queens – walking with my
books and mottled notebook getting gooey in my sweating hands:
the doorways dark and sinister because gangsters, thugs and mad
rapists hang in dark doorways honing their knifeblades on the brick
walls, waiting – and I pass a sad, broken down, slat structured,
tarpaper roof, shack flat, with paper shades torn and wounded
hanging yellow and smudgy over dusty windows – and the glass
doorway is covered with a kind of rotten doily curtain – it is late
for me to be home, I was hung-up goofing in the candystore,
bullshitting about all the pussy I was getting – me, a kid of maybe
twelve, maybe thirteen, jerking off at girdle ads – walking home
and that glass door opens and two chicks squeeze thru it – I know
those chicks, I mean I've seen them in school; one of them's got tits
pushing out of her dayglo pink-red cashmere sweater and not only
has she got big tits, and I mean big, round, pyramids poking and
filling out that pink-red fuck dayglo cashmere sex sweater with a
black tight skirt so tight you see the halfmoon bowl of her belly
and her hipbones and legs pushing thru the black fabric – not only
big tits, but she's got a huge Punch & Judy nose whose shadow
divides her ripe fat full lips painted layer upon layer with some
bright red lipstick that means business; – she's standing there
with another chick, the other chick's got on a white blouse whose
buttons are open halfway down her neck to reveal the black rim of
her bra and her small flesh swell of titmeat heaving and undulating
– they wiggle their fingers at me, their fuck-cock fingers, and giggle, and wiggle their hips, and the big nosed one does a bump.
They shut the door and peek out thru the rotten doily door curtain
to see if I'm going to cross the street and go in; – the problem
being that the big-nosed one with those mysteriously huge tits has
got two brothers who everybody says are killers: silent, nonverbal
cats who don't do anything but kill – kill with their fat-knuckled
hands, strangle, punch to death, hack to death – or thumb-out
your eye or Eastern secret hand-defense you right in the central
heart-nerve button – or they use their hands to hold knives or guns
or, worse yet, tommygun, blamblamblamblam – vomit of bullet
explosion light in the darkness and all the bullets in a beautiful
dotted sequence to my guts. I see the two chicks go into their

bedroom and open the paper shade. The paper shade rattles up faster than I can twitch and I see them bouncing up and down on the bed. Crosses all around the room, the Virgin Mother, the blond long-haired Christ arising out of a thorn-banded liver-like heart – bouncing on the bed and hiking skirts up to their 1) lavender panties 2) black panties. Me without a fuck to my time, good at getting the fuckdumb freaks horny with my words, man, even then, with my words, my love's on my tongue – me, fuckdumb and horny, dream jerkoff novice, I think to myself as the dusk begins to darken the grimy street all the more – I think that it's time that I did something about it and maybe now is the time. And I walk across the street, and as soon as the chicks see my form move over the rutted cement, the windowshade is pulled down over the window and then they're peering thru the funky doily door curtain. The front porch is of rotten wood slats that my sneakers sink into like wet sand. Big nose opens the door, giggling and grabbing at my fly. – C'mon in, baby, she says, and breaks up in laughter along with the girl in the white blouse now open to her navel. They both laugh as I stand there. White blouse dances out the door and gets behind me and pushes me into the arms of big nose. The tit impact against my chest, how they seem to cave into a flesh custard, and her puffy cunt mound bounces into my crotch, and her breath is of onions and garlic and her nose looks like it's going to curve into her mouth like a pipestem. – C'mon, baby, there ain't much time. – What d'you mean? – Not much time before my brothers get back from work. Everybody knew they worked in the steel foundry. Some said they could toss molten steel up into the air with their bare hands. Molten steel lassoes in the dark tropic air of the plant. – Touch me, says big nose, you know where. Don't you want to? she asks moving in on me while white blouse pushes her small tits and cunt into my rump so that I lurch into big nose and drop my books. Big nose sticks the tip of her tongue out and lets it slide along the bright red painted ridges of her lips. – Touch me. Kiss me, she orders, and also, at the same time, she snickers when the white bloused chick begins to chortle. No more to the story, friends, because I heard heavy boot-scrapes on the porch steps and froze into an instant snowman – something out of a movie cartoon about a fucked-out, freaked-up, cat leaping off a canyon's edge and stopping halfway in the air to test the ground with a toe that touches sky – and he freezes there, like a photograph, before divebombing

into the faraway canyon floor – slide whistle sound – screen jars –
crash of Pandora's box being dumped down an elevator shaft.
No more to the memory other than me grabbing up my schoolbooks
and racing past the brother standing in the doorway with his
dullblack lunchpail held loosely in a catcher's mitt paw of a hand,
hairy and bloated with power. – What the fuck, he said – but I
kept my face away from his keen hawksharp eyes and raced down
the street nearly bumping into the other brother who was standing
at the corner talking with a buddy of his in a leather jacket flipping
a .22 caliber bullet into the air and catching it.) – Sing us a song. –
Muff, muff. Trying to pump out some of my come plume into her
hot mouth cave but it's like being constipated – the white cosmos
wants out, mad itching at the burning cocktip – sucked on like that,
I see it all flushed and raw-looking, shining with her spittle – but
Norma doesn't care, she can suck me off until eternity pushes our
bones away and sweeps us all out of the universe.

III

Shlink's at it again. A man like Shlink needs more than security to
make him sure of tomorrow. No matter how much money he has
in his pockets – no matter how much money he has in the banks
– he worries that it isn't enough, that it'll be taken away from
him. Somebody, some Them or They, will rob him of his fortunes
because of not paying for a TV set bought thru a mail-order house,
or for not paying for all those magazine subscriptions he's been
sending out for all these years. All of these petty concerns, these
surface irritants, ramble and scramble about in his head, in one
crummy furnished room of his mind.

They conceal the great fear shadows that blot out his thought.
Suddenly, in an instant, he's an old man trying to break down the
closet doors with his impotent fists. – Let me out, let me out, he
whispers, his voice lost, all words turn to powder. Maybe Shlink's
in jail where he was once before. In the Tombs on Riker's Island.
Because he was two months late on alimony payments. God spare
your heart no agony, Zelda Gerndel, no agony, you incredibly
asinine, lemon-cunted wretch of a bitch. In jail in the Tombs in the
cell where the stone walls were wet with East River water seeping
thru. Shut up. Incognito. Don't fuck around with love, the officer

says, laughing like he was choking on newspapers stuffed down his
throat. Don't fuck around with love. And Shlink, penniless Shlink,
shrunken Shlink, slinking thru his agonies, fist raised in messianic
wrath against all systems that jail a man. Law is revenge. It doesn't
protect me. I can't afford it. In the Tombs, his cellmates a trio of
tortured fools and lumpenlouts groaning in unison with Shlink. –
Innocent, we are

> innocent, we are innocent.
> Innocent of law, we stand in awe
> before shut rooms. Shut rooms
> mean shut doors. Open up.
> Feed us air and light. Set us loose.

The spade, a ten-time alimony loser, blabbing because he'd
gotten strung-out on a sleeper habit. Nobody knew the trouble
he knew. The other cat, an agonizingly dumb wop who had these
stubby hands that looked as if they'd work wonders grabbing and
digging up earth, kept muttering about how he didn't understand
what it all meant, they don't do things like this to a man in his
country, after he married some bullet proof harpy-whore trump
after his wop gold which turned out to be as phony as a plaid sunset,
and she, a hustler too dumb to get married because her fucking
prime time was done with, turns him in for passing counterfeit and,
the agonizingly dumb wop got the money from his not-so-dumb
Uncle in Italy to get to America. The Uncle, thoughtfully, laid
a English-Italian dictionary on him, a dictionary of less than a
hundred pages, bound in a plastic cover. The trollop jockstrap
girlscout got ahold of the wop thru the mail, some dream-fraud
lonely-hearts club. Spade babbling, wop groaning and slamming
his chest, and Shlink intoning the ancient chant of betrayal that
started long before Moses, even in Shlink's memory of it. They'll
never get me in jail again. He worries about money because he wants
to buy concepts and it takes a lot of money to do that. I want to buy
freedom, he tells himself, in a cab, cross-town, over the bridge, into
Brooklyn, a sister act, two chicks fresh out of parochial school, who
might just catch on. Anyway, a good second act for Moses. Already
he is promoting and building a huge network roadshow of singers,
bands and stars. Solomon Factor Shlink Present THE TOP TEN.
Very good. Thrilling concept. If the acts are right. Got to have

all the bands and singers in the top ten at that moment. Got to have enough money to buy that moment. Got to have enough money to break out of time's prison. Got to have enough money to buy time.

IV

The dream begins before dreams are known and mingle with the new thoughts and I, the child, a fisherman of small seas, saw her flanks of golden coins, and heard her pink voice sing of Atlantis, and saw into the mystery of her blue eyes.

V

Out of the window the skyline is a shadow form beneath the burning sunset sky. He keeps the window open to feel the cold air and hear the whip and whine of wind outside. On top of the city, the clouds pass thru my window everyday. It's coming, the song is almost done, and it's right that it should end just when night crawls over the city and drowns the streets in the new scene. Yellow light blinks on and off furiously on the controlboard. Hot line. Pushes a green button. – Yeah? – Hey, it's Raven. (The band's lead-guitarist.) – Yeah, yeah, what the fuck is it, man, I'm right in the middle of a song. – They took my amps away. – Who took your amps away? – The goddamned motherfucking music store thugs did. – Well, shit, why did that happen? You get paid every week. You should be able to make the monthly payments. (Even when Raven's pissed his voice is soft, one tone, the stone-tone.) – Man, you know how it is, I just forget that's all. What am I gonna do for the gig tonight? – Shit, you need a mamma, a lawyer, an accountant, and some goon to roll for you. Call Shlink. – He isn't at the office. – Why the fuck isn't he at the office? – How the hell should I know, man? (Raven is six-foot and weighs in at one hundred and fifty pounds, stands in a stork-like slump, his long straight hair down the chakras to his mid-spine, like some incredible concentration camp saint, his delicate white long thin fingers all over his Les Paul, gold-finish, Bigsby, ivory binding, mid-fifties' $500 guitar. The chicks think

he's so sinister that they're always trying to gangbang him and he
doesn't mind at all, and pass the joints and go mining the limits
of their collective/individual cervixes.) – He must've stepped out
for a sandwich. – No, man, no, says Raven, his soft monotone
rising up and sliding down his limited vocal hills, the graph of
his speech, no, I been trying for hours. Hours, man. – What
the fuck good is he? Fuck it. How much do you owe? – Two
hundred and forty-seven dollars and thirty-two cents. – Is that
for one month's rental? – No, it's for almost three months. –
Where the hell's your head? – Oh, man, you know how it is,
some things just don't manage to get into it, you know? – Have
them call me. (There's a bad pause between the flow of talk. He
can sense Raven's beautiful skull mask face move into a shaded
place.) – The store is closed. (As if he knew, before Raven said it,
and again to realize the enormity of circumstance's levels: they've
got to be at the hall at seven-thirty – it's nearly six now – and
spend a while with the band getting straight on the sound-level –
and Raven knows all this up front but, as usual, stones out time
– another revolutionary: – time isn't for me, man, I ain't buying
a clock for my soul &tc. &tc. – and Shlink not around at a time
of crisis – the precious mystic balance of preparation once more
tilted. He feels like a yogi in deep meditation being nudged and
pushed to move over, watch out for the steamroller coming down
your mountain slope to flatten it out, for the future, beautiful, new,
Now, Holy City being built for a spectacle movie called, as it were,
Holy City: – *Alternate take*: tightrope walker looking straight ahead
(classic warning: Don't look down, that's all right), straight ahead,
spotlight centered in your eyes; then to realize there's something in
your shoe and you want it out, a fucking pebble, maybe a mound
of sawdust . . . Circumstance, the foundation of his glory and the
band's glory, once again steps in to betray his art – for a moment,
the sunset, the wind, all of it lead his frenzy, his trance. Now
shattered.) – Goddamit to hell, Raven, don't you know anybody
that'll let you use their amp for tonight? I'll pay 'em for it, for
Chrissake. – Hey, that's a cool idea, man, yeah, yeah. I'll try some
of the cats in the Dark Forest. But, says Raven, pausing again,
the effort of organizing an extended plan proving too much for his
stone-age mind basin, but how are we gonna get the amps from
one place to another? – Call Ezra, for God's sweet asskissing sake!
– Right, right, sighs Raven. – Cool, says Raven, as an afterthought,

okay, all I gotta do now is make some phone calls. – Hey, Raven? –
Yeah? – Be there at seven-thirty. – What if something happens? –
Don't call me. Just be there. Call Ezra. Okay? – Yeah, yeah, sure,
too much. – Later. – Yeah.

And the show is over.

VI

Orf is Shlink's first client. The only one, so far, to make money,
to hit it big. Shlink suffers from the hunger that devours him,
feasts on his greed which in return eats on the hunger. Two acts
in one day!

Shlink is haunted by Brian Epstein. Haunted by Epstein's
incredible fame, haunted by his sad wasted death. Vows never
to drink and take pills. To keep straight. The kids can kill themselves. They're replaceable. Shlink to Shlink is beyond caricature
or duplication. An original like Epstein. Brian's timely death was a
cosmical transferring of karma to karma, mantle to mantle. (I wear
it proudly.) But still Shlink wears cheap suits. Klein's racks clothe
his lumpy frame. Wears cheap shirts, and Thom McAn shoes he
finds outside in the bargain bins. Shlink's hair defies time's bleach.
Every morning he applies shoepolish (two for 29c at Walgreen's:
Black Beam) to his white and gray greasy strands threaded thru
his thinning mane. Buys odd condiments at a spade voodoo shop
in Harlem which knows he's coming five blocks before he arrives.
The black tribal sucker drums boomalaying like a shower of silver
dollars on a tight drumhead. – Shlink's coming to fight time off.
One major clause of the Great American Dream (has there every
been a minor arcana to the American Dream?) is never to grow
up, never to grow, ugh, old. A critic in a book once called it the
Peter Pan Syndrome. Keep young. Young is where it's at. Shlink
opens the green door, heavily painted with a ridgy thick glossy
Kelly green. Hoodoo, voodoo bells attached to the door ring and
chime a fast black mass tone-row. – Mr Shlink, says Immanuel
Confucius Malta Samedi/Erzulie Sloane. (Confidants, cronies, call
him Sloane.) Mr Shlink, how good, sir, to see you again, sir,
dragging out "sir" in a parody of Robert E. Lee handing his
well-polished Excalibur to General Ulysses S. Grant. – What can
I, sir, do for you, sir?

Incense and sachets stationed in every shadowy nook and shelf. Powerful stench. It's a small shop. Some shelves on a wall, then the counter: a wood frame, glass paneled counter covers the width of the shop, except for a narrow passage for Sloane to move thru. A beaded curtain behind the counter leads into Sloane's living-quarters. Above the beaded curtain in bloodred scrawl on goathide parchment: a rune.

Shaded by a metal disc is a green lightbulb which makes a murky blotch upon the powders, fluids, twigs, stems, bark, threads, parts, fragments, seeds, &tc. contained in hundreds of small chamois sacks, woven medicine bags, &tc. Sloane's backroom: a pale and transformed shadowplay because of the red lightbulb lighting its interior.

–What can I do for you? Sir.

–The same. The hair. The cock. The usual. Good Fortune . . .

–Wait, sir, wait. The same is 23. Hair is 40. Sexual apparatus . . . sir, what did you have in mind?

On the wall is a splayed and dried salt-white sea-creature turned into a bat shape. Sloane, or his master, has decorated the sinister white shape with black and red X's.

On the floor are rugs and underneath the rugs are crunchy objects which Shlink, when he shifts about on his Thom McAn's, mangles and snaps and cracks.

–I want to . . . it's hard to say, mumbles Shlink.

–What, sir? Is it about Power, Success, Fame?

Shlink nods.

–Perhaps a woven basket for your member. The hemp used to weave the sheath is made of a sacred grass found only on one side of one slope of one almost unobtainable mountain in, sir, Tibet. Tibet.

Sloane catches the flare that blasts off bright in Shlink's mouse-like round dark eyes. Tibet.

–Sir, you know, of course, the powerful magic in Tibet . . .

–Yes, yes, mumbles Shlink, but will it fit?

–Guaranteed, sir, says Sloane.

–How much? asks Shlink, embarrassed at the edge in his voice when money is articulated.

–I'll put it on your bill, sir. Now, let me touch your scalp, sir.

And Sloane puts on a leather glove like a home-made baseball mitt and plops it on Shlink's head. Grease from Shlink's lubricated locks

has formed, forever thru the ceremonial repetition of this occasion,
a forever-damp stain in the leather.

   –Mm. You're popping off, sir.

   –You mean, more hair is going?

   –Yes, sir, the hair is going. Have you been usin' Mother Charm's
elephant-fat salve and tiger balm regular?

   –I'm a busy man, whines Shlink.

   –Do you massage the front hair-guards regular?

   –When I can.

   –Regular, sir?

Shlink sighs that repentant, humble gush of chastised lung
fumes. The very heart that holds him together becomes a coddled
fragile anagram.

   –No, I haven't had time . . .

   –What you need, sir, if I may advise you, is the special Astral
Multiple Fix-All . . .

   –Yes, yes, you're right . . .

   –One pill to take care of all your physical problems . . .

   –Of course, right, automation . . .

   –But, sir, the price is beyond belief.

   –I'll believe it. I'll pay . . .

Somewhere in that small closet of a shop, a crisp gong is bonged.
Its brass echo shimmers and reverberates thru the room. Some
items tip and tumble off the shelf.

   Drums begin to mesmerize their drummer somewhere. A regular
rolling Monogram Lost In Africa soundtrack. Bead curtains rattle
with the vibrations. Hand drums. Shlink imagines a giant spade
congo drummer, shirtless, charcoal black, sweating, hills of muscles
rippling, pounding out the instant truth to all the other tribes who
pause, spears before them, to listen, to break the code down.

   –Astral Multiple Fix-All is so precious that it demands sacrifice
in order to obtain it.

   (Re-cap for motivational clarity. Shlink, the grub, hoards Shlink,
the divine. It is thru grubbing we affirm our sacred nature.
Sometimes. Now Sloane, a fast-thinking, slow-walking, ghetto
eccentric, is democratic towards whomever he filches loot from.
– Asshole simple, he says to the boys, – get what you can from them
that's got and who want to give it to you. Well, the cronies goggle
on this, slapping cards around, passing about a half-pint of off-label
whisky, and regard Sloane as half-devil, half-man, but, most of

all, they regard Sloane as a cool operator, which is what Sloane considers his scam to be. Nothing to it. Just thirty-nine years of eating shit in order to convert it back into a new paste to further clog the wanting hearts of stooges requiring home-brewed flimflam.

Shlink wants desperately to survive. Half-assed tries to do the latest exercises every morning. Gotta keep the body alive. Breaks his flabby form's tender muscle-spread to do those push-ups which, after two of them, he foregoes in order to serve the more sensible needs of his stomach. An English muffin, lots of margarine, spoons of orange marmalade, a cup of coffee, lots of cream, sugar, sunnyside-up eggs, hash-browns, served up, for the last year, at the Riker's around the corner from his furnished room. – After fueling the gut, Shlink tells himself he'll exercise but, after the load in the tubes, he slows down for a mid-morning snooze. Visions of Atlas flex in his groggy skull. To fight time, to buy power, to endure, one has to consider many things. Sloane knows a patsy when a patsy breathes mortality-fear all over his glass-covered counter. Shlink can't face the occult with the same buzz-saw edge he faces promoters and bankers with. His life is at stake. Gotta keep going. Visions of a Yankee Stadium sell-out Top Ten Concert. The whole world calling him day and night begging for his advice, his artists.)

–I'll pay. Anything, moans Shlink as if in the zenith of a rare orgasm, submerged in a dim erotic slow-motion water world. – Anything.

Sloane smiles. Steps on the floor-buzzer. The gong goes off. The drums stop. The voice of a woman comes moaning and mumbling thru a hidden speaker.

RAP: 1

– I don't suppose I think much about the future; I don't really give a damn.

The only thing I'm afraid of is growing old. I hate that. They get old and they've missed it somehow.

John Lennon

WAK! TOTAL INFORMATION! THE ULTIMATE STANDARD OF TOTAL AMERICAN RADIO NEWS! W! A! K! THE HAPPENING NOW POP ROCK AND POP NEWS STATION!

booms forth. Transistor god. The godhead in the ear plugged

in that way. Echo-chamber basso-profundo resonance of the news-caster, his voice surrounded by Morse Code and teletype locust chatter.

–19-year-old Mervin Winter partner in the Greenleaf High School Marijuana Ring was found hiding out in the Greenleaf Hills with one and a half pounds of Marijuana and a few ciggies which were immediately confiscated by the arresting officers.

EVERYTHING YOU DO FEELS BETTER IF YOU'RE ON TOP! COKE GIVES YOU A LIFT!

THINGS GO BETTER WITH COKE! COKE! THE WAY TO GO!!

–Make it to the 10th Annual Teen-Age World's Fair: Karate exhibitions, stock-car races, band contests, dance contests, fashion shows, and more, MORE, MORE!!

–Ruby Small killed her husband by sawing off his legs to fit into the small cedar trunk in their bedroom. Mother of three, she said she killed her husband because he made her dance in the nude and consume benzedrine tablets.

–Hey. Y'wanna avoid the Draft?

–Yeah.

–Join the Army.

GO STEADY WITH A CLEAR SKIN! POLISH OFF BLEMISHES, CLEAN OUT PORES.

DEFEND YOURSELF WITH KETSUGO!

KETSUGO GIVES YOU ALL THE COMBINED ARTS OF SELF-DEFENSE FOUND IN JUDO, ATE-WAZA, AKIDO, YAWARA, SAVATE, KARATE AND JIU JITSU.

–500,000 more troops sent to West Thailand's Buddhist-infested mountain village of Hip Yang . . . Kills his nine children, his wife, then kills himself . . . Those on the ground watched in horror as his chute failed to open and he rocketed to earth at the Sky Diving demonstration given earlier this afternoon . . .

HEAR WIDESPREAD SECRET CONVERSATIONS THRU SOLID WALLS! 500 SHOT AUTOMATIC SLING-SHOT!

DEVICE PICKS UP 2-WAY CONVERSATION WITHOUT CON-NECTING TO THE PHONE!

"Out of about two-thirds of a million people in both cities, over a quarter of a million died as an immediate result of the bombings:

Daytime	Population	Deaths
Hiroshima, 1945	400,000	200,000
Nagasaki, 1945	270,000	122,000

The injured will continue to suffer and die in the indefinite future."

VII   The Setting-up, the Rehearsal

Raven's late, but he's got an amplifier. It's carried onto the stage by a kid with lemon-custard skin blotted with pimple clusters that look like so many squashed nits. – Hey, says Raven, let the kid stay. He's Arnold's brother and he's letting me use the amp for a freebie to the gig tonight. I sort of told him it would be cool. – Sure, sure, just get set up. – Yeah. Right. Say? – Yeah? – We don't have to lay out any bread for it. – Right. Set up, all right? – Man, it was a scene getting that motherfucking amp into the cab, man. You know how tight ass cabbies are when you bring anything into their cabs. Wheeww.

Raven's long hair and clothes smell of potsmoke.

Ezra's set up the other equipment. Their amps are six: bass-amp, lead-guitar amp, rhythm guitar amp, drum mike fed thru separate amp, two microphones going into two speaker columns run by Ezra at the board, balancing the sound of voice against the electronic band-roar, and his own amplifier.

Tim is the drummer and he is the first to arrive. He carries an old cloth satchel stuffed with sticks, mallets, brushes, screws, screwkeys, hardware for the drum that clanks when he sets the bag down by his stool. Tim uses two bass drums, two snares, four tom-toms, and six cymbals including the hi-hat. He sits on his stool before the drum set and begins to tap the top drumheads with his fingertips, adjusting the heads' tension with a small chrome key – the tone, the tone, thinks Tim, a dream of arranged tones, a drumset set upon a Cinema Scope stage, and each drum tuned to a special tone, and chimes, and rows of wooden blocks with individual tones, and maybe a card table lined with glasses filled with water up to varied levels to strike each rim, like the beggar in front of the Newsreel movie on Friday night (hits the glasses with the vibrato of a mandolin player); – Tim sees himself in a motorized drumstool, able to jet from drum to block to glass to gong – freaks his head to think of using on a stage-high gong the tip of a phoenix feather, then pick up a special Louisville Slugger Supen Drummer batdrumstick and bop the huge stage-high gong in its black center – Tim turns twenty next week and time, except keeping it, eludes his conceptual considerations: In High School he was called Mr Drums – in class, takataktak-ta-tak-a-ta on the desk or finger drumming on different books, like, History of America's Beautiful & Ultimate Arc Into Heaven, had a good hollow thud sound to the fingertips – then Tim would switch to Algebra I, a blue, dark blue, buckram covered tome with silver stamping on the spine, and the math book gave off a nice contained ringing brittleness which sounded cool in contrast to the history book – & so on, on, and on – all the teachers, one time or another, responded outrageously to the fingerdrumming Chinese torture – Mr Drums in the High School Marching Band, on parade, the bright aluminum helmets of the ROTC blinding him, the heads in the band having a tough time keeping on their feet – the hip bandsmen got stoned in the basketball court before going to the Band Room – like Indians who chew odd roots, Tim smokes odd herbs in order to endure the physical demands of his work and to transcend them whenever possible and, also, to be high was to be holy, or, at least, closer to the rhythm God keeps;

  checks-out his bass-drum footpedals – boom boom boom boom – thinks of maybe having a rack built to attach, say, four pedals to a single pole and control each pedal's release by tapping the toe on a fast-action lever that'd trip each pedal into slamming hide; – incredible bass drum runs and riffs while Tim is busy pulling out all the tones possible on the upper drumset; – maybe an electric foot-pedal to trip the pedals, set to, say – yeah, this is it! – say it's an all electronic, computer-set, connected to a weird metronome whose slot is fed interchangeable printed circuits – and all of it's controlled by pressing a button on the floor – boom boom boom boom;

  begins a nervous series of drumrolls, thumps, tattoos, rattles, throbs, attacks. Tim keeps warming-up until he's called to stop and rehearse the new song.

Second on the scene is Cal, the rhythm guitarist. Cal's a small fellow with a full-beard. He is very neat. Bathes twices a day. Always smells of soap and bath-lotion, shaving lotion and deodorant. The other guys in the band stopped kidding him about being Mr Clean after Cal got uptight, did a lot of jaw-clenching, and turned a bit pale around his lips which were sealed on a secret dream of, perhaps, clean white towers and pure air – who knows?

Cal opens his immaculate hardshell guitar case, as new and unscuffed as the day he bought it. Unwrapping the cloth around the guitar's neck, then unravels the cloth around the guitar's body. Cal's guitar is a custom-neck Gibson Super 400 CES. – Sure, man, I sent it to the Factory to have them remake the neck for me – and this impressed Raven no end because Raven had never thought of such extravagant connections. Cal wipes the neck off with a special cloth inside the small box in his case.

With his coil chord plugged into the guitar and into his amplifier, Cal begins to strum a fast sequence of chords, and repeats them over and over while the amplifier warms-up and, suddenly, the sound of Cal's guitar and the chord-pattern come crashing ahead. Tim keeps drumming an assortment of time counts, rhythm fucking, work-out nervous diddles and dawdles.

Lost in the sound of his sound. Cal plays a mellow guitar, that's why Raven insists on having him back him up. Raven plays wild demon guitar and Cal is always behind him with mellow, fat-toned chords and a solid rhythm sense.

Teddy Roy Burk, the bassist, comes in while Cal and Tim are busy in their trances of sound. Teddy Roy's from Texas and is almost as tall as Raven, almost as thin. But Teddy Roy looks short because of the way he slumps around, bent over like an old monk. Teddy Roy slams his case on top of his amp and pulls out his funky-finished Fender Precision bass. – Aww, fuck, he grumbles. – Fuck, fuck, shit, he grumbles again.

I'm the all-time, all-out, clap-trapper. (It's the fifteenth time in three months that he's had to get massive shots to fight off venereal disease.) What do you all want to know about puspissing clap? Huh? I'm an authority on the matter. What d'you want to know: Gonorrhea. Gonococcus. I mean I memorized the fucking medical dictionary. Which motherfucking teeny weeny tight cunt gave it to me again? They're all so wild looking. Knees stamped with moonfaces, minis nudging no-panty covered crotch/cunt/fuckholes, smelling sweet, clean as a laundered sheet – all of 'em, incredible to look at and just right, if you know what I mean – they come

crawling to me off stage, trying to ooze under doorways, moaning
– O Teddy Roy, fuck me, fuck me. – Now, hell, what do you do
when there's maybe half a dozen of these rainbow teenys – and
some of 'em ain't too tiny no more neither – knocking on your
door, a sweet holy chorale of them – Fuck me, fuck me – like this
one chick, after all the makeup was scrubbed off in order to put
new makeup on, says to me that it's how I hold my goddamned
bass that drives her onto the walls, it's so, it's so – cocky, she
squeals, and her face is a young girl's face, nowhere near a lady –
but, oh man, her tight cunt squeezed every drop of baby-juice out
of me; – Fuck! if it's her – Shit – It's always "her," and ain't that
true? – always the sweet, sister-type with tiny tits and a burning
box and all you think of is, My God, am I tearing her apart, and
she's groaning and moaning and all you see beneath her fluttering
eyelids is a mysterious white flash.

The Doctor, a dude with hair slapped thin on his shiny dome,
parted in the middle, his breath smells of old food stuck in his
teeth, tells me that if I have anymore fucking penicillin shots that
they won't stick. I'll get immune to the drug. – Well, fuck, Doc,
I say, what the fuck am I gonna do?

The Doc smiles, man – he's got a lot of gold in his mouth! – the
Doc smiles and tells me to quit messing around with dirty chicks.
And I ask him, – Shit, Doc, they all look clean to me. How can
you check?

It seems incredible to ask a chick the instant before you're ready
to slam your rod into her crack whether or not she's gonna give you
the clap? How do you do it? There you are, rockin' and a rollin' (like
the song says, man), out of the breathless mumble and movement,
my drone comes forth: – Say, baby, you got the clap? Now, what
chick is gonna take that lightly? spread out like a poem, nipples
twitting, belly moving in lust, juices steaming out of her cunt.

–Doc, you don't know what you're saying.

He jams the needle into my tracked ass.

–You're lucky we don't stick into your cock's eye, he says,
chuckling, pulling out the needle rather abruptly. – We used to.
Boy, let me tell you about World War Two. – Huh? – Man, don't
you remember World War Two? Hitler, Tojo? – My father does.
That's all he talks about. Dumb cow. All the time, goin' to them
mind-screaming war movies, where everybody dies well and kills
real fine, ten to a bullet, and my old man is there in the fucking

movie, the only fucking movie in Pearl, Texas, sweating in the air-conditioned closet, getting his fucking rocks off watching some moronic muscle-brained flab-gut like John Wayne come charging a fucking fox-hole, dumping tons of grenades into it, and man, what a band, playing big brass march bullshit music – KAP – LAMM! POW! SMASH! – and my old man, for Christ's sake, in the movie-house with a fucking Smith & Wesson .32 Police Special in a hip holster. If it ain't war movies, it's cowboy movies that really blow his brain, and get him to rubbing and touching the handle of his S&W while a shit-chip head like Charlton Heston spurs down the dusty street of Doom, Texas looking for some cool moron like oh Jack Palance or, maybe, another real mean looking zombie in black – and my old man sits there, grabbing onto his gun, drooling and grunting in the afternoon, while kids cutting school are fingerfucking in the balcony and copping tit-grabs in the loges – and my old man's drinking beer and grunting, – Get 'em, Sheriff, get him – and the kids are all wondering what the fuck kind of dumb pig noise that is – and my old man doesn't care – shit, he's Charlton Heston, Duke Wayne, all of 'em, walking down that level escalator, endless street of Showdown, USA – Blam! blam! blam! And after the show is over, after he sees it maybe three times, he goes over to T.J. Flight's pad and they target practice for hours, drinking beer, telling dirty stories, getting raunchy with T.J.'s wife whose got new muscles in her legs from spreading them so much.

Then T.J. and the old man start rapping until dawn about the war and war movies until, I'm sure, there's no difference and old T.J.'s wife is back upstairs in the bedroom, where she belongs, spreading and sighing as, maybe, Clint Harper, a local pinball champ, is fucking her silly.

Gets his bass on, plugs it in, starts a few thumping runs, trying to, somehow, relate his instrument to the other guys busy in their peculiar warm-up musical spasms.

So cocky, right, thinks Teddy Roy, who has two habits hard to break. One is passive and has to do with his awe of his T-for-Texas cock which erupts from his flesh like a bull's horn and seems, when fully hard, too huge for his frame. He rightly feels that his muscular member is a cause for celebration and demands all chicks to spend a great deal of time praising it with their mouths and dictionaries. His other, more active habit, is a proud record of having a chick every night of the year, not mattering what kind of circumstances, trances, fevers, &tc, he finds himself in. Some of the most painful ejaculations known to man have been endured by Teddy Roy Burk in order to maintain his record.

Raven yanks out his old Les Paul, gold finish, ivory binding, Bigsby, &tc, and plugs it into the borrowed Fender Twin-Reverb. Pot-cake invades his head. Too much. Outa sight.

Volume's up full notch on the Twin-Reverb and he balances the volume dials on his guitar. Flips the pickup-switch, checks out volume intensity on both settings. Guitar set, amp ready, Raven plays a wild hair-raising run, pushes the guitar's face into the Twin-Reverb. Feed-back overtones rumble the stage beneath his feet. Too much. The pot-cake is a cloud slowly covering his brain's continent. All its hills and centers are shadowed in the cloud's passing.

–Hey, man, let's try this, he says, and slams out the chord-riff intro for *Mighty Mountain Blues*.

The band pulls into it immediately.

ALMOST TRANSPARENT BLUE

Ryu Murakami

Translated by Nancy Andrew

IN THE MIDDLE of Oscar's room, nearly a fistful of hashish smoldered in an incense burner, and like it or not, the spreading smoke entered one's chest with every breath. In less than thirty seconds I was completely stoned. I felt as if my insides were oozing out through every pore, and other people's sweat and breath were flowing in.

Especially the lower half of my body felt heavy and sore, as if sunk into thick mud, and my mouth itched to hold somebody's prick and drain it. While we ate the fruit piled on plates and drank wine, the whole room was raped by heat. I wanted my skin peeled off. I wanted to take in the greased, shiny bodies of the black men and rock them inside of me. Cherry cheesecake, grapes in black hands, steaming boiled crab legs breaking with a snap, clear sweet pale purple American wine, pickles like dead men's wart-covered fingers, bacon sandwiches like the mouths of women, salad dripping pink mayonnaise.

Bob's huge cock was stuffed all the way into Kei's mouth.

Ah'm jes' gonna see who's got the biggest. She crawled around on the rug like a dog and did the same for everyone.

Discovering that the largest belonged to a half-Japanese named
Saburō, she took a cosmos flower from an empty vermouth bottle
and stuck it in as a trophy.

Hey, Ryū, his is twice the size of the one ya got.

Saburō raised his head and let out an Indian yell, then Kei seized
the cosmos flower between her teeth and pulled it out, jumped on
the table, and shook her hips, like a Spanish dancer. Flashing blue
strobe lights circled the ceiling. The music was a luxuriant samba
by Luiz Bon Fa. Kei shook her body violently, hot after seeing the
wetness on the flower.

Somebody do it to me, do it to me quick, Kei yelled in English,
and I don't know how many black arms reached out to throw her
on the sofa and tear off her slip, the little pieces of black translucent
cloth fluttering to the floor. Hey, just like butterflies, said Reiko,
taking a piece of the cloth and spreading butter on Durham's
prick. After Bob yelled and thrust his hand into Kei's crotch, the
room filled with shrieks and shrill laughter.

Looking around the room, watching the twisting bodies of the
three Japanese girls, I drank peppermint wine and munched
crackers spread with honey.

The penises of the black men were so long they looked slender.
Even fully erect, Durham's bent fairly far as Reiko twisted it. His
legs trembled and he shot off suddenly, and everyone laughed at
the sight of his come wetting the middle of Reiko's face. Reiko
laughed too and blinked, but as she looked around for some
tissue paper to wipe her face, Saburō easily picked her up. He
pulled her legs open, just as if he were helping a little girl to piss,
and lifted her onto his belly. His huge left hand gripping her head
and his right pinning her ankles together, he held her so that all
her weight hung on his cock. Reiko yelled, That hurts, and struck
out with her hands, trying to pull away, but she couldn't grab on
to anything.

Her face was getting pale.

Saburō, moving and spreading his legs to get more friction on
his cock, leaned back against the sofa until he was lying almost
flat and began to rotate Reiko's body, using her butt as a pivot.

On the first turn her entire body convulsed and she panicked.
Her eyes bulging and her hands over her ears, she began to shriek
like the heroine of a horror movie.

Saburō's laugh was like an African war cry, as Reiko twisted her face and clawed at her chest. Squeal some more, he said in Japanese, and began to turn her body faster. Oscar, who'd been sucking Moko's tits, Durham, who'd placed a cold towel on his wilted prick, Jackson, who wasn't naked yet, Bob on top of Kei – all gazed at the revolving Reiko. God! Outasight! said Bob and Durham, and went over to help turn her around. Bob took her feet and Durham her head; both pressing hard on her butt, they began to spin her faster. Laughing, showing his white teeth, Saburō then put both hands behind his head and arched his body to drive his cock in even deeper. Reiko suddenly burst into loud sobs. She bit her own fingers and tore at her hair, because of the spinning her tears flew outward without reaching her cheeks. We laughed harder than ever. Kei waved a piece of bacon and drank wine, Moko buried her red fingernails in the huge butt of wiry-haired Oscar. Reiko's toes were stretched back and quivering. Her cunt, rubbed hard, gaped red and shone with mucus. Saburō took deep breaths and slowed down the spinning, moving her in time with Luiz Bon Fa's singing of "Black Orpheus". I turned down the volume and sang along. Laughing all the time, Kei licked my toes while lying on her stomach on the rug. Reiko kept on crying, Durham's semen dried on her face. With bloody tooth marks on his fingers, sometimes growling like a lion from the pit of his stomach – Oh-h, I'm gonna bust, get this cunt off me, Saburō said in Japanese and thrust Reiko aside. Get away from me, pig! he yelled. Reiko grabbed at his legs as she fell forward; his come shot straight up and splattered and sprayed on her back and buttocks. Reiko's belly quivered and some urine leaked out. Kei – she'd been smearing her own tits with honey – hurriedly slid some newspaper under Reiko.

That's jes' awful, she said, slapped Reiko's butt and laughed shrilly. Moving about the room, twisting our bodies, we took into ourselves the tongues and fingers and pricks of whoever we wanted.

I wonder where I am, I kept thinking. I put some of the grapes scattered on the table in my mouth. As I skinned them with my tongue and spat the seeds into a plate, my hand felt a cunt; when I looked up, Kei was standing there with her legs apart, grinning at me. Jackson stood up dazedly and stripped off his uniform. Grinding out the slim menthol cigarette he'd been smoking, he turned toward Moko, who was rocking away on top of Oscar.

Dribbling a sweet-smelling fluid from a little brown bottle on Moko's butt, Jackson called, Hey, Ryū, bring me that white tube in my shirt pocket, OK? Her hands held tightly by Oscar, her bottom smeared with the cream, Moko let out a shriek: That's co-old! Jackson grasped and raised her buttocks, got his cock – also thickly coated with the cream – into position and began thrusting. Moko hunched over and screeched.

Kei looked up and came over, saying, That looks kind of fun.

Moko was crying. Kei grabbed her hair and peered into her face. Ah'll put some nice mentholatum on ya afterwards, Moko. Kei tongue-kissed with Oscar and laughed loudly again. With a pocket camera, I took a close-up of Moko's distorted face. Her nose was twitching like a long-distance runner making a last spurt. Reiko finally opened her eyes. Perhaps realizing that she was all sticky, she started for the shower. Her mouth was open, her eyes vacant, she tripped again and again and fell. When I put my hands on her shoulders to lift her up, she brought her face close to mine. Oh, Ryū, save me, she said. An old smell came from her body. I dashed to the toilet and threw up. As Reiko sat on the tiles getting drenched by the shower, I couldn't tell which way her reddened eyes were looking.

Reiko, ya big dummy, ya'll jes' drown. Kei shut off the shower, thrust her hand in Reiko's crotch, then squealed with laughter to see Reiko jump up in panic. Oh, it's Kei. Reiko hugged her and kissed her on the lips. Kei beckoned to me as I sat on the toilet. Hey Ryū, that cold feels good, right? Since I was cold outside, I felt hotter inside. Hey, ya got a cute one. She took it in her mouth as Reiko pulled back my wet hair, sought out my tongue like a baby seeking the breast, and sucked hard. Kei braced her hands against the wall and thrust out her butt, then buried me in her hole, washed free of mucus by the shower and dried. Bob, his hands dripping sweat, came into the shower. There're not enough chicks, Ryū, you bastard, taking two of them.

Swatting my cheek, he roughly dragged us, dripping, just as we were, into the next room and threw us on the floor. My prick, still tight inside Kei, twisted as we fell. I groaned. Reiko was tossed like a rugby pass up on the bed and Bob leaped on top of her. She struggled, raving, but she was pinned down by Saburō and a chunk of cheesecake was crammed into her mouth, choking her. The record music changed to Osibisa. Moko wiped her butt, her face twitching. There were traces of blood on the paper. She showed them to Jackson and muttered, That's awful. Hey Reiko, that cheesecake's good, huh? Kei asked, lying on her stomach on the table. Reiko answered, Something's thrashing around in my stomach, like I'd swallowed a live fish or something. I got up on the bed to take her picture, but Bob bared his teeth and pushed me off. Rolling to the floor I bumped into Moko. Ryū, I hate that guy, I've had it, he's a fag, right? Moko was on top of Oscar, who rocked her while he gnawed a piece of chicken. She started to cry.

Moko, you're OK? It doesn't hurt? I asked. Oh, I don't know anymore, Ryū, I just don't know.

She was rocked in time with the Osibisa record. Kei sat on Jackson's knee, sipping wine, talking about something. After rubbing her body with a piece of bacon, Jackson sprinkled on vanilla extract. A hoarse voice yelled Oh baby. A lot of stuff had ended up on the red rug. Underwear and cigarette ashes, scraps of bread and lettuce and tomato, different kinds of hair, blood-smeared paper, tumblers and bottles, grape skins, matches, dusty cherries – Moko staggered to her feet. Her hand on her ass, she said, I'm famished, and walked to the table. Jackson leaned over to apply a band-aid and a kiss.

Pressing her chin on the table, breathing hard, Moko attacked a crab like a starving child. Then one of the blacks stuck his shaft in front of her, and she took that in her mouth too. Stroking it with her tongue, she pushed it aside and turned again to the crab. The red shell crunched between her teeth, she pulled out the white meat with her hands. Piling it with pink mayonnaise from a plate, she put it on her tongue, the mayonnaise dribbling onto her chest. The odor of crab flowed through the room. On the bed, Reiko was still howling. Durham pushed up into Moko from behind. Her butt jiggled, she held onto the crab, her face twisted, she tried to drink some wine but with the rocking of her body it went into her nose and she choked, tears in her eyes. Seeing that, Kei laughed loudly. James Brown began to sing. Reiko crawled to the table, drained a glass of peppermint wine and said loudly, That tastes good.

"Haven't I told you over and over not to get in too deep with that Jackson, the MP's are watching him, he's going to get caught one of these days," Lilly said as she snapped off the TV picture of a young man singing.

Oscar had said, OK, let's finish up, and opened the veranda doors. A piercing cold wind blew in, a fresh wind, which I could still feel.

But while everyone was still lying around naked, Bob's woman Tami had come in and gotten into a bad fight with Kei, who'd tried to stop her from hitting Bob. Tami's brother was a big gangster, and since she'd wanted to run and tell him, there was nothing I could do but bring her along here to Lilly's place. I'd heard Lilly was a friend of hers, she'd talk her around. Until just a few minutes ago, Tami had been sitting over there on the sofa, howling, I'll kill them! Her side had been raked by Kei's nails.

"So don't I always say you better not bring in punks who don't know anything about this Yokota territory? What would you have done without me, huh? You wouldn't have got off easy, Ryū, Tami's brother is real bad."

She drank a swallow from a glass of Coca-cola with a lemon slice floating in it, then passed it over to me. She brushed her hair and changed into a black negligée. Still seeming angry, she brushed her teeth and shot up on Philopon in the kitchen with the toothbrush still in her mouth.

"Aw, come off it, Lilly, I'm sorry."

"Oh, all right, I know you'll just go and do the same thing tomorrow . . . But listen, you know, the waiter at my place, a guy from Yokosuka, is asking if I want to buy some mesc. How about it, Ryū? You want to try it, don't you?"

"How much is it, for one tab?"

"I don't know, he just said five dollars, should I buy it?"

Even Lilly's pubic hair was dyed to match. They don't sell stuff to dye the hair down here in Japan, she'd told me, I had to send away for it myself, got it from Denmark.

Through the hair over my eyes, I could see the ceiling light.

"Hey, Ryū, I had a dream about you," Lilly said, placing her hand around my neck.

"The one about me riding a horse in a park? I've heard that one before." I ran my tongue along Lilly's eyebrows, which were growing out again.

"No, another one, after the one in the park. The two of us go to the ocean, you know, a real pretty seaside. There's this big beach, wide and sandy, nobody there except you and me. We swim and play in the sand but then on the other side of the water we can see this town. Well, it's far away, so we shouldn't be able to see much, but we can even make out the faces of the people living there – that's how dreams are, right? First they're having some kind of celebration, some kind of foreign festival. But then, after a while, a war starts in that town, with artillery going boom, boom. A real war – even though it's so far away, we can see the soldiers and the tanks.

"So the two of us, you and me, Ryū, just watch from the beach, sort of dreamy like. And you say, Hey, wow, so that's war, and I say Yeah, right."

"You sure have some weird dreams, Lilly."

The bed was damp. Some feathers sticking out of the pillow pricked the back of my neck. I pulled out a little one and stroked Lilly's thighs with it.

The room was dimly gray. Some light stole in from the kitchen. Lilly was still asleep, her little hand, with the nail polish off, resting on my chest. Her cool breath brushed my armpit. The oval mirror hanging from the ceiling reflected our nakedness.

The night before, after we'd done it, Lilly had shot up again, humming deep in her white throat.

I just keep using more, no matter what, I've got to cut down pretty soon or I'll be an addict, right? she'd said, checking the amount left.

While Lilly had been rocking her body on top of mine, I'd remembered the dream she'd told me about, and also the face of a certain woman. As I'd watched the twisting of Lilly's slim hips . . .

The face of a thin woman digging a hole right next to a barbed wire entanglement around a large farm. The sun was sinking. The face of a woman bent down to thrust a shovel into the earth, beside a tub full of grapes, as a young soldier threatened her with his bayonet. The face of a woman wiping away her sweat with the back of her hand, hair hanging over her face. As I'd watched Lilly panting, the woman's face floated through my mind.

Damp air from the kitchen.

Is it raining? I wondered. The scene outside the window was smoky, milk colored. I noticed the front door was ajar. Yesterday, since we were both drunk, we must have gone to bed without closing it. A single high-heeled shoe lay on its side on the kitchen floor. The tapering heel stuck out, and the curve of firm leather over the front was as smooth as part of a woman.

Outside, in the narrow space I could see through the open door, stood Lilly's yellow Volkswagen. Raindrops stuck to it like goose bumps, and then the heavier ones slid down slowly, insects in winter.

People passing like shadows. A mailman in a blue uniform pushing a bicycle, several school children with book bags, a tall American with a Great Dane – all passing through the narrow space.

Lilly took a deep breath and half turned her body. She gave a low moan and the light blanket that had covered her fell to the floor. Her long hair stuck to her back in an S shape. The small of her back was sweaty.

Scattered on the floor was Lilly's underwear from the day before. Far away and rolled up small, the garments were just like little burn marks or dyed spots on the rug.

A Japanese woman with a black shoulder bag looked around the room from the doorway. Her cap bore some company insignia, the shoulders of her navy jacket were damp – I thought she must have come to read the gas or electric meter. When her eyes got used to the dim light, she noticed me, started to speak, seemed to think better of it, and stepped outside again. She glanced back once more at me, naked and smoking a cigarette, then went off toward the right, her head cocked to one side.

Through the space outside the door, now open a little wider, passed two grade-school girls, talking, gesturing, wearing red rubber boots. A black soldier in uniform ran by, leaping over the muddy spots just like a basketball player dodging a guard to shoot.

Beyond Lilly's car, on the other side of the street, stood a small black building. Its paint was peeling in places; "U-37" was written in orange.

Against the background of that black well, I could clearly see the fine rain falling. Over the roof were heavy clouds, looking as if someone had smeared on layer after layer of gray pigment. The sky in the narrow rectangle that was visible to me was the brightest part.

Thick clouds swollen with fever. They made the air damp, made Lilly and me sweat. That's why the crumpled sheets were clammy.

A think black line slanted across the narrow sky.

Maybe that's an electric wire, I thought, or a tree branch, but then it rained harder and soon I couldn't see it anymore.

The people walking in the street hurriedly put up umbrellas and began to run.

Puddles appeared on the muddy street even as I watched and widened out in a series of ripples. Played on by the rain, a big white car moved slowly along the street, almost filling it. Inside were two foreign women, one adjusting her hairnet in the mirror, and the other, the driver, watching the road so carefully that her nose was almost pressed against the windshield. Both were heavily made up; their dry skin appeared to be caked with powder.

A girl licking an ice cream bar passed, then came back and peered in. Her soft, blonde hair was plastered to her head, and she took Lilly's bath towel off the kitchen chair and began to wipe herself dry. She licked ice cream off her finger and sneezed. When she raised her head, she noticed me. Picking up the blanket and covering myself, I waved at her. She smiled and pointed outside. Putting my finger to my lips, I signaled her to keep quiet. Looking toward Lilly, I laid my head on my hand to show she was still sleeping. So be quiet, I gestured again, my finger to my lips, and grinned at her. The girl turned toward the outside and gestured with the hand holding the ice cream. I turned my palm upward and looked up in a pantomime of noticing the rain. The girl nodded, shaking her wet hair. Then she dashed outside and came back drenched, carrying a dripping bra that looked like one of Lilly's.

"Lilly, hey, it's raining, do you have washing hanging out? Get up, Lilly, it's raining!"

Rubbing her eyes, Lilly got up, saw the girl, hid herself behind the blanket, and said, "Hey, Sherry, what are you up to?" The girl tossed the bra she was holding, yelled in English "Rainy!" and laughed as her eyes met mind.

Even when I gently peeled the band-aid off her ass, Moko didn't open her eyes.

Reiko was rolled up in a blanket on the kitchen floor, Kei and Yoshiyama were on the bed, Kazuo was by the stereo, still holding tight to his Nikomat, Moko lay on her stomach on the carpet, hugging a pillow. There was a slight bloodstain on the band-aid I'd peeled off, the hurt place opened and closed as she breathed, reminding me of a rubber tube.

The sweat beading her back smelled just like sex juices.

When Moko opened the eye that still had false eyelashes, she grinned at me. Then she moaned when I put my hand between her buttocks and half turned her body.

You're lucky it's raining, rain's good for healing, I'll bet it doesn't hurt much because of the rain.

Moko's sticky crotch. I wiped it for her with soft paper, and when I stuck in a finger, her naked buttocks jiggled.

Kei opened her eyes and asked, Hey, so ya stayed over last night with that whore-lady?

Shut up, stupid, she's not like that, I said, swatting at the little insects flying around.

Ah mean Ah don' care, Ryū, but ya got to watch about getting a dose, like Jackson said, some of the guys around here have got it real bad, ya could rot to pieces. Kei pulled on just her panties and fixed coffee, Moko stretched out a hand and said, Hey, give me a smoke, one of those mint-flavour Sah-lem.

Moko, that's Say-lem, not Sah-lem, Kazuo told her, getting up.

Rubbing his eyes, Yoshiyama said loudly to Kei, No milk in mine, OK? Then he turned to me – my finger still in Moko's ass – and said, Last night when you guys were messing around upstairs, I got a straight flush, you know, really right on, a straight flush in hearts – Hey, Kazuo, you were there, you can back me up, right?

Without answering him, Kazuo said sleepily, My strobe's gone somewhere, somebody hiding it?

Jackson said I should wear makeup again, like I'd done before. That time, I thought maybe Faye Dunaway'd come to visit, Ryū, he said.

I put on a silver negligée Saburō said he'd got from a pro stripper.

Before everybody arrived in Oscar's room, a black man I'd never seen before came and left nearly a hundred capsules; I couldn't tell what they were. I asked Jackson if he might have been an MP or a

CID man, but Jackson laughed, shaking his head, and answered, Naw, that's Green Eyes.

"You saw how his eyes are green? Nobody knows his real name, I heard he'd been a high school teacher but I don't know if it's true or not. He's crazy, really, we don't know where he lives or whether he has a family, just that he's been here a lot longer than we have, seems he's been in Japan an awful long time. Don't he look like Charlie Mingus? Maybe he came after he'd heard something about you. He say anything to you?"

That black man had looked very uptight. I'll give you just this much, he'd said, then rolled his eyes around the room and left as if he were making an escape.

His face hadn't changed even when he saw Moko was naked, and when Kei asked him, How about some fun? his lips had trembled but he didn't say anything.

"You'll get to see the black bird sometime, too, you haven't seen it yet, but you, you'll be able to see the bird, you've got them kind of eyes, same as me." Then he'd gripped my hand.

Oscar said not to take any of those capsules, because Green Eyes had once passed around laxatives. He told me to throw them out.

Jackson sterilized a battlefield syringe. I'm a medic, he said, so I'm a real pro at shots, right?

First they shot me up with heroin.

"Ryū, dance!" Jackson slapped my butt. When I stood up and looked in the mirror, I saw what looked like a different person, transformed by Moko's painstaking, expert makeup technique. Saburō passed me a cigarette and an artificial rose and asked, What music? I said make it Schubert and everyone laughed.

A sweet-smelling mist floated before my eyes and my head was heavy and numb. As I slowly moved my arms and legs, I felt that my joints had been oiled, and that slippery oil flowed around inside my body. As I breathed I forgot who I was. I thought that many things gradually flowed from my body, I became a doll. The room was full of sweetish air, smoke clawed my lungs. The feeling that I was a doll became stronger and stronger. All I had to do was just move as they wanted, I was the happiest possible slave. Bob muttered Sexy, Jackson said Shut up. Oscar put out all the lights and turned an orange spot on me. Once in a while my face twisted and I felt panicky. I opened my eyes wide and shook my body. I called out, panted low, licked jam off my finger, sipped wine, pulled my hair, grinned, rolled up my eyes, spit out the words of a spell.

I yelled some lines I remembered by Jim Morrison: "When the music is over, when the music is over, put out all the lights, my brothers live at the bottom of the sea, my sister was killed, pulled up on land like a fish, her belly torn open, my sister was killed, when the music is over, put out all the lights, put out all the lights."

Like the splendid men in Genet's novels, I rolled saliva around in my mouth and put it on my tongue – dirty white candy. I rubbed my legs and clawed my chest my hips and my toes were sticky. Gooseflesh wrapped my body like a sudden wind and all my strength was gone.

I stroked the cheek of a black woman sitting with her knees drawn up next to Oscar. She was sweating, the toenails at the end of her long legs were painted silver.

A flabby fat white woman Saburō had brought along gazed at me, her eyes moist with desire. Jackson shot heroin into the palm of Reiko's hand; maybe it hurt, her faced twitched. The black woman was already drunk on something. She put her hands under my armpits and made me stand up, then stood up herself and began to dance. Durham put hash in the incense burner again. The purple smoke rose and Kei crouched down to suck it in. At the smell of the black woman, clinging to me with her sweat, I almost fell. The smell was fierce, as if she were fermenting inside. She was taller than I, her hips jutted out, her arms and legs were very slender. Her teeth looked disturbingly white as she laughed and stripped. Lighter colored, pointed breasts didn't bounce much even when she shook her body. She seized my face between her hands and thrust her tongue into my mouth. She rubbed my hips, undid the hooks of the negligée, and ran her sweaty hands over my belly. Her rough tongue licked around my gums. Her smell completely enveloped me; I felt nauseated.

Kei came crawling over and gripped my cock, saying, Do it right, Ryū, get it up. All at once spittle gushed from one corner of my mouth down to my chin and I couldn't see anymore.

Her whole body glistening with sweat, the black woman licked my body. Gazing into my eyes, she sucked up the flesh of my thighs with her bacon-smelling tongue. Red, moist eyes. Her big mouth kept laughing and laughing.

Soon I was lying down; Moko, her hands braced on the edge of the bed, shook her butt as Saburō thrust into her. Everyone else was crawling on the floor, moving, shaking, making noises. I noticed that my heart was beating terribly slowly. As if matching its beat, the black woman squeezed my pulsing prick. It was as if only my heart and my cock were attached to each other and working, as if all my other organs had melted.

The black woman sat on top of me. At the same time her hips began to swivel at tremendous speed. She turned her face to the ceiling, let out a Tarzan yell, panted like a black javelin thrower I'd seen in an Olympic film; she braced the grayish soles of her feet on the mattress, thrust her long hands under my hips and held tight. I shouted, felt torn apart. I tried to pull away, but the black woman's body was hard and slippery as greased steel. Pain mixed with pleasure drilled through my lower body and swirled up to my head. My toes were hot enough to melt. My shoulders began to shake, maybe I was going to start yelling. The back of my throat was blocked by something like the soup Jamaicans make with blood and grease, I wanted to spit it up. The black woman took deep breaths, felt my shaft to make sure it was deep inside her, grinned, and took a puff on a very long black cigarette.

She put the perfumed cigarette in my mouth, asked me quickly something I didn't understand, and when I nodded she put her face to mine and sucked my saliva, then began to swivel her hips. Slippery juices streamed from her crotch, wetting my thighs and belly. The speed of her twisting slowly increased. I moaned, getting into it. As I screwed both eyes shut, emptied my head, and put my strength into my feet, keen sensations raced around my body along with my blood and concentrated in my temples. Once the sensations formed and clung to my body, they didn't leave. The thin flesh behind my temples sizzled like skin burned by a firecracker. As I noticed this burn and the feeling became centered there, I somehow believed I had become just one huge penis. Or was I a miniature man who could crawl up inside women and pleasure them with his writhing? I tried to grip the black woman's shoulders. Without slackening the speed of her hips, she leaned forward and bit my nipples until blood came.

Singing a song, Jackson straddled my face. Hey, baby, he said, lightly swatting my cheek. I thought his swollen asshole was like a strawberry. Sweat from his thick chest dripped onto my face, the smell strengthened the stimulus from the black woman's hips. Hey, Ryū, you're just a doll, you're just our little yellow doll, we could stop winding you up and finish you off, y'know, Jackson crooned, and the black woman laughed so loudly I wanted to cover my ears. Her loud voice might have been a broken radio. She laughed without stopping the movement of her hips, and her saliva dribbled onto my belly. She tongue-kissed Jackson. Like a dying fish, my cock jumped inside her. My body seemed powder dry from her heat. Jackson thrust his hot prick into my dry mouth, a hot stone burning my tongue. As he rubbed it around my tongue, he and the black woman chanted something like a spell. It wasn't English, I couldn't understand it. It was like a sutra with a conga rhythm. When my cock twitched and I was almost ready to come, the black woman raised her hips, thrust her hand under my buttocks, pinched me, and jabbed a finger hard into my asshole. When she noticed the tears filling my eyes, she forced her finger in even deeper and twisted it around. There was a whitish tattoo on each of her thighs, a crude picture of a grinning Christ.

She squeezed my throbbing cock, then plunged it into her mouth until her lips almost touched my belly. She licked all around, nipped, then stroked the tip with her rough pointed tongue, just like a cat's. Whenever I was on the verge of coming, she pulled her tongue away. Her buttocks, slippery, shiny with sweat, faced me. They seemed spread almost wide enough to tear apart. I stretched out a hand and dug my nails into one side as hard as I could. The black woman panted and slowly moved her butt from side to side. The fat white woman sat on my feet. Her blackish-red cunt hanging down from under sparse golden down reminded me of a cut-up pig's liver. Jackson seized her huge breasts roughly and pointed to my face. Shaking the breasts that lay on her white belly, she peered into my face, touched my lips split by Jackson's prick, and laughed Pretty in a soft voice. She took one of my legs and rubbed it against her sticky pig liver. My toes were moved around – it felt so bad I could hardly stand it – the white woman smelled just like rotten crab meat and I wanted to throw up. My throat convulsed and I nipped Jackson's prick slightly; he yelled terribly, pulled out, and struck me hard on the cheek. The white woman laughed at my bleeding nose, Gee that's awful; she rubbed her crotch even harder against my feet. The black woman licked up my blood. She smiled gently at me like a battlefield nurse and whispered in my ear Pretty soon we'll have you shoot off, we'll make you come. My right foot began to disappear into the white woman's huge cunt. Again Jackson thrust his prick into my cut mouth. I desperately fought down my nausea. Stimulated by my slippery, bloody tongue, Jackson shot his warm wad. The sticky stuff blocked my throat. I heaved pinkish fluid, mixed with blood, and yelled to the black woman, Make me come!

SMALL DEATH IN VENICE

Sean O Caoimh

THEY CALL IT the small death but this, he thinks, is a long drawn-out agony.

He lies there, the grand horizontal, and she rides him hell for leather. He tries to stay hard and it obliges, taking its own pleasure. He watches it going in and coming out, a thing apart, working away, shining and flushed with pride. Remote as it is he wills it to pulsate, to twitch, to throb.

She says – You're marvellous, the best lover I've ever had.

He thinks – That's something. Score out of ten? The latest ten?

Outside the barges hit the pilings of San Trovaso. Rumble of diesels, shouts, hooting of vaporetti on the Grand Canal. In the Galleria dell'Accademia next door the cast out lady in Giorgione's *Tempest* sits naked under the town called Paradise.

Inside Room 12 of the Pensione Accademia she sits on his erection and heaves up and down and undulates like a turbulent sea. He lies there unmoved.

She says – I love it.

He looks up at her. Her face is contorted by her intense concentration. It's red and blotchy and sweat streaks her forehead. Eyes bloodshot, the whites veined in pink. She has the grim, tight-faced determination of a pained jogger or a cyclist leaning into a steep hill. She holds her breasts in her hands

and throws her head back in military jerks in time with her
hips.

He fills her. He matches her spasms with his convulsions.
It's remote, detached, with a life of its own, but obedient to
the cause.

He thinks – Now I'm just a cocksman. No lover no more.

She says – I want you to come.

He thinks – I'm saving it for Christmas.

He's irreverent, almost indifferent.

It wasn't always like this.

The meeting on the mountain at Verbier. The exchange of looks.
The instant knowing. The trembling. In the village next day –
Come to Venice. – Yes. Later that evening, the Visitation. His
room filled with her fragrance, his bed with her lace, her skin,
her delectable wetness. Her long hair brushing his cock. – It's
beautiful. Is it mine? – Forever. What a laugh.

The small death and the resurrection. Again and again.

She says – I can't come any more. And comes again.

He's hooked. In deep, in love with her body, erotic love that's
like drowning.

The narcosis of the cunt.

His desire: to be better than the rest.

A week later in Venice. Looking at the Veronese in the Palazzo
Ducale. Europa abducted by the Bull. Her lips parted, her face
in ecstasy, a wayward breast, abandonment. And the first shock.

He says – I'm like a bull when you make love with me.

She says – I fuck. I don't make love.

But she smiles and squeezes his bulging trousers.

In Room 12, disarray. She light and airy like an *île flottante*, her
skin tasting as cool and fresh as the first salmon of the season
and the first green peas. Him addicted. Lust into love and no
protection. Compulsive touching. She holding his hard under the
Titian in the Frari. His fingers inside her going up the steps in
San Rocco.

Then, the illusion. The re-living of the moments, endowed with
romantic love, profane yet sacred. The manic lift every time. The
letters. The midnight calls: I miss you. And more. Each word

remembered and inflated. The rerouting of life around her. The
fitness of it; the certainty. The almost religiosity of it. Yes, the
grand illusion.

Now she's alone, masturbating herself on him. And he's away in
the Palazzo Labia coming off on the Tiepolos.
   She says – I'm coming.
   He thinks – Great. Best out of three?
   He looks at her lumpy stomach. The sucked-in diaphragm, the
tensed-up muscles running like a mountain range from ribcage to
pubis. A flat-topped ridge criss-crossed with deep ravines. The
folded-up layers of flesh lined like the neck of an old sea turtle.
Or a concertina. Everything in motion, sinews stretched, thighs
lifting and falling like the connecting rod of a ship's reciprocating
engine. And down there the beauty mark just above the crease
of the V.
   She says – I love it.
   She leans over to watch herself as she pumps away, her hair
mercifully hiding her face: she can't see his apartness, the falsity
of his act. Now she reaches up, throws her head back, her mouth
open, beginning to sound. She drops a hand and grabs his. She
rubs it against her mons, her fingers touching his slippery cock.
   She says – I want to kiss it.
   She falls off and turns and kneels, *soixante-neuf*, and takes him
in her mouth and offers him her sex. He extends a tentative tongue.
He has lost the taste.
   He remembers. The dunes. The golden sand in her golden hair.
The taste of salt, of honey, of delicious cunt.
   He thinks – How I loved her. Was there always hate underlying
the love? It's too sophisticated for a bog Irishman with his prick
still in the confessional.
   She's on her way now. Eating him like a ripe mango. Her nether
region vibrating in synch with her mouth and tongue. She holds
nothing back. Always over the top. Gluttony in all orifices.
   The small death. How did it expire?
   With humiliation.

It keeps coming back. When she turned up with the finger bruises
inside her thighs. Up by the slit. Black and blue from violent
fucking. From learning to dive, she said, not caring that it was

an obvious lie. Not important enough for a decent deception. Not caring.

She wants more than he can give. He had thought no one could give her more. He was naive. He asked her if she wanted two men, wanting her to be angry. She only laughed and said – The only aphrodisiac is variety, Baby. Lighten up.

By the pool. Raoul working on the fence. She beckoned. Then the three of them in the water, her holding them both. Raoul sitting on the side, her head between his legs and himself entering her from behind. Her laughing and him sick to death.

Upstairs. Her guiding him into the forbidden place while she lowered herself over Raoul. He could feel the intruder. The shit on the sheets.

She said – It's just a game. It doesn't count.

But it did. It does. Now she is there, all by herself. She raises her head, squeezes his prick hard, locks his head into her cunt, floods his face.

She cries – Oh, God! Oh, darling!

He thinks – Oh, balls. Change the record.

She lies on top of him and tries to eat his mouth. She tastes of cunty ashes. He tries to turn away. She pulls his head back. She's angry.

She says – You don't love me any longer.

He thinks of the old joke – Loves you? Of course I loves you. I fucks you, don't I?

He says – Let's go to the island of San Michele. With the mist and the cypresses.

She says – Yes, let's. It sounds sexy.

He wishes he could get a funeral gondola, all black and gilt, with four oarsmen and angels with wings spread on the stem and the stern, a black canopy with tassels, and cushions where the coffin lies.

The taxi-boat arrives at the ornate gate of the cemetery of San Michele. It's twilight. Long shadows, black water, smell of mud and putrescence. The lights of Murano filtered through the mist. Rose walls and sinister cypresses. They step ashore. He tells the man to wait. The man says it's closing soon. To hurry.

She says – It looks like a graveyard.

He says – Yes. A burial ground. L Ile des Morts. It was once a prison.

She says – It is sexy.

He says – All the best people come here. Stravinsky. Diaghilev. Ezra Pound.

She asks – Who was he?

He says – A mad poet. We have to pay our respects.

They go to Ezra Pound's grave. It has a white stone and a white urn filled with fresh flowers. He stands. He turns to her. He lowers his hand. He unzips himself. He pushes her head down, not gently. She squats. She extracts his penis. It's hard. She sucks him, he helps her by pulling it next to her mouth. His hand hits her teeth. Now she is excited. It's a new experiment. It's the kind of bizarre situation she likes.

He pushes her away and ejaculates over the grave.

She cries – Why did you do that?

He says – A benediction. He wrote about you: "Your mind and you are our Sargasso Sea."

She says – What does it mean?

He says – Weeds, darling, we're mired in weeds. Putrid, rotten, all passion spent.

He turns and walks away.

Small death in Venice.

Dead and buried.

R.I.P.

NEEDLESS TO SAY

Lisa Palac

THE FROZEN VEGETABLE display made Angelique's nipples hard.
She was choosing between a carton of chopped spinach and a bag
of carrots, broccoli and cauliflower otherwise known as California
Medley.

California . . . California. Just the sound of the word made her
wet. The home of indigenous blonde bimbos and vacant surfer
dudes who drenched themselves in various pore-clogging palm
oils, then panted like rabid dogs as they slid around the back
seat of their cherry '77 Cutlass convertibles. The acme of hot-tub
orgies with big dicks from the Hollywood Hills, cellular phone sex
and fuchsia teddies with nipple cut-outs. The Land of Porn.

Angelique dreamed of performing incredibly nasty acts on a
Naugahyde couch while the videotape rolled. She and some
greased-up stud would pump and munch on each other like
snacks, eventually sliding down onto the lime shag carpet, while
the slightly balding director with a roll of fat hanging over his Elvis
– The King! abalone belt buckle shouted, "That's it BAYbee! Show
it all to me BAYbee! Ye-he-hes!"

She could make the Oooh Yeah Face better than Ginger Lynn
and she could be making a million fucking dollars at it too, but it
wasn't going to happen in Milwaukee.

Angelique threw the bag of frozen nuggets on top of the
bratwurst. Her high heels clicked against the waxed checkerboard

floor of Giuseppe's Finer Foods as she pushed the shopping cart down the aisle, wiggling her ass seductively for all of her regulars to see. She could make those pimply-faced, nervous stock boys cream in their pants if she wanted to. All that teenage testosterone ready to explode like a nuclear warhead at the mere sight of a pubic hair. Out of the corner of her eye, Angelique could see them straining to keep their eyes glued to her luscious ass.

She wore her favorite red cha-cha heels today and they made her butt stand out like a ripe bubble. Her legs were longer than Route 66 with directions to the Tunnel of Love posted every mile. The leopard lycra spandex skirt barely covered her back door and a cut-off T-shirt revealed that her man-made 34C tits didn't need a bra. A turgid mass of bleach-blonde hair, glued in place by an entire can of Aqua-Net Firm Hold, shot up toward the ceiling, then fell around her shoulders. Her eyes were circled with tons of thick black eyeliner and her lips were colored California Orange.

Wiggle it, Angie. She bent over just a little bit, pretending to check something in the cart, and rotated her firm cheeks. Surreptitiously, she glanced over her shoulder just in time to catch the stock boys turn their drooling faces back to a freezer full of frozen food.

Bending over wasn't the only talent she had. She knew all the poses from grinding along with Tony's (her now ex-boyfriend and total jerk) porno tapes and thumbing through copies of all his *fucking* fuck magazines. Next to laughing at the homemade Polaroids of all the flabby-assed sluts in the swingers' section, Angelique liked the letters from readers the best, and was dying to know if they were real. They were always saying things like, "The two virgin pizza delivery girls, needless to say, were begging to suck my cock!" or "Needless to say, I shot my biggest load watching her screw my brother and his Latvian lesbian Bingo tutor in the tool shed!" If these letters were real, then why didn't something like that happen to her? Why, why, why? Her bottom lip began to curl down into a little pout. She could screw in a tool shed better than any other Slavic lesbo, if she only had half a chance. Life was so unfair.

To cheer herself up, she wheeled the cart into the Shampoo/Toothpaste/Feminine Hygiene aisle. For Angelique, shopping was a confession of faith; a cold cash belief that the proper combination of fake tan, garter belts and the right deodorant would ultimately lead her to Porn Star status. Or at least the simulated adventures of one.

Angie Lee flipped on her Walkman. How do they expect people to have a meaningful shopping experience when the air is filled with this nauseating Muzak? she thought.

I'm burnin' up, burnin' up for your luh-uv . . .

Madonna's breathy squeals blasted through the wires. This crotch-grabbing, mattress-humping, Catholic Italian who liked to be spanked was Angelique's absolute idol. Angie had all her records, but her favorite was still the first one. "Burnin' Up" was her manifesto and The Boy Toy, her fearless leader. That woman had balls . . . and great tits, too. Angelique wondered what kind of douche she used.

She sang along with the superstar. She shook her head with such raging abandon, her hair actually moved. She pranced down the aisle, submersed in a distorted MTV wet dream.

. . . I'll do anything, I'm not the same, I have no shame . . . I'm on FIRE!

The music pounded away like an insatiable hard-on, while her eyes scanned the myriad products available for today's woman: feminine deodorant sprays, suppositories, intimate cleansers, disposable douches and douche bags; maxi pads, mini-pads, tampons on a stick and tampons on a string; pills to avoid bloating, crabbiness, over-eating, pimple-production, fatigue, iron deficiency, depression, moodiness and temper tantrums, which when unchecked could lead to frenzied fits of murder!

C'mon let go!

Madonna was insistent. The vocals ripped apart Angelique's hesitation and with a sweeping motion, she dumped the entire shelf into her cart. Shit, she broke a nail.

The cart was overflowing with goodies now. Time to go. Happily, she made her way toward the check-out. Okay, was she obsessing? Maybe there was one box too many of panty shields. Maybe she should wear two at a time. One time Tony asked her why a chick would need to wear a pad everyday.

"I thought that thing only happened once a month, unless ya got knocked up or somethin'. Whaddaya get? Some fuckin' clam disease? Haw, haw, haw." Stupid asshole.

Or the time when Tony was laid off from the meat-packing plant and he listened to those Springsteen records all fuckin' day and would whip out his cock whenever some ugly babe got rejected on "Love Hook-Up," the dial-a-date show.

"Come and get it, Fido! Here, Barky!" he'd say, dangling his dick in front of the TV and swallowing a pisswarm Meister Brau.

What a low-class scum-sucking shit. He thought he was so great, and he didn't even know he had pimples on his ass and left skid marks in his underwear. Breaking up with him was the smartest thing she ever did – besides buying those refrigerator magnets on sale.

No matter what line Angelique picked, it always turned out to be the longest one. There was always some old lady who picked an item without a price tag or insisted on digging for exact change in the bottom of her purse. To help the century pass, Angie grabbed the latest issue of *Charm* magazine and scanned the headlines on the cover: Where Men Like to be Licked, Lipstick Tricks, Bolivian Fashion Rage, Money: How to Get It, Find Your G-Spot in Minutes. She had a few minutes. She flipped to page 53.

She rested her elbows on the rail of the cart and arched her back so that her succulent plumbutt stuck way out. She slid off one high heel and slowly began to rub her bare foot against the inside of her other leg as she began reading the sexy instructions. Wash hands . . . two fingers . . . insert deeply . . . pressing forward . . . may feel like a small almond. Angelique pressed her creamy thighs together and gave a teensy little moan. She drew the magazine closer to her, shielding her face with the glossy pages. Gingerly, she ran one finger around the outline of her wet pink lips, then drove it into her mouth like a garden spike. She rammed one finger, then two, in and out of her lip service until they were completely covered in her sweet stickiness. She was just about to try and sneak them down to her pussy when she noticed the spy.

Two lines over Angel saw Mrs Alfaromeo. She kept glancing and pointing at Angelique, then whispering to her prune-faced old man. That nosy bitch, thought Angel, everybody probably knows about my abortion now. Mrs Alfaromeo's daughter, Carmella, worked at the clinic and provided the entire neighborhood with abortion gossip. Somebody should gag that prissy little Carmella I-Have-No-Cunt.

Mrs Alfaromeo was now smiling and waving and flapping her gums frantically; obviously trying to cover up her spying blunder with some forced conversation.

Angel lowered the magazine and pulled the headphones away from her ears.

"What," Angie gave her best Bored Bitch imitation, "are you saying?"

"I say, how you feeling?"

Fuck. She knows. Angelique gave the geriatric an indignant stare.

"I feel pretty horny after watching your daughter give some black guy a blow-job on your front porch last night!"

The old woman took a big swallow of air and slammed a can of tomato paste down on the conveyor belt with deliberate rage. She prayed to the fluorescent ceiling lights and told her wrinkled porker that he should have worn his hearing aid if he wanted to know what was going on. Smiling, Angel flung the magazine in with the other treats, pushed her cart up to the register, and began unpiling her load.

Angelique couldn't resist flashing the bag boy. She made sure to give him a good view of her braless silicone wonders with every item she placed on the moving black belt. *You want a show, honey?* she thought, *I'll give it to you and you can pay me later.*

"Total's 83.94." The gum-chomping check-out girl was barely understandable.

Angie Lee tried to focus on counting her cash, but couldn't keep her eyes off the nubile flesh who was just finishing packing up the paper bags with the last box of vaginal suppositories. She imagined the growing desire in his pants and licked her lips in anticipation.

"That's 83.94."

She made the transaction and slung her purse over her shoulder. Meanwhile the pulsing behemoth put the bags into an empty cart, preparing for their departure.

"I need some help puttin' all this stuff in my car." Oh, Angie you coy bitch. "Could you help me?"

"Sure," he said. Wasn't he sweet? A little bit of acne but great hair.

He followed Angie out into the parking lot. Click, click, click. Her plastic heels tapped the black tar surface.

She made sure to walk in front of him, not beside him, so that he could revel in her perfect *perfect* ass. She also wanted to give him the opportunity to rub up against her when she bent over to slam the key in the lock. But he didn't take the bait when she opened up the trunk of her 1989 Buick Riviera. What the hell was this throbbing glob of hormones waiting for?

She spun around and slammed her lips into his. Snatching a fistful of his crusty gelled hair, she slurped and slobbered all over his adolescent face, smearing it with California Orange. Her tongue desperately searched for the way into his love-licker, but he would not open his mouth.

"Open your mouth, baby," Angie Lee cooed. "Open up for Mommy."

The bag boy stood motionless. His face was more frozen than the bag of California Medley, which was now melting in the suffocating Wisconsin sun. Only his eyes were bulging.

"Lamby-pie, open your mouth and let my slippery snake in," she hissed. Still no response. "I said open it, you little shit!" Angie yanked his bottom lip down with one hand and pried his teeth apart with the other. Her pointy tongue darted in and out of his cavity-filled mouth with a winner-take-all fury. And this conquest was only the beginning.

She began grinding and writhing against his filthy green Giuseppe's apron. Her hungry crotch humped his leg while she grabbed his ass with both hands and pounded his scared stiff body against her loose slutty self. She clawed at his face with her painted talons and dug her teeth into his never-been-kissed flesh.

"Owww!" he screamed. The sound of his sudden yelp made her lose her balance and she practically twisted her ankle when her cha-cha heel gave way.

"Damn it you lovely little virgin bastard, you hot horny teen-ager," she whispered into his waxy ear, "I'm going to rip you up."

Angie Lee stuffed her sex plans into his brain. Detailed descriptions of coital exploits were flooding his head, but bag boy had a one track mind: If he didn't get back soon, he'd lose his fifteen-minute break. With anxious tenacity his head kept snapping back in the direction of the grocery store, straining to see who might be witnessing his possible de-flowerment, until Angelique put the iron grip on his boner-to-be.

"I am a bitch in heat!" she cried, enunciating every word like a Pentecostal preacher. "And you're gonna cool me off." In a smooth move, she caught his crumpled black tie and dragged him around to the side of the car.

He was flat on his back in the back seat when Angie ripped off her T-shirt and produced two perfect melons. Straddling him, she began playing with her overripe fruits, making little circles around her rock hard nipples.

"Aren't you dying to touch me?" Sugar poured out of her mouth. "Aren't you . . .?" She paused, eyebrows raised, waiting for his name.

"Sergio . . . but . . . uhm . . . like my friends call me Sam."

"Oooo Sam. I like Sam. Oooo, yeah." She tweaked her nipples harder and harder and sucked in a lot of air every time she said Oooo, yeah. Just like in the movies.

She reached out and tugged on his zipper, but he grabbed her wrist.

"What's the matter, Sammy?"

"You're not sick or anything are you? I mean you bought all that weird stuff."

Suddenly her eyes narrowed into evil slits. "What *weird* stuff?" She spit the words out through her clenched teeth, now just inches away from his petrified face.

"All that stuff, for like when girls get infections."

"I don't have any infections. All of that *stuff* keeps me smelling fresh and feminine. You want me to be feminine, don't you?"

"Yeah . . . I guess so."

"Tell me what else you want." He shrugged his shoulders. "I'll tell you what you want! You want my honey pot! My carnal canal! My shaved slice of sin! MY PUSSY!" Her fingernails tore into his stained white bag-boy shirt, releasing a shower of buttons.

"You want to see my cunt riding up and down on your virginal cock, don't you? You want to see me rub my clit? Do you know what that is? My clit? I bet you don't, you naive slave-boy. See, Oooo I'm rubbing it now. Oooo yeah. Ooooh oooh ooooh you want to hear me scream when I come and keep on screaming as I take more and more of your thick pud deep deep and deeper inside me. You want to see me explode again when you shoot hot lava blasts from your volcanic rod deep inside my mammoth crater! Don't you? Oooo yeah, oh here it comes baby, here it comes! I'm showin' it to you, baby! Oh! Oh! Oh! OOOOooo YEAH!"

She heard the buzz droning in the distance. Her vibrator must have gone off accidentally in her purse, she thought. She opened her eyes. Instead, it was the annoying signal telling her the car door was ajar. He was gone.

She adjusted the rear view mirror and checked her lipstick at the same time. Some idiot behind her was beeping their horn. The light was green. Fuck you, asshole. She gave him the finger. Her tires squealed when she rammed the pedal to the floor. In her mind, she was already composing the letter: "I was doing my weekly shopping, when this totally gorgeous stock boy, who was also a virgin, offered to take my groceries out to the car. He ended up packing my trunk in more ways than one! Needless to say, I never thought it could happen to me . . ."

TRUCK STOP RAINBOWS

Iva Pekarkova

Translated by David Powelstock

I LAY NEXT to the road – and only the sensations I desired had permission to approach me. But a hostile, disturbing sound invaded my pleasant and harmonious space, and began to come nearer along the highway feeder road. At first it sounded like the buzzing of a bumblebee somewhere in the distance, but then this bumblebee began growing and getting closer, until its buzz became the unmistakable sound of a motor.

The sound did not go whizzing by me – the car stopped, and I lazily prepared to open at least one eye: it was probably some kindhearted guy who wanted to give me a ride and would ask me envious questions about my vacation; I'd have to explain that I was sunbathing at the moment and wasn't interested.

I raised an eyelid.

Two cops stood next to the ditch. Each one had the sun in his hair and one flat shoe half-imbedded in the clay; they looked at me with a suspicious expression that struck me as kind of cute. I smiled, at both of them.

(The main thing is not to resist. Don't be insolent, just pretend you're an adorable, ditzy, idiot, Fialinka . . .) One of them said, "What are you doing here? Where are you from? Were you headed somewhere for vacation? Alone? Let's have a look at your Citizen's Identification Booklet; yes, a routine check . . ."

He said it diffidently, abstractly – it really was kind of cute the way the practiced, subtly threatening tone that saturated the voice of every law officer was shrouded by his charming Brno accent . . . Let's have look – he said it as if there were syllables in L written at least a fourth part higher on the scale: *Let's have a look* . . . Oh, Brno.

(Be careful, Fialinka, blush; most important, don't be a wise-ass, for God's sake, don't be a wise ass.)

"Comrades" – but just slipped out – "I just *adore* the way you Brnians talk. Say something else for me. Let's have a a look at my ID . . . *Let's have a look* . . . It's so refreshing, comrades, I just can't get over that Brno accent, I just can't . . . Let's a have a l – "

They released me from the police station in the center of town about three hours later. It was recommended that I head straight home and not even think of hitchhiking on the highway – the comrades would be keeping an eye on me. I was told that my behavior was extremely suspicious and that the comrades in Prague would be checking up on my studies. So I shouldn't be surprised when they called . . . Do you understand, comrade *student*?

I took the tram (without buying a ticket, of course) that ran most directly out to the Southern Road. A tight-lipped, severe, not very pretty smile of determination was ripening on my lips. A sneer.

My mind was made up. I was on my way to look for that wheelchair for Patrik.

The sun had been at its zenith a long time already when my tram finally jolted up to the end of the line. I worked my way over to the prohibited highway through the honeycombed mire of dried and cracked puddles. I ran down from the overgrown embankment and took a look around. No cops in sight. And as soon as the promisingly Western silhouette of an Intertruck appeared on the horizon, I thrust out my chest and stuck out my arm. Not the usual supplicant gesture of humble, honorable hitchhikers everywhere, I stretched it out seductively and imperiously, like a girl who had the price of admission.

The rig began to slow down almost immediately, and the screech of brakes in that cloud of swirling dust on the shoulder added to my self-confidence. I didn't sprint the few meters to the cab as usual. I picked my pack up out of the ditch deliberately and approached with the slow step of a queen of the highway. I caught sight of a face reflected in the side mirror. The driver backed up right to my feet, jumped out, and ran around to open the door for me.

And since I'd noticed a little D next to the truck's license plate, I cleared my throat and said: *"Fahrst du nach Pressburg?"*

I didn't add *bitte* or anything like that – I chose the informal *du* over *Sie* without even being at all sure how old he was.

It made no difference anyway.

He smiled (pleased I spoke German), nodded, and, when I added a regal *danke* after he lifted my pack up into the cab, he observed cheerfully, *"Aber du sprichst Deutsch sehr gut!"*

And that was the beginning of the long period, maybe too long, when I decided to become what almost every cop already assumed I was.

I had decided to get Patrik that wheelchair.

After twenty kilometers of small talk I was pleasantly surprised at my long-untested German. I smoked Marlboros (somehow convinced that without a cigarette clasped between my delicately outstretched fingers – even though they were still smeared with dirt – the impression wouldn't be complete) and, with a few successfully composed complex sentences, brought the conversation around to the difficulty of life in a socialist state. Kurt (we'd long ago exchanged names) steered with the barest touch of his left hand and, with his face turned toward me, nodded attentively. He was taking the bait. I don't know if he was listening, probably not, but he still kept saying how much he admired my German: God knows now few of these highway girls knew anything more than *bunsen*, the German word for fuck. He doesn't look unsympathetic, and I could do worse for my first time, I thought to myself. I babbled on cheerfully – and contemplated what would probably happen. This was not like an adventure that comes to you. This was not the work of my old friend Serendipity. I still wasn't used to my role – and I knew that I was going to have to take matters into my own hands.

Kurt asked, "Are you hungry? Do you want to eat with me? *Willst du essen?*"

"Sure," I said. "*Warum nicht? Ich will fressen,*" I added, replacing the verb "to eat" with the verb "to feed" (like an animal).

Kurt burst out laughing and leaned over to clap me on the shoulder. His hand slipped down by my breast.

"*Aber du sprichst Deutsch sehr sehr gut. Wo hast du alles gelernt?*"

"Right here," I lied, and pointed over my shoulder to the well-appointed little Intertruck sleeper. "*Hier . . . hier habe ich alles gelernt.*"

Kurt was already sitting almost next to me on the seat and weighing my tits on his palm. "*Du bist so fantastisch! Ist das möglich?*"

Everything is *möglich*, I thought for a second, everything is possible, you horny, half-assed imperialist bastard. But right now you're going to have to wait, old boy, because first we're going to discuss the terms.

I rolled that word "terms" around on my tongue and suddenly felt myself endowed with a power and strength I'd never known before. I was a girl who had the price of admission.

At a rest area Kurt got out and went around to the food pantry he had on the side of his cab. He returned with bread, a hunk of cheese, and a big salami such as I'd never seen in my life: like Hungarian salamis, only more tender . . . and the smell, God, how good it smelled! My stomach started rumbling.

Then Kurt showed me how to lift my seat and haul out from under it a huge storage chest of drinks in cans; I almost went blind gazing at all the different brands and types of juices, colas, beers, and soft drinks. I reached for one completely at random and opened it, careful not to aim it at myself. When it popped and a couple of drops sprinkled on the floor, Kurt gave me a congratulatory smile, almost like the one you give a good doggy when he offers you his paw. Oh God, how gifted I am! I can even open a soda can!

"I'd like to take you somewhere for lunch," he said apologetically, "but I don't know of any decent restaurant around here. And besides . . . in Czechoslovakia, actually anywhere in your Eastern Europe . . . well, I really don't like to eat at any of the places, I like to bring everything with me . . . Otherwise, I get sick, and I can't afford that, you see?"

He said it as if apologizing, but at the same time it didn't occur to him that he was speaking with someone who practically never saw anything but the local food . . . It never made me sick, I was used to it . . . It suddenly hit me that he saw Czechoslovakia as something like a pigsty – even though I, poor little piglet, was cute enough, he wasn't about to stick his snout into the slop that sustained me from day to day. It could make him sick.

The Southern Road, by the way, unlike the Northern Road, was definitely not lined with homey, warm and smoky, cozily bespattered taverns. On the Northern Road you could have a plate of gristly goulash for a fiver or soup for two crowns – and that's what we ate up there. The Southern Road, on the other hand, was lined with a bunch of so-called first-class restaurants, where trying to eat for less than fifty crowns was considered to be in bad taste, and the waiters, all spoiled by hard-currency tips, would give the cold shoulder from on high to any piddling Czech who happened to stray in there. In short, the places on the Southern Road were specially designed for the filthy-rich drivers of Western semis.

Kurt unwrapped the enticing yellowish-brown loaf of imperialist bread and a packet of margarine. He sliced the salami and cheese on a paper tablecloth stretched out across the space between us – and meanwhile I spread margarine on some slices of bread. Perfect teamwork . . . I didn't hesitate for a second that day: I was hungry – And good manners? Ha! Why pretend, girl? After all, is this guy really worth being proper? Is anybody really worth all those contrived social lies?

I started stuffing myself with salami and cheese. I was dimly aware that this was the best salami and cheese I'd tasted in my life – and the bread with margarine was substantially better than if it had been smeared with socialist "Fresh Butter of the Highest Sort". I was pigging out without mercy, and Kurt, taking only an occasional bite, looked at me agreeably and hospitably, as if he were feeding his favorite dog. He injected, "*Gut?*"

I nodded with my mouth full and bit off another piece of bread. I suddenly found myself in the middle of a dream. Or – if I had any inclination toward acting – I would say I found myself in the middle of a theater piece. I'd plunged headlong into one of the leading roles, without a clue as to how the whole drama (or was it a comedy?) began or ended. I hadn't learned my lines, I wasn't thinking in advance about what to say the next second, and there was no time to recall what I'd said a minute ago. I was standing

in the middle of an unfamiliar stage – and yet it was as if sometime
long ago I'd played this role a hundred times before. I didn't know
what I was supposed to say, what would happen or what the male
lead would say to me. But a prompter (not the one who poked
her head out occasionally from a booth below the stage, but one
that was fixed somewhere in my head and was speaking to me
directly), an unfamiliar prompter always assigned me just the
right line or gesture at just the right moment to fit my part. I
could see everything from the inside and the outside at the same
time, evaluating my dramatic performances as I went and finding
it satisfactory. As for the rest, the director and the audience were
irrelevant. The main thing was that I was completely satisfied with
my role, that I was comfortable in it; it seemed to me that it had
been tailored especially for my body, that the author of the play
had written it for me and nobody else but me, for this second
Fialinka, for a worse and more cynical I. I knew that I would
never have wanted this to be my everyday existence – but I had
always known that such a person lived somewhere within me, and
it was intoxicating to be able to act out my second I . . .

Who am I now and who had I really been before? I had *always*
been playing a part, I, the notorious seeker of truth. I had lied. I
had deceived with my body . . . Was I deceiving any more than I
had before? I adapted to Kurt, my fellow player, I made myself the
way he wanted me to be: supple, just the slightest bit unlike the
others, not stupid, but not overly clever either, with a superficial,
suggestive wit . . . a promising girl, who's easy to get to know.

I stuffed myself with bread and margarine, greedily sucked at my
fingers, still stained with Brno clay (my entire back and the back
of my pants were caked with clay, but that made no difference at
all at the time) – and the precise, perfect prompter in my head
kept telling me what to do next. The prompter determined what
I was to say, how to act, what faces to make, how to move my
hands, my body. She decided what I was to think about. *How* I
was to think.

(You're a shitty actress, Fial, Patrik used to say to me. You
don't know how to transform yourself, and if someone ticks you
off, you insult him right to his face. If only you could just pretend
a little for the pigs. Just the tiniest bit . . .)

And now I could feel within myself dozens, hundreds, maybe
thousands of potentially possible lives, from which I'd chosen just

one at some point long ago (and God only knows if it had even been I who'd chosen it). It was embarrassing: at some point I had developed into a compete personality, fully balanced according to all the psychiatric norms. But those ten thousand voices were arguing, fighting, and voicing their opinions inside my skull, and it was making my head spin. And those hundreds of complete, plausible, legitimate lives – each of which wanted to be lived – were locked in a battle for their rights. I was feeding on West German bread and perfect, moist salami, more delicately seasoned than any I'd ever tasted – and I allowed one of those other lives to grow and dominate. I gave it permission to be lived.

No, this was no longer just a prompter. A little sadly, I closed my eyes (from the outside it looked like a blissful fluttering of the eyelids from tasting the salami) and plunged headfirst into metamorphosis.

After a good lunch, one needs a rest, observed Kurt. He drew the curtains closed, and the atmosphere in the cab, heated by the summer sun, suddenly became erotically sultry. The curtains were red and turned my little German's cheeks pink. The remains of lunch had long been carefully cleared away. After rolling them up in the paper tablecloth, this great lover of order had chucked the whole mess out the window and instructed me to do the same with the juice and beer cans. (A guy who had until then been sitting idly nearby in his little Skoda MB had immediately shot out to scoop up this rare prize.) A few last crumbs that had slipped out of the paper were now itching me under my back as this person pulled me over next to him and started sounding the depths with his hot, impatient hands. Actually, he wasn't doing much sounding. He was quite sure of himself.

I let him fondle my breasts a little – just through my T-shirt – and then I pulled away and got right to the point: "*Ich brauche Geld.*"

(This time the prompter in my head seemed to have made a small mistake – even though Kurt had probably heard those words a million times, my tone didn't quite fit the image of the average highway hooker. I said it too significantly with too much urgency: I was going to have to make a lot of money – as much as possible in hard currency – in order to get Patrik that wheelchair.)

Kurt was a little taken aback. Just the tiniest bit. Then he reached into the glove compartment. He opened it a crack, just enough to stick his hand in (I wasn't supposed to see everything he had in there, I realized), and groped around. He pulled out a large bottle of shampoo. "*Willst du das? Willst du?*" He turned the fine container around in his hands, like a shopkeeper displaying his merchandise. Look, little girl, how shiny! Now, how 'bout a feel of those titties? The shampoo really did glimmer beautifully; it was tempting stuff: even from where I was sitting I could smell its sweet apple scent. "You have such beautiful, wonderful hair, Via . . . This will be a little something just for you . . . Just a sort of small gift. Out of friendship. Would you like it?"

I shook my head – and I suddenly felt pretty awkward. I couldn't explain my desire to him at all, why I needed cash. There was no time to go through the whole story about Patrik. He wouldn't have listened – and if he had, he still wouldn't have believed it. Any long-distance trucker could tell you that every single Czechoslovakian girl had, as a rule, all kinds of relatives and at least two dozen best friends, all on their deathbeds with terminal diseases.

I didn't feel like going into that whole story. He simply wasn't worth it.

(Oh yes, if we had met under different circumstances, I would have run up to your truck . . . refused your cigarettes . . . I would have used the formal *Sie* with you, at least at the beginning . . . and we might even have talked for real. Actually communicated. But I had already decided that my words were not going to communicate anything; I would use them only to weave a web, in which I had to catch at least a few West German marks. Perhaps we could even have gotten along, Kurt, you don't look stupid. But you have been chosen, selected for this beginning, and you can't change a thing about it now. Neither of us can. It's impossible.)

"*Ich Brauche Geld*," I said. With shocking offhandedness (shocking to me), I pulled a Marlboro out of his pack – and without making even the slightest move to light it for myself, I waited for him to lean toward me with the lighter flame.

"Do you understand?" I said through the cloud of smoke. "I don't need your damn shampoo. If you want it . . . if you really want it . . . then I need cash."

With no less shocking offhandedness, I undid the button of my jeans and the fly unzipped by itself. (The majority of zippers of Czechoslovakian manufacture immediately leaped at such opportunities to unzip themselves – Patrik always claimed that this was one of the methods by which Czechoslovakian manufacturing enterprises contributed to the campaign to encourage population growth.) I undid the jeans sort of casually. They peeled away from my hips a little.

"*Wieviel?*" he whispered. He was getting to the point.

(It occurred to me later that this must have been monotonous for him, to say the same words to various girls. *Veefeel?* – this much some of them must have understood. *Veefeel? Veefeel?*)

He didn't look as if he wanted to pay very much, even though at the moment, by all appearances, he was longing to make love to me. Christ, why put it so delicately – I mean, he wanted to fuck, it was clear from certain physical signs. Impressively obvious physical signs, I couldn't help thinking, and the not-for-profit part of my physical instinct had already begun looking forward to it, more or less. The commercial part asked, "How much can you give me?" and it repeated, "I really need cash, get it, I need cash."

This was a sport, a game, I was gradually realizing. Kurt was definitely not poor, and even though he probably picked up some girl on every trip he made through Czechoslovakia and had to pay for it, I was sure he could afford to hand me a couple of hundred marks. It was a sport: pick up as many girls as possible in the East and then outdo all the other drivers bragging about who nailed what girl for how little. Supposedly, the consensus among Western Intertruckers was that "Czech whores are good whores, the cheapest whores on earth" – and except for a few insignificant cases, the truckers tried not to spoil them . . . it was a sport. I remember this one Dutchman, a pretty nice guy, who once gave me a lift on the same route I was riding that day, but under different circumstances: he gave Fialinka Number One a lift, while today a newborn second Fialinka rode that highway. He told me how he and his friend once made a bet on who could score a Czech highway girl for the lowest price. I had one for five marks, the Dutchman said modestly. I couldn't get breakfast for that in the Netherlands. But my friend, he outdid me. He bargained this one girl down to one mark, *one mark*, can you imagine, howled the

Dutchman, and she wasn't all that bad. True, she gave him the clap . . .

I'd always laughed at those prices, determined more by location and nationality than by the quality and appearance of the girl. And sometimes I was ashamed for my countrymen – still, it'd simply never occurred to me just how damn personally those highway prices could affect me. "*Verstehst du mich?*" I repeated. "*Ich brauche Geld.*"

And poor, dear Kurt (in different circumstances I certainly could have gotten along with him and, God knows, maybe even have made love to him on an entirely different philosophical basis), this Kurt stared at the strip of tummy below my T-shirt, sighed, and said, "*Funfzig Marks? Ist das okay?*"

I thought it over, then nodded.

The red curtains were made for lovemaking (that is, if this particular act didn't call for a change of terminology); the conditions were almost brothel-like. The sun, already substantially lower in the sky, shone straight into the cabin and illuminated it perfectly. Redly. Shamefully. Maybe red actually is the only color for this, I said to myself, and I noticed the shadow of the fabric pattern on that other face; maybe only red light will do, because suddenly there was not a trace of shame in that cab.

I'd never done anything like that in the cab of a truck during the day before; not that I needed darkness for such acts, quite the contrary; but that clear summer day outside somehow didn't seem right. Actually, I just didn't feel like it – even the other one, the buyer, didn't show any special enthusiasm. Any real desire. He was simply buying himself a whore and he'd just closed the deal with her . . .

He quickly kissed me: tongue thrashing in my mouth, a kiss supposedly passionate but in reality commercial and lukewarm. I guess he figured it was his duty.

He hurriedly checked the swaying folds of the curtains, to make sure no prying eye could look in. "*Gut,*" he said, satisfied.

Then he pulled down his shorts.

The prompter in my head, that precise, intrusive internal voice, never let go of my hand. I knew exactly what to do, even though I'd never slept with anyone under these circumstances before: it had always started with my consciousness becoming pleasantly, mistily bedewed by someone I liked, so that the pleasurable feelings were always clear and unambiguous. But today I didn't even know whether I liked Kurt or not – and it made no difference at all. I had always wanted to be warmly intoxicated with perfectly mellowed (though perhaps only transient) desire; I would let myself dissolve into pleasant reverie – and the truckers who caught on were then allowed to come after me. Come into me. Pay a tender, longed-for, intimate visit. Always for a limited time.

But now – now I saw everything with perfect and loathsome sobriety. Without ardor. Without desire. I examined the shameful lighting in our little cab without shame: everything had perfectly clear, absolutely sharp outlines; gone was that undulating, dewy translucence I needed so badly during my Nights of Distances, my Nights of Instants. I was stone sober and wide awake: I was an actor on the stage of my own private theater, and the role was translated by my lips and movements with perfect precision. It became the way I could seductively (like a typical easy woman) slip out of even that clay-caked T-shirt. It became the bowing of the head I used to inconspicuously avoid direct eye contact; the precise and realistic movements of body, hands, lips. I knew exactly what to do, although I had never behaved this way before. And he didn't get it. How could he have guessed I had a prompter directing me from inside my defenseless-looking head? He surrendered himself to my hands and lips without the least sign of surprise. I did exactly what he anticipated. I did exactly what he expected and wanted, and if anything especially turned him on, it was that he didn't have to ask for anything. He was not so experienced that I couldn't surprise him. I was functioning. I didn't try to assess him, to figure out whether I liked him at all. I paid attention only to myself – concertedly, critically. I did everything I could think of doing – and although I'd never studied what was most pleasing to (average) men, my intuition helped me. I kissed him deeply, a kiss no less clinging than the one he had given me before – and I let him sigh blissfully. Or semi-blissfully. It was an experienced and wet kiss, well calculated – but still just a sort of half-kiss. Everything was halves and semis . . . Our semi-rapport. Our semi-commercial exchange. The half-light. Semi-desire. And we were half-human. We were marionettes, waving our hands, moving, living according to the puppet master's nimble fingers . . . And when that large, actually very large, and hard piece of flesh (*Fleisch*, it occurred to me, *Fleisch*) plunged into me, I realized that even this time I would feel pleasure. Semi-pleasure. I was making my acting debut on the stage of the Southern Road – and the sun had shifted slightly in the sky, so that the shameful lighting colored my rival's face. (Yes, he was my rival, though not my enemy.) Perhaps all my old sins and loves returned to me and aroused me as I conscientiously, attentively (and no doubt artfully), rode him like a hobbyhorse, rocking and plunging. Men like it when they don't have to exert themselves too much, reasoned the prompter in my head. And I was willing to provide good service for good money. I rocked and plunged, more vigorously and deeper, to the point where it hurt – and through the filter of perfectly sober thought I felt my eyes becoming moist and saw the same voluptuous moisture in my rival's eyes and my thighs quivering with the first tendrils of pleasure that were beginning to spread from my crotch, after all . . . After all . . . ? No, there was no after all about it, this was the approach of a powerful, compact, nearly painful orgasm, its potent, absolutely unfeigned spasms gripping my rival like a velvet vice. I bit his shoulder and neck to stifle the moans and the scream that struggled to leave my throat. We weren't the only ones parked at that rest area. I gripped him again and again in the velvet vise and looked with my misty but perfectly sober eyes directly into his; I observed how his face twisted, how he cried out and groaned and pulled me toward him, his nails digging into my buttocks, one hand on each, spreading them. He pulled me toward him and his face twisted with the animal grimace of genuine ecstasy: the quivering spread to my thighs and groin and down my legs . . . I knew the convulsion would come soon – and it would be a painful one – but payment had been made. I held on, and when I felt the hot liquid streaming into me like a firehose into a burning house, I calmly realized how perfectly my prompter had everything planned: these were my safest days of the month . . . Soon the convulsions stopped in my thighs, replaced only by a trembling exhaustion, and my rival, or sexual partner, was still quivering too. He was overcome. And lying next to him afterward, tired, trembling, my prompter did not forget to speak up and show me precisely how to place my hand on his heaving shaggy chest so that it would seem intimate without applying too much pressure –

though, of course, this meant nothing at all. I was still trying to catch my breath in the sultry atmosphere of the shamefully lit cab. That was good, solid lovemaking, it occurred to me.

A good fuck.

SWEATING PROFUSELY IN MÉRIDA: A MEMOIR

Carol Queen

THE BOYFRIEND AND I met at a sex party. I was in a back room trying to help facilitate an erection for a gentleman brought to the party by a woman who would have nothing to do with him once they got there. She had charged him a pretty penny to get in, and I actually felt that I should have gotten every cent, but I suppose it was my own fault that I was playing Mother Teresa and didn't know when to let go of the man's dick. Boyfriend was hiding behind a potted palm eyeing me and this guy's uncooperative, uncut dick, and it seemed Boyfriend had a thing for pretty girls *and* uncut men, especially the latter. So he decided to help me out and replaced my hand with his mouth. That was when it got interesting. The uncut straight guy finally left and I stayed.

In the few months our relationship lasted, we shared many more straight men, most of them – Boyfriend's radar was incredible – uncircumcised and willing to do almost anything with a man as long as there was a woman in the room. I often acted as sort of a hook to hang a guy's heterosexuality on while Boyfriend sucked his dick or even fucked him. My favorite was the hitchhiker wearing pink lace panties under his grungy jeans – but that's another story. Long before we met him, Boyfriend had invited me to go to Mexico.

This was the plan. Almost all the guys in Mexico are uncut, right?

And lots will play with me, too, Boyfriend assured me, especially if there's a woman there. (I guessed they resembled American men in this respect.) Besides, it would be a romantic vacation.

That was how we wound up in Room 201 of the Hotel Reforma in sleepy Mérida, capital of the Yucatán. Mérida's popularity as a tourist town had been eclipsed by the growth of Cancún, the nearest Americanized resort. That meant the boys would be hornier, Boyfriend reasoned. The Hotel Reforma had been recommended by a fellow foreskin fancier. Its chief advantages were the price – about $14 a night – and the fact that the management didn't charge extra for extra guests. I liked it because it was old, airy, and cool, with wrought-iron railings and floor tiles worn thin from all the people who'd come before. Boyfriend liked it because it had a pool, always a good place to cruise, and a disco across the street. That's where we headed as soon as we got in from the airport, showered, and changed into skimpy clothes suitable for turning tropical boys' heads.

There were hardly any tropical boys there, as it turned out, because this was where the Ft Lauderdale college students who couldn't afford spring break in Cancún went to spend their more meager allowances, and not only did it look like a Mexican restaurant-with-disco in Ft. Lauderdale, the management took care to keep all but the most dapper Méridans out lest the coeds be frightened by scruffy street boys. Scruffy street boys, of course, is just what Boyfriend had his eye out for, and at first the pickings looked slim; but we found one who had slipped past security, out to hustle nothing more spicy than a gig showing tourists around the warren of narrow streets near the town's central plaza, stumbling instead onto us. Ten minutes later Boyfriend had his mouth wrapped around a meaty little bundle, *with* foreskin. Luis stuck close to us for several days, probably eating more regularly than usual, and wondering out loud whether all the women in America were like me, and would we take him back with us? Or at least send him a Motley Crüe T-shirt when we went home?

Boyfriend had brought Bob Damron's gay travel guide, which listed for Mérida: a cruisy restaurant (it wasn't) and a cruisy park bench in the Zocalo (it was, and one night Boyfriend stayed out most of the night looking for gay men, who, he said, would run the other way if they saw me coming, and found one, a slender boy who had to pull down the panty hose he wore under his jeans so Boyfriend could get to his cock, and who expressed wonder because he had never seen anyone with so many condoms; in fact most people never had condoms at all. Boyfriend gave him his night's supply and some little brochures, about *el SIDA* he'd brought from the AIDS Foundation, *en español* so even if our limited Spanish didn't get through to our tricks, a pamphlet might).

Damron's also indicated that Mérida had a bathhouse.

I had always wanted to go to a bathhouse, and of course there was not much chance it would ever happen back home. For one thing, they were all closed before I ever moved to San Francisco. For another, even if I dressed enough like a boy to pass, I wouldn't look old enough to be let in. But in Mérida perhaps things were different.

It was away from the town's center, but within walking distance of the Hotel Reforma. Through the tiny front window, grimy from the town's blowing dust, I saw a huge papier-mâché figure of Pan, painted brightly and hung with jewelry, phallus high. It looked like something the Radical Faeries would carry in the Gay Day parade. Everything else about the lobby looked dingy, like the waiting room of a used-car dealership.

Los Baños de Vapor would open at eight that evening. They had a central tub and rooms to rent; massage boys could be rented, too. I would be welcome.

The papier-mâché Pan was at least seven feet tall and was indeed the only bright thing in the lobby. Passing through the courtyard, an overgrown jumble of vines pushing through cracked tile, a slight smell of sulfur, a stagnant fountain, we were shown up a flight of concrete stairs to our room by Carlos, a solid, round-faced man in his midtwenties, wrapped in a frayed white towel. The room was small and completely tiled, grout black from a losing fight with the wet tropical air. At one end was a shower and at the other a bench, a low, vinyl-covered bed, and a massage table. There was a switch that, when flipped, filled the room with steam. Boyfriend flipped it and we shucked our clothes; as the pipes hissed and clanked, Carlos gestured to the massage table and then to me.

Boyfriend answered for me, in Spanish, that I'd love to. I got on the table and Carlos set to work. Boyfriend danced around the table gleefully, sometimes stroking me, sometimes Carlos's butt. "Hey, man, I'm working!" Carlos protested, not very insistently, and Boyfriend went for his cock, stroking it hard, then urged him up onto the table, and Carlos's hands, still slick from the massage oil and warm from the friction of my skin, covered my breasts as Boyfriend rolled a condom onto Carlos's cock and rubbed it up and down my labia a few times and finally let go, letting it sink in. He rode me slow and then hard while the table rocked dangerously and Boyfriend stood at my head, letting me tongue his cock while he played with Carlos's tits. When Boyfriend was sure that we were having a good time, he put on a towel and slipped out the door. Carlos looked surprised. I had to figure out how to say, in Spanish "He's going hunting," and get him to go back to fucking me, solid body slick from oil and steam; if he kept it up, he would make me come, clutching his slippery back, legs in the air.

That was just happening when Boyfriend came back with David. He was pulling him in the door by his already stiff penis, and I suspected Boyfriend had wasted as little time getting him by the dick as he usually did. He had found David in the tub room, he announced, and he had a beautiful, long *uncut* cock. (Boyfriend always enunciated clearly when he said "uncut".) David *did* have a beautiful cock, and he spoke English and was long and slim with startling blue eyes. It turned out he was Chicano, second generation, a senior Riverside High who spent school breaks with his grandmother in Mérida and worked at Los Baños de Vapor as a secret summer job. We found out all this about him as I was showering the sweat and oil off from my fuck with Carlos, and by the time I heard that he'd been working at the Baños since he turned sixteen, I was ready to start fucking again. David was the most quintessentially eighteen-year-old fuck I ever had, except Boyfriend's presence made it unusual; he held David's cock and balls and controlled the speed of the thrusting, until his mouth got preoccupied with Carlos's dick. David told me, ardently, that I was beautiful, though at that point I didn't care if I was beautiful or not, since I was finally in a bathhouse doing what I'd always wanted to do and I felt more like a faggot than a beautiful *gringa*. But David was saying he wished he had a girlfriend like me, even though I was thirty, shockingly old – this actually was what almost all of Boyfriend's conquests said to me, though I suspected not every man could keep up with a girlfriend who was really a faggot, or a boyfriend who was really a woman, or whatever kind of fabulous anomaly I was.

Then someone knocked on the door and we untangled for a minute to answer it, and there were José and Gaspar, laughing and saying we were the most popular room in the Baños at the moment and would we like some more company? At least that's how David translated the torrent of Spanish, for they were both speaking at once. Naturally we invited them in, and lo and behold, Gaspar was actually *gay*, and so while I lay sideways on the massage table with my head off the edge and my legs in the air so I could suck David while José fucked me, I could watch Boyfriend finally getting *his* cock sucked by Gaspar, whose black, glittering Mayan eyes closed in concentration, and I howled with not simply orgasm but the *excitement*, the splendid excitement of being in Mexico in a bathhouse with four uncut men and a maniac, a place no woman I knew had gone before. Steam swirled in the saturated air like superheated fog, beading like pearls in the web of a huge Yucatán spider in the corner; David's cock, or was it José's or Carlos's again, I didn't care, pounded my fully opened cunt rhythmically and I wished I had her view.

You know if you have ever been to a bathhouse that time stands still in the steamy, throbbing air, and so I had no idea how long it went on, only that sometimes I was on my back and sometimes on my knees, and once for a minute I was standing facing the wall, and when Boyfriend wasn't sucking them or fucking me, he was taking snapshots of us, just like a tourist. The floor of the room was completely littered with condoms, which made us all laugh hysterically. Rubber-kneed, Gasper and David held me up with Carlos and José flanking them so Boyfriend could snap one last picture. Then he divided all the rest of the condoms among them – we had more at the hotel, I think that week we went through ten dozen – and got out his brochures. He was trying to explain in Spanish the little condoms he used for giving head – how great they were to use with uncut guys 'cause they disappeared under the foreskin – and I was asking David what it was like to live a double life, Riverside High to Los Baños, and who else came there – "Oh, everybody does," he said – and did they ever want to fuck him – of course they *wanted* to – and did he ever fuck them – well, sure – and how was that? He shrugged and said, as if there were only one possible response to my question, "It's *fucking*."

When we left, the moon was high, the Baños deserted, the warm night air almost cool after the steamy room. The place looked like a courtyard motel, the kind I used to stay in with my parents when we traveled in the early sixties, but overgrown and haunted. The Pan figure glittered in the low lobby light, and the man at the desk charged us $35 – seven for each massage boy, four each to get in, and six for the room. Hundreds of thousands of pesos – he looked anxious, as though he feared we'd think it was too much. We paid him, laughing. I wondered if this was how a Japanese businessman in Thailand felt. Was I contributing to the imperialist decline of the third world? Boyfriend didn't give a shit about things like that, so I didn't mention it. In my hand was a crumpled note from David: "Can I come visit you in your hotel room? No money."

THE BUTCHER

Alina Reyes

Translated from the French by David Watson

NEITHER OF US said a word. I watched the movement of the windscreen wipers. I grew sluggish with the smell of my wet hair next to my cheeks.

He opened the door, took me by the hand. My sandals were full of water, my feet squelched against the plastic soles. He led me to the lounge, sat me down, brought me a coffee. Then he turned on the radio and asked me to excuse him for five minutes. He had to take a shower.

I went over to the window, pulled the curtain open a little and watched the rain falling.

The rain made me want to piss. When I came out of the toilet I pushed open the bathroom door. The room was warm and all steamed up. I saw the broad silhouette through the shower curtain. I pulled it open a little and looked at him. He reached out a hand but I pulled away. I offered to scrub his back. I stepped onto the rim, put my hands under the warm water and picked up the soap, turning it over between my palms until I worked up a thick lather.

I began to rub his back, starting at the neck and shoulders, in circular movements. He was big and pale, firm and muscular. I worked my way down his spine, a hand on each side. I rubbed his

sides, moving round a little onto his stomach. The soap made a fine
scented froth, a cobweb of small white bubbles flowing over the
wet skin, a slippery soft carpet between my palm and his back.

I went up and down the spine several times, from the small of
the back to the base of the neck up to the first little hairs, the
ones the barber shaves off for short haircuts with his deliciously
vibrating razor.

I set off again from the shoulders and soaped each arm in turn.
Although the limbs were relaxed, I felt bulging knots of muscle.
His forearms were covered with dark hairs; I had to really wet
the soap to make the lather stick. I worked back towards the deep
hairy armpits.

I lathered up my hands again and massaged his buttocks in a
revolving motion. Though on the big side, his buttocks had a
harmonious shape, curving gracefully from the small of the back
and joining the lower limbs without flab. I went over and over
their roundness to know their form with my palms as well as with
my eyes. Then I moved down the hard solid legs. The hairy skin
covered barriers of muscle. I felt I was penetrating a new, wilder
region of the body down to the strange treasure of the ankles.

Then he turned towards me. I raised my head and saw his
swelling balls, his taut cock, straight above my eyes.

I got up. He didn't move. I took the soap between my hands again
and began to clean his broad, solid, moderately hairy chest.

I began to move slowly down over his distended stomach,
surrounded by powerful abdominal muscles. It took some time
to cover the whole surface. His navel stood out, a small white
ball outlined by the rounded mass, a star around which my
fingers gravitated, straining to delay the moment when they would
succumb to the downward pull towards the comet erected against
the harmonious round form of the stomach.

I knelt down to massage his abdomen. I skirted round the genital
area slowly, quite gently, towards the inside of the thighs.

His penis was incredibly large and erect.

I resisted the temptation to touch it, continuing to stroke over
the pubis and between the legs. He was now lying back against
the wall, his arms spread, with both hands pressed against the
tiles, his stomach jutting forward. He was groaning.

I felt he was going to come before I even touched him.

I moved away, sat down fully under the shower spray, and with my eyes still fixed on his over-extended penis, I waited until he calmed down a little.

The warm water ran over my hair, inside my dress. Filled with steam, the air frothed around us, effacing all shapes and sounds.

He had been at the peak of excitement, and yet had made no move to hasten the denouement. He was waiting for me. He would wait as long as I wanted to make the pleasure last, and the pain.

I knelt down in front of him again. His cock, already thickly inflated, sprang up.

I moved my hand over his balls, back up to their base near the anus. His cock stood up again, more violently. I held it in my other hand, squeezed it, began slowly pulling it up and down. The soapy water I was lathered with provided perfect lubrication. My hands were filled with a warm, living, magical substance. I felt it beating like the heart of a bird, I helped it ride to its deliverance. Up, down, always the same movement, always the same rhythm, and the moans above my head. And I was moaning too, with the water from the shower sticking my dress to me like a tight silken glove, with the world stopped at the level of my eyes, of his belly, at the sound of the water trickling over us and of his cock sliding under my fingers, at the warm and tender and hard things between my hands, at the smell of the soap, of the soaking flesh and of the sperm mounting under my palm.

The liquid spurted out in bursts, splashing my face and my dress.

He knelt down as well, and licked the tears of sperm from my face. He washed me the way a cat grooms itself, with diligence and tenderness.

His plump white hand, his pink tongue on my cheek, his washed-out blue eyes, the eyelids still heavy as if under the effect of a drug. And his languid heavy body, his body of plenitude . . .

A green tender field of showers in the soft breeze of the branches . . . It is autumn, it is raining, I am a little girl, I am walking in the park and my head is swimming because of the smells, of the water on my skin and my clothes, I see a fat man over there on the bench looking at me so intently that I pee myself, standing up, I am walking and I am peeing myself, it is my warm rain on the park, on the ground, in my knickers, I rain, I give pleasure . . .

He took off my dress, slowly.

Then he stretched me out on the warm tiles and, with the shower still running, began planting kisses all over my body. His powerful hands lifted me up and turned me over with extreme delicacy. Neither the hardness of the floor nor the pressure of his fingers could bruise me.

I relaxed completely. And he placed the pulp of his lips, the wetness of his tongue in the hollow of my arms, under my breasts, on my neck, behind my knees, between my buttocks, he put his mouth all over, the length of my back, the inside of my legs, right to the roots of my hair.

He lay me on my back on the ground, on the warm slippery tiles, lifted my hips with both hands, his fingers firmly thrust into the hollow as far as the spine, his thumbs on my stomach. He placed my legs over his shoulders and brought his tongue up to my vulva. I arched my back sharply. Thousands of drops of water from the shower hit me softly on my stomach and on my breasts. He licked me from my vagina to my clitoris, regularly, his mouth stuck to my outer lips. My sex became a channelled surface from which pleasure streamed, the world disappeared, I was no more than this raw flesh where soon gigantic cascades splashed, in sequence, continually, one after the other, forever.

Finally the tension slackened, my buttocks fell back onto his arms, I recovered gradually, felt the water on my stomach, saw the shower once more, and him, and me.

He had dried me off, put me in the warm bed, and I had fallen asleep.

I woke up slowly to the sound of the rain against the tiles. The sheets and pillow were warm and soft. I opened my eyes. He was lying next to me, looking at me. I placed my hand on his sex. He wanted me again.

I wanted nothing else but that. To make love, all the time, without rage, with patience, persistence, methodically. Go on to the end. He was like a mountain I must climb to the summit, like in my dreams, my nightmares. It would have been best to emasculate him straight away, to eat this still hard still erect still demanding piece of flesh, to swallow it and keep it in my belly, for ever more.

I drew close, raise myself a little, put my arms around him. He took my head between his hands, led my mouth to his, thrust his tongue in all at once, wiggled it at the back of my throat, wrapped it and rolled it over mine. I began biting his lips till I tasted blood.

Then I mounted on top of him, pressed my vulva against his sex, rubbed it against his balls and his cock. I guided it by hand and pushed it into me and it was like a giant flash, the dazzling entry of the saviour, the instantaneous return of grace.

I raised my knees, bent my legs around him and rode him vigorously. Each time when at the crest of the wave I saw his cock emerge glistening and red I held it again and tried to push it even further in.

I was going too fast. He calmed me down gently. I unfolded my legs and lay on top of him. I lay motionless for a moment, contracting the muscles of my vagina around his member.

I chewed him over the expanse of his chest; an electric charge flowed through my tongue, my gums. I rubbed my nose against the fat of his white meat, inhaled its smell, trembling. I was squinting with pleasure. The world was no more than a vibrant abstract painting, a clash of marks the colour of flesh, a well of soft matter I was sinking into with the joyous impulse of perdition. A vibration coming from my eardrums took over my head, my eyes closed. An extraordinarily sharp awareness spread with the waves surging through my skull, it was like a flame, and my brain climaxed, alone and silent, magnificently alone.

He rolled over onto me, and rode me in turn, leaning on his hand so as not to crush me. His balls rubbed against my buttocks, at the entry to my vagina, his hard cock filled me, slid and slid along my deep walls, I dug my nails into his buttocks, he breathed more heavily . . . We came together, on and on, our fluids mingled, our groans mingled, coming from further than the throat, the depths of our chests, sounds alien to the human voice.

It was raining. Enveloped in a large T-shirt which he had lent me I was leaning on the window-sill, kneeling on the chair placed against the wall.

If I knew the language of the rain, of course, I would write it down, but everyone recognizes it, and is able to recall it to their memory. Being in a closed space while outside all is water, trickling, drowning . . . Making love in the cramped backseat of a car, while the windows and roof resonate with the monotonous rain drops . . . The rain undoes bodies, makes them full of softness and damp patches . . . slimy and slobbering like snails . . .

He was also wearing a T-shirt, lying on the couch, his big buttocks, his big genitals, and his big legs bare.

He came over to me and pressed his hard cock against my buttocks. I wanted to turn round but he grabbed me by the hair, pulled my head back and began to push himself into my anus. It hurt, and I was trapped on the chair, condemned to keep my head pointing skywards.

Finally he entered fully, and the pain subsided. He began to move up and down, I was full of him, I could feel nothing except his huge monster cock right inside, whilst outside the bucketing rain poured down pure liquid light.

Continuing to jerk himself in me, to dig at me like a navvy while keeping my head held back, he slid two fingers into my vagina, then pulled them out. So I put in my own and felt the hard cock pounding behind the lining, and I began to fondle myself to the same rhythm. He speeded up his thrusts, my excitement grew, a mixture of pain and pleasure. His stomach bumped against my back with each thrust of the hips, and he penetrated me a bit further, invaded me a bit further. I wanted to free my head but he pulled my hair even harder, my throat was horribly stretched, my eyes were turned stubbornly towards the emptying sky, and he struck me and hammered me to the depths of myself, he shook up my body and then filled me with his hot liquid which came out in spurts, striking me softly, pleasurably.

A large drop would regularly drip somewhere with the sound of hollow metal. He let go of my hair, I let my head sink against the casement and began to sway imperceptibly.

I had him undress and stretch out on his back on the ground. With the expanders on his exercise machine I tied his arms to the foot of the bed, his legs to those of the table.

We were both tired. I sat down in the armchair and looked at him for a moment, spread-eagled and motionless.

His body pleased me like that, full of exposed imprisoned flesh, burst open in its splendid imperfection. Uprooted man, once more pinned to the ground, his sex like a fragile pivot exiled from the shadows and exposed to the light of my eyes.

Everything would have to be a sex; the curtains, the moquette, the expanders and the furniture, I would need a sex instead of my head, another instead of his.

We would both need to be hanging from an iron hook face to face in a red fridge, hooked by the top of the skull or the ankles, head down, legs spread, our flesh face to face, rendered powerless to the knife of our sexes burning like red-hot irons, brandished, open. We would need to scream ourselves to death under the tyranny of our sexes, what are our sexes?

Last summer, first acid, I lost my hands first of all, and then my name, the name of my race, lost humanity from my memory, from the knowledge of my head and of my body, lost the idea of man, of woman, or even of creature; I sought for a while, who am I? My sex. My sex remained to the world, with its desire to piss. The only place where my soul had found refuge, had become concentrated, the only place where I existed, like an atom, wandering between sky and grass, between green and blue, with no other feeling than that of a pure atom-sex, just, barely, driven by the desire to piss, gone astray, blissful, in the light, Saint-Laurent peninsula, it was one summer's day, no it was autumn, it took me all night and the next morning to come down, but for months afterwards when I pissed I lost myself, the moment of dizziness that's it, I draw myself back entirely into my sex as if into a navel, my being is there in that sensation in the centre of the body, the rest of the body annihilated, I no longer know myself, have no form nor title, the ultimate trip each time and sometimes still, just an instant, like being hung head down in the great spiral of the universe, but only you know what those moments mean, afterwards I say to myself "is that really who I am?" and "how beautiful the world is, with all those bunches of black grapes, how good it is to go grape-picking at the height of summer, with the sun catching the grapes and the eyes of the pickers, the vines are twisted, how I'd love to piss at the end of the row!", and there are all sorts of stupid things like that in our bodies, so good do we feel after that weird dizziness which we miss a little, nevertheless, already.

I got up, knelt with my legs apart above his head. Still out of range of his face, I pulled open my outer lips with my fingers and gave him a long look at my vulva.

Then I stroked it slowly, with a rotating movement, from my anus to my clitoris.

I would have wanted grey skies where hope is focused, where quivering trees spread their fairy arms, capricious, hot-headed dreams in the grass kissed by the wind, I would have wanted to feel between my legs the huge breath of the millions of men on earth. I would have wanted, look, look at what I want . . .

I pushed the fingers of my left hand into my vagina, continued to rub myself. My fingers are not my fingers, but a heavy ingot, a thick square ingot stuck inside me, dazzling with gold to the dark depths of my dream. My hands went faster and faster. I rode the air in spasms, threw my head back, weeping onto his eyes as I came.

I regained the armchair. His face had turned red, he grew erect again, fairly softly. He was defenceless.

When I was small, I knew nothing about love. Making love, that magic word, the promise of that unbelievably wonderful thing which would happen all the time as soon as we were big. I had no idea about penetration, not even about what men have between their legs, in spite of all those showers with my brothers. You can look and look in vain, what do you know, when you have the taste for mystery?

When I was even smaller, no more than four, they talked in front of me thinking that I wasn't listening; Daddy told about a madman who ran screaming through the woods at night. I open the gate of my grandmother's garden, and all alone with my alsatian bitch I enter the woods. At the first gap in the trees, on a mound of sand, I lie down with the bitch, up against her warm flank, an arm around her neck. She puts out her tongue and she waits, like me. No one. The pines draw together and bend over us, in a tender, scary gesture. In the middle of the woods there is a long concrete drain, bordered with brambles where blackberries grow, and where one day a kart driver hurtled violently off the track in front of me and put his eyes out. There is a blockhouse with a black mouth disguised as a door, and right at the end a washing plant devoured by moss and grass. Preserved in the watercourse is the hardened print of an enormous foot.

I went and lay on the ground next to him, laid my head on his stomach, my mouth against his cock, one hand on his balls, and I went to sleep. Certainly the footprint in the wet cement was of a big, strong, blond and probably handsome soldier.

When I woke up next to his penis I took it in my mouth, sucked it in several times with my tongue, felt it swell and touch the back of my throat. I massaged his balls, licked them, then returned to his cock. I placed it in the hollow of both my eyes, on my forehead, on my cheeks, against my nose, on my mouth, my chin, my throat, put my neck on it, squeezed it between my shoulder blades and my bent head, in my armpit, then the other, brushed against it with my breasts till I almost reached a climax, rubbed it with my stomach, my back, my buttocks, my thighs, squeezed it between my arms and my folded legs, pressed the sole of my foot against it, until I had left a trace of it over the whole of my body.

Then I put it back in my mouth and gave it a long suck, like you suck your thumb, your mother's breast, life, while he moaned and panted, always, until he ejaculates, in a sharp lamentation, and I drink his sperm, his sap, his gift.

BEAUTY'S PUNISHMENT

Anne Rice

I The Auction in the Market-Place

THE CART HAD come to a stop, and Beauty could see through the tangle of white arms and tousled hair the walls of the village below, with the gates open and a motley crowd swelling out onto the green.

But slaves were being quickly unloaded from the cart, forced with the smack of the belt to crowd together on the grass. And Beauty was immediately separated from Tristan, who was pulled roughly away from her for no apparent reason other than the whim of a guard.

The leather bits were being pulled out of the mouths of the others. "Silence!" came the loud voice of the Commander. "There is no speech for slaves in the village! Any who speak shall be gagged again more cruelly than they have ever been before!"

He rode his horse round the little herd, driving it tightly together, and gave the order that the slaves' hands should be unbound and woe to any slave who removed his or her hands from the back of the neck.

"The village has no need of your impudent voices!" he went on. "You are beasts of burden now, whether that burden be labor or pleasure! And you shall keep your hands to the back of your necks or be yoked and driven before a plow through the fields!"

Beauty was trembling violently. She couldn't see Tristan as she was forced forward. All around her were long windblown tresses, bowed heads, and tears. It seemed the slaves cried more softly without their gags, struggling to keep their lips closed, and the voices of the guards were miserably sharp!

"Move! Head up straight!" came the gruff, impatient commands. Beauty felt chills rising on her arms and legs at the sound of those angry voices. Tristan was behind her somewhere, but if only he would come close.

And why had they been put out here so far from the village? And why was the cart being turned around?

Suddenly she knew. They were to be driven on foot, like a gaggle of geese to market. And almost as quickly as the thought came to her, the mounted guards swooped down on the little group and started them forward with a rain of blows.

"This is too bitter," Beauty thought. She was trembling as she started to run, the smack of the paddle as always catching her when she did not expect it and sending her flying forward over the soft, newly turned earth of the road.

"At a trot, with heads up!" the guard shouted, "and knees up as well!" And Beauty saw the horses' hooves pounding beside her, just as she'd seen them before on the Bridle Path at the castle, and felt the same wild trepidation as the paddle cracked her thighs and even her calves. Her breasts ached as she ran, and a dull warm pain coursed through her sore legs.

She couldn't see the crowd clearly, but she knew they were there, hundreds of villagers, perhaps even thousands, flooding out of the gates to meet the slaves. "And we're to be driven right through them; it's too awful," she thought, and suddenly the resolves she had made in the cart, to disobey, to rebel, left her. She was too purely afraid. And she was running as fast as she could down the road towards the village, the paddle finding her no matter how she hurried, until she realized she had pressed through the first rank of slaves and was now running with them, no one before her anymore to shield her from the sight of the enormous crowd.

Banners flew from the battlements. Arms waved and cheers rose as the slaves drew closer, and through the excitement there came the sounds of derision, and Beauty's heart thudded as she tried not to see too clearly what lay ahead, though she could not turn away.

"No protection, nowhere to hide," she thought, "and where is Tristan? Why can't I fall back into the flock?" But when she tried, the paddle smacked her soundly again, and the guard shouted to her to go forward! And blows were rained on those around her, causing the little red-haired Princess on her right to break into helpless tears. "O, what's to happen to us? Why did we disobey?!" the little Princess wailed through her sobs, but the dark-haired Prince on the other side of Beauty threw her a warning glance: "Quiet or it will be worse!"

Beauty couldn't help but think of her long march to the Prince's Kingdom, how he had led her through the villages where she had been honored and admired as his chosen slave. Nothing like that was happening now.

The crowd had broken loose and was spreading out on either side of them as they neared the gates. Beauty could see the women in their fancy white aprons and wooden shoes, and the men in their rawhide boots and leather jerkins, robust faces everywhere alight with obvious pleasure, which made Beauty gasp and drop her eyes to the path before her.

They were passing through the gates. A trumpet was being sounded. And hands reached out from everywhere to touch them, pushing them, pulling at their hair. Beauty felt fingers brush roughly across her face; her thighs were slapped. She let out a desperate scream, struggling to escape the hands that shoved her violently forward, while all around came the loud, deep, mocking laughter, shouts and exclamations, random cries.

Tears were flowing down Beauty's face and she hadn't even realized it. Her breasts throbbed with the same violent pulse she felt in her temples. Around her she saw the tall, narrow half-timbered houses of the village opening broadly to surround a huge marketplace. A high wooden platform with a gibbet upon it loomed over all. And hundreds crowded the overhanging windows and balconies, waving white handkerchiefs, cheering, while countless others choked the narrow lanes that led into the square, struggling to get close to the miserable slaves.

They were being forced into a pen behind the platform. Beauty saw a flight of rickety wooden steps leading to the boards above and a length of leather chain dangling above the distant gibbet. A man stood to one side of the gibbet with arms folded, waiting, while another sounded the trumpet again as the gates of the pen were shut. The crowd surrounded them, and there was no more than a thin strip of fencing to protect them. Hands reached for them again as they huddled together. Beauty's buttocks were pinched, her long hair lifted.

She struggled towards the center, desperately looking for Tristan. She glimpsed him only for a moment as he was pulled roughly to the bottom of the steps.

"No, I must be sold with him," she thought and pushed violently forward, but one of the guards shoved her back into the little cluster while the crowd hooted and howled and laughed.

The red-haired Princess who had cried on the road was now inconsolable, and Beauty pressed close to her, trying to comfort her as much as to hide. The Princess had lovely high breasts with very large pink nipples, and her red hair spilled down in rivulets over her tear-stained face. The crowd was cheering and shouting again now that the herald had finished. "Don't be afraid," Beauty whispered. "Remember, it will be very much like the castle finally. We will be punished, made to obey."

"No, it won't be!" the Princess whispered, trying not to move her lips visibly as she spoke. "And I thought I was such a rebel. I thought I was so stubborn."

The trumpet gave a third full-throated blast, a high echoing series of notes. And in the immediate silence that fell over the marketplace, a voice rang out:

"The Spring Auction will now commence!"

A roar rose from all around them, a near-deafening chorus, its loudness shocking Beauty so that she couldn't feel herself breathe. The sight of her own quivering breasts stunned her, and in one sweeping glance she saw hundreds of eyes passing over her, examining her, measuring her naked endowments, a hundred whispering lips and smiles.

Meantime the Princes were being tormented by the guards, their cocks lightly whipped with the leather belts, hands plumping their pendulous balls as they were made to "Come to attention!" and punished with severe cracks of the paddle to the buttocks if they did not. Tristan's back was to Beauty. She could see the hard perfect muscles of his legs and buttocks quivering as the guard teased him, stroking him roughly between the legs. She was miserably sorry now for their stolen lovemaking. If he could not come to attention, she would be to blame.

But the booming voice had sounded again:

"All those of the village know the rules of the auction. These disobedient slaves offered by our gracious Majesty for hard labor are to be sold to the highest bidder for the period of no less than three months' service as their new Lords and Masters shall see fit. Mute menials these incorrigibles are to remain, and they are to be brought to the Place of Public Punishment as often as their Masters and Mistresses will allow, there to suffer for the amusement of the crowd as much as for their own improvement."

The guard had moved away from Tristan, giving him an almost-playful blow with the paddle and smiling as he whispered something in Tristan's ear.

"You are solemnly charged to work these slaves," the voice of the herald on the platform continued, "to discipline them, to tolerate no disobedience from them, and never an impudent word. And any Master or Mistress might sell his slave within this village at any time for any sum as he should choose."

The red-haired Princess pressed her naked breasts against Beauty and Beauty leaned forward to kiss her neck. Beauty felt the tight wiry hair of the girl's pubis against her leg, its moisture and its heat. "Don't cry," she whispered.

"When we go back, I will be perfect, perfect!" the Princess confided, and broke into fresh sobs again.

"But what made you disobey?" Beauty quickly whispered in her ear.

"I don't know," the girl wailed, opening her blue eyes wide. "I wanted to see what would happen!" and she started to cry piteously again.

"Be it understood that each time you punish one of these unworthy slaves," the herald continued, "you do the bidding of her Royal Majesty. It is with her hand that you strike the blow, with her lips you scold. All slaves once a week are to be sent to the central grooming hall. Slaves are to be properly fed. Slaves are to be given time to sleep. Slaves should at all times exhibit evidence of sound whipping. Insolence or rebellion should be thoroughly put down."

The trumpet blasted again. White handkerchiefs waved, and all around hundreds upon hundreds clapped their hands. The red-haired Princess screamed as a young man, leaning over the fence of the pen, caught her by the thigh and pulled her towards him.

The guard stopped him with a good-natured reprimand but not before he had slipped his hand under the Princess's wet sex.

But Tristan was being driven up to the wooden platform. He held his head high, hands clasped to the neck as before, his whole attitude one of dignity despite the paddle soundly playing on his narrow tight buttocks as he climbed the wooden steps.

For the first time Beauty saw beneath the high gibbet and its dangling leather links a low round turntable onto which a tall gaunt man in a bright jerkin of green velvet forced Tristan. He kicked Tristan's legs wide apart as if the Prince could not be addressed even with the simplest command.

"He's being handled like an animal," Beauty thought, watching.

Standing back, the tall auctioneer worked the turntable with a foot pedal so that Tristan was turned quickly round and round.

Beauty got no more than a glimpse of his scarlet face and golden hair, blue eyes almost closed. Sweat gleamed on his hard chest and belly, his cock enormous and thick as the guards had wanted it, his legs trembling slightly with the strain of being so widely spread apart.

Desire curled inside of Beauty, and even as she pitied him, she felt her organs swelling and pulsing again, and at the same time the terrible fear, "I can't be made to stand up there alone before everyone. I can't be sold off like this! I can't!"

But how many times at the castle had she said these words. A loud burst of laughter from a nearby balcony caught her off-guard. Everywhere there were loud conversations, arguments, as the turntable went round again and then again, the blond curls slipping off the nape of Tristan's neck to make him appear the more naked and vulnerable.

"Exceptionally strong Prince," cried the auctioneer, his voice even louder, deeper than that of the herald, cutting through the roar of conversation, "long-limbed, yet sturdy of build. Fit for household labor certainly, field labor most definitely, stable labor without question."

Beauty winced.

The auctioneer had in his hand a paddle of the long narrow flexible leather kind that is more a stiff strap almost than a paddle, and with this he slapped Tristan's cock as Tristan faced the pen of slaves again, announcing to one and all:

"Strong, attentive organ, capable of great service, great endurance," and volleys of laughter rose everywhere from the square.

The auctioneer reached out and, taking Tristan by the hair, bent him from the waist suddenly, giving the turntable another whirl while Tristan remained bent over.

"Excellent buttocks," came the deep booming voice, and then the inevitable smacks of the paddle, leaving their red blotches on Tristan's skin. "Resilient, soft!" cried the auctioneer, prodding the flesh with his fingers. Then his hand went to Tristan's face, lifting it, "and demure, quiet of temperament, eager to be obedient! And well he should be!" Another crack of the paddle and laughter all around.

"What is he thinking," Beauty thought. "I can't endure it!"

The auctioneer had caught Tristan by the head again, and Beauty saw the man lifting a black leather phallus, which hung from the belt of his green velvet jerkin by a chain. Before she even realized what he meant to do, he had thrust the leather into Tristan's anus, bringing more cheers and screams from all quarters of the marketplace, while Tristan bowed from the waist as before, his face still.

"Need I say more?" cried the auctioneer, "or shall the bids begin!"

At once they started, bids shouted from everywhere, each topped as soon as it was heard, a woman on a nearby balcony – a shopkeeper's wife, surely, in her rich velvet bodice and white linen blouse – rising to her feet to call her bid over the heads of the others.

"And they are all so very rich," Beauty thought, "the weavers and dyers and silversmiths for the Queen herself, and so any of them has the money to buy us." Even a crude-looking woman with thick red hands and a soiled apron called out her bid from the door of the butcher's shop, but she was quickly out of the game.

The little turntable went round and round slowly, the auctioneer finally coaxing the crowd as the bidding grew higher. With a slender leather-covered rod that he drew from a scabbard like a sword, he pushed the flesh of Tristan's buttocks this way and that, stroking at his anus, as Tristan stood quiet and humble, only the furious blush of his face giving his misery away.

But a voice rose suddenly from far back in the square, topping all the bids by a broad margin, and Beauty heard a murmur rush through the crowd. She stood on tiptoe trying to see what was happening. A man had stepped forward before the platform and, through the scaffolding beneath it, she could just see him. He was a white-haired man, though he was not old enough for such white hair, and it sat upon him with unusual loveliness framing a square and rather pacific face.

"So the Queen's Chronicler wants this sturdy young mount," cried the auctioneer. "Is there no one to outbid him? Do I hear more for this gorgeous prince? Come on, surely . . ."

Another bid, but at once the Chronicler topped it, his voice so soft it was a wonder Beauty heard, and this time his bid was so high that clearly he meant to shut off all opposition.

"Sold," the auctioneer cried out finally, "to Nicolas, the Queen's Chronicler and Chief Historian of the Queen's village! For the grand sum of twenty-five gold pieces."

And as Beauty watched through her tears, Tristan was roughly pulled from the platform, rushed down the stairs, and driven towards the white-haired man who stood composed with his arms folded, the dark gray of his exquisitely cut jerkin making him look the Prince himself as he silently inspected his purchase. With a snap of his fingers he ordered Tristan to precede him at a trot out of the square.

The crowd opened reluctantly to let the Prince pass, pushing at him and scolding him. But Beauty had only a glimpse of this before she realized with a scream that she was herself being dragged out of the gaggle of crying slaves towards the steps.

II Beauty on the Block

"No, it can't be happening!" she thought, and she felt her legs give out from under her as the paddle smacked her. And the tears blinded her as she was almost carried to the platform and the turntable and set down. It did not matter that she had not walked in obedience.

She was there! And before her the crowd stretched in all directions, grinning faces and waving hands, short girls and boys leaping up the better to see, and those on balconies rising to get a more careful look.

Beauty felt she would collapse, yet she was standing, and when the soft rawhide boot of the auctioneer kicked her legs apart, she struggled to keep her balance, her breasts shivering with her muffled sobs.

"Lovely little Princess!" he was calling out, the turntable whirling suddenly, so that she almost fell forward. She saw behind her hundreds and hundreds crowded back to the village gates, more balconies and windows, soldiers lounging along the battlements above. "Hair like spun gold and ripe little breasts!"

The auctioneer's arm wound round her, squeezing her bosom hard, pinching her nipples. She let out a scream behind her closed lips, yet felt the immediate surge between her legs. But if he should take her by the hair as he had done Tristan . . .

And even as she thought it, she felt herself forced to bow from the waist in the same fashion, her breasts seeming to swell with their own weight as they dangled beneath her. And the paddle found her buttocks again, to the screaming delight of the crowd. Claps, laughs, shouts, as the auctioneer lifted her face with the stiff black leather, though he kept her bent over, spinning the turntable faster. "Lovely endowments, fit surely for the finest household, who would waste this pretty morsel in the fields?"

"Sell her into the fields!" someone shouted. And there were more cheers and laughter. And when the paddle smacked her again, Beauty gave out a humiliating wail.

The auctioneer clamped his hand over her mouth and he forced her up with her chin in the air, letting her go to stand with her back arched. "I will collapse, I will faint," Beauty thought, her heart pounding in her breast, but she was standing there, enduring it, even as she felt the sudden tickle of the leather-covered rod between her pubic lips. "O, not that, he cannot . . ." she thought, but already her wet sex was swelling, hungering for the rough stroking of the rod. She squirmed away from it.

The crowd roared.

And she realized she was twisting her hips in horrid vulgar fashion to escape the sharp prodding examination.

There was more clapping and shouting as the auctioneer forced the rod deep into her hot wet pubis, calling out all the while, "Dainty, elegant little girl, fit for the finest lady's maid or gentleman's diversion!" Beauty knew her face was scarlet. Never at the castle had she known such exposure. And as her legs gave out from under her again, she felt the auctioneer's sure hand lifting her wrists above her head until she dangled above the platform, and the leather paddle slapped at her helpless calves and the soles of her feet. Without meaning to, Beauty kicked helplessly. She lost all control.

Screaming behind her clenched teeth, she struggled madly as she hung in the man's grip. A strange, desperate abandon came over her as the paddle licked at her sex, slapping it and stroking it, and the screams and roars deafened her. She did not know whether she was longing for the torment or wildly trying to shut it out.

Her own frantic breaths and sobs filled her ears, and she knew suddenly that she was giving the onlookers precisely the kind of show they adored. They were getting much more from her than they had from Tristan, and she did not know whether or not she cared. Tristan was gone. She was forsaken.

The paddle punished her, stinging her and driving her hips out in a wild arc, only to stroke her wet pubic hair again, inundating her with waves of pleasure as well as pain.

In pure defiance, she swung her body with all her force, almost pulling loose from the auctioneer, who gave a loud astonished laugh. The crowd was shrieking as he sought to steady her, his tight fingers biting into her wrists as he hoisted her higher, and out of the corner of her eye Beauty saw two crudely dressed varlets rushing towards the platform.

At once they bound her wrists to the leather chain that hung from the gibbet above her head. Now she dangled free, the auctioneer's paddle turning her with his blows as she sobbed and tried to hide her face in her upstretched arm.

"We haven't all day to amuse ourselves with the little Princess," the auctioneer cried, though the crowd urged him on with shouts of "Spank her," "Punish her."

"Calling for a firm hand and severe discipline for this lovely lady, what am I bid?" He twisted Beauty, smacking the soles of her naked feet with the paddle, pushing her head through her arms so that she could not conceal her face.

"Lovely breasts, tender arms, delectable buttocks, and a sweet little pleasure cleft fit for the gods!"

But the bids were already flying, topped so quickly he did not have to repeat them, and through her swimming eyes Beauty saw the hundreds of faces gazing up at her, the young men crowded to the very edge of the platform, a pair of young women whispering and pointing, and beyond an old woman leaning on a cane as she studied Beauty, raising a withered finger now to offer a bid.

Again the sense of abandon came over her, the defiance, and she kicked and wailed behind her closed lips, wondering that she didn't shout aloud. Was it more humiliating to admit that she could speak? Would her face have been more scarlet had she been made to demonstrate that she was a thinking, feeling creature, and not some dumb slave?

Her sobs were her only answer to herself, her legs pulled wide apart now as the bidding continued, the auctioneer spreading her buttocks with the leather rod as he had done to Tristan, stroking her anus so that she squealed and clenched her teeth, and twisted, even trying to kick him if she could.

But he was now confirming the highest bid, and then another, and trying to coax more out of the crowd until she heard him announce in that same deep voice:

"Sold to the Innkeeper, Mistress Jennifer Lockley of the Sign of the Lion, for the grand sum of twenty-seven pieces of gold, this spirited and amusing little Princess, surely to be whipped for her bread and butter as much as anything else!"

III The Place of Public Punishment

THE SUNLIGHT was too bright for a moment. But Beauty was busy folding her arms and marching, lifting her legs as high as she could, and finally the square became visible as they entered it. She saw its shifting crowds of idlers and gossips, several youths sitting on the broad stone rim of the well, horses tethered at the gates of the Inns, and then other naked slaves here and there, some on their knees, some marching as she was.

The Captain turned her with another one of those large soft spanks, squeezing her right buttock a little as he did it.

Half in a dream it seemed, Beauty found herself in a broad street, full of shops much like the lane down which she had come, but this street was crowded and everyone was busy, purchasing, bargaining, arguing.

That terrible feeling of regularity came back to her, that all of this had happened before, or at least that it was so familiar that it might have. A naked slave on her hands and knees cleaning a shop window looked ordinary enough, and to see another with a basket strapped to his back, marching as Beauty was being marched, before a woman who drove him with a stick – yes, that too looked regular. Even the slaves, bound naked on the walls, their legs apart, their faces in half-sleep, seemed just the ordinary thing, and why shouldn't the young village men taunt them as they passed, slapping an erect cock here, pinching a poor shy nether mouth there? Yes, ordinary.

Even the awkward thrust of her breasts, her arms folded behind her to force her breasts out, all of that seemed quite sensible and a proper way to march, Beauty thought. And when she felt another warm spank she marched more briskly and tried to lift her knees more gracefully.

They were coming to the other end of the village now, the open marketplace, and all around the empty auction platform she saw hundreds milling. Delicious aromas rose from the little cookshops, and she could even smell the wine that the young men bought by the cup at the open stands, and she saw the fabrics blowing in long streams from the fabric shop, and heaps of baskets and rope for sale, and everywhere naked slaves at a thousand tasks.

In an alleyway, a slave on his knees swept vigorously with a small broom. Two others on all fours bore baskets full of fruit on their backs as they hurried at a fast trot through a doorway. Against a wall, a slender Princess hung upside down, her pubic hair gleaming in the sun, her face red and flushed with tears, her feet neatly tethered to the wall above with wide tightly laced anklets.

But they had come into another square opening off the first, and this was a strange unpaved place where the earth was soft and freshly turned as it had been on the Bridle Path at the castle. Beauty had been allowed to stop, and the Captain stood beside her with his thumbs hooked in his belt, watching everything.

Beauty saw another high turntable, like that at the auction, and on it, a bound slave was being fiercely paddled by a man who worked the turntable round and round with a pedal as the auctioneer had done, whipping hard at the naked buttocks each time it spun to the proper position. The poor victim was a gorgeously muscled Prince, with his hands bound tight on his back and his chin mounted up on a short rough column of wood so that all could see his face as he was punished. "How can he keep his eyes open?" Beauty thought. "How can he bear to look at them?" The crowd around the platform squawked and screamed as stridently as they had done at the earlier bidding.

And when the paddler raised his leather weapon now to signal the punishment was at an end, the poor Prince, his body convulsing, his face twisted and wet, was pelted with soft bits of fruit and refuse.

Like the other square it had the atmosphere of a fair, with the same cookshops and wine vendors. From high windows hundreds watched, their arms folded on sills and balcony edges.

But the turntable paddling was not the only form of punishment. A high wooden pole stood far to the right, with many long leather ribbons streaming down from an iron ring at the top of it. At the end of each black ribbon was a slave tethered by a leather collar that forced the head high, and all marched slowly but with prancing steps in a circle around the pole, to the constant blows of four paddle-wielding attendants stationed at four points of the circle like the four points of a compass. A round track was worn in the dust from the naked feet. Some hands were bound behind the back; others were clasped there freely.

A straggle of village men and women watched the circular march, commenting here and there, and Beauty looked on in dazed silence as one of the slaves, a young Princess with large floppy brown curls, was untethered and given back to a waiting Master, who whipped at the slave's ankles with a straw broom as he drove her forward.

"There," said the Captain, and Beauty marched obediently beside him towards the high Maypole with its turning bands of leather.

"Tether her," he said to the guard, who quickly pulled Beauty over and buckled the leather collar around her neck so her chin was forced up over the edge of it.

In a blur, Beauty saw the Captain watching. Two village women were near him and talking to him, and she saw him say something rather matter-of-factly.

The long band of leather running down from the top of the pole was heavy and carried along in a circle on the iron ring by the momentum of the others, and it almost pulled Beauty forward by the collar. She marched a little faster so that it would not, but it tugged her back, until she finally fell into the right step, and felt the first loud spanking blow from one of the four guards who rather casually waited to punish her. There were so many slaves trotting in the circle now that the guards were always swinging their bright ovals of black leather, Beauty realized, though she was blessed with a few slow seconds between blows, the dust and the sunlight stinging her eyes as she watched the tousled hair of the slave ahead of her.

"Public Punishment." She remembered the words of the auctioneer telling all Masters and Mistresses to prescribe it whenever they felt it necessary. And she knew that the Captain would never think, like her well-mannered, silver-tongued Masters and Mistresses at the castle, to give her a reason for it. But what did it matter? That he wanted her punished because he was bored or curious, that was reason enough, and each time she made the full circle she saw him clearly for a few moments, his arms at his sides, his legs firmly apart, his green eyes fixed on her. What were all the reasons but foolishness, she mused. And as she braced herself for another smart blow – losing her footing and her grace for an instant in the powdery dust as the paddle swept her hips forward – she felt an odd contentment, unlike anything she'd known at the castle.

There was no tension in her. The familiar ache in her vagina, the lust for the Captain's cock, the paddle's crack, these things were there as she marched, the leather collar bouncing cruelly against her uplifted chin, the balls of her feet smacking the packed earth, but still it was not that terrible quavering dread she had known before.

But her reverie was broken by a loud cry from the crowd near her. Over the heads of those who leered at her and the other marching slaves, she saw that the poor punished Prince was being taken down from the turntable where he had remained for so long an object of public derision. And now another slave, a Princess with yellow hair like her own, was forced into place, back arching down, buttocks high, chin mounted.

Coming round the dusty little circle again, Beauty saw that the Princess was squirming as her hands were tied behind her back, and the chin rest was being cranked up by an iron bolt so that she couldn't turn her head. Her knees were bound to the turntable and she kicked her feet furiously. The crowd was as thrilled as it had been by Beauty's display on the auction block. And it showed its pleasure with much cheering.

But Beauty's eye caught the Prince who had been taken down and she saw him rushed to a nearby pillory. There were several pillories, in fact, in a row in their own little clearing. And there the Prince was bent over from the waist, his legs as always kicked apart, his face and hands clamped in place, the board coming down with a loud splat to hold him looking forward and quite unable to hide his face, or for that matter to do anything.

The crowd closed in around the helpless figure. As Beauty came round again, groaning suddenly at an unusually hard crack of the paddle, she saw the other slaves, Princesses all, pilloried in the same way, tormented by the crowds, who felt of them, stroked them, pinched them as they chose, though one villager was giving one of the Princesses a drink of water.

The Princess had to lap it, of course, and Beauty saw the pink dart of her tongue into the shallow cup, but still it seemed a mercy.

The Princess on the turntable meantime was kicking and bouncing and giving the most marvelous show, her eyes shut, her mouth a grimace, and the crowd was chanting the number of each blow aloud in a rhythm that sounded oddly frightening.

But Beauty's time of trial at the Maypole was coming to an end. Very quickly and deftly, she was released from the collar and taken panting from the circle. Her buttocks smarted and seemed to swell as if waiting for the next spank, which never came. Her arms ached as they lay doubled behind her back, but she stood waiting.

The Captain's large hand turned her around and he seemed to tower over her, gilded with sunlight, his hair sparkling around the dark shadow of his face as he bent to kiss her. He cradled her head in his hands and drew on her lips, opening them, stabbing his tongue into her, and then letting her go.

Beauty sighed to feel his lips withdrawn, the kiss rooting deep into her loins. Her nipples rubbed against the thick lacing on his jerkin, and the cold buckle of his belt burned her. She saw his dark face crease with a slow smile and his knee pressed against her hurting sex, teasing its hunger. Her weakness seemed complete suddenly and to have nothing to do with the tremors in her legs or her exhaustion.

"March," he said. And turning her around he sent her with a soft squeeze of her sore buttock towards the far side of the square.

They drew near to the pilloried slaves, who writhed and twisted under the taunts and slaps of the idle crowd milling about them. And behind, Beauty saw closely for the first time a long row of brilliantly colored tents set back beneath a line of trees, each tent with its canopied entrance open. A young man handsomely dressed stood at each tent and though Beauty could glimpse nothing in the shadowy interiors, she heard the voices of the men one by one tempting the crowd:

"Beautiful Prince inside, Sir, only ten pence." Or "Lovely little Princess, Sir, your pleasure for fifteen pence." And more invitations like these. "Can't afford your own slave; enjoy the best for only ten pence." "Pretty Prince needing punishment, Madam. Do the Queen's bidding for fifteen pence." And Beauty realized that men and women were going and coming from the tents, one by one, and sometimes together.

"And so even the commonest of the villagers," Beauty thought, "can enjoy the same pleasure." And ahead at the end of the row of tents, she saw a whole gathering of dusty and naked slaves, their heads down, their hands tethered to the tree branch above behind a man who called out to one and all: "Hire by the hour or the day these lovelies for the lowliest service." On a trestle table at his side was an assortment of straps and paddles.

She marched on, absorbing these little spectacles almost as if the sights and the sounds were stroking her, the Captain's large firm hand now and again punishing her softly.

When at last they reached the Inn, and Beauty stood in the little bedchamber again, her legs wide, her hands behind her neck, she thought drowsily, "You are my Lord and Master."

It seemed in some other incarnation she had lived all her life in the village, had served a soldier, and the mingling of noises coming from the square outside was a comforting music.

She was the Captain's slave, yes, utterly his, to run through the public streets, to punish, to subjugate totally.

And when he tumbled her on the bed, spanked her breasts, and took her hard again, she turned her head this way and that, whispering, "Master, and then Master."

Somewhere in the back of her mind she knew it was forbidden to speak, but this seemed no more than a moan or a scream. Her mouth was open and she was sobbing as she came, her arms rising and encircling the Captain's neck. His eyes flickered, then blazed through the gloom. And there came his final thrusts, driving her over the brink into delirium.

For a long time she lay still, her head cradled in the pillow. She felt the long leather ribbon of the Maypole prodding her to trot as if she were still lost in the Place of Public Punishment.

It seemed her breasts would burst as they throbbed from the recent slaps. But she realized the Captain had taken off all his clothes and was slipping into the bed naked beside her.

His warm hand lay on her drenched sex, his fingers parting the lips ever so gently. She drew close to his naked limbs, his powerful arms and legs covered with soft curly golden down, his smooth clean chest pressed against her arm and her hip. His roughly shaven chin grazed her cheek. Then his lips kissed her.

She closed her eyes against the deepening afternoon light from the little window. The dim noises of the village, thin voices from the street, the dull bursts of laughter from the Inn below, all merged into a low hum that lulled her. The light grew bright before it began to fade. The little fire leapt on the hearth, and the Captain covered Beauty with his limbs and breathed in deep sleep against her.

IV Soldiers' Night at the Inn

FOR HOURS Beauty slept. And only vaguely was she aware of the Captain jerking the bell rope. He was up and dressed without an order to her. And when she fully opened her eyes, he stood over her in the dim light of a new hearth fire, his belt still unbuckled. In one swift movement he slipped it from around his waist and snapped it beside him. Beauty couldn't read his face. It looked hard and removed and yet there was a little smile on his lips, and her loins immediately acknowledged him. She could feel a deep stirring of passion inside, a soft discharge of fluids.

But before she could break through the languor, he had pulled her up and deposited her on the floor on her hands and knees, pressing her neck down and forcing her knees wide apart. Beauty's face flamed as the strap walloped her between the legs, stinging her bulging pubis. Again came a hard slap to the lips, and Beauty kissed the boards, wagging her buttocks up and down in submission. The licking of the strap came again, but carefully, almost caressingly punishing the protuberant lips, and Beauty, fresh tears spilling to the floor, gave an open-mouthed gasp, lifting her hips higher and higher.

The Captain stepped forward, and with his large naked hand covered Beauty's sore bottom, rotating it slowly.

Beauty's breath caught in her throat. She felt her hips lifted, swung, pushed down, and a little throbbing noise came out of her. She could still remember Prince Alexi at the castle telling her he had been made to swing his hips in this ghastly, ignominious fashion.

The Captain's fingers pressed into Beauty's flesh, squeezing her buttocks together.

"Wag those hips!" came the low command. And the hand thrust Beauty's bottom up so high that her forehead was sealed to the floor, her breasts pulsing against the boards, a throbbing groan choked out of her.

Whatever she had thought and feared so long ago at the castle didn't matter now. She churned her bottom in the air. The hand withdrew. The strap licked up at her sex, and in a violent orgy of movement she wagged and wagged her buttocks as she had been told to do.

Her body loosened, lengthened. If she had ever known any other posture but this she couldn't clearly remember it. "Lord and Master" she sighed, and the strap smacked her little mound, the leather scraping the clitoris as it thickened. Faster and faster Beauty swung her bottom in the circle, and the harder the strap licked her the more the juices in her surged, until she could not hear the sound of the strap against the slick lips, her cries coming from deep in her throat, almost unrecognizable to her.

At last the licking stopped. She saw the Captain's shoes before her and his hand pointing to a small-handled broom beside the fireplace.

"After this day," he said calmly, "I won't tell you this room is to be swept and scrubbed, the bed changed, the fire built up. You will do it every morning when you rise. And you will do it now, this evening, to learn how to do it. After that you'll be scrubbed in the Inn yard to properly serve the garrison."

At once Beauty started to work, on her knees, with swift careful movements. The Captain left the room, and within moments Prince Roger appeared with the dustpan, scrub brush, and bucket. He showed her how she must do these little tasks, how to change the linen, build up the wood on the hearth, clear away the ashes.

And he did not seem surprised that Beauty only nodded and didn't speak to him. It didn't occur to her to speak to him.

The Captain had said "every day." So he meant to keep her! She might be the property of the Sign of the Lion, but she had been chosen by its chief lodger.

She could not do her tasks well enough. She smoothed the bed, polished the table, careful to kneel at all times, and rise only when she must.

And when the door opened again, and Mistress Lockley took her by the hair and she felt the wooden paddle driving her down the steps, she was softened and carried away by thoughts of the Captain.

Within seconds, she'd been stood in the crude wooden hogshead tub. Torches flickered at the Inn door and on the side of the shed. Mistress Lockley scrubbed fast and roughly, flushing out Beauty's sore vagina with wine mixed in water. She creamed Beauty's buttocks.

Not a word was spoken as she bent Beauty this way and that, forcing her legs into a squat, lathering her pubic hair, and roughly drying her.

And all around Beauty saw other slaves being coarsely bathed, and she heard the loud bantering voices of the crude woman in the apron and two other strong-limbed village girls who went at the task, now and then stopping to smack the buttocks of this slave or that for no apparent reason. But all Beauty could think of was that she belonged to the Captain; she was to see the garrison. Surely the Captain would be there. And the volleys of shouts and laughter from the Inn tantalized her.

When Beauty was thoroughly dry, and her hair had been brushed, Mistress Lockley put her foot on the edge of the hogshead and threw Beauty over her knee and swatted at her thighs hard with the wooden paddle several times, and then pushed Beauty down on her hands and knees as Beauty gasped for breath and sought to steady herself.

It was positively odd not to be spoken to, not even sharp impatient commands. Beauty glanced up as Mistress Lockley came around beside her, and for one instant she saw Mistress Lockley's cool smile, before the woman had the chance to remember herself. Quite suddenly Beauty's head was lifted gently by the full weight of her long hair, and Mistress Lockley's face was right above hers.

"And you were going to be my little troublemaker. I was going to cook your little buttocks so much longer than the rest for breakfast."

"Maybe you still should," Beauty whispered without intention or thought. "If that's what you like for breakfast." But she broke into violent trembling as soon as she finished. O, what had she done!

Mistress Lockley's face lit up with the most curious expression. A half-repressed laugh escaped her lips. "I'll see *you* in the morning, my dear, with all the others. When the Captain's gone, and the Inn's nice and quiet, and there's no one here but the other slaves waiting in line as well for their morning whipping. I'll teach you to open that mouth without permission." But this was said with unusual warmth, and the color was high in Mistress Lockley's cheeks. She was so very pretty. "Now trot," she said softly.

The big room of the Inn was already packed with soldiers and other drinking men.

A fire roared on the hearth, mutton turned on the spit. And upright slaves, their heads bowed, scurried on tiptoe to pour wine and ale into dozens of pewter flagons. Everywhere Beauty glanced in the crowd of dark-clad drinkers with their heavy riding boots and swords, she saw the flash of naked bottoms and gleaming pubic hair as slaves set down plates of steaming food, bent over to wipe up spills, crawled on hands and knees to mop up the floor, or scampered to retrieve a coin playfully pitched into the sawdust.

From a dim corner came the thick, resonant strumming of a lute and the beat of a tambourine and a horn playing a slow melody. But riots of laughter drowned the sound. Broken fragments of a chorus rose in a full burst only to die away. And from everywhere came shouts for meat and drink and the call for more pretty slaves to entertain the company.

Beauty didn't know which way to look. Here a robust officer of the guard in his vest of shining mail pulled a very pink and pale-haired Princess off her feet and set her standing on the table. With her hands behind her head she quickly danced and hopped as she was told, her breasts bouncing, her face flushed, her silvery blond hair flying in long perfect corkscrew curls about her shoulders. Her eyes were bright with a mixture of fear and obvious excitement. There another delicate-limbed female slave was being thrown over a crude lap and spanked as her frantic hands went to cover her face before they were pulled aside and playfully held out before her by an amused onlooker.

Between the casks on the walls, more naked slaves stood, their legs apart, their hips thrust out, waiting to be picked, it seemed. And in a corner of the room, a beautiful Prince with full red curls to the shoulders sat with legs apart on the lap of a hulking soldier, their mouths locked in a kiss as the soldier stroked the Prince's upright organ. The red-haired Prince licked at the soldier's coarsely shaven black beard, mouthed his chin, then opened his lips to the kissing again. His eyebrows were knit with the intensity of his passion, though he sat as helplessly and still as if he had been tied there, his bottom riding up with the shift of the soldier's knee, the soldier pinching the Prince's thigh to make him jump, the Prince's left arm hanging loosely over the soldier's neck, right hand buried in the soldier's thick hair with slow, flexing fingers.

A black-haired Princess in the far corner struggled to turn round and round, her hands clasped to her ankles, her legs apart, long hair sweeping the floor as a flagon of ale was poured over her tender private parts and the soldiers bent to lap the liquid playfully from the curling hair of her pubis. Suddenly she was thrown standing on her hands, her feet hoisted high above, as a soldier filled her nether mouth with ale to overflowing.

But Mistress Lockley was pulling Beauty so that she might take a flagon of ale and a pewter plate of steaming food in her hands, and Beauty's face was turned to see the distant figure of the Captain. He sat at a crowded table far across the room, his back to the wall, his leg outstretched on the bench before him, his eyes fixed on Beauty.

Beauty struggled fast on her knees, her torso erect, the food held high until she knelt beside him and reached over the bench to place the food on the table. Leaning on his elbow, he stroked her hair and studied her face as though they were quite alone, the men all around them laughing, talking, singing. The golden dagger gleamed in the candlelight and so did the Captain's golden hair and the bit of shaven hair on his upper lip, and his eyebrows. The uncommon gentleness of his hand, lifting Beauty's hair back over her shoulders and smoothing it, brought chills over Beauty's arms and throat; and between her legs the inescapable spasm.

She made some small undulation with her body, not truly meaning to. And at once his strong right hand clamped on her wrists and he rose from the bench lifting her off the floor and up so she dangled above him.

Caught off-guard, she blanched and then felt the blood flooding to her face, and as she was turned this way and that, she saw the soldiers turning to look at her.

"To my good soldiers, who have served the Queen well," the Captain said, and at once there was loud stomping and clapping. "Who will be the first?" the Captain demanded.

Beauty felt her pubic lips growing thickly together, a spurt of moisture squeezing through the seam, but a silent burst of terror in her soul paralyzed her. "What will happen to me?" she thought as the dark bodies closed in around her. The hulking figure of a burly man rose in front of her. Softly his thumbs sank into the tender flesh of her underarms, as, clutching her tightly, he took her away from the Captain. Her gasps died in her throat.

Other hands guided her legs around the soldier's waist. She felt her head touch the wall behind her and she tucked her hands behind her head to cradle it, all the while staring forward into the soldier's face, as his right hand shot down to open his breeches.

The smell of the stables rose from the man, the smell of ale, and the rich, delicious scent of sun-browned skin and rawhide. His black eyes quivered and closed for an instant as his cock plunged into Beauty, widening the distended lips, as Beauty's hips thudded against the wall in a frantic rhythm.

Yes. Now. Yes. The fear was dissolved in some greater unnameable emotion. The man's thumbs bit into Beauty's underarms as the pounding went on. And all around her in the gloom she saw a score of faces looking on, the noises of the Inn rising and falling in violent splashes.

The cock discharged its hot, swimming fluid inside her and her orgasm radiated through her, blinding her, her mouth open, the cries jerked out of her. Red-faced and naked, she rode out her pleasure right in the midst of this common tavern.

She was lifted again, emptied.

And she felt herself being set down on her knees on the table. Her knees were pulled apart and her hands placed under her breasts.

As the hungry mouth sucked on her nipple, she lifted her breasts, arching her back, her eyes turned shyly away from those who surrounded her. The greedy mouth fed on her right breast now, drawing hard as the tongue stabbed at the tiny stone of the nipple.

Another mouth had taken her other breast. And as she pressed herself against the mouths that suckled her, the pleasure almost too acute, hands spread her legs wider and wider, her sex almost lowered to the table.

For one moment the fear returned, burning white-hot. Hands were all over her; her arms were being held, her hands forced behind her back. She could not free herself from the mouths drawing hard on her breasts. And her face was being tilted up, a dark shadow covering her as she was straddled. The cock pushed into her gaping mouth, her eyes staring up at the hairy belly above her. She sucked the cock with all her power, sucking as hard as the mouths at her breasts, moaning as the fear again evaporated.

Her vagina quivered, fluids coursing down her wide-spread thighs, and violent jolts of pleasure shook her. The cock in her mouth tantalized her but could not satisfy her. She drew the cock deeper and deeper till her throat contracted, the come shooting into her, the mouths pulling gently at her nipples, snapping her nipples, her nether lips closing vainly on the emptiness.

But something touched her pulsing clitoris, scraped it through the thick film of wetness. It plunged through her starved pubic lips. It was the rough, jeweled handle of the dagger again . . . surely it was . . . and it impaled her.

She came in a riot of soft muffled cries, pumping her hips up and up, all sight and sound and scent of the Inn dissolved in her frenzy. The dagger handle held her, the hilt pounding her pubis, not letting the orgasm stop, forcing cry after cry out of her.

Even as she was laid down on her back on the table, it tormented her, making her squirm and twist her hips. In a blur she saw the Captain's face above her. And she writhed like a cat as the dagger handle rocked her up and down, her hips spanking the table.

But she was not allowed to come so soon again.

She was being lifted. And she felt herself laid over a broad barrel. Her back arched over the moist wood, she could smell the ale, and her hair fell down to the floor, the Inn upside down in a riot of color before her. Another cock was going into her mouth while firm hands anchored her thighs to the curve and a cock pushed into her dripping vagina. She had no weight, no equilibrium. She could see nothing but the dark scrotum before her eyes, the unfastened cloth. Her breasts were slapped, sucked, and gathered by strong kneading fingers. Her hands groped for the buttocks of the man who filled her mouth and she clung to him, riding him. But the other cock pummeled her against the barrel, plugged her, grinding her clitoris to a different rhythm. Through all her limbs she felt the searing consummation, as if it did not rise from between her legs, her breasts teeming. All her body had become the orifice, the organ.

She was being carried into the yard, her arms around firm, powerful shoulders.

It was a young brown-haired soldier who carried her, kissing her, petting her. And they were all over the green grass, the men, laughing in the torchlight as they surrounded the slaves in the tubs, their manner easy now that the first hot passions had been satisfied.

They circled Beauty as her feet were lowered into the warm water. They knelt with the full wineskin in their hands and squirted the wine up into her, tickling her, cleansing her. They bathed her with the brush and the cloth, half playing at it, vying to fill her mouth slowly, carefully with the tart, cool wine, to kiss her.

She tried to remember this face, that laugh, the very soft skin of the one with the thickest cock, but it was hopeless.

They laid her down in the grass beneath the fig trees and she was mounted again, her young captor, the brown-haired soldier, feeding dreamily on her mouth, and then driving her in a slower, softer rhythm. She reached back and felt the cool, naked skin of his buttocks and the cloth of his breeches pulled halfway down, and touching the loosened belt, the rumpled cloth, and the half-naked backside, she clamped her vagina tight on his cock so that he gasped aloud like a slave on top of her.

It was hours later.

She sat curled in the Captain's lap, her head against his chest, her arms about his neck, half sleeping. Like a lion he stretched under her, his voice a low rumble from his broad chest, as he spoke to the man opposite. He cradled her head in his left hand, his arm feeling immense, effortlessly powerful.

Only now and then did she open her eyes on the smoky glare of the whole tavern.

Quieter, more orderly than before. The Captain talked on and on. The words "runaway Princess" came clear to her.

"Runaway Princess," Beauty thought drowsily. She couldn't

worry about such things. She closed her eyes again, burrowing into the Captain, who tightened his left arm about her.

"How splendid he is," she thought. "How coarsely beautiful." She loved the deep creases of his tanned face, the luster of his eyes. An odd thought came to her. She had no more care what his conversation was about than he had care to talk to her. She smiled to herself. She was his nude and shuddering slave. And he was her coarse and bestial Captain.

But her thoughts drifted to Tristan. She had declared herself such a rebel to Tristan.

What had happened to him with Nicolas the Chronicler? How would she ever find out? Maybe Prince Roger could tell her some news. Perhaps the dense little world of the village had its secret arteries of information. She had to know if Tristan was all right. She wished she could just see him. And dreaming of Tristan, she drifted into sleep again.

BEAUTY'S RELEASE

Anne Rice

1 Through the City and into the Palace

BEAUTY OPENED HER eyes. She had not been sleeping, and she knew without having to see through a window that it was morning. The air in the cabin was unusually warm.

An hour ago she had heard Tristan and Laurent whispering in the dark, and she had known the ship was at anchor. And she had been only slightly afraid.

After that, she had slipped in and out of thin erotic dreams, her body wakening all over like a landscape under the rising sun. She was impatient to be ashore, impatient to know the full extent of what was to happen to her, to be threatened in ways that she could understand.

Now, when she saw the lean, comely little attendants flooding into the room, she knew for certain that they had come to the Sultanate. All would be realized soon enough.

The precious little boys – they could be no more than fourteen or fifteen, despite their height – had always been richly dressed, but this morning they wore embroidered silk robes, and their tight waist sashes were made of rich striped cloth, and their black hair gleamed with oil, and their innocent faces were dark with an unusual air of anxiety.

At once, the other royal captives were roused, and each slave was taken from the cage and led to the proper grooming table.

Beauty stretched herself out on the silk, enjoying her sudden freedom from confinement, the muscles in her legs tingling. She glanced at Tristan and then at Laurent. Tristan was suffering too much still. Laurent, as always, looked faintly amused. But there was not even time now to say farewell. She prayed they would not be separated, that whatever happened they would come to know it together, and that somehow their new captivity would yield moments when they might be able to talk.

At once the attendants rubbed the gold pigmented oil into Beauty's skin, strong fingers working it well into her thighs and buttocks. Her long hair was lifted and brushed with gold dust, and then she was turned on her back gently.

Skilled fingers opened her mouth. Her teeth were polished with a soft cloth. Waxen gold was applied to her lips. And then gold paint was brushed onto her eyelashes and eyebrows.

Not since the first day of the journey had she or any of the slaves been so thoroughly decorated. And her body steamed with familiar sensations.

She thought hazily of her divinely crude Captain of the Guard, of the elegant but distantly remembered tormentors of the Queen's Court, and she felt desperate to belong to someone again, to be punished for someone, to be possessed as well as chastised.

It was worth any humiliation, that, to be possessed by another. In retrospect, it seemed she had only been a flower in a full bloom when she was thoroughly violated by the will of another, that in suffering for the will of another she had discovered her true self.

But she had a new and slowly deepening dream, one that had begun to flame in her mind during the time at sea, and that she had confided only to Laurent: the dream that she might somehow find in this strange land what she had not found before; someone whom she might truly love.

In the village, she told Tristan that she did not want this, that it was harshness and severity alone she craved. But the truth was that Tristan's love for his Master had deeply affected her. His words had swayed her, even as she had spoken her contradictions.

And then had come these lonely nights at sea of unfulfilled yearning, of pondering too much all the twists of fate and fortune. And she had felt strangely fragile thinking of love, of giving her secret soul to a Master or Mistress, more than ever off balance.

The groom combed gold paint into her pubic hair, tugging each curl to make it spring. Beauty could hardly keep her hips still. Then she saw a handful of fine pearls held out for her inspection. And into her pubic hair these went, to be affixed to the skin with powerful adhesive. Such lovely decorations. She smiled.

She closed her eyes for a second, her sex aching in its emptiness. Then she glanced at Laurent to see that his face had taken on an Oriental cast with the gold paint, his nipples beautifully erect like his thick cock. And his body was being ornamented, as befitted its size and power, with rather large emeralds instead of pearls.

Laurent was smiling at the little boy who did the work, as if in his mind he was peeling away the boy's fancy clothes. But then he turned to Beauty, and, lifting his hand languidly to his lips, he blew her a little kiss, unnoticed by the others.

He winked and Beauty felt the desire in her burning hotter. He was so beautiful, Laurent.

"O, please don't let us be separated," she prayed. Not because she ever thought she would possess Laurent – that would be too interesting – but because she would be lost without the others, lost . . .

And then it hit her with full force: she had no idea what would happen to her in the Sultanate, and absolutely no control over it. Going into the village, she had known. She had been told. Even coming into the castle, she had known. The Crown Prince had prepared her. But this was beyond her imagining, this place. And beneath her concealing gold paint she grew pale.

The grooms were gesturing for their charges to rise. There were the usual exaggerated and urgent signs for them to be silent, still, obedient, as they stood in a circle facing each other.

And Beauty felt her hands lifted and clasped behind her back as if she were a senseless little being who could not even do that much herself. Her groom touched the back of her neck and then kissed her cheek softly as she compliantly bowed her head.

Still, she could see the others clearly. Tristan's genitals had also been decorated with pearls, and he gleamed from head to toe, his blond locks even more golden than his burnished skin.

And, glancing at Dmitri and Rosalynd, she saw that they had both been decorated with red rubies. Their black hair was in magnificent contrast to their polished skin. Rosalynd's enormous blue eyes looked drowsy under their fringe of painted lashes. Dmitri's broad chest was tightened like that of a statue, though his strongly muscled thighs quivered uncontrollably.

Beauty suddenly winced as her groom added a bit more gold paint to each of her nipples. She couldn't take her eyes off his small brown fingers, enthralled by the care with which he worked, and the way that her nipples hardened unbearably. She could feel each of the pearls clinging to her skin. Every hour of starvation at sea sharpened her silent craving.

But the captives had another little treat in store for them. She watched furtively, her head still bowed, as the grooms drew out of their deep, hidden pockets new and frightening little toys – pairs of gold clamps with long chains of delicate but sturdy links attached to them.

The clamps Beauty knew and dreaded, of course. But the chains – they really agitated her. They were like leashes and they had small leather handles.

Her groom touched her lips for quiet and then quickly stroked her right nipple, gathering a nice pinch of breast into the small gold scallop-shell clamp before he snapped it shut. The clamp was lined with a bit of white fur, yet the pressure was firm. And all of Beauty's skin seemed to feel the sudden nagging torment. When the other clamp was just as tightly in place, the groom gathered the handles of the long chains in his hands and gave them a tug. This was what Beauty had feared most. She was brought forward sharply, gasping.

At once the groom scowled, quite displeased with the openmouthed sound, and spanked her lips with his fingers firmly. She bowed my head lower, marveling at these two flimsy little chains, at their hold upon these unaccountably tender parts of her. They seemed to control her utterly.

She watched with her heart contracting, as the groom's hand tightened again and the chains were jerked, and she was pulled forward once more by her nipples. She moaned this time but she did not dare to open her lips, and for this she received his approving kiss, the desire surging painfully inside her.

"O, but we cannot be led ashore like this," she thought. She could see Laurent, opposite, clamped the same as she was, and blushing furiously as his groom tugged the hated little chains and made him step forward. Laurent looked more helpless than he had in the village on the Punishment Cross.

For a moment, all the delightful crudity of village punishments came back to her. And she felt more keenly this delicate restraint, the new quality of servitude.

She saw Laurent's little groom kiss his cheek approvingly. Laurent had not gasped or cried out. But Laurent's cock was bobbing uncontrollably. Tristan was in the same transparently miserable state, yet he looked, as ever, quietly majestic.

Beauty's nipples throbbed as if they were being whipped. The desire cascaded through her limbs, made her dance just a little without moving her feet, her head suddenly light with dreams of new and particular love again.

But the business of the grooms distracted her. They were taking down from the walls their long, stiff leather thongs; and these, like all other objects in this realm, were heavily studded with jewels, which made them heavy instruments of punishment, though, like strips of sapling wood, they were quite flexible.

She felt the light sting on the back of her calves, and the little double leash was pulled. She must move up behind Tristan, who had been turned towards the door. The others were probably lined up behind her.

And quite suddenly, for the first time in a fortnight, they were to leave the hold of the ship. The doors were opened, Tristan's groom leading him up the stairs, the thong playing on Tristan's calves to make him march, and the sunlight pouring down from the deck was momentarily blinding. There came with it a great deal of noise – the sound of crowds, of distant shouts, of untold numbers of people.

Beauty hurried up the wooden stairs, the wood warm under her feet, the tugging of her nipples making her moan again. What precious genius, it seemed, to be led so easily by such refined instruments. How well these creatures understood their captives.

She could scarcely bear the sight of Tristan's tight, strong buttocks in front of her. It seemed she heard Laurent moan behind. She felt afraid for Elena and Dmitri and Rosalynd.

But she had emerged on the deck and could see on either side the crowd of men in their long robes and turbans. And beyond the open sky, and high mud-brick buildings of a city. They were in the middle of a busy port, in fact, and everywhere to right and left were the masts of other ships. The noise, like the light itself, was numbing.

"O, not to be led ashore like this," she thought again. But she was rushed behind Tristan across the deck and down an easy, sloping gangplank. The salt air of the sea was suddenly clouded with heat and dust, the smell of animals and dung and hemp rope, and the sand of the desert.

The sand, in fact, covered the stones upon which she suddenly found herself standing. And she could not help but raise her head to see the great crowds being held back by turbaned men from the ship, hundreds and hundreds of dark faces scrutinizing her and the other captives. There were camels and donkeys piled high with wares, men of all ages in linen robes, most with their heads either turbaned or veiled in longer, flowing desert headdresses.

For a moment Beauty's courage failed her utterly. It was not the Queen's village, this. No, it was something far more real, even as it was foreign.

And yet her soul expanded as the little clamps were tugged again, as she saw gaudily dressed men appear in groups of four, each group bearing on its shoulders the long gilded rods of an open, cushioned litter.

Immediately, one of these cushions was lowered before her. And her nipples were pulled again by the mean little leashes as the thong snapped at her knees. She understood. She knelt down on the cushion, its rich red and gold design dazzling her slightly. And she felt herself pushed back on her heels, her legs opened wide, her head bowed again by a warm hand placed firmly on her neck.

"This is unbearable," she thought, moaning as softly as she could, "that we will be carried through the city itself. Why were we not taken secretly to His Highness the Sultan? Are we not royal slaves?"

But she knew the answer. She saw it in the dark faces that pressed in on all sides.

"We are only slaves here. No royalty accompanies us now. We are merely expensive and fine, like the other merchandise brought from the hold of the ships. How could the Queen let this happen to us?"

But her fragile sense of outrage was at once dissolved as if in the heat of her own naked flesh. Her groom pushed her knees even wider apart, and spread her buttocks upon her heels as she struggled to remain utterly pliant.

"Yes," she thought, her heart palpitating, her skin breathing in the awe of the crowd, "a very good position. They can see my sex. They can see every secret part of me." Yet she struggled with another little flair of alarm. And the gold leashes were quickly wound around a golden hook at the front of the cushion, which made them quite taut, holding her nipples in a state of bittersweet tension.

Her heart beat too fast. Her little groom further frightened her with all his desperate gestures that she be silent, that she be good. He was being fussy as he touched her arms. No, she must not move them. She knew that. Had she ever tried so hard to remain motionless? When her sex convulsed like a mouth gasping for air, could the crowd see it?

The litter was lifted carefully to the shoulders of the turbaned bearers. She grew almost dizzy with an awareness of her exposure. But it comforted her just a little to see Tristan kneeling on his cushion just ahead, to be reminded that she was not alone here.

The noisy crowd made way. The little procession moved through the huge open place that spread out from the harbor.

Overcome with a sense of decorum, she dared not move a muscle. Yet she could see all around her the great bazaar – merchants with their bright ceramic wares spread out upon multicolored rugs; rolls of silk and linen in stacks; leather goods and brass goods and ornaments of silver and gold; cages of fluttering, clucking birds; and food cooking in smoking pots under dusty canopies.

Yet the whole market had turned its chattering attention to the captives who were being carried past. Some stood mute beside their camels, just staring. And some – the young bareheaded boys, it seemed – ran along beside Beauty, glancing up at her and pointing and talking rapidly.

Her groom was at her left, and with his long leather thong he made some small adjustment of her long hair, and now and then fiercely admonished the crowd, driving it backwards.

Beauty tried not to see anything but the high mudbrick buildings coming closer and closer.

She was being carried up an incline, but her bearers held the litter level. And she struggled to keep her perfect form, though her chest heaved and pulled at the mean little clamps, the long gold chains that held her nipples shivering in the sunlight.

They were in a steep street, and on either side of her windows opened, people pointed and stared, and the crowd streamed along the walls, their cries growing suddenly louder as they echoed off the stones. The grooms drove them back with even stricter commands.

"Ah, what do they feel as they look at us?" Beauty thought. Her naked sex pulsed between her legs. It seemed to feel itself so disgracefully opened. "We are as beasts, are we not? And these wretched people do not for a moment imagine that such a fate could befall them, poor as they might be. They wish only that they might possess us."

The gold paint tightened on her skin, tightened particularly on her clamped nipples.

And try as she might, she could not keep her hips entirely still. Her sex seemed to churn with desire and move her entire body with it. The glances of the crowd touched her, teased her, made her ache in her emptiness.

But they had come to the end of the street. The crowd streamed out into an open place where thousands more stood watching. The noise of voices came in waves. Beauty could not even see the end of this crowd, as hundreds jostled to get a closer look at the procession. She felt her heart pound even harder as she saw the great golden domes of a palace rising before her.

The sun blinded her. It flashed on white marble walls, Moorish arches, giant doors covered in gold leaf, soaring towers so delicate that they made the dark, crude, stone castles of Europe seem somehow clumsy and vulgar.

The procession turned to the left sharply. And, for an instant, Beauty glimpsed Laurent behind her, then Elena, her long brown hair swaying in the breeze, and the dark, motionless figures of Dmitri and Rosalynd. All obedient, all still upon their cushioned litters.

The young boys in the crowd seemed to be more frenzied. They cheered and ran up and down, as though the proximity of the palace somehow heightened their excitement.

Beauty saw that the procession had come to a side entrance, and turbaned guards with great scimitars hanging from their girdles drove the crowd back as a pair of heavy doors were opened.

"O, blessed silence," Beauty thought. She saw Tristan carried beneath the arch, and immediately she followed.

They had not entered a courtyard as she had expected. Rather they were in a large corridor, its walls covered in intricate mosaics. Even the ceiling above was a stone tapestry of flowers and spirals. The bearers suddenly came to a halt. The doors far behind were closed. And they were all plunged into shadow.

Only now did Beauty see the torches on the walls, the lamps in their little niches. A huge crowd of young dark-faced boys, dressed exactly like the grooms from the ship, surveyed the new slaves silently.

Beauty's cushion was lowered. At once, her groom clasped the leashes and pulled her forward onto her knees on the marble. The bearers and the cushions quickly disappeared through doors that Beauty hardly glimpsed. And she was pushed down onto her hands, her groom's foot firm on the back of her neck as he forced her forehead right to the marble flooring.

Beauty shivered. She sensed a different manner in her groom. And, as the foot pressed harder, almost angrily, against her neck, she quickly kissed the cold floor, overcome with misery that she couldn't know what was wanted.

But this seemed to appease the little boy. She felt his approving pat on her buttocks.

Now her head was lifted. And she saw that Tristan was kneeling on all fours in front of her, the sight of his well-shaped backside further teasing her.

But as she watched in stunned silence, the little gold-link chains from her clamped nipples were passed through Tristan's legs and under his belly.

"Why?" she wondered, even as the clamps pinched her with renewed tightness.

But immediately she was to know the answer. She felt a pair of chains being passed between her own thighs, teasing her lips. And now a firm hand clasped her chin and opened her mouth, and the leather handles were fed to her like a bit that she must hold in her teeth with the usual firmness.

She realized this was Laurent's leash, and she was now to pull him along by the damnable little chains just as she herself was to be pulled by Tristan. And if her head moved in the slightest involuntary way, she would add to Laurent's torment just as Tristan added to hers as he pulled the chains given him.

But it was the spectacle of it that truly shamed her.

"We are tethered to one another like little animals led to market," she thought. And she was further confused by the chains stroking her thighs and the outside of her pubic lips, by their grazing her taught belly.

"You little fiends!" she thought, glancing at the silk robes of her groom. He was fussing with her hair, forcing her back into a more convex position so that her rear was higher. She felt the teeth of a comb stroking the delicate hair around her anus, and her face flooded with a hot stinging blush.

And Tristan, did he have to move his head, making her nipples throb so?

She heard one of the grooms clap his hands. The leather thong came down to lick at Tristan's calves and the soles of his naked feet. He started forward, and she immediately hurried after him.

When she raised her head just a little to see the walls and ceiling, the thong smacked the back of her neck. Then it whipped the undersides of her feet just as Tristan's were being whipped. The leashes pulled at her nipples as if they had life of their own.

And yet the thongs smacked faster and louder, urging all the slaves to hurry. A slipper pushed at her buttocks. Yes, they must run. And, as Tristan picked up speed, so did she, remembering in a daze how she had once run upon the Queen's Bridle Path.

"Yes, hurry," she thought. "And keep your head properly lowered. And how could you think you would enter the Sultan's Palace in any other manner?"

The crowds outside might gape at the slaves, as they probably did at the most debased of prisoners. But this was the only proper position for sex slaves in such a magnificent palace.

With every inch of floor she covered, she felt more abject, her chest growing warm as she ran out of breath, her heart, as ever, beating too fast, too loudly.

The hall seemed to grow wider, higher. The drove of grooms flanked them. Yet still she could see arched doorways to the left and right and cavernous rooms tiled in the same beautifully colored marbles.

The grandeur and the solidity of the place worked their inevitable influence upon her. Tears stung her eyes. She felt small, utterly insignificant.

And yet there was something absolutely marvelous in the feeling. She was but a little thing in this vast world yet she seemed to have her proper place, more surely than she had had in the castle or even in the village.

Her nipples throbbed steadily in the fur-lined grip of the clamps, and occasional flashes of sunlight distracted her.

She felt a tightness in her throat, an overall weakness. The smell of incense, of cedar wood, of Eastern perfumes, suddenly enveloped her. And she realized that all was quiet in this world of richness and splendor; and the only sound was that of the slaves scurrying along and the thongs that licked them. Even the grooms made no sound, unless the singing of their silk robes was a sound. The silence seemed an extension of the palace, an extension of the dramatic power that was devouring them.

But as they progressed deeper and deeper into the labyrinth, as the escort of grooms dropped back a bit, leaving only the one little tormentor with his busy thong, and the procession went round corners and down even wider halls, Beauty began to see out of the corner of her eye some strange species of sculpture set in niches to adorn the corridor.

And, suddenly, she realized that these were not statues. They were living slaves fitted into the niches.

At last, she had to take a good look, and struggling not to lose her pace, she stared from right to left at these poor creatures.

Yes, men and women in alternation on both sides of the hall, standing mute in the niches. And each figure had been wrapped tightly from neck to toe in gold-tinted linen, except for the head held upright by a high ornamented brace and the naked organs left exposed in gilded glory.

Beauty looked down, trying to catch her breath. But she couldn't help looking up again immediately. And the spectacle became even clearer. The men had been bound with legs together, genitals thrust forward, and the women had been bound with legs apart, each leg completely wrapped and the sex left open.

All stood motionless, their long, shapely, gold neck braces fixed to the wall in back by a rod that appeared to hold them securely. And some appeared to sleep with eyes closed, while others peered down at the floor, despite their slightly lifted faces.

Many were dark-skinned, as the grooms were – and showed the luxuriant black eyelashes of the desert peoples. Almost none were as Tristan and Beauty were. All had been gilded.

And in a silent panic, Beauty remembered the words of the Queen's emissary, who had spoken to them on the ship before they left their sovereign's land: "Though the Sultan has many slaves from his own land, you captive Princes and Princesses are a special delicacy of sorts, and a great curiosity."

"Then surely we can't be bound and placed in niches such as these," Beauty thought, "lost among dozens and dozens of others, merely to decorate a corridor."

But she could see the real truth. This Sultan possessed such a vast number of slaves that absolutely anything might befall Beauty and her fellow captives.

As she hurried along, her knees and hands getting a little sore from the marble, she continued to study these figures.

She could make out that the arms had been folded behind the back of each one, and that the gilded nipples too were exposed and sometimes clamped, and that each figure had his or her hair combed back to expose the ears which wore jeweled ornaments.

How tender the ears looked, how much like organs!

A wave of terror passed over Beauty. And she shuddered to think of what Tristan was feeling – Tristan, who so needed to love one Master. And what about Laurent? How would this look to him after the singular spectacle of the village Punishment Cross?

There came the sharp pull of the chains again. Her nipples itched. And the thong suddenly dallied between her legs, stroking her anus and the lips of her vagina.

"You little devil," she thought. Yet as the warm tingling sensations passed all through her, she arched her back, forcing her buttocks up, and crawled with even more sprightly movements.

They were coming to a pair of doors. And with a shock, she saw that a male slave was fixed to one door and a female slave to the other. And these two were not wrapped, but rather completely naked. Gold bands around the foreheads, the legs, waist, neck, ankles, and wrists held each flat to the door with knees wide apart, the soles of the feet pressed together. The arms were fixed straight up over the head, palms outward. And the faces were still, eyes cast down, and the mouths held artfully arranged bunches of grapes and leaves that were gilded like the flesh so that the creatures looked very much like sculptures.

But the doors were opened. The slaves passed these two silent sentinels in a flash.

And the pace slowed as Beauty found herself in an immense courtyard, full of potted palm trees and flower beds bordered in variegated marble.

Sunlight dappled the tiles in front of her. The perfume of flowers suddenly refreshed her. She glimpsed blossoms of all hues, and for one paralyzing instant she saw that the vast garden was filled with gilded and caged slaves as well as other beautiful creatures fixed in dramatic positions atop marble pedestals.

Beauty was made to stop. The leashes were taken from her mouth. And she saw her groom gather up her own leashes as he stood beside her. The thong played between her thighs, tickling her, forcing her legs a little apart. Then a hand smoothed her hair tenderly. She saw Tristan to her left and Laurent to her right, and she realized that the slaves had been positioned in a loose circle.

But all at once the great crowd of grooms began to laugh and talk as though released from some enforced silence. They closed in on the slaves, hands pointing, gesturing.

The slipper was on Beauty's neck again, and it forced her head down until her lips touched the marble. She could see out of the corner of her eye that Laurent and the others were bent in the same lowly posture.

In a wash of rainbow colors the silk robes of the grooms surrounded them. The din of conservation was worse than the noise of the crowd in the streets. Beauty knelt shuddering as she felt hands on her back and on her hair, the thong pushing her legs even wider. Silk-robed grooms stood between her and Tristan, between her and Laurent.

But suddenly a silence fell that utterly shattered the last of Beauty's fragile composure.

The grooms withdrew as if swept aside. And there was no sound except the chattering of birds, and the tinkling of wind chimes.

Then Beauty heard the soft sound of slippered feet approaching.

2 Examination in the Garden

It was. not one man who entered the garden, but a group of three. Yet two stood back in deference to one who advanced alone and slowly.

In the tense silence, Beauty saw his feet and the hem of his robe as he moved about the circle. Richer fabric, and velvet slippers with high upturned curling toes, each decorated by a dangling ruby. He moved with slow steps, as if he was surveying carefully.

Beauty held her breath as he approached her. She squinted slightly as the toe of the wine-colored slipper touched her cheek, and then rested upon the back of her neck, then followed the line of her spine to its tip.

She shivered, unable to help herself, her moan sounding loud and impertinent to her own ears. But there was no reprimand.

She thought she heard a little laugh. And then a sentence spoken gently made the tears spring to her eyes again. How soothing was the voice, how unusually musical. Maybe the unintelligible language made it seem more lyrical. Yet she longed to understand the words spoken.

Of course, she had not been addressed. The words had been spoken to one of the other two men, yet the voice stirred her, almost seduced her.

Quite suddenly she felt the chains pulled hard. Her nipples stiffened with a tingling that sent its tentacles down into her groin instantly.

She knelt up, unsure, frightened, and then was pulled to her feet, nipples burning, her face flaming.

For one moment the immensity of the garden impressed her. The bound slaves, the lavish blooms, the blue sky above shockingly clear, the large assemblage of the grooms watching her. And then the man standing before her.

What must she do with her hands? She put them behind her neck, and stood staring at the tiled floor, with only the vaguest picture of the Master who faced her.

He was much taller than the little boys – in fact, he was a slender giant of a man, elegantly proportioned, and he seemed older by virtue of his air of command. And it was he who had pulled the chains himself and still held the handles.

Quite suddenly he passed them from his right hand to his left.

And with the right hand, he slapped the undersides of Beauty's breasts, startling her. She bit down on her cry. But the warm yielding of her body surprised her. She throbbed with the desire to be touched, slapped again, for an even more annihilating violence.

And in the moment of trying to collect her wits, she had glimpsed the man's dark wavy hair, not quite shoulder length, and his eyes, so black they seemed drawn in ink, with large shining beads of jet for the irises.

"How gorgeous these desert people can be," she thought. And her dreams in the hold of the ship suddenly rose to mock her. Love him? Love this one who is but a servant like the others?

Yet the face burnt through her fear and agitation. It seemed an impossible face suddenly. It was almost innocent.

The ringing slaps came again, and she stepped back before she could stop herself. Her breasts were flooded with warmth. At once, her little groom thrashed her disobedient legs with the thong. She steadied herself, sorry for the failure.

The voice spoke again and it was as light as before, as melodious and almost caressing. But it sent the little grooms into a flurry of activity.

She felt soft, silken fingers on her ankles and on her wrists, and before she realized what was happening, she was lifted, her legs raised at right angles to her body and spread wide by the grooms who held her, her arms forced straight up in the air, her back and head supported firmly. She shivered spasmodically, her thighs aching, her sex brutally exposed. And then she felt another pair of hands lift her head, and she peered right into the eyes of the mysterious giant of a Master, who smiled at her radiantly.

O, too handsome he was. Instantly, she looked away, her lids fluttering. His eyes were tilted upwards at the outsides, which gave him a slightly devilish look, and his mouth was large and extremely kissable. But, for all the innocence of the expression, a ferocious spirit seemed to emanate from him. She sensed menace in him. She could feel it in his touch. And, with her legs held wide apart as they were, she passed into a silent panic.

As if to confirm his power, the Master quickly slapped her face, causing her to whimper before she could stop herself. The hand rose again, this time slapping her right cheek, and then the left again, until she was suddenly crying audibly.

"But what have I done?" she thought. And through a mist of tears she saw only curiosity in his face. He was studying her. It wasn't innocence. She had judged wrongly. It was merely fascination with what he was doing that flamed in him.

"So it's a test," she tried to tell herself. "But how do I pass or fail?" And shuddering, she saw the hands rising again.

He tilted her head back and opened her mouth, touching her tongue and her teeth. Chills passed over her. She felt her whole body convulse in the hands of the grooms. The probing fingers touched her eyelids, her eyebrows. They wiped at her tears, which were spilling down her face as she stared at the blue sky above her.

And then she felt the hands at her exposed sex. The thumbs went into her vagina, and she was pulled impossibly wide as her hips rocked forward, shaming her.

It seemed she would burst with orgasm, that she couldn't contain it. But was this forbidden? And how would she be punished? She tossed her head from side to side, struggling to command herself. But the fingers were so gentle, so soft, yet firm as they opened her. If they touched her clitoris, she would be lost, incapable of restraint.

But mercifully, they let her go, tugging at her pubic hair, and only pinching her lips together quickly.

In a daze, she bowed her head, the sight of her nakedness thoroughly unnerving her. She saw the new Master turn and snap his fingers. And through the tangle of her hair she saw Elena hoisted instantly by the grooms just as she had been.

Elena struggled for composure, her pink sex wet and gaping through its wreath of brown hair, the long delicate muscles of her thighs twitching. Beauty watched in terror as the Master proceeded with the same examination.

Elena's high, sharply angled breasts heaved as the Master played with her mouth, her teeth. But when the slaps came Elena was utterly silent. And the look on the Master's face further confused Beauty.

How passionately interested he seemed, how intent upon what he was doing. Not even the cruel Master of Postulants at the castle had seemed so dedicated as this one. And his charm was considerable. The rich velvet robe was well tailored to his straight back and shoulders. His hands had a beguiling grace of movement as he spread Elena's red pubic mouth and the poor Princess pumped her hips disgracefully.

At the sight of Elena's sex growing full and wet and obviously hungry, Beauty's long starvation at sea made her feel desperate. And when the Master smiled and smoothed Elena's long hair back from her forehead, examining her eyes, Beauty felt raging jealousy.

"No, it would be ghastly to love any of them," she thought. She couldn't give her heart. She tried not to look anymore. Her own legs throbbed, the grooms holding them back as firmly as ever. And her own sex swelled unbearably.

But there were more spectacles for her. The Master came back to Tristan. And now he was lifted into the air, and his legs spread wide in the same manner. Out of the corner of her eye, Beauty saw that the little grooms struggled under Tristan's weight, and Tristan's beautiful face was crimson with humiliation as his hard and thrusting organ was examined closely by the Master.

The Master's fingers played with the foreskin, played with the shiny tip, squeezing out of it a single drop of glistening moisture. Beauty could feel the tension in Tristan's limbs. But she dared not look up to see his face again as the Master reached to examine it.

In a blur she saw the Master's face, saw the enormous ink-black eyes, and the hair swept back over the ear to reveal a tiny gold ring stabbing the ear lobe.

She heard him slapping Tristan, and she closed her eyes tight as Tristan finally moaned, the slaps seeming to resound through the garden.

When she opened her eyes again it was because the Master had laughed softly to himself as he passed in front of her. And she saw his hand rise almost absently to squeeze her left breast lightly. The tears sprang to her eyes, her mind struggling to understand the outcome of his examinations, to push away the fact that he drew her more than any being who had hitherto claimed her.

Now, to her right and slightly in front of her, it was Laurent who must be raised up for the Master's scrutiny. And, as the enormous Prince was lifted, she heard the Master make some quick verbal outburst which brought laughter from all the other grooms immediately. No one needed to translate it for her. Laurent was too powerfully built, his organ was too splendid.

And she could see now that it was fully erect, well trained as it was, and the sight of the heavily muscled thighs spread wide apart brought back to her delirious memories of the Punishment Cross. She tried not to look at the enormous scrotum, but she could not help herself.

And it seemed that the Master had been moved by these superior endowments to a new excitement. He smacked Laurent hard with the back of his hand several times in amazingly rapid succession. The enormous torso writhed, the grooms struggling to keep it still.

And then the Master removed the clamps, letting them drop to the ground and pressed both of Laurent's nipples as Laurent moaned loudly.

But something else was happening. Beauty saw it. Laurent had looked at the Master directly. He had done it more than once. Their eyes had met. And now as his nipples were squeezed again, very hard it seemed, the Prince stared right at the Master.

"No, Laurent," she thought desperately. "Don't tempt them. It won't be the glory of the Punishment Cross here. It will be those corridors and miserable oblivion." Yet it absolutely fascinated her that Laurent was so bold.

The Master went round him and the grooms who held him, and now took the leather thong from one of the others and spanked Laurent's nipples over and over again. Laurent couldn't keep quiet, though he had turned his head away. His neck was corded with tension, his limbs trembling.

And the Master seemed as curious, as fastened upon his test as ever. He made a gesture to one of the others. And, as Beauty watched, a long gilded leather glove was brought to the Master.

It was beautifully worked with intricate designs all the way down the leather length of the arm to the large cuff, the whole gleaming as if it had been covered in a salve or unguent.

As the Master drew the glove over his hand and down his arm to the elbow, Beauty felt herself flooded with heat and excitement. The Master's eyes were almost childlike in their studiousness, the mouth irresistible as it smiled, the grace of the body as he approached Laurent now entrancing.

He moved his left hand to the back of Lauren's head, cradling it, his fingers curled in Laurent's hair as the Prince stared straight upward. And with the gloved hand, the right hand, he pushed upward slowly between Laurent's open legs, two fingers entering his body first, as Beauty stared unabashedly.

Laurent's breathing grew hoarse, rapid. His face darkened. The fingers had disappeared inside his anus, and now it seemed the whole hand worked its way into him.

The grooms moved in a little on all sides. And Beauty could see that Tristan and Elena watched with equal attention.

The Master, meanwhile, seemed to see nothing but Laurent. He was staring right at Laurent's face, and Laurent's face was twisted in pleasure and pain as the hand moved its way deeper and deeper into his body. It was in beyond the wrist, and Laurent's limbs were no longer shuddering. They were frozen. A long, whistling sigh passed through his teeth.

The Master lifted Laurent's chin with the thumb of his left hand. He bent over until his face was very close to Laurent's. And in a long, tense silence the arm moved ever upward into Laurent as the Prince seemed to swoon, his cock stiff and still, the clear moisture leaking from it in the tiniest droplets.

Beauty's whole body tightened, relaxed, and again she felt herself on the verge of orgasm. As she tried to drive it back, she felt herself grow limp and weak, and all the hands holding her were in fact making love to her, caressing her.

The Master brought his right arm forward without withdrawing it from Laurent. And in so doing, he tilted the Prince's pelvis upward, further revealing the enormous balls, and the glistening gold leather as it widened the pink ring of the anus impossibly.

A sudden cry came out of Laurent. A hoarse gasp that seemed a cry for mercy. And the Master held him motionless, their lips nearly touching. The Master's left hand released Laurent's head and moved over his face, parting his lips with one finger. And then the tears spilled from Laurent's eyes.

And very quickly, the Master withdrew his arm and peeled off the glove, casting it aside, as Laurent hung in the grasp of the grooms, his head down, his face reddened.

The Master made some little remark, and again the grooms laughed agreeably. One of the grooms replaced the nipple clamps, and Laurent grimaced. The Master immediately gestured for Laurent to be placed on the floor, and the chains of Laurent's leashes were suddenly fixed to a gold ring on the back of the Master's slipper.

"O, no, this beast can't take him away from us!" Beauty thought. But that was the mere surface of her thoughts. She was terrified that it was Laurent and Laurent alone who had been chosen by the Master.

But they were all being put down. And suddenly Beauty was on hands and knees, neck pressed low by the soft velvety sole of the slipper, and she realized that Tristan and Elena were beside her and all three of them were being pulled forward by their nipple chains and whipped by the thongs as they moved out of the garden.

She saw the hem of the Master's robe to her right, and behind him the figure of Laurent struggling to keep up with the Master's strides, the chains from his nipples anchoring him to the Master's foot, his brown hair veiling his face mercifully.

Where were Dmitri and Rosalynd? Why had they been discarded? Would one of the other men who had come in with the Master take them?

She couldn't know. And the corridor seemed endless.

But she didn't really care about Dmitri and Rosalynd. All she cared about truly was that she and Tristan and Laurent and Elena were together. And, of course, the fact that he, this mysterious Master, this tall and impossibly elegant creature, was moving right alongside of her.

His embroidered robe brushed her shoulder as he moved ahead, Laurent struggling to keep pace with him.

The thongs licked at her backside, licked at her pubis, as she rushed after them.

At last, they came to another pair of doors, and the thongs drove them through into a large lamp-lighted chamber. She was bid to stop by the firm pressure of a slipper on her neck once more, and then she realized that all the grooms had withdrawn and the door had been shut behind them.

The only sound was the anxious breathing of the Princes and Princesses. The Master moved past Beauty to the door. A bolt was thrown, a key turned. Silence.

Then she heard the melodious voice again, soft and low, and this time it was speaking, in charmingly accented syllables, her own language:

"Well, my darlings, you may all come forward and kneel up before me. I have much to say to you."

3 Mysterious Master

A tumultuous shock to be spoken to.

At once the group of slaves obeyed, coming round to kneel up in front of the Master, the golden leashes trailing on the floor. Even Laurent was freed now from the Master's slipper and took his place with the others.

As soon as they were all still, kneeling with their hands clasped to the backs of their necks, the Master said:

"Look at me."

Beauty did not hesitate. She looked up into his face and found it as appealing and baffling now as it had been in the garden. It was a better-proportioned face than she had realized, the full and agreeable mouth finely shaped, the nose long and delicate, the eyes well spaced and radiantly dominant. But, again, it was the spirit that magnetized her.

As he looked from one to another of the captives, Beauty could feel the excitement coursing through the little group, feel her own sudden elation.

"O, yes, a splendid creature," she thought. And memories of the Crown Prince who had brought Beauty to the Queen's land and of her crude Captain of the Guard in the village were suddenly threatened with complete dissolution.

"Precious slaves," he said, eyes fixing on her for a brief, electric moment. "You know where you are and why you are here. The soldiers have brought you by force to serve your Lord and Master." So mellifluous the voice, the face so immediately warm. "And you know that you will serve always in silence. Dumb little creatures you are to the grooms who attend you. But I, the Sultan's steward, cherish no such illusions that sensuality obliterates high treason."

"Of course not," Beauty thought. But she didn't dare to voice her thoughts. Her interest in the man was deepening rapidly and dangerously.

"Those few slaves I pick," he said, his eyes traveling again, "those I choose to perfect and offer to the Sultan's Court are always apprised of my aims, and my demands, and the dangers of my temper. But only in the secrecy of this chamber. In this chamber I want my methods to be understood. My expectations to be fully clarified."

He drew closer, towering over Beauty, and his hand reached for her breast, squeezing it as he had done before, just a little too hard, the hot shiver passing down into her sex immediately. With the other hand he stroked the side of Laurent's face, thumb grazing the lip as Beauty turned to watch, utterly forgetting herself.

"That you will not do, Princess," he said, and at once he slapped her hard and she bowed her head, her face stinging. "You will continue to look at me until I tell you otherwise."

Beauty's tears rose at once. How could she have been so foolish?

But there was no anger in his voice, only a soft indulgence. Tenderly, he lifted her chin. She stared at him through her tears.

"Do you know what I want of you, Beauty? Answer me."

"No, Master," she said quickly. Her voice alien to her.

"That you be perfect, for me!" he said gently, the voice seeming so full of reason, of logic. "This I want of all of you. That you be nonpareils in this vast wilderness of slaves in which you could be lost like a handful of diamonds in the ocean. That you shine by virtue not merely of your compliance but by virtue of your intense and particular passion. You will lift yourself up from the masses of slaves who surround you. You will seduce your Masters and Mistresses by a lustre that throws others into eclipse! Do you understand me!"

Beauty struggled not to sob in her anxiousness, her eyes on his, as if she could not look away even if she wanted to. But never had she felt such an overwhelming desire to obey. The urgency of his voice was wholly different from the tone of those who had educated her at the castle or chastised her in the village. She felt as if she was losing the very form of her personality. She was slowly melting.

"And this you will do for me," he said, his voice growing even more soft, more persuasive, more resonant. "You will do it as much for me as for your royal Lords. Because I desire it of you." He closed his hand around Beauty's throat. "Let me hear you speak again, little one. In my chambers, you will speak to me to tell me that you wish to please me."

"Yes, Master," she said. And her voice once again seemed strange to her, full of feelings she hadn't truly known before. The warm fingers caressed her throat, seemed to caress the words she spoke, coax them out of her and shape the tone of them.

"You see, there are hundreds of grooms," he said, narrowing

his eyes as he looked away from her to the others, the hand still clasping her. "Hundreds charged with preparing succulent little partridges for Our Lord the Sultan, or fine muscular young bucks and stags for him to play with. But I, Lexius, am the only Chief Steward of the Grooms. And I *must* choose and perfect the finest of all playthings."

Even this was not said with anger or urgency.

But as he looked again at Beauty, his eyes widened with intensity. The semblance of anger terrified her. But the gentle fingers massaged the back of her neck, the thumb stroking her throat in front.

"Yes, Master," she whispered suddenly.

"Yes, absolutely, my little love," he said, crooning to her. But then he became grave, and his voice became small, as if to command greater respect by speaking its words simply.

"It is absolutely out of the question that you do not distinguish yourselves, that after one glimpse of you the great luminaries of this house do not reach out to pluck you like ripe fruit, that they do not compliment me upon your loveliness, your heat, your silent, ravening passion."

Beauty's tears flowed again down her cheeks.

He withdrew his hand slowly. She felt suddenly cold, abandoned. A little sob caught in her throat, but he had heard it.

Lovingly, almost sadly, he smiled at her. His face was shadowed and strangely vulnerable.

"Divine little Princess," he whispered. "We are lost, you see, unless they notice us."

"Yes, Master," she whispered. She would have done anything to have him touch her again, hold her.

And the rich undertone of sadness in him startled her, enchanted her. O, if only she could kiss his feet.

And, in a sudden impulse she did. She went down on the marble and touched her lips to his slipper. She did it over and over. And she wondered that the word "lost" had so delighted her.

As she rose again, clasping her hands behind her neck, she lowered her eyes in resignation. She should be slapped for what she had done. The room – its white marble, its gilded doors – was like so many facets of light. Why did this man produce this effect in her? Why . . .

"Lost." The word set up its musical echo in her soul.

The Master's long, dark fingers came out and touched her lips. And she saw him smiling.

"You will find me hard, you will find me impossibly hard," he said gently. "But now you know why. You understand now. You belong to Lexius, the Chief Steward. You mustn't fail him. Speak. All of you."

He was answered by a chorus of "Yes, Master." Beauty heard even the voice of Laurent, the runaway, answering just as promptly.

"And now I shall tell you another truth, little ones," he said. "You may belong to the most High Lord, to the Sultana, to the Beautiful and Virtuous Royal Wives of the Harem . . ." He paused, as if to let his words sink in. "But you belong just as truly to me!" he said, "as to anyone! And I revel in every punishment I inflict. I do. It is my nature, as it is yours to serve – my nature, when it comes to slaves, to eat from the very same dish as my Masters. Tell me that you understand me."

"Yes, Master!"

The words came out of Beauty like an explosion of breath. She was dazed with all he had said to her.

She watched him intently as he turned now to Elena, and her soul shrank, though she did not turn her head a fraction of an inch or move her steady gaze from him. Yet still, she could see that he was kneading Elena's fine breasts. How Beauty envied those high, jutting breasts! Nipples the color of apricot. And it hurt her further that Elena moaned so bewitchingly.

"Yes, yes, exactly," said the Master, the voice as intimate as it had been with Beauty. "You will writhe at my touch. You will writhe at the touch of all your Masters and Mistresses. You will give up your soul to those who so much as glance at you. You will burn like lights ın the dark!"

Again a chorus of "Yes, Master."

"Did you see the multitude of slaves who make up the ornaments of this house?"

"Yes, Master," from all of them.

"Will you distinguish yourselves from the gilded herd by passion, by obedience, by putting into your silent compliance a deafening thunder of feeling!"

"Yes, Master."

"But now, we shall begin. You will be properly purified. And then to work immediately. The Court knows that new slaves have come. You are awaited. And your lips are once again sealed. Not under the sternest punishment are you to make a sound with them parted. Unless otherwise commanded you crawl on hands and knees, buttocks up and forehead near to the very ground, almost touching it."

He walked down the silent row. He stroked and examined each slave again, lingering for a long time on Laurent. Then with an abrupt gesture, he ordered Laurent to the door. Laurent crawled as he had been told to do, his forehead grazing the marble. The Master touched the bolt with the thong. Laurent at once slid it back.

The Master pulled the nearby bell cord.

4 The Rites of Purification

At once the young grooms appeared and silently took the slaves in hand, quickly forcing them on hands and knees through another doorway into a large, warm bathing place.

Amid delicate tropical flowering plants and lazing palms, Beauty saw steam rising from the shallow pools in the marble floor and smelled the fragrance of the herbs and spiced perfumes.

But she was spirited past all of this into a tiny private chamber. And there was made to kneel with legs wide apart over a deep, rounded basin in the floor through which water ran fast from hidden founts and down the drain continuously.

Her forehead was once again lowered to the floor, her hands clasped upon the back of her neck. The air was warm and moist around her. And immediately the warm water and soft scrub brushes went to work upon her.

It was all done with much greater speed than at the bath in the castle. And within moments, she was perfumed and oiled and her sex was pumping with expectation as soft towels caressed her.

But she was not told to get up. On the contrary, she was bid to be still by a firm pat of the hand on her head, and she heard strange sounds above her.

Then she felt a metal nozzle entering her vagina. Immediately her juices flowed at the long-awaited sensation of being entered, no matter how awkwardly. But she knew this was merely for cleansing

– it had been done other times to her – and she welcomed the steady fount of water that suddenly gushed into her with delicious pressure.

But what startled her was the unfamiliar touch of fingers on her anus. She was being oiled there, and her body tensed, even as the craving in her was doubled. Hands quickly took hold of the soles of her feet to keep her firmly in place. She heard the grooms laughing softly and commenting to one another.

Then something small and hard entered her anus and forced its way in deep as she gave a little gasp, pressing her lips tightly together. Her muscles contracted to fight the little invasion, but this only sent new ripples of pleasure through her. The flush of water into her vagina had stopped. And what happened now was unmistakable: A stream of warm water was being pumped into her rectum. And it did not wash back out of her as did the douching fluids. It filled her with ever-increasing force, and a strong hand pressed her buttocks together as if bidding her not to release the water.

It seemed a whole new region of her body came to life, a part of her that had never been punished or even really examined. The force of the flow grew stronger and stronger. Her mind protested that she could not be invaded in this final way, that she could not be rendered so helpless.

She felt she would burst if she did not let go. She wanted to expel the little nozzle, the water. But she dared not, she could not. This must happen to her now and she accepted it. It was part of this realm of more refined pleasures and manners. And how dare she protest? She began to whimper softly, caught between a new pleasure and a new sense of violation.

But the most enervating and taxing part was yet to come, and she dreaded it. Just when she thought she could bear no more, that she was full to overflowing, she was lifted upright by her arms, and her legs were pulled even wider apart, the little nozzle in her anus plugging her and tormenting her.

The grooms smiled down at her as they held her arms. And she looked up fearfully, shyly, afraid of the utter shame of the sudden release that was inevitable. Then the nozzle was slipped out, and her buttocks were spread apart, and her bowels quickly emptied.

She squeezed her eyes shut. She felt warm water poured over her private parts, front and back, heard the loud full rush in the basin. She was overcome with something like shame. But it wasn't shame. All privacy and choice had been taken from her. Not even this act was to be hers alone anymore, she understood. And the chills passing through her body with every spasm of release locked her into a delirious sense of helplessness. She gave herself over to those who commanded her, her body limp and unprotesting. She flexed her muscles to help with the emptying, to complete it.

"Yes, to be purified," she thought. And she experienced a great undeniable relief, the awareness of her body cleansing itself becoming exquisite as she shuddered.

The water continued to flow over her, over her buttocks, her belly, down into the basin, washing away all the waste. And she was dissolving into an overall ecstasy that seemed a form of climax in itself. But it wasn't. It was just beyond her reach, the climax. And as she felt her mouth open in a low gasp, she rocked back and forth on the brink, her body pleading silently and vainly with those who held her. All the invisible knots were gone from her spirit. She was without the slightest strength, and utterly dependent upon the grooms to support her.

They stroked her hair back from her forehead. The warm water washed her again and again.

And then she saw, as she dared to open her eyes, that the Master himself was there. He was standing in the doorway of the room and he was smiling at her. He came forward and lifted her up out of this moment of indescribable weakness.

She stared at him, stunned that it was he who held her as the others covered her in towels again.

She felt as defenseless as she had ever been, and it seemed an impossible reward that he led her out of the little chamber. If she could only embrace him, only find the cock under his robes, only . . . The elation of being near him escalated immediately into pain.

"O, please, we have been starved and starved," she wanted to say. But she only looked down demurely, feeling his fingers on her arm. That was the old Beauty speaking the words in her head, wasn't it? The new Beauty wanted to say only the word "Master".

And to think that only moments ago she had been considering love for him. Why, she loved him already. She could breathe the fragrance of his skin, almost hear his heart beat as he turned her

and directed her forward. His fingers clasped her neck as tightly
as they had before.

Where was he taking her?

The others were gone. She was set on one of the tables. She
shivered in happiness and disbelief as he himself began to rub
more perfumed oil into her. But this time there was to be no
covering of gold paint. Her bare flesh would shine under the oil.
And he pinched her cheeks with both hands to give them color
as she rested back on her heels, her eyes wet from the steam and
from her tears, watching him dreamily.

He seemed deeply absorbed in his work, his dark eyebrows knit,
his mouth half open. And, when he applied gold leash clamps to her
nipples, he pressed them tight for an instant with a little tightening
of his lips that made her feel the gesture all the more deeply. She
arched her back and breathed deeply. And he kissed her forehead,
letting his lips linger, letting his hair brush her cheek.

"Lexius," she thought. It was a beautiful name.

When he brushed her hair it was almost with angry, fierce strokes,
and chills consumed her. He brushed it up and wound it on top of
her head. And she glimpsed the pearl pins that he used to fasten
it. Her neck was naked now, like the rest of her.

As he put the pearls through her ear lobes, she studied the smooth
dark skin of his face, the rise and fall of his dark lashes. He was like
a finely polished thing, his fingernails buffed to look like glass, his
teeth perfect. And how deftly yet gently he handled her.

It was over too fast, and yet not fast enough. How long could
she writhe, dreaming of orgasm? She cried because there had to
be some release, and when he put her on the floor her body ached
as never before, it seemed.

Gently, he pulled the leashes. She bent down, forehead to the
ground, as she crept forward, and it seemed to her that she had
never been more completely the slave.

If she had any ability left to think, as she followed him out of
the bath, she thought that she could no longer remember a time
when she had worn clothes, walked and talked with those who
did, commanded others. Her nakedness and helplessness were
natural to her, more natural here in these spacious marble halls
than anywhere else, and she knew without a doubt that she would
love this Master utterly.

She could have said it was an act of will, that after talking with

Tristan she had simply decided. But there was too much that was unique about the man, even in the delicate way that he himself had groomed her. And the place itself, it was like magic to her. And she had thought she loved the harshness of the village!

Why must he give her away now? Take her to others? But it was wrong to question . . .

As they moved along the corridor together, she heard for the first time the soft breathing and sighs of the slaves who decorated the niches on either side of them. It seemed a muted chorus of perfect devotion.

And a confusion of all sense of time and place overcame her.

TWO AT ONCE

Robert Silverberg

"YOU NEVER HAVE?" Louise asked. "Not ever?"

This was in the glorious seventies, when everyone was doing everything to everyone, in every imaginable combination. I was young, healthy, prosperous and single. And we were in Los Angeles, city of year-round summer and infinite possibility.

"Not even once," I said. "Things just haven't clicked the right way, I guess."

"Well," Louise said, "let me think about this."

What we were discussing – over Belgian waffles and mimosas at a favorite breakfast place of mine on the Sunset Strip – was my primo fantasy, the one sexual act – well, not the only one, but the only one that really interested me – that I had never managed to experience: making love to two women at the same time. Fucking one, amiably caressing the other, then switching, then maybe resting for a little while and watching as they amused each other, and then starting the whole cycle again, Ms. A. followed by Ms. B – the good old sandwich game, me as the filling, double your pleasure, double your fun.

Louise sipped her mimosa and thought about it. Her brow furrowed; her wheels were turning.

"Janet?" she said. "No. No, that won't work. Martine? Probably not. Kate?" She shook her head. Then: "Dana, maybe?"

It was maddening. Delicious possibilities flickered one by one in her eyes, rose briefly to the level of a bright gleam, and died away with a shake of her head just as each of the girls she named started to assume a thrilling reality in my mind. I had no more idea who Janet was, or Kate or Martine, than you do. They were only names to me; but for the single dazzling instant that they dangled in the air between us as potential members of our trio they were glorious names already turning into delectable flesh, and in the hyperactive arena of my imagination I could see myself rolling around in bed with lovely Louise and lissome Janet (blonde, leggy, slim-hipped) or luscious Louise and languid Martine (dark ringlets, heavy swaying breasts) or lascivious Louise and lubricious Kate (bright sparkling eyes, tiny tattoo on left buttock). But as fast as the tantalizing visions arose, Louise dismissed them. Janet had moved to San Francisco, she remembered now; Martine was in a relationship; Kate's motorcycle had gone into a ditch in Topanga Canyon the week before. Bim, bam, boom: all three vanished from my life just like that and I had never even known them.

"Dana, though," she said. Louise's eyes brightened again and this time they stayed that way. "Yes. Yes. Very probably a yes. Let me see what I can do about Dana, all right?"

"Dana's a female?" I asked uneasily.

Louise giggled. "For Christ's sake, Charlie, what do you think?"

"I knew a Dana in college once. A man."

"You said two women, didn't you? Come on, then." She tossed me a mischievous look. "Unless it's the other kind of threesome you were thinking of."

"Not exactly, Louise."

"I wouldn't mind that, you know."

"I bet you wouldn't. But I would."

"Well, then. All right." She winked. "I'll see what I can manage."

A hot little quiver of anticipation ran through me. Louise would manage something: I was sure of it. This was the giddy seventies, after all, when the whole planet was in heat. We were in Los Angeles, global capital of carefree copulation. And Louise, slim, agile, raven-haired, uninhibited Louise, was very resourceful indeed. She made her living setting up window displays for the innumerable little women's clothing boutiques that had sprouted up all over Venice and Santa Monica and West Hollywood, and she knew hundreds of women models, fitters, designers and boutique owners, nearly all of whom were young, attractive and single.

"Finish your mimosa," Louise said. "Let's go to the beach."

Louise did her window work between three in the afternoon and half past eight at night. Plenty of time for play, before or after.

"Isn't it too cool today?" I asked.

"The radio says it'll be seventy-five degrees by ten o'clock."

January 13th. Seventy-five degrees. I love L.A. in the winter. We went to the beach: the old nude beach at Topanga, the one they closed down around 1980 when the people in the expensive beach houses began to get tired of the show. The water was a little chilly, so all we did was run ankle-deep into the surf and quickly out again, but the beach itself was fine. We basked and chatted and built a sand castle – more of a bungalow, really – and around noon we got dressed and drove down to Louise's place in Venice to shower away the sand. Of course we took the shower together and one thing led to another, and between that and lunch Louise was a little late getting to work. Nobody would mind.

We were such good friends, Louise and I. We had known each other for three years and at least once a week, usually on a Tuesday or Wednesday morning, we had breakfast together and went to the beach. Then we went to her place and balled. We liked each other's company. Neither of us expected anything more than that from the other: company. She was twenty-eight; I was a couple of years older. Good friends, yes. I had met her at a bookshop on Melrose and we had liked each other right away and there we were. We didn't give a thought about getting married, either to each other or anyone else. What a nice decade that was! The stock market went to hell, the government was a mess, inflation was fifteen per cent, sometimes you had to wait on line for an hour and a half to buy gas. But for Louise and me and a lot of others like us it was the time of our lives. Yes. The time of our lives. Everybody young, everybody single, and we were going to stay that way forever.

Two days later she called me and asked, "Are you free Saturday night?"

"I could be." We rarely saw each other on weekends. "Why?"

"I talked to Dana."

"Oh," I said. "Well, then!"

"Will you spring for dinner for three at Le Provence?"

"I could do that, yes." Le Provence was a small and very

authentic French restaurant in Westwood that we liked. Dinner
for three would run me close to forty bucks in the quaint money
of the era, a nice bottle of wine included. But I could afford it. I
was writing continuity for Saturday morning TV then – Captain
Goofus and His Space Brigade. Don't laugh. Captain Goofus kept
me solvent for four seasons and some residuals, and I miss him
very much. "Tell me about Dana," I said.

"New York girl. Been here about a year. Medium tall, brown
hair, glasses, nice figure, very bright. Smokes. You mind that?"

"I can survive. Stacked?"

"Not especially. But she's built okay."

"How do you know her?"

"She's a customer at Pleasure Dome on Santa Monica. Came
into the store one night in November while I was setting up the
Christmas window. We've had lunch a few times."

"You sure she'll go for this, Louise?"

"Le Provence, Saturday night, half past seven, okay?"

My first blind date in years. Well, all right. Louise vouched for
her. The two of them were already there, sitting at a table in the
back, when I showed up at the restaurant. In half a minute I knew
that things were going to work out. Dana was around twenty-five,
slender, pleasant-looking if unspectacular, with big horn-rimmed
glasses and quick, penetrating eyes. Her whole vibe was New York:
alert, intelligent, fearless. Ready to throw herself joyously into our
brave new California world of healthy, anything-goes erotic fun. I
didn't sense any tremendous pheromonal output coming from her
that related specifically to *me*, no instantaneous blast of lust, just a
generalized willingness to go along with the project. But that was
okay. We had only just met, after all. Expecting a woman to fall
down instantly at my feet foaming with desire has never been any
prerequisite of mine: simple willingness is quite sufficient for me.

My ever-active mind began to spin with fantasies. I saw myself
sprawled out on the big water bed with Louise to my left and Dana
to my right, all of us naked, both of them pressing close against
me, squirming and wriggling. I imagined the sleek texture along
the inside of Dana's thighs and the feel of her cool firm breasts
against my hands while the rest of me was busy with Louise. And
then slipping free of Louise and turning to Dana, gliding into her
up to the hilt while Louise hovered above us both, grazing my back
with the tips of her breasts –

Back in the real world Dana and I started to make polite first-date chitchat, with Louise sitting there beaming like a matchmaker whose clients are going in the right direction.

"So, Louise tells me you write for television?"

"Saturday morning cartoons. Captain Goofus and His Space Brigade."

"Far out! You must make a mint."

"Half a mint, actually. It's not bad. And you?"

"A word processor," she said.

"A what?"

"Typist, sort of. Except I use a kind of computer, you know? In a law office in Beverly Hills?"

I didn't know. Computers were something very new then.

"Must be movie lawyers," I said. "They're the only ones who can afford a gadget like that."

She named the firm. Entertainment law, all right. But actually Dana wanted to write screenplays; the word-processing thing was just a way station en route to success. I smiled. This city has always been full of ambitious would-be screenwriters, two-thirds of them from New York. I expected her to pull a script out of her purse any minute. But Dana wasn't that tacky. The conversation bubbled on, and somewhere along the way we ordered, and I felt so up about the whole thing that I selected a nine-dollar bottle of Bordeaux. Nine dollars was a lot for a bottle of wine in those days.

We'd be done with dinner by nine, I figured, and it was a five-minute drive over to my apartment on Barrington just above Wilshire, and figure half an hour for some drinks, brandy or sherry or whatever, and a little music and soft lights and a couple of joints – this was the seventies, remember – and the clothes would begin to come off, and then the migration to the water bed.

Two women at once, at last! My dream fulfilled!

But then a waitress we hadn't noticed up till then brought the wine to the table and things started to go strange.

She was standing next to me, going through her elaborate bottle-opening rigmarole, cutting the red seal and inserting the corkscrew and all, paying all the attention to me because obviously I was the one who would be picking up the bill, when suddenly she happened to glance toward Dana and I heard her gasp.

"Oh, my *God*! Dana! What are *you* doing in LA?"

Dana hadn't looked at the waitress at all. But now she did and I saw a flush of amazement come over her face.

"Judy?"

They were both babbling at once. Imagine! Coincidence! Terrific to see you again! Old friends from New York days, I gathered. (High-school chums? Pals in Greenwich Village?) Lost touch, hadn't seen each other in years. Judy, an aspiring actress, just passing time as a waitress. Sure. Been here five years; still hoping. Must get together some time. Maybe tonight after work? Apartment on Ohio between Westwood and Federal, practically around the corner from here. Listen, see you in a little while – can't stay and gab. Is the wine okay, sir? Glad to hear it. My God, Dana Greene, imagine that!

Judy poured us our wine and moved along.

Dana couldn't get over it. Imagine – Judy Glass, waiting tables right in the restaurant where we were eating!

My guess was right on both counts: they had gone to high school together in the Bronx, hung out together in the Village afterward. Really close friends: wonderful to rediscover her. Three sips of wine and Dana jumped up and went across the room to talk to her newfound old pal some more. I didn't like that: diversion of interest. Broke the rhythm of mutual seduction. Little did I know. I saw them giggling and whispering and nodding. About what? I would have been amazed. You too. The chitchat went on and on. Old Pierre, the boss, scowled: get on with your work, Mademoiselle. Judy went in back. Dana returned to the table. Said something to Louise that I couldn't hear. Louise grinned. The two of them got up, excused themselves, went toward the bathroom together. Judy was still back there somewhere too. What the hell was brewing? Gone a long time. Louise returned; Dana didn't. I gave her a quizzical look.

Louise said, looking mischievous, "How would you feel if Judy comes home with us tonight, Charlie?"

That startled me. "Instead of Dana?"

"Also."

"Three women?" I was utterly floored. "Jesus Christ."

"Think you can handle it?"

"I could try," I said, still stunned. "God Almighty! *Three!*"

"Dana thought it might be fun. A really Los Angeles thing to do. She can be very impulsive that way."

It took a couple more bathroom conferences for them to work everything out. Somehow they thought it was crass to discuss the logistics in front of me. But finally it was all set up. The restaurant would close around eleven; it would take a little time for the employees to cash out, but Judy could be at my place by half past. A late evening, but worth it, all things considered.

The rest of dinner was an anticlimax. We talked about the weather, the food, the wine, Dana's screenwriting ambitions. But we all had our minds on what was coming up later. Now and then Judy, busy at other tables, shot a glance at me. Second thoughts? I wondered. Or just sizing me up? I shot a few glances at her. I felt dizzy, dazzled, astounded. Would I be equal to the task? A foursome instead of a threesome? A one-man orgy? Sure. God help me, I had to be equal to it. Or else.

We dragged the meal out till half past nine. I drove to my place, Dana and Louise following in Louise's car. Upstairs. Soft music, low lights. Drinks. Kept clothes on while waiting for Judy. Not polite to jump the first two ladies before number three shows up.

Long wait. Eleven-thirty. Quarter to. Judy getting cold feet?
Midnight. Doorbell.

Judy. "I thought we'd never finish up tonight! Hey, what a cool place you have, Charlie!"

"Would you like a drink? A joint?"

"Sure. Sure."

We were all a little nervous. The big moment approaching and nobody quite certain how to start it off.

Things simply started themselves off: a sudden exchange of glances, grins, nods, and into the bedroom we went and the clothes dropped away. And then we were one naked heap on top of the water bed.

So it began, this extraordinary event. The wildest fantasy you could imagine? Sure. But I'm here to tell you that it's possible to get too much of a good thing. Go ahead, laugh.

They certainly were gorgeous. Louise trim and athletic and darkly tanned, Dana pale beneath her clothing and breastier than she seemed when dressed, Judy plump-rumped, red-haired, freckled down to her belly. We were all pretty stoned and piled on each other like demented teenagers. I got my right hand onto one of Judy's soft, jiggling breasts and my left onto one of Dana's firmer ones and put my tongue into Louise's mouth, and somebody's hand passed between my thighs, and I brought my knee up between somebody else's thighs so she could rub back and forth on it, and then abruptly I was fucking Louise – start with the familiar one, work into it slowly – while trying to find Dana and Judy with my fingers or toes or anything else I didn't happen to be using on Louise.

The perfect deal, you say? Well, maybe. But also a little confusing and distracting. There were all sorts of things to think about. For example I didn't want to get so carried away with Louise that I'd have nothing left for the other two. Luckily Louise always came easily and quickly, so I was able to bring her to her pleasure without expending a lot of my own energy, and I turned to find one of the others.

But they were busy with each other. Licking and grappling, slurping away merrily. I realized now that they had been better chums back in the old New York days than they had mentioned. It was a turn-on to watch them, sure, but finally I had to slide myself between them to remind them I was here. I peeled them apart and Dana came into my arms and I went into Dana. She was heated up and ready, wild, even, and as her hips began a frantic triple-time pumping I had to catch her and slow her down or she would finish me off in six seconds flat. A little humiliating, really, having to ease her back like that. But for me the first come is always by far the best, and I didn't want this once-in-a-lifetime event to be over so fast. So that was something else distracting to think about. I clung to Dana for as much of the ride as I could take, but finally I had to pull out and finish her by hand, while sliding over into Judy. Louise was moving around in the background somewhere. She was one more thing to worry about, really, because I didn't want to ignore anyone even for a minute, and there wasn't enough of me to go around. I shouldn't have worried all that much. Louise could take care of herself, I knew, and would, and did. But I am a conscientious sort of guy in these matters.

I know, I make it sound like it was a lot of work, and there you are sitting there telling me that you'd have been happy to have taken my place if I found it all that much of a bother. Well, let me tell you, I know there are a lot worse things to complain about than finding yourself in bed with too many women at once. But it *was* a lot of work. Really. A stunt like that has problems as well as rewards. Still and all,

I have to admit it wasn't such a terrible ordeal. Just a little complicated.

I was in the rhythm of it now – you know how it is, when you get past that first fear of coming too soon, and feel like an iron man who can go on forever? – and I swung around from Judy to Louise again, and back to Dana, and on to Judy. While I was with Louise, Dana and Judy seemed very capable of keeping each other occupied. While I was with either of the other two, Louise improvised with one or another or all three of us at once. It went on and on. I was swimming in a sea of pussy. Wherever I moved there was a breast in my hand and one in my mouth and somebody's thighs wrapped around my middle. Our bodies were shiny with sweat; we were laughing, gasping, dizzy with the craziness of it.

Then I knew I would drop dead if it went on one more minute, and I reached for Louise and entered her and began to move in the special rhythm that brings on my orgasm. She knew at once what I was doing: she slipped into a reciprocating rhythm and whispered little encouraging things into my ear and I cut loose with the most gigantic come I am ever going to have.

And rolled off the bed, chuckling to myself, and lay on the floor in a stupor for I don't know how long while sounds of ecstasy came from the bed above me. Somewhere in the night I found enough strength to get back into the fray for another round or two. But by three in the morning we had all had enough, and then some. I opened the bedroom windows to let the place air out, and one by one we showered and the girls dressed, and we went into the living room, weary and dazed and a little sheepish, all of us stunned by everything that had passed between us this weird night. Dana and Judy left first. Louise lingered for one last joint.

"Well?" she said. "Satisfied now?"

"Am I ever," I said.

What I didn't tell her then, but will confess to you now, is that I wasn't. Not really. Three at once is a remarkable thing. Extraordinary. Unbelievable, almost. But not really satisfying, in terms of my original fantasy. It was too hectic, too mechanical, more work than play. Or so it seems to me, looking back on it now.

Is that hard to believe? Maybe I'm being too picky, I guess. Some guys are never satisfied with anything.

But really: all I wanted was *two*. Not three. Just two. Fucking one, caressing another – switching – switching back – calmly, attentively, sharing my bed with two lovely women, concentrating on them both, fully, without any extraneous distractions. Not an endurance contest or a circus event but a divine adventure in sensuality.

Well, it was never to be, for me. We set it up and then by accident a third woman got involved and I could never set it up again the right way. Louise met a real-estate tycoon a few weeks later and moved to Phoenix. I phoned Dana but she told me she was going back to New York. Le Provence closed and I don't know where Judy went. And the seventies ended and life got a lot more sedate for most of us, especially where stuff like threesomes were concerned. So I still haven't ever been to bed with two women at once, though I once did it with three. Ironic, I guess.

Two at once – I still fantasize about it.

I guess it's not ever going to come to pass. But I live in hope.

EMILIA COMES
IN MY DREAMS

Jindrich Styrsky

Translated by Iris Irwin

EMILIA IS FADING from my days, my evenings and my dreams. Even her white dress has darkened in my memory. I no longer blush as I recall the mysterious marks of teeth I glimpsed one night below her little belly. The last traces of dissimulation impeding the emotion I was ready to feel have disappeared. That troupe of girls is lost forever, smiling uncertainly and with indifference as they remember how their hearts were torn by passion and by half-treacherous humility. Even her face has been exorcised at last, the face I modelled in snow as a child, the face of a woman whose compliant cunt had consumed her utterly.

I think of Emilia as a bronze statue. Marble bodies, too, are not bothered by fleas. Her heart-shaped upper lip recalls an old-world coronation; the lower lip demanding to be sucked arouses visions of harlotry. I was moving slowly beneath her, my head in the hem of her skirt. I had a close-up view of the hairs on her calves, flattened in all directions under her lace stockings, and I tried to imagine what kind of a comb would be needed to smooth them back into place. I fell in love with the fragrance of her crotch, a wash-house smell mingled with that of a nest of mice, a pine-needle lying forgotten in a bed of lilies-of-the-valley.

I began to suffer from optical illusions; when I looked at Clara her body merged into the outline of Emilia's with the tiny heel. When Emilia felt like sinning, her cunt gave off the aroma of spice in a hayrick. Clara's fragrance was herbal. My hands are wandering under her skirt, touching the top of a stocking, suspender knobs, her inner thigh – hot, damp and beguiling. Emilia brings me a cup of tea, wearing blue mules. I can never again be completely happy, tormented as I am by women's sighs, by their eyes rolling in the convulsions of orgasm.

Emilia never tried to penetrate the world of my poetry. She looked at my garden from over the fence, so that everyday fruit and ordinary berries seemed the awesome apples of some prehistoric paradise, while I moved foolishly along the paths, like a half-wit, like a useless dog with its nose in the grass tracking down death and fleeing its own destiny. I was crazy, seeking to find again that moment when shadows fell across a paved square somewhere in the south. Leaning on the fence, Emilia sped on through life. I can see her so clearly: getting up in the morning with her long hair loose, going to the lavatory to piss, sometimes to shit, and then washing with tar soap. Her crotch made fragrant, she hurried to mingle with the living, to rid herself of the feeling that she was at a fork in the road.

Emilia's smile was a wonderful thing to watch. Her mouth seemed a dried-out hollow, but as you drew near to this upper lode of pleasure you could hear something trembling down inside her, and as she parted her lips for you, a knob of red flesh burst from between her teeth. Age fondles time lovingly. Morality is only safe at home in the arms of abandonment. Her eyes that never closed at the height of her pleasure would take on a gleam of heavenly delight, and looked ashamed of what her lips were doing.

In the corners where I seek my lost youth I come upon golden curls carefully laid away. Life is one long waste of time. Every day death nibbles away at what we call life, and life constantly consumes our longing for trivialities. The idea of the kiss dies before ever the lips meet, and every portrait pales before we can look at it. In the end worms will eat through this woman's heart, too, and grin in her entrails. Who could swear, then, that you had ever existed? I saw you with a lovely naked girl of astonishing whiteness. She lifted her hands and the palms were black with soot. She pressed one hand between your breasts and placed the other over my eyes so that I was looking at you as through torn lace. You were naked under an unbuttoned coat. That single moment revealed your life to me in its entirety: you were a plant, swelling and budding. Two stems rising from the ground grew together and from that juncture you began to wilt, but your body was already taking shape, with a belly, two breasts and a head where two entrancing pink weals swelled up. At that moment, though, the lower part of your body began to wither, and collapsed. And I grovelled before you, grunting with love such as I had never known. I do not know whose shadow it was. I called it Emilia. We are bound together for ever, irrevocably, but we are back to back.

This woman is my coffin, and as she walks I am hidden in her image. And so as I curse her I damn myself and yet love her, falling asleep with a cast of her hand on my cock.

On the first of May you'll go to the cemetery and there in Section Ten you will find a woman sitting on a gravestone. She will be waiting for you, to tell your fortune from the cards. You will leave her and look for explanations on the walls of boarding establishments for young ladies, but the girls' faces in the windows will turn into budding buttocks and tulip arses, and will quiver as a lorry drives past. You will be crazed with fear they're going to fall down into the street, fear that is close to the pleasure you felt at your first boyish erection and close to the terror you felt when your sister taught you to masturbate with a hand of alabaster.

Who do you think can console you now? Emilia is fragmented, torn scraps of her likeness have been borne away by the wind to places beyond your knowledge, and that is why you cannot call on her to be the medium of your calming, and anyway you have long ago learned not to mourn moments of farewell.

The sky slumbers and somewhere behind the bushes a woman moulded of raw flesh is waiting for you. Will you feed her on ice?

Clara always sat on the couch, wearing little, and expecting to be undressed. One day she took my revolver from a drawer, took aim, and fired at a picture. The cardinal's hand went to his chest and he fell to the ground. I felt sorry for him and later on whenever I visited brothels on the outskirts of the city, and paid the whores for their skills, I was always aware that I was purchasing a moment of eternity. Any man who once tasted the salt of Cecilia's cunt would sell his rings, his friends, his morals and all the rest, just to feed the insatiable monster hidden beneath her pink skirt. Oh, why do we never distinguish the first moments when women treat us as playthings, from the time when we drive them to despair? I woke up one night in the early hours, at the time flowers drop their petals and birds begin to sing. Martha was lying by my side, a treasure-house of all ways of making love, a hyena of Corinth, lying with her cunt spread open to the dawn. She caught the disgust in my eyes and surely wanted nothing better than to see me nauseated by the filth of her. I watched her sex swelling and pouring out of her cunt, over the bed and on to the floor, filling the room like a stream of lava. I got out of bed and fled madly from the house, not stopping till I reached the middle of the deserted town square. As I looked back I saw Martha's sex squeezing out of the window like a monstrous tear of unnatural colour. A bird flew down to peck at my seed and I threw a stone to drive it away. "You will be lucky, you will repeat yourself over and over again," a passer-by spoke to me and added: "your wife is just giving birth to a son."

Two little sparrows kept rendez-vous every noon behind the pale blue corsage of Our Lady of Lourdes: I was innocent when I entered the catacombs. The row of square boxes naturally aroused my curiosity. There were a few boys hanging by their bound feet from the tops of the olive trees, flames roasting their curly young heads. In the next room I found a bunch of lovely naked girls entwined in a single monstrous living creature like something from the Apocalypse. Their cunts were opening and closing mechanically, some empty, some swallowing their own slime. One in particular caught my eye, the lips moving as though trying to speak, or like a man whose tongue has turned to stone trying to crow like a cock. Another was a smiling rosebud that I'd recognize among a hundred specimens, to this day. It was my dead Clara's cunt, dead and buried, with nobody to wash her body with the mint-scented lotion she loved. Sadly I brought out my cock and stuck it aimlessly into the writhing mass, uncaring and indifferent, telling myself death always brings debauchery and misfortune together.

Then I put an aquarium on my window-sill. I had a golden-haired vulva, in it, a magnificent specimen of a penis with a blue eye and delicate veins on its temples. As time went on I threw everything I had ever loved into it: broken cups, hairpins, Barbara's slippers, burnt-out bulbs, shadows, cigarette ends, sardine tins, all my letters and used condoms. Many strange creatures were born in that world. I felt myself to be a Creator, and I had every right to think so. When I had the aquarium sealed up I gazed contentedly at my mouldering dreams, until there was no seeing through the mildew on the glass. Yet I was sure that everything I loved in the world was there, inside.

I still need fodder for my eyes. They gulp down all they get greedily and roughly. At night, asleep, they digest it. Emilia scattered her shocked scorn generously, arousing desire in all she met, provoking visions of that hairy maw.

I still remember something that happened when I was a boy. I'd just been expelled from high school and nobody would have anything to do with me. Except my sister. I would go to her secretly, in the night. Lying in each other's arms, legs entwined, we slowly dreamed ourselves into the dulled state of all those who lie on the knife-edge of shame. One night we heard soft footsteps and my sister nudged me to hide behind the armchair. Our father came into the room, shutting the door quietly behind him, and climbed into her bed without a word. That was when, at last, I saw how one makes love.

Emilia's beauty was not meant to fade, but to rot.

THE STORY OF NO

Lisa Tuttle

AT FIRST SIGHT I thought I knew him and felt my blood heat, my muscles loosen, the breath evaporate from my lungs.

The imprint of his touch rose like stigmata on my skin, and the memory of his tongue hungry in my mouth aroused a need I hadn't admitted to myself for a long time, a desire for the forbidden.

"What is it?" asked my husband. Startled, I looked across the restaurant table at the well-known face and remembered who and where I was: a wife in her forties staying in an elegant, expensive English country house hotel with her husband, the vacation our anniversary present to each other. "See someone you know?"

"No." For that was in another country, and besides . . . "He wouldn't be that young, if it was who I thought. He was that age *then*." The man I remembered would be my age still and maybe would still find me attractive. That young man couldn't be much past twenty. If he looked at me, he'd see someone old enough to be his mother, someone not worth noticing, sexually invisible. He turned his head, and his clear green gaze fell on me with a shock like cold water, and he smiled.

"You're blushing," said my husband with interest. "Was he an old boyfriend?"

"No. Oh, no. Just someone I met once in Houston. Do you want to taste my salmon mousse?"

Once. A single night. Yet the memory of it was with me always.

Many a dull or sleepless night I had pulled it out to comfort myself. I had used it so often it had come to seem like a story I'd read somewhere, and not something that had really happened to me. As a fantasy, I'd even shared it with my husband some nights in bed. But it was real – or had been, once.

I first saw him in a Montrose bar, drinking by himself. He had a tumble of black curls surrounding a long, clean-shaven face, with a sensuous mouth and startling green eyes. Only the overlarge, slightly crooked nose kept him from beauty, but his was a striking face and mine were not the only eyes drawn to stare at it. Nor was it only his face that attracted. He had a physical presence as disturbing as some rare perfume. His was not an outstanding body – nobody would have picked him to model for a centerfold – but it was long and slim and wiry. My husband, handsome, tall, and well-muscled, was certainly more attractive by objective standards, but I wasn't thinking of my husband as I admired the fit of the stranger's jeans.

I took a seat and ordered a drink. I wasn't looking for trouble. I hadn't been planning adultery. I was content, I thought, to look and not touch. I liked the way his lips curled around a cigarette and his eyes narrowed against the smoke. I liked his slender fingers, and the way he moved, shifting his weight or rolling the stiffness out of his neck and shoulders as unself-consciously as an animal.

I gazed for a time at his intriguing, less-than-classical profile, then shifted my stare, let it fall in a caress on his shoulders, his back, down to the ass which so nicely filled his tight, faded jeans. He turned his head lazily toward me as if he'd felt, and liked, my touch. I moved my eyes back up his body to meet his eyes, and I didn't smile. He was the first to look away. Then I did smile, but only to myself.

Someone else, a man, approached him, cigarette in hand, and he gave him a light and responded to his conversational ventures absently, his attention hooked by me. I could feel his senses straining in my direction even when his back was turned, his eyes fixed elsewhere, his ears assaulted by the blandishments of the cigarette smoker – who eventually gave up and took his need to someone else. Which was when my prey turned around and looked at me again.

I had to hide a smile of triumph. That I retained the ability to make a man desire me was reassuring. I had been feeling mired in marriage, as if my wedding ring had conferred invisibility, and his look sent a surge of well-being through me. As he straightened, flexing his shoulders and the muscles of his long back before moving away from the bar with an easy, loose-jointed motion, I imagined him naked and aroused and felt a tightening of my internal muscles.

He bought me a drink and then I bought him one. We sat and looked at each other. There were few words, none of importance. The conversation that mattered was conducted between our bodies, in minute shifts in posture and attitude, in the crossing and uncrossing of my legs as I leaned toward him and then back, in the way he stroked his own face with his long, slender fingers. He never touched me. I think he didn't dare. I tried to make it easy for him, resting my hand on the tabletop near his, moving my legs beneath the table. With every move I made I aroused myself more until finally, quite breathless and unthinking with desire, I reached out my hand beneath the table and put it on his denimed thigh.

The pupils of his strange green eyes widened, and I smiled. He put his warm hand on top of mine and squeezed.

"Can we go to your place?" he asked, his voice very low.

Confronted with reality, I lost my smile. What was I playing at? I pulled my hand away and stood up. He followed me so quickly that he nearly overturned the table.

"No," I said, but he followed me out of the dim, air-conditioned bar, into the parking lot. The hot, tropical night embraced us like a sweaty lover. Someone, in a book I'd once read, had compared the smell of Houston to the aroma of a woman, sexually aroused and none too clean. I drew a deep breath; spilled beer, gasoline, car exhaust, cooking fumes, perfume, after-shave, rotting vegetation, garbage, and, beneath it all, a briny tang that might have been a breeze wafted in from the Gulf of Mexico.

He was right behind me, following, and as I turned to tell him off, somehow instead I fell against him. And then we were clutching each other, breast to breast, mouth to mouth, kissing greedily. The need I felt when he first touched me, the intensity with which it rushed all through me was so powerful I thought I would faint. Then, slowly, resting in his embrace, I came back to myself, back to him. I had never known anything as sensually beautiful as his mouth; the soft, warm lips that parted against mine, dryness opening into wetness, a moist cave where the sly, clever animal that was his tongue lived and came out to nuzzle and suck at me greedily. His breath was smoky and dark, tasting of desirable sins, of whisky and sugar and cigarettes.

His hands, long-fingered, strong and clever, moved over my body as we kissed, at first shy, but then, as I clung to him fiercely, making no attempt to push him off, becoming bolder. He was quickly impatient with the barriers of my clothes, which were little enough: a cotton blouse, a short summer skirt and underwear, my legs bare, naked feet strapped into leather sandals. One of his hands, which had returned again and again to cup and trace lazy patterns of arousal on my bound and covered breasts, now began swiftly and without fumbling to unbutton my blouse, while his other hand, behind me, was pushing up my skirt and tugging at the elastic of my panties. In a matter of minutes, maybe seconds, he could have me stripped naked.

I wanted nothing better than to be naked in his capable hands, but not here, in public, surrounded by strangers – was he crazy? "No," I gasped and pushed him off and pulled away, struggling to refasten my buttons.

He reached for me again, and I slapped at his hands. He looked stricken. "I want you. Don't you –?"

I laughed. "Not here, be reasonable!" There were people all around us, getting in and out of cars, overflow customers from the bar and people from the neighborhood out for a breath of air, drinking beer from six-packs purchased at the convenience store across the street. This parking lot and the whole street was like a fair or a carnival, an impromptu, open-air party to celebrate summer in the city. I waved a hand to indicate the crowd passion had temporarily hidden from us, and as if I'd waved away smoke we both saw, at the same time, a man and woman locked in a fervent embrace just yards away from us. As I stared, I realized that the woman had one hand inside the front of the man's trousers.

My stranger grinned at me, a wide, white, wolfish smile. He put his hands on my hips and pulled me tightly to him. His erection felt enormous. His breath hot in my ear, he whispered, "Nobody's going to notice. Nobody'll care."

It was true nobody else seemed to notice the passionate couple, or, if they did, they politely pretended not to see. Other people had their own concerns; why should they care? Nor would it have been different if the lovers had been of the same sex. The Montrose was the most Bohemian and most sexually tolerant area of Houston, which was why I had chosen it for my escape that night. It provided a place where I could temporarily forget who and where I was and become a stranger, pretending I was a free woman at large in San Francisco, New Orleans, or Paris.

The smoky, spicy, sweaty smell of this other stranger, his body's heat and solid mass against me, the hands that caressed my hips and thighs and breasts, all wore away at my hesitation, as did his low voice, telling me a story:

"I was at a rock concert one time, thousands of people packed in close together, all standing up to see better, and moving, kind of dancing in place because there wasn't room to do anything else. I was with this girl . . . she had on a really short skirt, like yours, and one time when she dropped her purse and bent over to pick it up I saw she wasn't wearing any underpants. So . . . I got her to stand in front of me, and I unzipped, and slipped it in, and slowly, easily, pumped away. Nobody knew what we were doing. Even when we both came nobody noticed, because everybody was yelling and hopping around." He had pushed up my skirt at the back again and now snagged the elastic of my underpants – soaking wet by now – and began to ease them down.

"No."

Half of me wanted him to ignore my refusal, not to stop, to take me there among the crowds, even to be seen by disapproving, envious strangers – the other half of me was horrified. What if somebody who knew me came by, somebody I worked with, or one of my neighbors? So I said no again more fiercely, and when I pulled away he let me go.

"You're driving me crazy."

"What do you think you're doing to me?"

"Nothing, compared to what I'd like to do."

We stared at each other, hot and itchy with frustration. I grabbed his hand. "We'll find somewhere not so public. Come on."

I had nowhere in mind except to get away from the crowds. We walked away from the laughter and talk, away from the blare of amplified music and the bright blur of neon signs toward the quieter streets where there were no bars or all-night service stations, no massage parlors or convenience stores; quieter streets lined with trees where the buildings housed beauty parlors and dentists, small businesses that closed up at nightfall. On one such half-deserted

street he pulled me suddenly into the embrasure of a darkened
antique shop and pushed me up against the wall.

"No." I whispered the word, soft as a caress. I wasn't even
sure he heard. His hands were swift and urgent. My blouse was
unbuttoned, my bra undone, my breasts out, nipples teased and
kneaded to an aching stiffness. I surrendered, undone, melting,
and then quite suddenly I saw myself from the outside: some slut,
half undressed in a public place with a stranger, letting a stranger
do that to her – I woke up with a sickening shock. That couldn't
be me. I'd always been a good girl, even before I married I'd only
had two steady boyfriends; I'd never picked up strange men. Now
that I was a married woman this sort of behavior was unthinkable.
Sex was something that happened at home, in bed, not in a shop
doorway.

I tensed and fought off his hands. I twisted to one side and
struggled to push him away, but he pinned my wrists together
effortlessly, one-handed, and stared at me, a faint smile twitching
his lips.

"No," I said weakly, not meaning it. I suddenly wanted more
than anything to be overpowered, to be made to do what I wanted
to do, to have the guilt taken away. He gazed into my eyes and
read there what I wanted as he rolled an erect nipple between
thumb and forefinger. I felt fixed by his gaze, unable to fight.
I stood very still, quivering. He let go my hands and tugged my
skirt up to my waist.

"Take off your pants and spread your legs," he said.

I felt dizzy with desire. "No," I whispered. I didn't mean I didn't
want to, and I didn't mean I did. By my word I meant a different
kind of yes; meant make me do it, do it to me, I'm helpless now.

His eyes were unwavering on mine, but for a moment I was
afraid he wouldn't understand. Then he said, "Try and stop me."
He tugged at the waistband of my panties, and then gently peeled
them down my legs. When they reached my ankles, I stepped out
of them and stood passively, my sex exposed to his view.

A little sigh of pleasure escaped his lips as he looked at me.
Then he became stern again. "Up against the wall and spread
your legs."

I swallowed hard, then found my voice and the only word I had
left. "No."

He laughed. "No? No? What does that mean? Your body's saying something else." He slipped his hand between my legs. I gasped and quivered as he found my wetness. "Your body doesn't lie. Your body says yes." His touch was as soft as his voice, delicate and perfectly judged. I moaned and closed my eyes, unable to watch him watching me as he stroked my clitoris. I let him continue until his touch was too teasing, his fingering too delicate for my much harsher desire, and then I reached down to push his hand harder against me and his fingers inside me. He gasped as if he were the one penetrated, and I cried out with pleasure, a loud and violent "No!"

The wall was hard against my back. My thighs ached with strain as I rode his hand, the clever, stranger's fingers that knew me better, it seemed, than I knew myself, knowing just how to stroke and to probe together, knowing when a teasing gentleness should become more brutal. All this time he watched me, watched my face contort and read my desire as he murmured obscenities and endearments, commands and compliments alternating with a purpose like the hard-soft touch of his hand.

And then his other hand was on my ass, fingers probing the crack, and I moaned as he began to work me with both hands, back and front, and I cried out for more, still more.

Without taking his hands away, hardly faltering, he went down on his knees and began tonguing my clitoris, breathing hard with his own excitement. The warm, wet touch of his mouth was gentle, exact, and excruciating, and it was more than I could bear. Like lightning, white-hot, jagged, and intense, the orgasm flashed as I cried and yelled and clutched his curly head. "No," I cried, and "No" again, as if I must, in my last, desperate moments of pleasure, deny the force of that pleasure, or the reality of it – as if that word would keep it from being real to anyone but me.

Later, but still too soon, while I was rocked in the after-glow, unwilling to be disturbed, he caught my hand and carried it to his crotch, pressed it against the hard, warm bulge of his cock.

I have often wondered what I meant by that. Never in my life before that night had I said no meaning yes, but that night no was my word, my only word, and he had seemed to understand.

I pulled my hand away. "No."

Maybe I'd forgotten how to say yes. Maybe I wanted him to force me. Maybe I'd just had enough and wanted to send him away. Maybe, my own desire sated, I simply wasn't interested in his. Later, when I wanted more, I couldn't believe I'd meant I'd had enough then. I didn't want to believe I'd been selfish enough to send him away unsatisfied simply because my own immediate need had been met. Most of the time I preferred to believe that when I said no at the end I still meant yes, and that it was his understanding that failed him, and me.

Whatever I might have meant, whatever I'd wanted it to mean, he heard me say no, and took me at my word and left, and I made no effort to call him back.

I never saw him again, although there were nights when I went looking, and there has scarcely been a night since then that I haven't thought of him and longed for another chance.

After dinner, my husband and I took coffee in the large, yet cozy library, seated on one of the couches upholstered in leather as soft and supple as living skin, near the fire crackling in the hearth. We didn't talk to any of the other guests – we were being more English than the English on that trip – but we didn't have much to say to each other. Maybe we'd been married too long, maybe we were inhibited by the company. Certainly I was memory-haunted, aroused by the presence of the young man who looked so much like my long-ago stranger. Guilt made me uneasy in my husband's company, made me flinch when he touched me. My eyes kept sneaking across to him, and I pretended it was the books in the floor-to-ceiling bookcases that interested me. I felt him watching me, too, usually just as I looked away, but occasionally our glances would intersect, meeting for one highly charged instant before we both hastily looked away. Was it possible that this boy found me as desirable as had his look-alike of nearly twenty years ago? I hoped my husband wouldn't notice, but maybe it wouldn't be such a bad thing for him to know that another man wanted me.

It grew late, and we left the library, passed through the great hall, and mounted the grand staircase, our feet silent on the thick, pile carpet. I gazed up at the Pre-Raphaelite beauties who adorned the brilliant stained-glass windows but hardly saw them through my memories of warm, sensuous lips, long, clever fingers, and the cock I had never known.

I undressed slowly and dreamily in our luxurious room. I was down to the black silk teddy he'd surprised me with on Valentine's Day when my husband came up behind me and pulled me to him, his hands on my breasts, his breath warm in my ear. I could feel his erection, and I was as aroused as he was, but by the memory of someone else.

Guilt, or something else, made me whisper, "No."

He kissed me gently on my neck, and I moved my silk-clad bottom teasingly. His hands tightened on my breasts while his lips sought out the pulse in my neck. Caught up by rising excitement, again guilt mingled with desire and I breathed, "No," and he let go.

I remained rooted to the spot for a few moments in astonished disappointment, feeling the chill of his departure, hearing him sigh as he got into bed.

But what else could I expect?

No had never meant yes in our shared vocabulary. I had never wanted it to until now, just this moment, when I longed for a little telepathy.

Tingling with frustration, I peeled off my useless sexy underwear and climbed naked into bed.

"Goodnight, my darling," he said, and the chaste kiss he gave me forestalled my chance of letting him know, with my mouth on his, how I really felt. Of course I could have done something more obvious, or simply told him in words, but I couldn't think of the right words. I was in a mood to be taken, not to take, so all I could do was lie there wide awake, sulking about being misunderstood and horny, while he fell asleep with insulting ease. Surely, if he'd *really* wanted me he wouldn't have been able to sleep. Surely, if he'd really wanted me, he would not have walked away.

Time in darkness alone passes slowly. I thought again about that long-ago night and imagined I hadn't said no, but yes. Or that he had ignored my token protest, had pushed me against the wall and taken me, willingly against my will. Pleasure without guilt; I didn't want to, I couldn't help it, he made me . . . The game I had to play if I were to remain a happily married woman. Finally I got up. I thought I'd seen a copy of *The Story of O* on the bookshelves downstairs. With a little help from my hand, it might help me to sleep. I wrapped a silk kimono around my nakedness and left my sleeping husband.

The great house was silent, although not dark. Electric lights in the form of candles burned on the walls of the hall-ways, illuminating all the closed bedroom doors. I imagined all the other guests paired in pleasure except the solitary stranger, who might be lying awake now, as horny as I was, and for the same reason. I wished I knew which was his door.

In the library the fire still burned, casting enough light to show me that someone was there before me.

He must have had the same reason as I did for coming here. As I entered the room he turned in surprise from the bookcase, a book in one hand. He wore a short, flimsy robe, tied with a sash. Under it, I knew, he was naked.

We stared at each other without speaking for what seemed a long time. There aren't many times in life that you get a second chance. I knew I'd never forgive myself if I didn't take this one. I closed the door firmly behind me and walked into the room. When I was only a few feet away from him, standing in the full glow of the fire, I stopped, untied my kimono, and shrugged it off, enjoying the sensation as it slithered silkily down my naked body and settled on the floor, enjoying also the gleam of his eyes as he stared at me without speaking.

He made no voluntary motion, but I saw the rising of his heavy cock, and the blood-flushed, rounded head parted the silken curtain of his dressing gown, roused by my nakedness. I had never seen it before, and it was bigger and more solid than any of my fantasies.

I smiled and licked my lips. A few steps more, and I sank to my knees before him.

"No," he said. He caught me by the shoulders and raised me up. "I'm going to fuck you – the way I should have done years ago. You won't get away from me this time."

I was stunned. It wasn't possible that this was the same young man I'd picked up in a bar almost twenty years before – he wasn't old enough, and he spoke with an English accent. But if he wasn't the same man, how did he *know*?

His hands were on me, rougher than I remembered, and greedier as he felt and fondled my nakedness. Then he pulled me hard against him, the silk of his robe like the cool fall of water against my skin. His warm, firm cock butted at my sex, and he kissed me. How I could remember such a thing with any certainty after so long a time, I don't know, but his lips felt like the same lips, and his mouth tasted still of desirable sins: of whiskey and sugar and, very faintly, cigarettes. I nearly swooned with pleasure as his tongue moved in my mouth and his hands, gripping my hips, moved to caress and explore my buttocks and finally between my legs.

He laughed, finding me so wet and ready for his probing fingers. "You're hot, aren't you? Can't pretend you don't want me."

"No," I murmured into his mouth, agreeing. I wanted him, now, hard, fast, slow, any way at all.

Without letting go of me, his mouth fastened firmly, devouringly, on mine, his cock prodding me, he walked me backward and pushed me down on my back on the very same leather couch where I'd sat drinking coffee with my husband a few hours earlier.

The shock of memory, of sudden guilt, made me struggle up and exclaim, "No – I can't – "

"Oh, yes you can."

"No." I said it reluctantly as I struggled to rise, sorry that he wasn't stopping me, outraged that I wasn't stopping myself. But my freedom was an illusion. As soon as I had regained my feet he caught me in his arms and picked me up with a strength I had not known he possessed. Ignoring my feeble efforts to escape, he turned me around and pushed me down, face first on the couch. It was warm and solid, both yielding and supporting, covered in leather so fine that I had the sensation of having been pressed down on top of some other person. Before I could even catch my breath he was lifting me by the ass, a cheek in each hand, and then I felt his lips on my labia, his hot, clever tongue raking my clitoris.

All protest, all urge to flight, rushed out of me in a low moan of pleasure. He drew his head away with a low laugh. "Yes, you'd like that, wouldn't you? Let me do anything but fuck you . . . But that's what I'm going to do, and nothing you say can stop me."

I said nothing. I didn't think about what I wanted, or what was right. I lay still and let him position me for his pleasure. I was lying nearly flat, facedown on the broad leather-cushioned couch, my legs dangling over the edge. He lifted my ass and parted my legs and the head of his cock nudged at the slick lips of my cunt. I couldn't see him anyway, this stranger my lover behind me, so I closed my eyes and gave myself up to physical sensation.

He was very big and greedy in his lust. Although I was very wet and willing, he spared me no tenderness but thrust himself inside me hard and fast, using his hands to part the cheeks of my ass at the same time, as if he wanted to split me in two. Even as I welcomed and wanted this penetration, at the same time the sensation of being forced was strong, and I cried out, half fainting with the shock of it.

"No . . . oh, no . . ."

He laughed and thrust again, this time burying himself to the hilt in me. Withdrawing slightly, he thrust again. "No?" With each thrust he repeated the word which came out sometimes as a croon, sometimes as a gasp, and I echoed him.

"No . . . no . . . no . . ."

Our denials came closer and closer together as he found a hard, driving rhythm that satisfied both of us. I lost all sense of place and time and even of self as he drove into me and drove himself, and me, finally, over the brink into a fierce, all-consuming orgasm, with a final shout in which our two voices mingled.

A little while later I felt him withdraw. I made a small sound of protest but no move, too exhausted and happy where I was, sprawled facedown and legs spread on the couch. Until I heard the door to the library open.

Annoyed that he could leave me this way, I opened my eyes and raised my head just as the lights came on. There in the doorway, coolly surveying me and my lover, was my husband.

He looked at me, lying naked and flushed, and then at the man, also naked, his still-rampant penis glistening with our mingled juices. It was very quiet. And then, shockingly, he smiled.

"Happy anniversary, darling," he said. "I hope you enjoyed yourself?"

I began to push myself up, my mind whirling.

"Oh, no," he said. "Stay there, please. Or shall I ask our friend to hold you down?"

My erstwhile lover was beside me at once, his hands on my shoulders firmly keeping me from changing my position.

"I certainly hope you enjoyed yourself, because now it's my turn," my husband continued. There was a note in his voice that I had not heard in a very long time, and I suddenly realized that he had set this up, a sexual game of a sort I had never imagined he would want to play, an unexpected anniversary gift for both of us, and suddenly I felt more excited than I would have thought possible.

"You've been a naughty girl," said my husband. "So I've asked our friend to stay . . . I'm going to have to punish you first, before we can kiss and make up."

I began an ineffective struggle to get away, but the stranger had no trouble restraining me. "No," I whimpered. "Please. No."

A CARCASS OF DREAMS

Marco Vassi

There is no better way to know death than to link it with some licentious image.

DE SADE

THE DYING GYNECOLOGIST

THE DREAM OF LIFE was ending, and he was returning to the unformed state where consciousness could not follow. Having accepted the inevitability of this moment many years earlier, having made it a daily meditation, he was now without apprehension. If anything, he experienced a mild curiosity, faintly eager to experience the phenomenon of death.

For several hours he had lain in what appeared to be, to those gathered around his bed, a deep coma. But he was in fact fully awake. Having spent his entire career in the service of others, he gave himself permission to take these last few moments for himself, sinking lazily into his thoughts, savoring the voluptuous cadence of his breath, wandering down the corridors of memory to gaze upon the thing he had been, the infant, the boy, the man, and finally, the unencumbered organism coming to its predestined conclusion.

In the room sat his wife, his four children, his oldest friend. His favorite cactus plants had been moved in from his office so he might have the solace of their presence, reminiscent of the silences of the desert, the same silence he now prepared to enter. The six people waited, not speaking, wrapped in the wide calm that emanated from the man in front of them.

He felt no pain. The garment of flesh that had served him faithfully for so long had worn out and was ready to be discarded, to go back into the earth.

"I wonder what happens to the *I* in *me*," he said to himself, "to the intelligence that is even now asking the question. Is there any chance it might continue after the body ceases to function?"

As though in response, some strange sensation seized him, held him for an instant, and then disappeared.

"I'll know soon," he thought. "Or perhaps I won't know anything at all."

The situation amused him, and he smiled. The sudden appearance of the seemingly incongruous expression startled the others, who were watching him closely, half ashamed of their subliminal desire to have the whole thing over with. His eldest daughter leaned over and whispered in her mother's ear, "He must be a saint, to be able to smile on his deathbed."

"Wouldn't it be peculiar to die and find myself face to face with old Jehovah," the man thought. "Imagine all that nonsense turning out to be literally true. It's a mysterious universe, and anything is possible."

He chuckled, causing the hair on the necks of the people around him to rise.

The breath caught in his throat and his frame shuddered. There was no specific point at which he could grasp the unfamiliar process of passing away, but he knew that the moment of departure was very near.

"This is really very odd," he mused, "I can feel it happening, but it seems so distant, as though it had nothing to do with me at all. I don't feel like *I* am dying. There is just death going on, and I am one of the people observing it. The only difference between me and the others is that when it happens, they will stand up and walk out and I will be left lying here."

Then abruptly, as though he had fallen from a great height, he felt everything drop away from him. Time underwent a cataclysmic change, and he was swept by a sensation of rocketing through space at an exponentially increasing speed, until he was going faster than light itself. And yet, the faster he moved, the more still everything became. Opposites lost their identity.

One by one, his faculties shut down. Hearing, touch, taste, smell, all disappeared. His thoughts blew off his mind like shingles from a roof in a high wind. He opened his eyes for the last time.

"Sam," his wife said.

"Goodbye Constance," he croaked and saw nothing more.

Relinquishing everything he had ever imagined he might lay claim to in the universe, he bade farewell to himself. In a microsecond of utter clarity, he saw what an ironic play life was, what a strange dance of fantastic reality. Beyond all ability to apprehend his experience, he gave himself up to death.

But it was not yet time.

He lost awareness of the external world, and his breathing stopped, but the vital force which had animated the inert elements of his body and sustained the cohesion called existence had not yet dispersed. A doctor would have pronounced him dead, for his heart had stopped beating. But beneath the measurable manifestations, in the core of his being, the finest thread of electricity still hummed. All that he had been was now reduced to that single throb of energy.

Subjectively, it was like falling asleep, and into a dream. First, a total loss of self-consciousness, then a sentient blackness, and finally a slow discernment of form. A blank screen lit up, and on it appeared the thin line of a far distant horizon, such as the edge of ocean seen from shore. It separated sea from sky, both the same shade of deep cobalt blue.

For an eternity, nothing moved. And then, faintly, a dot emerged from ground into figure, balanced delicately on the line. Subtly, slowly, it grew larger, obviously coming closer to the shore where the man stood. Without any landmarks, there was no way to estimate its size. As the relatives and friend began to look at one another, attempting to decide who should approach the body to find out whether the end had come, the man began to hear the first low ripple of trumpets which seemed to accompany the object.

Now, measuring the thing against his own height, he was able to assess its scale. As the music swelled, a jagged burst of golden light shattered the scene, and he gazed up at what thunderously swept toward him, a thing a thousand feet high and perhaps a third as wide, taking up his entire field of vision. It flew forward with majestic ease until it stopped suddenly, a few feet in front of him, and his knees buckled when he realized what it was.

He looked up into the face of a giant, encompassing, and perfectly formed cunt, quivering in purple radiance, a great mandala enveloping him in its aura. He gazed upon it reverently. In smell, in texture, in pulsating vividness, it was the quintessence of cunt, ideal in its every fold, its every hue.

"My Lady," he whispered, and fell prostrate before it.

In the mind of the man within his mind, kneeling before his object of worship, he was twenty-five again, in his last year of medical school, wondering whether he should become a specialist or go into general practice. He was talking it over with a friend, when the young man told him, "Why don't you become a gynecologist. You're always complaining about how horny you are. If you become a cunt specialist, you won't have any trouble at all getting laid. Just think of all those women coming in and spreading their legs for you. And paying for it to boot!"

As the entire course of a great river can be traced to a tiny bend at its source, so his career was shaped by the offhanded bit of half-meant advice. He shaped his studies in that direction, giving his parents rationalizations which involved the greater profitability of that particular line of medicine, and within two years, he began practice.

His first patient had found him almost unbearably nervous. The woman was infected with some baroque venereal strain, and when she split herself apart on his table, the smell which seeped from the tainted organ caused him to retch. He was fortunate that she was a prostitute with no false modesty, and so was saved from embarrassment by her remarking, "Yeah, that's the way my clients feel. Can you fix it up, doc?"

He performed a series of tests, sent smears to the laboratory, and finally doused her with antibiotics, vaginal jellies, and suggestions for douching. A week later he saw her again and her cunt was as good as new. When he examined her the second time and pronounced her well on the way to cure, the gratitude in her eyes was as much payment as the money she gave him.

How many cunts had there been after that? Middle-aged housewives with bored cunts, young girls with puppydog cunts, whores with leathery cunts, nuns with pimply cunts, secretaries with pornographic cunts, witches with velveteen cunts, grandmothers with withered cunts, children with unarticulated cunts, passionate women with engulfing cunts. Cunts of a thousand eyes, cunts of a million moods. Smiling, pouting, shouting, brooding, yearning, burning, angry, gay, hungry, sad. Again and again the same single action – the legs swinging wide at his request, like the gates opening to the thief upon saying the magic words, "Open Sesame." He would first see the hair, sometimes sparse, sometimes thick, or coarse, or fine, or black, or golden, or red, or curled, or straight. And then the thing itself.

Where few men looked and few men touched, he prodded and pulled and stroked. He dove in with instruments, he slithered in with fingers. Sometimes he found disease, often he found nothing more than the desire to be entered. And when his hand came out it was not infrequently covered with secretions that were something other than the lubricating cream he had used to ease his penetration.

At the beginning he had kept what they had taught him in school was the proper professional distance. All the doctors had been trained to treat the cunt as something septic, something to be approached only with gloves on, with formal face and averted glance. Something to be pried apart with metal shoe horns. But he could not maintain that artificial pose for long. He loved cunts. That was the reason he had become a gynecologist: to see cunts, to touch cunts, to smell cunts, to heal cunts.

It was in the third month of practice that his first thrilling contact took place. The patient was the wife of a prominent psychoanalyst, in her early thirties. She came for a general checkup, saying she did it once a year and that his name had been recommended by a friend. She wore a tight sheath dress, outlining her ample buttocks, showing her bulging thighs, accenting her full breasts. She was a beautiful and sultry woman, and the doctor felt his cock stir at the thought that he would soon have her lying on her back, her legs hoisted over stirrups, and with what he knew would be a luscious cunt lying agape, waiting for him to minister to it. His lips trembled slightly as he spoke, so calmly, in such a sophisticated manner, saying all the lines proper to the doctor-patient scenario.

"It's amazing what you can get away with," he thought, "once you put it in a socially acceptable context."

In the examination room it went as he expected, except that when it came time for him to slip on his plastic gloves, he boldly discarded the gesture. When he touched the fragile edges of her pink cunt, it was with his bare fingers. He seemed to enter some sort of trance, his ratiocinative faculties mesmerized. He entered a world of brute sensation, and without his understanding the process as such, his hands began a complex communication with her cunt. He found he was talking to her as he moved inside her, in a way that augmented the medical patter, the stock phrases . . . "does that hurt? is it sore there? this seems fine." When he stroked her cervix, it was not sex, and yet it was not not-sex. It was like the perfect edge of good massage, in which the mode is tactile ambiguity, where meaning and message continually interpenetrate.

A sigh escaped her lips. "She's enjoying this as much as I am," he thought, "and for the same reasons." Her cunt was already wet and the aroma it gave off was unmistakably erotic. His eyes moved from her cunt up past her belly between her breasts and into hers. She was watching him.

"Yes," she said.

He took off his clothes and fucked her as she lay. He came standing up.

From then on he fucked on the average of two women a day. Once he had broken through the convention of professional coldness, he was able to see with mounting acuity that at least half the women who came to him came simply to be caressed.

"Where are the men?" he said to himself over and over again. "Why isn't anyone loving these poor women?"

At first he made some mistakes, occasionally pushing for a sexual encounter when one hadn't spontaneously arisen, and he succeeded only in frightening the women involved. He often had doubts as to what sort of danger he might be in; might not a complaint end his career, or even land him in jail? Finally, he made peace with the fact that if he paid attention to business first, the business being the diagnosis and cure of disease, then whatever plums fell his way were his right to eat, and no bad fortune would be attached to that.

The woman he married was frigid. He chose her precisely because she was frigid. Examining her one afternoon, he saw that she had absolutely no sensation in her vagina. Her pelvis was locked in a chronic muscular spasm and her entire attitude was one of distaste for anything carnal.

"She's perfect," he thought, "she'll never bother me with excessive demands."

He courted her and married her and within a week after the ceremony she was overjoyed when he suggested separate bedrooms. He only fucked her about a hundred times in over thirty-five years, in groups of about twenty-five each, to conceive children. She settled into the role of mother and housewife, and purred in constant contentment that her husband allowed her to remain chaste.

Meanwhile, back at the office, he fucked himself silly.

By the time he was sixty, he had fucked more than fifteen thousand different women and had had his hands in the cunts of at least five times that many. "This is the best job a man could ever have," he told himself often, as his door opened, and his nurse ushered in yet another woman, and he would look at her the way a man looks at a woman's body in the street, calculating its curves, imagining its charms. But with a crucial difference.

"In a few minutes," he would think, "you're going to spread your legs for me, and offer me your cunt. And it will all seem very proper until I touch you a certain way, and you will realize that, all social rationalizations aside, you are opening your cunt to the eyes and fingers of a total stranger, a man you have never seen before, and one who, you will comprehend with a delicious shudder, wants to fuck you. And will we fuck? Or will I eat you out? Or will you suck my cock? Or will I have you get on your hands and knees so I can 'examine' you from behind?"

As the darkness of his death deepened, the memories faded, and the immense cunt before his mind's eye began to tremble, and open. From its roseate serrated center another cunt emerged, and another from the center of that. Cunt after cunt opened from the cunt preceding it. It was an infinite progression, never fully reaching him, continually spilling forth. He strained forward, to be taken into the heart of the budding cunt machine. It was the baby attempting to return, it was the man diving into the mystery, it was both and all.

And as he reached up in revery, the body on the bed bent at the middle and sat bolt upright. The people in the room were shocked at what they thought was a corpse perform such a sharp strenuous act. His lids flew up, but he saw nothing. His lips moved. A single word leapt from his throat.

"Cunt," he said.

And from the depths of his desire, the face of death spun forward at lightning speed to snatch him in its jaws. What it looked like, no one will ever know, for death comes differently to each human being.

The gynecologist fell back on the bed. This time he was really dead. Those who heard his final word claimed that he had said nothing when people asked if he had said anything before he died. They did not understand what he meant, and ascribed it to delirium. It was given out to all his friends that he had died happy. As indeed he had.

In one of his notebooks there was found the notation, "There are too few doctors who remember the original reason for playing doctor."

SUBWAY DICK

HE MAY HAVE seen her hundreds of times before he noticed her. Every weekday morning for over four years he had reached the Christopher Street station at a little after eight o'clock and stood with scores of others waiting for the train to take him to the world uptown where he spent half his waking hours, sitting in a cubicle, performing obscure and largely meaningless rituals with thousands of sheets of paper. Like the millions who descended daily into the tunnels to be shunted back and forth like cattle, he was usually in a foul mood. But the woman changed all that.

She had just lost a dime in a gum machine, and was standing in front of it, fuming and banging at the coin slot, when he passed by. Something about the quality of her energy at that point arrested him and he stopped to look at her. He drank in her features with a single visual gulp. But the subway car came thundering in and braked to a halt with a sickening screech of metal against metal, and he was jostled out of his stance. He did not think about her further that day.

The next morning, he saw her again, and once more swallowed her whole with his eyes. He stopped, taking a more detailed look at her, scanning her jet black hair, worn in a pony tail, her thin nose with flaring nostrils. Her body was wrapped in a thick winter coat, protection against the February cold. To his surprise, she glanced at him, her eyes oddly troubling, and then looked away.

During the next few weeks, although he made no special effort, he ran into her almost every morning. She was beginning to take on the air of an acquaintance. Once he started to greet her before he checked himself, remembering the strict New York etiquette which absolutely forbids talking to, smiling at, or in an way being friendly to other people on the street. It took him a while to realize that he was coming to relish seeing her, that it added a spark of interest to an otherwise dull and tedious beginning to his days.

By the end of March, he knew a good deal about her. The range of her wardrobe, the texture of her moods, the rhythm of her walk, had all been openly accessible to his study. It was amusing to speculate. Judging from the quality of her clothing, she probably made no more than a hundred and fifty dollars a week. She was probably a secretary. She wore no rings of any kind, and almost certainly lived alone. She used a minimum of makeup, a faint flush of lipstick and light eyeshadow. Her reading taste was random, as she might carry St Augustine's *Confessions* one day and a popular book on astrology the next.

It wasn't until the first week in April that he felt a desire to get closer. The first day on which it was warm enough to do without a coat, she appeared in a tight skirt which outlined a full high ass and rounded thighs, and in a jacket which, when unbuttoned, showed breasts that were just large enough to fit into each of his cupped hands. The thinness of her mouth, at first glance giving her a prim look, now contrasted with the electric sensuality of her body. It occurred to him that it might be possible to fuck her.

That galvanized him into action.

From the status of a charming novelty to add a touch of mystery to his mornings, she became a goal, a prize for him to win. He began to get up earlier each day, in order to shower, to choose his clothes with care, and prepare his mood. He went through the mating ritual which is common to birds and fish and beasts that share the same biosexual heritage as humans. He thrilled to his own sense of purpose, and attempted to calculate whether she might find him attractive. Without describing it as such, he began to court her.

Hers was the stop before his. As the weather grew warmer and her clothing grew lighter, he arranged it so he stood closer to her in the tightly packed car. He was finally able to smell her perfume, mingled with the crisp aroma of her firm flesh. He was able to perceive the delicate whorls of her ears, the slight tensions in her throat as she swallowed. He wondered what her name was. He even became aware of her imperfections, and could judge from her complexion on which days she had her period. He also thought he could detect, from a general looseness and jauntiness in her manner, when she had fucked the night before. One Wednesday, he actually touched her, feeling the rough tweed of her skirt against the tops of his knuckles. His knees sagged and he had to grab the hanging support strap to keep from falling to one side.

That evening he pondered talking to her. It maddened him that, while on one level he knew her intimately, in terms of social intercourse they were total strangers. He had watched her walk across the platform and knew the way her buttocks jiggled as she moved, and yet he had not yet heard her voice. He considered that were he to speak to her, he might find her terribly ignorant. Too often in the past he had desired a woman's body and had his lust shrivel upon coming in contact with her mind.

"What if she is shallow?" he said to himself. And in the end decided not to make any overture just yet.

Wondering whether it was cowardice or wisdom that chose his course of inaction, he worked toward more physical contact without any formal introduction or exchange. The following morning he moved with the force and agility of a star halfback in arranging it so that he stood behind her without having drawn undue attention to himself. Sliding and jostling with consummate skill and experience, he followed her through the densely packed crowd until she stopped at one of the vertical support bars in the center of the car. He eased in close.

It had been subwaymanship of the first water, and no knight jousting for a lady's favor could have performed better. As the train pulled away from the station with its customary lurch and everyone in the car swayed with it, he looked down the length of his body. Her buttocks were less than an inch away from his cock.

"So near and yet so far," he thought. He dared not move.

The train gathered speed as it clanged toward Fourteenth Street. It hit a curve and once again the mass of humanity within its iron confines, like fluid in a container, rolled to one side. Unbelievably, and to his stinging joy, the twin mounds of her ass cheeks swung pendulously back and nestled for a brief tingling second in the hollow of his crotch. Fire alarm bells went off in his groin, and he was almost instantaneously erect, the bulging cock straining the fabric of his pants.

She did not touch him for the rest of the ride, and when he got to his office he went directly to the john where he sat, massaging his cock with quiet frenzy until the autonomous ejaculation relieved him of the almost unbearable pressure. The fleeting contact was enough to serve as fuel for the most outrageous fantasies. He imagined that her cunt was endowed with a special heat-generating faculty, that merely to be near it would be enough to trigger orgasm in an army of men. He went through the rest of his day in a stupor, relegating the tasks to be done to his instinctive center, and saving his intellectual ability to enrich the pictures in his mind.

The next day was a Saturday and he was too overwrought to spend the weekend alone. He knew he was at the edge of some mammoth foolishness, but he could not help himself. "I only rubbed against a woman on the subway," he repeated to himself. "I mustn't let it get blown all out of proportion." But the woman had been transmogrified into an *idee fixe*, and he was succumbing to its magnetic power. To ease his tension, he called an old girl friend and fucked her five times in the sixty hours he had to wait before he would see the lady of the subways again.

And when he did, he knew he was lost. She wore a skirt so tight, with material so thin, that both the outline and color of her panties could be seen. Her blouse was diaphanous, and he could make out the pale gold of her skin beneath it on both sides of the brassiere which cupped her breasts in its white plastic grip. Despite the debauch of the weekend, desire boiled in his blood.

The train moved smoothly, and he cursed the efficiency of the engineer. But just before Thirty-third Street, it stopped altogether, and the lights dimmed. There was a two-minute wait before the conductor's voice rasped over the loudspeaker, "There's a train stuck ahead of us, and we'll have a short delay." It was a crashing stroke of good luck.

His strategy was to try the *mano morte*, the deadhand technique used by the Italians. The fingers are allowed to rest against the body of the target woman in such a way that there is no suggestion of attack. If she seems not to notice, the pressure can be gradually increased. If she fidgets, he can take refuge in the fact of the extreme crowding to silently plead innocence of wanting to have touched the delicious skin in front of him.

The middle knuckle of his middle finger came to rest exactly in the center between her buttocks, where the skirt pulled tautly over the valley. For a number of seconds he dared not even allow himself to feel the sensation, so delicate was his approach. Then, she shifted her weight, going from one leg to the other, and her cheeks moved, suddenly, grandly, sweeping across the width of his hand. A burbling moan of pleasure chugged to his lips, but he suppressed it sharply. He waited a short while, and then put his hand against her once more. Again she shifted, and again the treasured ass slid beneath his touch.

Now he was in a quandary. Was she unconscious of what was happening and moving randomly, or aware of his touch and showing her annoyance, or aware of his touch and cooperating in the encounter? It seemed as though his entire manhood was on the line. He had waited a very long time, and now was the moment to test their relationship. Boldly, he pulled back his hand and with a sense of historical finality, shuffled forward two tiny inches, just enough to ease the front of his body against her back.

Sheet lightning played over his sensorium. He was as alert and balanced as a man on a tightrope. She might whirl around and say something ugly, something terribly ugly, and inflict a wound on him that would take a long time to heal. Or she might respond to his overture. He waited, tortured by the suspense.

And upon that, quite easily, simply, and gently, she relaxed into her heels, throwing her weight back, and let her body rest with utter passivity against his. She had accepted the touch.

The train leapt forward just as his erection began to poke into the space between her legs. They rode that way until reaching her stop, his cock sizzling with the secret contact in the packed subway car, while his face remained calm, his eyes darting about to see if anyone saw, and finding nothing but the stunned gazes of the city's wage slaves being transported to another day of empty drudgery. When they came to her station she stepped away from him quite deliberately and before getting off looked once over her shoulder and into his eyes. He could not tell what her expression meant.

It escalated rapidly after that. He was soon pressing into her very tightly, pushing his pelvis with tiny surreptitious strokes as she squeezed her buttocks and released them. On some days she wore no panties and he gave up his boxer shorts altogether. He almost screamed the day she reached behind her and caressed his cock with her hand.

They took to meeting at the back of the subway car so she could lean into the corner while he covered her. If he kept his raincoat on he could slip his cock out of his fly with no one seeing. One morning she wore slacks and he put his erection between her legs, coming in her woolly crotch as the train slugged its way uptown.

They suffered a near fatal accident one morning when a young schoolboy, recklessly making his way from car to car, opened the connecting door and they almost pitched forward into the narrow platform. He had a wild impression of gleaming tracks before he recovered his balance and pulled himself back in, grabbing her waist to keep her from falling. The boy caught a glimpse of his cock and blinked in disbelief before a slow smile spread over his face and he whispered, "Sorry to crash in on your party, mister."

Still, he was loath to speak to her. "What can I possibly say at this point?" he thought. "We've already progressed beyond conversation." And then, "Why spoil a good thing? If we start dating, instead of being the most extraordinary experience of my life, she'll show up as just another woman."

He was amazed that the affair had progressed from discovery to infatuation to consummation to cynicism so effortlessly, and all within the parameters of an eight-minute subway ride.

Yet, what could be accomplished in the crowded car was painfully limited, and he was bursting for a more total encounter. Then one morning, as he waited for the train, he saw her standing next to the women's toilet. She nodded, and he edged toward her. She backed up, put a nickel in the slot, and opened the door, beckoning him to follow. Like one in a trance he moved past her into the tile room. She slammed the door behind them and jammed the lock with a piece of metal.

They were alone in the white gleaming cubicle.

"This is insane," he hissed, the first words he had ever spoken to her.

By way of reply she peeled off her clothes. He watched mesmerized as the long-desired body appeared before him. When she was naked she abruptly threw herself at his feet, begging him to fuck her. She tugged at his pants and licked his shoes, rolling across the filthy floor. The woman of his dreams lay before him, a panting slut, fingering herself shamelessly.

Propelled from the mundane to the baroque with such rapidity that the pulse in his temples began pounding painfully, he tried to put the event in some context. But it was all exploding too quickly, too forcefully. The girl groaned with desperate want and he could do nothing but succumb to the moment.

The many months of slow building broke in the instant, and for the following five minutes they did practically everything possible for a man and a woman to do together, playing out Krafft-Ebing and the Kama Sutra at high speed. At one point she lay bent over the porcelain pissoir, her face in the water, as he whipped her with his leather strap. Some instinct told him he would never have another chance with her and that he had to get it in all at once. And it was not until he found himself foolishly ejaculating in her right ear that he came to his senses, aghast at the situation he found himself in.

He stepped back and leaned against the wall; he was slightly delirious. The woman dressed. When she was ready, he fumbled for something to say before they left the john. But his eyes grew wide as she reached into her purse and pulled out a police badge and a .357 Magnum revolver.

"You're under arrest," she said. And added, "I've had my eye on you for some time now."

The case, when it finally appeared, was thrown out of court. The city, due to the uproar being raised by Gay Activists' Alliance, was enjoying a spell of liberalism in what were technically considered sex crimes. The judge ruled that the man was a victim of vice squad entrapment, and, as such, his arrest was unconstitutional.

He was so shaken by the entire course of events that he moved to San Francisco. He was just recovering from his ordeal when he learned they were planning to build a subway there. He then jumped off the Golden Gate Bridge.

The woman began another long lonely vigil, seeking sex offenders in the tunnels beneath the city, riding the rails until some man touched her, and then rubbed his cock against her, letting him have his way until he was fucking her and stomping her and pissing on her and doing god-awful things to each of her orifices, at which point she would arrest him. She felt that sex was holy, and had chosen her job to keep it that way.

LAND OF THE SPERM KING

IN THE VALLEY not far from where the mythical realm of Shangri La was reputed to have been, there flourished a people who lived for almost three thousand years without a government. They had no laws, no organization of any kind, and were guided by a spiritual leader who was chosen from among the children born on the day of the winter solstice, each serving for life, and then passing the mantle on to whichever of the eligible candidates gave the wisest answer to the secret question, which only kings and queens could ask. The leader, when he or she was close to death, would have all those born on the shortest day over the years of his or her reign gather in the wood outside the village, see them one by one, and decide who was to succeed to the position of eminence.

It was a strange role, for in no one's memory did the guide ever have to do anything. There were never more than several thousand people in the land; children were considered such rare and wondrous creatures that there was a trembling hesitancy about bringing them into the world. Everyone ate the same thing: fruits and nuts which fell from the trees, and a form of yoghurt made from goat's milk. They all drank the highly mineralized water that flowed from the mountains. They never killed anything. Their clothes were made from the skins of animals that had died a natural death. They did not work, except to fashion garments and cups, and build shelters to live in. They had no formal sports, although wrestling was popular, as was reindeer riding, climbing, and swimming.

Among them were a few who grew up with a deep inner distance from the others, and they spent most of their time alone, fashioning drums and flutes from wood and hides, giving the others music. Some made strange shapes out of clay and gave the others images to ponder. Some appeared periodically to tell long stories in hypnotically rhythmic language, speaking of things no one had ever experienced but which sounded mysteriously familiar.

When the spirit moved the guide, he or she would begin to dance, and then a feast would take place, the people making a fire and brewing tea from a grass that grew on the far side of the mountain that overshadowed their land, a drink with magic powers of intoxication. Sometimes the celebration would last for days, until the entire population had been so perfectly unified in a vortex of energy by the sacred dance and the sheer power of their massive gathering, that the field they moved in became the scene of a single orgiastic organism, pulsing in ponderous and quickening tempo.

Generally, however, they spent their time contemplating the wonder of creation.

The guide possessed one idiosyncrasy as a mark of office; he or she ate nothing but sperm. In fact, to the degree that the people had a formal culture at all, it centered around providing the guide with enough to eat. Since sperm is a perfect food, the guide needed nothing else. And since the people lived a rarified existence, eating only the purest foods, drinking only the most vital water, breathing only the sharpest air, and since they were exposed to nothing but peaceful manifestations of the life energy, they were as sensitive as flowers in their capacity to take nourishment directly from the sun. It is not surprising that the guide's daily intake was relatively small, usually amounting to no more than the combined volume of seventeen ejaculations.

Over the span of history, of course, different guides developed individual feeding habits. The conventional method was for male guides to use the cunts of young maidens as cups, having the day's male volunteers mount the female volunteers and make love lustily until orgasm, at which point the guide would put his mouth to a succession of still hot trembling vaginas and suck the sticky deposit from the freshly fucked lips. Most of the female guides took their sperm straight, lying languidly on a couch while the day's complement masturbated over her and at the moment of climax putting the spurting cocks into her waiting mouth. There were what the people called "interesting" guides, men who sucked the sperm directly from cocks, and women who preferred using cunts as a vehicle.

Occasionally there would be a guide who developed more esoteric tastes and might request a daily dollop of yak sperm. One guide took a fancy to tiger sperm, and since the people were so gentle they could approach the fiercest beasts and coax the vital fluid from them, the wish was able to be granted. That particular guide was legendary for his sexual prowess, for after half a cup of tiger sperm he was able to fuck twenty women to satiation without stopping once. Another guide, a woman, ate only hummingbird sperm, and before she died had become totally transparent.

It never occurred to anyone at any time that things should be different. They were the only people in the history of the species who did not let the acquisition of language rob them of their primal simplicity, and so they attained true human dignity. Possessing wisdom, they had little use for knowledge; living in a state of tranquil bliss, they had no inclination to intensity of purpose. They watched the universe in its constant infinite turnings and workings, understanding that they were blessed just to be alive and know the wonder of it all. In touch with the primordial realities of the cosmos, they were beyond the superficialities of civilization.

It is conjectured that they were the descendants of a small band of people that followed Lao Tzu out of China after he wrote his *Tao Te Ching*. Instead of going to the mountains to die, as legend has it, he went to live. Leaving China at the age of eighty-five, he continued for another sixty-three years, teaching the people non-ado. So powerful was his influence that it sustained them for almost three millennia.

In the seventeenth century of the Christian era as measured by western calendars, they were visited by two Dominican priests who came upon their valley by accident. The men were scandalized by what they considered obscene rites and general godlessness. They attempted to preach the gospel, but were met by a respectful indifference. They became an odd sight, flapping furiously about in their black and white robes, brandishing crucifixes, waving their bibles in the air, shouting at the people to put their clothes on and repent. It must be admitted that it was difficult to preach hellfire and brimstone to a people who had no concept of sin except "doing what is unnecessary," a faculty the priests excelled in. But the people were willing to let them be, viewing them as merely one of the more bizarre manifestations of the unfathomable universe.

The missionaries were able, however, to test the tolerance of even this ultimately benign people, first by chopping down living trees to make a dead church, and then by running through the grove where the guide was awaiting his daily meal and lashing the backs of the happy fuckers who were preparing his food. The people, for the first time in centuries, were confused, and they asked the guide what they should do, an action no guide in anyone's recollection had been asked to perform.

He thought about it a while and requested that the priests be restrained. Then, hoping to pierce to the core of the situation, he asked two of the young maidens to draw forth some sperm from their bodies so he might take their measure. The priests howled with outrage at the tender ministrations being given them by the gentle fingers and loving tongues of the women. And when they came, it was with horrible curses mingled with terrible prayers.

The king tasted each of their deposits and retched violently.

"These men are . . ." he began to say, and then paused, not having a word for the concept "depraved." He spit out the sperm and pondered for a while. "Take them to where the eagles nest," he said at last, "and push them from the mountain."

The priests were disposed of and the people remained undisturbed for another three hundred years.

Yet, their time was marked. In one of the wars which continually erupted about them, their valley was discovered by a platoon of Chinese soldiers. Shortly thereafter, they were descended upon by a delegation from the People's Republic, and told that they were to be liberated from the chains of spiritual autocracy and introduced to the wonders of democracy.

"You will be removed from your primitive state," the directive read, "and given factories and schools and police. Women will be free and allowed to work side by side with men. Everyone will learn to read and illiteracy will be eliminated." Finally, they were informed, they would elect their own representative to sit in the People's Assembly in Peking. Beyond that, they would be taught how to farm, pen animals, make iron, and build roads.

The people were stunned. The night the representatives left, with word that they would return in a week with soldiers, planners, teachers, officials, and anthropologists, the guide summoned the entire village.

"There is no way to know why these things happen," he said.

"It is like watching the night sky and seeing a star suddenly plunge into the darkness of space. It is our time to be destroyed, and there is nothing we can do."

He stroked his wispy beard. "For myself, I will not live to serve those smiling and well-intentioned brutes who think their primitive machinery is superior to our formless understanding. I will go to the place of the eagles and throw myself into the air which is the sustainer of us all. You may come with me, or you may stay here, and learn to survive amidst the stupidity which is fast descending upon us."

He sat silent for a long while and then his face brightened. "Yet, we still have seven sunrises and seven sunsets. Time enough for eternity." And with that he jumped to his feet and began to dance.

The morning of the day when the delegation was scheduled to arrive, the entire people, spent from the continuous orgy of the previous week, went to the nearby mountain top. They sat in a loose circle and entered a state of communion, sharing their vibrations, sharing their breathing, their awareness. Finally, the guide stood up and walked to the edge of the precipice. As he stared down, a small boy's voice called out to him.

"Before we all return to the flow, can you tell us what the secret question is?"

The guide turned around and looked into the child's open face. "There is only one question," he said slowly, "and that is this:

"Why are there no questions at all?"

The boy's lips began to move and he started to speak. But then as though a light had gone on within the light of the sun, his entire expression changed and became one of perfect understanding. His face relaxed and his eyes grew soft. He looked back at the guide, and said nothing.

The guide smiled.

"Yes," he said to the boy and to the whole people, "the answer is not to say the answer, but to be the answer." Then to the child alone, "You might have been guide after me."

And with a cry of rapture, he threw himself off the cliff.

One by one and two by three they followed, until the last man and woman stood looking down at the rocks below.

"When we die, there will be no humans left," she said.

"Then so be it," he told her. "It is as the guide has said: it is our time to be destroyed."

They too flew into the void, and when the Chinese arrived that afternoon they could not make sense of what had happened. They made an official report to their headquarters, and by the time the sun had set they had planted their flag and given the place a name, something that no one had ever bothered to do before.

NO WOMAN OF MAN BORN

SHE STARED INTO the mirror for a quarter of an hour, taking inventory, integrating the perceptions.

The legs are long and muscular, the shoulders broad, the hips narrow. The skin on her face is delicately etched, the result of two years of electrolysis. Straight black hair to the base of her neck, covering her ears, curling around her throat. Breasts curved like soft sherbet, the children of injected hormones. She is a handsome woman, as once she was a pretty man. Her ass is androgynous, and between her thighs the infolded scrotal sac.

"I have done it," she thought. "At last I have a body to match my desires."

She ran her hands over her belly and cupped her breasts, stroking the nipples with her fingertips. They wrinkled, and stretched taut. She smiled.

"Alexandra," she said out loud. "Men will want you." And with that did a slow bump and grind for her reflection in the glass, all the while hugging heself with satisfaction.

As with all transsexuals, her road had been painful and difficult. For her entire youth and young manhood, she was unable to understand herself as anything but a homosexual, a condition she despised. Impotent with women, she had been, as a man, wretched in her need for men. And after many years of therapy, she came to accept that the condition of homosexuality was intractable.

The conclusion that followed, while logically ineluctable, had been for a long time too frightening to consider seriously. The existential force of having one's penis cut off shook her to the roots of her being. But her torment knew no surcease, and the choice between radical change and suicide became quite clear. She opted for the former.

She began tentatively, making enquiries, writing letters of application to doctors who had performed the process of transformation. Before long, the fantasy began to precipitate a reality, and she found herself having interviews with psychologists, talking to other transsexuals who had come out the other side, several in each of the two directions, and finally entered the actual mechanics of transition, beginning with hormone shots, hair removal, special counseling, and on one unforgettable day, the first operation. And with all this, lessons on how to dress, how to move, how to speak, how, in short, to behave like a woman.

It had taken three years to reach this point, watching the final result in a mirror. A miracle had been performed, and it seemed to throw open a sparkling new world. She could enjoy men at last, as she always had, but now freely and openly, without the homosexual guilt she had never been able to shake off. She understood that from a certain viewpoint, her present condition might be considered even more pathological than the former one. But she didn't *feel* ashamed, and it is one's feeling about oneself that, in the last analysis, is the basic criterion for all judgement.

Now, when she flirted with a man, it would be as a woman. And when she gave head, it would be a woman's lips around the cock she sucked. Her face would be smooth, powdered, her mouth slightly rouged. Her chest would hold a woman's breasts for a man to fondle, and while the nipples would never yield milk, that would make no difference to her or to the man who was taking his pleasure with her. And when a man fucked her, it would be as a woman that she received him, and not as a "pervert," the word she had always used to describe herself. And after all this, she had, instead of the embarrassing penis, a cunt opening into her body, not as pretty as a real cunt, nor with a real cunt's smells and juices, but for all that, something that would serve. Its very artificiality, in fact, might give it a power of attraction and appeal that no real cunt could have.

"After all," she reasoned, "there can't be more than a couple of hundred artificial cunts in the whole world." She consoled herself that rarity overshadowed any intimations of the grotesque.

She opened the closet door on which the mirror hung, and began to choose her attire for the day. While recuperating from the final operation, she had not gone out or seen anyone, wanting to make her entrance into society all at once, whole and resplendent. She dressed beyond her usual simple taste, knowing that she was overdoing it, but unable to resist the temptation to go out in full drag.

"But it's not drag any more," she exclaimed. She was no longer a man, and the nylon stockings and panties and garter belt and brassiere and slip and dress and earrings and nail polish and lipstick and pumps and eyeshadow were now her legitimate clothing. A rush of excitement surged through her as she thought of bathing suits and the beach, of tight slacks and swinging her hips as she walked.

And for an instant, she even thought of Ralph, her friend for so many years, the man she loved more than anyone in the world, but to whom she could never venture a physical overture. Ralph had known that she was homosexual, and it had not affected their friendship, which was based on an intellectual affinity. Still, he had made it clear that he could not consider her sexually. During the time she was undergoing her transformation she had asked him, "Do you think you might desire me when I am a woman?" And he had not replied for a long time, then answered, "It might be possible. I don't know. It's extraordinary just to think about, but I won't know until I see you in your new body."

Now, glorious in full regalia, she looked at herself once more, and a well-dressed, very attractive woman of about thirty-five looked back, and winked. She was feeling just the tiniest bit randy already.

"Would you like to go for a drink?" Alexandra said to her image.

"And perhaps meet a man?" the image asked.

"Or should I call Ralph?" Alexandra replied.

"Not yet," her image told her, "you need some experience first."

Alexandra felt a shiver go down her spine as the impact of the reality she had become grazed her deepest sense of self. She checked herself out one last time, picked up her handbag, and walked out the door to see what the world had to offer.

As she stepped into the street, apprehension gripped her. At the back of her mind was the thought that someone would notice, would point to her and say, "Look, there's a transsexual." She glanced down to see if her slip was showing, and the already conditioned gesture of a woman brought her new courage.

She attracted no attention at all, except the routine stares of men who looked at her breasts as she approached and at her ass as she went by. She had to suppress her exuberance which threatened to propel her into long striding steps, and remember to walk as her coach had taught her, keeping her awareness on the sensation of her thighs rubbing against one another.

"Stay with your feeling of sensuality," he had told her, "that will keep you from reverting to masculine mannerisms."

Feeling more and more secure, strolling down the sidewalk as though she were a queen dressed as a commoner, her royalty apparent to no one but herself, she turned into one of those small dark restaurants which dot midtown. She stood uncertainly in the doorway for a moment, and was taken with a small edge of panic when the floor manager came up to her and said, "Will there be just yourself, madame?"

Madame!

She smiled graciously. "Just a drink, please, I won't be having lunch," she said, using the voice the same teacher had coached her in, making her sound a little like Marlene Dietrich with a bad cold.

He led her to a tiny round table, and she lit a cigarette to steady her nerves as the waiter brought her a Brandy Alexander, a drink she had always felt diffident about ordering when she went about in a man's body. She sipped slowly, relishing the fact that she left lipstick marks on the glass. Her joy was total, and she was torn between wanting to weep and wanting to throw up her arms and shout with pleasure.

Instead, she looked around discreetly, and several tables away a man of about forty, dark and rugged, wearing a very expensive suit, was looking at her with an unmistakable glint of desire. He was exactly her type, the kind of man who, when she had been a man, she would have done anything to have, and then have felt guilty about wanting. But now she could accept his overture, talk to him, and swim in his hunger for her. She would have to go slowly, waiting for the proper mood to tell him that she was a transsexual. And if he still wanted her, then she would have him, have a man at last, freely, openly.

She began to return his stare, but felt herself floundering in her response. She could not smile, nor lower her lids, nor shift her body, nor give any of the clues women use when they want to tell a man they're interested. She looked away in confusion.

"What's wrong?" she wondered. "Why don't I respond?"

She was about to ascribe it to nervousness in her new role when she realized that she was not really reciprocating his desire, and could find no feeling upon which to mount even a seductive glance. Intellectually, she could tell herself why she should desire him, could remember that there was a time when she would have been attracted to him, but now, he had no more sexual appeal to him as a woman than women used to have for him as a man.

She bent her head over her drink, pondering the strangeness of the situation, and was lost deep in thought when she sensed someone sitting across from her, at her table. Her heart skipped as she guessed it might be the man, and she didn't know how to deal with him.

But when she looked up, she found a woman looking back at her. A slim, well-groomed, utterly composed woman, who wore no makeup, and was dressed in a tightly cut suit. Her hair was short and her eyes were very very knowing.

The woman smiled, an expression that flushed through Alexandra like the embrace of a hot bath after a long stiff walk on a winter day. Her limbs grew weak, and the rest of the restaurant faded into distant obscurity, behind the irresistible magnetism of the woman who sat before her.

"I've been watching you," the woman said. "It was clear that you had no interest in that man who's been trying to catch your eye."

Alexandra knew at once that the woman was a lesbian, knew at once that she was making an overture, and knew at once, with stomach-shrinking certainty, that her new body was responding.

The homosexuality had pursued her through the entire change of gender, and in her transformed loins there flickered the familiar flame of an old forbidden desire.

THE ORGANIC COPROPHILIAC

WENDY DELICATELY SHADED the corner of her mouth with her lipstick brush, took a long deep look at herself in the professional makeup mirror with the tiny frosted bulbs all around the edge, and smiled radiantly. From her sequined shoes to her beehive hairdo, she was perfectly rendered, ready to win all glances at the Senior Prom. The other men would neglect their dates just to have a dance with her, and she would flirt outrageously with them, knowing all the while that no matter who held her in his arms, only Jeff could hold her in his heart.

"Jeff," she whispered, and her fingers trembled at his name. Tall, rugged Jeff, with his lopsided grin and his playful blue eyes, his electrifying figure on the football field and his deep love of humanity which would one day earn him the initials M.D. after his name. She rubbed the pin he had given her just six months earlier, on that night when the moon had lit up the waters of the reservoir as they sat in his Maserati and he spoke those fateful words in her ear.

"Be mine," he had said. And hot scalding tears of joy had spilled from her eyes.

Now she stood up, regarding her young figure in the glass. The wide gown hid her long shapely legs, shaved and oiled for the night's special date. Her waist was narrow and flared quickly to pearl-white breasts that swelled over the tops of her bra cups. No man had ever seen her nipples, or put his hands on the sweet mound between her thighs. She was more than a virgin; she was a consciously constructed landscape of hesitant delights, nurtured and guarded, prepared for the appearance of the single gardener who would enter some day to gather up the fragile buds of her tender flowers. She had been kissed so few times that her lips still tingled when another mouth brushed hers. And no

fingers had ever traced the luscious curve between her firm full
buttocks.

"But tonight," she breathed, and trembled over the expanse of
her entire body at the thought of what the night would bring.

There was a light tap at the door and her mother came timidly
into the room. The two women looked into one another's eyes
through the mirror, and then Wendy turned.

"Mother," she gushed, "I'm so happy."

"And I'm happy for you," her mother replied. "It seems just
like yesterday that I was standing where you're standing now,
thinking about the man who was to become your father."

"We've lived in this town a long time, haven't we?" Wendy
asked in that solemn voice which always overtook her when she
thought of her American heritage.

The older woman swept forward and held the young girl by the
arm. Her face was troubled. She had the look of a person who
was about to enter into a necessary but difficult conversation.

"There isn't much time before Jeff gets here to pick you up,"
she began, "and there's something I need to talk to you about."

"I think I know what it is," Wendy said, spinning out of
her grasp.

"You're thinking of letting him do it tonight, aren't you? You're
planning to go *all the way!*"

"Please, mother," Wendy pleaded, "I'm a grown woman. It's
time I decided these things for myself. And I do love him. Don't
spoil it by trying to argue me out of it."

"No, no, it's not that. I would be the last to try to dissuade you.
After all, I did . . . the same thing, the night of my Senior Prom."

"You?" Wendy asked, aghast.

"I was young once too," her mother said. She eased Wendy into
the rocking chair that had been in their family for a hundred and
twenty-seven years. "I just want to be sure you're careful. And
perhaps if I tell you a little story, it will help you understand." The
woman sat down opposite her daughter, and began a tale which her
mother had told her, and had been told by her mother before her,
insuring that each generation was aware that its children did not
lose the historical continuity which kept the blood line strong.

"It was your great grandmother who was first seized by the
seemingly irrational desire to eat shit," the older woman said. "In
those days, people didn't have the enlightened attitudes we have

today, and what with killing Indians and chopping down trees, there just wasn't time for bedroom finesse. Lil was seventeen when she got married, as cheery a cherry as you are right now. Her husband was a good man, dependable, but boorish. She didn't even know how to broach the subject of her secret desire to him.

"One day, while he was off on a four-day hunting trip, a knife-grinder came by their house. She describes him in her diary as gaunt and salacious, and adds, 'just what I was looking for'. She invited him in for lunch, and when they were finished eating, she blurted out what she wanted from him."

Wendy paled. Like many young people, it was almost inconceivable to her that what she had looked upon as an intensely private urge might be common place to the rest of humanity. Her mother's voice went on, describing what their ancestor had done, but she heard little of the narrative, her own mind being filled with the image she had cherished for so long.

She saw herself lying on a couch, her skirt hiked up over her thighs, her cunt redolent with pungent slime, toes curled in anticipation. Above her, his piercing eyes boring into her tender flesh, Jeff bears down, his great buttocks crushing her cheeks, his terse anus pressing against her sweet innocent lips. And then, with a subtle shift, the passage begins. She gasps, she moans, she faints, and in succumbing, her mouth falls open. He pushes down, and with a fanfaronade of aggressive thoughts, voids his bowels on her immaculate face. She tried to escape, knowing all the while that she does not want to escape. She chokes as the hot suffocating mass slides onto her tongue, into her throat, and down her chest, scorching her lungs and filling her body with the vile and glorious fulfilment she had always understood would be hers. She cries out and rises to actively cover the pulsing hole, stretching her lips until they crack, sucking the final product of the body she loves until she almost bursts from lack of breath, as she combines the lowest servility with the highest daring, the profoundest love with the most scarifying sensuality.

She looked up out of her revery and into her mother's smiling face. The woman seemed to be reading the pictures in her mind. Wendy blushed.

"There's no way to explain it, really," she said. "Doctor Cory thinks that the desire is an inherited characteristic. It just seems to run in the family."

Wendy began to speak, hesitated, and then began again. "But

I'm not the only one," she said. "Most of the other girls talk about the same thing."

"They're not allowing sex education in the class-rooms, are they?" her mother shot out, ready to be incensed at the notion that the board of education was usurping what she believed to be the duty of parents.

"No," Wendy told her. "We get together at the soda shoppe and talk about our feelings. You know how girls do. And just yesterday Clarissa asked me whether I thought it was all right to let a boy shit in your mouth on the first date."

"In my day a girl would want at least an engagement ring before she'd let a boy take such liberties."

"I think so too, and that's what I told her. I think a girl and boy should know each other for a few months at least, and be going steady, before they get that intimate. But at least half the girls think that's old-fashioned."

"Well, times do change," her mother sighed philosophically. "But they'll learn the value of holding certain things back unless a man is extra good to them. If a woman gives a man everything at once, she has nothing to manage him with. You may not think that's important now, but wait until you've been married a few years."

"I don't know if I can hold myself back," Wendy pleaded.

Her mother took Wendy's hands between her own and held them to her breasts. "Jeff's a good boy," she said, "and I'm sure he's serious about your relationship. Just be careful that's all."

"Will you give me some advice?" Wendy asked, capitulating at last to a recognition of superior wisdom in this area on the part of her mother.

"Well," the woman said, "make sure he doesn't eat spicy food or drink too much early in the evening. If he gets the runs it will ruin it for both of you. And don't get shit on your dress. It's almost impossible to wipe off and you'll stink all the way home. Make sure he doesn't think you're too easy or he'll lose respect for you."

Wendy put her head on her mother's shoulder. "I'm so lucky to have such an understanding mother," she said.

"My mother did the same for me," the older woman went on. "And you might as well start practicing how to cook from now on. After you're married you'll have to be very careful about his diet. See that he gets enough roughage. And feed him the healthiest food you can. You might as well be getting some good shit from him if you're going to get any shit at all."

Wendy's mother stepped back and the two women gazed at each other with moist eyes. "My little baby's going to be all grown up after tonight," the older woman said.

"You're the best mother a girl could ever want," Wendy told her.

Just then the door swung open and a man walked into the room. Portly, red-nosed, and kindly, he beamed at the picture before his eyes.

"Daddy!" Wendy squealed.

"That Jeff certainly is a lucky man," he said, looking at his daughter's shining face. And then he turned to his wife and in a gruff jocular tone asked, "Is there any chance of getting something to eat around here tonight?"

Wendy and her mother looked at one another for a few seconds, and then burst out laughing, leaving the man smiling in gentle confusion. He and his wife had had separate bedrooms for almost five years, and for him the ingestion, digestion, and elimination of food was no longer a process that held any trace of erotic passion.

BLUEBEARD'S INSTANT GRECIAN URN

PAUL THOUGHT HE knew why women resisted, and his unwilling-
ness to let any external reality alter the system of his perception
was, paradoxically, his greatest advantage over them. He lived
in a world of images, and ruthlessly imposed his projections
on everyone in his life in order to attain his ends. He had
no feeling for women as autonomous creatures, but worshipped
them passionately as objects of desire. He easily equated conquest
with caring.

For him, a woman's sexual response functioned exactly like a
neural synapse, in an all-or-nothing manner. In the same way that
a large number of electrical stimuli build a charge that, at a crucial
moment, fires the spark across the gap between nerve endings, a
series of fucks would mount a readiness until, with shocking speed,
the woman would surrender to her most uninhibited expressions.
Generally, women held back, even in orgasm, sensing that once
they let go, an unfathomable chasm would open up, and all that
could save them from dissolution would be the continued attention
from the man who brought them to that condition. They would
then be, for all practical purposes, in his power.

Paul was an expert at enticing women to disregard their warning
systems, their memories of broken hearts, betrayals, refusals; he
was a master at pushing them to the edge of the erotic abyss
and seducing them to leap. His was the knack of easing women
into insouciance, yielding their essence to his demand. For Paul,
only that moment of yielding counted. Before she surrendered to
her need in his arms, a woman was an object of dalliance; and
afterward, she had nothing further to reveal.

He possessed a rare combination of genius and lasciviousness.
He might have modelled himself on de Sade, except that he lived

in a technological era, and looked upon tying virgins to stone walls in hidden crypts with a certain condescension. He had more sophisticated machinery at his disposal.

From the first moment, when he was just nineteen, that a woman let drop the veils of her public countenance and revealed the terrible beauty of a face that had become no more than a pool within which to see the rigors of a soul in ecstasy, he knew that nothing else in life would have any real value for him. He dedicated himself to the elicitation of that brief moment when absolute openness flowered before his eyes. No priest ever served any god better than Paul the cultivation of women.

In the course of a decade he had found hundreds of them. He learned exactly how to manipulate himself to get them to offer their treasure to his insatiable eyes. He was handsomely endowed, a little over six feet tall, his body combining the best features of a lumberjack and a Martha Graham dancer. He wore his blond hair slightly long, and spent six hours each week at a gym, in narcissistic contemplation of his muscular development, as he lifted weights, swung on trapeze bars, or swam lustily in the pool. Otherwise, he was at work, doing a job which bored him, but which allowed him to live in fairly opulent fashion. After having taken a Ph.D. in molecular chemistry, he landed a position at Johnson and Johnson, joining a vast staff of laboratory workers whose projects included searching for ways to produce more long-lasting glue for Band-Aids.

At night, he fucked.

He continually looked forward to the bliss of having an attractive and intelligent woman squirming under him, his cock splitting her throbbing cunt, her fingers raking his shoulders, her legs shamelessly pulling him more deeply into her, and through it all her face a mask of capitulation to unholy joy. It was the face, more than the mere sensations of the act, which transported him. When the stilted mask of civilized appearance melted and the beast emerged, the angel could be born. And if she were, in her daily life, ultra-sophisticated, ultra chic, then when she broke, he was blessed with seeing the contrast between that artificiality and the ultimate gift that can ever be given to man: the perception of the naked female soul.

But it was all so fleeting! He might watch a woman edge her way toward frenzy, see her hover at the very brink, and then go wild with the joy of wanton release. As the deep-chested howls burst from her throat, he could hold her only a few seconds, using her entire body as a feedback mechanism to orient the angle and intensity of his cock and thrust so that he extracted the maximum response, before she slipped into an orgasmic fury so private that the shades came down once more over her eyes. There were never more than those few brief moments during which he could gaze upon her, with the rapt expression of a saint in the midst of a beatific vision. And then it was gone. Gone forever.

"If only there were some way to preserve the stickiness indefinitely," he heard a colleague say one afternoon during a seminar on the relationship between the respective surface tensions of skin and plastic.

"Preserve!" The word echoed in his mind.

"Yes," he thought, "if only I could preserve that instant."

That night he cancelled his date in order to ponder the implications of his insight. "What if I could," he mused, "freeze the woman at the very second she is producing the expression which is her most perfect, her highest manifestation of beauty?"

He thought of photography, but discarded the idea. A two-dimensional representation was not what he wanted. He desired the real thing. His mind leapt from personal to social ramifications. "I would not only possess the thing that is most precious to me in the world, but will have created a work of supreme art, and in the process have immortalized a woman who would otherwise have passed into oblivion unknown. Such a piece would make the Mona Lisa seem the work of a primitive."

He was quite mad, of course, but also extremely, brilliant, and with the resources of one of the nation's foremost chemical plants at his disposal, he was soon experimenting with a formula that would have the properties he required of it. It would have to be liquid, for he saw that he would need to use a syringe. It would have to work instantaneously, to keep the body he used it on in semblance of the full flush of life. And it would have to penetrate to every last cell of the person's physical structure.

Fired by the flames of monomania, he poured his genius into the project, and within a year he was ready to make his first try.

He decided to start with Cathy. He had been fucking her desultorily for several months, and she had peaked rather early in the affair. It was only a sentimental fondness for her that kept him seeing her. She was still capable of producing first-rate expressions, especially in the way her lips fell open after he came in her mouth, allowing his sperm to dribble down her cheeks and over her chin. He had seen that half a dozen times already. Her orgasm expression was neoclassic, the suggestion of pain in her furrowed brow contrasting exquisitely with the sucking gesture of her lips. After considering all contingencies, he decided to attempt to capture her reaction to being fucked in the ass. Primarily because the hypodermic would be easier to use if he was behind her, and secondly because during that particular variation she attained an attitude of licentious imbecility which he fancied.

When the moment arrived, he was very sad. His body and mind working with the skill of a master technician, he savored the depth of his emotions. In order to accomplish his aim he would, in effect, be killing the lovely woman now groaning under him.

"But, in a sense," he rationalized, "I am doing her honor. She would have died one day anyway, aged and infirm, her body a mass of sagging wrinkles. This way, I freeze her at the height of her beauty, and in the process make her immortal." It reminded him of the fact that the samurai chose the cherry blossom as their symbol because, unlike other flowers, it falls from the branch in the fullness of its fragrance, sacrificing itself so that others might know its precious scent.

It was with mixed feelings that he pressed the needle to the base of her skull, just as she tilted the pelvis backward to impale her buttocks on his thick cock. He slid into her, causing her to gasp, and at the moment he was imbedded completely between her cheeks, and the look of unutterable pleasure that he was seeking moved across her face, he injected the potion into her skin.

At once she was completely paralyzed. Even her heart stopped mid-beat. For an instant he was breathless at the transformation. She had become a statue. He pulled out slowly, his cock feeling as though it were stuck in a piston tube packed with axle grease. He knelt next to her and turned her over. He could scarcely believe his eyes.

She had been caught at the edge of becoming. Her face was a map of demon lust. As he gazed into her fixed stare, he had trouble convincing himself that she was dead, for even the glint of passion had been captured. For a few seconds he was chilled by the notion that she was still alive, imprisoned in that rigid coffin of flesh.

"But that's absurd," he said, as he went to get a saw.

It was not difficult to sever the head from the body, which he was not really interested in except as a curiosity. It was fascinating to observe that the entire inside of her cunt was flexed in an orgasmic spasm. He put the torso in the bathtub, where another brew of specially prepared chemicals neatly dissolved it.

He brought the head to a special laminating machine he had devised, and placed it in a hollow, where a fine electron mist covered it completely. It sealed the woman in a very delicate plastic, as securely as if she was a driver's license. When he took her out, she looked like a woman about to come, except that she had no body.

"You are mine forever," he whispered, "the real you, the true you, the you that lives eternally in beauty."

After that, his collection grew steadily. He became regular at most of the singles' bars on the upper east side, and each evening he left with yet another candidate for immortality. Most failed to meet his increasingly exacting standards. Only the best were considered for his hall of fame.

He became adept at discerning types amidst the confusing superficial appearances. With no research ever having been done in the area, he had to construct his own system of classification, a Linnaeus of the rapturous expression. He divided women in scores of ways, such as the various degrees of opening between their lips at certain crucial check points; whether they kept their eyes open or closed, whether or not their nostrils flared. The quality of the eyes was a world of exploration in itself, and he was able to distinguish fifty-three distinct shades of cheek coloration.

His most frequent mistake in the beginning, when he was still exuberant over his success, was to confuse the excitement of fucking with the nature of the expression produced. Some fucked so well that he forgot to watch closely enough. The best fuckers were not always the best lookers, and vice versa.

When he found one that seemed promising, he would not take her all the way on the first night, knowing that the longer he cultivated her, the more sublime would be her expression when she finally did let go. He would nurse her the way a gardener will care for young shoots. The ones who were fortunate enough, or unfortunate enough, to fail to meet his criteria, were shooed out the next day, unceremoniously, so they would know not to try to come back.

Each morning, as he sipped his coffee, he would stroll among his heads, kept in a room empty of everything except the pedestals they rested on, and talk to them. He would look from expression of unbearable bliss to expression of deeply tormented joy to expression of total giving, and say, "Well, I had hoped to have another friend for you girls to chat with, but she didn't turn out. For a while there, when she put her ankles around my neck, I thought she might produce a really fine expression, but she was too jaded for me to reach her. An airline stewardess. She later told me she had once been fucked by a mule in a Mexican stag bar. Her face barely lost its composure all night. Or, on those days when he had captured another woman, would proudly carry the head in and say, "This is Frances. Isn't she exquisite?"

And then would light a cigarette and say, "Well, another try tonight," and go up to each one and kiss her full on the mouth, whispering endearments, murmuring, "Remember the night you made it all the way, how good it felt, how close we were?" And then would put out the light and go to work.

His doom was nicely ironic. As he injected a Balinese Temple Dancer who was part of a troupe visiting the city, her cunt contracted in an esoteric convulsion known only to a few initiates of the cult she had been trained in. His cock was gripped in an unbreakable grasp that was meant to last for no more than a split-second and provide a totally unique sensation. But frozen as she was, he was trapped inside her, a paralyzing spasm of pleasure-pain coursing through his body.

He tried for over an hour to extricate himself, when he realized that gangrene was setting in. He saw the implications fully. To seek medical help would mean being charged with murder, for questions would be asked, his apartment would be searched.

He decided not to prolong the agony. He lifted her up and carried her into the room of heads. He took all his women down, one by one, and put them in a circle on the floor. He lay down in the middle, the woman of the night still in his arms. For a long time he looked from face to face, remembering, weeping. And when his heart was full, he took the instrument he had used on all of them and plunged it into his chest.

He died as he had lived, a slave to the beauty of women.

THE SICILIAN'S REVENGE

AT FIFTY-FIVE, there were few pleasures left to him. He enjoyed sleeping, he enjoyed drinking wine and talking with his friends, and he enjoyed renting young Irish prostitutes and having them take their clothes off before him as he watched, his eyes sardonically drinking in their flesh, knowing that they found him repulsive, and then directing them to kneel between his thighs and suck his thick cock until he came, usually not for at least an hour, all the while telling them stories of his childhood in Italy, and when they were finished, dismissing them abruptly. He never had any girl more than once; after he had seen a woman's ass, he lost all further interest in her.

On this day he was in a particularly pensive mood, almost philosophical, as the whore dutifully slavered over his cock. He had just concluded a fairly complex deal which involved the takeover of the Chase Manhattan Bank and all the Rockefeller oil refineries in New Jersey through his company. The Capa Tosta Concrete Corporation. From his offices on the hundred and tenth floor of the World Trade Center Building, he looked down over the grimy expanse of New York City.

His eyes narrowed when they rested on Central Park, Prospect Park, and all the other small sections where nature still had some small toehold. He estimated that he had twenty-five years of vigorous health left, and in that time would not rest until every square inch of the city was covered with cement. Until all five boroughs were drowned in buildings.

His gaze went west. There was still the rest of the United States. But that would have to be for his sons. For himself, he would be content if the city became a single giant mausoleum, a final testimony to his power. It would be a feat such as would make the pyramids of the Pharaohs pale into insignificance.

He patted the head of the girl sucking his cock. "You know, Irish," he said, "all those people down there, they are children. They are fools. Even the educated ones." He paused a moment and added, "Especially the educated ones. They don't know what's real."

His eyes grew watery and dim. "When I was a boy in Italy," he told her, his voice thin, its rhythms moving in cadence to her bobbing head, "we never had all this shit. Dirty air, filthy water, traffic jams, people unhappy all the time. We laughed and we fought. We sang songs and ate fresh fish. We had figs growing in the back yard and I drank goat's milk for breakfast. We lived near the sea, and in those days the sea was clean, the water sparkled. We swam every afternoon. And then there was the wine, and the bread fresh from the oven, and the stars at night, and making love in the hay. Oh, what a time that was! Every week we celebrated the birthday of some saint, and we even had a priest to remind us that there are higher things in the world than man. It wasn't like this pig pen, where the people roll around in garbage and think they are the kings of creation."

He sighed and gave himself over to the sensations produced by the friction of her delicate tongue around the tip of his cock. She swept forward and took the rod into her throat, held it until she gagged, and pulled back. There was something about the old man's calm, his quiet voice, which pacified her, nullified her initial feeling of distaste. The thing in her mouth was iron-hard, and gnarled like a De Nobili cigar. Sucking it was like sucking her thumb when she was a child; it was relaxing, easy, with the single difference that this experience was raked by spasms of such tingling sexuality that her toes curled. Despite her desire to remain detached, she had found herself blowing him with mounted excitement.

"But my stupid mother," he went on, "may the devil stick hot pitchforks in her ass, wanted to go to America. 'The streets are paved with gold,' she kept saying, until my poor father finally gave in, sold the farm, and moved us all here. There was no gold. Just misery, and poverty, and filth. And even if there had been gold, what good would it have been? You can't eat gold, it won't keep you warm at night, it has no love."

He beat his fist against the arm of the chair he was sitting in. "That's what's wrong with this country," he shouted, "there is no love here."

He put his hands on her hair. "Lick it at the tip," he said, and for a few moments he did nothing but watch as she lapped the glistening tool, and paid attention to the fluctuations of pleasure brought by each movement of her tongue.

"But an animal learns to survive wherever it is," he said after a while. "My father bought a grocery store, and we started a new life. It wasn't long before we were paid a visit by the Honored Society, and when I compared their methods of doing business and their success to my father's way of life, well, the choice was obvious. There's no point trying to be honest in the city; it's all based on lies anyway. I became a member of the Family, and today I am don of all the dons."

It struck the girl for the first time that the man whose cock she was sucking was perhaps the most powerful man she might ever meet. Most of her time was spent with fifteen-dollar-a-throw longshoremen, and while she wasn't destitute, she was far from any real financial comfort. The fact that she had been offered five hundred dollars for a few hours of work was astonishing in itself; that it was being paid by the highest Mafia chief in the country was almost too much for her to assimilate.

She had no way of knowing his reasons for picking her, that when he was nineteen he had been struck with an overpowering infatuation for a blue-eyed auburn-haired Irish girl whose fair skin made his dark Mediterranean blood boil. But when, after much trepidation, he had approached her, she had laughed at him, calling him a "spaghetti-stuffed garlic eater." Of course, he had shot her and thrown her body in the East River, but even that was not compensation enough for his wounded pride, and over a thousand times afterward, he had had his men scour the entire eastern seaboard for young Irish girls that he could subject to the – to his mind – degrading ritual of cock-sucking.

"The mayor, he thinks he runs the city," the old man continued. "But all he does is prance around and look pretty. Nobody with any real power listens to him. He's somebody to put in front of the television cameras so the cattle think their vote means something. No, it's the ones who control the life systems and the death systems who are in command, only most of them are so stupid, they don't realize it yet.

"Look at the police. Some of the commanders are beginning to figure out that they have thirty-thousand men, armed with hand guns, and with access to machine guns, horses, tear gas, tanks, grenades. But if they made a move, they'd have the state militia to contend with, and the federal government. They'll have to lie low until the whole nation is falling apart in chaos.

"But they are only the most obvious candidates. Think of the firemen who can allow the city to burn, or perhaps even burn it themselves. And the garbagemen, who only strike for higher wages, but could consolidate as a political force, threatening to let plague conditions arise if their demands weren't met. Still, none of these people have any political awareness."

The girl continued sucking. He had put his hands on the back of her head and was guiding her by imparting a momentum to her motions. She let her lips go slack and allowed his cock to bob in and out of her mouth, her tongue licking it each time it entered and each it left. She had begun to have fantasies that he might want her as his private whore, and drew pictures in her mind of a swank apartment, a complete wardrobe, a sports car, charge accounts, and trips to Puerto Rico in the winter. She dropped her reserve and worked up a feverish pleasure in what she was doing, giving herself up to wanton expressions, hoping he would be taken by the masks of lasciviousness she wore. The old man had seen all of this before.

"And even they don't strike at the heart of things," he went on. "Who controls the drinking water, the water to put out fires? Did you ever give a second thought to all those men you see climbing in and out of sewers? Everybody looks down on them, but no one stops to consider that they have access to switches which control the city's vital fluid. While the mayor makes speeches for the newspapers, grimy men with wrenches hold our destiny in their hands.

"But it doesn't end there. You can almost hear the people from Con Ed smirking. Do you remember the night of the great blackout? That was just a test to see if it could be done. It was fun for a few hours, but what would happen after a few days and nights without electricity? Suck it, Irish, suck it! No lights anywhere. Traffic snarled because the traffic lights didn't work. Refrigerators useless, food spoiling. No radio, no television, no elevators, no subways. We would be plunged back into the Stone Age in no time. Bands would form. The gun and the knife would be the law. And not too many would survive.

"And there are other possibilities," he said, waving his hands through the air. "Radicals blowing up the bridges, tunnels, subway tracks. Or the telephone company, operating the central nerve cord that runs through all city life. It is the indispensable tool of business, and without it business would fold. And without business, there is no New York."

He was approaching orgasm. The moment of climax was still five minutes away, but he could sense its beginning. With his body as calm as it was, he was able to give himself to sensation without tension, and thus truly savor the long deep swell which preceded ejaculation. Capable of dispensing with any consideration of the girl except as a tool for his pleasure, he could devote his undivided attention to his inner state.

"But not one of them suspects the overwhelmingly obvious truth as to what real power is." His voice held a tremor of excitement, partially from the growing heat in his loins, partially from the impact of articulating his vision. "And that is with *me*," he continued, "because the one thing they all have to do is *live here!* They must *spend their time here*. And I'm the one who decides what kind of place they get to stay in. No matter who's in command, no matter what form of government, no matter what the state of the economy, the most important reality of the city is its environment. And what makes the environment is the architecture. And I control the architecture."

His voice purred. "I'll make sure there is nothing left but concrete. Mile after mile of living earth has already been covered up, suffocated, and giant stone buildings loom where trees used to grow. There is almost nothing natural left. Most plant life has been destroyed, most animal life, most insect life. The people have nothing left but hard surfaces to walk on, to sit on, to lie on, to look at. Even the sky is hard to see. They are allowed some few cats and dogs and horses, and the pitiful specimens they put in the concrete prisons they call zoos. But that is all. And soon, even they will disappear. The pigeons will be killed. Only rats and roaches will remain. Rats and roaches and people.

"And as they become sicker and sicker, more and more confused and unhappy, they will never begin to guess what their trouble is, that's how unbelievably ignorant they are. They will blame the mayor, they will blame the police chief, they will blame drugs and permissive education. They will revolt, they will change leaders.

They will try everything. But the obvious will never occur to them, that they are slowly dying, being killed by the lack of life around them. They will go to their graves as blind as blind as when they were alive. And I shall win, I shall build everywhere. Cement will rule the earth!"

As he said the last words his thighs tensed and a voluminous spurt of sperm burst into the girl's mouth. She went through all the motions of swallowing it as though it were some kind of nectar, hoping to please the old man with her gusto. But the instant after he came he pushed her away, stared into her face for a moment, and shook his head to deny the memory which refused to let him rest.

"Go suck the boys in the back room," he said.

She began to protest, caught up in a swirling disappointment, but a glint in his eyes told her she had better not say a word. She stood up, licked a few drops of semen form her lips, and petulantly walked towards the door, her buttocks jiggling as she went, to the back room where seven men sat around a wide table playing cards. She would be told to crawl under the table, and go from cock to cock until she had done them all, and then be bundled out into the street, a half a thousand dollars and several insights richer.

The old man buttoned his pants and walked to the window. The city was practically invisible because of the thickly polluted air. Even from his great height he could hear the infernal roar, the din of triumphant machinery. Everywhere cars chugged like ancient beasts, spewing gases in their wake, and at a thousand sites the relentless momentum of construction, more and taller buildings rising to occupy even the samllest bit of free space. And through all this the people walked, their ears shattered by the noises, their nostrils pinched against the stench, their entire bodies incessantly punished by the crunch of crystallized finance. Seem from above, the scene resembled nothing so much as a *danse macabre* of zombies, hulks whose souls had long since been sucked dry.

"I will have revenge on you," he muttered, "for fooling my mother that there could be a good life here, for taking my father away from his land and causing him to die in an unheated tenement, away from the sea and the sky, and for forcing me to become such an evil man to survive. I will destroy you, and my children shall destroy your entire nation. Just by giving you what you want, more cement, more concrete, more steel. To cover the beautiful earth, to tear down the forests, to poison the lakes and the rivers.

"And for what? To build these human garbage dumps, these cities. To construct highways and bridges and dams and all the stupid structures that you worship."

He laughed, a horrible creaking sound.

"I will give you what you want, America," he shouted. "I will give you *progress*. And it will take you straight into the mouth of hell."

CIRCUS OF JADE

BUTCH MEDUSA LAY amidst the pile of bodies. There were eleven other women in the heap, the result of the most ambitious project she had yet undertaken. The group contained representatives of each of the world's races, and was a palette of wildly complementary skin colors and hair textures. Both tall and short were there, as well as fat and thin. Each of the women was from one of the sun signs of the Zodiac, and Butch had personally tested and tasted all of them for copiousness and flavor of vaginal secretions. But now, after all the drugs and music, after the hours of flirtation and foreplay, after the weeks of preparation and expectation, as asses and cunts and mouths and breasts and feet rolled and flashed in a continuous panorama of sensuality, Butch had to admit that she was bored.

"This orgy has no socially redeeming value," she said to herself as a lithe Ethiopian sword-dancer sucked one of her nipples between her lips. Loath as she was to admit it, Butch had come to the end of a cycle and was unwilling to garner the energy to break into a new phase.

She had begun her career one night by sweeping into a lesbian bar dressed in a suit of chain mail and carrying a mace. The place was instantly polarized, the more strident exponents of the new female image finding her intolerably outré, while the lustier women flocked to her side, glad that at least one person was still ready to champion unfashionable stereotypes. For five years subsequent to her coming out, she had run amok in the ultra-sophisticated circles of post-decadent tribadism, imparting a quality of aesthetic ruthlessness to a life style that had been foundering in sterile polemics. Among her vassals were many daughters of the wealthy, and she had no difficulty producing the money she needed to support her rampant metatheater.

The thought she had been suppressing for months now came to the surface of her consciousness. "To do what I want to do, I really need some cocks."

She blew a whistle and the writhing mass of bodies quivered once and fell still. She leapt to her feet, breasts jiggling.

"Sweet Sappho's pussy," she yelled, "is this the best you can manage? If I want choreography I'll find a bunch of fags. I want passion, goddamnit. And reaching behind her, she picked up a fourteen-foot bull whip with which she began to flay the women lying in front of her.

"What do I have to do to get some *feeling* around here?" she shouted, and laid about her with the thick ugly leather instrument.

The cries she extracted, however, were only bleats of pain, and she was no longer interested in mere sadomasochism, having had her fill one afternoon when she flogged three virgins into insensibility on the secluded grounds of a Connecticut estate an admirer had put at her disposal. She threw the whip down in disgust and went to her study to ponder.

"It's not their fault," she thought, "they're doing the best they know how. It's just that there's no sense of purpose." She lit a joint and settled back on her zebra-skin watercouch. Plunging into a deep trance, she found many of the fragments of a vision that had been haunting her coming into place. It was an idea so compelling that she hesitated even to think about it. But she was hungry for challenge, and within an hour knew what she had to do.

"It won't be easy." she mused, "finding the men I need for the job. The gays are free enough, but they don't really want to fuck women. And I have to have both male and female energy for the project. The straights are so crippled I couldn't even put an honest proposition to most of them. Aren't there any lovers left? Men who are pliable enough to take orders from a woman one moment and then throw her down and rip off a piece of ass the next? I need men with firm bodies and warm hearts, men with hard cocks and clear minds, men with fire in their blood and mercury in their egos. Where will I find them?"

The next day began a quest which was to take her over the entire nation and last for almost a year. She put her affairs in order and left a skeleton crew behind to answer her mail and maintain her Park Avenue duplex. And then she began her search.

The technique she used was simple. Whenever she saw a man she sensed was ripe for plucking, she would walk up to him and say, clearly and directly, "Would you like to fuck me?"

If he answered too quickly or was thrown into confusion, she abandoned him at once. She wouldn't consider any man who wasn't together enough to assimilate her approach instantaneously, take a moment to breathe and look at her, peer into her eyes and appraise her body, and respond from the core of some real impulse.

Those who passed the first screening were taken to her hotel room and allowed to fuck her. And as the man went through his motions, she registered impressions of his total being. If, at the end of the first fuck, she still thought he had potential, she would outline her scheme and offer him room and board to work with her. After she had hired her first helper, of course, the game became trickier, for the ensuing prospects would be confronted not only with a woman's asking him what no other woman had probably ever asked before, never so honestly and openly, but also with the man standing next to her.

At the end of three months she had found four men.

The movement began to grow interesting as a spirit of camaraderie seized the group. It was the first time Butch had seen America and was amazed at how much of it was still unspoiled by urbanization. In Santa Fe she picked up a deaf mute, and she took her band into the surrounding hills for a retreat.

That night Butch found herself lying naked on her back, bent over a bedroll, as the men played poker and drank coffee around a fire. Every once in a while one of them would stroll over to fuck her. For her part, it was pleasant to enjoy the cool night air and look at the stars, letting her mind drift, to have her revery interrupted only by the sweet penetration of a cock or by a mouth on one of her breasts or by a hand under her buttocks.

The men, on their part, enjoyed a kind of friendship almost impossible for men to know any longer. Free from financial worries, they could allow themselves to relax. With a woman they could fuck at any time they wanted, they were liberated from sexual tension. And since they all shared the same woman under the same conditions, they had no cause for jealousy, and the bond among them grew unhampered. And it was just the strength of the bond that Butch relied upon for the realization of her vision.

At the end of a year she had gathered seventeen men and returned to the city. The power of their circle was enormous and she was ready to try the next level of operation. She got back in late August, a month before the beginning of the New York season, and started her preparations at once.

First came the costuming. The men were all dressed alike, with short leather skirts, gold earrings in their right ears, and jade bracelets on their left wrists. She led esoteric psychophysical exercises and dances to coordinate their reflexes and cement their sense of unity. She gave lectures to pinpoint her objective. During that period they were allowed no sex so their lust would build.

And when they were at a fine edge, she brought in a victim for them to practice on, a nineteen-year-old debutante, slim, auburn haired, with only a handful of fucks in her experience and a literary infatuation with lesbian love. Butch picked her up at one of the consciousness-raising sessions that have superseded bars as cruising grounds, ravished her for an entire night, and primed her for the experience of being had by a band of men. Half hypnotized, half yearning to live out a fantasy she had been barely able to admit to herself, she agreed to cooperate.

"It's a shame to have to destroy her," Butch thought, "but the men have to be forged into a seamless unit, and only a ritual murder will really do the trick. Besides, once she is really opened up, it would be impossible for her to live in the world anyway."

The night of the affair, after the girl was fucked for the fifty-third time, the last edge of her resistance to madness cracked, and for the next five hours she screamed herself hoarse, pleading for more. "Fuck me, fuck me, fuck me," she shouted over and over again, a hundred times, a thousand times, ten thousand times, the skin of inhibition totally torn and the well of her inexhaustible sexuality yielding its waters.

Finally, Butch dispatched her cleanly, a single bullet through the temple, snuffing out the torment that had its roots in ecstasy, in the eternal restlessness of the flesh.

"This is the power we are going to tap," Butch told the men who looked at the corpse with wide eyes. "We have just begun to unleash the limitless force of sexual energy. When we can control that force and harness the power of the orgasm, we will have a weapon which will reduce all the atomic stockpiles on Earth to the status of toys. And then we shall impose peace on the world. But first, we have to get rid of the body."

Butch called on her reserve army of women, and found an equal number to match the men. There was another month of intense preparation, and then she was ready for her first test: the formation of a sexual cyclotron.

The women all knelt in a circle, their asses up and away from the center, while the men crouched behind them, their cocks at the openings of the cunts. Butch lay in the center, her head pointing north. At her signal, the men all entered the women at once, and began fucking with slow regular strokes. The women held hands all around, as did the men, so that from above, at a Busby Berkeley angle, the whole thing looked like a jellyfish pulsating at the edges. And at the brain of the superorganism was Butch Medusa, coursing all the vibrations through herself. The rhythm increased as a group consciousness began to form. Everyone was aware of the state of everyone else's being.

Gradually, control shifted from the individuals to the group as a whole. A power emerged that was greater than the ability of any single person to claim. It began to take over by itself, reducing the men and women to units in a conglomerate. Unity was achieved through adherence to the dictates of the over-soul.

Orgasm approached, a single orgasm which included the bodies of everyone in the circle. The men joined through their arms, the women joined through cock and cunt, all eyes on the body in the center, all minds empty of thoughts, and Butch gathering all the energy in a single sustained awareness, they came together. And at that instant, Butch was buoyed by a sheet of blue light and lifted six feet off the floor. She hovered for eight minutes and then drifted slowly back down to the rug.

For that period of time, through the city, all hostility in every human being was allayed. Policemen stopped with their fingers on the trigger, husbands and wives stopped mid-argument, taxi drivers stopped with curses on their lips. Not one violent act was committed. Everyone was enveloped in a euphoric cloud, and for weeks afterward scientists speculated as to whether some electronic mass hysteria was the cause. Many found grounds to reaffirm their faith in God. Some claimed that extraterrestrial beings were influencing the earth.

The group was giddy with success, but Butch calmed them

down. "We can't go too fast," she warned. "Too much joy all at once would destroy the fabric of every civilization in the world. People would revert to their simple animal state. Governments would collapse. And the havoc that followed would mean the death of millions. Let them get used to happiness little by little. And meanwhile, we can increase our numbers. One day we'll be able to sustain the effect indefinitely, and then we can open all the switches and fuck the species into survival."

The plan might have worked except for an unforeseen event. Butch Medusa fell in love. She met a man who filled her with all the inane and irresistible feeling such as used to propel teenagers into romantic raptures. The rational part of her realized that to give in to her emotions would destroy the final chance humanity might have to keep from going over the brink into total ruin. But she was helpless before the mood of surrender.

"It's what I get for fooling around with all those cocks," she said to herself bitterly. "Such a fate would never have befallen me if I had stayed a lesbian. This is what I get for trying to do good."

The man was not the kind who would tolerate her unbridled promiscuity, so she abandoned her commune. She moved to Long Island, where he worked as a professor of sociology at Stony Brook College. She had three children and spent her days at war with herself, hating the fact that she really enjoyed her new situation. She never spoke of her past even when the women in her bridge club began to talk about sex, revealing their fantasies and infidelities. Everyone thought her a model wife, which indeed she was.

The people in the duplex, without the unifying power of her vision, soon degenerated into a crowd of rowdy low-level orgiasts. The neighbors started to complain, and one night the place was raided. They were all booked on charges of indecent behavior, given suspended sentences, and told to leave the city. The body of the girl who had been shot had been smuggled out and buried on Staten Island, and thus was never found.

BOWEL BOOGIE

ONLY HER BODY was tied down; she could still move her head and look around the room.

It was ten feet high by ten feet wide by ten feet long. It was constructed entirely of tile. There was a vent in the ceiling to let in air, and a vent in the floor to let water drain out. A spout jutted from one wall, and over it was a shelf with various instruments.

She was chained to a table built of soft stone, held utterly immobile. Her wrists were manacled at her sides, a steel band went over her waist, and her feet were fastened to raised stirrups so that her legs were lifted and spread apart. She took a deep breath and closed her eyes.

The door opened slowly, a thick wooden partition with soundproof slats cemented to both sides. The doctor stepped in. He was one of the world's foremost therapists, having written a book called *The Secondary Stutter*, in which he traced all neurosis to the suppression of embarrassment people feel when farting. He closed the door behind him and beamed on the woman.

"Well, Ms Schneider," he said in a booming voice, "how good to meet you."

She looked up and gasped. The man wore hip boots, a long raincoat, and rubber gloves. His face was covered with a black mask. She had been told that he would want to remain anonymous, but it hadn't occurred to her that he would hide more than his name. The social worker at the clinic she had applied to for psychotherapy had explained that she might partake of an experimental program without charge, and in addition to having her difficulties cleared up, would be helping the march of science in its striving to obliterate all mental illness. She was told that the treatment would have to remain secret and that she would not know who would be treating her, in order to protect him from lawsuits. Ms Schneider had had her doubts, but she felt in desperate need of help, and couldn't afford to pay for it, so she agreed.

He walked over to the table. "Before we begin," he said, his voice deep and reassuring. "I'm sure you will have a few questions. But first I'd like to tell you a little about what we'll be doing."

The woman shifted her weight and he glanced at her through the narrow slits of his disguise. She was thirty-nine, worked as an elementary school teacher, and had never been married. Her body was slim, the flesh still firm. Uneventful legs blossomed into arched buttocks, and small breasts nicely graced her upper chest. Her pubic hair was sparse and her outer cunt lips were folded against each other like hands clasped in prayer.

"To put it most directly," he began, "my work is not a departure from, but the most recent development of, the psychoanalytic discoveries of Sigmund Freud. You've heard of Freud? The orthodox analysts would have me tarred and feathered if they knew what I was doing, but mostly because they are afraid to face the logical conclusions of their own theories. That is why I must say nothing about my work until I can prove that my technique is effective."

The woman opened her mouth to speak but he cut in before she could say a word. "Although I subsume the work of all the men and women who have gone before me, my approach is original, a totally new synthesis. And beyond the theoretical correctness is the fact that my technique is *absolute*." His voice rang with a strange vibration, sounding hollow beneath the mask. "You see, that has been the problem. All the great minds have understood neurosis and formulated their theories, but none of them could come up with a cure that would work in all cases. And this is to be my immortal contribution. The infallible cure for all mental and emotional disturbances."

He began pacing, but since the room was so small and the table took up the central space, he was forced to walk in a circle around the woman's body. She attempted to follow him with her eyes as he prowled. "The discovery of my technique, as with that of penicillin, was accidental. All the elements were present, and I just happened to be there to put them together. I remember the afternoon well, I had just finished reading the passage in *Function of the Orgasm* where Reich describes his basic insight into masochism. He found that what the masochist really seeks is the feeling of bursting open, of having his energy flow outward, through his armored self. The masochist doesn't enjoy pain itself, but hopes to find a release in pain.

"That was on my mind when I opened my mail and found a brochure from the Eulenspiegel Society, an organization composed of sadists and masochists dedicated to erasing prejudices about their condition. I was struck by the way in which life is always struggling to express itself in a positive fashion, even when it passes through what must seem like terrible aberrations.

"It was just then I felt the first peristaltic wave that signals a bowel movement. I went into the bathroom, closing the door behind me. As I turned the knob, however, I realized that there was no one else in the house! I was thunderstruck. My shame at such a basic biological activity was so deep that it led me to the most absurb behavior, closing the door against the censure of society when no other member of society was even present. I sat down and my eyes moved idly across the wall opposite and fell upon my wife's douche bag which hung from a hook. I don't know how to describe that moment. Choirs sang, and the room filled with light. It all came together in a crescendo of truth."

He stopped pacing and grabbed one of the woman's ankles tightly. "Do you see?" he said, his voice brimming with emotion. "Does it begin to make sense now?"

The woman thought he was stark raving mad. She did what people in rising panic often do, and reached into the recent past to recall the last moments of normality she could remember. The clinic was a highly respected institution, so when the nurse had asked her to remove her clothing and had fastened her to the table, there was still some sense of being connected to the workaday world, even though the trappings were bizarre. Ms Schneider had a fully conditioned faith in public organizations, and she drew on that to counter the brunt of her perception that she was helpless in a locked room with a maniac peering down at her naked body.

"I don't think I want to continue with this," she bleated.

"Ah ha!" he shouted. "That's the point. Very few people do. All other therapies have failed simply because at the point of greatest resistance the therapist allowed the patient to leave. I will change all that. My vision demands it. People must be saved in spite of themselves. That's the whole issue with neurosis. And nothing except my technique has any chance of curing neurosis, and of ultimately saving the world. Nothing else includes all the necessary elements. Bringing forth childhood repressions, it will allow that feeling of bursting so you will stop shrinking from life, and it will put you in touch with your need and your pain. It will allow you your full range of expression, and plumb to the core of your sexual nature. It will attack your most deep-seated inhibition, the one which grows from the cornerstone contribution of our civilization to the world, early toilet training."

The woman started to protest that none of this seemed connected to the relatively uncomplicated problems she had been dealing with, but he seemed to read her mind. "Your unhappiness is felt by you in one way, but its causes are beyond your awareness. You will see. You will fight me because I will show you your true self. You will scream, you will hate, you will cry, you will yearn, you will surrender, and you will win. You will have a total experience and for the first time in your life you will come alive. And nothing or no one will prevent you from achieving your goal, least of all yourself. I won't let you stop yourself from becoming healthy. I will force the neurosis out of you."

He reached to the shelf behind him and picked up a long hose with a plastic nozzle. "Ms Schneider," he said, "you have the honor to be the first patient to try the most revolutionary treatment in the history of psychology: Enema Therapy."

The woman sobbed openly. She could not believe that she had allowed things to go so far, that she hadn't stopped when she saw the room, or when the nurse tied her to the table.

"I don't want to," she cried out to the doctor.

"Of course you don't," he said cheerfully, attaching the hose to the spigot on the wall. "At least, the superficial part of you doesn't. But the deeper part, the part that brought you to seek help in the first place, is calling for help, and help it shall get."

He brought the nozzle level with the table top. He fingered some Vaseline from a jar on the shelf and delicately applied it to the woman's anus.

"No," she keened, now almost totally out of control.

"You'll see, you'll see," he crooned.

He placed the nozzle between her clenched buttocks and gently pushed, inserting it fully into her body. She tried to squirm away but was held too tightly. Her thighs bulged with tension. The doctor stepped back and viewed his handiwork.

"No matter what happens," he said, "just remember one thing: no physical harm can come to you here. Your own worse enemy is tied securely to the table. You may go insane for a while, but that's the only way to reach true sanity. There can be no reconstitution without regression, that's my motto."

He reached behind him and, taking a few seconds to appreciate the historic import of the moment, he turned the handle, beginning the flow of water into Ms Schneider's ass.

She filled up for almost twenty minutes. As the hot fluid entered her, she began to howl. Again and again she reached a point where she thought she could take no more and begged him to stop, but he was implacable. "It's all been measured ahead of time," he would say. Pain enveloped her in waves, giving way to a peculiar kind of pleasure, a sort of tingling release. She tried to back away from the nozzle, but her body was fixed in place. The doctor got an erection, watching her thrash about, her cunt winking lewdly above the phallic nozzle, but he maintained professional discipline and his stiff cock did not show beneath the heavy raincoat.

He maintained stoic composure. Even when she seemed on the brink of collapse, ready to faint or actually pass away, he never lost the necessary faith in his treatment. She was like a film shown by a berserk projector, her body threatening to burst as it yielded thousands upon thousands of repressed memories and feelings and thoughts locked in her muscles and brain cells. It was like a seven-year analysis gone through at the speed of sound, and with total abreaction. Her frame shuddered like a test plane in a wind tunnel. And she reached a state of such complete energy expansion that her hair stood on end, rising two feet from her scalp.

Finally, he turned the water off. It had begun to seep out around the edges of the nozzle and he knew that she was filled to the brim. When she felt the stoppage of flow, there was a momentary relief, but with astounding swiftness he pulled the nozzle out and stuck in a stopper, corking her as neatly as a wine bottle.

"Oh God," she wailed.

"We are going to remain like this for a little while," he said. "The first phase is over, and you have survived the initial trauma. Now the real work begins, for you will no longer be able to hide behind your freneticism and hysteria. In this treatment, all the masks of defense must be stripped and you must face your actual condition. We must go on until you are literally incapable of sustaining your experience, and your mind shatters with trying to rationalize it all. Then the unconscious will be liberated and the basic structural changes can take place in your character."

The following five hours were chaotic. She became feverish and then snapped into lucidity. She fell asleep and had bloated dreams. She babbled out loud. She tried again and again to expel the cork and push out the fluid, but was thrown back into helplessness. She entered the death state. For a while, she was raked with erotic flashes, and at one point began to grind her hips up toward the ceiling, running her tongue over her lips and moaning until she had an orgasm.

Occasionally the doctor added more water to replace what had been absorbed through the colon. Some of the sounds that ripped from her throat would have melted the heart of Satan himself, but the therapist was unshakeable.

"I must help her see it through," he said to himself. A lifetime of work was culminating in this experiment, and not only his reputation but his deepest definition of self was at stake. He hated neurosis the way a saint hates sin. His hope to rescue the world from destruction was wild enough to tax the limits of his rational mind, but some more primitive center within him goaded him on.

"The enema," he thought, "our only hope is in the enema."

He watched, waiting for the sign that the treatment was complete. He did not know what form it would take, but had unmoveable faith that she would come out the other side of her heightened anguish and go on into a life of freedom. All the while she seemed to be in the throes of unbearable suffering, radical internal changes were taking place, and he could do nothing but wait.

Finally, a profound shudder went through her. She had come to the end of her metamorphosis. Her soul had been scrubbed clean and brought to its basic grain. She was utterly naked. A lifetime of overlay had loosened and now floated inside her. Her characterological tensions had been dissolved and there was no portion of her mind which was any longer unknown to her.

"I've done it," he whispered, "I've accomplished in a few hours what therapists take years to do. She is cured. I can see it."

At that instant, the woman let out a wail that was indistinguishable from the cry a baby lets out right after birth.

"Love," the woman said, "I want love."

The doctor's eyes stung with tears. The woman had contacted the core of her being and been reborn. His approach was vindicated. He took a deep breath, and with a sweeping gesture, he pulled the plug.

She gushed for an eternity. Jet after jet of water burst from her. She vibrated with the release of all her sickness, the literal and metaphoric shit she had been keeping inside her. The brown fluid splashed on the walls over the floor, ran down the therapist's raincoat, poured down the drain.

"Free," he shouted, "you are free," and turned on the spigot again, this time to play the hose in a stream over her body as he undid her locks and chains. She sprang up from the table, pulsing with the river of new life that filled her, with the cosmic energy that was once more a part of her heritage. He put down the hose and the woman stood in front of him, her face radiant with happiness, a blue aura shining around her head.

"I don't know what to say," she said, "everything is . . . different now."

"I understand," he replied.

"I didn't realize how afraid I was. Not only on the table, but for my whole life. Afraid of everyone and everything. Why, I even used to be afraid to cross the street!"

She got dressed and the two of them talked in his office for a while. After removing his mask he proved to be a pleasant-looking man in his early fifties.

"Come back tomorrow," he said. "I want to take some psychological tests and tape your account of your experience. I'm going to present this to the world."

After she left, as he sat in silent enjoyment of his accomplishment, he heard a screech outside his window, followed by a hubbub of voices. Crossing the street bravely, the woman had been hit by a bus and was killed instantly. He rushed out. As he stood over her body a small tic developed at the edge of his mouth.

"It's always more complicated than one thinks," he muttered as he went back inside the clinic where he sat at his desk and began scribbling furiously in his notebook.

PRAY ON ME

"BLESS ME FATHER, for I have sinned."

"Yes, go ahead."

"It is the same. I have been looking at the Mother Superior again."

The priest sighed.

"Did it arouse you?" he asked.

The Pope looked up. "Arouse?" he repeated. "I'm almost eighty years old. I haven't been aroused since World War II."

"Then why do you keep going there?"

The old man shook his head. "I don't know," he said sadly. "I just find it compelling."

The confessor put his hand over his forehead. He was a Jesuit monsignor who had, after two years of special training, been given the delicate task of hearing the Pope's confessions. He could still remember the talk his own superior had given him on the first day he began his new duty. The head of The Society of Jesus, the man they called "The Black Pope," had impressed the seriousness of the task upon him.

"The Holy Father is the voice of God," he had said, "but he is also a man, subject to the same weaknesses which tempt all of us. You must not let his high office intimidate you. In the confessional you must treat him as you would any other sinner." Then he had leaned forward and whispered, "Should he let fall any bit of information which might be useful to *our* cause . . ." he began. The monsignor had jumped up in fright. "You are not suggesting that I break the seal of the confessional!" he exclaimed. "Of course not," said the superior, "but there is a difference between breaking and bending. I only suggest that you learn to bend, lest you yourself break. Or," he added, squinting meaningfully, "be broken."

"I curse the day I ever discovered that secret passageway,"

the Pope went on. "I searched the records and discovered it was Alexander the Second who had it built. And it was designed by Leonardo himself." He groaned as he recalled the night he reached for a rarely used book in the library of his private bedroom and discovered, deep in the corner of the shelf, a small switch. He pulled the lever and a small door opened at the back of the fireplace. Crouching, he entered, and found a candle that must have been made a hundred years earlier. He followed the tunnel for half a mile until he reached a narrow flight of stairs leading to a small platform. Standing on the ledge, he saw a space with two tiny discs hung from thin chains. He moved the bits of metal and was stuck by twin arrows of yellow light.

They proceeded from holes which opened into the bedroom of the Mother Superior of the order of nuns that serviced the Vatican, providing its cooks, cleaning women, and other menial servants. From the other side, the holes would not be noticed, since they were in the eyeballs of a painting of Saint Francis of Assisi, a huge masterpiece done by Michaelangelo, totally unknown to the outside world, and one of thousands of priceless art works casually strewn about the hallways of the global center of Christianity.

Peering through the holes, the Pope had looked upon a strange scene. The chief nun was lying on her cot, her knees up, her thighs trembling, her breasts heaving, her face a mask of joyful anguish, as with her hooked fingers she told the beads of her rosary. Her voice, as she recited the Ave Marias and Pater Nosters, rose and fell, at times almost indistinguishable from a deep moan. The Pope had scratched his head.

"If she wasn't saying the rosary," he thought, "I would swear she was having an orgasm."

He had looked in on her dozens of times after that. He had no way of telling what was going on in her mind, what baroque images cascaded upon her seared soul like scalding sperm from a celestial cock. It was several months before it occurred to him that he might, in some obscure way, be committing a sin. He told the story to his confessor who advised sealing up the tunnel, thus removing the temptation.

"But why do that unless what I'm doing is a sin?" the Pope argued. He did not want to stop his visits since they provided him with the only private excitement in an otherwise totally public life. Yet, he could not be at peace about them. Again and again he would kneel in the confessional and state, "I've been watching Sister Angela pray again."

They decided that since no sexual excitement was involved, and since the Pope had not had an erection for several decades, there could be no sin of lust. Individually and together they searched the lists of transgressions, going through the thousands upon thousands of thoughts, actions, and intentions which the Church had labelled as sin and for which a person could, with no qualms, be condemned to Hell. But not a single one seemed to cover the act of a Pope watching a nun say the rosary, despite the unorthodox way in which the prayer was said. They talked about mentioning the matter to the nun herself, but reasoned that if she were acting in innocence, their words might only raise scruples in her mind.

"If there's no rule in the books that says it's wrong, then why should I stop doing it?" the Pope asked.

"Why do you feel guilty about it?" rejoined the monsignor.

"Can't you advise me any better than that? You're my confessor."

"Well, you're the Pope," the monsignor answered, "why don't you ask God for advice?"

"I don't believe in God," the Pope said.

The priest felt as though he had been struck on the nose with a rubber mallet. "You too?" he said. "I thought I was the only priest who didn't believe in God."

"Nobody really believes in God," the Pope went on.

"Then why do we continue to do all this?" the confessor asked, his question taking in all of Catholicism.

"Well," the Pontiff drawled, his hands describing an arc in an Italianate gesture that seemed to subsume all the weariness of civilization, "this isn't such a bad job. We get enough to eat, a place to sleep, nice clothes to wear. And we don't have to knock ourselves out. I mean, it's not like digging ditches. You know what I mean?" He winked and nudged the monsignor in the ribs. "It's all a big game."

"But if you don't believe in God, why do you make such a fuss over your confessions?" The younger man was perplexed by the turn of events.

"Just because there's no God doesn't mean there's no sin," the Pope said. "A man still has to decide what's wrong and what's right for him. And he has to live by that if he is to respect himself at all. I bring these things up in confession because you seem like a sensible person and I enjoy talking to you." He stood up and walked to the window overlooking an immense, perfectly manicured garden. "I never cease being surprised at finding myself here," he said, his voice somewhat distant. "I was raised as a peasant. Becoming a priest was the easiest way to excape the drudgery of the farm. My promotions all took me by surprise, and by the time I was a bishop I realized that I was just a marker in the sweep of history, chosen by some quirk of destiny to rise to high office. When I was elected Pope I was no longer amazed."

He turned to face the monsignor, a gleam in his eye. "But the ones who gave me the office have had ample opportunity to wonder whether I am their ecclesiastic frankenstein monster. We all know that this complex of cathedrals is nothing but an elaborate stage set, and our daily rituals an empty charade. But I am the first to openly suggest it verbally, and they are beginning to worry. And the Council I convened is only the start."

The Pope went back and knelt on the *prie dieu* once more. "Since we are under the seal of confessional," he went on, "I can tell you something. A plan to completely overshadow what has gone before."

The monsignor blinked.

"Listen," the Pope told him. "I'm going to announce that on Easter Sunday of next year, I will issue my final dogma, *ex cathedra*. I will send a call throughout the world that I will speak from my highest spiritual authority and deliver a message directly from God Himself. I will advertise it for almost a year. I will say I have had a vision, a visitation from the Throne of Heaven, and on the given day, I will open the gates of Rome to the world. I will ask the heads of state to gather in the Vatican, and call in the leaders of all the religions of man. I will use radio and television. Saint Peter's will blaze in all its Renaissance glory, with lights, candles, torches, incense. The full Swiss Guard on display. The College of Cardinals, dressed in their finest livery, in attendance. And me on my most sumptuous throne, bedecked in gold and emeralds and diamonds and rubies. I will wear the Triple Crown on my head, and carry the mitre which signifies me as first among all the bishops of the earth. I will say High Mass and have a dozen choirs perform the most perfect works by Palestrina. And when all is prepared I will say the following:

God has spoken to me from the bosom of His infinite and mysterious wisdom. He desires an end to all false divisions between man and man. To this end, He declares all religions null and void. He will answer no prayer that is not spoken in absolute silence and privacy. As the Pope, obedient to His wishes, I hereby dissolve the Catholic Church, and urge all my fellow churchmen of rival faiths to do the same with their religions. Let us abolish formal religion in order to return to God. I speak this as an official pronouncement and declare that any Catholic who continues to profess himself or herself as a Catholic is automatically excommunicated from the Catholic Church which, from this moment on, doesn't exist any longer anyway.

The monsignor stared at the old man. "You're really going to do that?" he asked.

"Sure," said the Pope cheerfully, "why not? The trend is toward unity. And the best way to unify the world is to do away with all these silly religious organizations."

"But what about our jobs," the monsignor cried out.

"It will force a lot of people to earn an honest living for a change," the Pope told him. He was silent a few moments and then added, "But we still haven't decided anything about Sister Angela. I really want to come to some kind of decision about whether what I am doing is wrong. It really disturbs me."

The monsignor had difficulty tearing his attention away from the mammoth scheme the Pope had just outlined to turn to something he considered trivial, but it was not his hour. He pulled himself together. "What happened the last time you went there?" he asked.

"When she finished the last sorrowful mystery, she threw open her arms and screamed, 'Oh sweet Jesus, come and take me NOW,' and then sobbed for about five minutes, at one point so violently that she fell off the bed and began writhing about on the floor." He paused a moment. "She had nothing on under her robes."

"I see," said the monsignor, whose years did not prevent him from appreciating the more sensual aspects of the scene described.

"Oh, if only I were younger," the Pope said, "it would be a pleasure to sin with that woman."

The monsignor finally decided that the Pope was innocent of any wrongdoing, and what he felt as guilt was merely frustration. That afternoon he visited the Mother Superior himself, and with what he knew, coupled with the prestige of being the Pope's confessor, he did not find it difficult to suggest hearing her confession. As he suspected she might, she told him of her evening's activities, and he advised that he could not make any judgment on her behavior unless he saw it in person. They made an appointment for him to visit her quarters a week in the future. While she said the Act of Contrition, her gray eyes looked unblinkingly into his.

An hour later, he was closeted with the Head of the Jesuit Order, requesting that his confession be heard. He reasoned that if he revealed the contents of the Pope's confession in his own confession, he wouldn't, technically speaking, be breaking the seal of confession, but merely transferring it. And if the man he confessed to wanted to do something with the information, he would have his own conscience to struggle with. "Let him deal with his own seal," the monsignor said to himself.

Five days later, the Pope died under mysterious circumstances. During his brief illness he was kept inside his room and only a few cardinals, his doctor, and his confessor were allowed in.

"Tell me," the Pope said to the monsignor during his last confession, "are they poisoning me?"

"I really don't know," the monsignor replied.

"It feels like they're poisoning me," he said. "I wonder what sort of politics is buzzing around in their heads now. Do you know who's been fingered for succession?"

"I try to stay out of those things," the monsignor told him.

"Very wise," the Pope said. He took a deep breath. "You know, I looked at myself in the mirror the other day and I thought, 'To millions of people you are the Pope, the supreme spiritual leader. But to me you're like an old man dressed in drag, haunting this ancient marble theater.' And now, they're going to bring in a new act."

The Pope died feeling he had lived an interesting life. The monsignor went that same night to the Mother Superior's room, and discovered that she didn't believe in God either. But did have a sense of sin.

"Well, what the hell," he told her, "I can forgive sin. It says so in my contract."

He heard her confession and for penance told her to recite a rosary. And as she lay before him, her legs opening with each new level of rapture she reached imagining her Redeemer descending to fill her with His joy, the monsignor slowly took his clothes off, preparing to serve as a very real handle for her fantasy.

Finally he mounted her, and as she surged against him, her robes awry, her beads rattling, he whispered over and over again. "Your sins are forgiven you, go and sin some more," while behind him the eyes of the man who might have brought down the curtain on the entire show would never again appear to watch their scene through the holes in the ancient canvas.

YESTERDAY'S IAGO

NEITHER COULD REMEMBER how or where they met; they assumed it had been at a party. But suddenly, they were friends, and from the first shared an intimacy and trust which went deeper than anything they knew with anyone else, including their mates.

They experienced that rare and precious gift of total communion. They could sit for hours, holding hands, speaking or not speaking, attuned to a communication which went from words to silence and back to words without an interruption in the flow of meaning. Unaware of themselves, they often struck classic postures, and one might find them lost in one another's eyes, their fingers intertwined, sighing openly.

Albert was a poet, and chained to his dry despair. The wife and two children who inhabited his days seemed something of an afterthought, a footnote to his central concern. He held a job to support his family, and went through the motions of relationship, but it was only when he was alone, a beam of light transforming his desk top into a stage as he hunched against the glare of the white sheet of paper that challenged him, his hand holding a sharpened pencil hovering like a hawk about to strike, that he felt whole.

Until he met Margaret.

"You are as real to me as poetry," he told her, and she wept with the joy of recognition.

Through the years they came to comfort one another in times of crisis, to celebrate in times of plenitude. At first they attempted to integrate the singularity of their bond into their wider social contexts, but both her husband and his wife began to seethe with jealousy even though the two of them had not known so much as a kiss by way of sexual contact.

"I'd almost prefer it if you fucked her," his wife told him, "then you'd stop idealizing her and imagining that she's all that different from me."

Margaret's husband left her, and Albert began to visit her at her apartment regularly, lying to his wife about where he was. "It's strange," he said to Margaret, "you're like my sister, and I have to sneak off to see you."

At first they spoke mostly of her marriage, her suffering. Albert was a mountain of support, listening, guiding, caring. And leaning on him, she was able to effect the difficult transition from knowing herself only through the reflection of another to having a sense of identity as a single woman.

And as that took place, of course, she began to feel her need for a man once more, but this time promising herself that she would not allow herself to be vulnerable, but would take what a man had to offer by way of completion, and give back as good as she got. For her deeper aspects, she had Albert.

In this mood, her encounters with men began to take on an odd twist, for she discovered that she hungered for bad treatment. Her husband had known how to be mentally and emotionally cruel to her, and it was, in fact, his disgust for himself for falling into that trap which had prompted his leaving; but she could not find the same sort of punishment with men who were essentially one-night stands. A shift took place, subtle at first, but with rapid acceleration into clearly defined forms, until she recognized her craving for physical pain.

She didn't want to tell Albert, for fear she would repulse him, but one night she could hold it back no longer.

"I think I'm a masochist," she said.

"You've always been," he told her. "We've talked about that before."

"It's different now," she said. "It used to be passive and unconscious, but now I'm an active masochist. I openly ask for it."

She told him about the previous night. She had been sitting at home, knitting and listening to music, when a great restlessness seized her. Her legs trembled and she found her heart beating quickly. She went out into the street like a zombie, heading for the nearest bar. It wasn't too long before a man sat next to her, a grizzled dockworker in his mid-forties who looked as though he had been drinking steadily for the past thirty years. His very gruesomeness sent shivers of contorted desire through her, and while he was not cerebrally capable of formulating and articulating the nuances of the situation, his animal intelligence understood at once what was going on.

He grabbed her arm and led her out into the night. By that time she was quivering in anticipation and could barely stand. She dimly remembered lurching through obscure neighborhoods, and being half carried up a flight of stairs to his room. He flung her down on the bed and leapt up next to her. For a few moments he was pure frenzy, all the frustration of his lifetime pouring out on the willing woman who had given herself up to be used. He slapped and pawed and bunched her up, flinging her back and forth like a half-empty sack of flour. She could recall none of the details, only being aware that he might kill her, and not caring for anything except the brute energy that erupted from him.

"That's what I remember most clearly," she told Albert, "that I was sucking his energy from him, and I would do anything for that energy, even to letting him beat me."

"What happened then?" Albert asked, his voice calm and gentle, his mien serene, his attitude one of total compassion and acceptance.

"He ripped my clothes off," she continued. "And then it was sheer jungle sex. He had a cock like a policeman's billy, and he used it the same way, to beat me with. He didn't know what to do first, and he kept tossing me around in a dozen different ways, fucking me in the mouth, in the cunt, in the ass. All the while he kept slapping me and calling me the most foul names. And I . . . well, I enjoyed it so much it scared me. I just kept shouting, 'Yes, yes, this is what I want, this is what I've always wanted.'"

She paused. "When he came, I dug my nails a half inch into his skin and he didn't even feel it. Afterward we were both a little flabbergasted, and when I was leaving he said, 'I'm going to make believe this was a dream because this isn't going to happen to me again, and I don't want to start wanting it, because you aren't going to want me another time. Your type, you'll do this a thousand times with a thousand different men before you're through.' And I knew he was right. He was so dumb and sweet and sad that I got carried away and I went down on my knees and gave him a long, slow blow job. And I loved it. Being in that tawdry apartment sucking that stranger's cock after he had practically torn me apart."

She looked up. "What do you think, Albert? Am I sick?"

He stroked her hair and held her head in his hands and gazed deeply into her liquid eyes.

"I've only had one criterion in my life," he told her. "Anything which can be seen as poetry is its own justification. If you view it as something ugly, then that's what it becomes. If you can sing its beauty, then that is all there is. And your soul is the soul of poetry. If you remember that, you are free to do things which would horrify the timid and the trite."

Then he smiled, and added, "But none of that should let you forget that one time you might meet up with someone whose frustrations lie deeper than your dockworker's, and you could very well end up tied to a bed while some maniac tattoos your body with a razor blade, Or even less dramatically, but more probably, that same man loses his sense of proportion and smashes a fist into your mouth relieving you of a dozen teeth." He frowned, lit a cigarette, and went on, "But the real danger is more insidious. The body builds a tolerance for any sort of sensation, and if you take this path, you will start to need more and more violent behavior to achieve the same levels of stimulation. It's like heroin or any other drug."

She lay with her head against his chest and wept silently. "You are such a beautiful person and such a dear, dear friend," she said. "You care so much for me, and yet you leave me absolutely free. You never censor or blame."

"How could it be otherwise?" he replied.

The more lurid of the possibilities didn't come to pass, but the last one did. While Margaret didn't fall into the hands of a madman or receive any scars or permanent damage, she did enter an escalating cycle of sadomasochistic activity. Like so many in that particular endgame, she learned the value of choreography and expertise. She came to prefer a man who knew how to use a whip with discretion and skill over someone who struck out blindly and in rage.

In time she was introduced among a number of the formal and informal circles composed of people who shared similar tastes. She was initiated into more delicate forms of torture, including the judicious use of hot wax, the proper placement of needles, the hanging bar and nipple clips. She once spent a weekend as slave to an entire household, being used and abused by almost twenty men and women for three days. And, in logical progression, she developed a taste for what were called, in that clique, water games.

"It was extraordinary, Albert," she said. "There I was, my hands tied behind me, having just been fucked by three men at once, kneeling in front of a fourth. He told me to open my mouth and I thought he wanted me to suck his cock. But when I took it, it wasn't hard. The upper part of my face was covered with a leather mask, so I didn't know what was coming. Then this incredible sensation, a stream of hot liquid on my tongue. I still didn't know, and then the taste hit me. A fantastic taste, pungent and sweet and bitter and salty all at once. And then I knew. He was pissing in my mouth! And it drove me wild. I reached up and put his whole cock inside me and let him piss down my throat. And all the while my knees were shaking and I almost climaxed with excitement."

She looked at him, wondering whether this outrage would perturb him at all. Telling him was a treat, for she was able to experience her episodes at another level, but from time to time she became afraid of alienating his affection. But he only nodded and said, "Unless the person has some disease, urine is perfectly sterile. It can't hurt you. In fact, it's probably safer then the city's drinking water."

"Have you ever done anything like that?" she asked.

"I'm afraid my sexual tastes have always been suffocatingly pedestrian," he told her.

They continued in that manner for more than a year, and one night he arrived looking drawn. She tried to cheer him up with wine and stories of her week's activity but he became more and more glum. Finally he blurted out, "Susan left me. She's taken the children."

For the first time in their long relationship, she listened more to him than he to her. And after long, long hours of his pouring himself out, exposing a weakness and sensibility to pain that he had never shown before, at four in the morning, exhausted, he asked, "Do you mind if I stay here a day or two? I don't want to face that empty apartment just yet."

The two days stretched into four, and the four into a week, and finally he left. It was as though he didn't want to go, and yet felt extremely awkward staying longer. Her heart went out to him. After so many years, she had a chance to help him, to provide succor for his hurt.

But he did not call her for several weeks, and she could not reach him on the phone. Finally, she went to his apartment, and found

him drunk and disheveled, the place a shambles. She got him to
shower and shave, cleaned the house, and made a huge dinner for
him. Later, they sat on the couch and talked. It was the first time
that she knew him without his having his wife, and the difference
was palpable.

During a deep silence, something totally unforeseen happened.
He held her to him, as he so often had, but this time his arms
tightened until her face tilted up, and his lips covered hers in a
kiss that transmitted an unmistakable urgency.

Something profoundly deep within her melted. The transcendent
liberty she had discovered in her body blended with the hunger in
her heart, and in an instant she surrendered totally to him, on fire
with that unique melange of physical desire, emotional need, and
intellectual affinity to which is given the name love.

Instantly they were one, and without a thought they launched
themselves into a total lovemaking which thundered with the force
of so many years of waiting and building. The form was completely
constructed, their friendship was absolute, she could give herself,
give herself rapturously, having the abandon she had known in her
body with others and the fullness she had felt in her heart for Albert.
Now they were one, and it seemed as though her entire life had been
a preparation for this moment.

The next morning they decided to live together, and they moved
to a new neighborhood, wanting to make a clean break with
both their pasts. They found an apartment, and had a glorious
honeymoon of sorts for three weeks. And without marking the
moment as such, they passed into that space in which they were
grafted onto one another, and could not henceforth part without
a terrible tearing and rupture. In an informal and real sense, they
were married.

And one night, as they sat on the couch, reading, she felt a
strange vibration in the room. She looked up from her book and
found Albert watching her, his face slightly distorted.

With dire premonition she asked, "What is it, darling?"

His voice was hard, his eyes narrowed, "I was just thinking about
that dockworker you told me about," he said.

For a moment she couldn't think of what he was talking about.
And then it came to her. The dock-worker she had gone with shortly
after her husband left her.

"I was thinking about all the things you did with him," he went on, his voice thin and febrile, "letting him fuck you in the ass, sucking his cock."

And with a slow, mounting dread she realized that his entire system was laced with scorching jealousy and anger, a pervasive and unrelenting possessiveness, spiteful and thorough. She hoped it might be a momentary mood, but at a glance she understood that she was only seeing the tip of the iceberg. For he not only remembered that one night, but had catalogued in his memory every incident she had ever told him about. He knew every action, every feeling, every moan that had been hers for the past eight years. His control was absolute.

"But that was before . . ." she began to say and stopped. What was happening was beyond logic or reason. A cold clammy hysteria clutched her belly and fear flashed in her eyes like a trapped rat in a flooded cellar. The days of physical suffering were finished, and she was returning once more to the other kind of punishment, the emotional and mental murder. Her independent self began to crumble as she found herself once again at the mercy of her vulnerability. She felt a quick impulse to flee, but was helpless against the undertow of her conditioning.

Her friend had become her husband, and he wanted revenge.

FIST FUCKER

AT THE AGE of seven, Carl was taken into the old man's house, and after proper softening with ice cream, comic books, and discreet caressing, seemed to have no objection to holding the wrinkled penis in his mouth. He sucked it until it was hard, and when the sperm was plunked on his tongue, he tasted it ingenuously, not knowing that what had just happened would raise the unbridled fury of the caretakers of the world's official attitudes.

Ironically, the old man was a retired judge, and Carl's parents were pleased that their son should spend time in what they thought was an educational atmosphere. Until he was nine, Carl visited on the average of once a week, until his taste for the experience began to exceed the old man's ability to provide it. After his somber initiation into the realm of sex, he went in search of others.

His understanding of the role of sex in society was rudimentary and inchoate. Beyond the judge's admonitions that he must never speak about what they did except to tell his parents that the nice old neighbor had read to him and given him cookies to eat, he had no grasp of the hysteria which such simple behavior as cocksucking engendered. Yet, with animal instinct, when he began his forays into the wider world, he knew to seduce only those who he sensed were willing to be had.

By the age of twelve, Carl had thrilled scores of men with his surprising eagerness to service their unspoken desires. He developed a way of standing, of looking, which set up the necessary vibrations between himself and available provender. Playing with his schoolmates, he would often disappear for an hour and prowl strange streets, finding what he wanted, and consummating his quest in hallways or cellars or the back seats of cars.

Carl knew no genital excitement himself, and was somewhat perplexed that his ministrations would bring grown men to tears.

The gasps and moans which showered his ears as his delicate child's mouth would cover a cock and his tongue tingle intricate patterns over a thigh he appreciated only through empathy. What he did seemed to make others happy, and that was gratification enough.

He was first anally penetrated at the age of fourteen one summer afternoon. He was hitchhiking through the Long Island suburbs, sizing up the men who stopped for him, and either proceeding with them to a secluded space or perceiving rapidly that there was nothing to be had from that particular person. When the huge trailer stopped, the boy was taken with an unusual premonition that set him shivering. As he climbed into the cab, he was overwhelmed with an impression of muscular thighs and calloused hands. The man glanced at him once and seemed to know what Carl wanted before he even made an overture. He took the truck to a rest stop and led the boy into the back, where an entire household of furniture was stacked and being moved from South Carolina to Wyoming. It belonged to a nuclear physicist who, sickened at the corruption within the Atomic Energy Commission, had decided to become a sheep rancher.

The man pushed Carl onto a couch and stood over him, his cock straining against his pants. With expert fingers, the lad pulled the zipper down. Gently, he tugged the thickly veined tool out, and with a flutter of his eyelids, took it between his lips. He sucked for a long time, his thin young body gradually working up to a feverish pitch, tossing to and fro as he worked on the huge organ. Then, to his surprise, the man pulled back.

"Get on your stomach," the driver commanded.

Carl lay down, uncertain as to what would happen next. The man yanked his pants down, pulling them over his legs and past his feet, until the boy was naked below the waist, his slim virginal buttocks gleaming in the dull light. The man spit on his fingers and thrust them into the tiny anus, lubricating it slightly. Without a wasted gesture, he lowered his bulk onto the child and thrust his cock into the puckered opening.

A bolt of pain shot through the boy and he gasped for breath. But hot upon the pain came a flash of sweet burning, a tender yielding that brought tears to his eyes. Grunting and huffing, the truck driver fucked the boy a long time, putting him in a dozen different positions, maneuvering the small body with ease, using his brawny arms to arrange the slender limbs in the most open poses, and then bursting in with all the power and force he could manage.

He came as the boy knelt over the arm of the couch, his buttocks raised, his legs dangling, and himself crouching behind, half raised on his toes, his heels pressed into a chest-of-drawers for leverage. As he bucked into orgasm, he drove ruthlessly into the boy's bowels and lifted him half a foot into the air.

Not long after that, Carl left home. He had already begun to see that the semi-conscious world of home and school was a restricting and artificial facade imposed over the true facts of life. He was developing a wisdom which transcended the artifacts of conventional knowledge, and he could no longer pretend to possess the naiveté and immaturity expected of someone his age.

He went to San Francisco, where he discovered the baths. Because of his youth, his good looks, and his unbounded willingness to please, he soon became a favorite in gay circles. One night he was spotted by a faded millionaire who offered to house him with the others in the harem he had built in an effort to pique a glutted appetite. Carl accepted, and within a short time ascended to the status of superstar.

But none of this seemed to affect his basic humility, and his unabashed desire to provide sexual pleasure for others. By seventeen, he was a virtuoso in the art of passive homosexual performance, and highly skilled in all the nuances of surrender. His patron grew proud, and then jealous, of his charge, and forbade him to have contact with anyone but himself.

Soon after, he left the mansion, and on his way along a highway, accepted a ride from a bestial looking motorcycle rider who took him to his camp, where several dozen others lounged in snarling lassitude. The boy was thrown to them the way meat is thrown to lions in a zoo, and for several days he served as a slave to their every whim, catering to their surly need for stimulation.

On the fourth day, lying over a pile of sleeping bags, having been fucked by twelve men in succession, he was initiated into the form that he had been unconsciously evolving toward for his entire life. The leader of the pack, kneeling behind him, placed his bunched fist between Carl's buttocks. The boy gasped, and then relaxed, and the huge curled hand pressed tightly against his asshole. Slowly, he gave way, and the fist entered the hot opening. The universe seemed to crash about Carl's head as the man behind him continued to push, engulfing his hand, his wrist, and then his whole forearm up to the elbow. At that point, he stopped, and with a deliberate motion, flexed his entire arm, filling the pulsing channel completely with hard bulging muscle.

Carl smiled in ecstasy. After a decade of service, he felt he was finally being satisfied.

He continued drifting from adventure to adventure until one morning an eerie mood enveloped him. He was walking down a street and as he looked at the faces of the people who passed, he realized they were all asleep. He saw that, through his peculiar metamorphosis, he had become an utterly superior human being. By virtue of having lived in the realm of excess, where others were too fearful to venture, he had attained a depth of awareness that set him apart from the human herd.

Not intrinsically cerebral, and his formal education having ended early, he was not able to articulate the insight with any degree of precision. But as the bright western sun sparkled in his eyes, something like a religious revelation exploded in his brain. If it is true that a person who masters any one thing has mastered all of life itself, then he was a realized human being, for he had become an emperor of perversion.

Thereafter he wandered the country like a ghost. Men would encounter him and tell their friends of an apparition of startling beauty, who sucked cock and allowed himself to be laid and gave a pleasure that went deeper than the sexual, that ultimately soothed the soul. And if asked what he wanted in return, he would say simply, "Fist-fuck me, please," and would lie in rapture as the clenched hand went deeper and deeper into his entrails.

There is a photo of him, the only one in existence, in which he is suspended from a wooden crossbeam. He is shown being lowered onto two men, each of whom has one arm, up to the elbow, buried in his ass at the same time. The boy's eyes are closed, so it is impossible to tell what he is thinking. His face is in repose, and his body is in a state of complete relaxation. A Buddhist monk, seeing the picture, was heard to exclaim, "That is a man who has attained Nirvana."

He was found dead, at the age of twenty-four, wrapped in a mattress in a ravine outside of Los Angeles. No one knew his name or where he had come from, so he was buried in a public field. His life had been a total and selfless giving to others, and he was not known to have sought anything for himself, except the

blissful trance state which occurred whenever he was lovingly fist
fucked.

Several of the members of Troy Perry's Gay Church subsequently
began an official movement to have him proclaimed as their
first saint.

NICOLE

William T. Vollmann

THE NEXT THING Jimmy knew, he was on the street and it was dark and he was whore-hunting. He saw women dancing on the sidewalk; he was sure that they offered both acute and obtuse triangles; but they would not go to his hotel and he did not want to go to theirs because he did not like to feel trapped at the same time that he felt dizzy. – How fine the moonlight was, though! It made him retch. – He saw a whore leaning against the side of a reflective building, waggling her skinny knees although her high heels and her butt did not move and her head was cocked against her shoulder so that she could watch men out of the corner of her stupid little eyes. She said doll you want a date? and Jimmy said thank *you* for the offer but tell you the truth I'm looking for my friend Gloria you know the one with the big tits? – Oh that's just an *excuse*! sneered the whore, at which Jimmy cocked his head very wisely and said I never excuse myself except when I burp. Do you ever burp? Gloria doesn't. – Oh Christ, said the whore, who was as slender and unwholesome looking as a snake, and she stalked around the corner, heels clacking angrily. – Next he had several offers from a pimp who said he *knew* Jimmy would be satisfied, so Jimmy looked as dumb as he could and said wow pal sounds like a good one and you'll never believe this but I left all my money back at my hotel. – Don'tcha even have twenty on ya? said the pimp. – Jimmy said don't I wish but God's truth is

I got one hundred two hundred dollars back home in fact I got *lots* of money in fact I think I may even be a *millionaire*, so bring her by pal I only live two hours away from here what do you say? – When the pimp heard that, he didn't even bother to answer. He crossed the street, shaking his head, and Jimmy stood leaning up against a wall and laughing inside himself with snotty little gurgles like a bottle of Scotch pouring down the toilet. Finally he found a whore who would go with him. He looked around to make sure that the pimp wasn't watching and showed her forty dollars. Her name was Nicole, and she looked rather more than young, twenty-five maybe and strung-out, but not sharp and hard like a piece of broken glass, only used up like a dirty eraser, so he figured she would be OK with her lank hair curling around her ears and her ear-rings of white plastic pearls, so he said Well come on and Nicole looked at him tiredly with her skin stretched dry and tight across her forehead and Jimmy said Nicole your blue eyeliner's smeared you should fix it if you want to stay beautiful and Nicole rubbed her forehead and said she had a headache. He said well come *on* baby come with me then you can buy yourself a painkiller.

I don't usually go to the man's place, Nicole said. You promise you won't hurt me?

I promise, Jimmy said. If I wanted to hurt you, he explained to her very logically, you couldn't get away from me anyway.

That's not true, said Nicole. I could kill you easy.

Well see, said Jimmy grandly, you have nothing to worry about. You can kill me easy, so why be nervous?

He took her up the street and she kept asking how far it was. Three more blocks, said Jimmy. The light glowed in her hair.

The first thing she asked to do was use the bathroom. He heard her shit. I suppose she must be nervous, he said to himself. Jimmy had once been a reader, so he knew how in Auschwitz or Treblinka there was a ramp leading up to the gas chambers called the Road to Heaven where all the women had to wait naked and squatting while the men were finished being gassed (they went first because they did not need to have their hair cut off for the submarine crews), and while the sheared women waited they usually emptied their bowels and the guards laughed and laughed like hooded pimps in an alley and now history repeated itself as Jimmy stood nipping on a fresh beer and waiting for Nicole to complete the preparations for her little ordeal. Well, he said to himself, *I* can't help it if she's nervous. She's got a job to do.

Silently he said Gloria, are you still there? Gloria?

When Nicole came into the kitchen she was naked except for her red shirt. – You want a half-and-half? she said.

Sure, Jimmy said.

Will you *take care of me* first? she said smiling; her face glowed, she seemed so sweet like Gloria.

Sure I will, he said, what do you want me to do? (He thought she meant for him to jerk her off or otherwise *affect* her. He sometimes liked to fool himself.)

Will you pay me first? Nicole said patiently.

Oh fine, Jimmy said. He got the forty dollars out of his wallet and gave it to her.

Then Nicole sat down on the chair in the kitchen and took his penis in her hand and he saw how her arms were discolored everywhere with abscesses and needle tracks and he leaned forward a little so that Nicole could put his penis into her mouth and she began to suck at it smoothly, rapidly and Jimmy looked down at the top of her head and wondered if her eyes were open or closed and then he looked at the wall and watched a cockroach crawling down between the gas pipe and the sink, and he listened to the noises that her lips made sucking his penis, and he listened to the loud ticking of her cheap plastic watch. Jimmy was not thinking about anything in particular, but his penis began to get hard right away. As soon as it was entirely stiff like some dead thing, she took it out of her mouth and rolled a rubber onto it with her lined and grimy hands. – Now take your shirt off, Jimmy said. – He stepped back from her and dropped his clothes to the floor. Nicole sat wearily on the chair, rubbing her forehead. When she pulled her shirt over her head he saw that she had a cast on her left wrist. Her breasts were big and sad like owls' eyes.

You want my coat for a pillow? said Jimmy.

Nicole shook her head.

All right then, he said, get down on the floor.

The kitchen floor was black with dirt. Nicole lay down on it and raised her legs to make her cunt so nice and tight for him, and Jimmy stood over her watching the groping of those legs, which were speckled with boils and lesions, until her left ankle came to rest on the chair that she had sat on, while the sole of her right foot had to be content with bracing itself against Jimmy's refrigerator. Her breasts lay limp on her belly, as round as the faces of polished brass pendulums of clocks. Jimmy stood enjoying her for another moment, liking the way she looked as she lay there between the refrigerator and the wall, brown-skinned and almost pretty, with a white plastic cross between her tits.

Are you Catholic? he said.

Yes, Nicole said.

Jimmy strode around naked except for his socks, inspecting her cunt like an emperor. This was the best part. Nicole gazed up at him and pulled the lips of her slit taut and up to show him the ragged pear of pinkness inside, and her cunt-lips glistened under the kitchen lights with the brightness of metal foil. – Your pussy is just like a flower,* Jimmy complimented her; all the same he did not want to get his face too close to it. He got down on his knees; he leaned his weight on his arms as if he were doing push-ups (for Jimmy was always a gentleman who would not hurt a woman with his weight); then he stuck his penis into her. She had told him that he was her first date of the night, but her cunt seemed to be full of something viscous like come or corn syrup. Maybe it was just the lubricant she used. Anyhow, it stank. She had great black spots on her thighs that might have been moles or more probably the subcutaneous hemorrhages of Kaposi's syndrome as Jimmy well knew from his profoundly intellectual studies. Every time he thrust into her she grunted. He could not tell whether this was because he hurt her or because she did it to excite him and so get it over with faster. He did not feel that she hated him and her body was trying to expel him; more probably she just endured him and trusted to the frictionlessness of the corn syrup or whatever it was to protect her from being hurt by his thrusts (in direct proportion as *his* sensation was diminished), but the corn syrup did not much work anymore to soothe that red raw-rubbed meat between her legs, so Nicole just tried not to think about what was happening and grunted at Jimmy's every painful thrust and bit her lips whenever he grazed an ovary. She gripped his balls tightly all the time so that the

---

* "I still remember the effect I produced on a small group of Gala tribesmen massed around a man in black clothes," wrote Vittorio Mussolini. "I dropped an aerial torpedo right in the center and the group opened up like a flowering rose. It was most entertaining."

rubber wouldn't slip; she dug her fingernails into his balls, either by mistake or to make him come. But after thirty seconds Jimmy knew that he wasn't going to be able to come. Maybe if she'd just sucked him off he could have done it, but what with the rubber and the stuff in her cunt he couldn't feel much. Jimmy fucked and fucked until he got bored and then told her that he was done. – Call me, he said politely. – Later his prick started to itch, and he worried about disease.

MISSING THE BOAT

Elissa Wald

"I WANT TO play a game." These were my words, sly and reckless. It was a rainy night and I wanted something to happen.

"What kind of game?" Samantha – everyone called her Sam – asked. She and Sean were looking at me with interest.

"A sex game that will fuck up our friendship," I said, and laughed.

Maybe I was feeling this way because Sam had stayed too long. She was visiting New York and had been with me for over a week, so that I hadn't slept with Sean in all that time. But of course that wasn't all of it, there was more to it than just that.

Sam was the big brother I never had. I was eight and she was nine when I moved to her town, and she already owned the block. Back then she was a lean little tomboy – everyone thought she was a boy on sight – taller than me then, tougher, headstrong and bossy. She alternated between bullying me and protecting me, and I was in love with her.

She'd become a strange woman. Adolescence had stripped her of authority; puberty had distorted her image. No one would mistake her for a boy now. She's heavy, full-breasted, though she still keeps her honey-coloured hair cut short. She's quieter now, with the quiet of a trapped animal: careful, watchful, as if waiting for an escape to present itself. Still, I always have the feeling that the nine-year-old

Sam is inside her somewhere. And so I'm still a little afraid of her, and accord her the same skittish respect.

On the other hand, I had only known Sean for six months. I met him when I joined his karate class early in the fall. This visit gave Sam the chance to meet him, though I had told her all about him long before. To my surprise, they hit it off immediately, and better than I ever would have guessed. She even went down to his office one day while I was in school – I was taking classes part-time at NYU – and met him for lunch. I knew they had to be talking about me at least part of the time, and I wondered what she was telling him.

I had decided to take karate because I wanted to meet a martial arts master. And I was amazed to find, at the head of the first class I looked into, an almost exact replica of what I'd dreamed up. Sean might have been a Marine or a Navy Seal: just under six feet tall, hard and compact, with light brown hair buzzed to within an inch and cold blue eyes. His face habitually wore a grim expression: white-lipped, tight-lipped, severe.

He proved to be a good teacher, methodical and thorough. And he had the kind of presence I always imagined a karate instructor should have: commanding, close-mouthed, with an air of keeping plenty of contemptuous judgements to himself. The members of his class treated him with something like reverence. Within minutes I decided to put my money down, and signed up for six months.

I loved the *dojo*, which was actually a dancers' studio for most of the week. Even for an outsider, to cross that threshold was to step into another atmosphere, hushed and strange. The acoustics were like those of a temple: voices echoed, the air was charged with diligence. A hollow stillness enveloped the sound of bare feet on the wooden floor.

Sean ran a tight ship. His rules were simple and inflexible. Shoes had to be removed before entering the room, even if one was only visiting. Students who arrived early helped to mop the floor. Those who dared to come in late were to kneel at the back of the room until Sean acknowledged them formally, which he did with a nod in their direction and a single clap of his hands. The latecomers were then to bow, touching their foreheads briefly to the floor, before getting up to begin their stretches.

Sean didn't make up these rules. They're the standard rituals of

Shotokan etiquette which he himself obeyed, along with his fellow black belts, in his own master's classroom. Still, it was a thrill to see him enforce them, and I could never decide whether it was better to be early or late. I loved mopping the floor barefoot and in silence: head down, humble, a ship hand swabbing the deck. I loved wringing out the grey water, and leaving wide, shining arcs on the amber wood. But coming late might have been more exciting still. To slip to the back of the room and go to my knees. To lower my eyes, assuming a chastened, almost fearful, expression. To hold perfectly still, waiting for pardon. The longer Sean took to release me – the longer I knelt – the better. And then the signal clap like the crack of a short whip in the quiet, to which I would bend forward, put my forehead (and secretly my lips) against the floorboards.

Sometimes I thought he took longer to acknowledge me than he did anyone else. Watching him from beneath lowered eyelids, I thought he looked at me many times before clapping. Was it possible that he liked having me there, and in that position? The idea aroused me nearly to the point of pain.

For two months I lived for the Tuesday and Thursday evening classes where I flustered, stumbled, and temporarily lost the ability to tell left from right. It was an infatuation that literally kept me awake at night, staring into the dark, touching myself with a practiced hand and calling his image to my aid. I felt he was someone with whom there could never really be an equal relationship. I dreamed I could serve him; that he might allow this, even look for it. I never expected him to fall in love with me.

I remember the feeling of those nights, before he was mine. Emerging from the subway, across the street from the second-story classroom. It was dark and chilly out, but the light was always on in that window, and it seemed to emanate heat as well. Sometimes on my way in, with the other beginners, I'd overhear conversation about the impending class: rueful jokes, ironic despair, bruises being compared. I felt wholly outside these sentiments. I wasn't afraid of being hit or thrown. The blows absorbed by my body were part of a natural order; I took them as my due, as a weaker wolf will offer its throat to a stronger one in battle. To me, the *dojo* was the warmest, the safest haven; it held an inviolate hierarchy, with everything – everyone – in place. I couldn't wait to get there, and I was never ready to leave.

Sean asked me out on the last night of November. The karate class went out for pizza and beer on the last Thursday of each month; this was the second such outing since I'd joined. I was seated directly across from Sean and could barely eat. My skin tingled with longing and it was hard to swallow.

Afterward everyone crowded out to the sidewalk and milled around for a few minutes before taking their leave. I made small talk with several people, watching Sean out of the corner of my eye. Soon only he and I were left.

I made myself look straight at him. "I have so much work to do tonight," I said. "I hate the thought of going home."

"Been putting it off, huh?" he said.

"That's right," I said. "And I'd like to keep putting it off."

There was a light snow. Now, I thought. Now. Please.

"Well, you want to go get a cup of coffee?" he asked.

"I'd love to," I said. He hadn't smiled; I didn't either.

We went to a little Spanish dive. He liked his coffee strong, preferably Colombian; I made a mental note of this. It came; he drank it black, and then relaxed for the first time before my very eyes.

He did nearly all the talking, which shattered the cold, silent image I'd been nurturing all those weeks. He was easy-going, humorous, even gregarious, holding forth on a number of topics, including New York real estate, corruption in publishing, and all things political – he read at least three different papers every day. I held my cup of coffee in both hands for warmth and looked into his eyes. He was a regular guy. I felt the porcelain cool beneath my fingertips.

Dinner the following Saturday found him much the same. He liked me. I could see that he really liked me. And it was no longer impossible to believe. We'd eaten near my apartment and afterward he walked me home. I didn't invite him up. I didn't kiss him goodbye.

By Tuesday night, I was overwhelmed with schoolwork. I decided to sacrifice karate to do it. I had tentative plans with Sean after class, but I was ready to let them go as well. I made this decision on the street outside the *dojo*. The class wouldn't be starting for another few minutes; I decided to stop in quickly and let him know.

Sean was unlocking the broom closet when I walked in. I went right up to him.

"Sean."

He turned. "What are you doing in here with shoes? Take them off."

"I'm not staying," I protested. "I just wanted to talk to you a second."

"I don't care," he said. "Go back out and take them off."

Face burning, I retreated to the hall. Outside the door, I considered just leaving, bolting for home. Why had Sean been so cold? Had I offended him? I peered through the window. He was handing out mops. Apparently, I was the last thing on his mind.

I removed my shoes. My body was trembling for some reason. Had we really gone for coffee? Had dinner? Or was it only my imagination? I crept back into the room and stood timidly nearby as he advised a student about a swollen knee. It took a few minutes for him to notice me again.

"Oh, Cecilia. What did you want?"

"I, um – " I said. "I came to tell you I can't attend class tonight. Both of my final exams are this week."

He looked at me without any expression. It was the most awkward moment I'd ever experienced in that room.

"Fine," he said at last, as if wondering what the point was.

"But if you still want to get together later," I added in a rush, "I'm sure I'll have time to take a break. You could come by my apartment. I'd really like it if you would."

I was to see that it would always be this way. He was one man in the classroom, another out of it, and this sustained my attraction. I was gratified to see there was a part of him I'd never be able to touch.

I was comfortable with him before long. I stopped cleaning the apartment for his visits and no longer changed the sheets each time. I let him see me in my glasses and ratty old sweatshirts. In the beginning I liked to cook him time-consuming and exotic dinners; now I was more likely to make spaghetti. But in karate class, I still looked at him and couldn't believe he could belong to anyone, let alone me.

The other place I remained in awe of him was the bedroom – in the bedroom games that started right away. I pulled him into

them, but he knew instinctively how to play. I could give him the
briefest sketch of a fantasy, and he would pick it right up and run.
We created roles and inhabited them for a few hours.

   Once I called him at work. "Guess what I just did?"

   He sounded amused. "What did you just do?"

   "I wrote a personal ad. Just for myself, just for fun. I wanted
to see if I could do it – say who I am and what I want in around
forty words. I mean, of course what I wrote is just a fantasy. But
I had fun putting it down."

   "Well let's hear it," he said.

   I looked down at my notebook and read into the phone:

> Housegirl position sought.
> Vagabond wants to come home.
> SWF, wandering Jewess, charming
> waif, love slave will cook, clean, and
> entertain master of the house for
> room and board. I'll be your muse,
> masseuse, and charlotte russe.
> Take me in? Serious replies only.

   "I like that," Sean said. "Listen though, I have a meeting, have
to run."

   I hung up feeling vaguely let down.

   Half an hour later, the phone rang.

   "Hello?"

   "I'm responding to your ad in the paper," said a male voice.
There was no laughter in the tone, no irony. I knew it was Sean,
but my heart started to pound.

   "Yes, sir," I said.

   "I'd like to interview you for the position you're seeking, tonight
if possible."

   "Tonight is fine."

   "I'd like it to be on the late side. I have a lot going on
right now."

   "Anytime, sir. Your convenience."

   "I'll see you at ten o'clock then. Be on time." And he gave me
his address, as if I didn't know it.

   I arrived at his apartment that night in a blouse and skirt from the
Salvation Army. He answered the door in a sharply pressed white

Oxford shirt and dark trousers. Silver cufflinks were fastened at his wrists.

"Come in," he said. I followed him into the dining room where he indicated I should sit at the table. He sat at the head and I took the chair to his left.

"I'm Sean Cafferty," he said. "And you are?"

"Cecilia Fox, sir."

"How old are you, Cecilia?"

"I'm twenty-one."

"You're seeking a live-in position here with me?"

"Yes, sir."

"Where are you living right now?"

"I'm at the Ninety-fourth Street youth hostel. But my money's running out."

"I see. And before that?"

"I was with the circus."

"The circus," he replied. "And what were you doing there?"

"I groomed the cats, sir."

"The cats."

"There were two lions, five tigers and an albino leopard," I told him.

"All right. And your reason for leaving?"

"Unwelcome advances by the ringmaster, sir."

I watched him fight back a smile.

"Well, I'll explain my situation to you. I'm a busy man. I don't have a lot of time for housework. I need someone to pick up the slack for me, someone who'll do what has to be done without being told and make herself scarce when I need some space."

"I can do that. Sir."

"For instance, right now," he said. "What do you think needs to be done around here?"

I looked around the apartment. "I think the dishes need to be done, the floor has to be swept, and that you could use a Sloe Screw Against The Wall."

There was a blank pause. Then: "That's a drink," I added.

"Why don't we consider this evening a trial period," he suggested. "And let's see what happens. You can start right now."

I stood rather shakily. I was actually quite nervous as I went to the liquor cabinet and mixed this man a drink. I brought it to him in his armchair where he'd started to read one of the several papers he'd brought home. Then I found a broom.

It was calming to sweep. I found a rhythm and peace in it. I liked this apartment; I could see how it would be nice to land here after being rootless, adrift in the dead of winter. I was careful, fastidious; I evacuated the dust from every corner, angled the broom under each piece of furniture. And finally as I stood wreathed in steam, arms plunged into suds at the kitchen sink, I felt him come up behind me.

"Don't let me interrupt you," he said, and put a hand against the nape of my neck. I continued rinsing dinner plates and cutlery while he ran a possessive hand up the inside of my thigh. By the time the sink was cleared and the drying rack stacked, my underwear had been eased down several inches and he was penetrating me slightly, easily, with his fingertips. I was wet.

"Don't turn around," he said quietly into my ear.

"No sir," I murmured.

"Hold onto the edge of the sink."

I clasped the rim with both hands and closed my eyes.

"Little runaway," he chuckled. "Fleeing the evil ringmaster." I felt his lips against the back of my neck. "Are my advances . . . unwelcome . . . to you?"

"No sir," I whimpered.

"No? Tell me. Are they welcome? More than welcome, even?"

"Yes, sir . . . please."

"Please what?"

"Please, sir."

"Please, sir, what?"

"Please! Sir."

Still holding my neck, he bent me further over the sink and took me that way. I came before he did, came harder than I ever had before, and was hired on the spot. I slept that night across the foot of his bed.

We played out such scenes all the time. Sean understood the inevitable link for me between sex and submission, and was glad to oblige. He liked to hit, knew how hard to hit, and how many times. He knew how to secure a blindfold and tie a good knot. He understood what I wanted, which had little to do with pain and everything to do with mastery.

Our relationship was held together by sex. Usually when a relationship is described as mostly sexual, what's implied is "animal". Carnal. Not to be taken seriously. I have never understood this dismissal. Sex is, after all, a partnership – a recognition, communion – as legitimate as any other, and as essential.

The three of us – Sean, Sam, and I – were together nearly all week. Sam and I spent much of the time reminiscing out loud, as we liked to do whenever we got together, boring anyone else around us with a dozen years' worth of escapades. Sean, though, was attentive to every word, concentrated and serious, particularly when Sam had the floor. It was as if he were trying to glean something from her, something he needed.

"Cecy was such a *good* girl," Sam told him, with remembered distaste. "I *hated* her."

"Cecilia? A good girl?" Sean said. "I can't imagine it."

"Oh, please. Too good to be true," Sam said. "I was too rough for her. Too wild. Too filthy a mouth."

It was true. I had become friends with Sam more from a process of elimination than anything else. We both stood out in my new neighborhood, which was full of little rich girls, all of whom had their own phones and color TVs and canopy beds and designer jeans. I had never heard of designer clothing, and the idea of having my own television or phone was as incomprehensible to me as having my own house.

Sam lived two doors down from me. She was as much of an outcast on our streets as I was, because while all the other girls were playing with the new Barbie and Ken Condominium, Sam was up in a tree, or racing dirt bikes with the neighborhood boys. Her mother made her come over to meet me the day I moved in. I was in my room, sitting on the floor, playing with my new printing set and trying not to cry. I missed my old friends already and wanted to go back to Baltimore.

"This is Sam," my mother informed me. "She's going to take you to the park to meet some of the neighborhood kids." I was being delivered. My mother had never before spoken of another child as "taking me" anywhere. It was always *she* who had taken *us* places. This left me with some slight and unidentifiable panic.

"What are you doing?" Sam asked me after my mother had left the room.

"Making a newspaper," I answered.

She looked at me, then at my reams of paper; the stamp pad of black ink, and the rubber letters spread out on the rug. "What kind of fucking baby-toy is that?"

I stared at her in distaste. "Are you allowed to cuss?"

"Cuss? What's 'cuss'?" she demanded.

"You know. Like the f-word," I answered, thinking that she wanted me to trip up and say it.

"The *f-word?*" The f-word! You mean *swear?*"

But maybe because she didn't have another girl on the block for a friend, or maybe because I didn't own a single doll, she continued, grudgingly, to come over for the rest of the summer.

I accepted her company and her rule the way I accepted Mondays and Fridays, with the sense that these things were inescapable but not entirely lacking in promise. She was rugged, fierce, perpetually grass-stained. Dark blonde hair tumbled over her eyes, one of which was blue, the other brown. She came over nearly every afternoon, usually around four, for lack of anything better to do while her friends were doing their paper routes. She showed me around, taught me short cuts and good alleys for smoking and which stores were safest to steal candy from (not that I would ever have done these things, but I was learning not to say so). She always came to my house, I never went to hers. We made and consumed endless peanut butter and jelly sandwiches, washed them down with tall glasses of cold chocolate milk. I tagged along with her to the baseball diamond where there were heated games. Sometimes she would let me on her team, though I was never an asset. She liked my little brother, who was a year and a half younger than me, and often insisted to my dismay that we take him places.

We had two favorite activities. One was making a tent in Joey's – my brother's – room: an elaborate enclosure making use of all the blankets in the house. To enter it from outside, you had to crack open the bedroom door and crawl in on your hands and knees. This was particularly satisfying on rainy days, since we couldn't go outside anyway, and a storm added to the feeling of sheltering ourselves against the ominous. Our other favorite activity was simply called "Boat". It was a pretending game like "House" only we were on a ship instead. This always took place in my attic. We had seen the television movie, "Orphan Train", the night before this game was conceived, and we had adapted it, I'm not sure why, for a boat. My brother and I were the orphans and Sam was the captain, transporting us across the ocean to foster homes. En route, however, she, who was actually a "he", would decide to adopt us. (In any pretend game we ever concocted, Sam played a male and I, a female). The guest bed was her cabin. I got the sofa, and Joey got the walk-in closet. His role was always an innocent one; he was the good kid. I was the troublemaker to whom Sam had to lay down the law. When I stepped too far out of line, she would push me against the wall and take off her belt. Joey always pleaded for me but it was no use. She would crack the belt against the wall and I would pretend to cry. Occasionally, as if by accident, the leather would really meet the back of my legs, and whenever it did, I would fall silent, hold breathlessly still. This game left telltale black marks on the wall's white paint. Last time I was in that house, in December for the holidays, I went up to the attic to study and saw that they were still there.

"Your ass is mine. Boy." This was Sean's voice, affecting a Southern accent and soft in my ear. Sam was out – finally! – visiting some distant aunt to whom she'd promised an afternoon. Sean and I were alone at long last and I was getting my fix.

"Now this is your first day in the joint," he continued. "Maybe that's been enough time for you to see how it is around here, and maybe not. But a pretty boy like you ain't gonna last long without protection. You know what I'm sayin' to you?"

"Yes," I whispered. "Sir."

"Well you catch on nice and quick. You're gonna want to keep callin' me sir."

"Yes sir."

"Cause I ain't gonna take no disrespect. You got that? Now I'm gonna spell out the situation here." A pause while he took a fistful of my hair. "I been here five years now. I am the boss here. As far as you're concerned I'm the boss everywhere. In the cell, out of the cell. You do what I tell you."

"All right. Sir."

"That means you make up both these bunks every day, do my laundry when you do yours, and anythin' you get from the outside – cigarettes, stamps, whatever – it all goes straight to me. And there'll be other ways you'll be takin' care of me besides. Do you understand what I'm tellin' you boy?"

I was thrust onto my stomach, the men's boxer shorts I'd borrowed from Sean jerked down. No one had ever fucked my ass before him, but I was liking it more and more.

"Yes, I do, sir. I do understand."

"Good. 'Cause it been a long time – too long a time – since I laid eyes on a woman, and there ain't no point in thinkin' about how much longer it gonna be." His hand was on me now, smearing Vaseline. My breathing came hard and quick. "A man be somewhere for five, six, seven years, he gotta fuck somethin' or go out of his mind. Do you understand that, boy?"

"I understand sir." My voice low. He penetrated slowly, cleaving me inch by careful inch. It almost didn't hurt anymore. I whimpered partly in pleasure, partly in fear, then pleasure took over and I cried out involuntarily with each thrust. At these moments it was so easy to lose myself, to listen to my own cries as if to some intriguing and foreign orchestra.

"Oh, yeah?" Sean's tone went up in amused surprise. "Yeah? Is that right? Have I got myself a little faggot in here with me? Well what do you know?"

I was always fascinated with incarceration. I seized the opportunity to try it out in many childhood games. I loved being in "jail" in "Capture the Flag" – even though it just meant sitting under a tree, apart from the action. I even liked landing in jail in Monopoly, just enjoyed the fact of my little metal iron or shoe stuck in that box where a crudely drawn man clutched the bars.

Sam and I played a game where she was a motorcycle cop like in "CHiPs". This involved the forbidden use of an abandoned and near-dead little moped she'd found in a back alley. As a captured criminal I was forced onto the back and had to endure a few uncertain spins around the block before ending up in her backyard. Beside her garage there was a tall wooden shed where her family stashed the trash until garbage night. A sliding bolt locked it from the outside.

Inside there were metal trash cans and a cool cement floor. If I stood on tiptoe atop the aluminium lids, I could just see over the shed walls. Usually I was only imprisoned for about two minutes; there wasn't a whole lot for either of us to do while I was inside.

One fall afternoon, though, I remember hearing the bolt slide into place and suddenly knew the game was going to take a turn.

I stood for a moment pretending not to know. Everything within the shed was the same as always: solitary, silent, the interior slightly darker and chillier than the outside. I strained to see Sam between the slats of wood. She wore a strange expression, satisfied and glinting.

Time slowed as in a dream, each moment widening to contain a world. My skin prickled and all my senses were heightened. I could feel Sam through the wall as I hadn't been able to before in the open air. Sam was jealous because I could read twice as fast as her, and play the piano. She both loved and hated me for being a girly girl, for wearing dresses and having long hair and getting good report cards.

I clambered onto a trash can and peered over the shed wall.

"Sam?"

She was disappearing into a garage. I waited. In a minute, she emerged with a basketball under her arm.

"Sam," I tried again.

"You have the right to remain silent," she said, without really looking at me.

"When are you going to let me out?"

"When I'm ready." She set the ball to spinning on her index finger, a trick she was very proud of. "Maybe never," she added.

The top of the shed wall was very sharp, each wooden slat ending in a point. The structure was too thin to support any weight, and I was in no position to vault over, even if I dared. I lowered myself back down to the ground and resumed my position at the spyhole. Sam began practicing lay-ups against the backboard in her driveway.

I was surrounded on all sides yet I could till see the sky. My cell was cement- and wood-colored, but the ceiling was open and blue. I was quiet, taking in these details, marking the rhythm of Sam's basketball from within my prison. Panic was still at bay.

I didn't question why I was here. It was inevitable – hadn't I known it was coming almost before it happened? I was smaller and weaker and more than occasionally insufferable. What was unclear was how I was to appease her. Did she want me to beg, or would stoicism please her more? I didn't know.

Sam turned suddenly, without warning, hurling the basketball in my direction. I recoiled an instant before it crashed against precisely the part of the wall I'd been looking through. The entire structure trembled from the impact. I got the message: she didn't want me watching her. I just wondered how she knew.

I took a new position against the part of the wall farthest away from her, sitting with my knees drawn up, and studied the pattern of nail heads in the wood. All kinds of constellations were possible, depending on how you connected the dots.

What do dogs think about, chained in the yards?

Long minutes went by. The basketball pounded the concrete and swished in the net. I curled into myself and tried to fathom my transgressions. Sam and I had each been given a pair of grey mice by a boy up the street; I'd been allowed to keep mine, but Sam hadn't. We'd begun Hebrew school together some months ago, and I was already way ahead. In kickball the evening before, when our team already had two outs, Sam was on the third base when I kicked the ball straight to the pitcher.

I ascended the garbage can once again. "Sam?"

Silence. Scorn.

"Sam, what did I do?"

She spat in the dust.

"Say something," I begged her.

"Something," she said.

"Come on, Sam."

"Come on what?"

"I'll give you my Halloween candy," I said, thinking of how it irritated her that I'd saved it so long, eating a piece a day for weeks on end, my pink pillowcase still half full.

She spat again, like the ballplayers on TV. "I don't want a thing you've got."

Just then a fleet of dirt bikes, bearing five or six of the neighborhood boys, skidded into the backyard.

"Hey, Sam!"

She turned; I ducked. I felt it was important not to be seen.

I heard Vance DiCapriati, the leader of the pack, summoning her. "We're chicken racing Homestead down at the Birmingham Bridge. You comin'?" Homestead was a bordering neighborhood and the Birmingham Bridge spanned a steep ravine which the most daring kids negotiated on bicycles. Sam had braved it many times before. I would have loved to have gone along to watch, as I often did. It was with a fierce and possessive pride that I watched her descend amid clouds of dust into the canyon. I was usually the only onlooker who knew she was a girl.

I heard Sam get on her bike and leave with them.

It was late in the afternoon on a Thursday. I had homework I couldn't start, and there was a test the next day too. Evening would be falling in another half an hour; it would be dark. I wished I had my school books, wished in fact that I had any book. I wished I had a heavier coat. Already the temperature was dropping with the sun.

I sat, alone and shivering, and listened to the sounds of freedom around me. Shreds of conversation drifted over the fence; there was a rhythm of a hammer against some rooftop and trees rustling in the wind. I memorized every splintered board of my cell before the sky changed from blue to black. Not long afterward, a sweep of headlights afforded me a brief and hurtful moment of vision as Sam's parents pulled into the driveway. They were home from work.

Here was my chance to be sprung. All I had to do was hop onto a trash can and announce my presence. What kept me from doing this? I sat unmoving as the car doors slammed and my potential rescuers went inside without a clue. Leaving me alone with all the sounds of the night: crickets and distant traffic and my own muted whimpering.

I was there for hours. I was to find out later that Sam had forgotten about me. She had come home, flushed with triumph over a victory at chicken, and left her bike on the front porch. She had gone in to dinner and I never even came into her thoughts until the phone rang. It was my mother wondering where I was. Had Sam seen me at all that day?

Even then, it took Sam a minute to remember where I was and the realization was a sickening jolt. But she never let on; she never even blinked. No, she said, after appearing to think about it. She hadn't seen me at all. And then she made herself finish not only dinner but, to avoid suspicion, even dessert.

After putting down a dish of chocolate chip ice cream, Sam took the garbage out without being told for the first time in her life.

"Are you gonna tell?" is what she asked. Then, quickly: "I know you're going to." Her voice an attempt at flippancy. But I could hear everything: fear and anguish and regret, and most agonizing of all, her inability to show these to me.

I ran home without speaking to her. But when I got there I told my mother that I'd been in the library and had lost track of the time.

I can see the ways in which I've never changed. The blurred and broken line running down my life as on a highway – where the most ordinary, even dreary moment drifts, shifts, into the sublime – has never changed. And I'm in the backseat of the car, curled against the door and staring out, a passenger borne through the night. There are headlights, red and white: there are raindrops on the windowpane. There is coziness and safety. I don't want to drive. I never wanted to. I am seatbelted, rocked by the motion, lulled, contained. In a trance.

I might as well be on a boat – out in the middle of nowhere, surrounded by ocean, floating, suspended, anchored to nothing.

Children can instinctively make those journeys together. Sam and I could, anyway; we lost sight of shore for days on end. We had it all: ropes and rigging, cabins and chambers, flags, a plank, an upper deck and one below. We had it all and we knew where everything was.

When you grow up, something hardens around that world. It shuts like a shell. You can be left within it or without it, but what was once semi-permeable is now sealed off. Only the ones who mapped that original terrain can preserve some semblance of access.

To his credit, Sean recognized this, consciously or not. He paid as close attention as he could. He must have sensed he couldn't afford to do otherwise, if he wanted to get on board.

Over the years, my relationship with Sam became more equal. She no longer intimidated me as much, and I was more likely to challenge what she said and did. Occasionally the old dynamics would kick back in; like once when we were having a heated argument on her front lawn, and she told me to get out of her yard.

"Make me," I sassed.

And she picked me up and threw me over the hedges.

At other times she could be amazingly benevolent. She came on her bicycle some evenings to pick me up from swim practice, and rode me home on her handlebars. And she had a few words with some of the girls on the swim team. The ones who called me,

"The Scum from the South", and asked me, couldn't I afford a hairbrush? She had something to say to them, or maybe she just looked at them in her special way, but whatever it was, she said they wouldn't be bothering me again, and sure enough they never did. I was hers to bully; no one else was to have that privilege, if she could help it.

Defender or overseer: there was no telling which she might be, or how long each mood would last. Sometimes she would disdain both. One summer when we were about twelve, she suddenly stopped coming over in the afternoon. I was alarmed by her absence and called her on the phone.

"What are you doing?" I'd ask.

"Nothing much," she would say.

"Do you want to come over?"

"No, not today."

"Why not?"

"I just don't want to."

"But why don't you?"

"I just don't. No reason."

We had this conversation, or slight variations on it, every afternoon for several days.

"Well, when *will* you want to?" I finally whined.

"I don't know when. I can't tell you."

"Are you upset with me?"

"No, I just don't feel like doing anything with you. Okay? When I want to, I'll let you know."

This state of affairs made me thoroughly miserable.

At the beginning of that August, I went to my grandmother's house in upstate New York, where I spent a week nearly every summer. Every night there I lay awake, unable to get used to the silence and planning a strategy for getting Sam back. I would do something to get her attention, out in the street in front of our houses if need be, something she'd have to notice and be unable to resist. I'd set up a car wash with my brother, rake in big bucks, and she would beg to get in on it. I would construct a Japanese box kite, build a tree house. Some ostentatious thing she'd be dying to help with. As it turned out, none of these projects were necessary. The very night I returned home, she appeared at my back door with popsicles, asking if I wanted to see the new Clint Eastwood movie.

As I grew older, I became a dedicated student of the art of manipulation. I actually worked on this for its own sake; I thought it might be the most valuable skill one could cultivate in a lifetime. And most of the time, I was very successful. But not with Sam, never with Sam. She didn't seem resistant to my strategies as much as just immune. She called the shots and there was nothing to touch her. When she made up her mind, there was no swaying her decisions; when she said no, she meant no.

This wasn't true of Sean. He was easy to control. As long as you left him with the idea that he was calling the shots. I'd present him with two self-serving choices, for instance, and let him think he was making the decisions. If I wanted him to do something for me, I could usually, with slight pressures and hints, get him to think of it himself. I made the favors I asked for few and far between.

I saw early that he was afraid of my displeasure. This big man. The same one who ruled the *dojo*, the one who handed down orders all day as assistant manager of a major publishing company. He was anxious in my presence and tried to figure out what I might want before declaring himself in any way. "Do you feel like seeing a movie later, or not really?"

This was at once disappointing and convenient. Convenient because I did, after all, want my own way whenever I could get it. So I was careful, pulling the strings in silence, and averting my eyes so as not to watch him dance. It was a discreet collaboration; we were equally invested in his appearing to wear the pants.

He took me out frequently, and he cooked a lot more often than I did. He would iron my waitressing uniform if I was in a time crunch before work, and I soon came to rely on it. He would also come to the café to pick me up if my shift ended in the middle of the night, which was not unusual. This involved setting the alarm for 2:30 or 3:00 in the morning, even if it were a week night. By the time we got home, he'd have fully awakened and was likely to be aroused. I, on the other hand, would have just finished waiting on eight hours' worth of tables and my only lust was for sleep. Sometimes I'd indulge him. "Go ahead," I said to him once, "as long as I don't have to move." I recognized that sexual gratification ought to be his due for coming to get me. More often though, I let him go to bed frustrated, and he didn't push it. When fantasy was too exhausting to forge, I was the boss.

*   *   *

The long stretches where Sam withdrew from me, as she had that summer when we were twelve, recurred on a regular basis for the next several years. They bewildered and hurt me, but I learned to keep these feelings to myself, to put on a great show of indifference. I hardened myself against her, not wanting to give her the satisfaction of my pain. It got easier. We were changing.

Puberty was as infuriating to Sam as it was delightful to me. The metamorphosis I prayed for and wore padded bras to enhance brought Sam nothing but chagrin. She was no longer indistinguishable from the pack of boys she had run around with for so many years. At the same time, she seemed to have little in common with other girls. She scorned makeup and curling irons, cliques and gossip. I exulted and suffered through crush after crush; my romances were full of sexual initiation and high melodrama. Sam remained dateless and apparently indifferent through four years of high school. You couldn't say she was an outcast; you wouldn't describe her as a wallflower. She was simply a loner, standing more apart with every passing year.

She gained weight. Her clothes were always loose and ill-fitting, concealing her body: men's hiking boots with baggy jeans, oversized sweatshirts. She regarded my fashion experiments – the ongoing trials with lipsticks and eyeliner, tight sweaters and short skirts, fishnet stockings and spike heels – with the gruff amusement and fleeting interest one might accord a mildly ridiculous spectator sport.

During our periods of closeness it could feel as if we were travellers reunited by chance in a foreign country. The strange territory we'd ventured upon seemed to fade before our recognition. Small world, we might have said. It's been a long time; or: There's no place like home.

"What did you guys do for fun?" Sean asked at one point during the week.

I don't remember what we said; it was something vague about bar hopping, and the lame small town night scene.

Less and less: that would have been the correct answer.

Sean and I were alone in the apartment only one other time during Sam's visit. She'd said she was going out for a walk by herself. Lone walks were something she took quite frequently at home. We didn't protest, and we lost no time.

I had just stepped out of the shower and was standing, wrapped in a towel, in the middle of the bedroom floor, when Sean turned and stared at me for a moment, as if seeing me for the first time. Then: "Get dressed," he said, in that curt tone that means he's beginning something.

Hastily I dried off and drew on some underwear. Then I tried to think of what he'd want me to wear. First I chose a sheer pink negligée, then changed my mind and climbed into a black catsuit instead.

"Get in bed," Sean said coldly.

I went over and sat down cross-legged in the middle of the blue patchwork quilt.

"Kneel." It was almost a sigh. As usual, he was making me believe him. Whenever he talked to me in that abrupt, impersonal way, like a cop writing up his hundredth speeding ticket of the day, it was easy to forget we were playing a game. I knelt, trembling as much from apprehension as from my still-wet hair dripping down my back.

He stayed at the desk, pretending to be busy with something. He let me kneel there for about five minutes while he shuffled papers around, and then he came over.

"Back straight. Head up."

I complied, shivering. He sat down on the edge of the bed and regarded me, lifting my chin with two fingers and running his thumb over my mouth. With the other hand he popped the snaps which closed the catsuit between my legs. It sprang open. He put his hand there, as always, to feel the wetness, but something was wrong. There was another barrier where none should have been, a thin cotton sheath between his hand and my flesh. I'd forgotten to take off my underwear. It wasn't any sexy silk underwear either. It was a plain white pair, printed with pink flowers, that might have belonged to a six-year-old. Against the black lace of the catsuit, it was ludicrous. I felt heat rushing to my face.

"What is this?" San asked, ominously calm.

"It's my underwear."

"Why are you wearing underwear?"

"When I put it on I was going to wear something else," I said. "But then I decided to wear this and I forgot to take the underwear off."

"You forgot?"

"I'm sorry."

"You forgot. Can you tell me," Sean asked softly, "what you were thinking about – what it was you had on your mind – that took precedence over getting dressed for me?"

"I . . . I don't remember," I said.

"It must have been very important."

"No."

"Then how do you explain this?"

"I don't know."

Sean rose and disappeared into the bathroom without another word. He returned a moment later with a razor blade.

"Now tell me," he said in that same flat tone, "is this one of your better pairs of underwear?"

"No," I answered.

"Is there anything special about them? Any sentimental value here?"

"No, no . . ."

"That's almost too bad," Sean said, and with the razor blade he slashed a line through the white cotton. The material yielded easily, and a moment later was hanging in tatters around his invading hand.

I stared down at myself where his two fingers were disappearing inside me and felt inexplicably forlorn. I thought it almost would have been better if he had ruined a fancy pair of underwear – some article of lingerie which, by its lascivious nature, would have declared itself part of the game. To take such action against those pink and white flowers seemed a terrible and heedless cruelty: how could anyone want to slash and punish them? A stricken ache took over my body, pulsing outward from my heart, spreading through my chest to my arms and legs, and somewhere inside it was my orgasm, blooming like a dark rose. My eyes welled up and spilled over silently, but Sean was kissing my neck and didn't see this. For which I was grateful; I didn't feel capable of dealing with startled questions. I stared straight ahead, willing myself to breathe normally, and felt my tears drying, unnoticed and unexplained, in their tracks.

"I could never do those things," Sam told me, over dinner that week in New York. I was skipping karate to hang out with her, but we were going to the class just before the end, to watch the last fifteen minutes. She wanted to see how Sean taught. "Why deliberately bring pain into a relationship like that?"

"The pain is beside the point. I mean, it's there, it's fine, but it's only a means to an end."

"What end is that?"

"If you don't understand I don't know if I can explain. And anyway, if we both like it, what could be wrong?"

Sam was silent for a moment, regarding me. "The whole idea is just so strange, that's all. That that's all you two ever do. Don't you ever just want to make love?"

I thought about it before answering. I thought hard for almost a minute and then answered honestly. And I had to tell her no . . . no. "No. I really don't."

We slipped into the *dojo* where the karate class was almost over. Everyone darted furtive glances at us except for Sean. He was explaining the side thrust kick and was too intent on the class to pay us any mind. I felt the familiar thrill as we watched him demonstrating the techniques, correcting students individually on their stances, counting in Japanese. At the very end, he led the higher belts through an advanced *kata* which is what he does best. As always, I was awed by how gracefully he moved, how easy he made it look.

Sam leaned over and spoke into my ear. "I can't believe," she said, "that this is the same man I met downtown the other day for lunch."

"Yeah, I know," I said.

"Let's make a tent."

It was Sam's suggestion. We had been sitting in the apartment at a loss for what to do, having just tried to get into a movie which was sold out. It was raining outside, and still fairly early, nine o'clock on a Saturday night.

"Come on, like we used to do when we were little kids." She was already standing up, gathering the satin blanket to her body.

I felt a strange premonitory thrill. "Well, okay, why not?"

We started to work together. Sean watched with amusement for a while, then his boy scout instincts took over and he rather arrogantly took charge.

"No, put these two chairs back to back and secure the blanket between them, you see? Like this."

When we were done, the bed was canopied by my two quilts, the edges forming a heavy curtain which parted to permit entry. We crawled inside and lay down. I was between them. For a minute all three of us were very quiet. It was raining harder now, pelting the windows. Every now and then a blue flash of lightning lit the interior of the tent, and then we would hear the thunder. Finally Sean spoke.

"This is what you two used to do all the time, isn't it?"

"Right," I said. "Didn't you do something like this yourself, as a kid?"

"We made barricades with the cushions of the living room couch," Sean reflected. "And played a modified Cowboys and Indians."

"We made tents, and played Boat," I said. "It's amazing, the way we played. For hours on end, day after day. Sam, when did we stop? I mean, *how* did we stop? Did we wind down and play every other day for a while, then once or twice a week, or what? There had to be some final day when we played for the last time and we didn't know it. Does that seem strange to you, or is it just me?"

"No, I've wondered about that too," she said.

"Don't look back," Sean said, his tone heavy and mocking at the same time. "You can never go home again. Your playing days are over."

"But we play, Sean," I said. "We play all the time. Pretend games. Don't we?"

He was silent for a moment, then spoke seriously, as he hadn't before. "That's not playing for its own sake. That's sex."

"Was it ever for it's own sake? Aren't childhood games very sexual? Innocent, unrealized, or whatever . . . but essentially sexual."

"I think you're right," Sam said. "The way I always had to be the boy, and order you around. I loved doing it, too."

"Well, now you're making me jealous," Sean said lightly.

"And you're turning me on," I said. I wasn't completely joking, either.

"Oh, yeah?" Sean growled, pretending territoriality.

"Yeah . . . it's true," I murmured. I looked straight up at the ceiling, rather than at either of them. "So let's play a game."

"What kind of game?" Both of them were looking at me with interest.

"A sex game that will fuck up our friendship," I said, and laughed. "Let's play Boat!"

"I'm the captain," Sean said immediately, and we were all startled into silence. "I mean," he qualified quickly, "if we're actually going to play, I get to be the boss. You can be my sidekick," he added generously to Sam. "The ship's first mate."

"Then who am I?" I asked.

"You're our prisoner, taken in battle from the enemy ship. You can consider yourself lucky to be our slave," Sean continued. "It is only our incredible mercy that kept you from being thrown to the sharks."

I laughed at this. He wrapped his hand in my hair. "You won't be laughing for long," he said softly into my ear, and I stopped. He brought his other hand up to my face, made a fist, and lightly passed the knuckles over my cheek. Immediately my breathing grew rapid and shallow.

"Well, look what we've got here, mate," he said to Sam.

"Fine specimen of a wench, Captain," she replied with a straight face.

"That she is," he agreed. "But an enemy wench just the same."

"You're right, Captain. As usual."

"Well. What do you think? Should we have a look at our property?"

"I think that would be in order, Captain," the first mate replied.

"Let's strip her, then. Get her hands." Sam grasped my wrists and secured them above my head, and then Sean pulled off my tank top. I was wearing my favorite bra, strapless white lace with a circle of tiny imitation pearls in the middle.

"That's pretty fancy stuff this wench has got on. Too bad she won't be needing it anymore." Sean said, springing the clasp. The bra fell away, baring my breasts in the bluish light. Sean passed the palm of his hand over them casually, as he would stroke a cat, or a bolt of silk.

"Lovely," he said. "Mate, would you care to touch the wench?"

I looked at Sam. She seemed taken aback all of a sudden, as if my half-nakedness had woken her up to what was going on. She glanced at me, then quickly averted her eyes, and shook her head no. Sean was excited, though, that much I could see. He was in his element, didactic as ever, showing her the ropes, running the game. I looked at him and then at her, waiting to see what was going to happen. I felt suspended between them, calm, floating, open. Reasonable, flexible. I could have gone either way. Why not, I could only think to myself, much stranger things go on every day. I felt curious, devious, glinting, mocking. I was pleased also at having Sam all flustered. She didn't have the slightest clue what to do.

I was looking at her and thinking these things when all of a sudden she looked straight back, with a new expression I couldn't read. As if she could hear all my gloating thoughts and knew something I didn't. At any rate, it wasn't friendly.

"Go ahead," Sean urged her. "Look at her. She thinks you won't do it."

Maybe both of them could read my mind. Whatever the case, Sean's words seemed to release her. She reached over and twisted my nipple. I protested this by glaring at her and trying to squirm away. "Don't touch me," I challenged.

There was a frightening silence. Then: "What the fuck did you just say to me?" she asked.

I didn't answer.

"Can I do anything I want with this wench, Captain?"

"Do what you want," he told her. "I wouldn't let her get away with that," he added.

Her hand came back to my nipple. "Repeat what you just said," she ordered. For the first time I began to feel afraid.

"I didn't say anything."

She slapped me hard across the face. I saw stars, little orange bursts behind my eyelids. Amazement left me mute.

"How dare you lie to me," she hissed. "How dare you! You know what you said, now say it again."

Not knowing what else to do, I repeated myself, speaking low. "I said don't touch me."

"Can you believe this, Captain" Sam said, addressing Sean.

"She's a brazen little bitch. Let's strip her all the way down and see if a whipping changes her tune." Disbelief and excitement made me cold, and fear pricked my flesh. They pulled off my jeans. Sean went to my closet and took the riding crop from where it hangs on the hook inside. He came back to the bed, jerked my underwear down around my thighs, and handed the crop to Sam.

It seemed as if everything I had ever said and done with the two of them had led inevitably to this moment. My refusing to follow Sam around anymore, catching up to her, surpassing her. Now I was the one who was good friends with the boys, though for different reasons. I had become the athletic one, the bold one, the manipulator, the bully. But here she was; she had found me. She was holding the whip. And I wanted it. I could never remember wanting it so much before. Not with Sean, not with any man.

She beat me. Sean held my hands above my head and she wielded the crop, hitting me hard all the way down my back and legs. When I was striped from neck to ankle and crying with wild abandon, she stopped and regarded me with immense satisfaction.

"Now," she said, "there's a lot more where that came from, if you don't do whatever I tell you to do."

She made me kiss the whip. She made me kiss her feet. She made me go down on her, something I had never done to a woman. I could sense Sean watching from somewhere on the periphery of things; he seemed far away. I had a vague hope that he was impressed with what was either my inherent skill at this or considerable beginner's luck. Only after I had satisfied her this way three or four times did she deign to touch me in turn. It was all she had to do.

Through the open window came catcalls from the street. They could hear me eleven stories below.

"Write to me soon," I said to Sam on the way to the train. It was five o'clock in the morning, and the streets were bluish and still.

The morning after. I had expected, just before falling asleep, to be incredulous in the light of day, but I wasn't at all, and neither was she. We were calm, unsurprised and unapologetic.

"I will," she said.

"Tell everyone at home I said hello."

"Tell Sean I said goodbye."

That was the closest we came to even mentioning it. By the next time we saw each other, it would be just another episode in a dozen years' worth of memories.

I stood with her on the subway platform until the downtown IRT screeched into sight. We hugged each other and the train took her away. Then I climbed up to the street where day was breaking and instead of turning east toward my apartment, I found myself walking down to Riverside Park. I wanted an hour or so to myself before going home, where Sean was still asleep in my bed.

MOBIUS STRIPPER

Bana Witt

1 Hot Nazis

I was riding on the 7 Haight bus to my massage job downtown when I sat down next to a thin friendly blonde girl. She was on her way to the clap clinic. She said she had clap of the throat. She might have gotten it from a girl she had worked with on a porno film. I had never met anyone who'd done porn before, or even seen any for that matter. She said she was working for these really nice guys called the Mitchell Brothers and told me just to call their theater if I wanted to work.

I was very excited by the idea. I had just started to get into S&M: having boyfriends who liked to tie me up or spank me, biting hard, doing things that left marks and looking at my own marks after a long night. I thought I was about as kinky and decadent as anyone. I called after thinking about it for a few days. I went to an interview at the O'Farrell Theater and was confused by the incredible similarity between the two brothers. They were fine-boned, relatively small men, with a way of making the bizarre seem totally routine. The older brother was Jim, the younger, Artie. They asked me if I'd ever done this sort of work before and I said no, but that I was a masochist and loved to be beaten and they could really do it if they wanted. There was a list of other things they asked if I would do. I said yes to them all. They told me they were going to do a series of short, very hardcore films called *Ultra Core*.

A few days later I went to a large brick building in the Tenderloin. It's across from Hyde Street Studios now. I was overweight and not nearly as flashy as the other women, but much more enthusiastic. They had this outrageously beautiful makeup woman who was also from Fresno. Years later she would fall in love with my friend Patty at my wedding.

The title of the film was *Hot Nazis* and I was to play a lesbian Jew. I was very impressed when I heard Michael Bloomfield was writing the music. There were no scripts.

One room was a reproduction of a bleak concrete bunker. At one end was a large radio. On the wall to the left was a barbed wire cage filled with straw and bones, fresh bones from cattle legs. There was a large wiry German shepherd gnawing on one of the bones. Myself and a girl named Virginia were to be in the cage. I took her aside to find out if she really liked women. She did. She had done a lot of this work before. We were given torn thermal underwear to wear and smudged up a little. The first scene to be shot was of us getting it on in the straw. I had no idea having an audience would get me off so much. Virgina knew the ropes and nothing was faked. I was pretty submissive. She gave ferocious head and finger fucked me until I screamed.

The crew applauded our first scene. Then Artie (in retrospect I know it was Artie) asked me if I would fuck the dog. It boggled my mind. I wanted to be a trooper, but the dog! I declined and Virgina attempted to get the dog aroused. The dog growled. They left him alone.

The rest of the action focused around a tall gaunt man named Vernon, who played head Nazi and his girlfriend Enjil, a beautiful Nordic woman. There were several men playing Gestapo guards and a woman with dark hair named Monique. They did some scenes of the guards fucking one another and the girls, and then it was my turn again. I was to be held down on a table and screwed by Vernon. Everyone was doing hits off a full bottle of liquid amyl nitrate. I was lying on my back and he started out by running a riding crop across my body. Slowly he began tapping it on the insides of my thighs. He hit harder and harder, at which point my girlfriend was supposed to pull him off and he was to continue by screwing me. Only he wouldn't stop whipping me. Every time

he lifted the crop there would be a bright new red stripe on my
body. She tried to pull him off and he pushed her into the barbed
wire that was wrapped around the cage. He returned to continue
beating me now for real. He was laying the whip into my very white
skin as hard as he could. Finally Virginia yelled "CUT!" to the
cameramen. They realized we weren't just acting and subdued
Vernon. In the film the welts were unbelievable. Virginia's leg
bled real blood from the barbed wire.

They wanted just one final insertion shot on the table. I lay down,
face up. I asked Monique for a hit of the amyl nitrate. She tilted
the bottle and poured the whole thing up my nose and into my
eyes. The burning was unbelievable. I jumped up screaming, and
then I started rushing. It was like I'd shot speed and jumped off a
cliff at the same time. Everything was buzzing and my ears were
ringing and I couldn't get my breath. Jim had gotten water and
was flushing my face with it. I knew I was going to have a seizure.
I knew I was going to be blind. I knew I should go to the hospital.
It was the most total, complete panic I've ever had.

In the space adjacent to the *Hot Nazis* set was a room with
an elaborate bed. It had been used in a scene from the brothers'
film, *Sodom and Gomorrah*. I lay there for a long time while they
continued to shoot the movie. I finally realized I wasn't going to
die, that I was a lesbian Jew in a storage building in the Tenderloin
of San Francisco. Artie came in to see how I was. We had sex for
the first time and I finally felt the cord being cut from the tule fog
and tract houses that had been my home.

2 Dabbling in S&M

I never have liked going nude. I have rarely been thin enough to
be proud of my body. I'm thick through the waist. I have almost
no tits. I have great confidence in my face and legs, but as far as
my torso is concerned, I would just as soon leave it covered up.
I've had a few boyfriends who were very comfortable nude.

I also get cold very easily, but I just don't like people to look at
my naked body. It's not shyness. It is simply that I feel I cannot pass
muster. I've been with and around so many beautiful sexy women,
it has left me humble in that regard. A lot of men like to look at your

body, like when you're walking across the room. That bothers me. I never felt confident unless I was actually making body contact. I knew I was better at the tactile than the visual. I think my hating to be nude in front of people is why I got off so much on the movies. I got off from proving how hot I was, if not pretty, and because of the adrenaline from being terrified. I was lucky they didn't require any acting. I was way too scared to think clearly, but it made the sex great. The best part came afterwards, rehashing the films in my mind. I would be in retrospective bliss for weeks after a shoot.

When I was twenty-two I made up a list of everyone I could recall having had sex with. It was nearly two hundred people in length. Apparently I was active before the AIDS epidemic. I was unbelievably lucky on that one. Only two of them were real tricks, everything else was in films or for recreation.

Late in 1975 I answered an ad in one of the sex magazines that said they were looking for nude bondage models. It sounded like good, non-boring work. I called and talked to a man who seemed pretty lucid and straightforward. His name was Ron Reynolds or something close to that. Anyway, his initials were R.R. He had a little S&M Victorian in Oakland. I remember I'd never ridden BART, the local subway system, and I rode BART over from San Francisco. He picked me up in a stationwagon that smelled like a dog. He dressed like he sold cars, and seemed very gentle and polite. He wore very thick glasses with black frames that made his eyes look intense and maybe a little psychotic, but not enough to make me uncomfortable.

We drove to his house and I could still smell the dog. The place was divided into different torture rooms, with women attending them who dressed in leather, looked cold and unforgiving, and did domination scenes with men. There was never any standard sex. And this Ron guy was that way with me. Everyone I had done nude modeling for at that point had tried to fuck me, but he didn't try. It seems when sadists and masochists really become purist, The Scene is the whole thing, and the pain or the mood or the concept replaces orgasm and generic sexual activity.

We went to a room where he did photography. There was a large Irish setter sleeping in a shipping kennel. The door was open and she was very friendly, but she was the source of the omnipresent smell of dog. I was getting around fifty dollars an hour. The twisted pros of the industry really liked me even though I wasn't the standard tits-and-hair nude model. I was trusting, good natured, liberal, and incredibly submissive.

He had me model a number of weird leather arrangements. One was a leather hood with no holes in it, except one to breathe through. It pulled over your head like a falcon's hood. My hands were handcuffed behind me. I posed in a number of positions for about an hour: on my knees with my head bowed, or lying on my side on the floor under a floodlight, or sitting backwards in a chair. I never felt fear. It took me a long time to learn fear.

After the shoot he told me he really liked me. He had several live-in slaves and wanted me to join the crew. I thought it could be fun. It seemed like the beginning of an interesting cult.

On my second visit they began my initiation. He gave me a name with his initials in it: Morrow. All of his slaves had his initials in their name. Two pretty young girls came in, one was a young blonde with a gold ring through one lip of her pussy. I thought it looked great. I was told not to make eye contact with anyone and to always respond to Ron as Sir. That was hard to do with a straight face.

I was told to kneel in front of a bad painting of a woman with her head bowed. While I recited lines of devotion and submission, they whipped me. It was tremendously exciting and it hurt just enough. They had the line between pleasure and pain memorized.

They had a cool set-up for doing pain scenes. Beforehand they would give you a key word. If things ever got too heavy you could just say the word and things would stop.

I bellied up on living there. My main objection was that the place was tacky. If Ron had money or taste, I think I could have bought into it. But the furniture was ugly and old, the house smelled like that damn dog, and Ron was no prize. When I left that day, I thought, if I'm going to be a slave, I'm going to be a rich slave. *The Story of O* became my bible.

After seeing the blonde girl at Ron's and reading *The Story of O*, I decided to pierce my labia. I'd been working on films with a lot of other girls who had various piercings: labia, nipples, noses. I thought a gold ring looked pretty sexy. It was also like a badge showing how hardcore you really were. I didn't know any of the technicalities of correct piercing. I took a couple of pain killers and got out a large upholstery needle. I did clean it with alcohol.

I'd gotten a small gold self-piercing hoop to put in after I'd made the hole. My friend Patty came over to watch. She was intrigued. She and I had watched each other do some pretty bizarre things.

It was hard to get the needle to go through because the skin was very thick and rubbery. I had to really push and ended up having to put a cork behind it and then pushed it through. Bled like mad, got the earring in. Swelled so much in a day I wasn't able to walk. It was shiny and swollen and felt like red ants had nested there. I couldn't even think of wearing pants. By the third day I gave up, I pulled it out. It started healing within twelve hours and was completely healed in two days. It was miraculous.

I found out how to do proper piercing much later on. What you do is start on antibiotics a week before you do it and continue to take them for a week after. It cuts down on the grief I went through. I've met a lot of people over the years into ritualist piercing. They all used antibiotics.

3 Lower Haight

The most depressing place I've ever lived was at the bottom of Haight Street near Market. My apartment was in a three-story building that had originally been three flats, but they had been divided in half lengthwise to make six apartments. I lived in one of the back three where you had to use the outside stairs. I was living on SSI for being crazy, writing a lot of tortured poetry, taking drugs and screwing my brains out, like some people do on SSI.

I met Joanne while living on Lower Haight. She was the hottest woman I've ever known. When I met her we were both doing live all-girl sex shows at the O'Farrell Theater. My friend Artie took me to the dressing room on my first day and introduced us.

She was sitting on a table in front of a make-up mirror smoking a cigarette and wearing only a beat-up motorcycle jacket. With her laconic expression, her long naked legs, her short brown pubic hair, and her tiny nipples against the heavy gold zipper of the jacket, she looked like one of Warhol's women: jaded, bored and beautiful. She had gigantic cool and the prettiness of an East Coast socialite gone bad. She looked me up and down and sounding like Nico on valium, she said, "I can't wait to get to work."

It turned me on completely. From then on it was a competition to see who could be the most hardcore and the coolest. Doing shows with her was more fun than I'd ever had.

Our first time together was in the Ultra Room when it first opened. The Mitchell Brothers had come back from a visit to New York with the idea. The entire room was upholstered in black leather and measured about ten by fifteen feet in length. There were ropes and pulleys hanging from the ceiling with square mirrors set into the wall at eye level. All the girls could see their own reflection, but from outside the customers could see in. Two or three women would work the room at the same time, giving head to each other, using dildos, or just masturbating for the audience.

We started the show with three women in the room. We would flirt and kiss and hump each other, rapidly getting more and more bold until we were screaming and carrying on like mad women. I was on my period and Joanne gave me head. It wasn't pretty.

Here's what made it even more memorable: Herb Caen, a local newspaper columnist, had come to the O'Farrell that night. He brought a member of the Rockefeller clan, who had to go outside to throw-up after watching us. I'm sure it was better to do than see. The next day Caen said in his column that the show was the most disgusting thing he'd ever seen. Business tripled.

Joanne had a son who was six years old. He'd grown up around drag queens in the Castro District. He knew more about sexual aberrations than most adults, and would do gut-wrenching impersonations of drag queens trying to pick up tricks. Joanne got into angel dust, which I couldn't handle. But there was a lot of this other drug called MDMA around (now they call it Ecstasy). I would score it at Toad Hall on Castro Street. We shot it up a number of times and made love. It made you incredibly sensitive and horny. We thought we'd achieved sexual enlightenment.

We went to gay bars sometimes after work and would see how outrageous we could be, like I would give her head on the dance floor while she danced and held a martini in her hand. She loved being passionate in public, and so did I. Rumor had it Joanne had even fist fucked a gay guy on the bar at the Stud on Folsom Street. She made me feel like Pollyanna. I was in awe. I get total recall when I think of Joanne.

Also while living on Lower Haight, I befriended a strange photographer who called one night and asked me if I'd like to go meet his coke connection in the wine country and be like a present to him. I'd never been a present before and agreed.

The coke dealer was a big, gentle man who collected guitars and antiques, and had lots of dogs. The photographer also brought a beautiful girl who was about nineteen. She had thick chestnut hair and a Playboy Bunny body. Her name was Arrega. The two guys wanted to see us make love but she refused, and later asked me if she could come to my house the next day.

She moved in for a month and the photographer was crushed. It gave me great pleasure to watch men go nuts over her and then find out she was with me. She turned tricks on Polk Street occasionally while I was taking Isadora Duncan dance lessons at California Hill. We slept together but I was very jealous because she was still seeing men and ultimately threw her out.

After Arrega, I had an affair with a gangster and his wife. I first met them at a couples party in Oakland. We did three ways for a while, but as usual in those situations, I fell heavily for the woman. She was a tall, svelte submissive blonde he had rescued from the streets. I saw her alone for about six months while he was doing a short stretch of time in jail.

She disappeared and after he got out, while he was searching for her, I slept with him alone. He always had great drugs. He slept with a .357 Magnum under the pillow, which seemed kind of exciting to me for a while, then some remnant of common sense burst through when I heard at the bathhouse that the Hell's Angels had a contract out on him. Then Sonny Barger, the Oakland Hell's Angels leader, called my house to threaten him. I went back to my mother's house in Oroville for a while to chill out. I saw him on the Bay Area tv news, talking about his wife's disappearance through a voice processor with a mask on.

That was followed by a relationship with a fastidious hippie guy who worked for the Post Office, had been to Afghanistan (and never recovered), and could fuck like a man possessed. He was hunky but a little too chubby, with flawless auburn hair to his shoulders and a full beard. He decided to rescue me.

We'd been having polite dinners and good sex. He didn't shoot-up and had a nice apartment in the Avenues. I never cooked at my house and there were always dirty dishes in the sink. We'd had pizza one night and had slept at my place. For breakfast I'd decided to heat the pizza and blithely turned on the oven to heat, going into the other room for a few minutes. When I returned the entire top of the stove was covered with cockroaches. Big ones, baby ones. They were jumping around on the hot stove, and were so thick you couldn't see the top. I guess they'd been breeding in the oven.

I realized my life was grimmer than I really wanted, that maybe I had suffered enough for art, and moved into his apartment in the Avenues.

4 Tahoe

The first porno people I worked with besides the Brothers were from Los Angeles. The word around was that they were Mafia-backed. A lot of LA people came to shoot porn in San Francisco at that time because it was a lot less likely they would get busted here.

The people who "acted" in these films had a tremendous network going. I found I could call anyone who I'd worked with or even heard of and ask them about a potential employer. If someone didn't pay at the end of the shoot, or was horrible to work with, the word spread like lightning. I had about four pages of notes listing producers' names, and the opinions of other actors and their past experiences with them.

The first duo I worked with from LA were really sleazy. They wanted to make a ski-oriented film and were going to take the entire cast to Tahoe for a week. They also brought along a skiing coach, some camera men and the director's dad. We got a huge house at Northstar.

The director's dad liked to tell stories. He had been a hobo for a time and would tell about hopping freight trains and drinking sterno. I had never heard of such a thing. They would drain the fluid out of sterno cans used to heat food and mix it with Tokay grape wine. They called it Tokay and Squeezins. I couldn't believe he was still alive.

They had asked me to shave my crotch for the shoot, which I did but the second day I had broken out with razor burn. It was hideous. It looked like prime teenage acne all over my pubic area.

When we went skiing, it was a disaster. I had not skied since I was seven years old, and had very poor balance and muscle control. My dance teachers had always called it "your neurological problem", but it was a little more vague than that. My first time down the bunny hill I broke through the surface of a frozen-over creek and was totally drenched in ice water. The woman who played my favorite girlfriend in the film sprained her ankle and it became grossly swollen.

Our first scene together in the shower was shot the next morning around my razor burn and her ankle. Mostly I gave her head. The level of sexual excitement was so intense that everyone said they'd have to re-shoot the rest of the film to bring it up to our level. We could make each other come just by looking at each other.

We hung out together at the house when everyone else went out to the casinos at night. She had brought some heroin with her and we would smoke it and make love. It was like camp for decadent San Franciscans. I had never gotten to go to real camp because of my asthma.

On the third night there I had returned to my own bed to sleep and had a grand mal seizure. It was generally controlled by a drug called Dilantin, but I think the heroin cut right through. I woke up on the floor with a number of people I did not recognize staring down at me. I had wet my pants. I did not know where I was. It was several hours before my memory came back. The girl I had been with held me and stayed with me until I got reoriented. I had never had a seizure in front of strangers before but everyone handled it well.

I think the film was called *Snowballing* or something like that. I made a couple of hundred dollars a day and it was nice to get out of the city. I never saw the finished product.

Here's how I ended up with epilepsy:

I was a tremendously emotional, spoiled, asthmatic child who loved horses. I was stick thin and pale, and the floor of my room was stained from the ever-present vaporizer. My parents bought me a horse when I was ten to encourage me to be active, and to shut me up.

We found a totally wild, part-Morgan pinto mare up north in a town near Oroville called Bangor. We managed to tame her to some extent but she was always pretty crazy. She was even going over fences after about a year. I had a British ex-cavalry riding instructor who wasn't there the day of the accident, but my father was and some visitors from LA. I was jumping a course of fences about four feet high and wearing a helmet that was not appropriate for jumping. The real "brain-bucket" style has a wide leather chin strap. This had elastic. My horse took a bad fence, caught the pole above her knees, crashed on the far side and did a somersault. I was under her at the time.

They say the saddle held her weight off me and that I was probably hit in the head by a stirrup iron. When they took me to the Children's Hospital I was walking and talking but remembering nothing. The doctors sent me home. My mother was there and being a nurse, saw that my pupils were radically different from one another, a sure sign of a serious head injury. She took me to another hospital where it was determined I had a fractured skull. I didn't remember anything for three or four days. I returned home after a week in the hospital and this part I remember like a photograph. I was walking to the refrigerator for orange juice when I felt a big pressure on my forehead, then I felt tremendously drunk. I woke up with my face under the water heater, staring at thick dust motes and the pilot light, my legs wet with piss, and my mother saying, "You've had a seizure, just relax."

My body ached for days, as if I'd been bucked off a horse.

5 Highway 1

I came down the stairs with my little dog to answer the door at six in the morning, wearing only a long black and orange bathrobe. I was excited about seeing the man who was waiting there because I didn't get to see him very often, and then only at his whim.

He had called at 5.30, drug-crazed, belligerent and exciting, demanding that I throw out whoever was in my bed, which I did. His name was Artie Mitchell and I had met him when I worked on my first porno film. He had continued to call after the work was through. Being addicted to bizarre sex, he was the only person I'd ever met who had no fear of the physical or chemical edge.

There was an air of chaos and sleazy glamor that permeated his life, now confirmed by the silver limo at the curb driven by his hunky blonde cousin who smiled as I was pulled without resisting into the back seat littered with children's toys. I'd heard his wife was fertile.

I complained to him that I hadn't locked my apartment door and he told me with drunken gallantry that he would replace whatever was stolen. There wasn't much there anyway.

He had an uncommon ability for calling when I was on my period, but it wasn't really that hard because I was bleeding more often than not. We did some cocaine and soon were humping like mink on the approach to the Golden Gate Bridge. Being concerned about the nice gray velour seats I told him I was bleeding heavily. He told me he didn't care. We had hot, wet, mad menstrual sex on the bridge at sunrise, filling the back seat with orgasms while my little dog slept peacefully on the floor.

We took a break on the road to Mount Tam, where he pulled out a wad of money and wiped the blood off me and himself. He threw the bloody money on the floor with the dog and lit a joint.

Heading north on Highway 1, we picked up a suntanned girl hitchhiker with tangled blonde hair like the morning after. She was happy to be picked up by a limousine but after we'd started up again she saw the puppy and the blood money and got nervous. He teased her for being squeamish, and asked me to recite some poems. After she heard them, she asked to get out. We pulled over and left her by the roadside. We accelerated our intake of drugs.

We drove another hour up the perfect California coastline, then turned off on a dirt road that led to a little trailer with a small group of people standing around and sitting in lawn chairs drinking beer. We got out of the car and he told me they were his relatives. There was a sweet comfortable woman in her fifties who he said was his aunt. I was in my bathrobe with no shoes on. She was nice to me anyway.

The men had just been abalone diving. They were telling extravagant stories with their hands. I was astounded that my friend would ask anyone to meet relatives in my condition, but they took it well. They joked that they thought someone had died when they saw the limo in the driveway.

We stayed too long and he renewed his drunkenness with beer and hot sun well into the afternoon. When we finally left, we stood up in the open sunroof and made bird noises, calling to the crows.

We resumed our passionate fucking as we returned to the city. The tinted windows amplified the darkness, smudging the edges of things. It was late when we arrived and he wanted to eat, so we went to Japantown where they didn't care that I had no shoes. I ate sushi for the first time, and being so high it seemed to slither down my throat.

A week later I got a card from him: the ace of spades folded in a dollar bill covered with dried blood. I framed it and hung it on the wall.

THE PARIS CRAFTSMAN

Lucienne Zager

THE RUE DE L'ENTRANCE was to be found on the southern edge of the great city of Paris. It was an unimportant street of small dilapidated houses long past their best, if they had ever had a best. Cats sat on hot stones to drink in the noon sun and a midday silence more suited to a small village lay over the area. Alison parked her small red sports car as near to the building she sought as possible. She crossed the road to the paint-peeled door marked with a number nine. After hesitating, she knocked hard and waited. There was a long pause, and she had just raised her hand to knock again when she heard a noise from within. The man who opened the door to her was short, bent, old and foreign. "Herr Craftsman?" she enquired.

He nodded through half glasses.

"Alison Kwik," she said, extending a hand which he did not take. "Come in," he said in a thick German accent.

He led her into a dark and dirty hall. Instantly the cool air was full of the smell of leather, stacked along the walls were large rolled hides in many colours and ahead was a narrow staircase, equally ill lit. The old man went ahead and up the stairs and she followed. At the top he disappeared through a half-opened door. She slowly followed and found herself in a strange and crowded room. It was at the rear of the building and light flooded in through a large, dust-encrusted skylight set partly in the room. All around were cluttered work benches covered in strips of leather and gleaming tools polished with constant use. The sweet smell of leather hung heavily in the air, full of sensual animal power. Herr Craftsman had by now seated himself in a position of authority on a tall stool at a far bench.

"So you have come for one of my little toys?" He asked, his eyes sparkling with an excitement not suggested by this age.

Alison agreed with him, feeling both embarrassed and excited by the situation she found herself in. Though there was still a strong hint of the active male in the old man, there was also the professional detachment that all specialists cultivate. With the ease of long experience and complete familiarity with the difficulties almost all his clients found with the situation for the first time, he launched into his familiar routine. First he seated her by pointing to the only other chair in the room, then with delight he started to describe his service in detail. "You could have a half harness but that would not be for someone as beautiful and so well created by nature as you. No, for you" – here he paused to give effect to his consideration – "No, for you, a full and very elaborate harness is the only one. You are fit and young and would be a perfect body for something so wonderful and so demanding."

"Now," he paused again, holding his chin with his hand, "we must consider the most important of considerations. Will you require a female as well as a male extension?" Before Alison could even begin to answer, he answered for her.

"Yes, again you are someone who will most definitely want a female extension and, if you don't mind me being blunt, we will have to consider both size and shape. In fact to do this correctly and to give you my best work, I must be permitted to measure everything."

He held up his hand to suggest protection or reassurance. "My clients trust me, and I am sure that you will be no different. I have been recommended to you and for me to do my best for you, we must trust each other."

At this point Alison felt that she had better say something.

"Herr Craftsman, I would not be here unless I was willing to undertake what is necessary to possess an example of your extraordinary skill. I will, of course, be only too pleased to co-operate with you to achieve this."

"Good, good, we understand each other. Then we must get on. I regret, my facilities are very limited," he gestured around the room. "May I ask you to remove all your clothing. While you do this, I will get some things together so that I can take my measurements."

Alison found the moment and the request stimulating. This was certainly no doctor's surgery but the same detached pressure to conform was there and felt. She had undressed in front of many men but this was hardly that – more like a dressmaker but even then different.

Herr Craftsman turned away and started to gather together a number of obviously essential items. Alison set about undressing. Fortunately, she had on only casual clothes. First she looked around to find a place to put them. Seeing nothing obvious, she opted for the already crowded bench. With slightly false confidence, she pulled the tight cashmere sweater over her head. The soft material rubbed gently over her hard nipples. The cool air of the room felt fresh on her bare breasts. They delighted her and those who were allowed to play with them, male or female. Hard, high and very round, they were a little larger than her slim, long frame suggested. Next she unlaced her high-heeled boots, pulled them off and placed them neatly under the bench.

She had to stand to remove her tight jeans. She pulled them with difficulty down her long legs and had to hop to keep her balance. She was left with her small plain thong, the cord at the back disappearing between her round cheeky bottom, the thin material at the front cupping the distended mound and slightly moist where it slipped between the pouting lips.

The progress of the undressing had not escaped the alert eyes of Herr Craftsman, "Everything, please, young lady; everything." He made a slight movement of his hands and Alison looked down at the brief white covering and the pink pop socks.

"You can leave the socks on," said Herr Craftsman, as though such a concession would ensure her modesty.

Alison slipped her thumbs through the thin elastic and in one movement pushed the throng down to her feet, where she kicked it free. She stood up, legs slightly parted, to confront Herr Craftsman with the delicately trimmed and most minimal crowning of pubic hair over the powerfully displayed and lustful mouth of her vagina.

"Few," said Herr Craftsman, "of my many clients could be considered more worthy an owner of my talents than you." His eyes shone and his face beamed with the obvious appreciation of a connoisseur. Alison always liked a compliment, and smiled shyly back at him.

"Now to work. First we will measure the female requirement." He turned back to his bench and picked up a beautiful veneered box bound with brass corners. This he placed on a table and with care raised the lid. The long box was lined with dark blue velvet and held in individual compartments perhaps a dozen beautifully shaped red leather dildos in ascending order of size. Herr Craftsman repeated the display with another identical box. This, however, contained similar objects that differed in having exaggerated heads at the end of each of their lengths.

"We have, young lady, two choices in this department. First that of size and then between the one of even diameter and the one with the full head. The only way to choose is to try, otherwise I have found that sometimes a woman's eyes are bigger than, shall we say her, stomach. May I also hasten to assure you that though these samples have experienced many trials, they are always cleansed most thoroughly with surgical spirit.

"The leather from which they are made, and from which the one I make for you will be made, is of the finest quality, as soft as the place it must enter and yet almost totally waterproof. I fill the sheath with my own preparation, which permits some flexibility and feels most natural. You may also consider if you require the device only to fill the vagina or to be more dramatic and pass through the mouth of the cervix and beyond. You may also have one fitted to enter your rear passage as well."

Alison was by now very wet and very open. This almost clinical talk on such an erotic theme was deeply stimulating. Her hole, in fact holes, craved to be filled by the objects that she saw laid out so invitingly before her. It was like a sweet shop and she a child with pennies to spend. What to try first?

"I think I would like a head on the item, and I think that I would like one for my bum as well." She hesitated, hovering over the boxes.

"Take one," encouraged Herr Craftsman.

Her hand reached out and moved over the box, back and forth. Then, with decision, it alighted upon and removed a substantial dildo. Its leather was so inviting, warm to the touch and softer even than her cashmere. She brought it instinctively to her nose and breathed deeply of its rich smell. Her mind also visualized the pink, wet and hairy slits that this had already entered and she trembled at the thought of driving this hard monster in, pushing and twisting it as the recipient thrust back and twisted, skewered upon its attack. She moved it away from her nose, and as it passed her mouth her tongue licked out to caress the large round end.

Now oblivious of Herr Craftsman, and yet aroused by the audience, she brought its head down to meet her own cunt. To make the entry possible she arched her hips forward, bending and opening her legs.

This movement had the effect of opening her hole, and as she drew the soft leather between her lips for the first time, letting the liquids wet it, the need to plunge it in became very strong. Still, as though in a greeting, she let it rub against her clitoris and this touch sent its own messages throughout her body.

Then it was in. At first she felt that she had been too greedy. As her hand and arm forced it in and upward, she felt herself stretched as she had never been stretched before. She could feel it pass the inner gate with just a little pain and then it was onward. As only the last few inches of the massive device were left as a bright red circle framed in the distended mouth, she was aware of Herr Craftsman close by her.

"May I make some checks, young lady?" he said in his professional voice.

"Yes," agreed Alison.

He bent his head as she held her position, standing thrust forward with her legs well parted. She felt his hand touching and testing, then his skilled craftsman's fingers sliding between the dildo and the wall of her vagina, increasing the stretch significantly. Then the fingers were withdrawn and the hand moved with moist fingers up over her mound to the area of her womb. Here it pressed, just above the pubic bone. She was aware of his other hand on the end of the dildo and then its movement of the device, so that it pushed out hard against her skin. Still holding her in this way, he looked up at her face.

"If you were an adventurous girl, you could in my considered opinion get the greatest pleasure from the next size up. You are young and very accommodating. This one you would soon become comfortable with; the next size would always provide a challenge."

Without waiting for an answer, he gently pulled the dildo from her body with little twisting motions that thrilled her. Accepting that the matter had already been decided, he turned and placed the used dildo, now wet and gleaming, on a sheet of plastic and selected the next in line. There was a decided jump in the increments of size and this one looked quite impossible – more a device of punishment than of pleasure.

He handed it to Alison. "Go on, you will learn to enjoy it – even worship it. I know these things; it is my trade to know women's needs."

Alison took it and tried not to look. She knew that this too had been elsewhere and if another had been able to accept it then she would not be beaten and not admit defeat in front of this old man. It was worse and there was pain, but she had never contemplated the incredible feeling of being filled in this way; she could not restrain a gasp. She had not made this journey to this place, to this man, to find anything less than the total experience. This was an essential part of it, this size was to be hers. There were even larger ones in the box. Who they were for she dared not think. Herr Craftsman again went through his methodical examination. She cried out a little as his fingers distended, probed and searched.

"This is yours my dear, of this there is no doubt. In the future, when you are in your private world, you will thank me."

Alison believed that she would.

She sat back on the chair after removing the monster, to regain something of her composure. The old man searched for another item and produced a tube of proprietary genital lubricant. He now selected a red dildo – this one was quite small – and handed it to Alison.

"For the other hole, it is better that it is not too large, so that it can move freely as your body moves; this will give much more sensation."

He passed her the tube, and she anointed the small shaft with gel and, standing up again, she bent forward so that she could reach round and insert it.

"Don't lose it," cautioned Herr Craftsman. She smiled at this remark.

"Does it fit well?" he asked.

"Oh yes, very well," answered Alison. The strange and pleasurable sensation of anything pushed into her bottom was always a little joy.

She withdrew it and placed it alongside the other two on the plastic sheet.

"This one is best for your partners," he said, selecting a headed one of medium size. Unless you have a specific situation in mind, this size is usually universally acceptable in both positions. As it will be the active device, it is best if it is not too large, as men especially become frightened." A smile broke on his face for the first time as he made his no doubt often repeated joke.

He now picked up both a well-worn pad and an even more worn tape measure, together with a felt pen.

"Stand up very straight if you will, and part your legs. Lift your arms out from your sides and please keep very still so that my measurements will be exact."

Standing as she was instructed, the measurement was a further stimulating experience, for she could feel her juices trickling down her inside thigh and could smell her body even over that of the leather. Sweat, sex and leather made a heady perfume, she thought.

He was making little marks with the felt pen and running the tape across her skin. He missed nowhere. Even her hard nipples were marked and measured, the curve of her breast, the distension of her buttocks, down between to find her anus and on again to find her hole, marked for measurement in both cases by the insertion of his finger a little way.

When he was finished, he told her in a matter-of-fact way that she could get dressed. Alison was exhausted. She had been held at a pitch of excitement for quite some time and now felt as though she had been taken.

The selection of the harness style was undertaken from illustrations in a well-thumbed and dog-eared book. The different styles had been modelled by a blonde, attractively figured young woman, but indifferently photographed to create that slightly tacky feel to the images. Alison selected, with considerable and forceful advice, a harness that started with her head, which was to be encased in a box of leather straps. Provision was made for a gag to be incorporated if desired. A tight and high leather collar would encase her neck and then the straps would encircle her breasts, leaving the ends exposed. Dramatic and attractive straps fanned out and down her body, first to restrain the waist and then to lace across the curve of her womb, at the base of her mound. The male dildo would be directly mounted over her clitoris. Also positioned here was a special rubber pad with a cluster of little fingers that would press upon her button as she exerted her own force of the thrust. A wide and parting strap would pass between her legs, holding both her own internal devices. Movable fastenings ensured that these would be given some motion as the male dildo was used.

Alison could not wait to have this wonder in her possession, though it was some months before she received a small engraved card to advise her that it was ready for collection. The difference now was that the address for collection was quite different and the time was in the evening.

She arrived at a very select block of Paris apartments and took the caged lift to the third floor. The brass fitted door was opened by an attractive and smartly dressed woman.

"Alison Kwik?" she enquired with a French accent, and Alison answered that she was.

She was ushered into a small reception room of some quality. Herr Craftsman stood up to greet her. He now wore a moderately respectable suit.

"Ah, my dear young lady, such a pleasure to meet you again. Part of the substantial sum that my clients pay for my work is to provide them with an initial trial – should, of course, they so wish. Always I find that a little guidance is needed in the fitting of the harness and it is important to me at the level of satisfaction at which I desire to work that they feel that all is satisfactory and comfortable. This cannot be achieved without the practical use of the garment. Therefore, Madame Visage" – he gestured towards the woman who had opened the door – "helps me in this matter, in return of course for a professional fee for her special services."

Alison looked with now greater interest at the woman. She was perhaps in her middle thirties, with a slim and well-proportioned body. Her high cheek-bones, restrained dress and hair in a tight bun all gave her a look of refinement and quality edged with a touch of the severe.

"Are you happy with this arrangement?" the woman asked Alison.

"Oh yes, I am pleased to go along with whatever Herr Craftsman has arranged."

"Then please follow me," said Madame Visage and opened the door into the next room. The old man and Alison followed.

The room was a softly lit old Paris boudoir, rich warm and private. Alison saw immediately, laid across a divan, the object of the occasion – the red leather harness.

The woman took charge of the situation.

"Perhaps, Ms Kwik, you would be so good as to undress, so that Herr Craftsman and I can fit you with his special garment."

As with the first encounter, Alison felt detached and propelled along by the confidence and experience of others to whom this seemed routine. It was exciting, this surrender of choice. Tonight she had worn a dress, stockings and court shoes. While both the old man and the woman watched, almost impatiently, she undressed, placing her clothes with care and trying to retain some dignity. Even when she had removed her little silk top and matching knickers, she was still faced with the removal of her stockings and belt. This time she was completely nude, without even pop socks. The woman appraised her with a moment's detachment and then picked up the harness. It was quite beautiful, complex and even intimidating. The red leather organs that were intended for her looked even bigger than she remembered them to have been.

"We will proceed with the fitting, if you please. Stand leg-parted and arms out, and I will do the rest," instructed Madame Visage. Alison complied and Herr Craftsman sat down a little way away, no doubt to watch with craftsman's pride the demonstration of his work. The harness detached into two halves and Madame Visage started by fitting the top. Alison felt the initiate feeling of being encased as the straps were fastened around her head. The neck collar was drawn tight and she felt the way that it forced her head to stay erect. The woman worked quickly and with experience, the many little buckles fastened with ease in her nimble fingers. Alison could feel her torso being encased. Her breasts rose and were divided to point out to the sides. She saw how stiff the nipples had become and all around her was the smell of leather and the subtle perfume of Madame Visage. The woman now tightened the corset-like structure beneath Alison's breasts.

"Take a deep breath in and hold it, please," requested Madame Visage.

Alison complied and she felt the woman swiftly tighten the straps across her back so that now her waist was drastically pulled in.

Madame now reached for a tube of lubricant and methodically coated each of the organs.

"This will not be comfortable at first, so just relax. There will be a little pain but it will pass."

Alison did her best to ready herself for the entry of the large dildo. When it came there was no kindness in the entry used by Madame, but Alison knew that she would have enjoyed doing the same. Even so, a little cry, which must have given some satisfaction to the woman, passed her lips. It was worked in until Alison felt as though she would part with the filling force. The one in her behind was nothing like as bad and it slipped in to give her some pleasure.

Her crutch was forced wide open by both the device and the width of the harness. While the woman fastened and pulled up the lower section to the torso section, Alison was able to look down and see the large red dildo for the first time, erect and in front of her, curving up from the base of her mound like men she had so often seen. She was also aware that, at every tremor of the long organ in front of her, the rubber fingers at its base stirred her clitoris in a definite and stimulating way.

The woman now directed Alison's attention to a full-length ornate mirror against the wall. What she saw reflected was a remarkable and totally erotic sight that fired her in a way she had never experienced before. The muscles of her vagina started to work involuntarily on the distending solid leather within it and her sphincter tightened and gripped its plug. As she looked at herself, she became uncontrollably aroused. With difficulty, she turned sideways and saw pointed breasts and the penis in front of the thrusting buttocks. Her head was encased and warrior-like – indeed the totality was wickedly war-like.

Without further ceremony, Madame Visage, in the same flat tone, invited Alison to try the harness. As though she had done it a hundred times before – and perhaps she had – Madame Visage bent herself over the raised end of the divan. She reached backward and in one movement swept up the length of her dress and tucked it beneath her. Above her black seamed stockings, Alison could clearly see that Madame wore no knickers. The stockinged legs parted invitingly and were surmounted by a beautiful full bottom of firm white flesh. The legs ended in expensive, black, long-heeled shoes. Alison was taken aback by this display, for it was totally unexpected. Herr Craftsman watched from his seat.

"Do not hold back; please go ahead and try your new toy," came the voice of Madame Visage. "Either hole is permissible – whatever is your fancy – or both."

Alison moved forward, feeling the difficulty of walking, feeling the rub on her button driving her to greater heights. The dildo in front of her gleamed with the lubricant already rubbed on it.

She moved between the parted legs so that she was over the raised bottom. She could see the little hole clearly and in the darker place at the top of Madame's thighs she could see the hairy and wet rear of the vulva. Frightened but determined, Alison gripped the dildo in one hand and supported her weight with the other. She entered its round head into the soft lips that were presented. Then, remembering how the dildo had been forced into her own place, she thrust into the woman with all her force. She was successful in extracting a groan. With each successive thrust, she gained even more response. She held the woman's hips with her hands and moved her own with all her force. Though she was fucking, she was also being fucked and she could not restrain the mounting orgasm that was fed and driven by so many methods of stimulation in her own body.

When she had come, she withdrew and released the woman. She stood trembling and instantly wondering what it would be like to use on a man. The expression on her face was all the real thanks that Herr Craftsman needed. This work was so much more rewarding in his old age than the use of his supreme talents on the horses in old Vienna. The smell of this sexual young woman, which floated across the room, blended with his new leather. He was content.

ACKNOWLEDGEMENTS

"Desire Begins" by Kathy Acker, © 1974 by Kathy Acker. Excerpted from *I Dreamt I Was a Nymphomaniac Imagining*. Reproduced by permission of the author.

"Crash" by J. G. Ballard, © 1973 by J. G. Ballard. Reproduced by permission of the author, the author's agent Margaret Hanbury, and Farrar, Straus & Giroux Inc.

"The Age of Desire" by Clive Barker, © 1985 by Clive Barker. First appeared in *The Books of Blood 4*. Reproduced by permission of the author.

"A Long Letter from F." by Leonard Cohen, © 1967 by Leonard Cohen. Excerpted from *Beautiful Losers*. Reproduced by permission of Black Spring Press Ltd./Stranger Music Inc.

"Leone" by Régine Deforges, © 1988, 1993 by Régine Deforges. First appeared in *Lola et Quelques Autres*. Reproduced by permission of Franck Spengler.

"Equinox" by Samuel R. Delany, © 1973 by Samuel R. Delany. Excerpted from *The Tides of Lust*. Reproduced by permission of Rhinoceros Books.

"Pure Porn" by Dion Farquhar, © 1992 by Dion Farquhar. First appeared in *Fiction International*. Reproduced by permission of the author.

"Three Times a Woman" by Grushenka, © unknown. Public domain. First appeared in a private printing from Nafkeh Publications.

"Married Love" by David Guy, © 1991 by David Guy. Excerpted from *The Autobiography of My Body*. Reproduced by permission of the author's agent, the Virginia Barber Literary Agency, Inc.

"Lust" by Elfriede Jelinek, © 1989 by Elfriede Jelinek. First appeared in *Lust*. Reproduced by permission of Serpent's Tail.

"Watching" by J. P. Kansas, © 1996 by J. P. Kansas. Reproduced by permission of the author.

"We Like to Watch" by Donald Katz, © 1993 by Donald Katz. First appeared in *Esquire*. Reproduced by permission of the author.

"A Letter" by Jana Krejcarová, © 1962 by Jana Krejcarová. First appeared in *Yazzyk*. Reproduced by permission of Concordia, Prague, on behalf of the author's estate.

"Roses" by Evelyn Lau, © 1993 by Evelyn Lau. First appeared in *Fresh Girls*. Reproduced by permission of the author's agent Denise Bukowski and Hyperion Publishing.

"Oracle of the Thousand Hands" by Barry N. Malzberg, © 1969 by Barry N. Malzberg. Excerpted from *Oracle of the Thousand Hands*. Reproduced by permission of the author.

"Between Signs" by Cris Mazza, © 1993 by Cris Mazza. First appeared in *Fabric of Desire*. Reproduced by permission of the author.

"Her First Bra" by Cris Mazza, © 1996 by Cris Mazza. Reproduced by permission of the author.

"Boff" by David Meltzer, © 1996 by David Meltzer. Reproduced by permission of the author.